The Poison Priestess

KIRALYNN EPICS

The Silk & Steel Saga

Book One: *The Steel Queen*
Book Two: *The Flame Priest*
Book Three: *The Skeleton King*
Book Four: *The Poison Priestess*

Forthcoming books by Karen L Azinger

Book Five: *The Battle Immortal*

Additional books by Karen L Azinger
The Assassin's Tear

THE
POISON PRIESTESS

BOOK FOUR OF
THE SILK & STEEL SAGA

Karen L. Azinger

KIRALYNN EPICS

Published by Kiralynn Epics L.P. 2012

Copyright © Karen L. Azinger 2012

First published in the United States of America by Kiralynn Epics 2012

Front Cover Artwork Copyright Greg Bridges © 2012

Celtic Lettering used with permission of Alfred M Graphics Art Studio

The Author asserts the moral right to be identified as the author of this work

All characters in this publication are fictitious and any resemblance to real persons living or dead, is purely coincidental.

ISBN   978-0-9835160-8-8

Library of Congress Control Number: 2012921237

ACKNOWEDGEMENTS

My dream of an epic fantasy continues, and like the first three books, it takes a lot of people to make the saga come true. First and foremost, to my husband Rick, who is always keen for the next adventure and always believes no matter the odds. To my best friend, first reader and sword sister, Danae Powers, who listened from the very first chapter. To my writer friend, Peggy Lowe, a critique circle of one. To my alpha readers, Mike and Nick, your enthusiasm kept me going. To Greg Bridges for the totally awesome front cover and the book spine. To Peggy Lowe, graphic artist extraordinaire, for the back cover, the two maps and the logo, well done! To all of my readers who eagerly followed the saga to the fourth book, I write for you. If you like the saga, please write a review and tell your friends! And to my mom, for everything, I so hope you know.

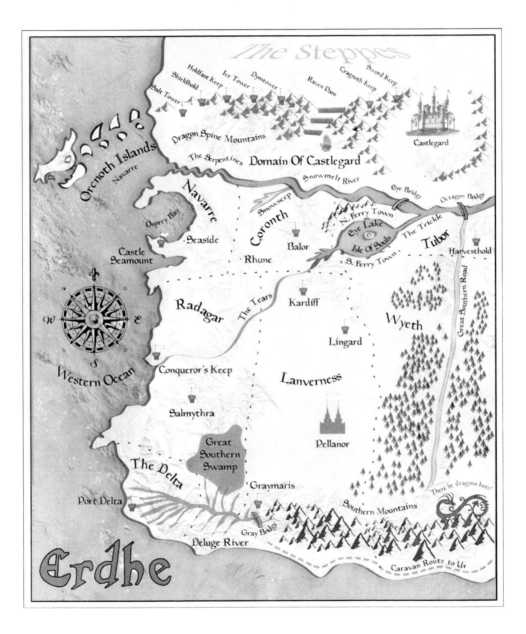

Prologue

The summons from the Grand Master came in the form of a whisper. *"Come!"* A subtle hand signal drew Rafe down the cloistered corridors towards a shadowy alcove, the whispered message passed with the barest of nods. "The Grand Master bids you to bear this." The monk opened his fist, revealing a fine-linked chain...and from that chain dangled a plain iron ring.

Rafe gaped like a novice. He'd heard of such rings, though he'd never dreamt of seeing one. Just a simple iron band inscribed with the All Seeing Eye yet this ring was the key to long guarded secrets. In any village marketplace it would fetch a single copper, nothing more than a worthless trifle, yet it was old and of incalculable worth, an heirloom of the monastery. He longed to accept it yet the truth could not be denied. "I'm not worthy."

"None of us are, yet you are called." The monk smiled, his face a crease of wrinkles. "Your protest proves your worth." He placed the ring and chain into Rafe's open hand, closing his fingers into a fist for safekeeping. "Bear it well."

Rafe clutched the ring. "Why me? I've worn the blue for less than a handful of years?"

The monk nodded, giving Rafe a kindly look. "Fresh perspectives are always needed, especially in times of prophecy." A chill shivered down Rafe's back, like a spectral hand leaving its mark. "Only twelve such rings remain to us. Eight are held by the wisest of the Order, masters in their fields of study. Two are reserved for the wanderers, monks who spend more time in the southern kingdoms than they do in the monastery. And two rings are rotated among the young, those with more promise than proof. By order of the Grand Master, this is yours to bear."

Rafe struggled to contain his excitement. "For how long?"

"Till you are unbidden...or until you leave the monastery."

Rafe hadn't yet made his decision regarding his future, whether to stay in the monastery and deepen his studies, or to become a wanderer and serve in the southern kingdoms. Both choices held their own allure, but to be asked to join the conclave was an honor undreamt. *To sit among the wise, to have his voice heard in conclave, a chance to change the future,* he clutched the ring, realizing how badly he wanted it.

"Your first conclave is tonight, at midnight."

Rafe gasped.

"Meet the others at the ironwood doors." The monk nodded. "Bear the ring well and tell no one. Secrecy remains one of our greatest strengths."

Astounded by the turn of events, Rafe slipped the slender chain around neck, hiding the ring beneath his midnight blue robes. Setting his hand to his robe, he pressed the ring against his heart, struggling to believe it was true. *Tonight, at midnight!* His first conclave, yet it seemed an ill-omened hour. But then he realized the frost owls flew at night, and all their messages brought grim tidings. Of late, the owls flew thick as starlings, bearing coded messages from monks seeded across the southern kingdoms. Knowledge flowed towards the Kiralynn Monastery like a river in flood, warning of ancient prophecies that rushed to be born. Rafe wondered if anything could stem the Dark tide.

The waiting proved hard. He paced his cell, seeking to meditate but inner peace proved elusive, his thoughts skittering like wild hares. At the appointed hour, he drew the slender chain from his neck, and set the iron ring upon his finger. Such a simple ring, yet it gave him access to the wise. He bowed his head, asking the Lords of Light for guidance. Raising the deep cowl of his midnight blue robe to signal a desire for seclusion, Rafe left his sleeping cell, his eagerness warring with his apprehension.

Like stepping from darkness to enlightenment, the change was always startling. Lamplight flickered along the hallway, cunningly set to illume the walls, so different from the simple austerity of his sleeping cell. Shimmering with gold and jeweled tones, vibrant swirls of intricate script filled the walls, a celebration of the written word. History was written upon the walls of the monastery, ancient truths mingled with pages of prophecy, the past and the future set side by side. As always, Rafe found the hallways intoxicating, seductive with knowledge and art, like living in the pages of an illuminated manuscript.

His gaze caressed the text as he made his way through the labyrinth. Each masterpiece held layers of meaning, from the words, to the entwined images, to the convoluted script. Legends said that if you stared at the script long enough, the complex patterns would unlock the mind's hidden doorways, revealing deeper truths. Rafe had long sought such enlightenment, yet for all his striving he'd never gained a deeper awareness.

The sweet scent of incense intensified and so did the silence, as if the hallways were steeped in thought. Stairs took him to the lower level, to the oldest part of the monastery, a relic built before the War of Wizards. Doors became scarce while the calligraphy lining the walls grew more ominous, depicting the darkest pages from the Book of Prophecy. Torchlight flickered along the mage-stone walls, casting shadows in his wake. Rafe felt as if he traveled backwards in time, to the very origins of the Order.

The long hallway came to an abrupt end. Two towering doors of ironwood painted a deep midnight blue blocked the way forward. Cold seeped through the ancient wood like a warning, casting a chill on the corridor.

Rafe found the others already assembled, eleven blue-robed masters, their hoods raised in seclusion. No words were spoken, for none were needed. He bowed towards them and then extended his right hand, revealing the iron ring. One at a time, the others mimicked his action, till each revealed a ring twin to his own, the twelve rings of conclave.

"By tradition, the oldest goes first." From a basket, the wizen master selected a candle as thick as a man's wrist and as long as a sword. Lighting it from a glowing brazier, he held the candle aloft and approached the double doors. A pair of iron Seeing Eyes adorned the wood. Pitted with rust, the ironwork was old and brittle; a testament to a thousand years of use, yet the workmanship was superb. Inset in the elaborate handle was a Dahlmar crystal, gleaming pale as chiseled ice, a warning and a test.

Rafe shivered to see the crystal, knowing the Order's oldest enemy had Awakened within the very walls of the monastery. He wondered if the ancient builders had foreseen the threat.

The master grasped the handle with his ringed hand, setting his bare palm against the crystal.

Rafe tensed, but the crystal remained dormant.

The master stepped back, waiting.

The ancient doors shivered opened of their own accord, just wide enough for a single man to slip through. A wintery gust burst through the narrow opening, snatching at braziers. Shielding the candle, the monk stepped into the beyond.

The doors shuddered closed, swallowing the monk whole.

Peace returned to the hallway, yet anxiety settled like a mantle on Rafe's shoulders. The monastery had ways of protecting its secrets; he wondered what trials lay ahead. Staring at the others, he silently pleaded for answers, but no one spoke. Rafe stifled the urge to pace, trying to mirror their apparent calm. Locked in silence, he waited as the others took their turn at the door.

One by one, the masters passed the test of crystal and stepped beyond the ironbound door. The last master, a woman with rich auburn hair, gave him a smile before gliding through the doorway. "Watch your step and do not falter." The door closed behind her and Rafe was left alone. With no one to watch, he began to pace, fidgeting with his ring, silently counting the beats of his heart.

A chime sounded signaling Rafe's turn. Choosing a tall candle, he lit it, and held it upright like a sword. He approached the doors, setting his ringed hand to the crystal. For half a heartbeat he wondered what would happen if the crystal flared red. Perhaps the door had a way of slaying harlequins, but thankfully his question went unanswered.

The crystal remained dormant and the ironbound doors shivered open.

Rafe muttered a prayer and stepped boldly into the unknown.

His boots slipped on ice. *"Bloody hell!"* He struggled to keep his footing. The doors closed behind him with a solid thud. His heart thundering, Rafe shuffled backward, clinging to the ironwood. Winter snatched at his robes. A cold wind howled around him, raising the hairs on the back of his neck. He stood outside the monastery, on a narrow ledge. A slender stone causeway, barely wide enough to hold a single man, arched across a bottomless abyss. Darkness lurked on either side, like a hungry maw waiting to be fed. Rafe leaned against the doors, a solid haven against the fatal drop. Refusing to look down, he stared aloft. A narrow slice of stars glittered overhead. Cold as ice chips in a moonless sky, the stars offered little comfort. In the dead of night, his candle provided the only light, a frail pinprick guttering in the wind. Fingernails digging into candle wax, Rafe took a steadying breath and stepped forward.

"Seek knowledge...Protect knowledge...Share knowledge," he whispered the Order's creed like a mantra, his words snatched away by howling wind. One foot in front of the other, he edged his way forward. Halfway across he wondered why the builders had not added a railing, but then he remembered something from his novice year. Rumors spoke of a stone bridge that would reject anyone who dared cross without the proper token, flinging the intruder to a terrible death. He wondered if this was the bridge. The monastery had ways of protecting its secrets...and testing the mettle of its monks, as if knowledge alone was not enough to join the conclave.

Rafe shuffled across the narrow span, wary of ice. A cold wind battered against him, pushing him towards the edge. Hunched forward, he rushed the last few steps, cursing the ancient builders.

A single door waited on the far side. Ancient ironwood, painted a deep midnight blue, perfectly fitted into the sheer cliff wall. Chiseled above the door, a pair of massive Seeing Eyes stared down at him. Icicles hung from the right eye, the frozen tears of winter. Rafe touched the door with his ring hand and it opened. Relieved, he rushed inside, pushing the door shut against the winter wind. A cold gust followed him. Candles guttered, sending the light dancing across midnight blue walls.

Silence returned with the closing of the door. A solemn stillness washed across Rafe, making his hasty entrance seem like a sacrilege. He bowed and smoothed his robes, trying to collect his dignity. Taking a deep breath, he raised his stare and was sundered by a sense of awe. Star constellations shimmered above each master like a halo. In the dimness of the rock-hewn chamber, the celestial lights hovered over each monk as if the very stars guided their thoughts.

The wind battered the door like a knocking ghost and Rafe realized he was gawking like a traveler fresh-come to the monastery. Embarrassed, he shuffled forward, not knowing what to do.

A kindly voice said, "The first seat to your left. Set your ringed hand against the backrest to awaken your star sign."

Rafe walked to the appointed platform, the one closest to the door. Eighteen raised wooden platforms circled the oval chamber. Five were forever shrouded in shadows, a testament to their lost rings. One glowed with a brilliant star sign, the one at the head of the chamber, yet the seat stood empty. Blue cloaked masters claimed the others. Sitting cross-legged, they remained statue-still, their blue robes puddled around them like still waters, their star patterns glowing overhead like guiding lights.

Humbled to be among the wise, Rafe set his ringed hand against the backrest. Crystals inset in the wood blazed alight, awakened by ancient magic. Placing his candle in a niche on the floor, Rafe took a seat beneath the glowing Hourglass, the symbol of time and the ever-changing seasons.

A solemn hush settled over the chamber.

"Each conclave starts with meditation. May the wisdom of the Lords of Light fill your minds."

Seeking to mimic the others, Rafe sat cross-legged, his blue robes pooled around him in warm folds. He tried to meditate, but his gaze leaped around the chamber, drinking in the details. Carved from sheer rock, the walls were painted a deep midnight blue, devoid of calligraphy or any adornment. A subtle cold seeped through the chamber, proof of the mountain's chilly embrace. Rafe shivered. So different from the mage-stone monastery, the chamber reeked of age and ancient intent, a secret hollow hidden from the world. And then his gaze found a deeper riddle, a small blue door cunningly set into the chamber's floor. *A trap door, perhaps to a hidden vault,* he wondered what it held. A chill shivered down his spine. Riddles wrapped in secrets, such was the Order's way, but sometimes it made him uneasy. His gaze sought the glowing star patterns, a comfort in the dark. Water dripped in the depths, like the pluck of a single harp string...or the heartbeat of a mountain. Lulled by the gentle sound and the soothing light, Rafe's thoughts drifted.

"A young one has joined us, a new ring bearer."

Rafe startled alert.

The oldest master spoke, his voice a dry rasp beneath the star sign of the Hermit. "As this is his first conclave, he must hear our rules. Within the Star Chamber, we have no names. We are known only by our star signs, a symbol that we leave personal ambitions behind." The Hermit gestured toward the empty seat. "As always, we serve at the bidding of the Grand Master."

Rafe stared at the empty chair with its glowing star pattern. As with all things in the monastery, the vacant seat held another, deeper meaning. By its very emptiness, the platform bestowed a unique power upon the Grand Master, the power of anonymity. Anonymity was something the southern kings would never understand and certainly never value; yet in many ways it defined the very nature of the Kiralynn Order. Cloaked in secrecy, the monks took the long view, using subtle means to achieve their ends. Staring at the empty chair, Rafe wondered how the Order's deep seated desire for concealment would influence the coming war.

The oldest among them struck a small gong. The sweet sound shimmered through the chamber like a blessing. "This conclave is now sealed."

The others made a graceful gesture, closing their hands in front of their mouths as if to catch their words and then pressing their fists to their chests, a silent vow of secrecy. Rafe hastily copied the gesture.

Rafe watched the others. He knew most of their names, but he followed the conclave's edict, thinking of them by their star signs. It said much that the oldest monk sat beneath the constellation of the Hermit.

The Hermit spoke first, his voice a dry rasp, full of age and authority. "The Grand Master has called a conclave to hear your wisdom. Another owl has come to the monastery, turning a page in the Book of Prophecy. The watch fires of the Octagon are lit."

Rafe swallowed a gasp, tasting his own fear. He'd never expected that prophecy to be fulfilled in his own lifetime.

"And what of the crystal dagger?" The question came from the Hunter, an auburn-haired woman of middling years. "We hoped to stop the Mordant before he came to his power. Has the blade bearer failed?"

"Yes and no." The Hermit answered. "A wanderer resides among the Octagon knights. It was his owl that brought warning this very night. The bearer of the crystal blade has crossed over the Dragon Spine Mountains, following the Mordant into the north."

The Hunter eased back in her seat. "Then there is still hope that the Mordant can be stopped."

The Weaver shook her head. "Do not be deceived by false hopes. The Book of Prophecy is clear." Her voice deepened, quoting the ancient text. *"When the red comet tears the sky and the watch towers of the Last Knights are lit, then war will come like a dark plague to Erdhe, even to the very gates of the Seeing Hand."*

Such an ill omen, Rafe shuddered to hear it spoken aloud.

"War at our gates." The Scorpion's voice was grim. "Darkness threatens to swallow all knowledge. But even if the southern kingdoms fail, the monastery will protect its own."

Rafe thought of the bridge he'd just crossed and realized the ancient builders had prepared for this very threat.

"Walls of Mist will not save us." The Weaver shook her head, her silver hair gleaming in the candlelight. "Never forget that the Mordant escaped with an amulet keyed to the Guardian Mist. Our best defense is lost." Her gaze circled the chamber. "The Kiralynn Order has ever fought the Darkness but we must also be prudent. The knowledge entrusted to us must not fall to the Dark. We must move deeper into the mountains, claiming a new sanctuary."

The Scorpion said, "The Dark Lord will loose more harlequins."

A grim pall settled across the chamber.

"The southern kingdoms have forgotten the harlequins."

The Hunter said, "They are learning, though it is a grim lesson."

"We must expose the reborn before they can betray those who serve the Light."

The Archer said, "A harlequin was seeded into the court of Lanverness, a traitor to lead the Red Horn rebellion...and we did not see it."

"They say his eyes glowed red when he was boiled alive." The Dragon scowled. "Boiled alive in front of half of Pellanor."

"I was there." The Hunter spoke, her voice grim with remembering. "While the rest of you hide in the mountains studying ancient lore, I have roamed the southern kingdoms seeking the enemy. I stood in the crowd and watched as the queen ordered the traitor's execution. The Lord Turner was the last to die. His parboiled corpse capered in the cauldron, his eyes glowing with the red light of hell. The queen caught more than she expected."

Rafe stared at the Hunter, unable to imagine the horror of meeting a harlequin.

The Hunter pressed her point. "A harlequin sat at the queen's council and none here suspected it."

"We are not infallible."

The truth sent a spike of fear through Rafe.

"Prophecies have a way of twisting to their own purpose."

"Yet we cannot afford mistakes, not when it comes to the reborn." The Hunter's gaze pierced the gloom like a hawk. "The Archer has the truth of it. The Dark Lord calls *all* his minions to battle. This will be no ordinary war. We must find the demons before they twist the future to Darkness."

"*And there will be a dark heart hidden among the princes of the sword.*" Everyone turned to stare at the Weaver. "The Book of Prophecies is rife with warnings of harlequins hidden among the royal houses. One quatrain in particular points toward the Octagon Knights. The Order must do more to expose the hidden evil."

The Hermit answered, "Aeroth was sent to Castlegard and the knights passed the test."

"Castlegard was not enough." The Weaver's voice snapped with warning. "The knights have holdings all along the Dragon Spine Mountains."

The Archer said, "And now an owl brings word that the Mordant has escaped into the north. Our most dire prophecies rush to be born. If the Mordant brings an army south, the Octagon must hold." His words fell like a threat, choking the air from the chamber like a hangman's noose.

The Hermit broke the silence. "The hidden harlequins must be found, starting with the Octagon Knights. The Grand Master will be so advised."

"So be it." Words of agreement circled the chamber.

Rafe huddled beneath his robes, feeling a sudden chill.

"The harlequins are not our only problem." The Archer spoke with grim certainty. "History tells us that the Mordant craves the powers of the ancient wizards.

The Hunter whispered what others refused to say. "*Soul* magic."

"Just so." The Archer nodded. "The Mordant is patient. Long has he scoured the land for lost magic, collecting focuses and hoarding them toward a dire future. Now, after a thousand years of preparation, the second cataclysm is nearly upon us. The Mordant has waited till all other magic has faded from Erdhe. With a single focus he can strike terror into the hearts of men." The Archer's gaze roved the chamber. "Swords alone will not defeat him. We must find a way to counter his magic or Erdhe will fall."

The Weaver shook her silvered head. "But most of our magic is peaceful in nature."

"Then we must be creative. And we must have a second testing."

Silence thundered through the chamber.

The Archer leaned forward, his voice intense. "You know of what I speak. The Order holds many focuses that remain unclaimed. We must test every monk, acolyte, and novice, hoping to waken more bonds."

"And what of the relics?" The Scales voice sounded like a doom.

For a dozen heartbeats no one spoke.

"We don't dare."

The Archer exploded in anger. "How can we *not* dare!" His dark gaze challenged the others. "The time of destiny is upon us. We must test the relics. We need to know if anyone here can wield them."

The Scorpion hissed, "Such power should not be wielded by mere men."

"The Mordant will not hesitate to use *all* his powers."

"And if we fight power with power the Order will become just as evil as the Mordant!" The Scorpion glared at the Archer. "Magic is dangerous and unpredictable. Once unleashed, it has a way of bringing unintended consequences. Remember the Deep Green...and the foul tales of the Pit."

The Hermit nodded, his voice reluctant. "In the War of Wizards, the Order underestimated how far evil would go to win. We must learn from our mistakes and prepare for the worst."

"But the *relics*?" The Scorpion shook his head. "I fear for Erdhe if the relics are unleashed."

"True, but the Mordant must be checked or Darkness will cover Erdhe."

The Scale's voice rang like a portent of doom. "Who knows what ancient magics the Mordant has hidden in his lair? We may face legends ere this war is ended."

"But the relics?" The Dragon entered the discussion. "I agree with the Scorpion and counsel for caution."

The Archer answered, "We've all read the prophecies and seen the signs. We are way past caution." He shook his head. "I'm not arguing for their use, only that we be prepared. Even the oldest relics may be needed...if any here can wield them."

The Hermit intervened, sounding the gong to end the discussion. "Is it the will of this conclave that the unclaimed focuses be tested?"

"So be it." The replies echoed through the chamber. Rafe lent his agreement with the others.

The Hermit nodded. "The focuses will be tested. And what of the relics?"

No one spoke.

Rafe's gaze was drawn to the seat reserved for the Grand Master. The star constellation of the Hierophant glowed bright above the empty chair. In the celestial hierarchy, the Hierophant served as heaven's guide to knowledge and wisdom, a fitting star sign for the leader of the Kiralynn Order. But the Hierophant also had a second, more obscure meaning, the wielder of arcane mysteries, the master of magic. Rafe wondered how much magic the Grand Master wielded...and if it would be enough to stop the Mordant.

The voting commenced but the conclave was evenly divided. The Hermit nodded. "The relics will remain untouched."

Rafe was secretly relieved, but he wondered if he'd cast the right vote. He glanced at the Archer, not surprised to find frustration glowering on his face, but he did not protest the outcome.

The Weaver said, "We should have done more to aid the bearer of the crystal dagger."

The Swan said, "Do not give up on the blade bearer. That one started as a pawn amongst knights but she will not remain a pawn for long. She has dared to cross into the north, into the very lair of the Mordant. The north will change her. She will become more...or she will fail." The words fell like a stone, like a prophecy...or a doom.

The Archer frowned. "She has gone beyond our reach. But I believe she will surprise us all, even surpassing the prophecies. Everyone save the Grand Master overlooked the princess of Castlegard. We all expected the crystal blade to choose a different bearer."

"The princess from Navarre."

"Just so." The Archer nodded. "That is why she was called here for her Wayfaring."

Rafe had watched the princess at weapons practice, spending long hours wielding her sword. He'd seen her determination and liked her for it.

"The Mordant attacked her when he made his escape, as if he recognized the threat."

"He could not have known what he did." The Scales shook his head, his gray hair peppered with a hint of black. "It had to be an accidental meeting, or the cursed luck of the Dark Lord."

"Either way, the girl survived. Recovered from her wounds, she petitions the Grand Master to be released from her Wayfaring."

"Yes, she speaks of *visions*, or are they merely an excuse to leave?"

The Archer glared at the Weaver. "You should know better than most. Perhaps the gods have gifted us with a second seer."

"But we've barely had time to train her." The Hermit's voice lashed with protest. "You'd loose another pawn into the great game?"

"The princess is bound by her Wayfaring. She must finish what she has started."

"But the Order owes her!" The words burst out of Rafe.

The others turned to stare.

Rafe swallowed, realizing he'd spoken out loud.

The Hermit said, "The Hourglass wishes to add his voice to this conclave."

The old man's glare could melt granite but Rafe refused to be cowed. "We invited her here. We promised her sanctuary, yet she was brutally attacked within our halls. A debt is owed to the princess of Navarre."

"And are you the one to pay it?"

Such an odd question from the Weaver, Rafe did not know how to reply.

The Archer said, "The Hourglass has the truth of it. She was attacked under our protection, a debt is owed." His stare circled the chamber. "I believe the Navarren princess has a part to play in the coming war. I served as the girl's inquisitor when she first arrived at the monastery, taking her interview in the garden of contemplation." His voice dropped to a hush. "So few women dare to take up the sword, it is almost a sign of greatness. Like the princess of Castlegard, I believe she is another touched by the gods. I agree with the

Hourglass and lend my voice to those who petition the Grand Master to release her. Loose the Osprey and see what damage she can do."

The Weaver said, "But she should not go alone." Her gaze turned to Rafe. "Since you petition the conclave on her behalf, will you join her quest?"

"Me?" Rafe was shocked by the question.

The Hermit said, "You should know that if you choose to leave the monastery you must forfeit the iron ring."

Rafe's hand curled into a fist.

The Dragon said, "Be warned. If you give up the ring it may never come your way again."

The Hermit smiled, but it did not reach his eyes. "Do you stand by your convictions?"

Rafe bowed his head, studying the iron ring. He felt the other's stares pounding against him, felt the weight of decision crushing his shoulders. He'd just gained the iron ring, a door to wisdom, a key to so many riddles, yet he felt the Order owed a debt to the princess. He'd always yearned to make a difference, perhaps this was destiny's way of pointing him in the right direction. "I will give up the ring to aid the princess."

A murmur of approval rippled through the chamber.

Rafe pulled the iron band from his finger.

The Hermit said, "Not yet." This time his voice held a measure of respect. "You will need the ring to safely cross the chasm."

So the rumors are true, Rafe settled the ring back on his finger. Stunned by his own decision, he heard little of the discussion. He was leaving the monastery for the chaos of the southern kingdoms. Dire prophecies stalked Erdhe, but perhaps he'd find a way to serve the Light. Regret warred with his sense of duty. He twirled the iron ring, wondering if his sacrifice would make a difference.

1

Steffan

Campfires swarmed the valley, setting the countryside alight. Twilight painted the darkening sky red, a fitting backdrop for the Army of the Flame, the red comet blazing overhead like a victory banner. So many campfires, enough to rival the gates of hell, Steffan studied the view, pleased by the numbers. The long march through Coronth had turned into a triumph. Village elders vied to feast his officers while the women threw themselves at his soldiers and the men gave up their plowshares for swords. Steffan took them all, the farmers and the blacksmiths, the devout and the ambitious, swelling his army of religious fanatics, an unstoppable force marching south to Lanverness.

They camped on the very border of queen's kingdom, just a short march away from first bloodshed. Expectation filled the night, the blessed eve before the holy war. Sixty thousand whetstones rasped against steel, filling the valley with a threatening hum like an infestation of angry wasps. While the soldiers prepared, the red-robed priests danced a frenzy around the bonfires, predicting victories for the Flame God. The valley throbbed with deadly intent, a horde of fanatics eager to be unleashed.

Steffan sipped brandy while waiting for the general. As the counselor to the Pontifax, his pavilion was set apart from the army, claiming the highest hilltop, the crimson silk glowing by torchlight. The deliberate distance created mystique...it also served as protection in case the Dark Lord chose to come again. Steffan preferred to avoid rumors caused by his screams. He rubbed his chest, remembering the agony of a fortnight past. He'd felt his god's displeasure, a molten fist squeezing his heart with a hellish heat, imprinting a warning and a threat. Something had gone terribly wrong in Balor, upsetting the Dark Lord's plans and drawing his ire. Steffan swore it would never happen again. He needed a victory in Lanverness, one lifetime was not enough.

Pip emerged from the pavilion, carrying a carafe of brandy. An orphan-thief rescued from the back alleys of Balor, the skinny red-haired lad had proved a valuable retainer, serving as a squire, a messenger, a collector of rumors, and a spy. "More brandy, m'lord?"

"Yes, and when the general arrives we'll sup outside. I like the view." He gestured to the inferno of campfires. "What's the temperament of the men?"

Pip flashed a smile. "Eager, m'lord." He carefully refilled Steffan's goblet with the amber liquid. "They're awed by the pyromancer's show. Most believe the god himself appeared in the flames, assuring every soldier salvation through victory. They're keen to wet their swords with the blood of infidels."

"Good." Steffan knew that war made soldiers superstitious. Hungry for omens from the gods, he gave them what they wanted most, the very reason he'd brought the pyromancer on campaign. Bonfires constructed with special reagents spewed sparks and erupted with colors, belching sulphur-laden smoke at just the right time, providing portents for the priests to read. And all the portents pointed to victory. Religious fervor was truly a beautiful thing. "With the Flame God on our side, how can we lose?"

Pip grinned. "Just so, m'lord." The lad moved to the spit and gave the handle a turn, ladling sauce over the goose. Grease dripped into the fire, releasing a rush of flames and a cloud of mouth-watering scents.

A horse galloped toward the hill, drawing Steffan's stare. Guards snapped to salute, holding the horse while a tall figure dismounted. General Caylib stalked up the hillside. A large brute of a man with short iron-gray hair, a pockmarked face, and an old scar that twisted the right side of his mouth into a perpetual scowl, the man looked more like a barbarian than a general. But looks could be deceiving. Steffan chose the man for his ruthlessness, his strict discipline, and his fervent loyalty. So far, he'd lived up to his reputation, but the first battle would tell all.

The general reached the pavilion, towering a full head over Steffan, a shadow in dark leathers. He offered a nod, his only sign of deference. "Evening, Lord Raven."

Steffan raised his goblet in salute. "An evening to celebrate, the eve of a holy war."

The general barked a laugh. "Save your devout blather for the men. Blood and plunder are good enough for me." He sprawled in a chair on the far side of the table, his boots stretched toward the fire.

"We'll have plenty of both before this war is done." Steffan took a seat across from the general. "Are the men ready?" He'd walked the camp in the guise of a simple soldier, but second opinions were often insightful.

"The priests have whipped the men into a holy lather. Give the order and they'll storm the very gates of hell."

Steffan chuckled. "Hell is safe from me, but not Lanverness."

"Aye," the general gave a wicked grin, "a kingdom ripe for the taking, the richest prize in all of Erdhe. And to think, it's ruled by a woman."

"Not for long. The queen will be their undoing."

While the two men talked, Pip laid the table, setting the roast goose on a platter next to a bowl of fried onions, potatoes, and leeks. The lad carved the bird into succulent slices but before he could serve the carvings, the general leaned forward twisting a leg from the goose.

Hefting the leg like a prize, Caylib grinned. "Good eating." He bit into the drumstick, grease running from the side of his mouth.

Steffan hid his annoyance. The general had the table manners of a pig. Perhaps the man truly was a barbarian but he had his uses. "So it starts tomorrow."

The general grunted, talking around a mouthful of goose. "The scouts report a village three leagues beyond the border, a prime place for our first assault." He reached for a tankard, taking a long swig of dark beer. "Bishop Taniff has asked to lead the vanguard. The mace-wielding cleric is frothing at the mouth for a taste of infidel blood."

"Then give him the honor. The men will see it as a sign of the Flame God's favor."

"Careful counselor, the bloody cleric has gained a following among the men. Grant him too many favors and you'll create a rival."

The general was shrewder than he looked. Steffan flashed a pointed smile. "Men have a way of dying in battle, even clerics."

The general barked a laugh. "You're a ruthless bastard, counselor."

"Aye, that's why we get along so well." He gestured to Pip and the lad refilled the general's tankard. "Any sign of the Rose Army?"

"Not yet." The general wielded the half-eaten drumstick like a dagger. "But mark my words, they'll run when they see us." He waved the drumstick toward the glowing campfires. "We have the numbers. No army in Erdhe can stand against us. Once they catch sight of us, they'll turn tail and run, seeking safety behind stone walls. Like mice, they'll scurry to their fortresses at Kardiff, Graymaris, Lingard, and Rosekeep. And once they shut the gates, they'll be hard to pry out." He stabbed the drumstick toward Steffan. "What'll you do then, counselor? Order a siege?" He hawked and spat a wad of gristle into the fire. "A siege is a bloody great waste of a good army."

"They'll be no siege." Steffan shook his head, remembering the Dark Lord's impatience. "Pellanor is the key. We take the capital and the capture the queen. Once we hold the queen the rest will fall."

"Straight for the plunder." The general barked a rude laugh, hefting his tankard in salute. "Sack the capital and kill the bitch-queen, I like it."

Hoof beats approached at a hard gallop. A half dozen horsemen rode to the base of the hill. The guards crossed their halberds, refusing entry. Angry words drifted up toward the pavilion.

A premonition shivered in Steffan's mind. "Perhaps it's the messenger."

The general threw Steffan a shrewd look. "Just as you predicted." He stood abruptly, knocking over his chair, "I'll see to it," and strode down the hillside.

His appetite forgotten, Steffan rose from the table and gestured to Pip. "I'll meet with them in the pavilion. Admit only the general and the messenger. And tell Olaff to keep the other guards well away. I'll have no rumors tonight."

Catching the seriousness of his mood, Pip gave a solemn nod, holding the silk curtain aside like the perfect servant.

Steffan stepped into luxury. Braziers lit the interior, casting a golden glow against pavilion's walls of crimson silk. He'd ridden to war but not without his comforts. The pavilion served as a shelter and a stage, meeting the needs of a warrior while providing the rich trappings befitting a lord and a conqueror. A table cluttered with maps stood in one corner, next to a stand holding his armor, and a chest for his clothes. Pip had a pallet on one side, while Steffan's bed filled the other, a lush mound of pillows and furs. Soft rugs lay strewn across the floor, a gilded chair waiting in the middle like a throne. A battle banner hung behind the chair, a golden flame on a field of red, a reminder his status in Coronth's religious hierarchy.

Steffan grabbed a goblet and filled it with brandy, his mind raging with possibilities. Taking a seat on the throne, he downed the brandy, anxious to learn the details behind the Dark Lord's wrath.

Pip swept the outer curtain aside. "General Caylib and a messenger from Balor to see you, lord."

"Enter."

The general strode into the pavilion, his words confirming Steffan's premonition. "The Black Flames intercepted a messenger from Balor."

A look of understanding passed between them. Steffan turned his gaze to the courier.

Mud spattered and weary, the messenger swayed on his feet. Falling to his knees, he proffered a sealed scroll with shaking hands. "My lord, I've killed five horses to bring this scroll with all haste. Balor is in chaos. The Keeper of the Flame needs you."

The Keeper, not the Pontifax, a chill raced down Steffan's back. He broke the seal and snapped the scroll open. Written in a shaky hand, the message was full of rants and demands...but little information, so typical of the burly Keeper. "What happened to the Pontifax?"

The messenger swallowed, wiping his hands on his red tabard. "Dead, my lord."

Dead! "How?"

"Burnt, consumed by the flames," the man shuddered as if he could not believe his own words.

"How?"

"Taken by the Flame God in a Test of Faith."

Steffan sagged back in the chair, stunned by the news. Little wonder the Dark Lord had been enraged. The Pontifax had died the worst possible death...the type of death that could unravel a religion. "But how did this happen? Did you see it? Were you there?"

The messenger nodded. "I was there that day. Like so many others, I went to witness the Test of Faith." He shuddered, his voice heavy with remembering. "The Pontifax prayed as he always did and then he entered the flames. Barefoot, he walked straight into the blazing inferno, a vision of holiness. At first the flames caressed him, proving the miracle of the Test of Faith...but then the prisoner leaped in." He shook his head as if in denial. "The sinner and the holy man grappled in the heart of the flames, locked in a struggle, as if good and evil fought before our very eyes...but then they broke apart." His voice shook in disbelief. "And the impossible happened. The Flame

God took the Pontifax! Bursting into flames, he burnt like a common sinner. He writhed in the flames, consumed by the God's Fire. I watched him die but I still don't believe it." The messenger gazed up at Steffan, pleading in his voice. "How could it happen? How could he die like that?"

The tale struck like a nightmare, worse than anything Steffan had imagined. "Who did it? Who was this sinner?"

The messenger shrugged. "No one. Just an old woman."

An old woman!" The shout sprang unbidden to his lips. The messenger cringed while Steffan struggled to contain his rage. How could an old woman foil so many plans? He stared down at the hapless messenger. "And then?"

The messenger swallowed. "The people went insane. They rioted, killing priests, killing each other. Somehow the Keeper retreated to the Temple, but the city remains a beehive of hate. Balor is a city divided, the rabble on one side and the Keeper on the other."

Steffan shook his head, the bloody Keeper was never meant to rule. Stupid and brutish, he'd make a mess of Coronth.

The messenger gestured to the scroll. "My lord, the army is needed in Balor. You must return and save the Keeper." He started to stand.

"I did not give you leave to rise."

The soldier shrank to his knees, a flicker of fear in his eyes.

Steffan locked stares with the general, sending a silent message. He gestured to Pip. "Give the messenger a drink, we have much to discuss."

The messenger grabbed the goblet, downing the brandy in a single long swill.

"Good. Now you're going to tell me everything you know. No detail is too small. Take your time and tell me everything." Steffan leaned back in the chair, plying the man with questions, sifting through details. Over and over, he asked about the old woman, about the Pontifax, and about the Keeper. Candles burned to stubs, yet Steffan kept digging. He repeated the most important questions, finding different ways to ask the same thing, always looking for discrepancies. Many details became clear, but there was never a single mention of the ruby amulet. Steffan assumed the Keeper did not have it. Satisfied that he'd wrung every drop of information from the messenger, Steffan leaned back in the chair. "You've done well. But I need one more duty from you."

The messenger eased back on his heels, his face relieved, as if the long ordeal were over. "Anything, lord."

"I need your silence."

The general was lightning fast, his massive hands encasing the young man's head. With a single twist, he broke the messenger's neck. The body slumped dead at Steffan's feet, a look of shock etched on the young man's face.

"Well done." Steffan prodded the body with his boot. "Word of the Pontifax's death can never reach the army. All religions need their icons, especially fanatics."

The general's voice was gruff. "What will you do?"

"Do?"

"Do we fight...or return to Balor?"

"An army of religious fanatics is a rare and wondrous weapon, not to be squandered on a mere mob." Steffan's voice hardened to steel. "The death of the Pontifax is unfortunate, but it will not deter us from our goal. The holy war starts tomorrow. Lanverness waits like a maid with her legs spread wide, eager to be raped."

"But with the Pontifax dead, you could rule Coronth."

Such shrewdness from a barbarian, but Steffan sought a larger prize. "I already rule Coronth."

"Then why not return and claim the throne?"

Steffan smiled. "I'll tell you a secret. Always give the rabble something to love and something to hate. Once the people of Balor get a true taste of the Keeper's brutality, they'll welcome the Lord Raven home with open arms. They'll beg me to assume the throne." He flashed a grin. "But only after we've conquered Lanverness. One throne is not enough."

The general laughed, a ruthless sound. "I like you, counselor." Sobering, he nudged the messenger's body with his boot. "This one's silence is assured, but they'll be more from Balor."

"The Black Flames will intercept them, just like this one." Steffan settled the scroll into a brazier, watching the Keeper's message blacken to ash.

"The death of a ruler is a hard thing to hide. You won't keep it secret forever."

Another shrewd observation from the barbarian. "I don't need to. Once the war starts, once we have a few victories notched on our swords, then I'll tell the army." Steffan paused to consider the possibilities. "Sometimes setbacks are opportunities in disguise." The grim details of the Pontifax's death ran through his mind. "The best lies are based on truth. We'll say the Pontifax entered the Flames and ascended straight to heaven. Too holy to walk amongst mere men, the Flame God called him home, ascending to heaven on steps of fire. More proof of the Flame God's divine favor."

The general barked a laugh, his voice gruff with disbelief. "And you expect the soldiers to swallow that tripe?"

"Of course, if it's told the right way. A few embellishments and the faithful will be keen to believe it. In fact, the more fantastic the story the more likely they'll cleave to it. The ascension of the Pontifax will become another miracle, enshrined in the hearts of the faithful, more proof of the power of their god."

"And when they learn the truth, what then?"

"My dear general, truth is a relative thing." Steffan chuckled. "It all depends on which version the faithful believe first. Once people believe something it is very hard to get them to un-believe. It's all about faith not logic. That's the beauty of religion."

"You wield religion like a sword."

"Exactly." Steffan leaned back in the chair, a satisfied smile on his face. "But enough of religion, we have practicalities to discuss."

The general nodded, pouring himself another brandy.

"The roads from Balor must be guarded. Every messenger must be intercepted and thoroughly questioned before being silenced."

"It will be done."

"And I need three of your best men for a special mission." Steffan considered the task, anxious to gain control of the ruby amulet. "Choose three Black Flames with a bit of thief in their background. Dressed as common mercenaries, they'll need swift horses to return to Balor."

"To help the Keeper?"

"No, to look for something that is lost. Something that now belongs to me."

"What?"

"A weapon of religion."

The general scowled, clearly disinterested...exactly the way Steffan wanted it.

"Send the men to me and I'll explain their mission."

The general nodded. "And what about this one?" He nudged the body with his boot.

"Olaff will take care of it. One of the advantages of having a bodyguard who is also a mute."

"Anything else?"

Steffan raised his goblet in salute. "To victory. To the start of the holy war."

The general raised his own goblet, a wolfish grin on his face. "To blood and plunder." He swilled the brandy and then tossed the goblet on the ground, striding from the pavilion.

Steffan scowled at the general's ill manners. The man truly was a barbarian, but every barbarian had his uses. Re-filling his goblet, Steffan stepped out into the night chill, gazing down at the army of campfires. The death of the Pontifax was disappointing, even shocking, but it could be handled, as long as he kept the news from the soldiers. In fact, the old charlatan's death might prove a blessing. Properly embellished, his death could serve to deepen the conviction of the faithful, to hone his soldiers to a killing rage. An army of religious fanatics was a fearful weapon, unparalleled in all of Erdhe...and it was his to wield. Steffan smiled, feeling destiny coalesce around him. The Dark Lord's plans would come to fruition and Steffan would reap his just reward. One lifetime was not enough.

2

Danly

Six steps to the edge of sanity by ten steps to hell, Danly paced his domain, but his cell always remained the same. Iron shackles clanged with each step, a bitter sound, but at least his cell had light. Torchlight from the hallway striped the floor with shadows. His jailors had moved him up out of the deep dungeon, delivering him from eternal darkness, giving him a cell with bars and torchlight. A straw pallet, a slops bucket, and a wooden bowl adorned his princely domain, the lord of all he surveyed, but he hadn't stopped dreaming of the Rose throne. A bitter laugh burst out of him. Danly scratched at his armpit, fingernails digging for lice, an infernal itch from his loyal subjects.

Whispers reached him even in the dungeon. He knew the rebellion had failed, but even the vaunted Spider Queen could not have caught all the conspirators. Like lice waiting to bite, there had to be more Red Horns hiding in the court, biding their time, waiting for the chance to put a king on the Rose throne. He clung to the hope, hoarding it like a starving man's last breadcrumb, a meager dish but it was all he had besides hate.

A roach scurried between the iron bars, heading for his food bowl, a marauder invading his domain.

"You didn't beg our leave." His voice sounded hoarse with disuse.

The roach continued its impudent march.

"Beg our leave or risk our displeasure!" Danly pounced, capturing the invader beneath his hand. "Beg our royal leave."

A tickle of many legs served as the only reply.

"Then *die* for your insolence!" He slammed his hand against the floor, crushing the invader. Brown gore clung to his palm. Wiping it on his tattered tunic, he resumed walking, repeating the command as he paced. "Die for your insolence!" The words had a lordly sound, a command fit for a king. A pity he couldn't enforce the same sentence on his royal mother, but that sweet pleasure would have to wait till the Red Horns rescued him, till he claimed his crown. His chains clanked as he paced, six steps by ten steps, still stuck in hell.

Somewhere down the hall an iron door clanged open.

Danly froze, listening.

Footsteps came his way, a lot of footsteps...too early for the morning gruel.

He scuttled to the corner, crouching in the shadows, setting his back against the cold stone wall. If he hid, maybe they wouldn't see him, just a shadow-prince hiding in darkness.

The footsteps drew near. Torchlight revealed soldiers in emerald green tabards...and amongst the soldiers, a tall man in black robes.

"*Nooo.*" The word shivered from his lips like a ghostly wail.

The soldiers stopped at his cell, a clatter of keys at the lock.

Danly couldn't face another session in the pit. "You don't want me. I've told you everything. No more names to tell, no more names."

The cell door swung open.

Panic gripped him. "You don't have leave to enter!"

But they came anyway, two soldiers, their faces grim, their hands gripping their swords, and between them glided the man in black, the queen's shadowmaster, the one he hated almost as much as his royal mother. Hatred gave him strength. "So the queen's cockroach comes crawling, what do you want?"

"Justice comes for you."

The words struck like a dagger, piercing him with a shiver of fear.

The Master Archivist drew close, his voice unrelenting. "Long overdue and more merciful than you deserve, but justice none the less."

The mention of mercy gave Danly a slim hope. "But there's been no trial!"

"Condemned by your own words in front of the queen, the traitor prince."

Danly tried another approach. His voice pleading, he took a step toward his enemy. "But I gave you names. I helped you defeat the Red Horns."

"Too little, too late." The shadowmaster's dark gaze was implacable.

Danly played his last gambit. "But...I've repented! I regret what I did." His gaze jumped from the master to the soldiers, desperate for sympathy. "I claim the clemency of the crown! Surely the queen's own son deserves mercy!"

"What you deserve is to be drawn and quartered."

Danly retreated, shrinking to a crouch, his back pressed against the cold stones.

But the master's words chased after him. "You deserve a public execution. Lashed to a butcher's block and dismembered by a skilled executioner, sliced bit by bit until the last thing you see is your traitorous heart beating in his hand."

"*No!*" A stream of hot urine gushed down Danly's leg.

Scorn washed across the master's face. "But I've come to give you a choice."

Danly grasped at the word. "A choice?"

The master nodded. "More mercy than you deserve." He raised his voice to a command, "Come."

More footsteps answered from the hallway. A red-robed apothecary, old and wrinkled, shuffled into view. A pair of soldiers in emerald green followed carrying a massive chopping block...and behind them, a black-hooded executioner bearing a gleaming axe.

"*Noooo!*" Danly scuttled into the corner. "*I don't want to die!*"

The master's voice cut through his panic. "I bring you a choice."

He clutched at the straw. "What choice?"

"Justice will be served." The shadowmaster was a stern pillar cloaked in black. "Even in the dungeons, the traitor prince is a threat to the queen and her rightful heir. That threat must be eliminated. So I bring you a choice, the axe or the knife."

Danly shuddered. "I d-don't understand."

The master gestured to the executioner. "The axe offers a quick and painless death, far more mercy than you deserve." He pointed toward the red-robed apothecary. "Or choose the knife. Keep your life but lose your manhood and be exiled from Lanverness on pain of death."

Danly covered his manhood with his hands. "That's no choice!"

"It's more choice than a traitor-prince deserves."

Danly's stare skittered around the cell, a trapped rat seeking escape, desperate for another way. The cell door gaped open, a tantalizing hope, so close but yet so far. Needing a diversion, he spit in the master's face and danced sideways, avoiding the soldiers while angling for the door.

"*Seize him!*"

Soldiers leaped to obey, but Danly was quick, squirming away from outstretched arms. Desperate for a weapon, he grabbed the chamber pot, hurling the brown sludge at the nearest guard. The stinking night soil struck the soldier in the face. Blinded by filth, the guard howled a curse, clawing at his eyes. Danly scampered past. Straining against his shackles, he lunged for the door. The white-whiskered apothecary blocked the doorway...but the old man chose to step aside.

Danly slipped past, sprinting for the promise of freedom...till a massive hand grabbed his neck. He squirmed but the hand tightened like a vise, dragging him back to the cell.

"*No!*" Danly fought, but the burly executioner yanked him to his toes. Shaking him like a rag doll, the executioner held him before the queen's shadowmaster.

The master's face was a mask of wrath. "Justice has finally caught you."

The soldier covered in brown stink drew his sword, his voice a smear of anger. "Let me gut him. This one doesn't deserve a quick death." He stepped towards the prince, his sword poised to strike.

Danly flinched from the hate in the soldier's eyes.

"No." The master's order stopped the sword stroke. "He'll have his choice." The shadowmaster's stare drilled into the prisoner-prince. "Do you know how Lord Turner died?"

Danly shook his head, knowing he did not want to hear this.

"He died screaming, cooked alive in a cauldron of boiling water, a parboiled traitor."

Danly's stomach convulsed but there was nothing to spew.

"You deserve the same fate, yet I give you a better choice." The master stepped close. "Decide." The word stabbed like a knife. "The headsman's axe...or the castrator's knife?"

Danly squirmed but the executioner held him fast. He stared at the shadowmaster but he knew he'd get no quarter there. His mind skittered in desperation, searching for a way out, and then it came to him. "The queen!" Danly thought he saw a flicker of hesitation in the master's cold stare. He latched onto the thought like a drowning man. "The queen wouldn't do this! Not like this! There'd be a trial, everything done above board and in the light of day." Laughter bubbled out of him, a mad sound tinged with desperation. "You're acting without orders." His voice dropped to a whisper, one conspirator to another. "Never usurp the Spider Queen's power. She'll turn on you...as she turned on me. My mother eats her own. She'll eat you alive."

A fist punched Danly square in the jaw. His head whipped back, an explosion of pain, yet the executioner held him firm. Danly coughed, spitting blood, realizing he'd bitten his tongue.

The master leaned close, his face enraged. "Never speak ill of the queen."

"You hit me!" Danly's words held a royal outrage, but then he realized the master's icy demeanor was shattered. He giggled. "You've slept with her! The whore-queen and her shadow-toy."

The master drew a dagger, a sharp sting beneath Danly's chin. "*Decide* or I'll decide for you. Your head or your cock?"

Death stared at him, cold and eager. Danly's thoughts fled. He gripped his manhood, his voice reduced to a weak croak. "Not my life..."

"You never were much of a man." The master stepped back. "Geld him."

"*No!*" Danly struggled, but the executioner held him firm. The shit-stained guard used a knife to cut away Danly's trousers, ripping them down his legs. A rush of cool air on his privates brought a new wave of panic. "*No, you can't do this!*"

Another guard knelt to unlock his leg-irons. The clink of iron sounded like a death knell.

"*No!*" Danly kicked and fought but the executioner was too strong. The big man muscled him toward the chopping block, pressing his back down on the bloodstained wood. Danly arched his back, struggling to wiggle free, but the executioner slammed him down, forcing his bare buttocks against the hard wood.

The red-robed apothecary leaned close, his voice dry as leather. "Spread his legs and hold him tight."

Soldiers grabbed Danly's legs, pulling his thighs apart, like a maid spread wide before the rape.

"No!" He could not believe this was happening to him. Danly's mind exploded in fear, a gush of stink erupting from his bowels. "*Don't do this!*"

The apothecary forced a wooden rod between Danly's teeth, his voice a calm whisper. "Two cuts and it will all be over. Two cuts to make a man into a maid."

Danly felt the knife against his privates, cold and keen. And then the screaming started...a scream from the depths of his soul, from the very depths of hell.

3

The Priestess

A fiery scent pervaded the market, leaving a searing heat on her tongue. The Priestess licked her lips like a cat tasting cream, *firespice,* a taste to burn away all others. For those born beyond Radagar's borders it was a formidable flavor, a remnant of the scorching desert brought to Erdhe by nomadic warriors, but although she was not native-born, she liked the heat.

Food sellers hawked their wares, offering roasted lizards skewered on sticks, grilled chicken hearts cooked with onions, and rounds of pan-fried bread, everything saturated with the all pervasive firespice. The Priestess wandered the clogged stalls of the royal market, enjoying the fiery scents. Rings on her fingers, golden sandals on her feet, she wore crimson robes of the finest silk and a veil across her face, a mark of wealth and refinement. A faint breeze ruffled the silk of her robes, just sheer enough to be almost indecent. *Almost,* she smiled feeling the piercing stares of greedy merchants and jealous women following in her wake.

Trailing a hand across bolts of silk, she admired the vibrant blues and exotic yellows, another echo of the desert past. From the sheer silk veils, to the scantily dressed pillow-slaves, to the exotic aphrodisiacs and the all-pervasive firespice, she took the pulse of the royal city. The market proved little had changed in the mercenary kingdom. Radagar's royalty liked their meals spicy and their pleasures hot. But pleasures were something the Priestess knew very well. A man's appetites often held the key to his defeat, especially a king's. The Priestess hid a knowing smile; she'd come to Radagar to turn up the heat.

Snapping her fingers, she summoned her steward, Otham. A tall imposing man with a bald head and a square jaw, he lengthened his stride and inclined his head, his voice a deep rumble. "Yes, mistress."

She gestured to a fabric seller. "I'll have the bolt of lame, the gold cobras stitched on sheer white silk."

"As you wish, mistress." Otham went to do her bidding, yet she was not alone. Three guards followed at a discrete distance, three of the thirty she'd brought from the Isle of the Oracle, all of them clad in ordinary fighting leathers, all of them excellent swords. She knew Radagar well enough to be wary; hence the guards trailing in her wake, yet the danger only heightened the market's pleasure.

So many sights and smells, the great market brought a rush of memories, as much a source of entertainment as trade. A muzzled bear danced for copper coins while a fire breathing juggler spouted gouts of flame. Sweat-stained mercenaries gave exhibitions of sword strokes, thrilling a cluster of small boys. Salt sellers hawked their wares amongst merchants selling toadstones guaranteed to thwart any poison. The exotic next to the ordinary, such was Salmythra, the capital city of Radagar, a boil of intrigues, poisons, and mercenaries...a place where the Priestess felt at home.

She flowed through the crowd to the market's heart, to stalls cluttered with bright bottles and stoppered flasks where the herb-witches and apothecaries plied their trade of potions. Rare elixirs and exotic ingredients held the promise of passion or death. Sensing a customer, a shrewd-eyed crone leaned from her stall, proclaiming the virtues of her brews. "A love potion to bind the heart of your paramour and keep him forever true!"

A competitor shouted, "An elixir of Calamint, pledged to cure your lover's wandering eye!"

"Ointment of Lady's Mantle to enhance the beauty of your breasts!"

"Tincture of Aarach to extend your man's stamina! Rampant like a bull in heat, he'll give you hours of pleasure for a single silver!"

Amused, the Priestess passed them with a knowing smile. Salmythra was famous across Erdhe for its aphrodisiacs, but nothing bottled or brewed could compare to the power of her own allure. When it came to the secrets of the bedchamber, she had no rivals, yet she'd come to the market for a purpose. Ignoring the sellers of potions, she finally reached the stalls of fresh ingredients. The market of Salmythra sold ingredients to healers or assassins, life and death sold side by side. She strolled among the stalls, surveying the offerings with a practitioner's eye. The market was well stocked despite the lateness of the season. Fresh leaves of purple belladonna, the rootstock of hellebore, bark shavings of black locust, and jars of the rarest snake venom all stood on display. So many poisons, so many cures, but nothing unique, nothing she did not already have in her own chest of ingredients, the harvest from her garden of deathly delights. Yet the Priestess persisted, needing something fresh, something with a double entendre, a message within a message.

Most flowers were out of season, so an herb or a poison would have to serve. A sprig of bright green caught her attention. Intrigued, the Priestess turned toward the stall. The leather-faced merchant was quick to fawn. "Madam has a keen eye." He fondled the leaves, extending a bundle toward her. "Old Latham offers the finest mistletoe in all of the great market. Strong enough to make a barren woman fat with child," he lowered his voice to a whisper, "or powerful enough to put passion to your lover's rod." He gave her a wicked grin. "A stiff rod is a good thing."

Her veil hid her smile. "How was this harvested?"

"Cut from the top boughs of a mighty oak and dropped into a white cloak." The merchant gave her a knowing look, "Old Latham sells only mistletoe that has never touched the ground, ensuring the full potency of the magic."

She gestured toward a bundle in the back. "Let me see that one."

"Ah, so the lady knows her lore." He offered the bundle with a wink and a nod. "White berries for healing, but the rarer red is best for passion."

She checked the leaves, lush and green, and the berries, ripe and red, a fine specimen. "Yes, this will do."

Otham stepped forward to pay the old man, not bothering to dicker. The Priestess turned away, intending to leave the market, but the seductive notes of a flute caught her interest. The sinuous melody led her to the market's edge, to a young boy sitting cross-legged before a basket. A pair of royal cobras, hoods flared, danced to the lilting song. Snake charmers were common in Radagar. The descendants of the desert-born were enthralled by the deadly serpents, but the boy displayed an uncommon gift, working two cobras at once.

Intrigued, the Priestess watched the performance, studying the boy. A long tumble of auburn curls hid his eyes, but beneath the filth lay a cherub's face, pretty enough for a harem, beauty wasted on the market. The tempo of the flute increased. The cobras hissed, fangs exposed, hoods flared wide, following the weave of the music. Death and beauty entwined...another double entendre. The possibilities were delicious. She gestured for Otham. He leaned close to hear her whisper. "I might have a use for this one. Clean him up and keep him near."

Otham nodded. "As you wish, mistress."

She turned, a veiled swirl of crimson and gold, and made her way back through the maze of city streets. One of her guards drew close, taking Otham's place, his hand on his sword hilt, his gaze alert. The streets were busy but none dared do more than stare, commoners making way for the veiled lady and her guards.

She reached the inn where she'd rented a nest of apartments and climbed the stairs to the second floor. Two guards stood watch on the balcony. One snapped a salute while the other rushed to open the door.

The bustle of the streets receded, replaced by a shadowed sanctuary of silks and incense. Her handmaidens, Tara and Lydia, sank to deep curtseys. She waved them away, along with the guards. "Leave me." Veils fluttered to the thick carpet, freeing her face. She shook out her long raven-black hair, a shimmer of darkness. Taking a deep breath, she entered the inner chamber, where the silver scrying bowl waited.

Shrugging off her robes, she knelt naked on the scatter of pillows, staring into the silver bowl. Water waited in the bowl, clear and placid. Taking slow deep breaths; she stilled her mind, reaching for the Darkness within. The Priestess closed her eyes, yearning for the touch of the Dark God. Her thoughts turned to the Isle of the Oracle, to the ancient well hidden in the hawthorn grove. Words of ritual sprang to her lips, invoking the ancient power. She swayed to the rhythm of desire, feeling the nearness of her Lord. The shadows coalesced. A weave of Darkness settled across her shoulders like a lover's embrace. Cold seeped into her skin, an inhuman touch. "Yours to use." Her breath misted in the sudden chill.

Darkness clasped her from behind, hard and insistent. Power spiked through her as the Dark Lord claimed his Priestess. She writhed with pleasure and moaned with pain, arching her back with each thrust. And then she was alone, abandoned on the pillows, a sheen of sweat like dew on her skin. The Darkness was gone but an undercurrent of power remained. She thrummed with sexual power, like molten lava coursing through her veins.

The Eye of the Oracle awoke.

A power throbbed between her breasts, a second heartbeat full of dark designs. She removed the slender chain from her neck, freeing the great moonstone from its clasp. The oval gemstone filled her palm. A legend of darker times, it glowed pale like a winter moon.

Bowing in homage, she settled the moonstone into the scrying bowl. The water hissed and churned, swallowing the gem with a clash of power. The Priestess held her breath, knowing the Eye had a reputation for claiming the life of the user...but not this time. The surface calmed and the waters turned midnight-black, a mirror of the Dark Lord's Oracle.

She leaned forward, her raven hair cascading around the bowl, creating a veil of shadows. The water lay dark and still, devoid of any reflection. She breathed on the surface, casting her power into the scrying bowl. "Show me the servants of the Dark Lord."

Colors swirled across the water, sharpening to images, giving her a bird's-eye view of a blond haired man escorted by soldiers in black and gold armor. A forked banner rippled overhead, midnight-black tipped in bright red, the dreaded Darkflamme, the battle banner of the Mordant. Needing to be sure, the Priestess focused her will causing the image tightened on his face...the same face she'd seen Awakened in the monastery. The Mordant reached for his armies in the north, but he was not yet crowned. There was still time to make her bid for power.

She blew a ripple across the water and focused her thoughts on another. The scene shifted to an arrogant man, dark and handsome, astride a roan stallion. Steffan rode at the head of a vast army. Halberds gleamed in the morning light as they marched south at a ground-eating pace. "Hurry, Steffan, now is the time to strike." He glanced aloft as if listening, but she knew it was only an illusion; communication was beyond the power of the Eye.

"Show me more." Ripples pulsed across the water, changing the scene. The Eye showed her a young man haggard with fever and pain, writhing on a straw-covered wagon bed. She recognized his face, *the eunuch prince released from the dungeons, a hidden dagger against the throne of Lanverness.* Plans percolated in her mind. She'd keep a close watch on the fallen royal, hoping he survived...but first she had another prince to catch, a contender for a different throne.

A wave of dizziness assaulted her. The Eye fed on her power, a relentless pull, but she was not yet done. The Priestess focused her will, drawing the last of her power, searching for a prince from her past. She saw him then, turbaned and proud, full of schemes and Darkness, his face achingly familiar. Once she'd served him, but that was before the Dark Lord. Soon the tables would be turned, the student now the master. She looked forward to this evening, to a triumph long awaited.

The scene shifted and she saw other faces, other minions of Darkness, but none interested her half as much as the first four. Her vision blurred. She gasped, sagging back on her heels, caught in a wave of dizziness. Her body was drained by the Eye. She needed to feed on a lover's passion. The dark waters bled to clear. The gemstone sat dormant at the bottom of the bowl, as dull as bone.

The Priestess reached for the gem. She cradled the moonstone against her breasts, whispering a promise. "Tonight, between silken sheets." The dizziness passed, as if appeased, and she rose to her feet.

She crossed the room and knelt to unlock the large rosewood chest. Turning the skeleton key to the left instead of the right, she avoided the trap of poison-tipped needles. The lock clicked open, releasing the familiar scents of dried herbs and dark ingredients. Her gaze caressed her secret hoard, taking a silent inventory. Honeycombed with drawers and hidden compartments, the chest held a lifetime of collected lore. Stoppered bottles, slender vials, and drawstring bags held her harvest from the Isle of Souls. She knew each component by name and by nature, so many ways to death, but her panoply of poisons would not be needed tonight. Instead, she released the catch on a secret drawer, removing a small velvet bag. Unwilling to risk the Eye at the prince's court, she slipped the moonstone into the bag and returned it to the drawer, a single treasure hidden amongst a hundred deaths.

Locking the chest, she reset the trap and then used a hand bell to summon her servants. Two handmaidens, one fair and the other dark, scurried into the room, dropping into deep curtseys.

"Tara, prepare my bath. A mixture of honeysuckle and sandalwood for tonight, sweetness leavened with the mystery of dark allure."

The golden-haired servant leaped to obey while Lydia helped the Priestess back into her robes, a swirl of crimson silk wrapped in artful folds.

"Have Hugo guard the rosewood chest. Let no one touch it on pain of death."

"Yes, mistress."

She found Otham waiting in her solar, her loyal steward bound by duty as well as passion. He gave her a half-bow. "All is as you ordered, mistress."

"The mistletoe?"

"Delivered on a silken pillow to the prince's palace."

"And the bribe?"

"Will see to it that your gift is delivered to the prince himself."

"And the boy, the snake charmer?"

"Bought for a handful of silvers. The guards will have him clean and ready for your pleasure."

She made her voice a purr. "You've done well...as always." Her fingertips played across his chest in a thoughtful tease. He was an accomplished lover...and her need was great.

Still as a statue, he gave her a smoldering stare, a cobra entranced by a flute.

Hunger reared within her, a fierce desire to take a lover, to drink his passion and renew her power. She bit her lip and forced it back...a tigress locked in too small a cage. "You may undress me."

His breath caught. He knelt and kissed her hand, a hunger of lips across her palm, a flick of tongue caressing her skin.

"Undress only."

His kisses stopped, his voice turning petulant, "Yes, mistress," but his hands continued their temptation, slowly drawing the silk away from her body. He made it a slow dance, lingering on each layer, till she stepped naked from a puddle of crimson silk. He stared, begging for more, his body betraying his need.

Taking pleasure from the tease, she let her hand brush against his straining manhood. "That will be all."

His jaw tightened. "Yes, mistress." Bowing, he took his leave, his face hungry with wanting.

She laughed, a throaty sound, and followed the scents of honeysuckle and sandalwood to the inner room. Easing into the steaming bath, she relaxed as her handmaidens rubbed oils into her skin, deft fingers running through her long raven hair. Desire pulsed through her, honed by Otham's tease, but the hunger would make her allure all the more potent, her victory all the sweeter. She looked forward to her night with the prince, to changing the destiny of a kingdom, to winning the Dark Lord's favor...forever more.

4

Liandra

So many ambitious men, her kingdom ran amok with them. The execution of the traitorous Red Horns had created vacancies in the Rose court, vacancies as high as the queen's council. From all across Lanverness, her 'loyal' lords had flocked to the palace, vying for her favor. She'd sifted through them, prizing intelligence and loyalty above all else...but all too often she compromised on both. Queen Liandra studied her counselors, the rich and the powerful, the grasping and the greedy. Like rutting stags, they competed for her attention, their voices clashing like antlers.

"Gentlemen, this argument does us no good." Her glare circled the council table, displeasure writ large across her face. "War is thrust upon us, an enemy army poised on our northern border. We need answers not arguments."

"But surely your majesty can see the wisdom of negotiations?" Lord Lenox was new to her council. A pinched-faced man with steel-gray hair, he replaced Lord Wesley as the new treasurer. "A delegation should be sent to Coronth to try and broker peace with the Pontifax."

The queen shot a subtle glance at Master Raddock, ensuring the silence of her deputy shadowmaster.

"*Peace!*" Prince Stewart made the word a curse. "Have you heard nothing? An *army* marches toward Lanverness! Without any declaration of war, without any provocation, yet they dare invade and you would have us sue for *peace!*" The prince glared daggers at the newly appointed treasurer.

Lord Lenox withstood the challenge with surprising poise. "Peace is always preferable to war."

"Platitudes against swords!" The prince shook his head, disgust ripe on his face. "Have you learned nothing from the refugees? Torture and atrocities are a way of life under the Pontifax." The prince clenched his jaw, making the freshly earned scar pulse along his face. "Steel is the only answer. We meet swords with swords...and heaven help us if we're not victorious."

Lord Lenox parried the argument with a flick of his quill. "Swords should be a last resort. Prepare the army but try negotiations first."

Major Ranoth, a craggy-faced veteran assigned as a military aid to the council, leaned across the table. "Me thinks the lord seeks to protect his holdings in the north."

The queen silently agreed, yet she let the interchange play out.

Lord Lenox sputtered with indignation. "How dare you! Everyone loses in a war." He appealed to the queen, his voice laden with reason. "Surely your majesty will agree to a delegation? After all, it is the *civilized* solution."

Twelve counselors turned their her way.

"Civilized, yes, and therein lies the problem." The queen fingered the strand of rubies at her throat, lessons from the Red Horns sharp in her mind. "Tell us, how does one fight a 'civilized' war? When barbarians storm the gates, do the defenders hurl words instead of rocks?" Her treasurer dared not meet her gaze. "War is not like chess. There are no rules." She nodded to her royal son, his handsome face marred by a saber stroke. "When it comes to war, perhaps being 'civilized' is a fatal flaw. Perhaps it will be our undoing?" Her gaze circled the table like a knight eager for the joust, but none had the wit or the courage to tilt with her. The silence lengthened, vexing her patience. She missed the Master Archivist. "It was not a rhetorical question."

Murmurs rippled around the table, but before her counselors could muster a reply, she turned her gaze on her new treasurer, deciding to skewer him on his own argument. "Lord Lenox," the sharp-faced lord sat straighter in his chair, "since you so vehemently sue for negotiations, we assume you will lead this delegation of peace?"

"Me?" The lord blustered like a ruffled rooster. "I'm no diplomat." His gaze raced around the chamber, seeking support. "Surely the Lord Treasurer is needed in the capital city?"

The queen answered with a dose of irony. "Surely."

Prince Stewart leaned forward, eager for the kill, but the queen stilled him with a glance. She surveyed her counselors, putting steel in her voice. "Make no mistake, gentlemen, *war* marches toward us. To deny the inevitable is nothing short of folly." She took note of the three lords who would not meet her gaze and wondered if she brewed another batch of traitors. "This council is summoned to answer a single question. How can an army of ten thousand defeat an army of forty thousand?"

"*Forty thousand?*" The threat echoed through the chamber.

The queen nodded, confirming the grim truth. "The latest estimate smuggled out of Coronth."

"Perhaps the estimate is wrong?" Lord Lenox was nothing if not persistent.

"Never underestimate the enemy." Her stare cut like a knife. "We trust you to count coins better than you do swords."

The treasurer blanched and looked away, chagrin on his face.

"What about mercenaries?" The question came from the far end of the table, from Lord Saddler, a goldsmith newly raised to the master of coin. The stout little man rarely spoke yet his sparse comments brought a breath of realism to the council chambers.

The queen favored him with a smile. "A good question. The Master Archivist is in Radagar as we speak; seeking to purchase the full might of the mercenary kingdom. Ten thousand bought swords will help...but it will not be enough." Her gaze settled on her royal son. "Strategy must triumph over numbers."

The prince nodded, his face grave. "The queen tasked me with this very same question. Since then, I have sought the advice of our generals, our veterans, and even our sergeants. The answers are as varied as the men. Some advocate making a stand at the border, hoping for a single decisive battle. Others argue that we should retreat to our strongest fortresses, letting stone walls compensate for numbers, daring the enemy to a lengthy siege."

Liandra kept her face impassive but she listened with pride. Her son had grown into the role of general, the battle scar adding gravity to his face. "And what does the crown prince recommend?"

"Neither. Given the numbers against us, a single battle is doomed to fail. And retreating behind fortress walls yields too much advantage to the enemy. So instead we shall wage a war of harassment, biting at the enemy's flanks, attacking his supply lines, fighting a series of ambushes at locations that best serve our smaller numbers. We'll seek a war of skirmishes, always retreating from a major battle."

"And the cost?" She'd discussed this with her son ahead of time, but the council needed to hear it.

He took a deep breath, as if plunging into the ocean. "This type of battle plan requires patience...and a lot of map."

Too many of her councilors looked confused. She prompted him for more. "Meaning?"

"The Rose army must constantly retreat, taking advantage of every hillock and valley, always nibbling at the enemy's flanks. Given the size of the enemy army, it will take many bites and many more leagues before the enemy is nibbled down to size." The prince twirled the gold signet ring on his right hand and then raised his stare to the queen. "With such a strategy, the war may come to the very gates of Pellanor."

"*No!*" Lord Lenox bellowed in outrage. "The capital must be protected at all costs!"

The prince bludgeoned the lord with cold hard facts. "Pellanor cannot be defended." Shocked silence met his words. "The city sprawls beyond its walls. Shops and houses crowd close to the battlements, negating their value. Castle Tandroth has become a luxury palace instead of a military fortress." His voice turned hard. "The city cannot be defended."

A grim hush settled over the council chamber.

The queen took a deep breath, chilled by the obvious truth. "Betrayed by our own prosperity." She shook her head. "Peace has civilized us beyond the memory of war."

Prince Stewart nodded. "Just so."

"But there must be something we can do?" It was Master Saddler, ever the practical one. "We can't just wait for war to come to Pellanor?"

The prince offered an answer. "I suggest the queen and her councilors move the capital to Kardiff, our strongest fortress. Set high on a hill, the walls of Kardiff Castle are built strong, a challenge for any army."

"No." Liandra stood at the head of the table, a shimmer of rubies and red velvet. "We are a symbol to our people. We will not retreat in the face of danger."

"But..."

She stilled her son with a single glance. "Courage must overcome the deficit of swords. The people will keep their courage if they see their queen standing firm." She made her voice a command. "The Rose Court will remain in Pellanor."

Storms raged across her councilors' faces...but they knew better than to argue.

The queen resumed her throne, smoothing the folds of her gown, her voice business-like once more. "We approve this strategy of skirmishes. But we must do more. We ask this council for suggestions."

Most of her lords stared at her, a mixture of shock and anger written large across their faces, while others murmured quietly among themselves. The truth had unsettled her loyal men, driving their wits from the chamber. Liandra missed the Master Archivist...in more ways than one.

Impatient, she tapped her ringed fingers on the tabletop. When no suggestions were forthcoming, she answered her own question. "An army must eat. We shall deny our enemy a full belly. Perhaps hunger will turn the soldiers of the Flame back to Coronth."

"How?" It was the Lord Sheriff this time, the leader of the constable force.

The queen replied. "The harvest was good this year, but instead of leaving it stored in barns and granaries dotted across the countryside, it must be collected and brought to Kardiff, Graymaris, Lingard, and Pellanor, to any castle or walled city that can protect the harvest and keep it beyond our enemy's reach."

Master Saddler shook his head. "Farmers will not easily give up their harvest. It's their livelihood and their winter stores."

"Yet they must give it up for the sake of the kingdom."

Lord Lenox blustered, "This is outrageous! A royal robbery! Surely the noble estates will be exempt from this thievery. Collect the harvest from the rabble farmers if you must but you dare not touch the estates of nobles, else you destroy the very fabric of the kingdom."

She gave the lord a withering stare. "Do you suppose the enemy will bypass your holdings, leaving your vineyards and orchards intact?"

"One can hope."

The man was deluded by greed. She regretted appointing him to her council. "There will be *no* exceptions."

Lord Lenox lowered his voice. "Careful madam, or your policies will breed enemies."

Gasps echoed through the chamber.

The Lord Lenox grew bold in his greed. She gave him a stinging stare, her voice cracking like a lash. "Enemies of the crown do not live long. Or have you forgotten the fate of the Red Horns?" She locked stares with her treasurer, like a pair of crossed swords...but it was the lord who flinched first, suddenly staring at the tabletop. "Pray that we win, Lord Lenox, else you may find yourself a landless commoner forced to take the test of faith."

A chill settled over the council chambers.

The queen studied her lords, staring at each in turn. Her policies would surely create enemies but first she needed to save the kingdom. Taking a deep breath, she smoothed the folds of her gown and returned to the business at hand. "The Rose army will be given a royal writ to collect the harvest. Farmers will be fairly compensated with one quarter of the market value in coin and the remainder in the form of a chit exchangeable for silver or food."

The lord sheriff replied. "And if they protest?"

"Then they break the queen's peace." Liandra made her voice hard. "We cannot feed the invaders." She nodded to the prince. "Start in the north and work your way south. Every sow, milk cow, and bag of grain must be removed from the enemy's path."

"My men will be stretched thin."

"We will *all* be stretched thin before this war is done. But we will place the constable force under your command, swelling the ranks of the army."

The prince nodded but the lord sheriff stiffened with displeasure.

"What about the villages? Why leave anything to succor the enemy?" The query came from Lord Mills, another recent appointment to her council. Wealthy and well connected, the dapper lordling had a smug smile on his handsome face. He could afford to be smug, seeing as most of his holdings were safe in the south.

"You offer a suggestion, Lord Mills?"

Dark eyes gleamed in a handsome face. "Poison the wells and burn the villages as the Rose army retreats south. Leave nothing for the enemy."

The queen suppressed a shudder. "We seek to save Lanverness not destroy it."

Lord Mills parried her glare with a sarcastic smile. "Perhaps the queen is too civilized for war?"

His words hit like a slap. "We will not become our enemy."

"What does a woman know of war?"

A gasp rippled through the chamber. Prince Stewart reached for his sword but the queen stilled him with a glance. Cold anger seeped through her. "Our sex has never diminished our achievements. Under *our* reign, Lanverness prospers beyond all memory." Steel laced her voice. "We rule with the body of a queen and the heart and stomach of a king. We warn you not to test our resolve."

"But you've only ruled in times of peace. Perhaps a king is needed in times of war, an iron hand to hold the sword."

"If we made a eunuch of you, Lord Mills, would your worth as a councilor be diminished or enhanced?"

Shock echoed from the faces of her lords.

"We dare wager your intellect would be enhanced."

Lord Mills flushed crimson. "Now the royal claws come out." The dark-haired lord gave her a twisted smile. "You're utterly ruthless with those who rebel, even with your own royal son." His voice held a nasty edge. "Why not turn that ruthless nature against the enemy?"

The barb made no sense, for she'd given no orders regarding Danly. The queen floundered for an answer.

Prince Stewart intervened, his eyes flashing with anger. "In Lanverness, even royal traitors get their just reward."

So the lordling's barb made sense to her son...yet Danly remained locked in prison, awaiting her decision. Understanding struck like a sword to her breast. Somehow Danly had faced justice...despite her indecision...and everyone in the council knew it. *Everyone save the queen.* Liandra reeled from the knowledge, forcing her face to remain impassive while her blood ran cold with fury. *Someone dared usurp her power, issuing orders behind her back. Someone she trusted.* Her mind ran wild with speculation...but she dared show no weakness before her loyal lords. Hiding her unease behind a cloak of royal anger, she confronted Lord Mills. "If you have any suggestions, we will hear them. But be advised, we shall use *all* of our power to preserve the land, the people...and *our* crown."

The dapper lord sketched a half-bow but his voice was full of sarcasm. "Your people expect no less."

The queen's voice dropped to a dangerous whisper. "Have a care, Lord Mills, else some may think you a Red Horn in counselor's clothing."

Lord Mills had the good sense to look away.

Anxious to end the meeting, the queen surveyed the rest of her lords. More than one had the sense to bow their heads in submission. "Any questions?"

The red-haired sheriff nodded, his face thoughtful. "You've ordered the harvest collected and brought to Kardiff, Graymaris, Lingard, and Pellanor. The first three have stout fortresses and are easily defended...but why Pellanor?"

"If the enemy reaches Pellanor, then the ploy of hunger has failed." Her words cast a pall on the chamber. "Now you know what we face." She rose from the throne, regal in rubies and red velvet. "Despite the odds, we shall prevail. We expect our lords to conduct themselves with courage and steadfast determination. Victory will be ours."

Twelve lords bowed toward their queen, "Victory to Lanverness," but the conviction in their words was mixed.

Anger flashed through her, leaching into her voice. "Prince Stewart, Master Raddock, with me." Turning abruptly, she strode from the chamber without giving her counselors a chance to take their leave, a sure sign of her royal displeasure.

A pair of guards rushed to open the doors. Courtiers and servants hovered outside but she waved them away with a frown. Anger laced her stride. Something was amiss in her court, something she did not understand. The queen outpaced her entourage, footsteps echoing in the marble corridors. Her thoughts raced ahead, replaying conversations, recalling faces, sifting through facts and rumors. The Spider Queen could ill afford to be outplayed, especially when war threatened her kingdom, but logic led Liandra to an answer she could not accept.

Guards snapped to attention while a young page rushed to open the doors to her private sanctuary. Liandra swept into her solar, instantly embraced by the scent of pine logs and the crackling warmth of a glowing hearth...but the simple comforts could not dispel her unease.

Lady Sarah stepped from the shadows, holding a tray of fresh-baked scones and honeyed milk. "I thought..."

The mere sight of food roiled the queen's stomach. "Perhaps later." Taking a seat on the carved throne set in front of the blazing fireplace, Liandra arranged the pleats of her gown to best accent her hourglass figure. Image was as much a habit as it was her armor.

A knock came from the outer door.

"The guards may admit Prince Stewart and Master Raddock, but everyone else is to be denied." Her voice brooked no argument. "We need time alone with our counselors."

"Shall I leave the tray?"

"No." The queen stared into the fire, considering the ambitions of her 'loyal' men.

Lady Sarah curtseyed and retreated from the solar. A moment later, Prince Stewart and the dark-robed deputy shadowmaster entered. The two men bowed and waited for permission to sit.

Permission was not given.

Liandra drummed her bejeweled hands on the throne, a sure sign of her displeasure, yet her two advisors remained stubbornly mute. "Knowledge is power, yet it seems knowledge has been withheld from your sovereign queen."

A warning glance passed between the two men but neither spoke. Liandra considered the two men. Tall with broad-shoulders, her royal son stood like a soldier on parade, his booted-feet spread wide, his right hand resting on the hilt of his blue sword, his gaze direct and uncomplicated. By contrast, the deputy shadowmaster slouched beneath dark robes, his gaze roving around the chamber as if searching for a threat...or an escape route. Short and barrel-chested, Master Raddock had the look of a back-alley brawler instead of a counselor to the wealthiest monarch in all of Erdhe. A smashed nose and an old scar ruined his pug face, a reflection of his low birth and shady past, yet the man had a cunning intellect that earned him the position of deputy shadowmaster, the right hand to the Master Archivist. The queen had approved Raddock's rise in power, recognizing that exceptional abilities often belied the circumstances of birth, yet sometimes she wondered if Raddock's loyalties resided with his sovereign queen...or with the lord who'd rescued him from the thieves' gallows.

Silence hung like a shroud in the room. The queen decided on a frontal attack. "We will hear a report on the fate of Prince Danly."

Neither spoke.

"Master Raddock, we will hear from you."

The master's eyes narrowed to dark pinpricks, like a cornered rat desperate to hide. "The traitor-prince," he cleared his throat, "everything was done according to orders."

His words stoked her fear, yet she held her voice steady. "Then you saw the orders, signed with our signature and affixed with our royal seal?"

"No..." his voice was hesitant, "the orders came...through the usual channels."

It was like prying teeth from hens. "And what were those orders?"

"To give the traitor-prince a choice." The spymaster's face hardened.

"A choice?"

"To lose his head...or his manhood."

The queen clutched the armrests, struggling to contain her shock. Statue-still, she harkened back to another conversation when the grim choice had first been proposed. Remembering the man who made the suggestion, her heart quailed. *Not you.* Struggling to keep her poise, her fingernails gouged the wooden armrests. "And?"

"The prince chose...to keep his head."

So her second son still lived, but as something less than a man, no longer a threat to her crown. "And where is he now?" She was surprised her voice remained so even.

"Chained to the back of wagon, heading west into exile. A ship waits for him in the Delta, to take him to the Serpent Isles."

So it was done...and beyond her control. A measure of relief swept through her but it did not abate her anger...or the pain in her heart. Liandra clenched her fists and steeled her face to stone. "And who oversaw the orders?"

The master's answer came in a flood of words. "Your majesty must know that your shadowmaster is loyal to the crown, always working to protect the Rose Throne against any threat."

"Your *queen* asked a question."

His face was reluctant, but he yielded the answer, his voice dropping to a rough whisper. "The Master Archivist, Lord Highgate."

Once spoken, the name struck like a dagger to her heart. Logic had not lied...yet the proof was bitter, so very bitter. The man she'd trusted above all others had dared to usurp her power. Pain pierced her. Her hands tightened into fists, her nails gouging her palms, but her will prevailed. She kept her face impassive and her voice steady, turning her gaze to her oldest son. "Did you know of this?"

"Not ahead of time, no." There was no guile in him.

"Then how did you hear of it?"

He shrugged. "Rumors abound, especially among soldiers."

The answer only fueled her anger. "So the whole court knows of this, yet the queen was not informed?"

Neither man answered.

"*Fools!*" Her voice was scalding. She took a deep breath, needing to hear it all. "What does the court think?"

Prince Stewart answered. "All the other traitors faced their fate months ago. Danly was the last of the Red Horns. Justice needed to be served. Even a prince is not above the queen's justice."

So the people believed the queen had issued the orders...her power remained intact...but what of her image? *A queen who castrated her own son,* Liandra suppressed a shudder. "And do you agree with Lord Mills, that it was a ruthless choice?"

Stewart's face flashed with anger. "Lord Mills does not deserve to sit on your royal council."

"Lord Mills is nothing but a yapping dog. He barks but has little bite...beware the ones who remain quiet and plot behind our back, for they are the real worry." She fingered the rubies at her throat, her voice growing hard. "Yet sometimes enemies have their uses, revealing more than allies." Her stare settled on his face. "Do you think it was ruthless?"

Her son looked away, staring into the blazing fire, his jaw clenched. "A terrible choice for any man, but was it ruthless?" He met her stare, honesty in his gaze. "Danly had a choice, which was more than the other traitors got...more than he deserved...yet justice was served."

The question slipped out. "What would you have chosen?"

The fire snapped and crackled, spitting a spark from the flames.

The Prince trod on the spark, leaving a burned smell in the room. "That's easy." His face dissolved into open admiration. "I choose to always be loyal to the queen."

His words proved a balm to her heart. At least she had one loyal son, one man she could trust. "You have grown into a fine general. We are pleased." She stared into the blazing fire, burying her emotions beneath a regal facade. "But we have much to do to protect Lanverness." She snapped her gaze to the deputy shadowmaster. "Tell the prince the latest news from Coronth."

Master Raddock nodded. "The flood of refugees has slowed to a trickle, but one man brought strange whispers from Balor. Weak from the journey, and perhaps delusional from his ordeals...yet he tells an odd tale, insisting that the Pontifax is dead, consumed by flames in a test of faith."

"What?" The prince gaped. "Is it true?"

The spymaster shrugged. "He is the first refugee to sing such a tale. Hard to say if it is truth or delusion."

"But this could change everything!" Hope radiated from the prince's face. "If the Pontifax is dead, then surely his religion must fall?" He stared at the queen, logic slowly strangling hope. "But you did not tell the council."

Her son was learning. Liandra nodded. "Religions rarely die so easy a death. Even if the Pontifax is dead, some zealous priest will surely leap to take his place." She sat straight in the throne, steel leaching into her voice. "As long as an army marches toward our border, we must prepare for war."

"And the council?"

"...need not hear the news, lest those who argue for negotiations blunt our preparations for war. The odds are already heavy against us. Divisiveness in our council will only hinder our efforts." The queen smoothed her gown, as if she could smooth away all opposition. "We will manage our council, and prepare our people...while you lead our swords against the enemy."

Her royal son stood straight and proud, handsome in the emerald tabard of the rose army. "What are your orders?"

"Take the army north and prepare for this war of skirmishes. When Lord Highgate returns from Radagar, we shall send the bought swords to you. Use the mercenaries as you see fit. Slow the enemy as best you can. Nibble at their flanks and perhaps your strategy of small bites will prevail. And while you fight, deny the enemy our harvest. Perhaps we can starve them back to Coronth." She eased back into the chair, tapping her ringed fingers on the carved armrests. "Perhaps hunger will work if swords do not." She gazed into the flames. "And when the monk, Aeroth, returns, we will see what aid the Kiralynn Order can provide. They owe us for Sir Cardemir." She turned her gaze back to her son. "Keep us informed of your victories...as well as any threats."

Prince Stewart nodded, his face troubled. "I accept the task...but?"

"Speak, we would hear your counsel."

"I'm reluctant to trust mercenaries."

"We have had this debate before."

"I respectfully ask that you hold the mercenaries in reserve, here in Pellanor. They can bolster the defense of the city and act as a rear guard."

"Agreed." She gave him a regal nod. "When will you march?"

"Within the week. There is no time for delay."

"All of Pellanor will see you off." Her voice softened. "We charge you to keep yourself safe. You are our firstborn, our royal heir."

He gave her a smile that revealed the boy within. "I'll stay safe, mother."

She would have said more but they were not alone. "The gods grant you victory."

"And you." She sensed his words were heartfelt.

The two men took their leave, bowing to kiss her emerald ring. She let them reach the door before her words struck like a lash. "Master Raddock, a word."

The shadowmaster stumbled to a halt while the prince escaped, the door closing behind him. Her deputy shadowmaster returned to skulk in front of the fireplace, his face closed, his shoulders hunched as if expecting a blow. She let him wait, feeling her royal displeasure. The fire snapped and crackled, burning down to a single log, and still she waited. If the shadowmaster felt discomfort, he showed no signs of it; the man had the nerves of an alley cat.

"You failed your queen."

"I obeyed orders."

"But not the *queen's* orders."

"I did not know."

"But you should have known. The fate of a prince requires a royal writ." Her words struck like swords. "Lanverness is a kingdom of laws. The *queen's* laws."

His eyes widened but he did not reply.

She shifted her attack. "Your daily reports contained no word of the traitor-prince."

"I thought..." his voice went hoarse. A struggle raged across his face but in the end his sense of survival triumphed, "The Master Archivist said he would provide a full report before he left for Radagar."

Her anger exploded. "How dare you withhold this from us! Ignorance is a state no monarch can afford, leastwise a queen." Her words cooled to a deadly edge. "How shall we treat with your silence? Shall we name it treason by omission? In most kingdoms, men hang for less."

A sheen of sweat soaked his face. "Not treason, never that!"

"Do you think the Master Archivist promoted you without *our* approval?"

He shook his head, like a man backed into a corner.

"We raised you up from a common back-alley thief." A glint of fear flashed across his face. "Oh yes, we know of your shady past, yet we accepted your service, and this is how you repay our trust?"

He fell to his knees, his face flushed. "Only in Lanverness could a man like me reach so high. Please, your majesty, let me serve you?"

Disgusted, she left him on his knees, turning her stare towards the glowing hearth. As the fires dimmed to embers, her anger slowly annealed to deadly logic. "We live in a world of knights and kings, where swords matter more than words. For a queen to keep her crown, she must be smarter and quicker than all those who seek to bring her down. And always the hounds nip at our heels...no matter what we achieve." She turned her gaze back to the kneeling shadowmaster. "We seek loyalty, intellect, and discretion in our shadowmen. Are you such a man?"

He nodded, his face contrite. "A queen's man."

At least he was smart enough not to swear...for he'd sworn once before. "We shall give you one more chance to prove your worth." She extended her hand, offering her emerald ring of office. "Do not fail us again."

He grabbed her hand and kissed her ring, fervent as a penitent grasping a holy relic. At least he groveled well. "And what shall we do with the one you serve?"

He sat back on his heels, staring up at her. "Lord Highgate?"

Even his name caused her pain. She nodded.

"He only meant to serve..."

She raised a hand, forestalling him. "We shall hear no excuses."

His gaze dropped to the floor, a war of emotions flashing across his face...but the queen did not relent, letting the silence lengthen, making him choose his loyalties.

He eventually raised his stare, his face pale. "Arrest him then. But hear his reasons before you pass judgment."

And there was the rub. The Master Archivist was a fine chess player, caging her with her own image. If she ordered his arrest, then the council, nay the whole kingdom, would know that the orders regarding Danly's punishment were not hers...and a queen could never appear to lose control, or the hounds would bring her down. "No, nothing so rash. This matter must be handled with great discretion."

He stared at her, his face wary.

"When Lord Highgate returns, you will take his report and then order him confined to his castle chambers, to await a summons from the queen. Rumors will be spread that he fell ill on his journey from Radagar, something in the food."

A chill settled over the chamber. "Will it be a fatal illness?"

So he thought her capable of murder. She made her voice hard, clutching the arms of her throne lest her hands betray her. "That will depend on Lord Highgate."

His face paled.

"In the meantime, you will continue to serve as our master of shadows." She extended her ringed hand. "Do not disappoint."

He kissed her ring without touching her hand, as if she might bite, and then he scurried from the chamber.

The door clicked shut and she was once more alone. *Always alone,* she paced in front of the fire, considering her loyal lords. Master Raddock, her thief turned shadowmaster, had a shrewd cunning but he was a pale imitation of his mentor and his loyalty remained in doubt, yet he would serve and she would make do. She always made do with lesser men. Her mind shied away from the Master Archivist. Perhaps there was no one she dared trust. A crown was a heavy burden, yet she would never give it up. She clenched her fists, staring at her royal rings, the great emerald and the gold seal gleaming in the candlelight. Lanverness prospered beyond the telling and the royal treasury was flush with gold. None of her ancestors had ruled half as well...yet she was the only queen among them, the only woman in a long line of kings. She'd achieved much, yet all her accomplishments seemed a thin comfort. Liandra stared into the hearth, but the embers had died, letting the chamber grow cold...as cold and bleak as her mood. Memories of him assailed her, nights filled with passion, stirring a raging need laced with hurt. She'd trusted him, letting him into her bed, letting him into her heart, yet he'd dared to usurp her power. Sex changed everything. She should never have slept with him. Power was too much temptation...for any man. *"Oh Robert, how could you do this to me?"* A single tear coursed down her cheek. Liandra bowed her head and linked her hands across her stomach. *"How could you do this to us?"*

5

Steffan

The day dawned red, a perfect omen for the start of a holy war. Banners of the Flame unfurled against the brightening sky, snapping in the breeze. Steffan rode at the head of the army next to General Caylib, surrounded by an entourage of bishops. A long snake of soldiers marched behind, red tabards competing with the morning sky. The men began to sing, deep voices raising a battle hymn, proof of their eagerness for war. Thousands of hobnailed boots kept time, drumming the sound of invincibility into the ground. They tramped through the autumn countryside, churning the dew-laden grass to mud. Fifty thousand foot and ten thousand horse marched into Lanverness unopposed.

The scouts proved their worth. As predicted, the village lay nestled at the foot of a steep ridge, quaint little houses made of timber and stone and thatch, surrounded by a patchwork of fallow fields and autumn forests. A handful of fat milk-cows grazed in a fenced pasture, but the farmers were not yet afield. Smoke rose in lazy curls from stone chimneys, a sleepy village lulled by a peaceful morning, soon to be shattered by war.

The army climbed the ridge, fanning out along the length like a second sunrise. Steffan and the general took the high ground in the center, the perfect vantage point for the carnage to come. Trumpeters, signalmen, and messengers surrounded the two leaders, awaiting orders. The battle plan was simple. Two divisions of foot made their way around the far ends of the ridge. Approaching the village from north and south, they executed a simple pincer formation designed to trap the villagers in the jaws of hell.

Horses nickered and battle banners snapped along the ridgeline, impatient for war. The general held the cavalry in reserve, watching as the two divisions emerged from the shadows. Sunlight broke through the morning clouds, streaming across the countryside, as if the Flame God gave his blessing to the battle.

Steffan drew his sword and stood in the stirrups, his voice booming along the ridge. "For the Flame God! Death to the infidels!"

A roar shook the ridge. *The Flame God!* Warhorses stamped and snorted. Soldiers shook their halberds and unsheathed their swords, howling for blood and victory.

Below the ridge, the two divisions broke into a run. Halberds gleaming, they hurtled forward, screaming their devotion to the Flame God.

The village stirred. Farmers emerged from their homes, some holding milking pails. Rubbing sleep from their eyes, they gawked at the soldiers, an unexpected nightmare.

A hungry growl rose from the soldiers, predators sighting their prey. Two lines of red converged like jaws snapping closed. Bishop Taniff led the charge. A tall, bearded cleric in blood-red armor, he waded into the villagers, swinging his mace in a deadly arc while bellowing prayers, the perfect fanatic.

Villagers erupted from their homes like ants kicked from a mound. Some tried to fight, wielding pitchforks and cudgels and scythes. The farmers showed uncommon bravery, a thin dike of homespun-brown holding back a relentless tide of red, but their valiant defense was fleeting. Halberds flashed in deadly arcs and the red advanced, reaping a bloody harvest. Bishop Taniff cut into the defenders, his mace carving a deadly path. Farmers fell beneath the onslaught while their women-folk screamed in horror.

General Caylib scowled. "Too easy. A bloody slaughter."

Steffan nodded. "Wars always start by killing the innocent. The true battles will come later."

Below, the resistance crumbled. The farmers broke and ran, retreating to their homes, as if oak doors could stop an army. Soldiers swarmed the houses like angry wasps seeking entry. Halberds broke windows and bit deep into oak doors. Wood gave way to steel, and the red tide poured in. A desperate few tried escaping out back windows, mostly women with babes in arms, but the soldiers cut them down. Flames erupted from some of the homes, a shout of victory from the soldiers. The fight became a ransack. The village gave up its spoils. Women were pulled from their homes to be raped in the fields. Soldiers emerged from houses carrying quilts, cured hams, iron tools, and sacks of grain while others prodded prisoners with their swords.

Terrified, the survivors cowered in submission. The peasants were herded into an empty paddock where soldiers gathered wood for a bonfire. A few women had sense enough to gather up their children and make a dash for the western woods. A handful evaded the soldiers, disappearing into the brush.

The general pointed toward the forest. "Sound the hunt. I want the strays captured."

"No." Steffan overruled the command. "Let them go."

The general growled, "Mercy's the last thing I'd expect from you, counselor."

Steffan laughed. "It's not what you think. I have my reasons." Turning in the saddle, he raised his voice to a command. "Let the trumpets sound our victory, the first of the holy war." He wheeled his sorrel stallion away from the ridge top, his black cape fluttering in the breeze. "Come, we have an offering to make to the Flame God."

They rode down from the ridge into the killing fields. Trumpets blared in triumph and battle banners streamed overhead. Steffan led them through the village to the paddock, his stallion stepping around broken bodies, most of them farmers.

Bishop Taniff waited at the gates, gore dripping from his spiked mace. The battle-cleric flashed a bloodthirsty grin, his voice booming in pride. "A holy victory, my lord!   The infidels are sweet to reap!"

Steffan nodded. "A fine start to the holy war. How many did we lose?"

"Three dead and five wounded. The Flame God protects his own."

"That he does. And now the god deserves his due." Steffan gestured to the wood pyre taking shape in the center of the paddock. "Consecrate the bonfire and prepare the brands."

The bishop grinned, a blaze of religious fervor in his dark gaze. "A righteous duty for a holy warrior." He made a half-bow and then turned and strode toward the mound, his baritone voice bellowing chants to the Flame God.

The bishop is a fanatic, but fanatics have their uses. Steffan stayed on his horse, surveying the scene.

The army encircled the paddock, victory exultant on every face. Soldiers climbed the fence, jostling for a better view. A detachment of soldier-priests approached the wood pyre. Distinctive in their mitered helmets and flame-embroidered baldrics, they waved braziers filled with incense. Purifying the ground around the pyre, they released plumes of blue-gray smoke while muttering a chant of prayers. The cloying scent choked the field, a prelude to the charbroiled carnage.

At the far end of the paddock, the surviving villagers huddled together. Shock and fear rode their faces, a pathetic cluster of two-dozen peasants, mostly women and children and a few graybeards too old to fight. The children cried, clinging to their mothers' skirts, but the adults were strangely silent. Steffan recognized the look. They'd passed beyond fear into a stupefying haze of disbelief, staring but not seeing, like cattle oblivious to the butcher. Another crop of souls sacrificed to his ambition.

The pyre was sanctified and the stage was set. Steffan gestured to a trumpeter. "Begin."

Horns blared in triumph, announcing the start of the sacrifice.

Bishop Taniff ignited a burning brand. Holding the flaming branch aloft, his baritone voice beckoned the faithful. "Behold the Flame God! The true source of our victory!"

Soldiers beat their shields, answering the call.

The bishop circled the pyre, his words full of holy enticement. "And the Flame God said unto the Pontifax, send your sinners to me in a burning pyre, a bonfire of your enemies. Take up your swords and cleanse the land of infidels. Make an offering of soot and smoke and souls, and the righteous shall be welcome in paradise!"

Soldiers took up the chant, *"Paradise! Paradise!"*

The bishop raised the fiery brand to the heavens and then slowly lowered it toward the wood. Drenched with oil, the pyre ignited with a whoosh of flames. Fire licked heavenward, releasing a blaze of heat.

At the far end of the paddock, the prisoners began to bleat.

Steffan signaled to the trumpeter. "Announce me."

The horns blared a trill of notes and Steffan rode into the paddock. Soldiers gave way, clearing a path before him. Circling the pyre, he rode towards the prisoners, his black cape billowing in the wind. "We've claimed the first victory for the Flame God!"

His men cheered, beating their swords against their shields.

Steffan raised his hands and the clamor stilled. "We've come to spread the true faith, and to liberate Lanverness from the abomination of a bitch queen!" He turned to address the prisoners. "We're on a holy mission and we've come to give you a holy choice! Our priests stand ready to hear your confessions. For those of you who will bend the knee and take our faith, you will find prosperity through service. For those who refuse, the Holy Flames await." Steffan gestured to the roaring pyre, the fierce crackling punctuating the silence. "A holy choice is upon you. Take the brand of conversion or the pyre of purification, yours to choose."

The soldiers beat their shields, "*Choose! Choose! Choose!*"

Red-robed priests approached, bearing brands of conversion.

Steffan waited on his warhorse, the breeze tugging at his cloak.

An old man stepped forward from among the prisoners. A gray-haired grandfather, he shook his fist in defiance. "We'll never take your god! You're nothing but a pack of murders and thieves! The Lords of Light save our queen!"

Steffan gestured to the bishop. "He has chosen."

Bishop Taniff grinned. "Take him!"

A pair of priests pounced. Dragging the old man from the paddock, they hurled him into the bonfire. For half a heartbeat, the old man stared from the fire, and then the flames struck. Fire claimed his hair, his beard, his clothes. Wreathed in flame, he capered atop the pyre, howling unearthly screams. Priests whirled around the bonfire, singing the glory of the Flame God. Soldiers cheered and banged their swords on shields, caught up in the ecstasy of an easy victory. But the old man had little stamina and the fire soon took its due. He slumped among the flames, reduced to a charcoal lump, black smoke billowing into the sky.

Bishop Taniff raised his arms in benediction. "Death to the infidel! All praise and glory to the Flame God!"

"*The Flame God!*" The soldiers echoed the bishop.

Once more, Steffan raised his hands for silence. He stared at the prisoners. Their faces chalk-white, the villagers shrank to a tight-knit cluster. Steffan suppressed a chuckle; certain none had ever witness such a horrible death. "The old man made his choice and our Flame God purified his sins." Steffan gestured to the flames. "Now you must choose. Will you bend the knee, swear fealty, and take the brand of conversion or will you embrace the Flames of purification. The choice is yours."

A woman answered, a mother with three children clinging to her skirt. "We'll swear your words and take your brand." She sank to her knees, dirt staining her skirt. Like sheep, the others followed, their knees bent, bleating for mercy.

Steffan gestured to the bishop. "Our first conversions of the war."

Bishop Taniff scowled, preferring the spectacle of sacrifice, yet he nodded toward Steffan. "They'll wear the Flame God's brand." He gestured and priests approached the kneelers, wielding iron brands glowing red with heat.

Steffan watched as the woman took the brand on her forehead. Her face grimaced in pain, but she did not scream. Leaving the prisoners to the priests, he stood in the stirrups and addressed the soldiers lining the paddock. "*Our first victory of the holy war!*" He raised his fist in triumph. "To the victors go the spoils! Burn the village and gather the cows. Tonight, we'll feast on Lanverness beef!"

The men cheered, a thunder of approval.

Steffan urged his stallion to a trot, seeking relief from the burning stench.

General Caylib cantered to join him. Drawing even, he gave Steffan a piercing stare. "Mercy, counselor?"

"Not mercy, but thrift. Never waste a resource. People are another form of plunder. They can curry horses, dig latrines, polish armor, and the women can serve as camp followers, keeping the men warm at night."

The general scowled, but Steffan could tell he was chewing on the answer. "The bishop did not like it."

"Bishop Taniff is a bloody fanatic who bears watching."

The general cocked an eyebrow. "More thrift?"

Steffan smiled. "For as long as he's useful."

The general barked a laugh. "I like you, Lord Raven. And I like that the war has finally begun."

"It has." Steffan smiled. "We've thrown down the gauntlet and sealed it with a bloody atrocity."

"You're forcing them to fight."

"Fight or submit. Either way, the Rose Crown will be mine."

"One thing puzzles me." The general studied Steffan's face, a wolf searching for weakness. "Why'd you let those strays escape?"

"To serve as heralds."

"But you've lost us the advantage of surprise!"

It was Steffan's turn to laugh. "*Surprise!* We never had it! Look behind you, general. The Army of the Flame raises a league-long dust cloud. The queen knows we're coming. By letting a few escape, we've traded surprise for terror. It only takes a few to spread tales. Terror is a mighty weapon, never underestimate its use. Create enough fear and our enemies will flee rather than fight."

"I like it." The general flashed a wolfish grin. "You're a shrewd one, counselor."

Steffan felt the pleasure of the Dark Lord, a rush of power flowing through him. "Fear will be the vanguard of our army. One way or another, Lanverness will be mine."

6

The Priestess

T he curtained palanquin swayed to the step of the bearers. Cocooned in silk, the Priestess reclined on pillows, peering between the curtains, observing the royal complex. Torchlight danced across marble columns and doors of beaten gold, each palace more extravagant than the next. An abundance of wealth crowded behind the protective walls, a royal sanctuary hiding a nest of princely vipers.

For those who had the wit to see it, the true nature of the mercenary kingdom was writ large across the royal compound. Each palace was owned by a prince of the blood. The glut of palaces was the product of the royal harems, a legacy of the distant desert. Instead of a single royal line, the harems spawned a war for succession. Over a hundred brothers and half-brothers vied for the Cobra Throne, intrigue and poison the weapons of choice. Centuries ago, the desert-born had crossed the seas to conquer a corner of Erdhe, but the culture of the sands proved their ultimate undoing. Locked in continual conflict, their descendants frittered away their power till Radagar was nothing more than a purveyor of mercenaries, poisons, and aphrodisiacs. Decayed to insignificance, yet the royal house continued with the deadly game of succession. Cunning and treachery were the true keys to the Cobra Throne. It was a game the Priestess knew very well, a game she intended to turn to her advantage.

The palanquin halted before a palace, an elegant exception to the surrounding extravagance. Moonlight shimmered on sandstone carved into graceful arches and bell-shaped domes, a confection of curves alien to the architecture of Erdhe. An arcade of slender columns created a shaded portico, echoing the pride of a desert past. Austere yet elegant, the palace reflected the complex nature of the man within, releasing a flood of memories for the Priestess.

Otham opened the curtains and offered his hand. She let him help her from the palanquin, a whisper of silk.

Just as she stepped to the cobblestone paving, the great cedar doors swung open. Servants dressed in silk emerged to bow a gracious welcome, but the Priestess knew soldiers watched from the shadows, scimitars guarding against treachery, a reality of a royal house.

A silver-haired seneschal with a close-trimmed beard stepped forward. Touching his brow and his heart, he gave the traditional greeting. "Welcome to the Royal House of Razzur. May you walk in the shade of peace and may your descendants be as numerous as the grains of sand in the deep desert."

The Priestess made her voice pure velvet. "May prosperity flow across this noble house like a spring that never runs dry." She lowered her veil, giving him a glimpse of her face. "It is good to see you, Hamid."

"And you, mistress." His smile was warm, but his gaze slid to her escort of guards, defining the extent of her welcome.

And thus the game began, before she even met the prince. She decided to make a gesture of good faith, a concession to the paranoia of a royal house. "My escort will remain here."

Relief washed across the old man's face. He gave her a half-bow. "You are wise in the ways of royal houses. I am to show you directly to the prince."

Inclining her head, she acknowledged the repayment of trust, pleased to gain entry without the usual search, a sign of favor from the prince. "I am eager to see him."

She settled the veil across her face and prepared to follow, but Otham hovered close ...too close. Turning, she threw him a daggered glance. "*All* of my escort will remain here."

His eyes flashed with anger, but he bowed to her will, his voice a low growl. "Yes, mistress."

The man was useful but his protective jealousy was wearing thin. She would deal with him later. Composing her face, she nodded to the waiting seneschal. He gave her a half-bow and led her into the palace depths.

Memories surrounded her like incense, so much remained the same. Pale walls of polished sandstone soared to arched ceilings, mimicking the colors and curves of the desert. Braziers lined the walls, throwing off heat to dispel the winter chill of Erdhe. Guards stood statue-still in the shadows, watching as servants slipped down the hallways. And everywhere, the babbling sound of fountains echoed through the corridors, a sign of wealth to the desert-descendants.

Elegance studded with luxury, the palace was a warren of rooms. She wondered which room the prince would choose for their meeting. An audience hall would be too cold and formal, a bedroom too presumptuous. As if reading her mind, the seneschal stopped at the entrance to one of the many garden atriums, a perfect choice, but then the prince was a man of many depths. Hamid bowed low at the columned archway, gesturing for her to continue alone. "The prince awaits you in the heart of the blue garden."

Another sign of favor, it boded well for her plans. She paused beneath the archway, her eyes adjusting to the moonlight. The atrium took its name from the ornate floor, an exquisite stylized garden depicted in blue tile, the vines and flowers woven together in a complex pattern pleasing to the eye. Designed in a square, the atrium stood open to the moonlight. Water cascaded down a tiered fountain, an inviting sound that drew her forward.

Silk whispered as she glided through the twisting pathways, so many memories, so long ago. She found him at the heart of the garden. Prince Razzur stood alone before the fountain, his back to her, a bold position for a contender to the throne. He wore a sapphire-blue turban and a pale robe of samite belted with a golden sash, no sign of any sword. Tall with broad shoulders and a tapered waist, he looked proud and strong even from the back. Memories shivered through her, igniting a fierce hunger rising in waves.

He turned, slowly, revealing the object of his attention. A gyrfalcon rode his gauntleted fist, a magnificent bird with white plumage and black banding on the folded wings. Belled and jessed, the gyrfalcon took strips of meat from her master's hand. The tamed raptor sent a clear message; the prince was an iron-willed man who trained hawks to his fist and women to his bed.

Lowering her veil, she met his dark gaze, remembering. A thousand and one nights, the length of her apprenticeship, the number of nights she'd spent in his bed, perfecting the art of seduction, plumbing the depths of every passion...but that was before the Dark Lord.

She studied his face, dark eyes and olive skin, further proof of his desert lineage. A hawk nose and a pointed chin, sharp cheek bones and a firm mouth, a man of many angles. His beard was close trimmed, black turned to pure silver, the only sign of change; he'd aged well despite the years. She smiled, wondering if he still had the stamina.

He flashed a rogue's grin, as if he knew her question, and then gestured with his free hand to the silken pillow resting on the fountain's lip. Her sprig of mistletoe lay upon the pillow, displayed like an offering. "Always a flower or an herb...but this time, after so many empty years, you send mistletoe." He proffered a strip of meat to the gyrfalcon, the sharp beak taking it from his fingers without breaking skin. "Mistletoe has a conundrum of uses. What is the message in this mystery? Depending on the preparation, the berries can be sure death...or a potent aphrodisiac." He stroked the breast of the gyrfalcon, his gaze as keen as the raptor's. "Which do you intend? Poison or passion?"

She gave him a throaty laugh. "Both."

"Hmmm." He cocked his head, a predator studying prey. "You were always...complicated."

"You know me so well." Her voice was low and husky. "Seduction *is* the ultimate poison." She took two steps to the left, her movements slow and languid, drawing his stare. "Passion seeps under a man's skin, becoming a need he can't live without," she stood with her back to a brazier, offering a silhouette backlit by fire, "a burning obsession that overrides logic, ambition, or even a sense of survival."

She felt his stare linger at her curves. "How is it you grow more enticing with age?"

She smiled, keeping her secret to herself.

He turned and settled the gyrfalcon on a perch, a flash of white wings and a jangle of bells.

"So you dare to fly the gyrfalcon, a bird reserved for kings?"

"I haven't flown her in a royal hunt yet, only trained her to the fist." He shrugged. "I've grown weary of peregrines. All my brothers have them."

"Still ambitious for the Cobra Throne." It was a statement, not a question.

He gave her a knife-edged smile. "Another passion. Or would you name it poison?"

"Only if you fail."

He laughed, a deep masculine sound sending a shiver down her spine. "Ah blossom, you never fail to amuse." He studied her, his stare changing to calculation. "What name do you go by these days?"

She never used her birth-name, a secret saved for a future conquest. "I haven't decided yet. Choose something you like. Any blossom will do."

He shook his head. "Not any blossom. Not for you." He circled her, slowly, studying the silhouette beneath the layers of sheer silk. "For you it must be something special, something rare, something with a double meaning." Leaning close, he breathed deep. "Sandalwood beneath honeysuckle, allure hidden beneath sweet innocence." He came full circle, standing in front of her, a hungry smile on his lean face. "I name you, Cereus, a blossom of the night."

"Cereus." She tried the name, liking the sound of it. "Is it real or myth?"

His gaze traveled her length, pausing at the lushness of her breasts. "Is your beauty real, or myth?"

"Perhaps you'll learn tonight."

"Perhaps it will take more than one night."

She made her voice a purr. "One night will be enough."

He raised an eyebrow in question.

She slipped the outer robe of silk from her shoulders, letting the wrap puddle to the floor, the first of many layers. "Tell me about this night blooming flower, this Cereus?"

"A rare desert blossom, yet the plant is said to look like nothing more than a dead shrub, a mass of brown twigs dried by the sun, but on one night of the year, on midsummer's eve, it blooms with exquisite flowers, a burst of delicate white petals surrounding a golden center. The blossoms last through the night, closing forever with the dawn's first kiss." He stepped close, meeting her gaze. "A single night of stunning beauty, enough to last a year."

She leaned toward him, her voice breathy with wanting. "Cereus...a year of passion in a single night."

His voice echoed her own hunger. "Why now? And why only one?"

"To help you gain the throne." Her answer fed his other passion, doubling the hunger in his stare.

"And how would you do that, my blossom?"

"Poison through seduction."

His breath caught. "You would dare?"

"If you have enough support among the other royals."

He gave her a terse nod. "I have the support but never an assassin clever enough to complete the deed, though many have tried."

"I will do this for you." Her voice was a low whisper. "Meet with Cyrus across the dice table and offer me as part of the bet. One night with the best of your karesh, a tempting wager, even for a king."

"You will be searched, and if the poison is found, you will lose your pretty head...or worse." His voice turned to stone. "You know the game, my rare desert bloom. The assassin always pays, never the prince. If you fail, even *I* will not be able to save you."

"The poison will not be found."

"How can you be so certain?"

"A man's appetites often hold the key to his defeat. I have studied Cyrus. I know his ways, his weaknesses."

"But do you know his strengths? The king is cunning and jealous of his throne. He will not be so easily fooled."

"He'll be a willing fool, especially when I offer him what he most wants, his secret pleasure, his guilty shame, his most hidden desire."

The prince looked intrigued but he did not ask. Instead, he reached out with a single finger to caress her cheek, a deft touch evoking memories of other nights. "And what do you ask in return?"

"Only a favor."

He barked a laugh. "I would hear this favor."

She loosened her silk mantle, revealing the plunging gap between the fullness of her breasts, a promise and a tease. "Cyrus has met with Rose Queen's councilor."

"The Master Archivist, a formidable man." He gave her a shrewd look, his hand caressing her face, a slow seduction.

"The queen's councilor bought the full mercenary might of Radagar."

A feather-light touch traced a trail down the side of her neck, following the plunge of silk to the shadowed cleft. "Yes, all ten thousand swords."

"The price was too low. I offer a better contract."

"The contract is already signed and sealed." His hand slipped beneath silk, cupping her left breast. "And the price was extraordinary."

She leaned into him, letting him feel the throb of her heart. "A new king, a new contract."

"So firm, so ripe, so taut." He thumbed her nipple. "Such a lush temptation...but a royal contract cannot be broken."

Need raged within her, but she held it in check. "Send the bought swords to Lanverness and collect the Spider Queen's gold, but give the officers different orders," her words became a purr, "...special orders."

He scowled, his hand a slow caress.

She made her voice a tease. "Honor among thieves?"

"Not thieves." His hand tightened in anger, capturing her left breast in a cruel grip. "The reality of selling swords."

She kept her voice level, the pain bordering on pleasure. "I offer a share of the plunder, a share of the rape of Lanverness."

His hand stilled, as if weighing the offer. "There is no plunder."

"If the mercenaries turn at the right moment, in the key battle, then there will be plenty of plunder. Enough to make this contract look like a mere pittance." She lowered her voice, a seductive whisper. "I offer you a chance to turn mercenaries into conquerors." She watched his dark eyes, baiting him with his own heritage, his own dreams. "I offer to restore the glory of the desert-bred." Disengaging his hand, she stepped away, just beyond his grasp, a tantalizing tease. "Will you dare to reach for the Cobra Crown?"

He stood statue-still, his face composed, but she knew him too well. Ambition smoldered in his dark gaze. "All or nothing?"

She nodded, waiting.

His voice cut like a sword. "Are you the falcon or the falconer?"

"Does it matter?"

He closed the distance, grabbing her waist. His fingers like steel, he clasped her close. "Whose fist do you fly to?"

She shook her head, sending a ripple through her long mane of raven hair, but she did not try to pull away. "Together we hunt a king. Does anything else matter?"

He stared at her, a hawk's piercing gaze, as if searching the depths of her soul.

She met his gaze unflinching, daring him to agree.

His grip eased. "Intrigue becomes you." Releasing her, he reached for her hand, raising it to his lips, a courtier's kiss, but his gaze never left hers. "Are you always this dangerous, blossom?"

"Only in bed."

He laughed but the sound held a heated edge. "Is that a challenge?"

Her voice was low and throaty. "You named me well." She ran a hand down his chest, past the sash at his waist, pressing against his rampant hardness. "Cereus, a year of passion in a single night."

He clasped her close, his lips bruising hers. "I'll take that challenge...and the throne."

Passion exploded between them. He swept her into his arms, carrying her to a divan sequestered by a lattice of screens. They tumbled across silken pillows, both striving for mastery. His hands were strong and sure, just as she remembered. Silk layers ripped away, leaving her naked. Bathed in moonlight, she made use of every weapon in her arsenal. Arching her back, she showed her curves to full advantage. He pounced on her, his hands insistent, his kisses intent. Such a skilled lover, he knew her every desire, but the balance of power had shifted. She gave him a ride like none he'd ever known before. Seduction, entrapment, enslavement, she led him on a wild dance, giving him the illusion of power. He rode her like a stallion claiming an entire herd. And all the while she wove a trap of scent and touch and skill, using her dark gifts to endow him with the stamina of ten men. Insatiable, his need raged like a storm throughout the night. They tumbled one on top of the other, taking turns at mastery and submission. He took her in every orifice, yet his need grew like a bonfire. By morning, the passion had seared to obsession, a poison lodged deep in his soul. Sprawled across silken pillows, he finally lay spent, sated with sex. She purred with satisfaction, knowing she'd ruined him for all other women. A year of passion in a single night, he'd named her well.

Brimming with power, the Priestess rose with the first light, tracing her true name in the sweat on his chest. He groaned in pleasure but never woke. Gathering her silks, she left him sprawled on the divan. She smiled, knowing she'd tamed a future king to her bed, another conquest for the Dark Lord, another step in the great dark dance.

7

Danly

B lue sky above...where before there'd only been stone. Danly squinted through a fever haze, his thoughts as sluggish as a frozen river. Clouds dotted the sky, sunlight warmed his face...but the world *moved*. He lay sprawled on his back, surrounded by the creak and groan of wood, the clop of hooves...and a terrible stink that assaulted his nose. He knew that smell, cold sweat and stale piss, the smells of pain and fear...the stench of the dungeon. *The dungeon!* He bolted awake, gasping with memories he didn't want; the Master Archivist's snide smile, the executioner's axe...and the red-robed apothecary with his knife.

"*No!*" The word was more a gurgle than a scream.

Blue sky above, proof he was free of the dungeon...but at what cost? Shaking, he refused to remember. He lied to himself, denying the pain at his groin. It couldn't be true, just a fever-soaked nightmare. He was a prince of the realm; they wouldn't dare do that to him...yet his fingers found a blood-encrusted bandage. Fear spiked through him. His hand hovered at the bandage; afraid of what lay beneath. Sweat poured out of him, but he had to know. His fingers wormed beneath, seeking his manhood.

"*Noooooo!*" The scream ripped out of him, a tortured howl. His mind convulsed and his body thrashed. They'd taken his manhood! They'd made him a maid! "*Nooooo!*" He howled like a thing possessed.

Cold water drenched his face. Danly sputtered for breath.

"Stop yer yammering." A guard glared down at him, a scowl on his face. "Keep quiet or you'll be wearing a gag."

Danly struggled to understand. He lay sprawled on the bed of a wagon, stale straw for a mattress...iron shackles chaffing his legs. *Iron shackles*...so he was still a prisoner. Horses followed behind, four guards in the green and white tabards, swords belted to their sides, their faces full of disdain. *So they knew!* Danly shut his eyes, seeking oblivion, hiding from the humiliation as much as the pain.

The wagon lurched over a rut. Startled, he jerked awake. Danly gaped at his surroundings, stunned to find nothing had changed. Chained to a wagon bed, he still wore his prison rags beneath a scratchy blanket, the reason for the stink. His beard was long and straggly, a measure of his time spent in the dungeon. *The dungeon,* his anger turned to a cold rage. Tugging on his beard, he wondered how long he'd wallowed in his own filth. He needed information...and a weapon, and a way to get free. Feigning a fever, he writhed beneath the blanket, his hands searching the straw for steel...but all he found was an empty bucket and a ladle. A ladle against six swords, he would have laughed if it wasn't so pitiful.

Danly laid still, breathing his own stink, staring up at the sky. The truth ate at his mind like a ravenous monster. They'd made a eunuch out of him. They'd stolen his manhood...and his chance to be king. A cold hatred raged in his soul. Somehow he'd find a way to repay his royal mother and her shadowmaster. Schemes of vengeance flooded his mind, each one more terrible than the last.

The wagon passed beneath a stand of trees, naked branches crisscrossing a darkening sky. Autumn or the brink of winter, where had the summer gone? He pulled the blanket close, seeking warmth.

The wagon ground to a halt, the clop of the horses falling silent. Danly lay still, watching through hooded eyes as the guards dismounted.

A blond-haired soldier climbed onto the wagon and nudged Danly with his boot. "Wake up."

Danly moaned, feigning a fever.

The soldier kicked harder. "Wake up and eat, or you can spend another night wallowing in yer own stink."

Danly glared at the soldier, his voice a weak croak. "Water?"

Another soldier snapped a command, "Carter, get him some water."

Danly hid a smile, still a prisoner but they meant to keep him alive.

The blond-haired soldier scowled, "I ain't a wet-nurse," but he climbed down from the wagon, returning with a water skin. Tossing the skin to Danly, he unlocked the chain binding him to the wagon bed. "Drink your fill and then get down from there if you want to eat."

Danly took his time, sloshing the cool water across his face, a balm against his fevered forehead. He tried to get clean, wiping his grimy hands on the dirty blanket. Filth smeared on top of filth, it was a hopeless task.

"Quit yer skulking and get down from there."

Danly realized he was stalling, the eunuch-prince cowering in the wagon, avoiding the company of real men. A breeze brought a whiff of roasting venison, juices dripping into the flames, waking his hunger, revealing a ravenous emptiness. Pulled by the smell, he inched forward, making careful movements, fearful of rousing the pain between his legs. Chains clanked around his ankles, a hindrance and a reminder. He reached the back and eased over the edge, wondering if it would hurt to walk. His feet hit the ground...and pain lanced his groin. A wave of dizziness assaulted him. His legs buckled and he nearly fell. Clutching the wagon, he bit his lip, refusing to scream. The dizziness passed and he stood on wobbly legs.

Six soldiers pinned him with their stares.

Danly's face reddened, but he refused to retreat. Taking mincing steps, he wobbled toward the campfire.

Someone snickered.

Someone else said, "All hail the eunuch prince!"

Danly flamed red, the words burning like a lash, but he kept walking, the clank of chains marking every step.

A dark-haired soldier laughed. "Does a eunuch squat to piss? Or do you just let it dribble down your leg?"

"Do you have anything left? Or did they shave you smooth like a maiden?"

Their mocking jibes came thick as arrows, every one finding its mark.

"Not much of a prince, are you?"

"That's enough." The leather-faced captain growled an order. "Get the prisoner a plate of food."

Danly made it to the fire, taking a careful seat on a felled log. A red-haired soldier with a pockmarked face handed him a plate of roast venison and a hard biscuit. Danly grabbed the venison and shoved it in his mouth, the hot juices running down his chin, fouling his beard. He nearly swooned at the taste. Ravenous, he ate like a hungry wolf, trying to fill the void in his stomach. Someone handed him a mug of tea. He longed for wine, or better yet brandy, but he gulped the bitter brew, holding the mug out for more. Licking the grease from his fingers, he ate a second serving. His hunger finally sated, he felt the soldiers' stares. Dark eyes stared his way, piercing him like spears tipped with scorn.

Danly hid behind a shield of words. "Where are you taking me?"

A stony silence was the only reply.

"What's to become of me?"

No one bothered to answer. Sitting ringed around the fire, the soldiers were all strangers despite their green and white tabards. Some sat on bedrolls, other leaned against logs...but all of them stared...as if he was a freak, or a monster...anything but a man.

The disdain on their faces wormed into his soul. Shame wrestled with rage, a tumult of anger building inside till he could take it no more. His rage exploded in a roar. *"Your head or your manhood?"* Like a gauntlet, he threw the challenge in their faces, spittle flying from his mouth. "What would *you* choose?" His finger stabbed at each soldier. "Choose! Choose! Your *head* or your *manhood*! Your *life* or your *cock!*"

A few looked away, but most stared back at him with cold hard faces.

Their silence melted his resolve. Swaying on his feet, Danly slowly sank to the ground, his voice hushed to a whisper. "You'd choose the same as me." He choked back a sob, his hands cupping his bandaged groin. "The same as me."

The fire snapped and crackled, spitting sparks.

The stern-faced sergeant drew his sword, scrapping a whetstone along the length of steel. "Not bloody likely."

The captain growled, "Enough of this. Carter, take the prisoner down to the stream and let him wash. He smells worse than a dung heap. And get him some fresh clothes."

The blond-haired soldier grumbled but he grabbed a saddlebag and then stood over Danly, his hand on his sword. "Get up."

The strength had gone out of him, like water run from a cracked jug.

"I said get up."

Danly struggled to rise, the chains clanking at his ankles.

"Hurry up." The soldier yanked him to his feet and shoved him toward the stream.

Danly stumbled and almost fell, the pain at his groin stabbing him with every step. He leaned against a tree, biting back a sob, wondering how it had all gone so wrong.

Behind him, the blond-haired soldier barked an order, "Move!"

Danly hobbled down the hill toward the rushing water. Something snagged the chain between his ankles. He tumbled forward, landing face-first in the stream. Cold water smacked him hard across the face, stealing his breath. Danly came up gasping, struggling to stand in waste-deep water.

Cruel laughter mocked him from the bank. "And to think I wanted you for my king."

The words hit harder than the water. Danly turned and stared at the soldier, his voice a whisper. "So you were a Red Horn?"

"And now I'm sworn to the queen. At least she has more balls than you." He threw a lump of soap at Danly, hitting him in the chest. "Get washed, before you kill us with your royal stink."

Suddenly numb to the cold, Danly fumbled with his wet shirt, peeling it from his skin, letting the rags float away in the current. Sinking into the water, he scrubbed hard, rubbing away the grime, rubbing away the horrors of the dungeon. And all the while the soldier's words burned in his mind, lighting a faint hope. *A Red Horn pardoned by the queen. Where there's one, there's sure to be more.* Perhaps the others remained loyal, waiting for their king. Leaderless, they lay dormant, seeded within the queen's court...waiting for his return. He'd kept his head...while all the other Red Horn leaders lost theirs. *He'd kept his head.* The realization gave him hope. The gods had spared him for a reason.

He cinched his prison pants and rose dripping from the water. "I need a shirt." His old voice had returned, command tinged with disdain.

The soldier stared, but he said nothing, tossing Danly a cloth bundle.

A butter-brown shirt, stained in the front, too long in the sleeves, scratchy wool instead of silk, but for now it would do. He was clean, he was alive, and he had a purpose. Danly stepped from the stream, striding to the limits of his chains. First freedom...then vengeance...and then the crown.

8

Steffan

A pair of scouts galloped down the hillside, their horses lathered and blowing. "My lord!" Riding straight to the column front, they reined next to Steffan. "My Lord Raven, we've captured the manor house you've been askin' for!"

"Intact?"

The scout looked befuddled.

Steffan rephrased the question. "Is the manor whole and unplundered?"

"It's whole enough," the scout grinned, "although the lads might have had a scullery maid or two."

"And the lord of the manor?"

The scout shrugged. "The lads were still searchin'. We thought it best to bring you word."

"Your names?"

"I'm Galbert and this is Tarnley."

Steffan turned to the general. "I've a mind to sleep in a bed tonight."

General Caylib quirked an eyebrow. "Getting soft?"

"Hardly. Swords are not the only way to capture a kingdom." Steffan quelled the general's questions with a look. "Bring two squads of Black Flames. I want the manor house secured and unplundered." He turned his gaze to the bishop. "Bishop Taniff, you have the army. Bring them at a quick march and have them camp around the manor. Tarnley will serve as your guide."

The bishop gave a curt nod while the general bellowed orders.

Eager to secure the manor, Steffan wheeled his stallion to the left. "Galbert, lead the way." The scout spurred his horse to a gallop. Steffan and his holy guard of thirty Black Flames followed. Banners streaming, they thundered up the hillside and into a copse of oak. The countryside looked peaceful enough, fallow farmland separated by wooded hillsides, but the sky told a different story. Columns of dark smoke speared the north, proof of past conquests. Steffan could almost smell the ashes of dead infidels, a threat and a warning. Grinning, he urged his horse to jump a fallen tree.

They rode for a handful of leagues before reaching the manor house. The estate was guarded by a ditch and a thick hedge, but the wrought iron gate stood open. They rode down the lane, unopposed. The fields looked well tended, fenced and plowed under for winter. Fat milk cows grazed in grassy pastures, fresh meat for his hungry army. Beyond the fields, a cluster of thatch and wattle cottages huddled together. Doors gaped open and one bloody corpse sprawled on the threshold, but if the tenants survived, he could not tell. At least the cottages remained intact, no scent of fire on the breeze. Steffan urged his stallion forward, keen to reach the manor house. The lane took them to the heart of the estate, a stone wall separating servants from the nobility. They clattered through a gatehouse and into a courtyard, sending a dozen chickens flapping in alarm. A pair of red-cloaked guards startled to a hasty salute while a third tupped a woman over a barrel. *"The Lord Raven comes!"* The cry echoed through the courtyard, more of a warning than a greeting.

Steffan dismounted. A handful of Black Flames surrounded him while the others hurried to secure the mansion.

One of the guards approached, hastily stuffing his manhood into his trousers. "Lord Raven, we've captured the manor house you've been wantin'."

"And the nobles?"

The guard flushed red. "I'll take you to the captain." He turned and led the way toward the manse.

Built of dressed stone with diamond-paned mullioned windows and a gabled roof, it was a grand house, befitting a wealthy lord. Carved double doors opened onto a great hall with a vaulted ceiling and a massive stone hearth. Four trestle tables ran the length with a fifth set on a small dais. Faded tapestries lined the walls with hunting scenes. Light speared through windows sending fractured rainbows across the floor. The great hall was large enough to seat three hundred, perfect for Steffan's intentions.

A pair of soldiers clattered down the stair. "Lord Raven," the captain saluted, "I see Galbert made good time."

"Your name?"

"Captain Humbolt, sir."

"You've done well to secure the manor house but what of the nobles?"

"Fled, sir. Nothing but nags left in the stables. They took the best horses, and as far as we can tell they took the gold and silver, but the larders are full and so is the wine cellar."

"And you did not think to follow?"

The captain blanched. "I was told you wanted the estate intact. With so few men, I thought it best to secure the mansion."

Steffan nodded. "Have the servants assembled in the great hall, I will speak to them. In the meantime, I want to see the lord's chambers."

The captain issued orders and then ushered Steffan and his guard up the stairs. The lord's bedchamber proved largely intact. A massive four poster bed piled high with embroidered coverings dominated the chamber. Clothing was strewn across the floor, the doors to the wardrobe hanging open, proof of a hasty retreat...or a quick ransack. The lord's solar held two more chests of clothing, rich velvets and brocades, both hastily stirred. The jewel box was empty and so was the sword rack, but the silver candlesticks remained.

"You've done well." Steffan hefted a candlestick and tossed it to the captain. "A reward for your diligence."

The captain grinned. "Thank you, sir!"

"I'll be staying here for the night. I want a woman, a hot bath, and the best bottle of the brandy in the cellar. Can you see to that?"

"Yes sir."

"Good man." Steffan strode from the solar and returned to the top of the stairs. Servants huddled below in the great hall, surrounded by soldiers. A few women wept and a few men bore bruises, but otherwise they looked intact. "I'm glad to find you in good health."

They stared aloft, trembling in fear, a dazed look in their eyes.

"We've come to spread the blessings of the Flame God. Your lives have been spared so that your souls can be saved. Tomorrow you'll be given a choice between the brand of conversion and the pyre of flames. I suggest you take the brand. But tonight, you will show your gratitude by serving a feast for my officers. Spare no expense, for your lost lords will not begrudge the largess. I want a feast fit for conquerors, your best wines, your best roast fowl and your best confections. Kill the fatted calf and open your cellars. Serve well and you will live well."

The servants gawked up at him.

"Get to work." Steffan glared down at them, "or I'll give you to the priests."

The outer doors banged open and the general clattered in.

The servants scattered like chickens fleeing the axe.

General Caylib crossed the great hall and climbed the stairs. A troop of Black Flames followed, halberds held at the ready. "The manse is secure and Bishop Taniff is bringing the army at quick march."

"Good. Have the army camp in the surrounding fields. Butcher the livestock and let the men raid the outer buildings but the manor house is to remain untouched. I'm holding a feast for the officers tonight. No priests, no bishops, just officers, and I want the best military men to be seated at your table."

The general scowled. "What are you up to, counselor?"

Steffan grinned. "Wielding my favorite weapon."

The general gave him a slanted look, but he asked no more questions.

A man of few words, he liked that about the general. Steffan returned to the lord's solar and found servants pouring pails of steaming water into an iron tub. A knock sounded on the door. "Come."

Pip entered, followed by Olaff bearing Steffan's travel chest. "They say we're staying the night."

"We are. I want fresh clothes laid out for the feast tonight and I'm expecting a woman."

Pip moved with practiced efficiency, supervising the bath and laying out a change of clothes. Steffan searched the lord's solar, looking for letters, writs, and other correspondence. He found the lord's seal, a fist clutching a lightning bolt, a pretentious symbol for such a minor lordling.

"Your woman is here, m'lord."

"Good. Send her in."

She entered with timid steps, walking with her head bowed, a flaxen-haired lass in peasants' clothing. He preferred dark-haired beauties, but a little variety now and then was a good thing. "Let me see your face."

She raised her head a finger's width, tears streaking her cheeks, a shy beauty.

"You don't want to do this."

She shook her head, her voice a whimper. "No, lord."

"But you've done this before."

"Yes," the smallest of whispers, "but only once."

He doubted her answer, peasant girls were bred early, but it made for a tempting illusion. "An army surrounds this manse, an army of men eager for release, but I'll give you a choice. You can stay the night and pleasure a lord, or you can walk out that door and a dozen soldiers will have you ere the sun rises. Yours to choose."

She stared at him with wide eyes. "I'll stay, lord."

"Good, now drop your clothes. I'll have a better look at you."

She stood in front of the fire, slowly shedding her layers. Steffan watched while sipping brandy. Her every movement was shy and demure, her very timidness enflaming his manhood. Her small clothes finally fell to the floor. Naked, she stood in front of the fire, her hands crossed in front of her breasts, peeking at him through a long tangle of flaxen hair. She was like a wood nymph, shy and unconquered. "Lower your hands." She obeyed and he got a good look at her breasts, tender buds waiting to be nibbled. Steffan yearned to pounce, but he knew the conquest would be sweeter for the waiting. "Now come and undress me."

She knelt before him, pulling off his dust stained boots. Her hands shook, fumbling with belts and buckles, her eyes too shy to meet his face. His manhood strained against his leathers but he did not help. When he finally stood naked before her, she flinched away at the sight of him. Her reaction only made him harder. "On your knees before the fire."

She obeyed, trembling before him. He knelt behind her. His hands cupped her breasts and stroked her flanks, like soothing a filly for the first saddle. When her trembling slowed, his hand delved her sex. So tight, he could not wait. He mounted her from behind, a deep thrust, over and over again. She writhed and bucked beneath him, but whether it was in pain or ecstasy, he did not care. He took her until he was sated, and then he turned her over. The second time was more languid, but just as satisfying. Finally spent, he lay on his back, staring at the coffered ceiling. She curled against him, tears streaking her face, yet she clung to him, her flaxen hair spread across them like a blanket.

"Will you keep me, lord?"

"So you liked that?"

"Yes, lord."

She was a tempting little thing, but he suspected her allure would vanish with her timidness. "What's your name?"

"Salmay, lord"

"If I keep you, you'll be one of many, never the one."

Her voice quavered, but she met his stare. "Yes, lord."

Already the timidness was fading, such a pity. "Then clean yourself up and choose a gown from the lord's trunks. I'll expect you in my bed tonight."

"Yes, lord!" He pulled away from her grateful kisses and strode into the lord's chamber. "Pip, I'll have my bath now." He settled into the tub. The water was lukewarm but it suited him. "The girl, Salmay, will be joining our train. See that she bathes and find her something suitable to wear. I'll have her in my bed tonight."

"Yes, lord."

"After the feast, I'll be meeting some officers in the solar. Have the fire stoked and a good bottle of brandy ready."

"Yes, lord."

He finished bathing and then dressed in black leathers, the red badge of the raven emblazoned on his chest. Belting on a jeweled sword, he swirled his cape around his shoulders. A knock came from the door.

"Come."

The general entered, still wearing his dust-stained clothes.

"Don't you ever bath?"

"I've a war to win."

"So do I."

"You have an odd way of fighting it."

Steffan grinned. "Is the army settled?"

"Encamped around the manse. They're butchering the livestock. They'll have their own feast, but the bishops and priests are not happy."

"The bishops can have their ceremony tomorrow, branding the converts and burning the infidels, but tonight I have plans to progress."

Questions glowered in the general's eyes but he did not ask them. "The officers are assembled in the great hall, and from the smells, I'd say the feast is ready."

"Then let's feast." He led the general down the hallway to the staircase overlooking the great room. Officers crowded the trestle tables, their red tabards stained by travel. Servants scurried between the tables filling tankards. Scents of cinnamon apples and roast beef wafted through the great hall. Someone spotted Steffan and pointed. The boisterous talk snuffed to silence.

Steffan descended the stairs and claimed the lord's seat at the head table. The general made his way to one of the long trestle tables. Steffan addressed the men. "We feast to celebrate a successful start to the holy war. Every opposition has been crushed and our baggage train swells with converts. Lanverness is ripe for the plucking. This feast is but a small measure of the largess that awaits you in Pellanor. Fight well and victory will be ours." He raised his tankard. "To victory and the Flame God!"

"Victory and the Flame God!" The cry thundered through the hall.

"Let the feast begin!" Steffan took a seat while platter-laden servants rushed to the head table. The delicacies were legion, oxtail soup and pigeon pie, buttered leeks and cinnamon apples, succulent piglets and crispy chicken and a side of roast beef that looked like half a steer. Red wine and ale flowed like rivers. Tankards were kept full and the serving platters kept coming. The officers reveled in the abundance. Steffan made the rounds, spending time at each table. Listening more than he spoke, he studied the officers, watching how they ate. The feast was a test of sorts, a chance to winnow the couth from the crude. Steffan spent the evening searching for those who sipped their wine rather than swilling it, for those who wielded a table knife rather than gnawing their meat straight from the bone. He found eight with table manners that could pass for nobles, but one had too many scars and the other was too devout, so he settled for six. Tapping them on their shoulders, he whispered instructions in their ears.

The desert course arrived with a flourish, dried fruits, and blackberry pie, and delicate marchpane confections. The men were in their cups, talking loudly and fondling the serving girls, bawdy jokes hurled between the tables. Steffan slipped away, retreating up the staircase. Six men followed.

He met with them in the lord's solar, a fire roaring in the hearth, a bottle of brandy breathing on the table. Taking a seat in front of the fire, he gestured for the others to sit. "I have a special task for you." Pip slipped from the shadows to serve the brandy. "Our victory is inevitable, but I wish to hasten the process. If Pellanor surrenders, we will save time and many lives. Why fight a war when you can win with deception?"

Tarkin, a gray-haired major, leaned forward. "What would you have us do?"

"I want each of you to take a string of horses and ride with all speed for Pellanor. Once there, I want you to pose as displaced nobles. To the commoners, I want you to speak of atrocities, spreading fear through the populous. But among the nobles, I want you to be bitter and angry. You will pose as minor lordlings, men who fought for their queen and defended their holdings, men who lost all to the superior numbers of the Flame Army. Outnumbered and overrun, you fled for your very lives, losing everything. But in your cups, you will speak with bitterness about other lords, the ones who surrendered to the Flame and kept their lands and their holdings. You'll condemn them for their turned cloaks and curse them for keeping their estates."

Understanding bloomed in their eyes.

"I send you to sow the seeds of surrender. You will spread the word that those who are swift to bend the knee will gain the most favorable terms."

The men grinned, enjoying the lie.

"Do your best to reach the ear of the queen's councilors. And when you reach them, I want you to whisper a rumor that you've heard from other refugees, a rumor that if the Flame Army reaches the gates of Pellanor, there will be no mercy, no surrender."

A chill settled over the chamber.

Tarkin asked the question. "Why us?"

"Nobles will be better believed than commoners." Steffan stared at them. "Do this for me and I will see you raised to lords."

Hunger sparked in their eyes. They looked at each other and nodded agreement.

"When do we leave?"

"On the morrow." Pip approached, handing each man a fat purse. "Coin enough to set you up in Pellanor." Steffan gestured to the lord's chests. "Take whatever fits, so you have the trappings of nobles. You'll have the pick of the horses, but leave every speck of red behind. Ride hard for Pellanor and spread your tales amongst the queen's lords."

Tarkin saluted and the others followed his lead. "It will be as you command."

Steffan raised his glass. "To victory, by sword or by deception!"

"*To victory!*"

Steffan downed the brandy and then left the men to ransack the chests. Satisfied with the night's work, he strode toward the lord's bedchamber. Scrubbed clean and clad in silks, Salmay waited for him in his bed. This time she was eager. Steffan loved the spoils of war.

9

The Priestess

L ike seduction, the Priestess took poisoning to an art form. Any assassin could slip hemlock into a flagon of wine but it took an artist to design the perfect death. Part of the secret lay in understanding the possibilities of each poison. Symptoms could range from the dramatic to the subtle, from tortured convulsions and visions of gods to falling deep into a fatal sleep. And then there was the choice of dosage, strong enough for an instant kill, or parceled out to appear like a lingering malaise. But the real finesse came in the delivery, like slipping into a garden to paint baneberry on an apple just before it was plucked, one bite away from death. The Priestess smiled. She prided herself on creative kills, death by design, the artistry of murder.

In the sanctuary of her scrying chamber, she considered the challenge of killing a king. It would have to be a quick poison, but the symptoms would need to be subtle, perhaps masked beneath a drunken stupor to allow time for escape. And then there was the delivery scheme, her favorite part. Rumors said over a hundred assassins had died trying to topple the cobra crown, a testament to the king's guards and his suspicious nature. She'd have to sneak the poison past a gauntlet of searches, fooling a royal court bred on intrigue. But the Priestess had advantages the other lacked. She'd studied the king in her silver scrying bowl, watching as he took slave girls and concubines to his bedchamber, releasing them after a night, a week, or however long they amused. But the women chosen for the king's innermost chambers saw a darker side to the royal pleasure, the king's secret shame. Soldiers discarded their bodies the next morning, strangled by the king's own hands, a lifeless tumble of soiled bed sheets sprawled in the midden heap. Women's lives were cheap to the desert-bred, their graves a repository for royal secrets. But the Dark Lord's Eye revealed the king's true weakness. The fetish the king killed for would be his undoing. The Priestess smiled, her solution held a delightful symmetry, her flair for the fatal satisfied.

Unlocking her rosewood chest, she surveyed the honeycomb of drawers, bottles, and boxes, her collection of deathly delights. Larkspur, wolfsbane, bloodroot, mandrake, she knew them all, by name and by nature, the harvest from her garden on the Oracle's Isle. Sown in the very shadow of the Dark Lord's influence, her plants had imbibed an evil potency far beyond the ordinary. A tincture of the least of them would fell a healthy giant. Smiling, she considered her lethal harvest. Of all the banes from her garden, purple nightshade was her favorite. Lethal in all its parts, she'd harvested the leaves, the blossoms, and the berries, but the root was by far the most potent. Opening a drawer, she selected a piece of root and shaved off wafer-thin slices. She took care with the knife, knowing the smallest cut of her skin would be fatal. Placing the shavings in a mortar, she added a dozen berries from the same plant. Known as devil's cherries, the red berries would add a sweet, enticing taste while deepening the poison. A tenth part almond oil and a dash of whiskey for flavor completed the ingredients. She ground the mixture to a fine paste, adding berries till she got the right shade of red. Satisfied with the results, she carefully applied the paste, starting with a thin layer and letting it dry before adding another. The application took half a day, but her patience was rewarded. The poison was hidden in plain sight, the vanity of a woman and the downfall of a king.

Washing her hands three times over, she left the inner chamber for her solar. Her two handmaidens sank to deep curtsies.

"Attend me."

Her women did their work well, scenting her dark hair with sandalwood and braiding it into a long coil before tying a single ribbon at the end. A deep red rouge was applied to her lips, the fingernails of her hands, and her nipples, a tantalizing surprise for her prey, and then they dressed her in layers of silk, shades of sheer green sequined with gold, the royal colors. Gold bracelets adorned her ankles, a bangle of small bells chiming with every movement, and on her feet, a pair of golden slippers. Every aspect of her appearance was planned, especially the slippers. Handcrafted from a thin cloth of gold, they conformed to the curves of her feet. Enticing yet simple enough to avoid suspicion, the slippers were the perfect foil. Well aware of the ancient taboo that proscribed the feet as unclean, she'd turn the desert culture against the king.

Her handmaidens finished and the Priestess studied her reflection. A dark-eyed courtesan stared back, a woman bedecked for pleasure, enticing enough for a king. Satisfied, she rang a small hand bell.

The outer door opened and Otham entered. His gaze widened at the sight of her, his voice dropping to a deep husk. "Yes, mistress?"

His reaction pleased her. "Is everything in order?"

"Everything is just as you commanded." His stare drank her in.

"And the guards?"

"Stationed outside the gates of the royal compound with fresh horses."

"And the boy, the snake charmer from the market?"

"Waiting outside with the palanquin."

She rewarded him with a smile. "Then it is time to hunt a king."

The words blurted out of him. "Must you take the risk?"

She laughed. "In the risk lies the pleasure."

His jaw clenched, his gaze spilling with anger. "There must be another way."

She rested a hand on his chest, forestalling his argument. "Obey my commands and all will be well."

He bowed his head. "As you wish, mistress." He reached for a dark green cloak and wrapped it around her shoulders. For a moment, he held her close, his manhood pressed against her, but she did not yield. Sighing, he lifted her into his arms and carried her out the door and into the noon sun. A palanquin surrounded by guards in the sky blue of House Razzur waited in the street below. The guards snapped to attention, one of them rushing to hold back the curtains of the palanquin.

Otham settled her on silken pillows. He gave her searching look and then closed the curtains. She heard him give orders to the guards and the palanquin lurched into motion.

Reclining on a mountain of pillows, she watched through the curtain slit. The streets were busy with the noon crush but the crowds thinned as they approached the royal compound. Her escort passed through the gate without incident, the guards showing deference to the royal crest emblazoned on the palanquin. Prince Razzur was a man of power, second only to the king.

The bearers struggled up the hill, past the glut of palaces, a competition of golden doors and gilded statues. In the afternoon light, the palaces seemed even more garish than they did at night, a triumph of wealth over taste. The Priestess smiled at the overweening decadence, a sure sign of a decayed power.

The palanquin lurched to the crest of the hill and stopped before a palace that outshone all others in terms of raw conceit. Massive marble columns supported a domed onion-roof gilded in gold. Larger-than-life statues stood between each column, desert princes wielding golden scimitars, inflated images of bygone heroes. And recessed beneath the shaded portico were a pair of golden doors embossed with hooded cobras, the symbol of the royal house, a throne held by poison, intrigue and fratricide.

Otham opened the curtains, helping her out. The Priestess stood straight and tall, hugging the cloak tight to hide her finery.

Ten royal guards stepped from the portico shadows. Wearing tabards of green and gold with royal cobras emblazoned on their chests, the soldiers gripped their swords, their faces full of suspicion.

The Priestess kept silent, deferring to the men.

Otham greeted the guards, bowing to the captain. "Lady Cereus, a member of Prince Razzur's karesh, has come to make a debt-payment to King Cyrus." He offered the captain a scroll sealed with the prince's emblem.

The captain inspected the scroll, throwing a speculative glance at the Priestess. "The lady is welcome but no guards from Razzur may enter."

Otham gave an obsequious bow. "The prince told us it would be so. I will remain outside with the guards, but," he gestured to the rear of the palanquin, "the lady has brought three servants that are included in tonight's payment."

The guards moved to inspect the others. The flute boy from the market stood with his head bowed. Scrubbed clean, he looked like a cherub, his auburn curls cascading around a heart-shaped face. Dressed in a short white tunic and gold sandals, he fidgeted from one foot to the other, nervously clutching his flute. Behind the boy, two muscle-bound bearers carried a large woven basket between them. Made of reeds, the basket was over four-foot tall, bowl-shaped to mimic the baskets used by snake charmers.

The captain scowled. "What's in the basket?"

Otham answered, "Nothing yet."

The captain snorted, giving the Priestess an appreciative glance. "They'll have to be searched." His voice deepened to a growl. "If anything is found amiss, you'll all pay the price."

Otham nodded, extending his hand to the captain, a small purse of golds hidden in his palm. "To compensate for your extra work."

The Priestess watched as the purse disappeared into the captain's belt. The bribe would not influence the guards' thoroughness but it would ensure the basket was not destroyed by an overzealous search.

The captain gave her a leering grin, "This way, m'lady." He strode towards a small side door made of beaten silver.

The Priestess swayed seductively with each step, following the captain into the marbled hallways. The palace interior mirrored the outside, a preening display of wealth. Green marble walls soared to beveled ceilings creating a faint echo of footsteps. Arched niches held rare vases and gem-encrusted figurines, each one worth a duke's ransom. Even the air smelled costly, gilded braziers releasing the rich scents of cinnamon and frankincense. And everywhere guards stood statue-still with hands on sword hilts, watching the movement in the hallways...the perfect blend of opulence and paranoia.

The Priestess kept her head bowed, hiding behind her veil, staying two paces behind the captain. Bells on her ankles marked each step, a soft chime as she memorized the twists and turns of the passageways. Servants bedecked in silk scurried past, but none glanced her way.

The captain showed her to a small but well-appointed chamber. Two cushioned divans flanked a round table laden with a flask of wine and a platter of dried fruits. Rich carpets covered the marble floor while a pair of braziers warmed the room. An ornate screen in the corner presumably hid a chamber pot. The only thing missing was a window.

"You are to wait here until the king calls for you."

She kept her voice demure. "And my attendants?"

The captain gave her a sly smile. "You will be re-united if you are deemed worthy to serve the king."

Bowing her head in acquiescence, she entered the room and took a seat on the divan, watching as the captain stood guard outside the open door. Tall and broad-shouldered, he stood with his hand on his sword hilt, his stare boring into her, distrust leavened with lust. Deciding to ignore him, she focused on the room instead. The divan was comfortable and the room beautifully appointed but it was nothing more than a gilded cage, a place to hold those who might be a threat to the crown. Suspicion was a way of life in the royal palace.

She kept her eyes downcast, studying the intricate pattern of the rug, playing the role of a mere woman, giving the captain no cause for alarm. Boredom threatened, but fortunately she did not have long to wait. A gray-haired matron and a moon-faced eunuch bustled into the room. Bowing, they gave her a speculative look, a pair of rogues gauging the mark before the fleece.

The Priestess waited, her head bowed in compliance.

The matron approached, beaming a gap-toothed smile that screamed of falsehood. "Well, deary, so you've come to entertain the king?"

The Priestess nodded.

"They say you're from Razzur's karesh?"

The question was heavily laden with gossip, a gossip she hoped infected the king. Hiding her smile behind her veil, the Priestess gave the smallest nod. "Yes."

"Well then, an experienced woman like your ladyship surely knows that certain measures must be taken to safeguard our royal master." The old woman winked. "We can't let a lady like you into the king's bedchamber without first checking a few things, now can we?" She rolled up her sleeves, revealing a pair of beefy arms. "So which will you have, m'lady, myself or Sal here?" Winking, she waved a meaty hand toward the whey-faced eunuch. "You know of course, that Sal is a palace eunuch so there'll be nothing untoward happening, no disgrace either way."

The Priestess made her voice meek, knowing the trial had to be endured. "Then perhaps Master Sal would be best."

The old matron threw her a shrewd look. "Well then, the choice is made. I'll be doing your clothes while Sal here does the honors." Her voice gained a serious edge. "Stand up, deary, and give us that lovely wool cloak."

The Priestess stood, letting the matron whisk the green cloak from her shoulders. While the old woman fondled her cloak, she darted a glance at the captain and found him leering in the open doorway. Feigning embarrassment she said, "Can you not close the door?"

The matron waved a dismissive hand toward the captain. "A member of the king's guard always watches. We always need a witness. It's as much for your protection as ours." Her meaty hands ran the length of the cloak, squeezing the fabric, looking for any hidden intent. "Good quality wool." Laying the cloak aside, she stared at the Priestess. "Let's have a good look at you then." The matron gave her a knowing appraisal. "Aren't you dressed like the queen of the harem?" She wagged a finger. "You best not be hiding anything under those silks, deary." She waved the eunuch forward. "Sal, you get started while I check the hair."

The matron moved behind her, kneading the Priestess's long raven braid. "Such beautiful hair." She gave the braid a harsh yank, the spite of old age confronting beauty.

The fat eunuch waddled close, his hands outstretched. "Pardon my touch, m'lady," but the rudeness of his grasp belied his words. Fingers fat as sausages traced her curves, crushing silk to flesh, ensuring nothing untoward lay beneath. Pawing her breasts, he pushed the silk aside to inspect. "Ah, rouge on your tits!" Brushing a finger across each one, he smeared the rouge and then sucked his finger clean, checking for poison. "And rouge on your lips, such a nice full mouth." His fat fingers traced her lips, another taste. "Now open wide." She opened her mouth and let him peer inside, feeling like a horse examined at auction. Satisfied, the eunuch knelt before her, his fat fingers groping between her legs. He touched and probed everywhere, licking his finger afterward, a royal taster of bedroom fare, more proof of the decadence and intrigue of the royal court. Through it all, the Priestess remained statute-still, bearing every indignity with stoic silence, all the while thinking of ten different ways to kill the fat fool.

The eunuch gave her bottom a final squeeze. "There's nothing but curves hidden beneath silk. She seems clean enough."

Her clothing in disarray, the Priestess made a show of restoring order to the intricate layers. The guard captain watched from the doorway, a leer on his face.

"Just one more thing, deary." The matron gave her a shrewd look. "Sit down and let Sal check those pretty slippers of yours."

The Priestess remained cool as still water. Taking a seat, she extended her right foot, relying on desert taboos to keep her secret safe.

The eunuch knelt and fondled each foot, but he never bothered to remove her slippers. "Nothing here." He snorted. "Pretty slippers, but you won't walk far in those without going lame."

The Priestess hid her triumph, moving her feet back under the divan, a woman trying to regain her modesty. "Are you done?"

The matron flashed a gap-toothed smile. "All but the waiting."

The Priestess had spent many nights studying the scrying bowl, learning the ways of the palace, but she hid her knowledge behind a façade of questions. "The waiting? What do you mean by 'the waiting'?"

"Didn't you ever wonder why you were told to present yourself at noon?" Clucking like an old hen, the matron settled on the opposite divan, and poured herself a goblet of wine. "The courtesans are always told to come early. Gives any poisons time to take effect." She waved toward the eunuch sitting cross-legged on the floor. "We'll just sit here, enjoy this fine repast, and see if Sal still feels well by the time the sun sets." Flashing a sly smile, she added, "You see, deary, if Sal lives then you live. Let's drink to his good health." Reclining on the divan, the matron sipped wine and nibbled on dried fruits, smiling like a cat sated with cream.

It was only then that the Priestess saw the hidden risk. "And Sal won't be having anything to eat or drink till sunset?"

The matron's smile grew. "That's right, deary." She made a clucking noise. "Wouldn't be a fair test otherwise, would it?" She waved a hand toward the platter. "Help yourself, deary, there's more than enough for the both of us."

The Priestess stared at the eunuch, considering the possibilities. The fat lump was safe from her...but what if he'd been poisoned ahead of time? She'd come as a debt-payment from Prince Razzur, the king's strongest rival. Poisoning the eunuch would be a shrewd way for a skilled player to eliminate a threat and damage the reputation of the prince. *Surely the king was not that shrewd.* Angry at the thought of being outmaneuvered, she pushed the risk from her mind, deciding to rely on the king's legendary lust. She'd gamble on Razzur's reputation, the most skilled and exotic courtesans in all of Radagar. Surely the king could not resist the chance to sample the best of Razzur's karesh? The question vexed her, but only time would tell. She studied the eunuch through narrowed eyes, willing the sands of the hourglass to flow faster, impatient for her chance to kill a king.

10

Liandra

The queen's councilors clamored to be heard. "They're raping the north! Whole villages put to the torch! Rumors say they take no prisoners."

"These religious fanatics fight like barbarians!"

"They must be stopped lest they reach Pellanor!"

The queen sat enthroned at the head of the council table, listening to the rantings of her loyal lords. Such small men, she despaired of getting good advice from any of them. "My lords," she raised her voice above the tumult, "this council was warned of war. Surely you expected no less from the enemy?"

Her words dampened their outrage. Deflated, their stares circled the table as if looking for a scapegoat.

Lord Lenox clutched a handkerchief like a white flag, wiping a sheen of sweat from his forehead. "We must retake the north! All that prime farmland cannot fall to the enemy."

Lord Mills snickered. "We all know where your holdings lie. A penniless lord is of little use to anyone."

"Enough." The queen intervened. "The entire kingdom is at risk unless we defeat the enemy." She gave them an icy glare. "We have come for advice, not argument." She gestured to her deputy shadowmaster. "Master Raddock, provide our council with a summary of the latest dispatches."

The chamber stilled, like a flock of vultures awaiting a meal.

The master cleared his throat, unaccustomed to speaking in council. "Dispatches from Prince Stewart confirm the enemy's numbers at nigh on sixty thousand."

"*Sixty!*" Lord Lenox looked like he would faint.

Lord Mills said, "We were told to expect forty thousand not sixty."

Master Raddock cleared his throat. "Our initial intelligence was wrong."

"But..." Lord Lenox made a strangled sound.

The queen glared. "Now you see the danger of underestimating our enemy." She gestured to her shadowmaster. "Continue."

"The Flame Army cuts a swath through the countryside. Burning villages as they march, they leave nothing but death in their wake. The Rose Army has engaged the enemy's raiding parties, seeking to cut off their supplies. The prince strives to empty the villages and remove the harvest to the nearest strongholds, but he warns that the enemy marches in a straight line. So far nothing blunts their progress, a spearhead aimed at Pellanor."

A grim hush settled over the chamber.

The queen studied her councilors. "There is more."

Master Raddock continued. "We've received a dispatch from the Master Archivist. Radagar's full might has been purchased. Ten thousand mercenaries march to Pellanor to take up the city's defense."

Master Saddler nodded. "Finally some good news."

Lord Lenox intervened. "Ten thousand will not be enough," he shook his head, "not nearly enough."

"No, it will not be enough." The queen agreed with her treasurer. "That is why we have summoned our full council. We seek ideas to defeat a larger army."

Lord Mills was the first to reply. Dark hair and dark eyes and rakish good looks, the lordling spoke with a certainty that far outstripped his years. "Give them what they want."

The queen drilled him with her stare. "Meaning?"

"Lanverness is attacked because of our wealth. So give them what they want." He smoothed his mustache, jeweled rings flashing from an elegant hand. "Offer them gold from the royal treasury. Pay them to sheath their swords and turn away."

"A bribe?"

"A crude word," Lord Mills offered a snake's smile. "Think of it as paying a ransom in order to save the kingdom."

"And what price would you put on our kingdom?"

The dapper lordling shrugged. "Perhaps half the treasury." Gasps rippled around the table, but Lord Mills stared them down. "Better to lose half than all."

How easily her lords spent her hard-earned treasury. "And once the gold is paid, what makes you think the enemy will march away?"

The lord shrugged. "Make them trade their swords for gold, without swords there can be no war."

"With so much gold, they can buy more swords." She gave the lordling a scathing glare. "You would have us surrender before the fight is barely begun." Her voice was laden with disgust. "Aside from Lord Mills, do any of you offer a suggestion to *win* the war?"

Major Ranoth, a craggy-faced veteran with a gruff voice, took up the challenge. "The dispatch from the prince says the enemy marches straight for Pellanor. Even with ten thousand mercenaries, the city will be difficult to defend." His voice dropped to a low growl. "Majesty, will you take the prince's advice and move your court to Kardiff?"

"We have been through this before." Liandra put steel in her voice. "The crown will stay in Pellanor as a symbol to our people."

"But majesty..."

She raised her hand, forestalling him. "We shall arm our citizenry, and offer weapons training to any who seek it. Let the people of this good realm fight to protect their city."

The major shook his head. "But majesty, the crown prince emptied the city of all able-bodied men. Aside from merchants too fat to lift a sword, there's none left to fight save graybeards and youngsters."

"Nevertheless, we shall offer them swords and pikes. The state of a man's beard does not preclude him from fighting. And if nothing else, it will allow the veterans to man the most critical posts."

The major nodded, "As you wish."

Lord Lenox intervened. "It will not be enough, not nearly enough."

"Lord Lenox, are you our treasurer or a doomsayer?"

"We need a diversion."

The queen looked up, catching the scent of a fresh idea. The statement came from the Lord Sheriff, a seasoned swordsman with a flamboyant shock of red hair, the man she thought of as her fox. "What do you mean?"

"If Pellanor cannot be easily defended, then we need to divert the enemy to another goal."

Her gaze pinned the sheriff. "Tell us more."

"Why does the enemy march on Pellanor? Is it for the gold of the treasury or the rose crown?"

"Both."

The sheriff nodded. "Then why not make them choose?"

"An interesting gambit." The queen took up the thought. "Move the treasury and they might split their army, or better yet, march to another city, perhaps one more fortified than Pellanor." She gave the lord sheriff her most gracious smile. "We like the way you think, Lord Sheldon. We will speak more on this matter."

The sheriff bowed and she turned her gaze to the other councilors. "Are there any other ideas worthy of consideration?" When none were forthcoming, she rose and extended her hand with her ringed hand. "This council is adjourned."

Her loyal lords leaped to take their leave, the lords Lenox and Mills lingering the longest, but it was the lord sheriff she favored with a smile. "Walk with us."

She swept from the chamber with the dashing sheriff at her side. "If we decide to move the treasury, where would you advise?"

"Kardiff is the most obvious choice. It has the strongest fortress but it is also the most northerly of your strongholds."

"If not Kardiff, then where?"

"Lingard or Graymaris, they are both strong city fortresses, protected by stout walls. Graymaris has the advantage of being the furthest south, making the enemy work for the prize."

"Your suggestion has merit. We want you to prepare to move the treasury to Graymaris. Plan the route and choose the men, but be discrete, and report only to us."

"How soon do you want the treasury moved?"

"Not until after the mercenaries arrive from Radagar, otherwise we will not have the men to spare."

He nodded. "I will need an inventory of the treasury."

"Master Raddock will assist you, but the other council members need know nothing. We will tell them ourselves when the time is ripe." She gave him a piercing glance.

"Understood, your majesty."

A pair of guards snapped to attention as they reached her solar. She offered the sheriff her ringed hand. "You have our every confidence, our cunning fox among the hounds."

Flashing a gallant smile, he kissed her ring. "Ever at your service." He lingered for just a moment, and then he turned and walked away with a jaunty swagger.

His reaction pleased her, a touch of brightness in a long weary day. She turned toward the doors and the guards rushed to throw them open. Warmth and brightness welcomed her. Liandra entered her solar, a sanctuary against the demands of court. She clapped her hands and her ladies leaped to attend. "We are done with the fineries of court."

Gentle hands unbound her hair, while others attended to the intricacies of her gown. So many hooks and buttons, Liandra sighed to be released. After a long day, her gown seemed constricting, the harsh demands of image. Settling into a plush velvet robe, she took her ease before the fire. As the other women retreated, Lady Sarah approached, balancing a small silver tray. "A bit of supper, majesty, chicken broth and a mug of mulled wine."

She had no stomach for food. "Take it away."

"But majesty, you must eat."

Liandra heard the subtle steel beneath the words. The queen capitulated. "Oh, put it there," she gestured to small side table, "you mother us like a hen."

Lady Sarah flashed a satisfied smile. "Someone has to." She set the tray on the table. "Will there be anything else?"

"No. Yes, keep us company."

With a curtsey, the petite auburn-haired woman settled into a small chair on the far side of the hearth. After more than a dozen years of service, Lady Sarah had the rare knack of providing companionship without the distraction of annoying chatter. The younger woman began to knit, weaving a steady rhythmic clacking with her needles.

Something about the sound was soothing to the queen. "What is it this time?"

"A scarf for my niece."

"Hmmm." The queen stared into the fire, her mind beset with worries.

"The seamstress shops of Pellanor will be busy this fall."

The queen's stare snapped to her senior lady-in-waiting. "Fashion is set by the queen."

"Just so," the knitting needles never missed a beat. "High waisted gowns, gathered just below the breasts, full and flowing. I expect a brocade will look best, or perhaps velvet, lots of rich velvets. Draping velvet can hide so much."

"You have a keen eye, Lady Sarah, pray that my councilors do not."

"Oh, men never notice such things till it hits them in the eye." She flashed a conspirator's smile. "Do you wish for a son or a daughter?"

Liandra laced her hands across the slight bulge of her stomach, indulging in a rare smile. "Oh this one will be a girl. The gods owe me a daughter."

A companionable silence settled between them, the knitting needles keeping time once more. It felt good to share her deepest secret, for she would need help keeping it. A royal secret kept hidden until the time was right.

"Will you tell the father?"

The question was softly asked yet it lanced the queen's heart. "Time will tell." Liandra looked away, staring into the crackling flames, the worries of a kingdom heavy on her shoulders. The Master Archivist was on his way back to Pellanor, bringing a small army of mercenaries. The mercenaries were welcome but not the man himself. Her stomach clenched at the thought of him, a conflict of duty and longing. She dreaded confronting him, but he'd made his choice. From the start, she'd made it plain she'd brook no threat to her crown. She'd never expected such a betrayal, not from him. Her mind shied away from the hurt, turning instead to the greater problem. The enemy showed no quarter, raping and pillaging her kingdom. She was desperate to defeat a larger army. Hunger was proving too slow a weapon and war had never been her province. Her fingers drummed the armrest. At least she'd gained one idea from her council. Perhaps the treasury could be used in more than one scheme. War was a sticky business, and she needed to weave plots beyond anything she'd done before. Something complex enough to preserve a kingdom and a crown, for Liandra knew there would be no one to save her if she failed.

11

The Priestess

The Priestess played the waiting game, studying the eunuch for signs of poison. Bald and fat, he sat cross-legged on the floor. A thoughtful look filled his moon-shaped face, as if he counted his own heartbeats, searching for a lethal flaw. A bellwether for treachery, the eunuch was safe from the Priestess, but a king's household is ever full of plots. She'd come to the palace under the banner of House Razzur, a rival to the king, so any treachery was possible. She loathed the idea of being ensnared by another's schemes, but she'd entered this viper's nest of her own accord. So she kept her face a mask of calm, keeping watch on the eunuch, knowing her life was tied to his, waiting for time to unravel the truth. Plots within plots, such was the business of killing kings.

The sands of the hourglass dragged, the afternoon stretching to forever. Without a window it was impossible to tell the true hour of the day or night. Just when she thought she could no longer bear the wait, a breathless page burst into the chamber. "The king commands entertainment!"

A startled look flashed across the matron's face but was quickly hidden beneath a scowl. Heaving herself off the divan, she offered the Priestess a gap-toothed smile. "Sal lives, so you live." She made a clumsy bow. "I hope you'll pardon us both for the search, m'lady."

Relief washed through her, the palace not nearly as devious as she imagined. "The king is well served by your efforts...but I need my companions in order to provide entertainment fit for royalty."

"The guards will bring them to you," the old lady's smile changed to a sour sneer, "assuming they've been found free of treachery." The matron bowed and ushered the eunuch from the chamber.

The Priestess watched them leave, wondering at the venom beneath the old woman's words. Perhaps it was the bitterness of old age confronted by beauty. Whatever the reason, she'd survived the gauntlet of searches, the first triumph of her plan. Stretching like a cat, she adjusted her silken layers, preparing for her performance.

Footsteps at the doorway announced the arrival of her servants. Two muscle-bound bearers carried the basket between them, the boy from the market following behind. She searched their faces. "Are you well?"

Rashid, the senior bearer said, "Yes, mistress. They searched us, just as you said, but we're fine."

"I didn't like it." The cherub-faced boy fidgeted, staring at the marble floor, clutching his flute in his hands.

Crossing the room, she cupped his chin, gently lifting his face till his dark stare met hers. "You've done well." She gave him a warm re-assuring smile, her voice like honey. "Neffer, are ready to play your flute for the king?"

A smile lit up his face, a cherub glimpsing heaven. "Yes, lady."

"Good." She brushed a playful hand through his auburn curls. "Play as you did in the market and you'll charm the entire court." Her voice dropped to a whisper. "Play your best for me and your reward will be great."

He nodded, his gaze bright with the desire to please.

She smiled; boys of his age were so easily charmed.

A guard at the doorway growled a warning. "The king grows impatient."

Releasing the boy, she turned to the two bearers. "You both know your orders?" Seeing their nods, she made her voice loud enough to be heard by the guards. "Then let's give the king a performance he'll never forget." She gestured toward the basket.

The bearers lowered the basket, tilting the opening toward her. Ducking low, she slipped inside, moving to the rear. Placing one foot against the back wall, she transferred her weight, tipping the basket upright. The bowl-shaped basket wobbled back and forth, finally settling in the vertical. Crouched at the bottom, she took a moment to orient herself by peering through the rough weave, spying on the guards hovering in the doorway. Bracing her hands against the sides, she said, "You may begin."

The bearers lifted the basket to their shoulders and followed the guards through the maze of corridors, the boy trailing behind. The Priestess braced against the basket's sway, like being set adrift in a rocky sea. She clutched the sides while trying to peer through the weave, eager to reach the king.

The din of male revelry announced their arrival. Royal princes clamored for entertainment, their strident voices refusing to be bored. Sizzling smells of grilled lamb laced with firespice wafted through the basket, proof she'd arrived as the dinner entertainment.

The basket was lowered to the floor, a sudden stop to the rocking motion. Pressing her face to the weave, the Priestess searched for the king. Opulence was her first impression. The royal hall was a vision of extravagance pushed to decadence. A forest of golden columns lined a dining hall paved with green marble and semi-precious stones. Turbaned princes reclined on gilded couches sipping drinks and sampling platters of sweetmeats. Scantily clad servant-girls scurried in the shadows, pouring goblets of wine and offering skewers of grilled meat. A feast set for princes, the king had a reputation for surrounding himself with royal sycophants; she'd have a full audience for her performance.

She moved around the basket till she gained a glimpse of the king. There was no mistaking the master of the Cobra Throne. Seated upon a raised dais, the king lounged on a golden divan large enough to hold a dozen people. Bald headed and olive skinned, King Cyrus was a giant of a man buried beneath rolls of fat. Bloated with power, he lolled across the divan like a python that had swallowed numerous rivals but digested none. The Priestess narrowed her gaze, considering her prey. In many ways, the king's glutinous appearance was a deception. Cyrus was a famed wrestler, strength hidden beneath obesity, a dangerous man in more ways than one. The bored look on his broad face hid a cunning cruelty. She smiled, wondering if the king had ever been bested by a woman. Tonight would prove an interesting challenge. She'd pit her poisonous elegance against his muscled bulk, trusting desire to be his downfall.

A stern-faced seneschal pounded his iron-shod staff against the marble floor. "The king has called for entertainment."

From the basket's heart, the Priestess watched as the two bearers and the boy fell prostrate to the floor.

The king gave a negligent wave and the seneschal said, "You may rise and address his majesty."

The three scrambled to their feet, keeping their heads bowed. The lead bearer, Rashid, took a step toward the king, his voice a deep rumble. "Lady Cereus, the best of Prince Razzur's karesh, has come as debt-payment to the king."

A ripple of excitement stirred the male guests.

Rashid kept his head bowed. "We humbly crave your majesty's permission to begin?"

The king made a curt gesture, his face a mask of bored indifference.

The two bearers bowed low, retreating to stand behind the basket. Neffer settled cross-legged on the floor. Without preamble, he raised the flute to his lips. A single pure note pierced the hall; a siren's call beckoning the attention of every man in the room. The boy held the note for a small eternity, and then he let it descend into a lilting melody, dissolving into the subtle weave of the snake charmer's song.

The Priestess watched from the basket's heart, waiting for flute's spell to take hold. An intricate weave of notes, the song teased the mind with mystery, tempting the imagination. Designed to enthrall a cobra, the ancient song bespelled her audience. Princes jaded with orgies sat forward, staring at the basket, curiosity naked on their faces. She kept them waiting...till their hands and heads began to sway, caught by the charm of the flute.

And then she struck. Holding fast to one end, she threw a coil of green ribbon up through the basket's mouth. Like a green snake uncoiling, the ribbon shot upwards, answering the summons of the flute.

Gasps of surprise rippled around the room...followed by a cascade of deep-throated chuckles.

Keeping her hands out of sight, she played the ribbon, making it dance to the flute, while slowly drawing it backwards.

The basket swallowed the ribbon...and the melody of the flute deepened, becoming more mysterious, more seductive.

Now it was her turn. She raised a single hand, a slow weave rising up out of the basket like a cobra caught by the flute. With each move, the bracelets on her arms chimed with feminine seduction.

"Ahhhh..." The princes sighed with anticipation.

Her hand wove an age-old spell, a subtle dance beckoning the men with a promise of more. The mood of her audience intensified, the men leaning forward on their divans. A sexual heat flooded the hall, setting them on edge. Her second hand joined the first, a pair of pale white cobras dancing to the music, the double entendre of death and beauty entwined, a lure to the desert-born.

And then it was time. Raising one slippered foot to the side of the basket, she pressed her weight forward, tipping it over. Tucking her knees to her chest, she rolled through the open mouth, leaping to her feet like a djinn sprung from a bottle.

"*Bak-her!*" Whistles and claps of appreciation rippled through the princes.

The dance began in earnest, her every movement liquid, her whole body weaving to the flute. She became the cobra, sinuous and hypnotic, full of sexual allure. With each twirl, layers of perfumed silk fluttered to the floor, revealing a flash of shapely thigh or a swell of pearl-white breast. Her ankle bracelets chimed to the rhythm of the dance. Light flashed from the crystals bedecking her slippered feet. She swirled, heat flushing her cheeks. Grasping her long braid of raven black hair, she wove it across her body like a snake, slithering across her lips and down between her breasts, reaching for her loins. And all the while, she kept her gaze fixed on the king, as if she danced for him alone.

Her dance had the proper effect. The king's stare followed her every movement, his gaze entranced by her slippered feet. His face flushed red as he leaned forward, the tip of his tongue darting in and out like a serpent scenting for sex.

She quickened the pace, loosing her dark skills into the dance. Her skin smoldered with heat, evoking temptation with every move. She called on the Darkness to deepen her allure. Power thrummed through her and the dance intensified. Sizzling with seduction, she swirled to the beat. Sexual need leaped through the men like fire to kindling. She felt their stares pounding against her and fed their need back into the dance. Empowered by their desire, she blazed with sensuality, promising a thousand delights. Her hands caressed her curves, making wanton gestures, a surrogate for the men. Silk swirled around her, a subtle mix of skin and tempting silhouettes. Like liquid desire, she flowed with the flute, weaving a spell of enchantment. The men gasped with need, but she kept her gaze fixed on the king.

The voice of the flute soared to a crescendo. The Priestess danced to the edge of the dais. Silk whispered from her hand, a soft lash teasing the king. Bells chimed on her wrists and ankles. Like a fantasy fulfilled, she stared into the king's eyes, offering a promise and a dare.

The flute reached the climax, stopping in mid note.

The Priestess melted to the floor, a flutter of silk draped across the steps, her open hand reaching up to the king.

"Huzzah!"

"Bak-her!" Cheers and whistles echoed through the hall, a thunder of male appreciation...but the Priestess held her pose, staring up at the king, making him the center of her world.

Cyrus stared down at her, his eyes dark pools of wanting. "Your name, my beauty?"

"Cereus, majesty, yours to please." The Priestess hid her smile, knowing she'd captured a king.

Cyrus reached for her, offering his hand.

"Don't touch her!" The cry sliced through the chamber like an assassin's sword. "The eunuch dies of poison! The temptress is a trap!"

The Priestess stifled a gasp, keeping her stare fixed on the king.

Annoyance flashed deep in the king's eyes but not surprise. Not surprise, the Priestess froze feeling the jaws of a trap. So the king ordered the eunuch poisoned to discredit his most bitter rival. Plots within plots, she was betrayed by politics. Rage flooded through her but she buried it deep.

Chaos erupted in the chamber. Guards sprang to the dais, their swords whispering from scabbards, but the Priestess did not move.

Cold steel pressed against her throat, the keen edge of death. The Priestess froze, staring up at the king, her gaze smoldering with sexual promise. She sent a fervent prayer to the Dark Lord, knowing her life depended on her allure.

12

Liandra

Five times Liandra changed her gown, finally settling on the gold samite with the deep neckline and the dagged sleeves. It was her most regal. Tonight, she needed to be pure queen.

A single guard waited outside her solar, Sir Durnheart, handsome in his emerald tabard, the hilt of his blue steel sword gleaming over his right shoulder, the one knight she could absolutely trust. She gave him the barest of nods and he fell into step behind her.

Candles lit the hallway, shadows merging with the last rays of sunlight. Tapestries lined the walls, exquisite carpets on the marble floors, but she saw none of it, her mind churning with arguments. Down the stairway and through a long hall, she reached the throne room. A pair of guards rushed to open the gilded doors.

She hesitated on the threshold, watching the last rays of light play across the long hall, and then she crossed the checkerboard floor, climbing the dais to her throne. Designed to impress, the throne was a massive confection of gold roses offset by emerald leaves. Worth a king's ransom, she considered it a fitting stage for a queen. She took her time arranging her gown, perfecting every line, her bejeweled hands glittering in the candlelight. Finally satisfied, she nodded to Sir Durnheart. "Bring him. And while he is here, let no one enter."

The knight saluted and made a smart pivot, striding the length of the hall.

The doors opened and shut with a resounding thud, echoing through the silence.

The queen sat alone with her thoughts. It had been almost two months since she'd last seen him, yet memories of their nights still burned with passion. She bit her lip, refusing to think of it. Tonight, she needed to be pure queen. Her fingers drummed the armrest. Minutes seemed like hours. Empty and cavernous, she held court to shadows, candles flickering the length of the audience hall.

And then the doors opened and her heartbeat spiked. Somber in robes of black, he stood on the threshold, tall and lean and dark as a shadow, her spymaster, her confidant, her lover. Their eyes locked. His glance struck like smoldering embers. Liandra gripped the throne's arms, forcing herself to remain statue-still.

Like her, he hesitated, as if considering his next move, but then he crossed the checkerboard, stopping at the foot of the dais. "You summoned me, my queen?" His dark gaze met hers, an intelligence as fierce as her own.

"Have you forgotten how to kneel?" She made her voice hard as ice, determined to ignore the weariness etched on his face.

"No, majesty." He sank to one knee, his gaze boring up at her. "But I wonder at your ire."

"You wonder?" Two weeks, the length of time she'd kept him waiting, locked in his own chambers, a political prisoner. She'd heard he'd worn a path in his carpet. "Surely, you know the cause."

"I sent you a report on the negotiations with Radagar. If you are unhappy with the price..."

She cut him off, "You know better." She gave him a cold stare, letting the silence reflect her displeasure.

His gaze narrowed, staring up at her. "I've heard rumors you've been unwell."

"Indigestion. A bout of bad trout."

He nodded, relief in his gaze.

How easily he accepted her explanation. Disappointment ambushed her, yet she refused to succumb. Staring down at him, she willed icy daggers into her glare.

Silence built like a wall between them. He broke first, uttering a weary sigh. "So, the traitor prince."

"Yes, the prince," her voice dropped to a deadly hiss, "how dare you usurp our power."

"Justice needed to be served."

"Justice belongs to the ruling sovereign." She filled her voice with disdain. "*We* wear the crown. *You* are merely our spymaster."

He catapulted to his feet, anger blazing on his face. "*Justice* needed to be served and *you* were locked in indecision."

"No, we considered the problem from all angles."

"You were *never* going to decide."

"Vacillation can be a tool of statecraft." She meant to be cold and calculating, but he brought out her claws, her words coming in a rush of heat. "Once removed, heads cannot be replaced. Shall we be hasty with *your* head? We're sure Sir Durnheart could take it in a single stroke."

"Madam, it had to be done."

"Without the queen's approval?"

"Even in prison, he was a threat to you! And the longer you delayed, the worse it looked!"

Rage threatened to engulf her. "You sleep with me and then you grasp for my crown!"

"It's not like that!"

"Then tell us how it is, for it looks like treason!"

His face paled. "No, not that, never that."

Once unleashed, her rage spewed like venom. "And we only learned of the deed in our council. *In our council!* A crown is a slippery thing and a sovereign can never be uninformed, especially not a queen."

"I never meant..." he shook his head. "You don't understand."

"Then explain before we pass judgment."

"I did it to protect you!" He began to pace like a caged beast, running his hand through his iron-gray hair. "It had to be done. Even imprisoned Danly was a threat to your crown. Justice needed to be served and this was the best solution. Dying, Danly might have become a martyr to the Red Horns. Unmanned, he proves he's not worthy of the throne. I knew he'd choose the coward's way, that's why I offered him a choice. It was the perfect gambit. Don't you see?" He turned and stared up at her, his hands spread wide in appeal. "Danly made his choice. Now he can live out his days as an exiled eunuch, with no threat to your crown, and no blood on your hands."

"But it was a decision only a sovereign could make." Her voice was cold and deadly, masking the pain of betrayal. "We *trusted* you, and you usurped our power, acting behind our back!"

"Yes, I did. I acted for you." He met her stare, his gaze as sharp and proud as an eagle. "I did it for Liandra, the woman beneath that cold crown. I sought to spare you the pain. For no woman, highborn or low, should ever be forced to condemn her own son to death. Such a thing leaves a scar on the soul. A burden you should never have to bear. So, yes, I did it for you." His voice deepened to a hoarse rasp. "I did it for us."

For us? His words struck like a hammer blow to her soul. She ached to tell him her secret, tell him about the longed for daughter, but she feared it would only give him power over her, a tool to be used against her. "How can there ever be an 'us', for I will yield the crown to no man."

"Madam, I never asked you to."

The sincerity in his voice almost overwhelmed her, almost. She closed her eyes, reminding herself of his rapier-wit, of his silver tongue. "We should never have put off the crown to be with you." When she opened her eyes, he was kneeling once more.

"Madam, you never did." The stark honesty on his face nearly blunted her anger. "To me you are always, and ever will be, the queen."

His words tugged at her heart. "Oh Robert," her voice threatened to break, "you should never have reached for my power. How can I ever trust you?"

"I serve you always." His stare smoldered into her. "We are bound by more than mere words."

The woman in her longed to believe him, longed to forgive her intellectual equal, her confidant...her lover. But she was also the queen, and this betrayal cut too close to her crown. "We cannot have those we trust act behind our back. A queen must be ever vigilant. We have made our decision." She made her voice cold and implacable. "Master Raddock is appointed our new shadowmaster. If you wish to serve, you will report to him, but henceforth, you shall be banished from our sight."

He gaped at her, openly hurt, an expression she'd never seen on his face.

His voice dropped to a hoarse rasp. "Don't make this mistake."

"It is *you* that made the mistake."

As if he aged a decade before her eyes, he slowly climbed to his feet. For the longest time, he stared at her, his eyes as dark as obsidian chips, drinking up the light, and then he bowed. "Ever yours," and turned and walked away, his back stiff and his shoulders straight, as if he wore pride like a cloak.

Her fingernails scraped against gold, her hands clutching the throne, but she refused to speak, refused to rescind her command. She watched as he walked the length of the throne room, crossing the checkerboard floor. The massive gold doors closed with a dull thud, swallowing him whole, and she was once more alone. *Alone with her crown.* Her hands laced across her stomach, knowing she had more than one crown to protect. A single tear escaped her eye. In her mind, she knew she'd made the right decision, the only decision a queen could make, but then why, oh why, did it hurt so much?

13

Danly

R ain fell like a plague, churning the road to mud. The wagon wheels clogged, slowing the horses to a dull plod...but Danly didn't mind. Speed was his enemy, taking him deeper into exile. Huddled beneath a sodden blanket, chains chaffing his ankles, the prisoner-prince considered his options. For the first time in his life, he had no gold in his pockets, no servants swarming to serve him, no loyal soldiers at his beck and call. Everything he'd valued had been stripped away, lost in defeat. Despair threatened to drown him...yet the need for vengeance persisted. A prince of the realm, he refused to go quietly into exile.

The journey gave him time to think. His fever abated and the pain at his groin lessened to a dull ache...but the loss of his manhood galled him. Memories of his past dalliances tormented him. *A eunuch prince,* Danly shuddered at the thought. To never know a woman's pleasures, forever scorned as less than a man...his hatred built to a rage, a black bonfire burning in his chest. Torn between hatred and despair, he realized he'd kept one thin advantage. He giggled at the thought. Perhaps his past could mortgage his future. The Spider Queen thought she'd taken everything from him, but Danly still had his reputation. His spending and debauchery had been legendary, the Prince of Excess, a patron of wine, women and gold. He wondered if it would be enough to win his freedom.

Captain Talcot kept them moving, a bark of orders at dawn's first light. Always heading west, the wagon creaked and groaned, passing through villages and farmland, his escort of soldiers staying close. Peasants gathered along the muddy road, gawking at the shackled prisoner. Bearded and bedraggled, wearing little more than rags, Danly sat hunched in the wagon, realizing how far he'd fallen. A few threw rubbish, but Danly saw no sign of recognition in their faces, just a common criminal paraded before the crowd. *Just a prisoner, not even a prisoner-prince,* the humiliation burned deep, branding his soul. The Spider Queen had much to atone for. Pulling the blanket close, he hid his face, thankful the wagon kept rolling.

On the captain's orders, they avoided the village inns and taverns, camping in the fields at twilight. But the rain made the nights miserable, the soldiers grumbling against their orders...all to Danly's advantage.

League after league, he studied his captors. Captain Talcot proved a stern-faced man wedded to duty. Danly suspected the captain was a queen's shadowman in soldier's clothing, a dangerous adversary. His second in command, the burly sergeant, was almost as bad, always sharpening his sword while keeping a keen eye on the prisoner. Carter, the former Red Horn, was full of spite, taking every chance to heap insults on the prisoner-prince. But among the other three soldiers, Danly found fertile ground for whispered words. One in particular, proved susceptible, Athon Baird, a peasant turned soldier, a young man with six kids and too many debts. The red-haired soldier enjoyed a good story and Danly sought every opportunity to spin tales of wine, women, and gold, trying to parley his past into a future.

Twilight threatened, streaks of red creasing a soggy sky. The wagon rumbled off the road and came to a stop under a stand of birch. Danly waited, feigning weakness, watching as the soldiers fell into their nightly routine. Splitting logs and collecting kindling they made camp, bedrolls spread around a crackling fire.

As he did most nights, Athon Baird finished his duties and then came to help Danly from the wagon. "Hungry?"

"Always." Danly eased toward the back of the wagon, his chains clanking with every movement. "And I need to walk. I'm stiff from too much sitting." Athon led him in a slow walk around the camp. Danly stretched, shuffling to the limits of his chains. "It's good to walk." The rain came to a stop but the ground remained sodden. Water leached through the rags wrapping his feet. *Rags instead of boots*, each soggy step reminded him of how much he'd lost. Danly swallowed his bitterness, struggling to keep his voice friendly. "Did I tell you about the time I bet a thousand golds on a single roll of the dice?"

"A thousand golds!" Athon grinned, eager for a story.

"Duke Anders had a fierce reputation as a gambler but I knew his luck was about to change, so I bet it all, a thousands golds, and I dared him to match the bet."

"Did he?"

Danly nodded. "I'd pricked his pride, challenging his reputation in front of his friends. The duke couldn't back down, but he didn't have enough golds to cover the wager, so he drew a ring from his finger, a gold ring with a ruby the size of a pigeon's egg."

Athon whistled. "A ruby that size would be worth a king's ransom."

"It was a family heirloom, a rare ruby of uncommon worth. I'd seen him wear it in the council chambers and I wanted that ring."

Athon flashed a grin, as if a common foot soldier could gauge the worth of such a ruby. Danly lowered his voice, drawing out the tale. "I passed the dice to the duke, giving him the first roll. Everyone gathered around to watch. The dice tumbled across the table...coming to rest on a ten."

Athon nodded gravely, "A hard throw to beat."

"Exactly, but lady luck was with me." In truth, he'd lost the throw and the ring to the Lord Raven but truth would not help his cause. "I scooped up the dice...and rolled an eleven!"

Athon took the bait, whistling in amazement. "Victory by a single pip! To gain a ruby like that for a mere throw of a dice." He shook his head. "Such a ring would change a man's life."

It was the response Danly had been fishing for. "Sometimes you have to take a chance, to risk everything when the prize is worth it...else your life will never change."

Athon snorted. "Chances like that are for princes...not men like me."

"No, my friend, I'm offering you just such a chance," Keeping his voice to a whisper, Danly lied with conviction. "I still have that ruby ring, and plenty of gold, all hidden in a safe place."

Athon stared at him, uncertainty in his gaze. "Where?"

"In Pellanor, with friends." His voice dropped to a whisper. "That ring could be yours...if you help me escape." Athon shied away, but Danly gripped his arm. "Think on it."

The redhead looked troubled but he did not pull away...and he did not rouse the others.

"Bradford might join us," Danly named the dark-haired soldier who always grumbled at the captain's orders. "There's plenty of gold for both of you. Enough to make you rich men." His voice dropped to a hush. "Just find a way to slip me a dagger and the three of us will do the deed while the others sleep."

Athon shook his head. "I don't know," but the seed was clearly planted.

"Just think on it. It's all I ask."

"Baird!" The captain's voice rang from the campfire. "Get the prisoner back here."

Athon jumped, startled like a thief caught with a stolen purse. "Yes, sir!"

Danly smothered his fear, praying the redhead would not give the game away.

Savory smells of beef stew wafted from a cast-iron cauldron, waking his hunger. Danly perched on a small rock, accepting a plate heaped with stew and a steaming mug of tea. He used a biscuit to sop up the gravy, shoveling mouthfuls of tender meat and chunky carrot. The others ate in companionable silence, all except for Athon. Sitting on the far side next to the sergeant, the redhead fidgeted with his food instead of eating. To Danly's eyes, he looked guilty as hell. Worried the others might notice; Danly contrived to lean sideways, spilling his tea.

"Hells below!" Carter roared with pain, frantically wiping the steaming tea from his crotch. "You clumsy oaf!" He aimed a vicious kick at Danly. "The queen should have taken your bloody head!"

Danly curled into a ball, pain throbbing through his side.

Captain Talcot growled, "Enough."

Carter glared. "He's up to something, I swear it."

Fear pierced Danly's hopes.

"Enough, Carter." The captain's voice brooked no argument. "Let the prisoner be."

"I'm watching you." Carter grabbed his plate and moved to the far side of the fire.

Danly grimaced, exaggerating the pain. Reclaiming his plate, he asked for a second serving. Keeping his shoulders hunched and his head bowed, he ate in silence, hoping to be ignored...but all the while he spied on the red-haired soldier, worried Athon's nerves would give the plot away. Danly scowled, knowing the fate of a prince should never depend on the courage of a peasant, but the die was cast, the bait was set, and all he could do was wait.

14

The Priestess

The royal audience hall erupted in chaos. Princes roused by the threat of assassination bellowed for their guards. Servants dropped platters and scantily clad women fled screaming. Grim-faced guards circled the king, swords drawn, providing a thicket of protection.

Amidst the chaos, the Priestess remained still as death. Draped across the marble steps like an offering, she held the king's stare, daring to speak despite the sword at her throat. "Sire, I am innocent."

The king barked a laugh but his gaze was drunk with lust.

A captain of the royal guard approached, his fist pounding against his gilded breastplate. "My liege, the eunuch writhes in convulsions, foaming at the mouth, death by poison. The temptress and her servants must pay the assassin's price."

A male voice yelled, "Give her to me, lord, I'll see that she pays!"

The Priestess studied the king, her mind frantic to unravel the plot. The eunuch had seemed healthy enough when she'd left the holding chamber, which meant that he must have been poisoned after she'd been summoned. If the king had ordered his own eunuch poisoned, then he knew she was free of threat. And knowing she was not a threat, he might succumb to lust. Drawing on all her Dark powers, she stared up at him. "Sire, you *know* I'm innocent." Her sultry voice held a thousand promises, her life depending on her allure.

King Cyrus flashed a cunning smile, a python swallowing a meal. "You came from Razzur, a debt payment from my dear half brother." He shrugged, his smile deepening. "Such a tempting opportunity, how could I not?" But his dark gaze brimmed with wanting, bitten by seduction's poison. "Now that I've seen you..." His voice sank to a hoarse whisper. "I want to taste you..."

"Then taste me." Her voice was low and sultry, stoking his need. "I'm only a woman...trained to please."

He licked his lips.

The captain of the guard intervened. "She's dangerous, sire. Let me kill her for you."

A male voice yelled, "I'll take her to bed! This one's too luscious to be wasted on a sword."

She stretched her hand out in supplication, the tips of her fingers brushing the king's sandaled foot. "Sire, take what you want." She gazed up at him. "You know I'm no threat." Her voice was low and throaty. "Do with me as you will but do not deny your needs."

The king's gaze darkened.

A second prince yelled, "Give her to us, Cyrus, we'll take the risk!"

The Priestess hid her smile, knowing the male rivalry helped her cause.

Another voice boasted, "I'll take her here, on the floor of the audience hall. We'll see how well she dances to *my* sword."

"Let me have her, sire! I'll plumb her secrets!"

"No, give her to me! I'll make her squirm!"

Anger flashed across the king's face. "*Silence!*" He roared like a lion brooking no rivals.

The pride of princes fell silent.

The king stood, hands on hips, a giant in height as well as girth. He glared at the assembly, his voice ringing with command. "House Razzur needs to be humbled. The two bearers and the boy shall pay the assassin's price. Take the bearers to the market and have them crucified."

Guards leaped to obey.

The boy screamed a piteous wail. "*No! Spare me!*"

"As for the boy," the king flashed a dangerous grin, "cage him in the market with two cobras. Add an additional cobra at every sunrise. We'll see how long his flute can keep the serpents at bay."

A prince yelled. "I'll wager he lasts three days!"

"Double the purse and I'll wager he lasts four!"

The Priestess shuddered, such a cruel court, and the king was the worst of all. The boy wept as they dragged him away. She regretted his fate, but pawns were often sacrificed for kings.

"As for the woman." He stared down at her, lust burning in his gaze. "Will you swear to serve?"

The Priestess drew on her power, her voice liquid allure. "*Anything* to please." She saw the fire stoked in the king's dark gaze.

A rumble of male approval echoed through the hall.

"And please me, you shall." The king gestured and the sword was removed.

She hid her triumph, reaching out to caress his foot. "Yours to command." Laying her head flat against the cold marble floor, she lifted his sandaled foot and placed it upon her head, the gravest insult to the desert-born, the gesture of a slave submitting to a master.

Shocked gasps echoed through the chamber. Women of the karesh were the third and fourth daughters of noble houses; they served but were never debased...at least not in public, but the Priestess knew her prey well, betting games of dominance and submission would ignite a reckless passion in her royal prey.

The king's voice rumbled with hunger. "You will attend me this very night." Removing his foot, he gestured for her to rise.

She sat at his feet, gazing up at him.

The king licked his lips, his face blazing with need.

A prince clapped. "Hazzuh!"

Another yelled, "Give her to us when you're done!"

The king's stare snapped to the pack of princes, scavengers hungry for the royal leavings. Annoyance washed across his face. "Be gone!" He waved a bejeweled hand, fat fingers thick with rings. "I grow weary of your chatter. You're all dismissed." Reaching down, he grasped her wrist and hauled her to her feet, urgency in his touch. "Come, my dark beauty, let's see how you dance in the royal bed chamber."

His grasp was like iron, cruel and unrelenting. Beneath the rolls of fat, Cyrus had strength enough to crush, to maim, to kill, a dangerous man to provoke. Clamping a meaty hand on her wrist, he led her down the dais to a side door. He half dragged her through a maze of hallways, his stride lengthened, full of purpose. Guards snapped to attention and servants bowed low, but the king paid them no heed.

Someone struck a gong while liveried servants rushed to open gilded doors. They entered the royal bedchamber, sending a bevy of servants to their knees.

The Priestess recognized the chamber from her scrying bowl. A sumptuous affair draped in green silk, every aspect lavish in scale and gilded with gold, a temple to decadence. Thick carpets covered the floor while gilded braziers lit the chamber, releasing a breath of frankincense. And in the center of the chamber, a massive divan dominated a raised dais. Large enough to hold an orgy, it was a bed befitting the appetites of an insatiable king.

Cyrus roared, "All of you out."

Servants scurried to obey, mice escaping through the only door. The king slammed the double doors shut, bolting them from within. Turning, he stared at her, a hungry smolder in his gaze. "Now, my dark beauty, I have you all to myself. What did you learn in Razzur's karesh?"

"How to dance." Her voice deepened. "How to tease." Tugging at a layer of silk, she offered a glimpse of cleavage. "A thousand ways to please." She knew just what he wanted, she'd seen it often enough in the scrying bowl. Steeling herself for what was to come, she held out her hand, beckoning him close. "Come, my king, let me show you the delights of House Razzur."

A predator gazed from his eyes, a conflict of hatred and wanting. Without warning, he charged, his quickness belying his massive girth. And then he struck, his hands coiling around her neck in a python's choke. Fat fingers squeezed with incredible strength, an iron grip choking her throat, his gold rings digging into tender flesh.

She gasped for breath, forcing herself not to fight, knowing submission was the only way to survive. Falling limp beneath his grasp, she gave him a liquid stare, her voice a hoarse rasp, *"Master?"*

He forced her to her knees. His eyes glazed, spittle foaming on his lips.

She stared up at him, trying not to struggle, knowing it would only push him past all reason. Desperate for breath, she wondered if she'd made a fatal mistake. So hard not to call on her magic, not to fight back...but then he released her. Gulping air, she crumpled to the floor. Sobbing for breath, she lay at his feet, playing her part in the charade, knowing the king needed to make a show of strength before he could be dominated.

"Get up." He nudged her with his sandaled foot, his voice hoarse with wanting. "Dance for me."

She dared a glance at his face. The raw hatred was gone, washed away by violence, leaving him free to indulge other emotions. Certain of victory, she rose like a cobra from a basket and began to dance. Hands and hips swayed as she moved around him, weaving a spell of enticement. Summoning the Darkness, she deepened her allure. Round and around she moved, brushing against him like a cat seeking pleasure. Slow and sure, she loosened his robes. Silk and samite fell discarded to the floor till the king stood naked, his face hungry with desire, his manhood rampant. Everything about him was thick and engorged, passion teetering on the brink of danger. She tightened her hold on him, fanning his desire while tugging him toward the bed.

A groan escaped him. The king reached for her, but she twirled away, leaving him panting. She shook her head. "Not yet." Pulling the ribbon from her braid, she released a cascade of raven hair, a rush of sandalwood scent. Tossing her head like a wild mare in heat, she struck him with her raven tresses, a thousand silken caresses across his naked skin, a sensual whip, an unrelenting tease. Round and round she danced, whipping him into a storm of need.

He groaned with pleasure, his manhood burgeoning with strain, his massive hands opening and closing, convulsive with need.

She evaded his grasp, pushing him onto the divan. The king toppled backward, a giant sprawled amongst a sea of pillows. Leaping onto the bed, she stood over him, slowly shedding her last layers. Each swath became a silken lash against his rampant manhood, whipping him into a frenzy. Naked, she knew just how to tease. His face turned deep crimson, his gaze dark with wanting...and then she took her chance. Setting her slippered foot on his chest, the gravest insult to a desert prince, she gazed down at him, lowering her voice to a seductive command, "My mighty king. My slave of the bedchamber."

Like many men of power, he longed to be dominated in bed. "Yesss..." He made the word a hiss of pleasure.

She pressed her foot into his chest. "What would you do to please me?"

His breathing deepened, his voice a hungry rasp, "Anything."

"Then kiss my foot."

His big hands captured her foot, slowly removing the gilded slipper. He gasped in delight. "Rouge on your toes!"

"Lick them. You know you want to."

Groaning, he gave into his fetish, his secret desire, his royal shame. Grasping her foot, he began to suck, making loud noises over each toe.

She hid her triumph, waiting for the poison to take hold. When he finished the first, a smear of red on his lips, she offered the second, a double dose. The harvest from her garden did not disappoint. Sweat erupted in rivers from his skin, pooling in the folds of fat. His gaze darkened and his voice became a hoarse croak, his manhood deflating to a limp sausage. Floundering amongst the pillows, he gazed at her, his eyes full of terror. *"What have you..."* but his voice faded to a wheeze, another advantage of nightshade.

The Priestess smiled, dropping all pretenses. "What have I done?" She traced her true name in the sweat on his chest. "I've killed a king."

He made one last grab for her, but his hands fell limp, his strength stolen by poison.

Laughing, she leaped from the bed and quickly dressed in her silken finery. While he wheezed on the bed, she ransacked his cedar chests. She took the first cloak she found, an expensive weave of dark blue wool, and twirled it around her shoulders. Next, she opened a small jewel chest. Emeralds, rubies, and diamonds, a fortune in jewelry glittered in the torchlight. Amongst the rings and pendants, she found one in particular that was worth her life, a golden broach fashioned in the shape of a rearing cobra, a pair of rubies for eyes. A sign of royal favor, Cyrus gave the broach to concubines he wished to see another night, a trinket to get them past the guards' scrutiny. She wondered how many women had worn the token only to die another night, killed for their knowledge of the royal fetish. This time would be different. She pinned the golden cobra to her cloak, prominently displayed above her heart, a token of triumph over a king.

Giving the jewel box a second glance, she decided not to waste the fortune. She emptied the chest into a pillowcase and twirled it into a roll, tying it around her waist, hidden beneath swirls of silk. Satisfied, she studied her victim.

Naked against a mound of pillows, his manhood shrunken beneath rolls of fat, the king lay sprawled across the divan. Soaked in sweat, he struggled for each breath. His struggle would be short-lived; the nightshade she'd used was particularly potent. In the meantime, he looked like a man sated with sex. The irony appealed to her, death by fetish.

Turning her back on the king, she eased the bolts on the door, slipping out of the royal bedchamber.

A pair of guards snapped to attention.

She started to close the door but the senior guard stopped her, his face full of suspicion.

Raising a finger to her lips, she glared a warning.

The guard ignored her, peering through the open doorway. The king chose that moment to issue a death rattle, a sound that was part wheeze, part snore.

She leaned toward the guard. "Wake him at your peril."

The guard paled and shut the door.

The Priestess hid her smile; fear was a beautiful thing. She decided to press her advantage. "Will one of you escort me through the palace?"

The guards' stare found the broach pinned to her cloak. "You've gained the king's favor but we dare not leave our post."

"Then I will see myself out." Gathering the cloak, she turned and swayed down the hallway, moving with a slow and measured pace, a woman with nothing to hide.

The broach proved an effective talisman, getting her past the scrutiny of royal guards. A thrill of triumph rushed through her as she reached the outer corridors, everything was going according to plan. The palace slumbered in the depths of night, ignorant of the king's fate. She planned to be well gone before the deed was discovered.

Reaching the outermost doorway, she paused; making sure the cloak covered her finery. Servants opened the door and she stepped into the night chill...and stumbled to a stop.

The palanquin was gone...and so were her guards.

The Priestess froze, cursing her servants. Noble-born women did not travel the streets of Salmythra alone, especially in the dead of night. Without her escort she couldn't leave, but if she stayed she'd be caught. The choice was easy; there was nothing to be done but brazen it out.

Summoning the bearing of a queen, she stepped from the doorway. Indifferent to the guards' stares, she walked beneath the portico, counting the steps to freedom. Twelve steps got her to the gilded statues. Five more steps and she reached the massive columns. Three more got her to the cobblestone street.

"Halt!"

So close, yet she could not run. She turned, a pillar of dignity, giving the guards a haughty stare.

A captain approached, followed by two guards. One of the guards carried a torch.

She searched their faces, relieved to find them strangers. "Yes, captain?"

Torchlight fell across her and the captain's eyes widen, staring at the cobra broach. "Lady, you should not wander the streets alone."

She sighed. "True, captain, but my escort has vanished and I must return home."

"It is unseemly." He shook his head, disapproval on his face. "Stay the night in the palace. Surely your escort will return with the dawn."

She'd killed a king yet she was too frail to walk the night. The Priestess kept her face serene, but beneath the mask, she seethed. The constraints of her sex threatened to trap her, but then she had a thought, deciding to turn his repressive culture against him. "My dear sister is heavy with child and I promised to attend the birthing. Her last child nearly killed her, a breech birth that tore something inside her, releasing a river of blood. She needs my skills in herb lore, I dare not tarry."

Scowling, the captain took a half step back as if she was unclean. Talk of birthing always made the desert-bred uneasy. "The king would never permit his mistress to wander the streets alone, especially in the dead of night." He gestured toward the palace. "If you must leave, let me assign an escort."

The desert culture threatened to be the death of her. "My dear captain..."

"My lady!" a deep voice called from the darkness.

"Ah, my escort." She pitched her voice to carry. "Tillot, is that you?"

Otham strode to the edge of the torchlight. Hovering in the shadows, he towered above the captain. "Pardon, my lady, but I fell asleep waiting."

The captain stared. "*This* is your escort?"

"Yes, captain." She gave him a sweet smile. "With Tillot by my side, surely no harm will come to me."

The captain glared at Otham. "You should take better care of your mistress."

Otham bowed low.

The Priestess made her voice low and soothing. "Do I have your permission to leave...or must I pester the king?"

The captain blanched. "I was only concerned for your safety." He made the hand gesture for a smooth journey. "May you walk in the shade of peace, my lady"

"And you, captain." She gave him a gracious smile and then turned toward the cobbled street. She was eager to be gone yet she forced herself to a lady's leisurely pace. With each mincing step, anger burned inside, her triumph of killing the king marred by the constraints of her sex. She understood why the Dark Lord chose men as harlequins, and she did not like it. Needing an outlet for her rage, she snapped at Otham. "What happened?"

He hovered close behind, his voice a low rumble. "I was nearly captured. Royal guards swarmed out of the palace, screaming about an assassination attempt, demanding the Razzur guards surrender. Razzur's men decided to fight. Most of them died rather than submit. In the heat of battle, I slipped away, hiding in the shadows, waiting for you." His voice caught. "I feared for you."

She sent him a sharp glare. "I killed a king, yet you 'feared' for me." Angry, she increased the pace, tired of being suffocated by men.

He followed, a hulking brute hovering at her shoulder. They walked in silence, making their way through the royal compound. By the time they reached the outer gate, the Priestess was limping badly, the cobblestones brutal on her slippered feet. She scowled, admitting the eunuch was right; the beaded slippers were beautiful but useless, like so much that filled most women's lives. Otham offered to carry her, but she silenced him with a glare.

The cobra broach got them through the guarded gate, out of the royal compound and into the city. The Priestess smiled, beginning to feel the triumph of the night.

Otham led her to a back alley where her people waited in the shadows. Clad in travel leathers and bristling with weapons, they held fresh horses. Hugo, the captain of her guards saluted fist to chest. "Was your evening a success, mistress?"

"Yes, but we need to be gone." As she talked, her handmaidens surrounded her, helping her change into riding clothes, supple leather breeches and knee-high boots. The boots felt like bliss after the hellish slippers. "Is my rosewood chest secure?"

"Secured with double bindings." Hugo watched her dress, an admiring smile on his bearded face. "Shall we expect trouble?"

She pulled on a leather jerkin, settling the king's blue cloak around her shoulders, the cobra broached pinned over her heart. "Not if we're beyond the city walls by dawn."

Her captain smiled. "Easily done."

"One more thing, have my bow strung."

Surprise shown from his face, but he did not argue. "I'll do it myself." He fetched her bow, bending the yew to the string.

"Mount up." She took the reins of a spirited black gelding and vaulted into the saddle. The horse felt good between her legs, better than most men. Gathering the reins, she asked the gelding for a trot, leading her people through the city's back ways.

Moonlight shimmered on empty streets, silvering the Cobra's city. The Priestess led her people through the alleyways, toward the eastern gate. The sound of a flute drew her towards the market. This late at night, the market stood empty, yet the pungent smells of trodden vegetables clung to the cobblestone. Torchlight shimmered at the far end, revealing a gruesome sight. Just as she expected, the two bearers were already there. Hung nailed to wooden crosses; they endured a slow and torturous death. Below the crosses, the boy faced a different fate. Caged with a pair of cobras, he played his flute, desperate to keep the serpents enthralled. Two brutal deaths and the third creatively cruel, together they'd send a potent message to royal assassins. In Salmythra, the king's retribution was both swift and terrible.

She paused, staring up at their agony. "My bow."

The captain eased his horse next to hers, handing over her favorite shortbow and a quiver of arrows. Controlling the gelding with her knees, she nocked an arrow and drew the bow to a kiss. She waited a heartbeat and then released. The arrow pierced the cobra's head. A second arrow took the second serpent. The flute fell silent and the boy began to sob. "Release him."

Two more arrows and the bearers were freed of pain. She wiped the bow dry and then handed it to her captain, a skill learned in childhood, as deadly if not as subtle as poison.

Her captain murmured, "Good shooting" but she did not bother to reply.

"Come, we have much to do." She'd had more than enough of Radagar. Wheeling the gelding to the east, she asked for a gallop. Letting the wind take her long raven hair, she gave herself over to the thrill of victory. She'd killed a king and changed the destiny of a kingdom, snatching victory from defeat. Power flowed through her, a feeling of invincibility, almost as good as sex. The stallion surged beneath her legs. She laughed, enjoying the ride, eager to win a place at the Dark Lord's side.

15

Liandra

Candles burned to stubs as Liandra reviewed the royal ledgers. War was a costly business but she persisted in chasing a profit. No sum was too small to escape the queen's notice. Numbers spoke to her, unveiling their secrets, whispering ways to multiply golds. Commerce was the lifeblood of her kingdom and she aimed to see it flourish despite the enemy. But war had an uncanny way of turning commerce on its head, making luxury items worthless and bare essentials scarce. Hoarded by the common people, the price of grain soared while silks and perfumes languished. At least she'd had the good sense to stockpile iron ore while luring half a dozen swordsmiths to her capital. By night and by day the sound of hammers rang through the city streets while wagons of grain rumbled through the gates. Pellanor was a beehive of activity, but it was a nervous commerce, fearful of encroaching war. At all costs, she needed to keep the enemy from the gates.

A knock sounded on the door.

Liandra leaned back, flexing fingers cramped from holding the quill. "Yes."

Lady Sarah appeared. "Supper is served and Lord Mills craves an audience."

"Another councilor suing for truce." They'd been at her door like a flock of frightened chicks, pecking away at her resolve. "Our loyal lords don't seem to understand that 'peace' under the Flame God is just another word for enslavement." She set the quill aside and stoppered the ink. "Tell the councilor the queen is otherwise occupied."

Lady Sarah nodded, but her face carried an odd look.

"Something else?"

The lady flushed, removing her hand from behind her back to reveal a sealed scroll. "Lord Highgate sends another scroll."

His name alone was a lance to her heart. Liandra stilled her face, staring at the scroll as if it were a viper. She was tempted to order it burned, but the man had a keen mind and an even sharper eye, and the times were troubled. Advice from her former shadowmaster could not be ignored, but it also took a toll on her resolve. "Set it on the mantle with the others."

Lady Sarah complied. "Will there be an answer?"

"No." The queen's voice brooked no argument, slamming a door on her heart.

"And supper?"

"Supper is welcome." She'd finally regained her appetite. "And our guest?"

"Awaits."

"Good." Setting aside the ledgers, the queen left her solar for the small round chamber that served as her private dining room. Servants scurried about the table, lighting candles and filling wine goblets. A fire crackled in the hearth, releasing a welcome warmth. Savory smells coaxed her to the table, roast pheasant with plum sauce, fresh-baked bread and apples laced with cinnamon, a feast of scents teasing her hunger.

A servant rushed to hold her chair. The queen took a seat, arranging the pleats of her gown, a lush emerald-green velvet embroidered with seed pearls. High waisted with artful pleats and a deep neckline, the new gowns were much more comfortable, and so much more concealing. Designed to her specification, the pleats obscured her waist while the low-cut bosom distracted prying eyes. The gowns set a new fashion for the rose court, protecting a royal secret. Only a handful of her ladies knew the truth, while her loyal lords seemed oblivious. Liandra smiled, a strange mixture of relief, amusement, and disdain.

Candlelight glinted off silver and fine porcelain, a show of opulence despite the war. Satisfied with the table, the queen gestured to the head steward, a tall balding man liveried in emerald green. "Oliver, admit our guest and begin serving once she is settled."

"Yes, majesty." He crossed the chamber and opened the far door, bowing a welcome to her guest.

Princess Jemma entered like a breath of spring. Fresh-faced and beautifully coiffed, the princess from Navarre executed a flawless curtsy, her dark eyes sparkling with hidden mirth, the perfect mix of royal duty and untamed spirit.

The queen gave her a welcoming smile. "You shall make an excellent queen one day."

"Your majesty is too kind." The princess took a seat opposite the queen, her petite figure perfectly accented by an elegant gown of midnight blue. "I always appreciate the chance to sup with you."

"The pleasure is ours. It is a pity duty too often intrudes." At a gesture from the queen, the servants began carving the pheasant, offering plump slices stuffed with garlic and slow roasted herbs. Baked yams caramelized with butter, oven-fresh bread and cinnamon apples completed the feast. The queen waited until the meal was served before dismissing the servants. A companionable silence settled between the two royal women. Liandra studied the princess; so confident in her beauty she did not wear a single jewel. "At our last supper, we set you the task of studying the commerce of war." The queen savored a taste of pheasant, the slice of dark meat accented with a crush of wild berries. "Tell us what you've learned?"

The princess smiled. "I did as you suggested, majesty, walking the markets of Pellanor, studying the ebb and flow of goods. Everything changed with the war. Not just the type of goods bought and sold, but the very feel of the marketplace. There's a tension in the people, an almost a feral desperation."

"Explain."

"When the food merchants open their stalls in the morning, the people flock in a buying frenzy. Most stalls turn barren in less than an hour, yet the harvest was good and the wagons keep coming."

"Hoarding. The people fear a siege, or worse."

"What will you do?"

"A fair question." The queen's bejeweled fingers stroked the wine glass. "We have resisted sending guards into the marketplace but perhaps it is time the crown enforced a fair price for grain and rations for all. The people must eat and the city must remain productive. Panic only serves the enemy." Liandra studied her guest. "What else have you learned? Where did you place your purse?" More than a month ago, the queen had gifted the princess with a heavy purse, seed money to invest in the commerce of Pellanor. It was a test of sorts, a trial by marketplace, and the queen was keen to learn the results.

The princess flashed a smile, her dark eyes sparkling, like a hawk rising to the challenge. "Food was the obvious choice, but the harvest was excellent and the scarcity is false. Sooner or later I knew the crown would step in to control the price."

"Just so." The queen nodded, pleased with her apprentice.

"Weapons were my second choice, but it seemed too obvious. Did you think of saddles, majesty? Every knight needs one. So I bought a share of a saddle shop and laid in a supply of seasoned wood and tanned leather. I suggested the master expand his trade into shields since they require similar skills." Pride flushed her face, like a hawk that had just caught the prize. "What do you think of my choice?"

"Very shrewd, so you'll turn a profit from the war?"

The princess stilled as if sensing a trap. "A fair profit for foresight, yes, but not usury, never that."

It was the perfect answer, the type of answer she'd expect from a daughter. Relieved, the queen smiled. "You have done well. The gift of multiplying golds is a very rare talent, a most valuable trait for a monarch, especially a queen. A rich treasury should reflect a rich kingdom, seeding prosperity back to the people. As queen, you should strive to be a boon to your kingdom, but beware, lest the lust for gold become a passion. Addiction to gold has long been the bane of many monarchs."

"Yes, majesty." The princess leaned forward. "But now I see how you use the royal treasury to bring new crafts and new trades to Pellanor. How you shape commerce to take advantage of the times."

The queen nodded. "Stagnation can be the death knell of a kingdom."

"Exactly! Stagnation is the very reason we have the Wayfaring in Navarre, so that each royal sibling can bring something different back to the seaside kingdom."

"Yes." The queen leaned back in her chair, her mind shifting to a different problem. "And what do you hear from Navarre?" She picked at the pheasant, but the bird had gone cold.

The princess turned grim. "The sea wolves return, raiding our coastline."

Her shadowmen had brought news of the raids but this was a chance to learn more. "Tell us more about these sea wolves."

"Like a plague, they show up every seven years or so, their great triremes plying the seas with impunity. They name themselves Mer-Chanters, fierce sea-going warriors who wield tridents and wear fish-scale armor. Father says they're like wolves who give the sheep time to fatten before returning to pasture to feed." Her face hardened. "But the sheep have grown claws, and they'll not make an easy meal of Navarre."

"Do they ever venture inland?"

"They might if a river is deep enough, but they never stray far from the sea, as if they are tethered to it."

For the first time, Liandra gave thanks that her kingdom was land-locked. "And what of the Army of the Flame?" The queen knew the answer but she asked anyway.

"So far Coronth ignores Navarre. But Father is worried, he keeps a close watch on the border."

"King Ivor does well to worry. If the Rose Army should fail, then the Flames will turn elsewhere." A grim stillness settled over the two women. "Navarre is famed for its archers. Your bowman might make all the difference."

"The army serves at the pleasure of the king."

Another perfect answer. "Just so. We have been in close correspondence with King Ivor and we believe he understands that it is far better to fight together than stand alone."

"And the sea wolves?"

"You have seen to the heart of the matter, for the king must also protect his own coastline. It is almost as if these sea wolves are in league with the Flame."

Princess Jemma shook her head. "Their attack does seem ill-timed."

"Perhaps a darker power meddles." The queen studied the face of the princess, a rare mix of beauty and intelligence. "But there is another alliance we would speak of, an alliance between the Rose and the Osprey. We would bind our two kingdoms closer with a royal wedding. Our eldest son, Crown Prince Stewart, has become an able general but in times of peace, Lanverness prospers by commerce. A queen who understands the way of multiplying golds would make the perfect wife." The queen's voice deepened. "We would have you as our beloved daughter-in-law, binding our two kingdoms in marriage."

A blush crept up the princess's face, but otherwise the young woman showed remarkable composure. "You honor me."

"The honor is mutual. We could think of no better bride for our son."

The princess stared at her hands, her face strangely guarded. Liandra had hoped for more emotions, perhaps a spark of joy, but duty had a way of smothering sentiment. "Of course, the marriage will depend on King Ivor's consent. Our swiftest courier carries our proposal to the king. Assuming he consents, it is our wish that you be married when Prince Stewart next returns to Pellanor. It will be a wartime wedding but it will not lack for pomp or ceremony."

"And the prince, is this what he wants?"

"Wants have nothing to do with a royal marriage. This is a marriage of state, an alliance between two kingdoms."

"But what of love?"

Softly spoken, yet the question hit like an arrow to the queen's heart. Liandra's breath caught, her own betrayal still too raw. "Love and crowns rarely mix. If you must choose, we advise you to take the crown and never let go. Erdhe is full of kings and knights but few queens. Men will try and use you for your beauty and your power. Take our advice and use them before they use you, for we would spare you the pain." The queen hid her own wounds beneath a mask of stone. "Besides, you were born to royalty. To women like us, marriage is a duty. If you are lucky, love may come later."

The face of the princess remained as brittle as glass.

Her stoic silence irked the queen. "Can you honestly say the crown of Lanverness does not appeal? You were born for the game of power, for the chase of golds. We have seen it in your face, heard it in your voice, as if you were our own daughter. You understand that it is not so much about wielding power as it is about making the greatest difference. Leadership is the ultimate proof that individuals matter. In Navarre, you are one of seven, competing for the throne, in Lanverness you will be the next queen."

The fire snapped and crackled, filling the silence between them.

The princess took a deep breath. "All that you say is true, *but*," her voice dropped a notch, "your son loves another, and that other is mine own sister."

So loyalty explained her reluctance, the realization made the queen want her all the more.

"A marriage between Jordan and the crown prince will do just as well, giving you the alliance you seek, the Rose wedded to the Osprey."

The queen stretched her memory. "Your sister, Jordan, the swordish one?"

"Yes." A note of defiance crept into her voice. "Jordan can dance the steel as well as any man, and she is loyal, brave, and true. And she has gone to the Kiralynn monks to learn the art of war."

"We do not seek a second son, but a daughter-in-law."

"Jordan will make a fine queen."

"Perhaps for Navarre." Liandra drilled the princess with her stare. "Do you honestly think she would wear the rose crown half as well as you?"

The princess stilled, her face pale, her gaze averted.

Liandra deliberately let the silence linger. The fireplace snapped and crackled, releasing a breath of pine, and still the princess would not meet her gaze. "Your silence shouts the answer."

"But..."

The queen raised a hand, forestalling the argument. "Your loyalty does you credit, but think of the greater good. And think of yourself as well. Name one other kingdom besides Navarre where the queen is anything but a broodmare."

The princess paled, her eyes turning dull as stones.

"We would spare you that fate." The queen's voice turned kindly. "We believe you are meant for greatness. To be a queen is to be a boon to your people. Tell us that you do not desire to be a powerful monarch?"

The princess flushed, her gaze retreating to her hands.

Liandra had her answer. "In time, you will see the wisdom of our words. Meanwhile, the decision rests in the hands of King Ivor. Trust him to make the right choice. Let duty be your guiding star."

Princess Jemma looked up then, her dark eyes as keen as any sword. "Is that what you've done, majesty? Followed duty or have you blazed your own trail?"

Another deep thrust to the heart. The princess was sharp and prickly, but she deserved the truth. "For a queen who rules, there is no timeworn path. Yet the welfare of our people is ever our goal."

"Always the queen, never the woman?"

The queen's breath caught, hearing an eerie echo of her lover's accusation. Liandra waited for several heartbeats before answering. "Our loyal lords all covet our power. Some hide it better than others, yet they are all hounds chasing the royal hind. Remove the crown for just one night and it is easily lost."

"It sounds lonely."

"Lonely...perhaps," the queen swallowed her own pain, "but never underestimate the difference a crown can make. In a world of kings and knights, women rarely matter, little more than chattel for the marriage bed. Yet look at us. None would dare say the Queen of Lanverness does not matter."

The princess nodded, her face solemn. "None, majesty."

"We will tell you a secret. Crowns *magnify*. They magnify the person, they magnify the actions. Once you have tasted a larger life it is hard to be diminished. We do not speak of opulence or the obedience of others, but rather the ability to employ all our intellect in order to make the greatest difference. To feel knowledge and purpose pulse through our veins, that is the very nectar of the gods."

"You speak of the crown as if it is a calling."

"Greatness *is* a calling. We hope you will dare reach for it."

The princess turned thoughtful. "You have given me much to consider."

"We hope you will choose wisely."

The princess's gaze sharpened to a sword thrust. "Do I have a choice?"

"A great queen always finds a way to have a choice."

The sparkle returned to the princess's eyes, the irrepressible glint of a challenge accepted. She bowed her head in homage. "Majesty, I have gained so much from this Wayfaring. No matter the future, I owe you a debt of thanks."

"Then repay us by becoming our daughter-in-law. Do not let destiny pass you by."

The princess did not reply. "Do I have your leave to go?"

"Yes."

The princess curtseyed, making a graceful exit, while the queen lingered at the table. Liandra sipped a glass of merlot while basking in the warmth of the fire, considering the conversation. Princess Jemma lacked experience but she was a rare gem of many facets. In the proper setting she would make a fine queen, especially under Liandra's tutorship. Assuming King Ivor approved, the queen expected duty to prevail. Then she would have two candidates for queen, a daughter-in-law and a daughter. Lacing her hands across the subtle bulge hidden by pleats of velvet, she stared into the crackling flames. But the question of succession mattered not, unless she won the war. And so far, the dispatches painted a grim picture, villages burned, her people murdered, and an invading army too numerous to count. Liandra's hands curled into fists. In a war against religious fanatics, the queen suspected there were only two possible outcomes, victory or annihilation.

16

Stewart

"Keep them moving!" Prince Stewart rode at the column's rear, keeping a close watch on the villagers as well as the new recruits, everything moving too slow for his liking. Farmers cracked whips and the oxen struggled to quicken the pace but the column limped south no faster than an old man could amble. Overloaded wains creaked and groaned, piled high with grain and dirty-faced children and chickens tied to tethers. Refugees clogged the dirt road, herding cows and goats and pigs and children. Pots and pans dangled from nearest wain, marking the leagues with a discordant clang. Dirt-stained and weary, the refugees from three villages trudged in a line straggling half a league long. His soldiers provided an escort, trying to hurry the exodus, but the oxen only walked so fast. Burdened with the fall harvest, the oxen teams held the column to a crawl. Frustrated, Stewart glanced skyward, worried the rising dust cloud sent a signal to the enemy.

"Keep moving!" Stewart beat the rump of a milk cow with the flat of his sword. The bovine bellowed in protest but then leaped back into line. Livestock had a tendency to wander, but at least the villagers needed no urging. Dark pillars of smoke scored the afternoon sky, rising above the distant hills like a doom. The enemy had a penchant for fire. Another village lost to invaders, but the Rose army could not be everywhere.

Anxious to quicken the crawl, he asked his stallion for a canter. A dozen officers kept pace behind him, his trusted aides and his escort.

Stewart cantered along the column, urging the people to haste. Despite their weariness, they looked up as he passed, especially the children. Most did not recognize his face, for he was as dust-stained as any soldier, but they cheered when they caught sight of his blue steel sword.

"The prince! The prince!" The chant rose from the children.

Standing in the stirrups, he unsheathed his longsword, flourishing it toward the heavens. Four feet of sapphire blue steel glittered in the afternoon light like a promise of protection.

Hope kindled in the eyes of the people. They raised a cheer, showing more heart than he'd seen in days.

Stewart watched their faces, always amazed by the power of blue steel. His mother had been right to commission the sapphire swords; he just prayed he was hero enough to wield it.

He topped a rise and got a better view of the column, a dark straggle stretched along the dirt road. Near the front, a wain had lost a wheel, slowing the column to a halt. "By the nine hells." If it wasn't one thing, it was another. Sheathing his sword, he urged his stallion to a gallop.

A knot of soldiers and peasants swarmed the wain, arguing over the problem. He nosed his stallion amongst them. "Why the delay?"

A young sergeant looked up. "The rear wheel's broke, m'lord."

"Then change the wheel and get the column moving. We've no time to waste."

A gruff-faced drover intervened. "Beggin' your pardon, lord, but it's worse than that. The axel's broke and there's no way to repair it."

Stewart swung down from his warhorse and peered beneath. Sure enough, the rear axel was snapped like a twig, sundered by an abundant harvest. He shook his head in frustration. "Unhitch the oxen and clear everything off. Leave nothing for the enemy." Villagers leaped to obey, but this was one of the granary wains, loaded to overflowing. Sacks and bushels and baskets could only hold so much, and all the other wains were already full to bursting.

A young sergeant approached. "My lord, it's still more than two-thirds full. Shall I set the wain afire?"

Every soldier knew the queen's orders. Nothing from the fall harvest was to be left behind.

"No fire." Stewart shook his head. "Set a fire to the wain and you'll invite the enemy to attack. Might as well send them a courier with our position."

"Then what sir? We haven't time to bury it."

He stared at the wain, knowing he couldn't risk setting it alight, nor could he leave it behind to succor the enemy, a vexing problem. Then he had a sudden thought. A devilish grin flashed across his face. "Piss on it."

Startled, the fresh-faced sergeant stared up at him. "What, sir?"

"I said, piss on it." Stewart swung down from the saddle and climbed into the wain. "If the enemy wants our harvest, then we'll serve it to them soaked in piss." He unbound his trousers and arched a golden stream into the grain. "May they choke on it and die!"

A cheer erupted from the people. Soldiers and farmers, young men and old, clambered up the side, eager to send a message to the enemy. It became an act of defiance. One gray-haired grandfather danced a jig as he arched a golden stream into the grain. Women gathered around, cheering the men on. The column began to move, swerving around the crippled wain, but every man, boy, and grandfather stopped to make a contribution.

The prince watched from his horse, cheered by the show of defiance. Beside him, Aubrey laughed, a young lieutenant in charge of the column. "By the time they're done, the grain will stink to high heaven! I'd like to see the enemy's face when they get a whiff of that!"

The prince glared at the lieutenant. "Better if we're long gone from here," but no one noticed his sharp rebuke, too caught up in the revelry of the moment. Stewart put spurs to his mount, asking for a gallop. His officers followed, riding at his back, a jangle of weapons and a flutter of emerald capes.

He reached the column's front and slowed his mount to a walk, his officers clustered around him. A dozen veterans served as his escort, but the rest were fresh-faced boys, barely old enough to shave, forced into uniform to fill the muster. Too few soldiers, too few veterans, yet they did the best they could. A sigh escaped him. After leaving a garrison of troops stationed in Pellanor, he'd divided his army into ten parts. His veterans, the Rose and the Thorn squads, harried the enemy, nipping at their flanks and attacking their scouting parties, while smaller squads of raw recruits scoured the countryside, escorting villagers and their harvest to the nearest castle. It was a risky gambit, splitting his army, but both tasks were equally important, slowing the enemy and keeping food out of their mouths. Stewart stretched in the saddle, scratching the stubble on his chin. The war was barely begun and already he was saddle-weary.

Lieutenant Aubrey spurred his chestnut mare forward, pulling even with the prince, a boyish grin on his face. "The bards will surely make a ballad of the wain! How the crown prince felled the enemy with his piss!"

"Not a ballad I'd sing to the queen. Or she'll wonder which sword I wield best." The men roared with laughter, especially the young ones. So full of spirit and bravado, they still saw war as a glorious adventure, while he wondered how many would live to become veterans. Stewart fingered the saber scar on his face, a grim reminder of his own brush with death. The ambush had been a close call, saved by a sixth-sense, or perhaps it was something else, something more. He touched the seashell broach pinned to his cloak, a gift from Jordan. It seemed forever since he'd seen her.

As if the men caught his melancholy mood, the banter from his officers died. They rode in silence, leading the straggling column through the rolling hills and fallow fields. Stands of trees dotted the hillside, the leaves turned russet and gold, brilliant in the waning light. The countryside was aflame with autumn colors; it would have been beautiful if not for the war.

"Shall we stop for supper?" Lieutenant Aubrey asked the question, pale blue eyes in a freckled face, too young to be in command, but recruits needed to grow up fast.

"No. We'll keep on till full dark. Tell the people to eat while they walk." Stewart frowned. "They won't be safe till we get them behind stout stone walls."

The lieutenant saluted and wheeled his horse, passing the command. The people grumbled but they did not stop, too many had heard tales of villages burnt, women raped, and children slaughtered. The Flame was a grim enemy. Somehow they had to turn the tide or Lanverness would be lost.

Aubrey returned, reining to the prince's left. "A hell of a way to fight a war."

"What do you mean?"

"This." The lieutenant gestured to the column. "Riding nurse-maid on a bunch of villagers when we should be attacking the enemy."

The young man's disdain was the very reason the prince spent time riding with the new recruits. Stewart raised his voice so the others would hear. "Do you consider siege warfare honorable service?"

Confusion flickered across Aubrey's face. "Yes."

"Then think of it as a siege."

"A siege?"

Stewart nodded. "In a siege, an army surrounds a fortress, putting a stranglehold on the people inside. In siege warfare, the weapons of victory are not swords or spears, but starvation and sickness. The enemy started this war when our fields were fresh harvested, hoping to plunder their way to Pellanor, feasting on the bounty of our farms. By denying them the harvest you make hunger *our* weapon." He studied their faces, watching as understanding dawned. "In a sense, you're waging a siege against the enemy. Do *not* underestimate the importance of your mission. What you do here is just as praise worthy as fighting, perhaps more so, since you save the lives of so many people."

He watched as his words sunk home. Their eyes gleamed with renewed determination and they straightened in the saddle, as they finally understood the value of their mission. If he did nothing else, his time with them was well spent.

Lieutenant Aubrey gave a solemn nod. "A good plan."

"The queen's strategy," Stewart quirked a smile, "and I've never met anyone who could best our queen at chess."

The men grinned with pride, restoring a sense of camaraderie and good cheer. Riding close, they peppered him with questions, begging for tales of the vaunted Rose squad and their engagements with the enemy. He did his best to answer without embellishing, trying to impart a sense of tactics with each tale.

The leagues passed and the sun lingered on the horizon, blazing to a golden glow. Stewart began to hope for an uneventful day, but then a scout appeared on the far hill. Standing in his stirrups, the scout waved a red pennant, a signal for danger.

"We've got trouble." He unsheathed his blue sword, raising it like banner. "Veterans to me! To me!" As the veterans rallied, he threw an order to the young lieutenant. "Choose a dozen men and set them to follow, while you keep the column moving. We need to get these people safe behind stone walls. Don't stop for anything."

Aubrey saluted, his face solemn. "As you command."

The lieutenant turned to roar a string of names, but the prince could not wait. Putting spurs to his mount, he galloped up the hillside, a dozen veterans riding at his back. Reaching the crest, he drew rein next to the scout. "What word?"

"A raiding party of at least thirty headed this way."

"Archers?"

"Mostly halberds and swords, a few crossbows."

Relieved, the prince nodded. "Then we'll be fairly matched, especially if they don't suspect we're near." He nodded to the scout. "Lead the way but I want to take them unawares."

Saluting, the scout wheeled his horse, galloping into the woods. A drum of hooves came from behind, the contingent of guards from the column, swelling their ranks to thirty-six. They rode two abreast, weapons held at the ready, stretching their senses for an ambush. Sunlight faded to twilight, leaving a tangled weave of shadows. It made for tricky riding, but the prince could not risk the enemy finding the column.

For half a league they followed the scout across a fallow field guarded by a raggedy scarecrow and then up a hill into a copse of oaks. A second scout slipped out of the trees, an archer with his face blackened with dirt. "Here, my lord."

It was just a whisper but the words seemed to carry. The prince angled his horse toward the archer. "Where are they?"

"In the next valley, looting a farmstead."

Before the prince could ask, the scout gestured to the brush. A farmer and his wife crouched by a felled log with three knee-high children clinging to the women's skirts. "I got the family out but there was no time to secure their stores."

Stewart nodded. "You did well. And the enemy?"

"I counted thirty-eight raiders, a scouting party scavenging for food. Last I saw, they were ransacking the farm."

"Then perhaps we can take them unawares." Stewart turned to his commanders. "Kelso, post a guard on the farmer and his wife. Mathis and Dane with me, the rest of you wait here, and stay sharp." He swung down from the saddle and tied the reins to a branch, before following the scout up the steep slope.

The scout set a swift stride, winding a path to the crest. Stewart kept pace despite his chainmail armor. Leaves crunched underfoot and brambles clutched at his cloak. Nearing the crest, they crawled till they had a clear view of the valley below. Torchlight glittered around the farmstead. The enemy ransacked the farm. Soldiers searched the outlying buildings, their red cloaks dimmed to black in the waning light. A horrible squealing filled the valley. *Torture!* "I thought you..."

The scout interrupted. "It's a pig farm, they're butchering the hogs."

Stewart nodded. "Then they'll be there a while." It was a small farmstead, dominated by a large pigsty, a sod-roof cottage and a stone smokehouse. "Let's take them while their hands are bloody." He turned to his commanders. "We'll use this ridge as a wall, pinning the enemy against it. Mathis loop around and bring your archers through the forest. Kelso will take the west road and I'll take the east." The others nodded. "We'll wait for a signal from Mathis, two hoots of an owl, and then we charge." He stared at his men. "Let no one escape."

His men flashed a feral grin, eager to wreck vengeance on the enemy.

They withdrew from the ridge and made their way back to the horses. Mathis, a grizzled veteran built like a tree stump, took charge of splitting the forces. Stewart prepared for battle, donning a solid oak shield emblazoned with crossed roses on a field of emerald green surmounted by a golden crown, the only sign of his rank. Setting a helm on his head, he mounted his warhorse. Unsheathing his blue sword, he summoned his men. "This way."

Twilight was gone, supplanted by night, but a silvery half moon provided just enough light. They made their way around the ridge and entered the woods. Torchlight lit the farmstead, the squeal of hogs and the laughter of soldiers filling the night.

Stewart cautioned his men to silence, waiting for the signal. Lowering his visor, he tightened his grip on his blue steel sword and touched his seashell broach for good luck.

An owl hooted twice.

A man's scream split the night; the first arrow had found its mark.

Stewart raised his sword to the heavens, urging his stallion to a gallop. *"For the queen!"* They charged up the narrow lane into the heart of the farmstead. Soldiers in red scurried before them, desperate to reach their halberds. Arrows thunked from the woods, a deadly rain. Stewart lowered his shield, riding straight for the nearest foe. Blue steel flashed in the torchlight, taking the soldier's head with a single swipe. The battle was joined, mounted knights fighting soldiers on foot, a clear advantage. Steel clanged and men groaned. A halberd slashed toward his face but he caught it with a parry. His warhorse lashed out, taking the enemy with iron-shod hooves. Stewart ducked another blow and slashed down with his sword. Stroke and parry, the battle became a blur.

"They're getting away!"

The cry caught his attention. Two enemy soldiers galloped for the open road. "Stop them!"

Stewart wheeled his stallion, giving chase. An arrow came from behind, taking the lead rider in the back, but the second rider did not slow. Stewart urged his horse to speed. The gap closed. The enemy glanced back, his face a grimace of fear. Stewart stood in the stirrups, blue steel raised for the killing blow. He leaned forward, controlling his horse with his knees. *Close, closer,* blue steel struck, cleaving chainmail and flesh with a single blow. The severed head bounced to the ground, the riderless horse squealing with fear. Stewart pulled his stallion to a halt. Blue steel gleamed cold and keen in the moonlight, a wondrous blade. Breathing hard, intoxicated by victory, Stewart turned his horse back to the farmstead.

The sounds of battle fell to a hush.

He emerged from the woods to survey the damage. Bodies littered the yard but most wore red cloaks. Flames engulfed the cottage, a raging bonfire casting warped shadows across the yard.

Mathis came forward to hold the reins of his stallion. The prince dismounted. "How many?"

"One dead, two wounded, one dying."

"And the enemy?"

"All dead."

"And the fire?"

Mathis shrugged. "A torch fell in the fighting."

Stewart nodded, but he worried it would serve as a beacon to the enemy. He sheathed his sword and unslung his shield. "I'll see the wounded."

"The dying man is asking for you."

"Who?"

"The young lieutenant, Aubrey."

"No!" He'd specifically ordered Aubrey to stay with the column. It was always the young and inexperienced who died first in battle. "Where?"

Mathis led him to the stone smokehouse. A cluster of men surrounded the young lieutenant. Propped against the sidewall, he lay still as death. They'd removed his armor, revealing a ragged sword thrust to his chest. The wound bubbled red with each breath, proof it pierced the lung. Pale and wane, the lad did not have long to live, yet he quickened when he saw Stewart. "My prince!"

Stewart knelt, taking the young man's hand, so cold to the touch.

"I know I disobeyed..."

"Too brave to stay behind," the prince intervened, "you only wanted to fight."

"By your side." Aubrey took short, shallow breaths, struggling to mask the pain. "A victory?"

"A clear victory, one for the bards. You fought with honor. Your name will be remembered." He gripped the young man's hand, willing him to live, watching as the light faded from his eyes. And then he was gone. Another young man consumed by war. Stewart bowed his head. Every loss felt personal, like chips of ice lodged in his soul. He tried to spare the young ones, but there weren't enough veterans. Leaning forward, he closed the lieutenant's eyes, murmuring a prayer to the Light.

"Shall we bury him, sir?" It was another raw recruit; a friend of the lieutenant's, but this one had survived his first battle.

"There's no time. In this war, the dead lay where they fall. But he will be remembered. His name will be honored." The mantle of command fell heavy across his shoulders. Stewart covered Aubrey with an emerald cloak. "Mount up!" Rising, he strode toward through the yard, his voice ringing with command. "Take their horses, and their weapons, and any food supplies. We need to get back to the column. This fire sends a signal to the enemy." Stewart strode toward his stallion. Climbing back into the saddle, weariness struck him like a war hammer. It was going to be a long hard war. He touched his seashell broach for luck. "Let's ride!"

17

Steffan

The army moved too slow, like a snake slithering through the autumn countryside. They'd shattered every foe they faced but gained little plunder and even less food, an unsatisfying start to the holy war. Steffan swiveled in the saddle, staring back at the long red line stretched over the distant hills. He'd hoped for a decisive victory, but the Rose Army refused to engage. They fought like cowards, striking at his flanks, attacking his raiding parties, nibbling away at his superior numbers. Their tactics galled him. He felt like a prize fighter with nothing to punch.

Lightning rumbled in the distance. Rain began to fall, spattering cold against his face, a prelude to winter. Steffan hunched beneath his cape; it was going to be a long slow war despite his superior numbers. Victory was assured, the sound of invincibility marching at his back, but he'd come to hate the slog of war.

He rode in the vanguard, surrounded by a handpicked guard of Black Flames, the most loyal of his holy warriors. Clad in silvered chainmail, a ruby-encrusted sword belted to his side, Steffan was dressed for war although the sword was never his best weapon. Battle banners snapped overhead, red and gold against an angry sky. Bishop Taniff began to sing, a deep baritone belting out another hymn to the Flame god. Resplendent in blood-red armor, a gold miter affixed to his helm, the bearded cleric proved as devout on the march as he was bloodthirsty in battle. The constant litany of prayers and hymns wore thin but Steffan could not gainsay them, especially when the Black Flames joined in. Perhaps the bishop grew too popular.

General Caylib flashed a knowing grin, his big black warhorse keeping pace with Steffan's roan. "Another god-awful hymn."

He sent the general a warning glance. "We're fighting a holy war."

"So we are. But we do more marching than fighting." The general's voice dropped to a low growl. "Lanverness was supposed to a plum ripe for the picking."

"And so it is, the richest kingdom in all of Erdhe, and it's drunk on too much peace. Wait till you see Pellanor. The capital city has grown beyond its walls, waiting for us like a whore spread wide across silken sheets. When we take Pellanor there'll be plenty of gold for all." Steffan grinned. "Don't worry, general, the queen's got a head for gold but no stomach for war. I'll wager her councilors are already soiling themselves, rushing to sue for peace."

"A bloody queen," the general gave him a baleful glare, "the bitch must be a sorceress. Her people and her crops seem to disappear overnight." The general hawked and spat. "Three villages and all of them empty. The men begin to grumble. No blood for their swords, no women for their loins, no plunder for their pockets...and worst of all, no meat for their bellies. Hungry and bored an army can turn on its masters."

Steffan considered the general's words while studying his escort. Burly men bristling with weapons, fearsome halberds of blackened steel riding their shoulders, black flames emblazoned on blood-red tabards, they sang war hymns with the conviction of true believers. The Black Flames were fanatics, elite fighters driven to a holy bloodlust. Religion might constrain the Black Flames but the ordinary foot soldier was not so devout. "Then we best feed them."

The general nodded. "Send for supplies from Coronth."

He couldn't do that. With the Pontifax dead, Coronth was in turmoil. The Keeper of the Flame sent a steady stream of messengers, demanding the army's return. None of the messengers lived to spread the tale. "No, we need to forage for supplies. We'll dine on the harvest of Lanverness."

"So you've said," the general snorted in disgust, "but the larder is empty. Every day raiding parties ride in all directions but the pickings are lean and a third of my men never return."

Steffan nodded, he'd heard the reports. "I'll order another bonfire tonight. The priests can read the portents. An omen of victory should bolster morale."

"Men can't eat portents."

"And I'll double the rations."

"What?" The general's outburst startled his warhorse. Yanking on the bit, he reined the stallion into submission. "What do you mean, you'll double the rations?"

"I'm betting on victory, general, all or nothing." His voice turned deadly serious, remembering the wrath of the Dark Lord. "Instead of four weeks of short rations, we'll have two weeks of full bellies, and in the meantime, I'll think of something. This war will not be won by swords alone."

"Then think fast, councilor, for a hungry army is a dangerous beast."

He gave the general a daggered glare. "In the meantime, *general*, you best find the enemy. Find the enemy and we'll find the stolen harvest."

The general bristled, but he did not argue.

Around them, the chorus of battle hymns ground to a halt, a rare stretch of blessed silence, the clop of hooves keeping time to the march. Steffan stood in the stirrups, scanning the hillside. A cold mist cloaked the hilltops. Autumn leaves fell from the trees, orange and red fading to brown. Fallow farmlands stretched between the hills, churned to mud by the rain, everything turning a dull brown. "Look at the countryside, general. This time of year, green should be easy to find."

"So you say," the general grunted, "but whoever leads the enemy fights like a fox, using the countryside against us."

"Then set a trap."

"How?"

The wind shifted and the rain came harder, big fat drops hitting Steffan square in the face. "You said the enemy shadows our army. Out numbered, they won't risk a direct attack, but instead, they nibble at our raiding parties, like fleas irritating a hungry lion."

The general grunted.

Steffan took it for agreement. "Then send a troop of Black Flames to shadow each raiding party. Ambush the ambushers."

The general grinned. "I like it. Send some cats to catch the mice."

"Exactly. But I want the enemy captured alive. Roast a few prisoners over a sacred bonfire and they'll soon tell us where the harvest is hidden. Find the harvest and we'll have no trouble feeding the troops. Feed the men and there's nothing to stop us from marching straight to Pellanor."

The general gave Steffan an appraising stare. "You look civilized, counselor, with your tailored cloaks and your sword inset with rubies, but underneath, you're just as ruthless and blood-thirsty as me."

"Anything to win, general. *Anything.*" Steffan spurred his horse to a gallop, impatient for victory. He had a crown to claim and another lifetime to gain, all in the name of the Dark Lord.

18

Danly

For two anxious days and three sleepless nights, Danly kept vigil, watching Athon's every move, wondering which way the dice would fall. All his life he'd believed greed would triumph over loyalty and now his very fate depended on it, but the red-haired soldier avoided his gaze, a nervous tick raging in his left eye. Plagued by worry, Danly wondered if he should have dangled a better reward...or perhaps chosen a different accomplice. Doubt gnawed at his stomach like a ravenous wolf but all he could do was wait. He'd never been good at waiting.

The sky cleared and the roads began to dry, making traveling easier. The horses quickened their pace, every league taking him closer to exile. Danly kept a close watch on the red-haired soldier, anxious for an answer, but Athon kept his distance. The affable soldier had turned surly and short-tempered, like a horse with a burr under its saddle. Danly thanked the gods that no one else seemed to notice.

The sun climbed high in the noon sky, a bright disc among the clouds. The wagon pulled off the road, coming to a stop in the shade of an elm. The soldiers dismounted, stretching from a long morning's ride. For the first time in three days, Athon approached the prisoner, his voice overly loud. "Do you need to piss?"

Danly nodded. "Thought you'd never ask. I'm near bursting with need." He scuttled off the wagon, struggling to keep pace with red-haired soldier.

Athon led him to a thorn bush. Fumbling with his pants, he released a golden stream.

Danly joined him, wondering if his fate would be decided over a piss.

"The golds are real, right? And the ruby ring?"

Danly's heartbeat quickened. "I stake my life on it."

Athon hawked and spit. "That's right, prince. If we get to Pellanor and there's no gold, then I'll take your life."

Danly suppressed a grin, marveling at the power of a well-told lie. "The gold will be there, I swear it."

Athon turned sideways, revealing the hilt of a hidden dagger. "I'll hide this in the straw. Bradford is with us. We'll do it tonight while the others sleep."

His words sounded bold, but the peasant-soldier reeked of sweat, the telltale smell of fear. Danly did what he could to bolster his courage. "Just remember, that ruby ring will change your life."

Athon grunted and turned away, the tick in his eye beating a fierce rhythm.

Danly followed, shuffling to keep pace, the chains rubbing his ankles raw. As he climbed onto the wagon, Athon shoved him from behind. "Get in there!" Danly sprawled in the soiled straw, but Athon neglected to chain him to the wagon. The prisoner-prince hid his grin, one step closer to freedom.

A whip cracked and the wagon lurched forward. Mounted soldiers followed close behind, a coating of dust turning their green tabards to a muddy brown.

Danly made a show of getting settled in the bouncing wagon all the while searching for the dagger. At first he couldn't find it...but then his hand closed on cold steel. He gripped the dagger, trying to keep the triumph from his face. His gamble had paid off, bartering bold-faced lies and a wastrel's past for a chance at freedom. Flush with excitement, Danly studied his escort, choosing his prey. He'd never killed with his own hands, always paying guards to do his wet work. He wondered what it would feel like. One of his men had sworn the rush of killing was nearly as good as sex. Danly hoped it proved true. A prisoner-prince turned judge and executioner, he studied his guards. His gaze settled on Carter, the repentant Red Horn with the snide smile. The blond-haired soldier had traded sides one too many times. Danly grinned at the thought of giving the arrogant bastard a second smile, a deep slit in his bloody throat. He fingered the dagger, anxious for the night.

A pale sun crawled across the autumn sky as if taunting him with delay. The small cavalcade traveled through harvested fields and into a forest. Dark green spruce and naked birch branches arched overhead, forming a tunnel of trees. *Another forest without a name,* Danly wondered where they were, how far from Pellanor, how close to exile? Forests and farms all looked the same to him, each village no different than the last. But whatever their position on the map, tonight he'd gain his freedom...or meet his death trying.

The wagon lurched to a sudden stop, the draft horses squealing in pain.

Danly was thrown against the wagon, bruising his arm.

The draft horses bucked in their traces, rocking the wagon. A whip cracked and a soldier shouted orders, but the horses were frantic. White-eyed, they reared in the traces, flailing their hooves. Danly gripped the wagon, afraid it would topple.

Crossbow bolts hummed from the forest, peppering his guard. Soldiers screamed, blood blossoming on their tabards. Danly cowered in the wagon, trying to make sense of the chaos. *Brigands on the road!* The sergeant drew his sword riding into the fray.

"Kill the prisoner!"

Captain Talcot leaped onto the wagon bed, his sword raised. "Die traitor!"

Danly scuttled backwards, a dagger his only defense. *"No!"*

A feathered shaft punched the captain's chest, blood spattering Danly's face. The captain tumbled backward. Danly stared in shock.

Something whispered past Danly's head. He cowered in the wagon, struggling to make sense of the attack. Feathered bolts punched the air, piercing armor and flesh. Men screamed and horses bucked. The road became a killing field. Desperate for cover, Danly slithered beneath the wagon, thankful Athon had left him unchained. Pain pierced his side. He jerked away, shocked to find he'd landed on a caltrop. Caltrops littered the road, their nasty spikes pricking flesh and hooves, the reason the draft horses had reared in pain.

A trap, they'd ridden into a trap, but were they friends or foes? Perhaps the Red Horns had come to his rescue.

Hoof beats galloped from behind, a bitter clash of steel.

Danly hid beneath the wagon, trying to make sense of the battle. *A weapon,* he needed a weapon. *He'd dropped the dagger!* Frantic, Danly scrabbled in the dirt, but it was gone. It must be in the wagon bed...but he couldn't move. Huddled beneath the wagon, he kept silent, watching while all around him men died.

A soldier fell next to the wagon, an emerald tabard skewered by three bolts. Athon turned his head and stared at Danly, pleading in his gaze. "Help...me..."

Danly looked away, refusing to be noticed.

A rearing horse squealed and then fell sideways, crashing his rider.

A sword gleamed in the dirt, only an arms length away. Danly wondered if he dared, deciding it was better to hide and hope he wasn't noticed.

The hail of bolts came to a sudden stop. The clash of steel fell eerily silent. Blood and bodies spattered the road. A horse nickered and a soldier moaned. A dozen horses milled on the side of the road, the victors inspecting the dead. A pair of brigands dismounted, slashing throats till the moaning fell silent.

Danly held his breath, wishing himself invisible.

Another rider dismounted, tall boots of subtle brown leather polished to a high gloss...the boots of a wealthy nobleman, or a successful brigand. The stranger knelt by Athon. The red-haired soldier stretched his hand back toward Danly's hiding place, his voice a breathy whisper. "I'm the prince's man..." but Danly said nothing. A quick slash and it was over.

The boots drew near, blood dripping from a dagger. The brigand crouched and peered beneath the wagon. A swarthy face stared at Danly, black hair, dark eyes, and a thin shaved mustache...a handsome man of middling years, no emblem of any type on his leather armor. "The prince I presume." He tossed a set of keys at Danly. "For the shackles."

Danly gaped like a fish pulled from the sea. "Who are you?"

"Your best hope." The man flashed a grin. "Come, we must be gone from here." He straightened and the boots strode away, mounting a horse.

Confused, Danly fumbled with the keys. His hands shook. It took three tries to open the lock, the chains eventually falling from his ankles...and all the while he wondered if he'd gained or lost by the ambush. Stunned by the sudden change in fortune, he hesitated...but hiding would do him no good. Taking a deep breath, he crawled from beneath the wagon.

A dozen mounted men stared at him. Bristling with weapons, their armor and cloaks a mixture of black, brown and dark green, but Danly could not find a single heraldic device among them. Brigands then, or perhaps mercenaries...but whom did they serve? Danly swallowed, struggling to keep his voice steady. "Who are you? What do you want?"

The dark-haired leader extended a gloved hand. "Come if you want to live."

Danly hesitated; sweat beading his brow.

"You're still within the Spider Queen's reach."

The threat decided him. The enemy of his enemy...perhaps he'd gained by the ambush. Danly took the offered hand and swung up behind the leader. The stallion snorted and took off at a fast canter, forging a path into the forest, the other brigands following close behind. Danly clung to the leader's cloak, stunned by the change in fortune, wondering if he was a prisoner, a prince...or a pawn.

19

Jordan

Snow came early to the southern mountains. While the valleys clung to their gilded leaves the jagged peaks clashed with ice. A wall of mountains reared overhead like the ramparts of a frozen citadel, but Jordan refused to be daunted. Setting a brisk pace, she followed the path through the dusky pines, a sense of urgency driving her upwards.

A dozen monks from the Kiralynn Order joined her in the trek. Wrapped in thick fur cloaks, using their quarterstaffs as walking-staves, they looked more like itinerant trappers than monks, not a speck of blue among them. Behind the monks, came the reindeer burdened with food and bedding, a clang of bells marking their progress.

Strung out in a line, they followed the path, climbing into the snow before they'd escaped the autumn foliage. Such a low snowline did not bode well for above, but Jordan refused to turn back. Studying the ground, she looked for familiar landmarks, but the snowy blanket changed everything, obscuring the path and erasing footprints. A pity the past could not be so easily erased. It was only last spring that she'd dared the mountains with Kath and Duncan and the others, coming to the monastery for her Wayfaring. It seemed forever ago. If only she'd been more wary that fateful night. Her stomach clenched, remembering the pain of the knife, a dagger thrust in the dark. She'd counted Sir Cardemir as a friend, yet he'd betrayed her, corrupted by the Mordant. The monks had healed the wound but not the memory. She longed for vengeance, but the gods had other plans. Plagued by nightmares, she'd begged the monks for release from her Wayfaring. Some argued the mountains were too perilous in autumn but she dared not tarry for the changing seasons. Finally the Grand Master relented, giving her leave to go. She fled the monastery with her escort, daring the ice-bound pass. Staring aloft, Jordan gripped her sword hilt, praying she was not too late.

By noon they reached the tree line, passing from dusky green into a bleak world of gray and white. After the jewel-bright monastery, the sudden lack of color seemed ominous. Turning her back on safety, she headed for the perils above.

The snow deepened, exacting a stiff toll. Sweat ran in rivulets down her back, her breath freezing to frost plumes. Plodding through the snow proved hard work, more than she was used to despite her daily sword practice. Jordan paused to catch her breath, staring up at the ice-bound peaks.

One of the monks drew near. "The snow's unusually deep this year, it foretells a bad winter." Rafe stood at her shoulder, a tall auburn-haired monk with startling gray-green eyes. "The snow gives warning, the pass will be dangerous. Perhaps we should return to the monastery?"

Jordan shook her head. "I can't turn back."

"Is it worth your life?"

She stared at him, startled by the question. "Yes."

He gave her a searching look and then nodded. "You've broken trail for long enough. Wait here and join the end of the line."

Jordan waited as the others trudged past, finally falling into line just ahead of the pack reindeer. Behind her, the stag's bell clanged with every step. She found herself moving to the steady toll, counting the never-ending beat. The path snaked upwards through a desolate landscape of snow and ice and rock. The snow gradually deepened, cold-white tugging at her boots. She stayed within the monks' footsteps, thankful for the respite. After each switchback, the lead monk shuffled to the back, letting another break trail. Jordan grinned, acknowledging the wisdom of their ways. It seemed the monks did nothing without thinking.

Time slowed to a dull slog, an eternity of up. Twice she found herself at the front, forging a path through the deepening snow, yet the icy peaks seemed no closer. Numb with weariness, Jordan let her guard down, her thoughts wandering to Stewart. Conjuring his face, she longed to touch him, to be with him, but then the daydream changed to a nightmare. His face turned bloody and battered, his gaze spiked with horror. *"No!"* She stifled a scream, her cry snatched by the wind. Stumbling, Jordan gripped her sword hilt, gulping deep breaths of knife-cold air. *Always the same look of horror in his eyes,* she made the hand sign against evil, taunted by a future she'd vowed to change. The Grand Master had named her visions a blessing, a gift from the gods, but they seemed more like a curse. Time teased her, every passing moment a bitter delay.

They reached another switchback, and it was her turn to lead. Snow lapped above her boot tops, cold and wet, like chains dragging her feet. Her muscles ached, forging a path through the cold white.

"Wait!" The call came from behind.

Jordan staggered to a stop and turned.

Rafe approached, snow dusting his furs. "Yarl found the cairn." He pointed back toward the last switchback, to a pyramid of rocks peeking above the snow.

"So?"

Rafe grinned. "Wait and see."

Three monks peeled away from the main trail, forging a fresh path to the east. The others gathered around the reindeer, removing their burdens. Rafe beckoned to her. "Come, the reindeer will flounder in the deeper snow. It's time to send them back to Haven."

Leather-bound packs were removed from the reindeer, one for each of the travelers. Released from their burdens, the reindeer bounded back down the trail, the stag's bell clanging a merry retreat. Jordan realized she'd miss the cheerful beat. Lifting one of the packs, she shrugged it onto her shoulders. It seemed heavier than when she'd packed it, perhaps she was more tired than she thought.

A bitter wind whipped around them, snow pelting their faces. Laden with packs, they stood in a huddle, waiting for the others to return. Jordan stamped her feet, trying to keep warm.

Ellis, a stunning brunette with hawk-sharp eyes, handed her a flagon. "This will help."

Jordan took a long swig of mulled wine. A river of heat flooded through her, the taste of autumn apples lingering on her tongue. Grateful, she stoppered the flagon and returned it. "Thanks."

The other returned carrying large bundles wrapped in worn oilskins. They knelt to untie the bundles, revealing strange teardrop-shaped hoops.

"What are those?"

Rafe laughed. "They're snow-walkers." He took a pair and handed them to her. "You wear them on your boots."

The workmanship was amazing, staves of wood bent to a teardrop shape with wicker webbing strung across the center. She'd never seen their like. "But what are they for?"

"For walking on snow." Rafe set a pair on the ground and then stepped onto them, lashing the leather bindings across his boots.

Jordan laughed. "You look like a furry duck!"

He flashed a grin. "A duck that walks on snow."

And then she realized it was true. Like magic he walked atop the snow instead of floundering through it. "How do you do that? Is it magic?"

"Not magic, but knowledge." He gave her a slow smile, a gleam of pride in his gray-green eyes. "Seek knowledge, Protect knowledge, Share knowledge."

Jordan gave him a sloe-eyed glance; the monks were full of surprises. She'd lived amongst them for a short while, yet she'd barely plumbed their depths.

"You best get those on."

She followed his example, stepping onto the strange teardrops and lashing them to her boots. At first they proved awkward, her stride hampered by the wide webbing, but she eventually settled into a waddling gait. The walkers proved a boon, much easier than plowing through the heavy snow. Jordan grinned, wondering what other surprises the monks harbored.

Reveling in the snow-walkers, she set off at a brisk pace, but the steep trail soon took its toll. After two switchbacks, she moved to the end of the line. They walked until twilight, the gray sky seeming to merge with the snow-capped peaks as if they climbed towards oblivion. One of the monks called a halt. They gathered in a huddle, keeping their backs to the wind, sharing a flask of lukewarm cider while Yarl went exploring. Jordan sipped the cider, her gaze following the burly monk across the rugged slope.

"Where's he going?"

Rafe answered. "To find a burrow."

"A burrow?" She studied the steep slope seeing nothing but tumbled boulders and snow.

"You won't find it."

"Then how do you know it's there?"

"We passed another cairn, the rocks indicate a nearby burrow."

She scowled, realizing she hadn't noticed it.

He laughed. "No, you wouldn't"

It was as if he read her mind. Before she could say anything, he explained. "The mountains are our fortress, our first line of defense. We know them like you know the battlements of your home castle."

She nodded; more proof the monks were shrewd, turning even the mountains to their advantage. They'd make formidable allies for Navarre if they weren't so damn reclusive.

A sharp whistle drew their attention. Yarl waved, beckoning them forward. One at a time, they left the trail for a narrow footpath. They scrambled across a steep scree slope, loose rock beneath snow, a dangerous passage. Jordan took her time, careful to walk in the other's footsteps. Rounding a boulder, she found Rafe waiting for her. "You'll need to remove your pack and snow-walkers." A dwarf-sized doorway was set into the mountainside. *A door into the mountain,* Jordan smothered her surprise. Shrugging off her pack, she knelt to unlace her snow-walkers, and then pushed her pack and the walkers ahead of her before crawling through the tiny doorway.

Warmth greeted her like a welcoming hug. Her eyes adjusted to the gloom, revealing a single chamber with a very low ceiling, thick rugs spread across the floor. Snug as a rabbit burrow, the small room delved into the mountainside, the timbered ceiling just a finger's width above her head. The low ceiling provided enough height to crawl or sit but not to stand. Stacking her snow-walkers near the door, Jordan shrugged off her boots, and then joined the others, finding a space for her bedroll along the far wall.

Rafe joined her, worming into the narrow strip between her and the earthen wall. "It's tight but cozy. Better than risking death on the mountain."

Once again, the monks surprised her. "How many of these burrows do you have?"

"Enough"

Always a cryptic answer, but she let him keep his secrets. Lulled by the warmth, Jordan leaned against her bedroll, content to take her ease.

With so many bodies crammed into such a small space, the burrow soon heated to a toasty haven. Shucking her furs, she watched as Yarl worked a small stone hearth in the outer wall, setting a paddy of dried dung to smolder. Sweet smoke swirled through the chamber, adding a pungent smell.

The dung fire surprised Jordan, something a peasant would use. She leaned towards Rafe. "Why dung instead of tinder?"

"Dung's really just dried grasses pressed together. Easy to carry and easy to store, a single large paddy will smolder all night. And if this were springtime, the smoke would keep the biters and bloodsuckers at bay."

"How do you know so much..." but then she checked herself, mentally answering her own question.

He flashed a grin but then sobered. "Knowledge is not just a weapon, it makes life easier. Another reason the monastery must never fall."

"But why do you hide? Most people consider the monks a legend."

His face stilled, as if a thousand thoughts swirled through his mind, but he did not answer.

"Tea?" Yarl handed her a brimming cup.

Her hands cradled the earthenware mug, letting the fragrant steam bathe her face. Breathing deep, she inhaled the delicious scent. Sitting cross-legged, she sipped the tea. Warmth spread through her, a subtle brew of mountain herbs with a hint of lemon thyme.

"Do you like it?" The big monk stared at her, dark eyes set in a head as smooth as an eggshell.

She'd never liked tea before the monastery, but she'd come to appreciate the subtle flavors. "It's very good."

Yarl grinned and filled the other cups, serving the rest.

Rafe leaned close, dropping his voice to a whisper. "You've just made a friend. Yarl prides himself on his brews."

She stared at the monk, a beefy chunk of a man hunched over the tiny hearth. Baldheaded with hands the size of shovels, he looked more like a brawler than a scholar. "A good man to have around."

"More than you know. Yarl is the quarterstaff master for the monastery."

So many contradictions, she wondered if she'd ever understand the blue-robed monks. "And what about you? What are you a master of?"

"Me? I'm just a fledgling by comparison, not really a master at all." But in his eyes she saw a host of secrets. She gave him a searching stare and then looked away.

Yarl crouched over the cook pot, adding ingredients like an alchemist. A rich savory smell swirled through the burrow, waking a ravenous hunger. Jordan leaned forward, her mouth watering, willing the pot to simmer.

Beside her, Rafe said, "I guess it's true what they say about a watched pot never boiling"

Jordan laughed, tearing her gaze from the pot.

It seemed a small eternity before Yarl handed her a bowl. "Eat well."

She spooned a mouthful of hot stew, nearly swooning with pleasure. Chunks of potato and tender venison in a savory gravy, so filling and warm and perfectly salted. Perhaps it was the altitude, but everything tasted delicious. She finished the last spoonful and then licked the bowl clean. With her stomach satisfied, she leaned back on her bedroll, succumbing to exhaustion.

Yarl collected the bowls and everyone crawled into their bedrolls. Lying close like rabbits snug in a den, Jordan felt safe and protected. Too weary to fight sleep, she succumbed to the cozy warmth. At first her dreams were welcoming. Entwined with Stewart on the snowcat fur, she remembered their first night together. She moaned with pleasure, enthralled by his touch, but her dreams quickly turned to nightmares. Visions intruded, full of bloodshed, deceit, and death. Like a grim foretelling, she watched Darkness tightened like a noose around those she loved...and they did not see the threat. *They did not see it!* Terror strangled her, holding her down, forcing to watch as her loved ones died. She railed against the visions, desperate to intervene. Her heartbeat hammered as she tried to run, but something held her back, binding her legs.

A scream shivered out of her.

A weight pinned her down. She woke to find a man on top. Thrashing against his weight, she reached for her sword.

"Shhhh, you're safe. It's just me, you're safe."

In the dim light, she saw Rafe's face close to hers. "You screamed in your sleep."

"Oh." Soaked with clammy sweat, she knew he spoke the truth. "I'm fine now."

He rolled onto his side, still within his bedroll.

She blanched, embarrassed by her nightmares. A quick glance proved most of the others still slept, a chorus of soft snores filling the burrow. Blankets shifted and a few tossed and turned, perhaps they feigned sleep. She bit her lip, hoping they wouldn't think less of her.

Rafe's voice was close, an insistent whisper. "What haunts you?"

She avoided his stare but he was persistent. "Was it the attack in the monastery?"

They all knew about the attack, about the dagger in the dark, but they did not know she hadn't seen the Mordant, hadn't sensed a thousand-year-old evil lurking in the shadows, near enough to touch. A shudder raced through her. Jordan thought of herself as a warrior of the Light, yet she'd never sensed the true threat. "No, not that."

Rafe was persistent. "Then what troubles you?"

He sounded so sincere, and she needed a friend. Sighing, she tried to explain. "The dreams started after I woke from the healing sleep. Dreams like none I've ever had, so real but all of them terrible." She'd fled the monastery, obeying the urgency of the dreams, but it seemed they wanted more from her. "I must get across the mountains. I must go back." She looked at him, hoping he'd understand.

"Why?"

The single word held a thousand questions. But the answer was just as complicated, a wild tangle of visions. "I have to...make a difference." It seemed a thin answer, but it was all she could give.

Rafe nodded. "So do we all."

His answer surprised her.

He leaned close, his voice a whisper. "Dire prophecies rush to be born in the southern kingdoms, yet some of us believe in your visions. We've come to help."

So she wasn't alone, the offer of aid nearly brought tears to her eyes. She stared at him, needing someone to confide in. Her fear blurted out of her. "Do you think a warrior of the Light can meet evil and not know it?" She held her breath, wanting to withdraw the question, yet anxious for his answer.

He met her gaze, his voice a low whisper. "Evil deceives."

The truth of his answer echoed in her soul.

"It's what evil does best."

"Just so."

"But having met evil, you will know it better the second time."

"May the gods make it so." She gave him a grateful nod, praying his words proved true, and then she turned away, burrowing into her bedroll. Jordan closed her eyes, but sleep eluded her. A deep urgency throbbed within her mind, prodding her to cross the mountains and return to the southern kingdoms. Darkness threatened the ones she loved, and only she could save them.

20

Liandra

The queen consulted the royal archives, but her recollections proved true. Over eighty years had passed since the last delegation from Ur. The empire chose an odd time to come calling, as if they somehow sensed her kingdom's vulnerability, but Liandra intended to show no weakness. In times of war, pomp and ceremony seemed a trivial concern, but the queen knew the value of appearances. She decreed a royal welcome, summoning the full splendor of the Rose Court.

Ur had long been the wealthiest trading partner to Lanverness, very wealthy, very distant, and very mysterious. Rumors ran wild about the distant empire. Merchant caravans traveled for more than twenty moon turns to reach the veiled kingdom, a long and arduous journey around the southern mountains, but the goods they brought back were beyond compare. Exotic spices, the finest brandy, the rarest healing brews, and the most vibrant silks all came from Ur. Liandra could ill afford to offend the royal delegation. Ever curious about her fabled trading partner, she'd dispatched six shadowmen to Ur early in her reign, but only one returned, stricken with a terrible wasting sickness. She'd listened to his report; never certain if the tales were true or the delusional rantings of a fever-racked mind. Thwarted by her shadowmen, the queen quizzed returning merchant caravanners, but they proved even less helpful, spinning wild tales of orgies and magic. The queen knew full well their fantastic tales only increased the value of their goods. Considering their prices, perhaps she should spin a few tales of Lanverness, something to consider. Liandra drummed her fingers on her throne, struggling to contain her curiosity. Rumors of the delegation had swirled through her capital city like a bonfire, raising a fevered-interest in the formal welcome. The queen found she was not immune to the rampant curiosity.

Liandra surveyed the audience hall. Lords and ladies bedecked in rich velvets and stunning silks preened like peacocks before the throne. Candlelight shimmered through the great hall, reflecting off marble floors and gilded mirrors, a jewel box setting for her court. Musicians played in the corner, providing a stately melody full of pomp and ceremony. Expectation thrummed through the hall.

She caught the sharp-eyed stare of her loyal lords, a pretentious contingent swirling around Lord Mills. They hid their daggers well; keen to oppose her policies on the war, yet for the sake of trade they wore their best courtiers' smiles. Greed pulled them to the surface, like sharks after chum. She nodded in their direction, a veiled warning in her glare.

Liandra shifted upon the golden throne. Bedecked in a low-cut gown of emerald velvet, she wore all the jewels of state. The Rose crown gleamed upon her brow, rings glittered on all her fingers, and the royal scepter sat nestled in the crook of her arm. Clad in the armor of state, a vision of wealth and majesty, she'd come to impress, knowing the importance of appearances when it came to trade negotiations.

Her two advisors stood closest to the throne. Master Raddock stood three steps down on the left. Swathed in somber robes of black, he looked like a crow squatting on her dais. At least his wits outshone his looks, but he proved a poor substitute for the master archivist. *Oh Robert,* she bit her lip, refusing to think of him. Seeking distraction, the queen turned her gaze toward Sir Durnheart. Her knight protector stood tall with broad shoulders, resplendent in shimmering mail, the hilt of his great blue sword rearing above his right shoulder, a vision of knightly splendor.

The stage was set. Like a rose in full bloom, Liandra sat between her two thorns, one stalwart and the other sneaky, both deadly in their own ways, another message for the delegation. Impatient, she tapped her fingernails against the throne. "Where are they?"

Her shadowmaster heard her whisper. "Shall I go and hurry them along?"

Before she could answer, the gilded doors opened to a blare of trumpets.

Her lords and ladies moved aside, opening a path across the checkerboard floor.

Tumblers erupted from the doorway. Three jesters in green and white motley tumbled the length of the checkerboard floor, executing daring leaps and thrilling summersaults. Bells affixed to their boots and hands chimed with every movement. Tossing ribbons to the crowd, they cavorted the length of the hall, providing a sprightly entertainment. Delighted applause rippled through her court, but Liandra considered it a strange opening to a foreign delegation. She watched in puzzlement as they came to rest below her throne. Two were dwarves, their teeth filed to nasty points, while the third had the face of an older man, yet his muscle-sculpted body was stunted like a lad of twelve years. She wondered at the message hidden beneath the jesters.

The three jesters bowed in unison and said, "Oh great Queen of Lanverness, we bring tokens of esteem from the Prince of Ur. Please accept these gifts in the spirit in which they are given."

A rumble of drums came from the doorway. The crowd gaped as a procession of muscle-bound bearers entered. Tanned bronze from the southern sun, they wore flowing skirts of white linen, their naked torsos glistening with oil. Silver cuffs gleamed at their wrists and around their necks a silver collar bore the symbol of Ur, a mystical Ouroboros, a dragon eating its own tail. Kohl lined their eyes creating a strange mix of masculine and feminine, but despite their exotic appearance, the bearers were outshone by their gifts. Balanced on their heads, they bore wooden casks branded with the mark of Ur. Liandra assumed they held Urian brandy, the finest liquor in all of Erdhe, known to merchants as liquid gold. After the brandy came bolts of silk, saffron and cinnamon-colored, the rarest of hues, laid like tribute at her feet. And finally, four bearers struggled to carry an immense wooden chest, their bulging muscles betraying the great weight of their burden. A hum of excitement rippled through the crowd. Her lords and ladies craned to see, but the chest remained closed, an intriguing tease set at the foot of her throne.

Trumpets sounded and three nobles emerged from the double doors. Tall men draped in flowing robes of darkest purple, the great dragon of Ur gleamed in silver on their chests, but their faces were strangely pale, as if they shunned the sun. One walked in front of the others, gliding across the checkerboard floor, his head shaved smooth as polished marble, a silver ring piercing his left nostril. A chain ran from the nose ring to a silver collar at his throat.

Liandra suppressed a shudder. She'd heard whispers of the Chained Servants of Ur, but she always considered them a myth, a merchant's exaggeration. She wondered what other myths might walk through her doors.

The three nobles reached the foot of her dais. They gave her a regal nod but they did not bow. The chained-one stepped forward. "We bring greetings to Liandra, the White Rose, the sovereign Queen of Lanverness, from his majesty, the Twelfth-fold Prince of Ur. Please accept these gifts as tokens of his royal esteem." He gestured and the bearers opened the chest.

Gasps rippled through the crowd. Liandra could only stare. Gold coins filled the chest, enough to buy a kingdom, or bribe it into submission.

The chained-one smiled. "The prince bid me give you this." Reaching within the folds of his robe, he removed a long slender box, just big enough for a dagger.

The queen gestured and Master Raddock stepped forward to inspect the gift. Opening the box, his eyes widened. Closing the lid, he proffered it to the queen.

Liandra accepted the box, slowly opening the lid. Nestled in velvet sat three uncut gems, a diamond, a ruby, and an emerald, each the size of a large man's fist. Gems of incalculable worth, she'd never seen their like. Liandra struggled to keep her face still as stone. "Such magnificent gifts, we are astounded."

The chained-one nodded, a hint of satisfaction in his thin-lipped smile. "The Twelfth-fold Prince of Ur wishes to ensure a hearty welcome."

"And has the prince come to our court?" Her shadowmen said otherwise, but she half expected to see a jewel-bedecked prince stride into her halls.

"Not yet, majesty. We have come to prepare the way. Look for him at the turn of the seasons, after the coldest winter's day but before the dawn of spring."

"And may we know his name?"

Something dark glittered in the chained-one's eyes. "Lord Magnum Bale."

The name meant nothing to her, yet she felt that it should, as if she played a strange form of chess and these were the opening moves. "And why has a prince of Ur risked such an arduous journey?"

"Long has my master been fascinated with the kingdoms of Erdhe, ordering his servants to question those who dare to cross the Serpent Sea. One merchant spoke of the custom of Wayfarthing. Intrigued, the prince deemed it advantageous for the royal family to learn the ways of our most distant trading partner. Emperor Faylon the Magnificient, the twenty-third emperor of the sunrise lands, agreed with his twelfth-fold son."

Know your enemy, the queen nodded. "The custom is called Wayfaring, and it is part of the succession for the kingdom of Navarre."

"But Navarre is a such little kingdom while Lanverness holds the wealth of Erdhe."

She wondered if she'd gained a strange ally, or another vulture come to sup on her kingdom. "We look forward to meeting your lord. In the meantime, we offer you and yours lodging in Castle Tandroth."

"No need." A strange smile played across his lips. "The prince has charged us with purchasing a manse within the city. We must see to our lord's orders."

A twitter of whispers raced through the hall. Liandra hid a smile, knowing the price of property in Pellanor had just quadrupled. For the minion of a great trading kingdom, the chained-one was less than shrewd. "As you wish, but first we've ordered a feast to welcome you to our kingdom. We wish to hear more of the Empire of Ur."

He inclined his head. "Yours to serve, but first I must ask, do you accept the gifts of my master in the spirit in which they are given?"

Such an odd question, as if a poisoned dagger lay hidden beneath his words, but such wealth could not be spurned, especially in times of war. "Yes, they are accepted with our thanks."

He bowed then, a flicker of a smile across his face. "My master will be pleased."

Sensing she'd been outplayed, the queen surveyed the gifts arrayed below her dais. Among the tribute, knelt the three jesters. *Green and white, the colors of Lanverness,* she should have read the intent in their motley. Amongst all the glitter and gold she'd accepted three spies into her court. She kept her face as smooth as sculpted stone. "You represent your prince, yet you have not given us your name."

"My name is insignificant."

"Yet we would know it."

He blinked as slow as a snake. "Frederinko, a Chained Servant of the Twelfth-fold Prince."

Gasps spiked her audience hall.

So the chained servants are more than just a fearsome fable, she'd have to tread lightly. "Dine with us, Master Frederinko, for we wish to hear of your prince and the kingdom of Ur."

"As you wish." He nodded, waiting for her at the bottom of the dais.

The queen stood, sending a ripple of bows and curtseys through the chamber. She descended the dais, Sir Durnheart and Master Raddock forming a guard at her back.

"Captain Blackmon," she singled out a guard from her waiting escort. "See that our gifts are conveyed to our private chamber. And triple the guard. The jesters should be given rooms in the Sword Tower."

The captain gave a smart salute.

"Come," Liandra gestured to the Urian lord. "We hope you will enjoy the delicacies of our court."

Instead of offering his arm as any well-bred lord might, her guest folded his hands within his robes and walked beside her.

The queen led him across the checker board floor, her court falling into deep bows to either side. She entertained her guest by explaining the architecture of Castle Tandroth while her mind considered the meaning buried beneath the gifts. Her treasury would brim with Urian gold, but then the meaning hit home. *Flaunted wealth,* like a gauntlet thrown at her face, the Urian prince had issued a ghostly slap. Liandra shivered, *and they bring spies to my court.* Warnings buried beneath treasure, she wondered what game they played...and she sensed it did not go her way. Liandra clenched her fists, knowing she needed to understand this new player. Queens prevailed...or they were toppled from the board.

21

Stewart

The village seemed peaceful enough, but Stewart knew peace could be deceiving. Smoke puffed from a single chimney, but otherwise he saw no sign of life. A dozen stone buildings hugged a central dirt road, a small wayside hamlet probably best known for the hospitality of its inn. "You're sure this is the place?"

The scout nodded. "They came yesterday, riding down the road bold as brass, forty raiders in red tabards. But instead of setting the village aflame, they ransacked each house, as if they were looking for something. Judging by the smoke, I'd say they decided to stay."

Stewart crouched in the muddy damp. The countryside held little cover, the thicket and trees bare of leaves. Their best protection was the morning fog, a sparse cloak of misty white hugging the ground. "If the raiders spared this village, then they've have changed their habits. I like it not." He had a bad feeling, a sixth sense that scratched at his mind, but forty raiders was the perfect bite for his men, a hard prize to ignore. "Gedry," he gestured to the scout. "Go count the horses again. I want to be sure of their numbers."

"Yes, lord." The scout scuttled forward, crawling through the damp leaves, his brown homespun disappearing into the muddy countryside. He'd ordered his scouts to abandon their emerald tabards for rough homespun. Stewart considered ordering the same for his knights. Emerald green had become a deadly risk in the naked forests, but the knights were too proud to give up their tabards, and pride was an important part of winning, especially against greater numbers.

A broken branch crunched to his right. Stewart whirled, his hand on sword hilt.

"Just me." Tall with broad shoulders, dark hair, and laughing eyes, Dane approached to crouch by his side. The eldest son of a duke, he'd been fostered to the Rose Court at the age of eight to become the sparring partner for the crown prince. Stewart could ask for no better swordsman to guard his back.

"Are the others ready?"

"Awaiting your orders. Will we break our morning fast on the enemy?"

"Most likely."

Dane grinned. "Nothing like a little bloodshed in the morning to make a man feel alive." His face turned serious. "How many?"

"Forty, but I sent Gedry to check the horse count." Stewart pointed toward the village, two bowshots away on the far side of the field. "Judging from the smoke, they seemed to be quartered at the inn."

"There's justice for you. The invaders sleep in beds while the heroes have rocks for pillows."

Stewart grinned, glad to be back among the Rose Squad. "Are you complaining?"

"Only to the gods." Dane's smile faded. "But you've got a bad feeling about this."

Stewart sobered. "You know me too well."

"Then let's ride past and fight another day. I've come to trust that battle sense of yours."

"No." Stewart scowled. "Time serves the enemy. We need to take as many bites from their numbers as we can. And forty is a good mouthful." A grimness settled over him. "But it's not nearly enough." He'd seen the campfires of the enemy, like a plague spread upon the land. "We're running out of map. We need to find a way to hurt them, to make them pay for invading Lanverness."

Dane grunted ascent but he offered no answers.

Stewart fell silent, the enormity of the problem falling like a mountain on his shoulders. He took a deep breath, telling himself to fight one battle at a time.

The two men kept watch on the village. Nothing moved except for the chimney smoke. The dawn proved murky and wet, a cold and dismal morning. Gray light filtered through low hanging clouds, and then it began to rain, a few drops at first, growing to a steady drizzle. Stewart stared skyward, through branches naked of leaves. Fat raindrops splattered his face like an insult, a cold trickle running down his back. The autumn trees gave little shelter, a miserable season to wage war.

"Damn the sky." Dane cast an angry glare to the heavens. "Paulie just got the rust out of my chainmail."

Stewart looked at his friend and struggled to stifle a laugh. Always the dapper nobleman, the war had taken a toll on his friend's lordly guise. "Look at you. Unshaven, bedraggled and mud spattered, the women of Pellanor would never guess you're a lord."

Dane glared. "You're one to talk." Leaning close, he took an exaggerated sniff. "What's that royal stink you're wearing? Essence of horse? Or is it sweat and mud?"

Stewart had to laugh, the tension melting from his shoulders. "War's not what we dreamed it would be."

"No. It's far too muddy, too wet, and too cold," Dane flashed a roguish grin, "but we're damned good at it."

Stewart clapped him on the back, his brother of the sword. "At least the mud and grime will hide the green of our cloaks. Mud might just save your sorry hide from an enemy arrow."

Dane made a mocking scowl. "Brown was never my color."

They both grinned, remembering the finery of the Rose Court.

The cry of a whippoorwill cut through the morning stillness. A pair of men slunk through the muddy field, short bows strung across their backs. They joined the two lords and gave their report. "No change in their numbers. We counted thirty-nine horses. They've set one lookout at each end of the village, but otherwise everything is quiet as a graveyard." Gedry grinned. "It seems we've caught them abed."

"Good." Stewart nodded. "The sentries need to die."

"Already done." Gedry made a slashing gesture across his throat.

"And still no alarm?"

Gedry flashed a gap-toothed smile. "None, lord."

"Then it's time to wet our swords." Stewart rose from a crouch, threading his way back through the woods. A horse nickered and armor jangled. The sounds seemed loud in the morning stillness. The others waited beyond the woods, sixty of his best knights, handpicked from the Rose Squad. They came alert as soon as they saw him. Tough-faced men in mud spattered tabards, bristling with weapons and armor. "Do we fight, my lord?"

"We fight." He climbed into the saddle and shouldered his shield, explaining the plan as the others gird for battle. The knights split into two groups, while the scouts prepared a dozen firebrands. Stewart led the main host back through the woods, Dane riding at his side. They ducked beneath low branches, emerging into the soggy field. His men spread out in a line, keeping their warhorses to a slow trot, approaching the village from the rear. Firebrands sizzled in the falling rain, the scouts kept pace with the knights. Stewart touched his seashell broach for luck, and then unsheathed his sword. Steel whispered from forty scabbards, like the deadly hiss of a many-headed snake. They crossed the muddy field without fanfare, or trumpets, or battle banners, a line of knights intent on death, rain drumming on their armor.

Stewart slowed his stallion to a walk, circling to the front of the inn, a cozy two-story building roofed with thatch. A weathered sign named it the Jolly Tankard, a reputation that was soon to be ruined. Turning his stallion to face the inn's door, he tensed, waiting. Nothing stirred save the chimney smoke. With his men in position, he nodded to Dane. "Time to ruin their morning."

Dane flashed a feral grin. Sheathing his sword, he reached for a firebrand and urged his horse toward the door. On command, the warhorse reared, ironshod hooves lashing out, drumming against the door. The door crashed inward and Dane hurled the firebrand inside. *"For the queen!"* Glass shattered across the inn, as scouts hurled firebrands through broken windows.

Shouts erupted from inside. Half-dressed soldiers burst from the open doorway, brandishing swords and halberds. Black smoke billowed from the windows, adding a burnt stench to the confusion. An arrow thunked into the ground near Stewart's horse while another whistled past his head. His warhorse reared, hooves lashing out, and the battle was joined. He leaned from the saddle, his sword slashing toward the nearest enemy. Blue steel cut through leather and bone, slaying the nearest enemy. He turned his warhorse, seeking another. The battle became a rout, mounted knights fighting against men on foot, slaughtering the invaders as they poured from the inn. Victory seemed assured, but then a horn sounded.

Dane yelled, *"Behind you!"*

Stewart whirled as a halberd rushed toward his face. He raised his oak shield, catching the half-moon blade on the edge. The force of the blow shuddered through his shoulder, nearly knocking him from the saddle.

"Black Flames! It's an ambush!"

The halberd attacked with a deadly fury. Stewart struggled to recover. Part spear, part axe, the halberd whistled toward his face. Stewart swung his sword around, blocking the blow. Steel clanged against steel. Unable to find an opening, Stewart wheeled his warhorse left, trying to bring the ironshod hooves into play, but the halberd slashed at his stallion's neck. Blood fountained and the warhorse screamed, rearing away. Stewart toppled backward, hitting the ground hard. The warhorse crashed next to him, hooves thrashing in an agony of death.

"It's an ambush! Fall back!"

Stewart scrambled to his feet, dodging deadly hooves. From the corner of his eye, he caught a glimpse of red-clad soldiers pouring from the other houses, far more than the forty they'd counted. Stewart gripped his sword and turned to face the teeth of the trap.

A rush of blackened steel swung toward his head. His oak shield took brunt of the blow. Staggered by the brute force, he slipped in the mud, but he kept his shield raised.

A whirlwind of blows rained against his shield. *"Die infidel!"*

His shield shattered, splintering into a thousand shards. He threw the remnants away, feeling naked with just a sword in his hand. For half a heartbeat, Stewart stared at the enemy, a mountain of a man with hatred glaring from his eyes.

"Now you die!"

Stewart parried the halberd.

A horse thundered near, bright steel cleaving the air.

The enemy's head flew from his shoulders. Blood sprayed across Stewart as the headless body staggered for two steps before toppling to the mud.

Dane reined to a halt, flinging the reins of a spare mount to the prince. "Time to flee. We're outnumbered."

"Sound the retreat." Stewart vaulted into the saddle. *"To me! To me!"* He raised his blue sword, standing in the stirrups, shouting over the din. The knights rallied around, hacking a path through the red tabards.

A horn blared and hooves thundered from the right. A line of emerald knights crashed into the enemy's rear. Lances couched, his reserve slammed into the enemy, a mounted battering ram of emerald green. Men screamed and fell, red tabards churned into the mud. They were still outnumbered, but the shock of spears opened a path in the fighting, a slender corridor of escape.

Stewart stood in the stirrups. *"This way! Follow me!"* He spurred his horse forward, but then he spied Gedry. Fighting on foot, the scout was outmatched by a Black Flame. Stewart threw a glance at Dane, "Get them out!" and then he swerved his horse to the right, crashing into the enemy. His blue sword swung in a mighty arc, cleaving through chainmail and flesh, killing the enemy with a single stroke. Reining the horse to a stop, he offered Gedry a hand. "Mount up!" The scout swung behind him, clutching tight. Enemy hands reached for the prince, trying to pull him from the saddle, but Stewart beat them away.

He spurred his warhorse to a gallop. *"Retreat! Retreat!"* He galloped for the narrow opening, but a black halberd swung toward him. Pain struck his chest like a lance. The blow took him unawares, knocking him from the horse. Stewart hit the ground hard. Stunned, he clutched his chest expecting blood, but there was none, saved from death by his chainmail. Gasping for breath, he staggered to his feet. All around him, the battle raged as the emerald knights beat a hasty retreat. He reached for his sword, but his scabbard was empty. And then he saw it, a gleam of sapphire-blue steel lying in the mud, a horse-length away.

He scrambled for the sword, but a half-moon blade swung toward his head.

Without sword or shield, Stewart could only stagger backwards, watching death slice toward him. He tripped over a corpse and fell hard.

The half-moon blade followed him, stopping a thumb's width from his throat. "Surrender or die!"

Stewart stared at the crescent-shaped blade, stunned by the reversal of fortune.

The sounds of battle dimmed as the last of the emerald knights escaped.

A bearded enemy glared at him. "Surrender or die!" The half-moon blade kissed his throat, a promise of death.

Stewart spat the hateful words. "I yield."

Hands grabbed him from behind, forcing his wrists together, binding them tight with strips of leather. Yanked to his feet, Stewart's gaze darted across the churned mud, frantic for his blue sword. A pair of red-cloaked soldiers fought over it. Rage thundered through him, but Stewart could only watch. Someone grabbed his hand, yanking his gold signet ring from his finger, while another took the dagger from his belt. A third ripped his seashell broach from his cloak.

"Not that!"

A gauntleted fist crashed into his jaw, smashing him to the ground. Blood filled his mouth. For a moment, the world went black, but then a hand gripped his hair, dragging him to his feet, and he realized the nightmare was real. "Obey or die." Despair washed over him, how could this happen? Prodded from behind, Stewart staggered through the mud, a prisoner of the Flame.

22

Danly

Danly wore no chains yet he was still a prisoner. They'd given him a horse to ride, a nag of a rundown mare that was sure to drop dead at the first hard gallop. As if the nag was not message enough, every day his captors proved their prowess, shooting game for the cook pot. His mount was too old to escape and his guards too accurate with their crossbows. Cruel iron no longer bit his flesh yet Danly remained well and truly shackled.

Still, his lot had improved, clearly gaining by the ambush. His new captors called him 'prince' and gave him decent clothes to wear, good leather boots and a warm wool cloak of butternut brown. One of the men cut his hair while another lent him a razor and a looking glass. The looking glass proved a shock, his eyes sunken like pits, his cheeks hollowed from the meager prison fare, but the worst jolt came from the streaks of gray in his beard. Gray...like the frosted beard of an old man. The sight drove him into a smoldering rage. Not content with stealing his manhood, the Spider Queen had taken his youth as well. The bitch had much to atone for.

Danly hacked at the beard, desperate to find the dashing prince beneath...but the reflected face remained a stranger. With the beard gone, the scars on his face became dominant. Five claw marks furrowed his left cheek, the raking nails of a prostitute's revenge. He decided he liked the scars, a badge of his manhood, proof of his prowess with women. Every morning, he borrowed the razor, scraping his face smooth, determined to keep the last vestige of his manhood in plain sight.

He kept to himself when he made his morning toilet. If his captors knew he was a neutered eunuch, they never said a word...but then again, they never said much of anything. A tight-lipped crew of seasoned soldiers, they refused to answer his questions. Twenty men, all of them bristling with steel, yet he could not spy a single emblem or heraldic symbol among them. Wearing a mixture of chainmail and leather, they carried a medley of weapons, swords, axes, war hammers and crossbows, always keeping them close at hand. Their speech held a smattering of accents, but nothing Danly could recognize. He guessed they were mercenaries, but whatever lord they served remained a mystery.

Riding by day, they camped at night, always avoiding villages and towns. Haste did not seem to matter. Neither did the direction they rode. Some days they rode north, others west, but then they'd turn south again. If there was a pattern, Danly could not see it.

He spent most days riding next to the leader, peppering the man with questions, trying to solve the riddle of his captors. Danly kicked his sway-backed mare, trying to keep even with the captain's stallion. "That ambush was well planned. Caltrops planted on the road, but how did you find us?"

Braxus flashed a smile, a swarthy man in dark leathers. "We have our ways."

Danly resented the dark-haired leader's surly wit, yet he persisted with his questions. "Did you follow the wagon from Pellanor? Is that how you found me?"

"So many questions, prince." Braxus laughed, a flash of white teeth in a sun-drenched face. "Can't you just enjoy this fine autumn afternoon?"

Frustration clawed at Danly. "But we don't seem to be heading anywhere. One day we canter north, the next day we trot south, yet you never consult a map. What are you looking for?"

Braxus shrugged. "We're looking for nothing." A sly smile spread across his face. "Merely waiting to be found."

"Waiting to be found?" The answer made no sense. "But why did you rescue me? If you're with the Red Horns, just say so."

The steady clop of hooves was his only reply.

"Then you're not with the Red Horns." Annoyance leached into Danly's voice.

"I've told you, prince, it's not for me to answer your questions." Braxus flashed a devilish grin. "You'll just have to be patient."

"Princes are rarely patient."

"So I've noticed."

Danly tried another tack. "I have gold, you know. Enough to make you and your men wealthy."

"And where is this gold?"

Danly tried to keep the eagerness from his voice, hoping the well-told lie would serve him once more. "In Pellanor, safe with friends."

Braxus gave him a sly smile. "Ah, of course."

Danly's frustration boiled over. "If not gold, then what do you want?"

The leader turned serious, his dark eyes full of warning. "Be careful, prince. There are more powers in this world than you know."

A shiver raced down Danly's spine.

A ring-tailed pheasant broke from the brush, a flutter of wings rising into a crisp blue sky. One of the brigands raised his crossbow. A single bolt thrummed aloft. The feathered shaft struck its mark. Skewered, the pheasant plummeted, dinner for the cook pot.

The lesson was not lost on Danly. He glanced at the leader. "You're men are good."

"Of course they are." Braxus sat straight in the saddle, his right hand resting on his sword hilt, looking like a brigand-prince. "To succeed in this

world, you must either be born to privilege or be very good at what you do."
His dark stare bored into Danly. "Which are you?"

The question hit like a slap. Danly sputtered with indignation. "Royalty is ordained by the gods. Kings and princes are always set above their people. It is the natural order of things."

The brigand's voice dripped with sarcasm. "Is that why we found you in rags and chains, stinking of shit, cowering under a wagon?"

Anger pulsed through Danly. "I'm still a prince."

"And your mother's still a queen, yet you'd take her throne."

"Women are not fit to rule."

The brigand gave him a snide smile. "Then you don't know many women."

Danly wanted to punch the smile from the brigand's face, but he settled for words and superior blood. "I'm a royal, a prince of Lanverness."

Braxus made a mocking bow. "Of course you are. Otherwise you'd have no value."

Danly glared. "What makes you so insolent?"

Braxus laughed. "I'm good with my sword...but I thought you figured that out."

"Who are you?"

The brigand leader turned serious, his dark eyes glinting in the sunlight. "Born a commoner, I used my wits and my sword to find a way to power."

"But whom do you serve?"

"Can't you guess?" His mouth twisted into a grin. "Someone powerful." Braxus laughed, spurring his stallion to a gallop.

Danly coughed, choking on the brigand's dust. He drove his heels into his horse's flanks, but the nag ignored him, stumbling along at the same slow trot. Danly glared at the brigand's back, sputtering with rage.

Days turned to weeks. Danly kept hammering the brigands with questions, like chipping away at a block of ice, yet he never got any answers. Travel became a dull routine. Forced to saddle his own horse and take turns cooking meals, Danly felt like a common soldier. Calluses appeared on his hands, dirt and grime beneath his fingernails. Appalled, Danly feared he looked more like a brigand than a prince. Trapped in some kind of nightmare, he stumbled through the days...till he was toed awake to a fog-filled morning.

"Come, prince, today you'll gain your answers."

Danly glared from his bedroll. "In this fog?"

Braxus laughed. "A perfect day for it."

Danly rose with the others, made a hasty toilet and then saddled his horse. Mist shrouded the forest, so thick he could barely see. Braxus grabbed the reins of Danly's horse, putting the nag on a lead. "Just in case you decide to stray."

They rode single file, weaving through the forest. The naked trees loomed like shadows, skeletal hands grasping at the swirling clouds. Danly pulled his cloak tight against the chill, peering through the fog.

A strange stillness settled over the forest, as if the mist strangled any sound. Wary of ambush, Danly swiveled left and right, looking for substance in the swirling white. The fog seemed unnatural, like a curse smothering the woods. Danly shivered, wishing for a sword. Just when he thought they were alone in the mist, he caught the faint sound of a flute. Simple notes, like a child's lullaby beckoned them forward.

Braxus turned toward the flute. "I think we've been found." He urged his horse to a trot.

They followed the notes, a slender thread leading through the mist. The flute grew louder, a simple peasant's song. Danly caught a glimpse of a campfire. Silhouettes appeared in the mist, soldiers and horses and tents. Sounds rushed to fill the white void, the whinny of a horse, the rasp of steel against stone, the snap and crackle of burning wood. A bearded soldier in dark chainmail sat cross-legged in front of a campfire, the player of the flute. He set the flute aside and rose to his feet, a welcoming smile on his face. "Ah, Braxus, you've been expected."

Braxus dismounted and clasped forearms with the bearded soldier. "We came as soon as we were found."

More riddles. Danly stayed on his horse and surveyed the camp, teasing details from the fog. He counted another thirty soldiers, a nest of brigands in an odd assortment of armor, all of them heavily armed. Escape just became that much harder.

The bearded man was speaking again. "And this must be the prince?"

Braxus nodded. "Rescued from a grim exile yet he shows little gratitude."

Danly prickled at the insult. "Was I rescued or merely re-captured? It's hard to tell the difference."

"See what I mean." Braxus held his horse. "Come, prince, the answers you crave are close."

Danly dismounted and stepped to the fire, warmed by the blaze. The bearded soldier whispered something to Braxus, gesturing into the mist. Braxus nodded, a hint of surprise on his face. "So soon." He clapped Danly on the back. "Come, you've been granted an audience."

"You speak as if I'm meeting royalty."

Braxus grinned. "Fate leads a merry dance."

Danly was reluctant to leave the warmth but it seemed he had little choice. "Where are you taking me?"

"You'll soon see." Braxus turned and strode off into the mist, leaving Danly to follow. They walked through the camp, past a ring of tents, and out into the bare-branched forest. Swirling mist quickly swallowed the camp sounds, muffling the forest with a cold dampness. Danly kept close to the brigand, wishing he had a sword. Braxus came to a sudden stop, pointing toward a scuffed dirt path. "Just follow the path. You are expected."

Danly gave the path a suspicious glare. "Alone?"

Braxus nodded.

"And if I run?"

"Then you'll never get your answers."

Danly knew they'd never let him walk free. He suspected archers lurked in the mist, waiting for him to stray. His shoulders twitched, but he took a step forward. One step and then another, he followed the path. Mist closed around him like a fist, a damp chilliness. The world turned white, like a blank parchment waiting for a tale. He walked alone, no guards at his back, no servants at his beck and call, no gold in his pockets. Stripped of everything, he wondered if he still had a destiny. Something caught his foot. He stumbled and nearly fell. His gaze darted back along the trail, half expecting to find a claw thrust up from the soil...but no, it was just a root.

Straightening his jerkin, he kept walking, amazed that no arrows struck him from behind. Trees loomed out of the mist like misshapen hands. The trail meandered up a hill, through a stand of cedar trees. The mist thinned and he caught a glimpse of a pavilion. Purple silk with golden phases of the moon embroidered around the sides, like something from a vision. Purple, the color of royalty, but the heraldry was unfamiliar, another riddle. Perhaps he'd found the lord of the brigands. Determined to gain some answers, he pulled the curtain aside and stepped within.

A woman!

His footsteps faltered. Not just any woman...a siren conjured from the songs of bards. Like a vision, she lay draped across a low divan. Purple silk clung to her sultry curves, a deep slit revealing a glimpse of long shapely legs. His gaze drank her in. Her dark hair cascaded to creamy shoulders, dark as midnight, lustrous as a raven's wing. Danly longed to run his hands through her hair, but then he saw her eyes, deep green like bottomless pools, and her lips, red and lush and full of temptation, begging to be bruised. Bewitched, he staggered forward. "Am I dreaming?"

"Would it be such a bad dream?" Her voice was low and throaty, a tease to his every desire. "Come warm yourself by my fire."

Her scent reached out to enfold him, musk, and sandalwood, and something else, something he yearned to possess. He staggered forward, drawn towards her fire. Pillows lay strewn across the floor, creating a soft bower of colorful silk. A low brazier sat in the middle, casting a crackle of flames...but the fire could not compete with heat of the woman. "Who are you?"

"Whom did you expect?"

"The leader of the brigands."

"Oh," her words were a purr, "such meager expectations." She leaned back and her robe parted, revealing a spill of curves, a deep cleft between her breasts. "I'm so much more than that." Her fingers traced the cleft. "Don't you think?"

He found himself kneeling amongst the pillows, struggling to think. "Where are your guards?"

"Guards?" Her throaty laugh feathered down his spine. "I have no need of guards." Her hand cupped his face, so soft yet so sure. "Are you such a fearsome warrior? Should I tremble in your presence?" She rose with an elegant grace, the swaying silk revealing more than it hid. He watched, spellbound, as she moved behind him, her fingers teasing the hair at his neck. Her breath whispered against his ear. "I've killed men before...with my own hand."

Danly tried to control a shiver. "But you're only a..."

"...woman? You have much to learn, prince." Her voice deepened. "Look down."

He stiffened in surprise. Her jeweled hand threatened his throat, a needle exposed on her ring like a serpent's fang. He quivered, hiding his fear beneath indignation. "Poison is for cowards and..."

"...women?" Her voice held a hint of amusement. "See, you're learning already."

His stare remained fixed on the needle. Somehow the danger only added to her allure.

She flicked her hand, working a subtle hinge, and the needle disappeared beneath the golden serpent, a mere ring once more.

Danly took a steadying breath. "What do you want?"

Her words whispered in his ear. "A throne, of course."

"It seems I've lost mine."

"With my help, it could be found." She pressed against his back, brushing against him like a cat in heat. "Do you want your throne?"

"I need an army."

"Such a small request." She loosened his cloak, letting it fall to the ground. "And what else?"

"Your charms won't work on me."

"Oh, I think they will." Her arms encircled him, her fingers tugging on the bindings of his tunic. Her scent enfolded him, making it hard to think. "Don't you want to be a king?"

He had to stop this before she embarrassed him. "A king needs heirs, and I'll never beget any."

Another throaty laugh, "Surely a prince like you sowed many wild seeds." She caressed his face, her fingers lingering on his scars. Her fingernails matched the lines. "I'll wager these scars are from a woman," her voice turned deep and throaty, "a woman scorned."

"So?"

"So find an old conquest, a healthy peasant girl with a babe at her breast and claim the brat as your own."

Danly gasped, such a simple idea.

"One son is all a king ever needs. One son to continue your name and your lineage."

Danly shivered, as if the woman peered into his very soul.

Her voice thrummed in his ear. "What else?"

Scents of sandalwood enveloped him. Sandalwood and something else, something musky and alluring, surrounding him like a haze. He shook his head, wondering if he was lost in a dream. "What are you, some kind of female djinn granting three wishes?"

She knelt behind him, her curves pressed into his back, her teeth biting the lobe of his ear. "Oh, I'm so much more than that." Her fingers worked the bindings of his trousers. "Give me your soul and I'll grant your third wish."

He flinched away. "Only the gods could grant such a wish."

She persisted. Deft fingers slowly unlaced his bindings. "As it happens, I have the favor of a god."

Danly laughed, drunk on her scent, intoxicated by her possibilities.

Her fingers brushed his groin. "Speak and you shall have it." Her voice dropped to a throaty whisper. "What do you desire?"

The words rushed out of him. "My mother took my manhood."

"Such a naughty mother. But with me, you can be a man again."

He hadn't been with a woman since they'd cut him. He wondered if he could. "For that, I'd give anything." He turned and lunged at her. Silk ripped beneath his hands, freeing the curves beneath. So lush and full, he grabbed with both hands, kneading her warm globes with his fingers, squeezing hard.

"No!" She stuck like a snake, her hand slapping his cheek.

The slap stung like a thousand nettles. For a moment, Danly feared she'd used the ring. He touched his face but there was no blood.

She gave him a shrewd look. "You'll live, for now, but you have much to learn."

He sagged back on his heels, confused. Even with her robe torn, she still looked regal, part siren, part temptress, part queen. He rubbed his cheek and looked away. "Nothing but a limp threat anyway." Bitterness washed over him. "I've seen gelded stallions. Once the balls are cut, the spear is done."

She knelt next to him, offering a seductive smile. "Not with me." Her hands trailed a path down his chest, lingering at his belt. "With me, you will be a prince among men, a stallion among mares."

He breathed deep, enthralled by her scent.

"You can be a man again, but it must be done my way."

He was desperate to believe. "Anything."

She shrugged the torn silk from her shoulders, revealing her true promise. Lush curves and silky smooth skin, he moaned with anticipation. Leaning close, she whispered. "Let me show you." She pushed him down into a nest of silken pillows, her dark hair cascading around his face like a curtain. "Let me teach you the way of a thousand delights." Straddling him, she slowly removed his clothes, covering his skin with teasing licks of her tongue, working her way down to his groin.

Lost in a feast of senses, he surrendered to her touch, to her intoxicating scent. At first it was merely pleasant, a dalliance of slow delights...but then the heat began to build. A bonfire of wanting woke within him. A moan escaped his lips as he burned within, as his loins quickened with heat. His spear stood triumphant, urgent with need. He gasped, as if the dead had risen to life. "By all the gods!"

Her voice was a low whisper. "No, just one."

He rolled on top but she held him at bay.

"Will you swear your soul to me?"

"What?"

"Will you swear your soul to me?

His manhood strained for release. "Yes, anything."

She gave a throaty laugh. "Then I grant your wish."

He fell on her, sheathing himself in her moist lushness, reveling in being a man once more. And with each wild stroke, he swore in his soul he'd do anything to have her again and again and again.

23

Liandra

Liandra retreated to her solar, a haven from the prying eyes of the Rose Court. Swathed in robes of ermine, she took her ease before the fire, examining the gifts of Ur. Opening the small narrow box, she held the uncut ruby up to the candlelight. "Look at this."

Princess Jemma and Lady Sarah both stared in awe.

She turned the stone, examining it from every angle. Flashes of deep red glinted in the light. "Flawless. A priceless gem."

"Is it real?"

Liandra gave the princess a wry smile. "Oh yes. This queen knows her jewels. A perfect flawless ruby of deep color, blood red, the size of a large man's fist." She shook her head in wonder. "We've never seen its like, and we *own* ruby mines."

"But why gift you with such wealth? What does Ur owe Lanverness?"

"Nothing, and therein lies the question. Lanverness and Ur have been trading partners for centuries, but we've never had a formal alliance." Liandra considered the gem. "Gifts of such magnitude always incur obligation." Her gaze pierced the princess. "What did you think of the delegates from Ur?"

"Strange, odd, secretive, yet their show of wealth is amazing, even overwhelming."

"Wealth flaunted in our court." Liandra frowned. "Perhaps the wealth is meant to distract."

"A diversion."

The queen nodded. "They strike us as scorpions trying to hide their stingers." She pondered the gem. "The trick is to accept the gift without being stung to death by obligation."

"Or subterfuge."

Liandra gave her apprentice a smile. "Exactly."

"Well I don't like them and I don't trust them and neither should you." Lady Sarah poured tea and then took a seat on the far side of the fireplace. "That chained one gives me the shivers, his skin as pale as a dead fish."

"What have you heard?" Her lady-in-waiting kept a close ear to the rumors of the court, a valuable resource for the queen.

"They say he's a *sorcerer*," Lady Sarah leaned forward as if sharing a great secret, "a wizard of black arts. As long as silver pierces his flesh, he can't work magic." She nodded like a sage. "That's why the king keeps him chained with silver piercing his nose, keeps him bound like a dog on a leash."

She'd heard tales of silver suppressing magic but she'd always considered them a fairy tale. "Magic is rare in the lands of Erdhe, we doubt he is a sorcerer. A king would not easily part with a servant of such power." She nestled the ruby back in the box. "No, the one that worries us is the mind behind the message, an unseen player, yet to show his face."

"The prince?"

"Perhaps." Liandra gestured towards the massive wooden chest set on the far side of the chamber. "Take a good look at the coins."

Princess Jemma crossed the room to open the chest. A wealth of gold glittered inside, a stunning sight. Burrowing her hand deep within, she removed a handful of coins. One at a time, she examined them, letting them fall like chimes back into the mound. "They're all different, and some are worn so smooth they're almost blank."

"They reek of age." The queen nodded. "Even *we* have never seen some of them, and we've always had a fondness for coins."

"But Ur must have vast trading webs, to kingdoms we've never even dreamt of."

"True, but some coins are more than three centuries old, from kingdoms long conquered and nearly forgotten." Liandra considered the treasure. "A message lies within the coins, more than mere wealth, yet we do not see it. Almost as if we are being taunted."

The princess gave a visible shiver and closed the lid. "At least the gold will help with the war."

"True. Yet the timing seems more than pure coincidence."

Lady Sarah huffed. "Well, I don't like those jesters, especially the dwarves, with their nasty pointy teeth, what horrid little men. Like something from a nightmare." She shuddered. "What a strange gift to give a queen."

"Not strange, crafty." Liandra fiddled with the rings on her fingers. "Dazzled by wealth, we accepted spies into our court. But we intend to turn the tables on the gift-givers. My shadowmen will keep watch. Perhaps the spies will teach us something of this twelfth-fold prince."

"Ur is such a strange land, with so many rumors and legends it's hard to know what to believe."

"Great distance will do that. In the absence of fact, the mind is free to run toward the fantastic." Liandra smoothed her robe across her expanding belly. "But it is the close-at-hand that troubles us. The Urians set us a problem of another sort. Flaunted wealth is always dangerous. Such casual largess will embolden our noble lords. It is so much easier to rule a kingdom when the treasury is fat."

The princess looked thoughtful. "Then you must remove the temptation."

"Exactly." Liandra smiled. "It is time to play a different gambit, one that might ensnare the Flame and my unloyal lords, all in one fell move."

The princess leaned forward, a keen look on her face. "When?"

"Tomorrow, at our council. We'll set the bait and see who takes it." Liandra gestured toward the treasure chest. "This chest gives new meaning to the notion of staggering wealth."

Lady Sarah tittered. "Did you see the muscles on those bearers?" She rolled her eyes. "In they marched, bold as brass, wearing nothing but those flimsy linen skirts. Quite the eyeful." The princess blushed and Lady Sarah laughed. . Liandra felt the tension melt from her shoulders, enjoying the company of honest women.

A knock came from the door, short and sharp.

The laughter died, both women looking toward the queen.

Liandra sighed. "Duty calls. Go and see who dares disturb us at this late hour."

Lady Sarah turned formal. Giving the queen a slight bow, she stepped to the door, shielding the opening with her body.

"I need to see the queen."

Liandra heard the urgency in Master Raddock's voice. "Show him in."

The black-robed master slipped through the door, like crow come late to the party. He sketched a hasty bow, his voice gruff. "Majesty, a visitor asks to see you."

"At this late hour? Surely the Urians have not returned?"

"No, majesty, but you said you wanted to be told at once."

Liandra's patience was running thin. "Well out with it then. Who seeks audience at such late an hour?"

"A newcomer, majesty. He claims to be a monk of the Kiralynn Order."

The news struck like a deep-sounding bell, resonating in her soul. "We will see this newcomer. Show him in."

Her shadowmaster bowed, slipping back through the door.

Princess Jemma rose as if to leave.

"No, both of you stay. Lady Sarah, our hair." Liandra basked in the warmth of the fire while Lady Sarah dressed her hair, adding combs adorned with seed pearls, a striking addition to her raven-black tresses. "And the emerald." The lady went to the jewel box, returning with a gold necklace set with an immense pear-shaped emerald, a statement of wealth in its own right, wealth she'd earned by the strength of her own intellect. Bedecked in furs and jewels, the queen awaited the late night visitor.

Another knock on the door.

"Come."

Lady Sarah slipped into the shadows while Princess Jemma remained seated by the fireside. Master Raddock returned. Behind him came a stranger, a man of middling height dressed in robes of midnight blue. He stood in the firelight, a hawk nose set in a tanned face, his dark hair flecked with gray. Two gray streaks flared away from his temples like wings, but it was his eyes that captivated, dark and brimming with intelligence, eyes that dared to be reckoned with. "I bring greetings from the Grand Master." He gave a half bow, but his gaze never left her face. "I am Fintan, a master of the Kiralynn Order."

"Welcome to our court...yet you come at such a late hour."

"Late hours are often a cloak for discretion."

More riddles wrapped in secrecy, Liandra nodded, knowing she needed to be sharp. "You are the second member of your Order to seek an audience. Master Aeroth comes and goes like the wind. You monks are too mysterious by half."

He gave her an odd smile. "Secrecy can be a weapon, or a shield, but the usefulness of both is dwindling. Darkness stirs in the north, threatening the lands of Erdhe."

"The north?"

"I have come in dire times. The Mordant seeks to reclaim his power."

Liandra suppressed the urge to make the hand sign against evil.

"When he has secured the north, he will turn his armies to the south."

Another army to contend with, the words struck like blows to her soul. "Your Order is full of dire warnings."

"To be forewarned is to be forearmed."

"We know the value of spies." Her words snapped with anger. "But we need more than warnings. Invaders from Coronth march across our lands, too numerous to count."

"The Army of the Flame. That twisted religion harbors another form of darkness."

"The Flame must be defeated ere we can contend with the north." Liandra's stare drilled the monk. "Do you come bearing dire messages or do your come to offer aid?" She dared to hope the rumors were true, her voice dropping to a whisper. "Do you bring magic to our court?"

He met her stare. "I bring knowledge, long protected by the Kiralynn Order. I'm told you are a queen who values knowledge."

A hint of challenge rode his voice, a challenge laced with intelligence. Liandra decided she liked him. "Come sit with us. We would learn the knowledge of the Kiralynn monks."

He took a seat amongst them, spinning a tale of knowledge and prophecy, a tale that stretched back through the ages, a story of war and magic, an immortal battle of Light against Dark. Liandra sat captivated, absorbing every word, gaining insights to age-old mysteries. The fire burned to embers and still they talked. Tales of the past colored the problems of the present. Liandra began to see a larger pattern. By the time sunlight glinted on the windowpanes, a plan began to take shape in her mind. She had more enemies than she'd ever suspected...but perhaps the monks could make a difference. Plots within plots, she'd find a way to save her kingdom.

24

Jordan

Jordan stumbled down the trail, shocked to find fall leaves still clinging to the valley below. A pageant of orange and gold flamed amongst the dark green firs, so much color it dazzled her. After the treacherous mountain passes, she'd begun to believe all of Erdhe lay locked in winter.

A cold wind clawed at her back, as if the mountains refused to relinquish their hold. Clutching her cloak, Jordan struggled to keep pace. The monks led the way, leaning on their quarterstaffs, shaggy as bears in their fur cloaks. Strung out in a line, they staggered down steep switchbacks, footsore and starving. Crossing the pass had been a nightmare of avalanches and blizzards, testing their resolve and exhausting their supplies. For the last three days they'd gone without food; nothing to fill their bellies save thinly stretched tea. Jordan felt hollow like a ghost, but she refused to give up. Licking her cracked lips, she stumbled down the trail, wondering if they'd crossed the mountains only to die of starvation.

Guilt gnawed at her, knowing the monks had joined in the ordeal because of her dreams. Without their lore, she'd never have survived. She shivered, remembering the glacier, one slip away from an icy death. But now they faced another peril, not a crust of bread among them. Hunger proved a merciless tyrant, gnawing at her insides. It still surprised her that the monks had so miscalculated the food supplies. For all their knowledge, they made mistakes. It did not bode well for the trials ahead.

Plagued by weariness, her mind slipped sideways, escaping into daydreams. Like precious jewels, she relived her nights with Stewart, especially Midwinter's Eve. Every facet of their first night was special, the memory blazing like a Yule log in her heart. Suffused with heat, she imagined his touch, but other images intruded. Without warning, her daydreams twisted to nightmares. Ghastly visions seared her mind. Like flashes of lightning they struck, one after another, hitting her with a fury of blows. MerChanter raiders swarmed the Navarren coast, sacking seaside villages, raping and pillaging till the shore ran dark with blood. The image changed and she saw Stewart bedraggled in tattered clothes, running through a bare-branch forest, armed soldiers chasing the hare. Lightning cracked and she saw a severed head stuck on a spike, staring down from a battlement. Faster and faster the images came. A shattered tower, red as blood, reared above a winter forest. Her sister, Juliana, barked orders on her ship's deck, desperate to outrun the MerChanter fleet. Her father sprawled dead at the base of Castle Seamount, his body tossed to the rocks like dross. A scream tore out of her. "No!" Refusing the visions, she hurled her protest to the gods. *"No!"*

"NO! No! No." Her cry echoed against the mountains, a mockery of her protest.

Hands gripped her from behind. "I've got you."

She struggled against the bonds.

"You're safe."

Reality returned in a rush. She stood on the edge of a precipice, staring down at a thousand foot drop. *"Oh!"*

Rafe held her from behind. "I have you."

Jordan stepped back from the edge and disengaged from his arms. Flushed with embarrassment, her face burned red. "Must be the hunger."

He gave her a knowing look but he did not gainsay her. "Have a drink." He handed her a water skin. "Water will fool your empty stomach, at least for a while."

Uncorking the skin, she took a long swallow of crystal clear snowmelt. Her stomach growled, but she had nothing to feed it. "Thanks."

Returning the water skin, she followed the others down the trail, struggling to close the gap. Shaken by the nightmares, she gripped her sword hilt, determined to avoid any daydreams, yet the visions haunted her. Such terrible images, such dire consequences, she did not understand half of what she saw, yet she felt compelled to act. Destiny tugged at her, pulling in too many directions. She shook her head, raging against the tumult.

"What did you see?" Rafe walked close as a shadow.

Her embarrassment doubled. "Nothing."

"The Grand Master believes your visions are gifts from the gods, memories from your time between."

"The time between?"

"You nearly died. Master Garth's magic pulled you back from the brink. Locked in a healing trance, you lingered between life and death, close enough to hear the gods." His voice dropped to a whisper. "Many masters would give much to know what you saw."

He'd saved her life more than once in the mountain pass...she owed him an answer, but it was such a jumble. "Light, I remember a warm light...and a feeling that everything made sense. I tried so hard to remember...but it slipped through my mind like clutching sand on a beach."

"And now?"

"Nothing but nightmares. Visions so terrible they can't be real."

"Perhaps they're futures you're meant to change."

Her frustration broke like a wave. "But I don't understand half of what I see! All I know is that it cannot be." Jordan glanced his way, but he had no answers. Exhausted, she fell silent, locked in misery once more. They straggled after the others, rounding another switchback. Another steep slope, it seemed as if the mountains had no end.

By midmorning they reached the tree line. Stunted pines and twisted firs provided a break from the biting wind. Jordan scanned the green fringe, hoping for late berries, wondering if pine needles would fill her empty belly, or just give her the runs. Ignoring the thought, she forced herself to keep walking, the last in a line of footsore travelers.

Midday came and went without a meal and still they walked. Her boots shuffled down the slope, barely clearing the rocky trail. Twice she tripped, the fall waking her from a daze. She picked herself up and pressed forward, surprised to find the forest had thickened. Pines and firs and a few aspens crowded the trail, a touch of autumn gold brightening the deep green. *Almost down*, Jordan breathed deep the scent of pine, desperate to ignore her ravening hunger. At least her hunger kept her visions at bay, a minor blessing.

The trail rounded a bend and a stranger stood in their way. A silver-haired woman cloaked in robes of midnight-blue. "What kept you?"

Another monk, Jordan sank to the ground, too weary to take another step. She glared at the newcomer, disappointed that the woman came alone, without horses or supplies, without food. But then she caught a tantalizing scent. She breathed deep, intoxicated by the scent of fried bacon wafting up the trail.

"Come, we have a camp set up below." The woman gestured down the trail.

Jordan found herself trotting down the trail, her nostrils flaring wide, following the scent of sizzling bacon.

The trail grew level and then widened into a small clearing. A horse nickered, a line of thirty mounts picketed along the trail. Beyond the horses, a circle of tents surrounded a campfire. Ravenous, Jordan followed the scent to the cook fire.

A stranger in brown leathers handed her a plate heaped with thick slices of bacon, pan-fried bread and roasted onions. "Lenore said you'd be here in time for supper."

"Thank you." Jordan took the plate and sank to the ground, stuffing a whole slice of bacon in her mouth. Nearly swooning, she groaned in pleasure, grease running down the side of her mouth. Her hands shook as she ate, so desperate to fill her belly. Wrapping the onions and bacon in a flat bread, she devoured the meal, licking her fingers clean of the salty grease.

"Another plate?" A stranger with russet hair and a thick beard offered seconds.

Jordan almost said yes, but then she realized she was full. "No, but you saved my life."

The stranger grinned. "Happy to be of service."

A contented silence swirled around the campfire. While her companions ate, Jordan studied the strangers, six men all in leathers, bristling with weapons, not a lord's emblem among them. They moved with a feral grace, clearly accustomed to wearing swords. Soldiers, or mercenaries, or perhaps thieves, yet they seemed at ease with the monks.

Jordan leaned toward Rafe, keeping her voice to a whisper. "Who are they?" But the russet-haired stranger had ears like a bat.

"Name's Thad Tokheart."

"Thad?"

"Short for Thaddeus."

Such an odd name, it must have shown from her face for he barked a laugh. "I know, it's such a scrollish name for a man who lives by the sword, but my parents were both monks and they dreamt of raising a scholar." He gave her a wry smile. "We don't always get what we want."

"No, we don't." *His parents were monks?*

He took her empty plate. "Find a place for your bedroll. We'll sleep here tonight and then get an early start at first light. Lenore says we'll have good weather tomorrow."

"Lenore?" Her mind seemed muddled.

"The monk who met you on the trail." She followed his gaze to the monk with silver-blonde hair. Lenore had a stately dignity about her, so at odds with the brigands seated around the fire. "You ride with a monk?"

"Sometimes. You'd best get to your bedroll, we've an early start tomorrow."

"You said that before...an early start to where?"

Thad barked a hearty laugh. "Wherever it is you're going."

"You're coming with me?"

"Of course, lass." His grin deepened. "The Grand Master said you might be needing a few swords, and what the Grand Master asks for, he gets."

Another riddle, but Jordan was too tired to figure it out. Spreading her bedroll near the campfire, she crawled inside. Exhausted, and sated with good food, she finally slept, untroubled by nightmares.

25

Steffan

Something in the night pierced his senses. Steffan snapped awake but he did not move. Feigning sleep, he watched through hooded eyes, seeking the disturbance. Darkness held sway, the fire in the brazier burned down to embers, nothing but a dull red glow. His gaze roamed the pavilion. Everything seemed in order, till he caught a glimpse of a shadowy figure lurking in the far corner. His heartbeat spiked. Fearing the guards would be too slow to stop an assassin, he kept his body still, his right hand creeping toward the dagger hidden beneath his pillow.

A throaty laugh arrested his hand. "Don't you know me?"

She stepped into the red light of the embers, raven-black hair tumbling around a heart-shaped face. Dark eyes and full pouty lips, she appeared like a vision from his dreams. "You!"

"Of course." She circled the brazier, a slow, sultry pace, slits of silk revealing a glimmer of shapely white thigh. "I promised I'd come."

"But how did you find..."

"Shhhh..." Her dark gaze glittered in the dim light. "Do you want to talk?" She prowled towards him. "Or do you want something more?" Her smoky voice hinted at forbidden pleasures, like fingernails caressing his spine.

He threw back the furs, inviting her to his bed.

And then she was in his arms, like he'd dreamed a thousand times, but this was so much more potent, so much more...consuming. Her fingertips blazed a path down his chest but he could not wait. Emboldened by her scent, by her touch, he gave into to his desires. Pulling her close, he rolled on top, pressing his need against her. He kissed her hard. Her tongue flicked within his mouth, bold and daring, igniting a bonfire within. Ravenous to have her, he ripped at her silks. Skin to skin, his hands claimed her, caressing every curve, delving every shadowy crevice, but it only deepened his desire. Rearing above her, he saw his own hunger mirrored in her face. Like an unquenchable sword, he took her without preamble, thrusting deep and hard and full of need. He came with a roar, his back arched, his skin slick with sweat.

But even after the first rush, he did not stop. Keeping a slow steady rhythm, he stoked the fires, letting the passion build between them.

A smile flicked across her face, like a cat tasting cream.

Something about her smile irked him, pricking his pride. Steffan swore that he'd make the second time last, that he would not come till she screamed. He slowed the rhythm to a tease, his tongue flicking along her skin, smitten by her sandalwood scent, by her salty taste.

She laughed, a silken sound that sent shivers down his spine. And then she rolled on top, her long legs gripping him tight, her dark hair forming a curtain against the night. She rode him, setting her own rhythm. "There's a fine line between pain and pleasure. Dare to walk the line?"

Her throaty challenge almost brought him to a climax. *Almost.* With a roar, he tipped her off the bed and onto the floor, and then he pounced, rolling to get behind her, to feel the swell of her buttocks against his loins. But she moved like dark lightning, fingernails raking across his back. Like two lions grappling for dominance, they rolled across the carpet, a ball of passion laced with pain. As if she knew his every secret, her touch quivered through him, pushing him to the limit of his endurance. Refusing to give in, Steffan found stamina he never knew he had. Back and forth, they stoked the fire between them, till he thought he'd burst into flame. Desperate to end it, he threw her across the bed and took her from behind. She arched her back and screamed and he finally found release, as if his very soul rushed from his body into hers.

Spent, he collapsed to the carpet, sodden with sweat.

She joined him; her head resting on his shoulder, nestled against him like a contented kitten.

It was only then that he noticed the first hint of dawn light filtering through the pavilion. "How do you do that?"

"Do what?"

"Make it last so long?"

She gave a throaty laugh, her fingers playing with the hairs on his chest. "A woman's charms."

He suspected it was far more than a mere charm but he wasn't going to complain. The Priestess was incomparable, beyond his wildest dreams, but he hoped he gave as good as he got. Catching a sudden chill, he pulled a fur from the bed, spreading it across them. Burying his face in her raven-black hair, he drank in her scent, an alluring mix of sandalwood and violets and something else, something mysterious, something that teased his mind. "It was your scent that woke me."

"Hmmm." She gave a sleepy murmur.

Warm beneath the fur, he held her close. He must have dozed, awakened by a flash of sunlight on his face.

Pip entered the pavilion, a silver tray held in his hands. "I've brought your..." The boy stumbled to a halt, his gaze feasting on the Priestess.

"Yes, put it there." Naked, Steffan emerged from the fur. Shivering against the morning chill, he reached for a discarded tunic "And stoke the brazier. It's cold in here." He pulled on a soft white cambric shirt more suited to a royal court than a war camp.

Pip set the tray on a low table, the tantalizing smell of fried bacon filling the pavilion, and then he leaped to add more coals to the brazier, his wide-eyed gaze returning to the Priestess.

She lay curled on the floor, one corner of the fur turned back, revealing a creamy shoulder and the full swell of a magnificent breast. Even asleep, the woman was a temptress, but then Steffan noticed the bright gleam of eyes beneath dark lashes. She stretched, as if just waking, and the fur slipped further down.

Pip swore, spilling unlit coals across the carpet. *"Damn!"* He leaped to recapture the coals.

Steffan chuckled, appreciating the lad's discomfort. "Fix the brazier and then go tell the general that we'll be camping here for the day."

"Here for the day?"

The lad was clearly addled. "Yes, light the brazier and then tell the general we won't be marching till tomorrow." Steffan reached for a mug of mulled wine. "I'm giving the army a day of rest, the priests a day of prayer, and the general a day to sharpen his swords. Just tell them I'm not to be disturbed." He settled on the floor, next to the Priestess, and gave the lad a dismissive look. "That will be all."

"Yes, m'lord." Pip straightened his tunic, and backed toward the entrance, his face flaming as red as his hair. Casting one last mooncalf-stare at the Priestess, he bowed his way out of the pavilion.

The Priestess chuckled, a warm throaty sound. "Your squire?"

"Squires are for knights." He leaned forward, tugging on the fur till both breasts were revealed, lush and full and perked against the morning chill. "Pip's a street urchin, part thief, part spy, part servant. He's useful enough, but you, my dear, enjoyed the tease."

"And you enjoyed showing me off."

He could not deny it.

She sat up, letting the fur puddle around her waist, and reached for his mug of mulled wine. Taking slow sips, she stared at him with dark, mysterious eyes. The woman was pure allure. Everything about her was seductive, but a part of him suspected she was a trap, a very delectable trap. Tearing his gaze away, he reached for the silver tray, and set it between them like a barrier. The smell of fresh-fried bacon hid her scent, rousing a hunger of a different sort. Wrapping a generous serving of bacon and fried eggs in a flatbread, he began to eat. "You came here unannounced, slinking into my pavilion in the dead of night. What if you'd found me in bed with another woman?"

Unruffled, she reached for the table knife, skewering a fried potato. "Then I'd have sent her away."

"Just like that?"

She gave him a sloe-eyed smile. "Just like that," and then she consumed the fried potato spear, enveloping it in one long mouthful.

He watched, mesmerized, knowing just how deep she could swallow.

Like a taunt, she held his gaze as she finished the potato and then she took a long drink of mulled wine, a single drop lingering on her lips. Her tongue flicked out, licking the drop. Red wine enhanced the color of her lips, so deep and lush and full. He tore his gaze away, realizing it was hard to think around her.

The brazier snapped and crackled, releasing a breath of heat.

"So why have you come?"

"We had an agreement, remember?"

Images of that steamy night in Coronth filled his mind. "You stayed but one night. I almost thought it a dream."

She gave him a languid smile, her hand brushing his thigh. "Oh, I'm so much more than a dream." But then she pulled away, lying back amongst the furs, her face changing from temptress to conspirator. "The Mordant reaches for power in the north. And once he secures that power, he will come south."

"How do you know this?"

"I have my ways." She skewered another potato, but this time she took small dainty bites. "We have but a single season to secure our claim to the south and prove our worth to the Dark Lord."

A chill settled across his shoulders. "Surely the Mordant will not interfere with our conquests?"

"Never underestimate the Mordant. As the eldest among us, he is the most favored by the Dark Lord, and the most ruthless, and his gaze has ever been fixed on the south."

"The north is a long march away."

She gave him a sharp look. "Not for the Mordant."

"What do you counsel?" He stared at her; shocked to realize that he truly wanted to hear her thoughts, though he seldom sought the advice of women.

"A swift victory in Lanverness." She seemed not to notice his scrutiny; her dark eyes alight with cunning. "Claim the strongest castles, put a crown on your head and rule with an iron fist. Solidify your power and hope to hold your winnings when the Mordant comes south. If you are strong enough, he may accept you as a vassal king."

Anger reared within him. "I do not do this for a vassal's crown."

"No, you do this for more lifetimes," her gaze skewered him, "for the favor of the Dark Lord."

Her rebuke cut deep. "As do you."

She nodded. "As do I. It's what makes us perfect allies. We have an understanding between us," leaning forward, she brushed his thigh, her voice low and sultry, "among other things."

Heat rose within him, but before he could act, the cunning look returned to her gaze, sharp as any sword. "How goes the war?"

"Slowly." Avoiding her stare, he parried her question with one of his own. "As I recall, you promised allies against Lanverness, yet I've seen no sign of any help. Have you brought an army with you?"

"No, something better."

"Something better?"

Shrugging off the fur coverlet, she stood naked in morning light. Subtle shadows accentuated her curves, beauty enough to take his breath away. He lay back on the carpet, enjoying the show. Lithe and graceful, she crossed the pavilion, wearing her nakedness like a crown.

"You're magnificent." The words poured out of him.

She gave him a sloe-eyed glance, "More than you know." She reached for a leather sack in the corner. Opening the sack, she withdrew a long length of sky-blue silk. Staring at him, she drew the silk across her body, under and around her breasts, a slow sensual tease.

Aroused, he leaned toward her. "You've got my attention, lover, but how is this better than an army?"

She flicked the silk and it unfurled, revealing the signal in the center, a black scorpion on a field of pale blue. "A battle banner?"

"The key to ten thousand traitors."

"How?"

"The Spider Queen has purchased the full might of Radagar, ten thousand mercenaries to swell the ranks of her army."

"*Ten thousand?*" It narrowed the odds, shrinking his advantage. "And how does this help?"

"There's been a change of kings in Radagar."

His eyes widened. "You've been busy."

"Just so." She gave him a satisfied smile.

"And this?" He plucked at the pale blue silk.

"The private banner of House Razzur. Raise it during the height of battle and the mercenaries will turn against the Rose."

The woman was full of surprises. "And how did you arrange this?"

"I made the new king a better offer."

"What?"

"A throne."

"You're dangerous," but somehow her danger only deepened her allure. He reached toward her but she moved away, settling on the far side of the silver tray, nestled among the furs.

She nibbled the last piece of bacon. "Tell me about the war."

How easily she dampened his ardor, but he wanted this woman, in his bed and in his schemes for power, so he bridled his anger. Sitting cross-legged, he considered her question. "You came at night, so you've seen our campfires. Our numbers are invincible. We smash through Lanverness like a battering ram, crushing every opposition, but the Rose Army will not engage. They fight like cowards, harrying our rear, nipping at our heels and attacking our scouting parties. Like flies they annoy but I cannot land a killing blow."

"Smart flies."

He gave her a venomous look.

"What else?"

He gaze narrowed; the woman was well informed. "The damnable Spider Queen has emptied the countryside of food. Instead of finding barns and granaries laden with the fall harvest, they stand empty, and the livestock moved. My army eats like a plague of locusts and the rations grow thin." He dropped his voice to a low growl. "A hungry army is a dangerous beast."

"Then feed them."

His anger flashed to irony. "My lady is oh so glib."

Annoyed, she threw him a daggered glance. "Don't be churlish. If your army hungers then turn it toward the nearest city."

He barely kept his anger in check; women were so ignorant of war. "The nearest city is fortified with thick walls and protected by a stout castle. I need a victory in battle, not a long drawn out siege."

Her gaze narrowed to dark pinpricks. "Your army hungers. The fall harvest has been moved, undoubtedly to a secure place. The nearest city is fortified, and most likely stocked with food. Yet you cannot afford a siege?"

"My army would starve faster than the defenders." He reached for the mug, refilling it with the last of the mulled wine. "A siege is not the solution, but at least you see the problem." The wine was cold, the spiced dregs floating on top, but he drank it anyway.

A slow smile dawned on her face. "If you cannot gain something by direct means...then be devious."

He sputtered, almost choking on the wine. "Deceive a city into opening its gates?"

"Why not?"

Something in her face told him she was serious. "What do you suggest? Seduce them into submission? Or offer them a throne?"

"Perhaps a bit of both."

"You have a plan." It was a statement not a question.

"The beginnings of one, but I need some time alone."

"Alone?"

She gave him a knowing glance. "Each dedicate gains certain gifts from the Dark Lord. Some of mine require privacy."

So he was not the only one with special gifts. He wondered what powers she held.

"Do not ask."

He gave her a sheepish grin. "And what am I to do in the meantime?"

"I've brought a prisoner with me, but you should think of him as a royal guest."

"Royal?"

"Yes, Prince Danly, second son of the queen of Lanverness."

The woman was a wonder, full of endless surprises. "So you've captured the spare heir?"

She raised an eyebrow in reply.

"He should bring a hefty ransom."

"Not from the Spider Queen, but he may have other uses."

More twists and turns; the woman's mind was like a labyrinth. "I met him once in Pellanor, a randy young man with a penchant for gambling. As I recall, he had terrible luck at dice. But how did you come to capture the spare heir?"

"I've had my eye on him for some time. A young royal with so many vices offers great opportunities."

"Especially for a woman of your talents."

She ignored his barb. "I need him to be well treated. With a pavilion, and fine clothes, and women, especially women. Chose the best of the camp followers, see that they're cleaned up and offer them to the prince. The nights are cold and he'll need someone to warm his bed." She flashed him a devilish grin. "Someone to show him just how much he's lost."

"Another one of your schemes?"

"Of course."

"Does this mean you'll be staying more than one night?"

Her gaze darkened, her voice breathy. "More nights...and more days." She leaned toward him, her hand tracing a path up his inner thigh. "No need to waste a single moment."

The woman was insatiable. But Steffan was happy to oblige.

26

Liandra

Her ladies-in-waiting fluttered about, putting the final touches on her appearance. Liandra sat statue-still, studying the mirror, reading the messages embedded in royal finery. She'd chosen a velvet gown of emerald green trimmed with ermine, a regal reminder for her loyal lords, a plunging neckline providing an added distraction. For jewels, she chose a diamond tiara and the pear-shaped emerald necklace glittering at her throat. Both were statements of wealth created since her ascension to the crown. A pity the message would most like be lost on her loyal lords, yet a queen needed her armor, and Liandra never hesitated to use all her tools.

"We are pleased. You may go."

Her women curtsied and began to withdraw.

"Not you, Lady Sarah." The petite auburn-haired woman avoided her stare, busying herself with the vials of perfume. The queen waited till the chamber was empty. "Tell us."

Brown eyes glinted her way, yet the lady remained silent.

The queen softened her voice. "Tell us what you've heard. You've been avoiding us all morning."

Lady Sarah wilted, sinking to a puddle of silk beside the queen. "Majesty, the rumors have started." Her voice dropped to a whisper. "The servants begin to wonder if you are with child."

Liandra's breath caught. "So soon." The queen covered the swell of her belly, a protective gesture. "This one is smaller than my sons, as if she knows to hide. We'd hoped for more time."

"I've tried to quash the rumors, yet they persist."

"Servants are often shrewder than lords, but we may still have time. Dissuade the rumors but do not lie, we'll not have your good named sullied."

"But once it is known?"

The queen chuckled. "Then my loyal lords will need to gain the courage to ask us, for we shall say nothing." She smoothed the velvet of her gown. "Until the question is asked and answered, it is only a rumor. The cowardice of our lords will buy us more time."

"Yes, majesty," her voice was troubled, "But when they ask, they will press you to name the father."

"The father only matters if the child is a son. A daughter will be discounted, overlooked, but she shall be mine, a daughter destined to learn the way of golds." Liandra cradled the swell of the child, an unexpected boon.

Lady Sarah gave her a sheepish look, removing a beribboned square of folded parchment from her bodice. "He still sends letters, and begs an audience. Will you not meet with him? Tell him of the child?"

Liandra hardened her heart, staring at the folded parchment as if it held a viper. "Put it on the mantle with the others."

"But he suffers, I see it in his face. I hear it in his voice. He pines for you."

She closed her eyes against the sudden assault of memories, his voice, his touch, his companionship. His absence left an aching chasm in her soul. *Oh Robert, how could you betray me?* It hurt too much too bear. She built a barrier against the memories, walls of duty surrounding her heart. She imagined a perfect fortress, without doors or windows or even a key. Snapping back to her solar, she made her voice as hard as steel. "We are the queen. He pines for our power."

Lady Sarah looked as if she would argue, but then she capitulated, bowing her head. "Yes, majesty."

"We thank you for your honesty." She raised the lady's face. "Never fear to tell us the truth."

"Yes, majesty."

"Now come," she rose to her feet. "We have a council to attend, and you have secrets to keep and rumors to harvest. A woman's work is never done."

Lady Sarah flashed a small smile. "Yes, majesty."

"That's better. We'll have no dour women in our entourage."

"As you say, majesty."

Liandra adjusted the folds of her gown, using thick pleats to hide the growing bulge. "Wish us luck."

"Luck, majesty."

The queen swept from the chamber, into a hallway crowded with courtiers. Ambushed by her sudden appearance, the gaggle bowed low as she passed, but her loyal courtiers were ever quick to attack. Assembling into a flock of brightly plumed lords, they trailed in her wake, chirping petitions and requests laced with flattery. She let them talk, plucking insights from their chatter. Men were easily judged by their wants. Down the staircase and into the grand hallway, she led them a merry chase till a pair of guards snapped to attention before the council doors.

Confronted by guards, the courtiers fell away. The queen passed through the double doors, entering the relative calm of the council chambers.

Ten loyal lords surged to their feet, and then bowed, some with honesty, others with cunning. She knew them all by name and by weakness. Greeting them with a nod and a smile, she swept to the head of the table. She'd barely gained her seat when the assault began.

"Majesty, word of the war is not good. Our northern provinces burn and the enemy advances unchecked."

Trust the weasel to start the attack. "And what does a treasurer know of war?"

Lord Lenox turned purple, his voice sputtering in outrageous. "Majesty, I've lost more than anyone here! All my estates are in the north, set to the torch by the advancing army. This war is ruining me!" His voice turned frantic. "You must do something!"

"We wage war." She gave him a frosty stare. "What else would you have us do?"

His voice turned desperate. "But we can't give up the north, not without a fight."

"We give up *nothing*." She gave him a disdainful glare. "Did you think only peasants would suffer? War is a costly business. At least you still have your lordship and your life."

"For now." Lord Mills dared to enter the fray. "Prince Stewart fights but he does nothing to stop the advance."

"He is outnumbered." Anger flashed in her eyes. She defended her son and her strategy. "He empties the north of food, making hunger the ally of Lanverness."

"But it is not working."

"He needs time." She glared at her loyal lords. "Did the prince not say in this very chamber that the strategy required a lot of map?"

Lord Lenox rung his hands. "The strategy is not working. We're running out of map!"

Lord Mills flashed a sinister smile. "Then sue for peace."

She scoffed at the notion. "Sue for peace with a monster? We've seen how religious fanatics wage war! They don't even keep what they conquer! They *burn* it!"

"Then bribe them with gold. The Urian gift alone would make a tempting ransom, enough to win a kingdom."

So predictable, she knew the Urian bounty would make them bold. How easily they spent her treasury. "You'd have us pay murderers?"

"Heed the advice of your council." Lord Mills was nothing if not persistent, his voice as smooth as snake oil. "Offer them a payment of gold and perhaps they'll leave."

"Like dangling meat before a lion, it will only make them hungry for more."

Lord Lenox returned to the fray. "But majesty, we can at least try. Send heralds with offers to negotiate. At the very least, it will buy us more time."

"Only if we trust them to stop fighting while we talk." She glared at her the pinch-faced treasurer. "Do you trust the priests of the Flame? Do any of you trust them to keep their word?"

They wilted under her stare.

"Nevertheless, the danger is real." Major Ranoth hefted a rolled map, asking for the queen's permission. Liandra nodded and he spread the map across the table, a map she'd seen before in the privacy of her solar, yet she studied it as if for the first time. Arrows of red showed the advance of the enemy army, a deadly spear aimed at the heart of her kingdom.

"According to the latest dispatches, the enemy is here, at the village of Darmooth." The major used a dagger as a pointer, indicating the red stain blotting the map. "Prince Stewart harasses the enemy's flanks and destroys his scouting parties, but he has yet to blunt the enemy's advance. So far, the enemy steers clear of our major strongholds at Kardiff and Lingard. Instead he drives through our farmland, heading straight for our capital city." The dagger drew a line from the red blotch straight south to Pellanor. "The capital city sprawls beyond its walls. If the enemy reaches Pellanor, the city will be lost."

A grim hush circled the table.

"What do you suggest?"

"Move the capital, majesty."

"Where?"

"Lingard might still be possible. The walls are formidable and Baron Ragnold keeps his own garrison of knights. But the safer bet is farther south," his dagger traced a line from Pellanor to the southwest corner of her kingdom, "to Graymaris, a strong fortress built to check the threat from Radagar."

Liandra eased back in her chair, a frown on her face, waiting to be persuaded. She wanted the idea to be owned by her loyal lords. The silence lengthened.

Lord Lenox was the first to break, using a white handkerchief to mop sweat from his brow. "It makes sense, majesty. Move the treasury and the court out of harms way."

She wondered how she'd ever chosen such a weasel for her court, but then she'd assumed a weasel might be shrewd at multiplying golds, a failure on both counts.

Lord Quince, a blunt-faced man with his better years behind him, seconded the motion. "Majesty, the major's recommendation makes sense, move the court to Graymaris. At least this way, you will be safe."

Her gaze roamed the table, noting the nods of agreement. "And what signal shall we send to our people if the queen flees her capital city?"

Lord Lenox blustered. "Not flight, majesty, a strategic withdrawal, suggested by the military."

Lord Hutchins nodded. "We dare not let the queen be captured, else the war is lost."

"Graymaris makes the most sense."

"Move the capital beyond enemy's reach."

Lord Cadwell added his slippery voice. "You must do what is best for queen and council. Only by preserving the government do you preserve the kingdom."

Liandra smothered a sneer, such a cowardly crew. How badly they sought to save their own skins. None seemed to notice that her staunchest supporters, the Lord Sheriff and Sir Durnheart remained oddly silent. The queen turned her gaze toward Lord Mills. "And you, Lord Mills, what is your advice to us?"

Her handsome lord spread his hands in resignation. "If you will not sue for peace then you must flee the capital."

"Your very choice of words condemns us."

"No slight intended, majesty, but you leave us no other choice. Since you cannot win by dint of arms, you must either negotiate or withdrawal."

She bowed her head as if capitulating. The silence stretched, she could almost hear them sweat. "You have convinced us."

An audible sigh rippled around the chamber.

"We will give the enemy a choice, daring him to split his army."

Some of her councilors squinted as if sensing a trap.

"The whole of the treasury, and those of my councilors who wish to go, shall be moved to the safety of Graymaris. The queen shall stay in Pellanor, as a symbol to our people, proof that our army will prevail."

Astonishment shown from more than a few faces, but their silence said it all. No one protested her choice. Liandra hid her contempt. Her puffed-up lords looked like toads offered a meal of juicy flies. Of course she'd handed them what they most wanted, a chance to save their lives while keeping the pride and the power of the treasury. She gave them a steely stare. "We shall issue orders to move the treasury within the fortnight. The sooner it is done, the better. Who among you will dare the trip to Graymaris?"

Lord Lenox could hardly contain his glee. "The treasurer needs to keep close to the treasury."

Liandra nodded. "Assuredly," one less weasel in her council, "And what choice do the rest of you make?"

The answer was predictable. The lords Lenox, Cadwell, Quince and Hutchins all chose to leave, rats fleeing a sinking ship. Only Lord Mills surprised her.

"I choose to stay, majesty."

Perhaps the man's ambition outweighed his common sense, or else he played a deeper game. "As you wish." Her gaze circled the table, meeting the stare of each lord. "The decision is made. The treasury will leave within the fortnight, be sure you are ready to travel."

Liandra rose, extending her ringed hand to her loyal lords. One at a time, they came forward to take their leave. She stared the hardest at the fleeing rats, their plans writ large across their faces. The cowards believed Pellanor was doomed, throwing the city like a sop to the Flames. And once the Flames consume their rightwise queen, her loyal lords would broker a peace from Graymaris, trading Urian gold for an end to a war. But Liandra knew one does not broker peace with monsters, and she had no intention of being consumed by Flames. Plans within plans, she'd long ago decided to let the cowards flee her capital, ridding her court of disloyal lords while setting a gilded trap. In the queen's court nothing was ever wasted, not even a pack of disloyal lords.

27

Fintan

Secrecy was second nature to a monk of the Kiralynn Order. Fintan waited till the dead of night, for the shroud of sleep to take the castle. Swirling a midnight blue cloak around his shoulders, he slipped through the gilded hallways, seeking the shadowy staircase of the western tower. Castle Tandroth lived up to its reputation, a warren of wealth and intrigue crisscrossed with confusing hallways, but after a week of exploration, he was beginning to learn its ways and its queen. He entered the staircase and began to climb. So many steps, his left knee began to ache, an old injury aggravated by cold. The tight spiral led to a stout oak door. Cold seeped through the door, a prelude to winter. He eased the door open and peered into the moonless night, relieved to find the crenellated battlements empty of guards. Clearly the queen trusted her city more than her loyal councilors.

Clouds scudded across the sky, masking the stars, but the inky darkness only made the city more impressive. Sprawling below, the city lapped at the very gates of the castle, ten thousand pinpricks of lights, candles, lanterns, and torches, enough to rival the very stars. In all his wanderings, he'd never found a city more worth saving, a beacon of light against the gathering dark.

A sound disturbed his musings, a faint scuff against stone.

He stilled, listening, and then whirled, a hand on his dagger, but he found nothing, only darkness and the bone-cold night. Wary, he prowled the tower top, but the sound, real or imagined, was gone. Since coming to the castle he'd felt the sting of watching eyes, a vague sense of unease riding his shoulders, but his gaze never found the stalker. Perhaps it was merely this strange new openness. Wearing the Order's blue robes beyond the southern mountains created a sense of unease. Perhaps the Order's cloak of secrecy was not so easily put off. Keeping his hand on his dagger, he took a position on the north side of the tower, keeping watch on the sky. He did not have long to wait.

White wings emerged from the clouds, a great frost owl soaring toward the tower as silent as snowfall. Though he'd seen it a thousand times, the gift of flight never failed to inspire awe. Fintan watched spellbound as the great owl circled the tower. Alighting on the battlement, a faint nimbus surrounded the owl, stretching and blurring till a blue-robed monk stood in its place.

Fintan stepped from the battlement, embracing his friend. "Aeroth!"

The dark-haired monk returned the greeting. "It is good to see you."

Knowing the cost of magic, Fintan pressed a flask of mulled wine into Aeroth's hands. "For you." He studied his friend as he drank, noting deep shadows beneath his eyes and more gray feathering his hair. The price of duty took its toll. They moved out of the wind, sitting with their backs to the battlement, sharing the wine.

"How do you find the queen? As formidable as they say?"

"Impressive, the woman has an intellect as sharp as steel." Fintan grinned. "She'd make a daunting addition to the Order were she not already a queen." He sobered. "The Grand Master did well to send us. The queen is worth saving. I only hope we are not too late."

Aeroth nodded. "And the others?"

"After so many years it is hard to shed the cover of secrecy. Gilbert and Aster chose to remain hidden, taking rooms at the Golden Tankard. The others are with the wagons, still three weeks from the city."

"The wagons?" Aeroth's gaze narrowed, his words a hiss. "Then the Grand Master approved its use?"

"We face the worst of times. Evil rises in all its forms. We must do what we can."

"I know. I've seen it." Aeroth's voice sounded as if it came from the grave.

"Tell me."

"The Knights of the Octagon muster for war. The Grand Master sent me to warn the king, but a harlequin was already among them."

The news chilled Fintan to the bone. "Another prophecy proves true."

Aeroth nodded. "The harlequin wore the face of a prince, masquerading as the king's own son. Once revealed, the evil one threatened the life of another son. Both princes died, spitted on the marshal's sword, but I fear the harlequin will be reborn, rewarded for sowing fear and distrust among the knights." Aeroth grimaced. "It all happened so fast, I could not stop the killing. And then the king in his grief turned on the messenger. The owl saved me, though I've never had to change while falling from a tower." Aeroth shuddered, taking a deep pull from the flagon. "A cold night."

"A cold season."

"Prophecies rush to be born."

"And we few must do what we can to avert the Dark."

"So you're here to save the queen?"

Fintan nodded. "First the Flame must be defeated, darkness of another sort, hence the wagons."

"Fight fire with fire." Aeroth shook his head, "but such a terrible weapon. Rumors say it has grown more potent with age."

"I witnessed the test. It burns with a fearsome heat, but once used there will be no more, the recipe is lost to the ages."

"Some knowledge is better forgotten."

Fintan shrugged. "Who can say, but for now, we use what we have."

"Any message for the others?"

"Only that I've arrived and I've heard strange rumors about a delegation from Ur."

"Since when does Ur meddle with Erdhe?"

"Exactly. It reeks of another hand."

Aeroth finished the wine and then got to his feet. "I'll pass the word." They clasped arms. "Stay well."

"And you." Fintan stood by the battlement, watching as his friend shimmered and changed, transforming back into the frost owl. A few flaps and the great bird took flight, soaring out over the city. Fintan watched for a time and then made his way back to the doorway and down the stairs, his mind riddled with worries. Even the warmth of the castle could not dispel his chill. He prowled the empty hallways, returning to his chambers in the eastern wing of the castle.

Latching the door, he stoked the fire, adding pine logs to the blaze. Heat beat against him, but a deeper chill persisted. Standing with his back to the fire, he considered the news from the north. Another prophesy fulfilled. Darkness was moving too quickly, spreading tentacles across the lands of Erdhe. He wondered if another harlequin hid within the queen's court. He scowled, feeling naked without a Dahlmar crystal, but at least he had magic of his own. His hand touched the focus nestled in his pocket, a small coin carved of malachite, inscribed with ancient runes. He fingered the coin, gaining a measure of calm.

*Tap, tap, tap...*came from the windowpane.

Puzzled, Fintan turned to stare. His chamber was on the fifth floor, nothing beyond the windowpanes but darkness.

Tap, tap, tap.

Perhaps Aeroth returned. He crossed to the window and stared through the mullioned panes, nothing but night on the other side. Releasing the latch, he opened the windows, but the sill was empty. Puzzled, he leaned outward, staring down at the castle wall, a deadly drop to the courtyard below.

Something stung the back of his neck. He slapped at the stinger, shocked to find a needle embedded in his flesh. He pulled it free, blood and a bitter smell upon the slender pin. Confused, he staggered back from the window.

Something dropped onto the windowsill. It looked like a four-legged spider dressed in skin-tight black, but it had a face, a man's face in a lad's stunted body.

Fintan's legs gave out. Weak as a babe, he collapsed to the floor, a cold creeping sensation claiming his body. He tried to scream, but the spider-man pounced, pressing his hand to his mouth. "No need to scream, your death is already sealed."

Fintan struggled to move, to reach for the focus in his pocket, but a strange languidness froze his limbs.

The spider-man grinned. "Sting of the Assassin."

Panic seized him. He'd heard rumors of the poison, but he'd always thought it a sinister myth. Fintan fought to move, sweat erupting from his skin. He didn't want to die, not like this, but his wishes made no difference.

"*A blue robed monk,*" the assassin hissed, making the words a curse.

He'd always known openness would have a price, but he'd never expected to pay for it with his life.

"Your time is done." The assassin removed his hand, grinning into Fintan's face. "You cannot move, you cannot breathe, yet you will feel everything." Hands searched his robes, turning out his pockets, feeling for jewelry at his neck and wrists. "They told me you reek of magic. Is this it?" The assassin grinned, holding the malachite coin aloft like a prize. "Yes, your eyes tell me it's true."

Fintan tried to turn away, but he was helpless as a worm, trapped within his own body. A scream built inside of him, but nothing came out.

"Nothing can defeat my master. Not your Order, not the Lords of Light." The assassin drew a long sleek dagger. "You will feel your death. You will feel every cut. Even your severed head will serve my master, bringing fear to the queen." The assassin leaned close, a twisted grin on his face. "Fear is the handmaiden of Darkness. I will enjoy taking your life."

Steel sliced across Fintan's throat. Blood fountained upwards. The first cut brought a burning pain. A scream roared inside Fintan, caught on a tidal wave of terror. Trapped in his body, he felt every ragged cut, every jagged saw of the blade. He could not breathe, he could not scream. Pain claimed him...and then there was nothing but darkness.

28

Stewart

Rain pelted his face with cold indifference, as if the gods shunned him. Stewart hunched against the downpour, struggling to keep pace. Trussed like a goat led to market, he walked in a line of twenty-six prisoners, all of them mud-stained and miserable. Three days of captivity and still he could not believe it. One swing of an enemy halberd and his war changed forever. Stripped of weapons, armor, and surcoat, they left him nothing but a quilted jerkin and boots. At least he kept his boots. More than half the prisoners plodded barefoot through the mud. Many bore wounds, blood oozing from makeshift bandages. Stewart saw their wounds as a mark of valor, an excuse for capture, while he was largely unscathed. Shame and anger dogged his steps in equal measure.

His captors had never even asked his name. Eager to pilfer his belongings, one officer stole his gold signet ring while two others fought over his blue steel sword. A Black Flame claimed his sword as a spoil of war, wrapping the tell-tale hilt with leather. Rage thundered through Stewart, quaking at the loss of the sword. At least his seashell broach was still within reach, tucked in the sergeant's belt pouch. The broach marked the man for death, if only Stewart could get his hands free.

The rope tugged forward, a relentless pull. He shuffled behind the others, his boots caked with mud, weariness warring with anger. Ropes burned his wrists, bound so tight his hands felt the sting of a thousand nettles. He strained against the bonds to no avail. For the thousandth time he scanned the woods, hoping to glimpse emerald among the bare branches, but rescue never came. The answer lay beneath his feet. Mud churned to a confusion of prints. In such a muddle even the best scouts could not sort enemy boots from the footsteps of a captive prince. Frustration beat against him, if only he'd blocked the halberd's blow.

The man in front slipped and fell.

Stewart hissed, "Get up, Gedry!" He willed the wounded scout to stand, knowing laggards died under the lash.

A whip cracked, "Keep moving, scum." A bearded guard leaned from his mount, wielding a cat-tailed whip. Bloody welts scored the scout's back, driving him to the ground.

"Keep moving!"

Gedry floundered in the mud, taking another lash.

"Filthy infidels," the guard made the words a snarl, "march or die!" He lifted the whip, poised for another strike.

Stewart stepped forward, glaring up at the guard. "Untie my hands and I'll carry him."

The guard stayed the whip, an ugly sneer on his face. "A hero? So you'll take the lash for him as well?"

Stewart stood his ground, meeting the guard's stare.

"You insolent dog." The whip snaked toward Stewart, a snarling whistle heralding pain. Stewart braced for the blow, his head bent, struggling not to flinch. Agony lashed along his left arm and across his back, burning like a red-hot poker. Stewart staggered, fighting not to scream.

The guard laughed, flicking the whip for another strike. "Cat-o-nine stings like hell! Not such a hero now."

Gedry struggled to his feet, his shirt stained with blood. "I'm standing! I'm standing!"

The guard sneered. "So you can both feel my lash." He coiled the whip for another strike.

Hoof beats galloped in the mud. The sergeant drew rein. "What's holding up the line?"

The guard changed his tone. "Two prisoners too lazy to walk."

Stewart kept his head bent, hiding the rage smoldering in his eyes.

The sergeant's horse churned the mud, his voice an angry command. "Keep them moving, Dalbris, and keep them *alive*. The priests want this lot for the Flame God. Disappoint the red robes and they'll take you instead. Now get them moving." The sergeant spurred his horse, cantering toward the front.

The guard's voice sank to a snarl. "I'm watching you two." The whip cracked but it did not strike. "Now march!"

The line staggered forward, mud sucking at each step. Stewart followed the tug, keeping pace with the others, but his mind mulled over the sergeant's words. *Wanted for the Flame God!* Panic flashed through him, he'd heard too many tales of Coronth not to fear the fire. Perhaps if he told them he was a prince, but a sixth sense warned him to keep quiet. Yet time was running out. He needed to escape, but not without the others. Thirty guards against twenty-six prisoners, the numbers were nearly even, but sometimes numbers lied. Everything was against them. Mounted and armored the guards were well fed, while every day's march sapped the prisoners' strength. Mud and muck took a heavy toll on a man's body, turning hardened soldiers into shambling wrecks, yet he had to find a way. Stewart flexed his shoulders, testing his bonds, but the rope held tight.

Whips cracked as the guards prodded the prisoners like cattle to market. Stewart focused on putting one foot in front of another, struggling not to trip. Footsore and weary, the day seemed to stretch forever, an endless slog through the mud.

At sunset they stopped, herded off the side of the road to a copse of naked trees. Stewart barely noticed his surroundings. When the line stopped, he sank to the ground, indifferent to the mud. A guard circled among them, checking their bonds.

"Food, give me food." A few men begged to be fed, but all they got for their courage was a cuff to the head.

The weather worsened with the rain falling in sheets.

Drenched and shivering with cold, Stewart tilted his head to catch the rain. Gedry sat beside him, shoulder to shoulder, sharing an arm's length of warmth. The scout whispered. "My lord, you should tell them."

"Shhhhh." Stewart hissed a warning.

"Tell them the truth and they'll have to treat you better."

Stewart shook his head, grim with doubt. By tradition, noble prisoners were ransomed for gold, but he did not trust the soldiers of the Flame. "I fear they'll use me against the queen. I'll not be a dagger held to the queen's throat."

"Yes, m'lord."

"And don't call me that, I'm merely a captain."

Gedry gave him a hard look. "Then don't take a lash for me...*sir*. It ain't right."

The scout was a man of pride. Men of pride deserved to be saved. The prince nodded. "You're a good man, Gedry. Gods willing, we'll see our way out of this."

Someone hissed a warning. "*Guards,*" and the two men fell silent.

Two guards approached carrying a steaming kettle and a bulging water skin. The men sat up, like dogs begging to be fed. Each prisoner received a single bowl of gruel and a cup of murky water. Stewart struggled not to lunge at his allotment. Carefully holding the bowl with both hands, he licked the spill from the side, desperate for every mouthful. Watery and full of grit, the porridge was at least warm and slightly salty. A piece of gristle floated on top, a rare prize. Stewart gnawed on it, his stomach growling, knowing he wouldn't feed such slop to his hunting dogs. Ravenous, he licked the bowl clean and then drank the water, holding the mug to the rain for a second cup.

All too soon the guards collected the bowls and the prisoners settled down to sleep. Huddled together like pigs in the mud, they sought any scrap of shared warmth. Some fell deep asleep, exhausted by the long march, while others whimpered and coughed, trapped by misery. Stewart remained quiet, his mind seething for a way to escape. Exhaustion threatened, but he held it at bay, racking his mind for a plan. The guards were well fed and well armored while the prisoners barely survived, desperate to make it through the day. And then he realized he had his answer. Desperation was their only advantage, the frenzied madness of men fighting for their lives versus guards who merely followed orders. And the key to unleashing such desperation was the truth.

He pressed his mouth close to Gedry's ear. "Pass the word. They mean to give us to the flames. Spend tomorrow's march searching for a sharp rock or a dropped knife, anything to cut the ropes. We escape or we die."

Gedry nodded and leaned toward the next man in the huddle. Whispered words flashed through the men, raising a hum of tension. *Fight or die*, it was the only weapon they had. Stewart prayed to all the gods it would be enough.

29

Steffan

Screams echoed up from the valley below, the twisted howls of the damned. Steffan watched from the hilltop. Priests stripped the captive naked and then hung him from an iron spear, raising and lowering him over the flames. A sea of red surrounded the pyre, soldiers chanting prayers to the Flame God, writhing in a frenzy of worship.

"Do you always have entertainment in the morning?" The Priestess emerged from Steffan's pavilion, her dark hair tousled, her hourglass figure seductive in a robe of deepest purple.

His gaze traveled the length of her, lingering on the lush cleft between her breasts. "Only for you, my sweet." He extended a hand and she joined him, staring down at the valley. "Behold the power of religion."

"Even from here I can feel the raw force of it," she shivered, "almost bestial in its intensity." She studied the ritual, a thoughtful look on her face. "Who is the victim?"

"An enemy solder. I've ordered my Black Flames to set traps for the enemy ambushers, bringing the captives back for questioning. The first few are tortured and the rest are eager to spew their darkest secrets."

She arched a dark eyebrow. "Torture?"

"To learn where the harvest is hidden."

"And does the fire make them sing?"

"Always. The infidels don't know fire the way we do. The first victim is usually stoic...till the flames take him in their embrace. Having watched the first man roast to death, the second always weeps like a babe, begging for release."

"And do you spare them when they sing?"

"And waste all this power?" He gestured to the army below, writhing like a kicked anthill. "Religion is a fearsome beast but it needs feeding now and then."

"Little wonder the Dark Lord is pleased with you." Her dark gaze studied him like a hungry hawk. "And where is the harvest?"

Steffan retreated to the awning of his pavilion, to the large oak table strewn with maps. He found the one he wanted. "We're here, a month's march from the gates of Pellanor. But here to the east, is Lingard, the nearest enemy stronghold." His finger tapped the map. "We'll find the harvest behind Lingard's stout walls, enough to feast my men for the final march to Pellanor."

"Lingard." Her gaze turned inward, her beautiful features locked in thought.

Steffan watched her. Not for the first time, he wondered what dark powers she held.

"Lingard, I know this city." A slow smile spread across her face. "The baron is loyal to the queen, but the captain of the guard can be twisted. His name is Vengar, a big ruddy man with red hair and a thirst for gold. Show him a flash of gold and he'll serve the highest bidder."

"I like the way you think. And is there a lady baron?"

"A wife dead over ten years ago."

"Even better." He gave her an appraising look. "How do you know this?"

She answered with a seductive smile. "A woman has her ways."

Steffan nodded, gaining a clue to her powers. Either the priestess had the ability to soul-sense, or else controlled an extensive spy network. Either way the woman was formidable, both in and out of bed. He reached for her, feeling a sudden need.

She raised a hand, forestalling him. "Not yet."

"Why?" His voice was more of a growl than he wanted.

"First the prince."

"Ah, the prince." He'd done as she asked, giving the captured prince a pavilion of his own, and his pick of the camp women, and enough guards to make sure he did not escape. But otherwise, Steffan had left the prince alone, surrendering him to the tender mercies of the Priestess. "Won't he follow your bidding?"

"Yes, but this is your army." She gestured to the seething mass of red roiling around the bonfire. "The prince must respect your command, and adopt your religion." Her gaze turned inward as if she listened to another voice. "This religion of yours is important." Her voice deepened, carrying the ring of prophecy. "So primal it turns the souls of men to hungry beasts. Never neglect the religion of the Flame, for it is part of the Dark Lord's plans, part of his victory over Erdhe." Her eyes closed and her head leaned back, a cascade of long dark hair shimmering in the morning light. A sigh escaped her, as if she were locked in the throws of passion. "I feel his pleasure. The Dark Lord revels in the pain of human sacrifice, in the raw power of twisted beliefs magnified across a multitude."

Steffan watched her, enthralled.

Her hand flashed out, taking his hand, pressing it to the cleft of her breast, skin against skin. Passion jolted through him. He staggered back a step, gasping with need. "What are you?"

Her gaze smoldered. "The Priestess of the Oracle." Something dark lurked in her gaze, something wild and untamable and brimming with power. "See to the prince, and then come to me if you wish to worship." She turned, regal as a queen, and disappeared into his pavilion.

As if released from a spell, Steffan sagged against the oak table, remembering to breathe. The woman was dangerous. A feral smile flashed across his face, but the passion was worth the risk. He reached for a goblet, draining the wine in a single long draught. Cold and overly spiced, the mulled wine had lost its appeal, but he refilled the goblet anyway, draining it dry a second time.

"My lord, let me heat that for you." Pip appeared, rushing to set the metal ewer over the flames.

"Where have you been?" The lad looked disheveled, his tunic rumpled, his red hair as straggled as a bird's nest.

"Spying on the prince, just as you ordered."

"And?"

"He's a surly one. Nothing pleases him. Not the wine, not the food, and not the women, not even Melinda," an odd look crossed his face, "and she's the best of them. Breasts like ripe melons and hair the color of wild strawberries." His words stumbled to a halt as if he realized he'd said too much. Flushing bright red, he busied himself with the mulled wine.

"And how would you know this?"

"You told me to spy."

"How?"

Pip stirred the wine as if it was of the greatest importance, but Steffan's relentless stare pulled the words from him. "A pinprick in the back of the pavilion, lord. I worried it till it was just big enough to look through."

"And will I find a pinprick in the back of *my* pavilion?"

"No!" Pip's eyes flared wide and his face turned pale. "No, lord, never that."

Steffan smothered a smile; pleased with the lad's reaction. A little fear was always healthy in a servant. "Good. Then you'll keep watch on the prince and let me know if any of the women ever please him."

Pip looked down, his voice dropping to a mumble. "Only her."

"What?"

Pip shuffled, his voice a low whisper. "Only *her,* lord." The lad darted a frightened glance toward the pavilion and back to Steffan. "But I never watch."

"Then how do you know?"

His face flamed red. "From the sounds, lord." The lad added more wine to the ewer, his hands shaking.

Steffan nodded, well aware of the Priestess's power. Another man might have been jealous, but somehow it only multiplied his hunger for her. Steffan knew she held the eunuch-prince in thrall, all part of a greater plan, but when the Priestess wanted pure pleasure, it was his bed she came to, over and over again. Just this morning, she'd howled like a cat when he took her. Her musky scent still lingered on his skin like a promise...or a goad.

"More wine, lord?"

"No. My cloak."

The lad scurried away, returning with his black wool cloak, the blood-red raven boldly embroidered on the left breast. He twirled the cloak across his shoulders. "Keep the wine warm. And I'll want a meal when I return."

"Yes, lord."

"And Pip," the lad looked up from the wine. "Serve me well and Melinda will share your bed."

The lad gaped like a puppy slavering over a bone. Speechless, he bowed toward Steffan, his face flaming red.

Steffan chuckled. It was past time the lad plumbed the pleasures of a woman, and besides, every vice was another means of control. Amused by Pip's eagerness, Steffan turned and sauntered down the hill. A lone pavilion sat nestled on the far hillside, far enough away so that sounds would not carry. A dozen Black Flames surrounded the pavilion, fierce fanatics wedded to their halberds, the best of his army. They snapped to attention as he approached.

A muffled scream came from inside the pavilion, followed by a loud slap. The curtains parted and a half-naked woman emerged. Sobbing, she nearly ran into Steffan. Her eyes widened at the sight of him, tears streaking her face. "Not my fault, lord." Bowing low, she scurried away, her torn dress doing little to hide her swaying breasts.

"I told you to leave!" Danly's voice was a low snarl within the pavilion.

Steffan parted the curtains and slipped inside. He stood in the shadows, comparing the past with the present. Gaunt from his ordeal, Danly lay sprawled on a divan, a goblet in his hand. His dark hair was unkempt and he reeked of sour sweat and spilled wine, looking more like a drunken wastrel than royalty. Old scars lined his left cheek, five deep furrows, the claw marks of an angry woman, a strange set of scars for a eunuch-prince.

"I said, be gone!" Danly's voice snapped with a nasty waspishness, but then he spied Steffan and his expression changed to sudden wariness. "Is it really you?" He stood, the empty goblet tumbling from his hand. "They told me you command here."

Steffan strode into the light. "Yes, we meet again, but much has changed since Pellanor." Steffan offered the prince a benevolent smile. "It is my army that protects you from the Spider Queen."

The prince gave him a twisted grin. "It seems fortune favors the raven. As I recall, you had the Dark Lord's own luck with dice."

Steffan chuckled. "If you only knew."

"What?"

Steffan covered his lapse with a smile. "My good fortune can also be yours."

Danly gave him a shrewd stare. "How?"

"We share a common enemy, both seeking to unseat a queen."

The prince stood in the center of the pavilion, unshaved, unwashed, stains of wine on his robe, looking anything but regal. "Tell me more."

Steffan gestured toward the divan. "You have my leave to sit." He hid a smile as Danly sank back down onto the pillows, how easily he established dominance. "You don't care for the camp women?"

The change in topic ambushed the prince, revealing a sudden flash of anger. "No, they don't suite me. They're all clumsy whores." He pulled his silk robe tight, hiding his mangled manhood.

Steffan hid his smile. "But a crown would suit you better."

"I was born to wear a crown and I almost had it."

"So I heard, but it slipped from your grasp."

Anger simmered on Danly's face, but he had the good sense not to answer.

"I've come to offer you another crown."

His gaze sharpened. "A king's crown?"

"No, a prince's, but it comes gilded with vengeance."

"Only a prince?"

Steffan shrugged, the lie coming easily to his tongue. "My army conquers in the name of the Pontifax. You will be a vassal prince, owing allegiance to Coronth." Steffan smiled. "Better a prince than a prisoner, and vengeance will come with your crown."

"What must I do?"

At least he was shrewd enough to know there was a price. "Start by offering your soul to the Flame God."

Danly's face turned sour. "I've heard the screams. I want nothing to do with your religion."

"The screams come from infidels, not the faithful. The faithful have nothing to fear. And since you are a guest in my war camp, I don't want you to fear."

Danly blanched at the threat but still he hesitated.

"It's for your own protection, you know." Steffan made his voice congenial. "A simple ceremony in front of the troops and you'll be dedicated to the Flame God." Steffan studied the princeling, annoyed by the sullen silence. "It's only a few words, a simple oath. Is your god so dear that you'd forfeit a crown?"

"I never expected *you* to speak of gods." Danly shook his head, a stubborn look on his face. "The gods are nothing but a pack of lies told by priests to keep the common people in thrall."

Steffan's gaze narrowed. "You'd best keep that thought to yourself. Heretics and infidels are burned alive in this camp."

Danly shuddered, making a warding sign. "Does it really matter that much?"

"Only if you value your life. You can't expect my holy warriors to protect an infidel-prince. My army marches under the banner of the Flame."

Danly reached for a pitcher, pouring a slosh of red wine into his goblet. "So I'll worship the Flame, what else do you want?"

How easily the princeling gave up his gods. "When Lanverness is conquered, the people will be given a choice, to worship the Flame or to die by it."

Danly shrugged. "I never cared a fig for the people. That malady belongs to my royal mother." His gaze sharpened. "I trust you intend to kill the bitch?"

"Oh yes."

"Good." Danly gulped a swig of wine. "What else?"

The prince was so compliant; perhaps he should geld all his captives. "What can you tell me about the city of Lingard?"

"Ah! Now we come to it." Danly sneered. "The chance to play the traitor prince!"

So the eunuch-prince was not as stupid as he looked.

Danly took a long swill of dark red wine. Wiping his mouth on his sleeve, he stared at Steffan. "What do you want to know?"

"Tell me about the city's defenses."

Danly shrugged. "If it will hurt the queen, why not?" He refilled his goblet and leaned back on the divan. "Lingard has formidable defenses. Unlike Pellanor, Lingard will be a tough nut to crack. The old baron believes in a strong defense, keeping the city from growing beyond its walls." Danly flashed a wicked grin. "You'll have to cross the moat and then scale thirty-foot walls. And then there's the catapults and trebuchets mounted atop the battlements. A steady rain of boulders can be a killing storm, even for an army as great as yours." The prince smirked. "If you want Lingard, your army will pay a steep price for it."

"When was the last time you visited the city?"

Danly shrugged. "Three years ago, or so. The queen makes a periodic progress around the kingdom, visiting each major city and stronghold to renew the bonds of fealty. As princes of the realm, my brother and I were both required to attend."

"So the baron knows you?"

Danly nodded. "Baron Rognald is a crusty old bastard, totally loyal to the queen." A snide smile played across his face. "I know you, Lord Raven, you'll try to trick your way into the city. But your bribes won't work this time. You'll have to play the soldier instead of the weasel." Danly drained the goblet and reached for more, snickering at his own words. "Loyalty defeats the weasel."

"Enough!" Steffan knocked the goblet from the prince's hand, spilling wine across the carpet. "I need a prince not a drunkard."

Danly glared but then he stood, his hand gripping the divan for support. His legs shook but a glint of fire still burned in his eyes. "You don't understand what it's like. What they did to me. What they took." His voice deepened to a hungry rasp. "How much I lost." He looked away. "I want the witch woman, the goddess with raven hair, no other woman will serve."

Steffan studied him like a bug beneath his boot. "Do you want the woman more than a crown?"

The prince wavered. "Both, I want both. I'm not a man without her."

So it was like that, an addiction of another sort. Steffan hid his contempt. "If you want the woman then you need to serve."

The prince nodded, a hungry glint in his eyes. "Anything."

More proof the Priestess's skills. The woman had sunk her claws deep. "Then listen closely." Steffan told him the plan, explaining the part he was to play.

Danly listened, sagging back onto the divan. His face turned pale. "It won't work. Rognald will have my head."

"It *will* work, if you believe."

"And where will you be, Lord Raven, while I risk my head? Safe with your army?"

"I'll be riding right beside you."

Danly stared up at Steffan, as if trying to read his soul. An odd grin spread across his face. "You're a tricky one, Lord Raven. Tricky enough to make it work. And you've the luck of the Dark Lord." He nodded. "I'll do it." His gaze narrowed. "For a crown *and* the woman."

Steffan nodded. "From now on, you'll be drinking only watered wine." He emptied the flagon onto the brazier, causing the flames to flare. "I need a prince not a drunkard. Play your part well, and a crown will be yours." Steffan turned and strode from the pavilion.

Cold air buffeted his face, cleansing him of the prince's stink. He climbed the hill to his own pavilion. A brazier glowed from inside, illuminating the red silk. The Priestess stood within, a tantalizing silhouette. Anticipation hastened his steps. He brushed the curtains aside and entered.

She stood waiting for him, her dark hair unbound, her lips moist and red. "Did he agree?" Her smoky voice ran like fingers down his spine.

"Of course."

She loosened the robe from her shoulders, letting the dark purple puddle to the carpet. Stepping naked from the silk, shadows and light played across her curves enhancing her allure. A vision of earthly delights, she opened her arms wide, his goddess of desire. "Come and worship. Come and celebrate the Dark Lord's triumph."

Passion throbbed through in him like a heartbeat. He crossed the pavilion and took her in his arms and nothing else mattered.

30

Liandra

*M*urder in our court, the words thundered through the queen's mind. There'd been murders before, but never of a new-found ally, and never in such a ghastly manner. The queen hoped to contain the murder before gossip spread like wildfire, setting panic alight in her court.

Clad in a simple gown of smoky gray velvet, Liandra made her way through the back halls of Castle Tandroth. Accompanied by Sir Durnheart, Master Raddock, and a pair of shadowmen, she insisted on viewing the scene for herself. Sometimes a queen needed to see things without the filter of advisors. The monk was important and his murder a bitter blow. An enemy hid within her court, a murderer masked in friendship, and the queen meant to learn his name.

Candlelight flickered on gilded hallways, portraits of her ancestors keeping watch over the castle. Master Raddock led the way. "This way, majesty."

A pair of shadowmen lurked in the hallway. They made their presence known and then disappeared back into alcoves. Master Raddock unlocked the door, ushering the queen inside.

Liandra entered the chamber and came to a sudden stop. *He* was there. Shock struck her like a slap to the face. Robed in black, he stood with his back to the door, his hair longer and grayer than she remembered, his shoulders tense with thought, every line of his body bent with purpose, *Robert!*

He turned as if he'd heard her very thoughts. His eyes widened, running the length of her, drinking her in, but then he gasped, a flash of emotions racing across his face. His keen eyes saw what other lords did not. Liandra knew the child was revealed, and he knew it was his. *He knew!*

The Master Archivist knelt, his gaze burning into hers. *"My queen!"*

Such fervor, she almost faltered, almost reached for him, but then the others crowded into the chamber, consuming all the air. Choked by emotion, she turned away. "Leave us."

"But majesty..."

She glared at Master Raddock and he had the good sense to back away. The others left without argument. The door clicked closed and she found she could breathe again, but she wasn't ready to face him. She ran a finger along the mantle, idly noting the dust. "I should have known you'd be here."

"Any threat to my queen."

She took a deep breath and turned. "What have you learned?"

He remained on one knee. His gaze flicked to her waist, lingering long enough to ask the question. Her hands replied, protectively covering the swell, but she said nothing, unready to speak of the child. He bowed his head, as if assenting to her unspoken rules, and then he stood, all emotion wiped from his face. "The murder happened last night." The tone of his voice was pure business, assailing her heart with a potent mixture of relief and sadness. "The body was found here, sprawled by the window. The severed head was over there." He pointed to a chest placed awkwardly before the door. "It was displayed on the chest, a horror confronting anyone who opened the door."

Her gaze lingered on the chest, wiped clean of blood. The gruesome bits were gone, removed by her shadowmen for discrete burial, yet the queen could imagine the severed head, the monk's eyes vacant with death. "The positioning of the head tells us the murderer meant to instill terror."

"Exactly. And it was crudely done, hacked from the neck."

The queen shivered at the gross brutality. "Such an awful death."

"Yet some of the details do not ring true."

"Tell us."

"There was no sign of a struggle."

Her gaze circled the room, noting the clothes dumped from a chest, the rumpled bed, and the toppled chair.

He studied her, interpreting the passage of her gaze. "The room was searched, yes, but the signs of struggle were missing from the body."

Her gaze snapped back to his.

"I examined the body before they took it away. There were no bruises, no broken fingernails, no skinned knuckles, no sign of a struggle from the monk."

"Then he was unconscious or dead before the head was taken."

"But the body bore no wounds, no clues to death other than the severed head."

"Poison?"

He nodded. "Possibly."

"Subtlety hidden beneath brutality, a dangerous combination."

"Precisely."

"Death and terror combined."

"Perhaps you've gained a new enemy?"

An ominous thought, yet she liked the way their minds fit together, solving the riddle. "There's something else?" She read it in the tension of his shoulders.

"Yes." He acknowledged her insight with a nod. "The door was not locked, but it was latched from inside."

"From *inside?*"

He nodded.

She crossed to the mullioned windows. "Were these latched?"

"Closed but not latched."

She opened the windows admitting a breath of cold morning air. Leaning out, she gazed below. Dawn lingered on the horizon, yet she spied the cobbled courtyard below, a death's drop away. She turned, craning for a view above. The windows on this side of the castle were unevenly spaced and the walls smooth-cut stone, no easy way to climb from one room to another. Puzzled, she closed the windows against the chill. "What did he do, fly?"

Their gazes met across the room.

"Rumors say the monks wield forgotten magic."

"And the enemy of the monks might wield the same."

He nodded, his face grim.

"And the monks' true enemy is Darkness." Liandra shivered. She could almost feel tentacles of evil reaching for her throne.

"At the very least an assassin of great skill lurks within your court."

An assassin of great skill, the words thundered through her mind.

"Majesty, you must take great care, for yourself...and the child."

And the child, the words echoed between them, something spoken that could no longer be hidden by gesture or subterfuge.

"Majesty, your secret is safe with me."

Her hands folded protectively across the swell of her belly. She wanted this child, wanted a daughter to learn her ways, but she would not have the babe used as a chain to bind her to any man. "We'll wear no man's yoke."

He waited, his face carved of stone.

Her voice held a dangerous edge, a monarch trapped by the nature of her sex. "Will you swear to relinquish all paternal rights to this child, so that it is *our* child, and *ours* alone? Never to be claimed? Never to be spoken of again?"

As far as she knew, he had no other issue from his loins. It was a lot to ask of a man...but she was a queen.

His voice dropped to a harsh rasp. "Madam, by all the gods, the child is yours, as is the throne."

He understood!

An edge of desperation crept into his voice. "But do not banish me from your service...do not keep me from your side."

The ice surrounding her heart cracked. *"Robert!"* She went to him.

He took her in his arms, a haven of strength and wanting. Lighting leaped between them. She knew he felt it too. He hugged her close and then he knelt, taking her ringed hand. "For the queen," he kissed the great emerald, but then he turned her hand, pressing an ardent kiss to her palm, "and for the woman," and then he leaned forward, placing a tender kiss on the telltale swell of her child, "and for the child that belongs to the queen."

A shiver ran through her. *"I've missed you so."*

He rose and took her in his arms. "You are always my queen. Always."

Such strong arms, providing protection without a claim of possession, she let herself lean against him, soaking up his strength. For a hundred heartbeats she reveled in his touch, but the crown was always there. Duty called and she stepped away. He did nothing to hinder her.

Liandra turned and walked to the fireplace, cold with ashes, cold as her royal bed. She ran her hand along the mantle, keeping her back to him, buying a breath of time. "The monk's death is a grievous blow." She turned to face him, the queen once more. "He came offering an alliance of knowledge, bringing warnings against the Mordant. This assassin strikes at the worst possible time, depriving us of a much needed ally."

"Perhaps not."

Her gaze snapped to his, reveling in his rapier-sharp mind.

He finished his thought. "The worst time would have been *before* the monk met with you."

She nodded. "Proving the assassin reacts instead of plotting, he plays catch-up. He is not as devious as he first appears."

Her shadowmaster nodded. "Just so," but his voice held a warning, "He is still very dangerous and very skilled."

Plots within plots, her mind traveled a different path. "It might be best if our alliance remains hidden."

His dark gaze snapped to hers. "One can see the advantages..." but she heard the catch in his voice.

"Lady Sarah will know the truth, of course, as will Master Raddock."

He nodded.

"Meanwhile this assassin must be found. We will know the hand behind the dagger."

He gave her a formal nod. "As you command."

She lingered, her gaze drinking him in. "We will find ways to meet."

Hope quickened in his gaze.

"But in public, we will continue to show our displeasure."

He flashed a conspirator's smile. "I will endeavor to weather the royal storm."

She could not help but smile, she'd missed him so. He kissed her hand, a wealth of promises in his touch. Liandra longed to linger, but duty called. Assuming a regal mask, she turned and opened the door. Her entourage snapped to attention, startled by her sudden appearance. She threw a scathing glance into the room, her voice crackling with anger. "Do not pester us with unproven theories. We are not pleased." Turning in a swirl of velvet, she swept down the hallway, her loyal lords struggling to keep pace.

Her mind thrummed with possibilities. A powerful ally was dead, murdered by an unknown assassin, but another ally was returned to her, a stalemate of sorts. But crowns were not preserved by stalemates. Plots within plots, Liandra needed to unmask the enemy, the assassin, and the mind behind him. Time choked tight like a noose around her throat. Too many enemies gathered around, she dare not make a single mistake.

31

Stewart

Someone kicked him awake. A guard growled, "No rest for the wicked, move your bones." Stewart groaned and found himself lying in the mud, huddled between Gedry and Timmons for warmth. Cold and aching, he stretched and sat up; a prisoner roped in a line of misery.

"Sam's dead."

"Got a deader here!" The guard moved down the line, kicking and prodding as he went. When he reached the dead man, he hacked the body with his halberd. Stewart shuddered at the gruesome sound of cleaved meat, but the dead man made no protest.

"Yep, he's a deader."

Stewart looked away; even the dead found no rest among the servants of the Flame.

A pair of guards approached, passing out bowls of gruel and cups of water. Stewart gulped his down, licking the bowl clean despite the sour taste. All too soon, the bowls were collected and the prisoners prodded to their feet. They made a quick toilet, another indignity. Guards jeered while the prisoners dropped their pants, but Stewart took advantage of the roped shuffle to whisper a command. "Look for something sharp, we escape or die in the flames."

Whips cracked and the guards herded them onto the road. Roped in a line, the prisoners began their shuffle north, another long day of slow agony. Fifth in line, Stewart scanned the road as he walked, his head swinging from left to right, desperate to find something sharp, something metal, anything to cut his bonds. At first he stayed alert, searching every footprint and wagon rut, but then he fell into a weary rhythm, his muscles aching, his eyes glazing over.

Pain flared across his back, the biting sting of a whip. Stewart flinched, stifling a scream.

"Faster, you heathen dogs!"

Stewart shambled faster while muttering a thousand curses. Hatred burned in him like a bonfire. Any religion that could make men so cruel did not deserve to exist. The queen was right; they fought a war of annihilation. If he ever got his blue sword back, he'd rid the land of the cursed Flame, but first he needed something sharp, something metal, anything to cut his bonds. He sent a prayer to Valin asking for aid, but the gods ignored him. The day dragged on, the sun creeping across a soggy sky and still he found nothing.

Hoof beats approached at a gallop. Hope surged in Stewart. He lifted his head, straining for a glimpse, but instead of emerald green, all the tabards were red.

"Off the road! Move, you sinners!" Whips cracked, and the prisoners scrambled to get off road. A few crouched, taking advantage of the unexpected rest. Stewart kept his head down, sneaking glances at the approaching riders. Red tabards emblazoned with black flames, the worst of the enemy. A cleric led the troop, a stern-faced man, his rank denoted by his strange mitered helm. The sight of the cleric sent a spike of fear through Stewart.

The cleric pulled his horse to a halt. "Who's in charge here?"

The sergeant answered. "I am, Sergeant Bernier of the Fifth."

"Any lords among your prisoners?"

The sergeant barked a rude laugh, but he quickly sobered under the cleric's harsh glare. "Just infidel dogs, my lord, soldiers taken in battle, nothing but muddy scum."

The cleric turned his gaze to the prisoners. "Any lords among you? Speak up, and you'll get better treatment, decent food and the hope of ransom."

Stewart slouched, hearing nothing but lies in the cleric's words. He kept his gaze on the ground, praying the others kept his secret.

"Straighten up!" Whips cracked and the guards moved among them. "Answer the lord bishop!"

Stewart wiped his face, smearing mud across his cheek.

The cleric urged his stallion to a walk, surveying the line of prisoners. He rode past Stewart, but then he turned back, the horse coming to a halt in front of the prince. Stewart felt the cleric's stare, like a brand searing into him, but he kept his head bowed and his eyes averted. "You there, with the coal-black hair, what's your name and rank?"

Stewart remained mute, wishing the cleric gone.

A sword poked him in the back. "Answer the lord bishop or I'll lop your ugly head off."

Keeping his gaze fixed on the mud, Stewart blurted his middle name, "Arthur", and quickly added, "a foot soldier."

"You seem like more."

Sweat erupted beneath his tunic. Stewart kept his gaze lowered, uncertain how to escape the bishop's scrutiny, but then Timmons shuffled forward. "I'm the one you want. I'm the bloody duke of Kardiff!"

Down the line, Dalt stepped forward. "I'm the earl of Graymaris!"

Owen yelled, "I'm the baron of Lingard."

Beside him, Gedry shouted, "And I'm the prince of roses! Send *me* to Pellanor and you'll have wagons full of bloody gold!"

Pride warred with gratitude; Stewart swore he'd find a way to win their freedom.

"Liars! Liars the lot of you." The bishop yanked on the reins, making the stallion stamp and snort. "Infidel dogs! You'll all burn in the Flames for your lies!"

Whips cracked and the guards laid into the prisoners, a fury of blows. Stewart hunched with the others, taking stripes across his back. The cleric rode away, a gallop of hooves tearing up the road. Stewart kept his head down, enduring the lash. But then he saw it; a gleam of metal churned into mud, a bit of broken spur.

Guards moved among the prisoners, wielding whips with a savage vengeance. In the confusion, Stewart sidled next to Gedry. "Look, on the far side of the road." He gestured with his gaze.

"I see it."

The prince shared a look of triumph with the scout. "Pass the word."

"Back on the road!" The sergeant rode up and down the line, bellowing orders. "Get moving, you scum! You're all fodder for the Flames!"

Guards herded them back onto the muddy road.

Stewart hissed, "To the far side!"

The others answered, surging across the road. Stewart pretended to trip, lunging for the bit of metal. Gedry and Timmons fell with him, a tangle of prisoners. Stewart palmed the broken spur. Whips cracked, and Stewart felt the sting across his back. Gedry screamed, catching a lash in the face. They struggled to their feet, keeping their heads bowed.

"Get moving, you filthy scum!"

The rope tugged forward and they were moving again, a shamble of muddy prisoners herded north, but one hid a smile. Stewart kept his head bowed, the broken spur clutched in his fist. It seemed the gods had heard him after all.

32

Liandra

Soldiers filled the courtyard, most of them mercenaries, red cobras emblazoned on a field of pea-green, the emblem of Radagar. Liandra watched from the battlement as the final preparations were made.

Twelve wagons laden with heavy chests formed the heart of the cavalcade, the massive chests secured with ropes and thick tarps imprinted with the royal seal of Lanverness. The queen sent the bulk of her treasury south to the fortress of Graymaris, along with four lords from her council, a dozen lesser nobles, and the entire troop of mercenaries.

Foreign soldiers in our castle, Liandra shuddered, feeling a sudden aversion to the mercenaries. Soldiers trained in Radagar, bought for the price of gold, she was glad she'd decided to send them south, although it would leave her capital woefully short of defenders. Plots within plots, she traded one gamble for another, betting wits could still defeat swords.

A cold wind battered the castle. Liandra hugged her silk shawl tight, wishing for her ermine cloak.

Below, the swirling chaos resolved into order. Her loyal lords, dapper in armor and velvet, sat atop caparisoned stallions as if they rode to war, when in truth, they led the retreat, leaving their queen to hold the capital. Contempt roiled within her, but Liandra kept it hidden. Far better to let them have their petty illusions, men served best when they thought themselves heroes.

"Our loyal lords," her voice echoed through the courtyard, every face lifting toward the battlement. "We charge you to take our treasury south to Graymaris. Keep it safe and march with all haste, for the wealth and hope of Lanverness rides with you." She spread her arms wide in a gesture of blessing. "May the Lords of Light grant you safe journey."

Her lords made courtly bows from their saddles, proud beneath their battle banners.

"For the Queen!" A single foot soldier cheered and the others took it up. "*The Queen!*" The cheer echoed through the courtyard, tempered by the silence of mercenaries.

Liandra gestured to the gates, convinced she'd made the right choice.

The great gates swung open and the horses spurred forward. Her loyal lords rode first, resplendent beneath snapping banners. Behind them, the wagons rumbled to motion, pulled by teams of massive draft horses. The great weight of the chests held the cavalcade to a slow walk, but such was the burden of wealth. Finally the mercenaries began to march, a long slither of pea-green following the wagons, boot heels tramping in unison against the cobblestone streets. Liandra shivered as if caught in a cloud of prescience, the sounds of war marching through her capital, the very thing she sought to avoid.

"Majesty?" Sir Durnheart stood at her right shoulder, his voice full of concern.

She raised a hand, forestalling him, needing to listen. Something was wrong; something was missing. And then she realized it, beneath the sounds of marching, the people were silent. Fearing abandonment, they watched but they did not cheer. Their silence put the cavalcade in a new light, highborn rats escaping a sinking ship.

She gathered her skirts, a rustle of bright silks, and made her way along the battlement to the barbican above the castle's outer gate. Mounting the stairs, she stood at the crenellated wall, staring down into the city streets. Her people crowded the streets, their faces sullen, watching the procession of wealth, somber as a funeral. She needed to give them hope. Removing her shawl despite the cold, she released it to the wind. It sailed out above the crowd, a twist of emerald silk, bright as any battle banner. A few looked skyward, staring at the length of the shimmering green. One boy spied the queen, pointing to the barbican. *"The queen stays!"*

Faces turned her way, full of skepticism, but then they saw her, emerald silks standing proud upon the castle walls. The queen watched as their faces came alight, a cheer rippling through the crowd till it became a roar. *"The queen stays!"* A thousand voices echoed the refrain, a tidal wave of hope.

Their cheers pierced her heart. She clutched the battlement, knowing this was the reason she schemed and fought. The gratitude of her people outweighed the worth of any amount of gold. Liandra drank in their cheers, storing them away like a secret strength. For two hours, she stood upon the battlement despite the cold, letting her people see their queen. Only when the last of the cavalcade disappeared into the streets, did she retreat from the barbican.

Her steps faltered, numbed by cold. Sir Durnheart leaped to her side, "Majesty!"

She waved him away, refusing to show weakness. Her hands and feet felt numb, yet she glowed with the gratitude of her people. She made her way along the battlement, grateful to reach the inner warmth of the castle's hallways.

Courtiers approached, but she waved them off, unwilling to sully the day with the pettiness of politics. She took the shortest route to the Queen's Tower, yearning for the sanctuary of her solar.

Her women were waiting, offering the queen a deep courtesy.

Lady Sarah beamed, "We heard the cheers from here." She waved the others forward, working to divest the queen of her silken finery. Lady Sarah touched her hand, recoiling in shock. "Majesty, you're nearly frozen!"

Liandra smiled. "No, on this day, we are kept warm by our people."

Lady Sarah scowled. "Little good it'll do if you catch your death of cold." She issued orders to others. "Quick, the ermine robe."

They'd warmed the robe by the fire. Liandra luxuriated in its plush warmth.

Lady Sarah clucked like an angry hen. "You should have worn the velvet instead of the silk."

Liandra smiled, content with her choice. "The emerald silk was bright like a banner. Sometimes show exceeds substance."

"Should have worn the velvet." Lady Sarah frowned, her fingers busy with fastenings.

Her women worked like bees around her, trading silks and jewels for plush robes of soft lambs' wool. One combed her raven hair while another placed fur-lined slippers on her feet. The fire crackled and snapped, a welcome warmth blazing from the hearth.

Liandra whispered a warning. "He will be here soon."

Lady Sarah caught her meaning, ushering the others from the queen's solar. "Her majesty needs her rest." The doors closed and the two women were alone. Lady Sarah began to fuss at a teapot set before the fire. "I set a pot of tea to brewing but its been sitting for a fair spell, probably over steeped. You took longer than I expected. Shall I pour another pot?"

"No, a cup of strong tea is just what we need to chase the chill away."

A tapping came from the secret door. Liandra's heartbeat quickened; she'd entrusted him with a key to the castle's secret ways. A moment later, the hidden doorway swung open and the Master Archivist stepped into the room. His face alight, he crossed the chamber to kneel by her side. "You were magnificent!"

"So you watched?"

His eyes glowed with praise. "Always."

"From the shadows?"

"As we agreed."

"And what did you learn?"

His face sobered and she regretted the question. "You did well to send the mercenaries."

She nodded. "So you saw it too."

"And you're well rid of those lords, weasels and silver tongues the lot of them."

"Yes, but Lord Mills chose to remain."

Her shadowmaster nodded. "Which only deepends my suspicions."

"That one plays a deeper game. Worth watching."

Lady Sarah poured tea, handing the queen a cup. Liandra laced her hands around the delicate porcelain, soaking up the warmth, too hot to drink. "Any luck with the assassin?"

"Not yet." His voice was a dangerous growl.

Lady Sarah sat by the fire. "This tea tastes bitter. Perhaps I should brew another pot?"

A sudden gust of wind rattled the windows in their lead casings. A window banged open, admitting a breath of cold.

Lady Sarah jumped. "I could have sworn I latched those!"

The queen's gaze snapped to her shadowmaster, her fears echoed in his face. He sprang to the windows, a dagger in his fist. Leaning out, he stared above and below. "Nothing." He latched the windows and then turned to scan the room, his gaze laden with suspicion. "The *tea!*" He leaped forward, knocking the cup from the queen's grasp. Porcelain shattered on the hearth, leaving a telltale puddle.

Lady Sarah stood, her voice indignant. "Why..."

"Poison."

Her brown eyes widened. She slowly set her teacup on the table as if it might bite.

The Master Archivist lifted the cup, sniffing and then dabbing his finger for a taste. "Have you left the teapot unattended?"

Lady Sarah blustered in confusion. "Well yes, her majesty took longer than expected. I poured the tea and added logs to the fire, but then I had other duties to attend to." Her voice faded. "Why?"

"An assassin stalks the queen's court, a master of poisons."

The lady gasped, but the queen's voice held steady. "What poison?"

"Judging from the taste, and from the use, I'd say Tansey."

Tansey, she knew this poison, a weed used by herb witches to abort unwanted babes. *"Tansey!"* Shock gripped Liandra, her hands clutching the swell of her child. "He seeks to murder our daughter!" She began to shake, a mixture of rage and fear. "You must find this murderer, this assassin of babes." Her hands whipped out, hitting the teapot, sending it shattering against the wall. "We'll have his head and we'll know the master he serves! Now go!"

Lady Sarah fled, and the Master Archivist took his leave, his face as dark as thunder, but the queen barely noticed. She paced in front of the fire; her fists clenched tight, her fingernails drawing blood. "They dared to reach for our child! *Our unborn child!*" Anger coursed through her, tainted by fear. Her court was suddenly more dangerous than ever before.

33

Jordan

The smell of fresh-baked biscuits pulled her from sleep. Jordan woke to find the camp struck, the horses saddled, and the others sitting around the fire sharing a morning meal. She stretched; surprised to find the sun at midmorning. Rafe approached, handing her a steaming mug. "You had an uneasy night. We decided to let you sleep."

Memories of her nightmares crashed against her, visions of death and despair. "Oh." Embarrassed, she took the mug, thankful for the warm brew. She drank the tea in one long pull and then rose from her bedroll. Belting her sword around her waist and swirling her checkered cloak around her shoulders, she slipped into the forest to make her morning toilet. Distracted by her dreams, she took a while returning. When she emerged from the trees, the soft murmur of voices died like a snuffed candle. Self-conscious, she took a seat near Rafe. Thad handed her a plate heaped with biscuits and crisp slices of bacon.

"Thanks." Suddenly ravenous, she pounced on the meal. The bacon tasted ambrosial and the biscuits soft as clouds. She took the edge off her hunger and then slowed, realizing they all stared at her. Her appetite fled. Setting the plate aside, she cradled a mug of tea, avoiding their stares.

Lenore was the first to speak. Wrapped in a cloak of midnight blue, the silver-haired monk held an aura of authority. "Have you decided?"

Jordan's gaze skittered around the others. Yarl sat hunched forward like a bear waiting to strike, while the beautiful Ellis watched with a hawk's steely gaze. Even Rafe studied her like a newfound scroll. She felt their gazes boring into her. The monks were fierce with intensity while the soldiers were keen with eagerness. Avoiding their stares, she found refuge in Thad. His blue-eyed gaze was warm and steady. "It's your decision, lass."

Anger sparked through her. "Who am I to deicide who lives and dies?"

"You won't be deciding who dies," his gaze held hers, "only who lives. Do nothing and they all die."

The truth cut like a sword.

Thad tugged on his russet beard, his gaze full of understanding. "Tis always the way with evil. Darkness expects the Light *not* to act."

Yarl leaned forward. "You've been given a rare gift, though it may seem like a curse, a chance to see what evil intends, a chance to thwart Darkness."

"Child," Lenore's voice carried the authority of the Order. "The gods gifted you with these visions for a reason." Her amber-colored gaze pierced Jordan, as if her eyes saw more than most. "Think of them as a sharp-edged sword. You must seize the sword and strike a blow against the Dark, for in this war our advantages are few."

Jordan nodded. "Seize the sword," it was advice she could appreciate. "But the visions are so confusing, how do I know which to choose?"

"Choose the one that is most dire."

Jordan shook her head. "They're all about death and deceit."

Thad said, "Follow your heart."

Jordan studied the big warrior, surprised by his advice.

Beside her Rafe said, "Remember how we talked about the stack of logs, choose the right one and they might all tumble."

"Good advice, but which one is the key?"

Rafe shrugged. "Perhaps the one you see the most?"

"A plague of nightmares," Jordan shook her head in frustration, "pulling me everywhere at once."

Lenore gave her a knowing smile. "The Order can reach many places. You need only tell us who to warn."

The monk's words brought spark of hope. "But even the fastest horse will take months to reach them."

"We have our ways." The silver-haired monk held her gaze, not a shred of doubt on her face. "To be forewarned is to be forearmed. Knowledge is the sharpest sword."

"All right then," Jordan made her decision. "Warn my father, the king of Navarre. Treachery and deceit stalk the seaside kingdom. Someone means to murder him but I don't know who."

Lenore nodded. "Who else?"

"Stewart, the prince of Lanverness. I see him running through a winter forest, stripped of arms and armor, enemy soldiers chasing him." Desperation leached into her voice. "You have to save him."

"The army of the Flame marches toward Lanverness." Lenore frowned. "Do you see defeat for the Rose kingdom?"

A hiss circled the fire.

Jordan blanched. "My visions aren't like that, just pieces of the puzzle."

Lenore nodded, her golden gaze implacable. "Who else?"

"An older baldheaded man, someone important, beheaded, his head stuck on a pike above a castle gate."

"Who is this man? Do you know his name?"

Jordan shook her head in frustration. "I don't know. I've never seen him before, but I know he's important."

"Anyone else?"

"No...yes. My sister Juliana, she's at sea, she needs to return to Navarre. And Navarre needs to be warned, the MerChanter fleet is coming, a bloody plague on our shores."

"MerChanter ships already raid the coast."

The biscuits turned to a lump in her stomach. Jordan clenched her sword hilt, feeling sick. "So my visions are true...and I'm already too late."

"Too late for some, but not for others." Thad put a steadying hand on her arm. "Do not give up. Despair is the handmaiden of Darkness."

The fire snapped and crackled. The others stared at her, but Jordan had no more to answers to give, everything else just a confusing jumble of images.

Lenore stood straight and solemn in her robes of midnight blue. "The king of Navarre, the prince of the Rose, and the sailing princess will be warned, but for the stranger, we can do nothing."

Jordan felt a cold stab to the heart, as if she'd failed.

Lenore's amber gaze was unrelenting, boring into her like a bird of prey. "And now you must decide, where will you take your sword?"

Jordan took a deep breath, her gaze going to the others. "Who's with me?"

Yarl nodded. "Rafe, Ellis, and I will join you, the other monks have their own missions."

Thad's voice was a deep rumble. "You'll have our swords, six of us at your back. And we brought spare mounts so we'll make good time."

Jordan gave him a grateful nod. Seven swords and three monks, she wondered how much difference they'd make, but she supposed they had to try. At least she wouldn't be alone.

"Time to decide." Lenore's voice was as hard as steel. "Waiting only serves evil."

Jordan sighed. "My heart tells me to seek Stewart, but the winter woods in my vision could be anywhere." Searching for Stewart would be like looking for a single grain of sand on an ocean beach, a futile effort while others paid with the lives for her delay. The truth hurt but it could not be denied. And then there was that other vision, the one of Stewart marrying Jemma in the gilded halls of Castle Tandroth. Shaking, Jordan pushed that nightmare from her mind. Opening her eyes, she felt the others' stares.

"Well?" Lenore cocked an elegant eyebrow.

Jordan took a deep breath, deciding to trust the gods. "I'll take Rafe's advice and follow the vision I've seen the most often."

The others leaned forward, their faces' expectant.

"I keep seeing a shattered tower, the stones as red as blood, rearing above a winter forest. It's very old, reeking of age, a ruin of some sort, but I don't know where it is, and I don't know what it means. I've never seen it before, yet the broken tower haunts my dreams."

Lenore and Thaddeus locked stares, an unspoken message passing between them. "It could be the Crimson Tower."

Thad nodded. "I know it."

Lenore turned her amber stare back to Jordan. "A curious choice."

"Why?"

"The Crimson Tower is an ancient ruin, a blasted remnant from the War of Wizards," her voice deepened, "once a stronghold of the Star Knights."

A shiver of certainty ran down Jordan's back. "Where is it?"

"In the heart of Lanverness, but you won't find it on any map."

"Why?"

"I know how to find it." Thad's voice was full of quiet confidence. "A broken tower used by thieves and ne'er-do-wells and wild things of the forest, shunned by local villagers as a haunted place. Legends swirl around the bloody tower, keeping honest folk at bay."

A conviction grew in Jordan. "That's where we need to go."

"Then the decision is made." Lenore nodded to Jordan, her face solemn. "The warnings will be sent and the Grand Master informed. May your sword serve the Light."

"Inform the Grand Master?" Jordan gave her a puzzled look. "You'll travel back across the mountains? I wouldn't wish that on an enemy."

Lenore gave her a knowing smile. "Do not underestimate the Kiralynn Order." And then she began to change, a faint nimbus of light glowing around her. The light flared, transforming the silver-haired woman into a giant white frost owl. "*Whoooo.*" The great owl took flight, a flap of snowy wings soaring toward the mountaintops.

"*Bloody hell!*" Jordan could only stare, watching as the great owl disappeared into the clouds. She turned to find the others dousing the fire and getting ready to ride, as if nothing out of the ordinary had happened. She grabbed Thad's arm, staring at the swordman's face. "Did you see that? Did you know that?

He gave her a quiet smile. "We all serve the Order."

Rafe approached. "Lenore trusted you. Now you know one of our long-held secrets. Do not betray our trust."

Jordan stared at the monks. "Can you all...turn into owls?"

Rafe shook his head. "It takes a special focus." His face turned grim. "Only two such rings are left to the Order. Our power wanes, yet we do what we can to stem the Dark tide."

She felt the weight of his words, another burden added to her shoulders, but the secret also brought hope. The monks were more than they seemed, and the Light needed every advantage. It was time to cast uncertainty aside, to act on her visions, to reach for her sword. She swung into the saddle, pulling her sword from its scabbard. A war cry burst from her. "*For the Light!*" The others mounted up, catching her need to be away. They set a hard pace, galloping down the mountains, heading for a broken tower in the heart of Lanverness.

34

Liandra

"We must find a way to protect our capital." The queen met with her small council, maps of the city strewn across the table. "When it comes to war, we shall hope for the best and plan for the worst. Pellanor must be protected." Six lords instead of the usual ten ringed the council table, diminished in numbers by the exodus of her treasury, yet the queen found the quality of her council much improved, save for Lord Mills. Dapper in a doublet of green velvet, the handsome lord listened but said little, much to the annoyance of the queen.

"Lord Mills, we will hear your opinion on this matter."

He gave her a courtly nod. "Majesty, my skills run to commerce not warfare."

"Yet you have a keen mind." She gave him a piercing glare. "You could turn it to more than one matter."

He met her stare with a glint of defiance. "Then my keen mind suggests you ask the military."

Their stares locked like crossed swords, until the lordling had the good sense to look away. Liandra smothered her anger, wondering why the slippery lord chose to stay instead of scuttling away with the rest of the rats, but that was a question for another day. She turned her gaze to the veteran at the far end of the table. "Major Ranoth, perhaps your opinion would provide more insight."

The leathery-faced major snapped to attention but his voice carried the tone of regret. "Majesty, your ancestors built Castle Tandroth as a stronghold, but the military value has long been eroded by the city's encroachment and the pursuit of luxury." He shook his head in a weary gesture. "Your castle has become a palace. It cannot be defended."

"Yes, yes, we have heard all this before." A touch of annoyance laced her voice. "We know our castle better than most, but it is the city we speak of."

The major grimaced. "Cities are best protected by deep moats and stout walls topped by catapults. With such defenses a small force can hold off an army, but Pellanor has none of these, and no time to build them. Against an army, the city cannot prevail."

But the queen was unwilling to accept the answer, her mind racing through a labyrinth of thoughts, desperate for a solution. Her bejeweled fingers drummed the tabletop. "Then if you cannot win, at least buy us time."

The major looked puzzled. "Time, majesty?"

"Yes, time, that rarest of commodities. Time creates possibilities, gives us options, a chance for allies to come to our aid, a chance for wits to foil swords." She seized the idea, certain of its rightness. "If you cannot fight for victory, then fight for time."

The major nodded, his face thoughtful. "Walls of any sort would at least slow the enemy."

"Exactly." The queen leaned forward, studying the map of the city. "What if we consider the city as a castle. Homes and shops are so closely built, they almost form a wall." Her finger traced a blockish outline around the most populous part of the city. "Seal the smaller roads and alleyways with barriers the height of the buildings and you begin to have a wall. Larger roadways can be fitted with wooden gates. Use the city's buildings as the backbone of your wall and you'll soon have a defensible rampart."

The major studied the map, his voice leavened with caution. "Such walls might slow an army but not stop them. It will buy time but not victory."

"Then buy us time." The queen's words snapped with confidence, steel beneath velvet. "Give us time enough and we shall find a way to victory."

Her confidence rippled through her lords like wind to a battle banner. "It might work." Nods of assent circled the table.

Master Saddler rarely spoke in council, yet he said, "The people will gain heart to see their city defended."

The portly lordling looked almost astonished at his own words, yet the queen gave him a warm smile. "You are exactly right, Master Saddler. That is why you shall work with Major Ranoth to construct the wall."

"*Me*, majesty?" His face flushed red. "But I am merely a goldsmith turned coin counter. I know nothing of walls."

"Yet you know our people, for you are closer to them than most of our lords, and you are honest, a rare combination. You shall work with Major Ranoth to define the wall and purchase those buildings that will become the city ramparts. Pay a fair price for the homes and then enlist the people's help to build the wall."

"But the treasury is gone to Graymaris."

"Not all of it. We would never leave ourselves without coin."

His eyes widened. "As you wish, majesty."

The queen nodded. "Now let us see a map of Lanverness. We need to know the nearness of the enemy."

Major Ranoth unrolled a second map across the table, a brightly painted vellum marked with villages, forests, strongholds and castles. Emptying a drawstring bag, he positioned lead soldiers on the map showed the changing locations of both armies. "Their main army presses south, about a moon's turn march from Pellanor."

A moon turn, it seemed such a slender sliver of time. The queen considered the map. "And has the prince emptied the north of food?"

"As you ordered." The major nodded. "His troops harass the enemy's supply lines, seeking to deprive them of all food, forcing the enemy to march hungry."

"Let us hope hunger blunts their drive south. Another reason we need time." The queen's fingers drummed the tabletop. "But it will not be enough, not nearly enough. We need to do more." Desperation was a goad to her mind. She stared at the lead soldiers painted bright red. "Soldiers of the Flame, religious fanatics, an army of believers, but how do we defeat an army of religious fanatics?" Her mind turned to Coronth. Reports from her shadowmen said the refugees defeated the Pontifax, yet his army still marched south. Perhaps the army did not know the truth? Yet the reports were certain, the Pontifax had died, burned in his own flames, causing riots in the streets. "We must defeat belief with doubt."

"What, majesty?" Major Ranoth gave her a puzzled stare.

"Defeat belief with doubt." She fastened on the thought. "This is no ordinary army. Doubt can shatter beliefs, destroying an army based on faith."

"But how, majesty?"

"This is not a matter of swords but a matter of shadows." Her gaze turned to Master Raddock but she knew his intellect was not equal to the task. She would need to raise the matter with Robert, her true shadowmaster.

A knock came from the door.

"Enter."

A guard peered inside. "An urgent message for the queen."

Liandra waved permission. The guard stepped aside to admit a dust-stained courier, a messenger from the army, but she did not like the fear in his eyes.

The lad fell to his knees, offering her a sealed scroll. "I rode as fast as I could."

She accepted the scroll, but her heart quailed when she saw the waxy imprint, a rampant griffin holding a sword aloft, the heraldic symbol of the dukes of Kardiff. A cadency mark overlaid the griffin, indicating the seal of the duke's eldest son. Her breath caught. Dane served as the second commander to her son, yet the army's dispatches always came under her son's royal seal. Breaking the wax, she opened the scroll, amazed that her hands did not shake. She skimmed the words till a single phrase pierced her heart. *The prince is captured, taken by Black Flames, unknown if he still lives.* "No! Not my son!" She gripped the table, finding it hard to breath.

Sir Durnheart moved to her side. "Majesty, what news?"

Liandra leaned against the table, gasping for breath, desperate to hold back the tears.

Sir Durnheart took her arm. "Majesty?"

Duty claimed her. Liandra struggled to find her royal mask. "It is nothing." She glared at her lords. "You will speak of this to no one." She took a step toward the door and nearly crumpled to the floor. Pain pierced her like a sword thrust to the abdomen. *"No!"* She clutched at the swell of the child. "Not both, not either." She railed against the gods, but the pain came again, sharp as any dagger.

"Majesty, what is it?"

The queen struggled to master her own body. Straightening her back, she forced herself to walk, the scroll crumpled in her fist. "Nothing. You are dismissed." She reached the door, each step a force of will. The hallway seemed to stretch to forever. Another stab of pain left her gasping, yet she forced one foot in front of the other, desperate for the haven of her solar. *At least my waters have not broken;* her mind repeated the words like a prayer. She bit her lip against another stabbing pain. *It's too soon!* She clutched her belly, desperate to keep the child. Just when she thought she would swoon, *he* was there, emerging from the shadows to scoop her into his arms, her Robert.

She clung to his dark robes, clung to his strength. "Must save the child."

"Shhh." He carried her up the stairs and into her solar, his shout scattering servants like frightened geese. *"Get the queen's healer!"* He laid her on the great bed, a rustle of silks.

Pain pierced her, another sword thrust. She gripped his hand. "Don't leave me!"

"I'm here, I'm always here." He gazed down at her, smoothing the sweat-damp strands of her hair.

She pressed the scroll into his hands. "Save our child, we must have an heir." Another wave of pain took her, and she wondered if she might die. Panic seized her, panic for her people. "Robert, you must save our kingdom!" She gripped his hand with all her might, desperate to tell him. "Doubt defeats belief! Find a way to defeat the Flame! You must do this for me."

His face blazed with determination, an anchor in a sea of pain. "For you, I will do anything."

She forced the words out, needing to be sure he understood. "The Flame Army, they don't know the Pontifax is dead! Doubt will defeat belief."

"I understand." His words were soothing. "The kingdom needs its queen." He kissed her hand. "And so do I."

And then the healer was there, holding a golden goblet to her lips. "Drink."

She drank the potion, falling back into silken sheets, claimed by a fog of pain.

35

Steffan

The morning dawned bright and fine, just enough wind to unfurl the banners, a perfect day for deceit. The horses pranced, tossing their manes, enlivened by the sunshine. Steffan rode in the vanguard with Prince Danly and the Priestess, a hundred soldiers riding in escort. Pennants rippled overhead, held aloft on long lances, and every one was green, emerald green. From a distance, the pennants served the deception, but in truth they were merely strips of cloth cut from the tabards of dead soldiers. Steffan spied bloodstains on one or two, a token of war. His escort was similarly disguised, a troop of Black Flames hidden beneath the enemy's emerald surcoats. He'd hoped to bring two hundred, a fitting escort for a prince, but too many surcoats were rent with sword cuts and soaked in blood, ruined beyond repair. So he settled for one hundred, the lesser number adding spice to the risk.

Steffan held his roan stallion to a brisk trot, fast enough to acknowledge the threat of war, but slow enough for royal dignity, all part of the ruse. Dressed in his finest court clothes of deepest black, he hid his raven badge beneath a bearskin collar, a thick chain of silver links marking him as the prince's counselor.

Beside him, the Priestess wore a stunning gown of crimson velvet, the plunging neckline revealing a tantalizing glimpse of cleavage. As the consort to a prince, she rode sidesaddle on a black gelding, tall and statuesque, a flash of jewels on her hands. An accomplished horsewoman, Steffan could not help but admire her seat.

To outfit the prince, they'd both ransacked their wardrobes for jewels and trims of fur. Danly wore a captured emerald cloak trimmed with ermine, a hastily forged circlet of silver set upon his brow. A burnished breastplate and a bejeweled sword marked him as a prince of war. Even the scars striping his face added experience to the effect, making him look older.

A half dozen guards with crossbows rode close behind the prince. An honor guard of sorts, they kept their crossbows loaded, providing surety to the prince's oath, but Steffan doubted they'd be needed. The Priestess kept the prince in thrall, bound with the silken leash of sex. Danly rode tall in the saddle, a smile on his face, clearly buoyed by the pomp of his princely trappings.

They rode for the better part of the day, through fallow farm fields and naked stands of maple and oak, the bright sunshine dispelling the dreary autumn chill. The countryside looked almost peaceful till they passed a tattered column of refugees, men and women pushing handcarts loaded with pots and pans, blankets and chickens, their bedraggled children following behind.

"Spare us a crust of bread!"

"Give us protection!"

"Keep us safe!" A few begged for help, but most were too exhausted or too defeated to raise their heads.

Steffan cast a sideways glance at the prince, but he seemed indifferent to their plight, his face as cold as stone, content to give them nothing but dust. Steffan urged his horse forward, eager to gain some distance from the wretched rabble.

By mid afternoon they topped a rise and got a first glimpse of the walled city. Lingard was formidable by any measure. Protected by stout stone walls and a daunting moat, the city kept safe within its defenses. Catapults and trebuchets studded the walls. Banners fluttered overhead, most of them emerald green but a few were bright gold emblazoned with the mailed fist of the baron, a heraldry that bespoke stubborn resistance and an iron resolve. Steffan studied the walled city and knew the general had the truth of it. Entire armies could batter themselves to death against Lingard's walls, all to no avail. Force would never capture such a fortress, and sieges took too long. But where force would never win, trickery and deceit might prevail. Steffan smiled, intrigued by the challenge.

The prince's horse shied, stepping sideways, fighting the bit, betraying the nerves of his rider. Steffan gave the prince a piercing look. "My lord, are you well?"

Danly yanked on the reins, bring the horse to heel. He cast a desperate glance at Steffan, his voice a low hiss. "What if they know?"

"The Red Horns were punished with ne'er a mention of a traitor prince." Steffan smiled. "The queen's own pride will defeat her, skewered by her own secret. With this act you reap your own revenge."

"But the Red Horns know!"

"And most of them are dead, executed by the Spider Queen."

"It only takes one and our ruse is blown."

"Life is about chances. Sometimes you have to roll the dice." Steffan flashed a rogue's smile. "Lingard is far from Pellanor, the odds are in our favor." His voice turned stern. "Play your part well and earn your crown."

Danly's eyes widened like a bolting horse, but the Priestess leaned forward, laying a soothing hand on his arm. "Be the prince and you will succeed." Her voice deepened. "You were meant to wear a crown. I see royalty in you." Her words put iron in his spine. Danly straightened in the saddle, the silver circlet gleaming against his raven hair.

Steffan looked away, burying his annoyance beneath a mask of calm, marking the prince for death if he betrayed the plan.

They rode in silence, approaching the city at a brisk trot. The drawbridge was lowered but the gates remained closed, sending a mixed message. Since the catapults remained stationary, Steffan assumed the cold welcome was merely a precaution of war. Pulling his horse to a halt, he stopped the column within bowshot of the walls. He took a moment to survey the fortress, considering the risks and rewards. Death versus victory, Steffan grinned. "Let the dice roll."

The Priestess gave him an odd look but Steffan just laughed, he never lost at dice. He turned and waved a herald forward. "Announce us."

Bedecked in emerald green, twin roses on his surcoat, the herald cantered toward the ironbound gates. Wheeling his horse beneath the gates, he threw his voice against the walls. "Open the gates for his majesty, Prince Danly of Lanverness! Open the gates for your sovereign prince!"

Soldiers milled on the battlement, all of them garbed in golden-yellow surcoats, the household guard of the baron. A bearded knight gave answer. "We had no word of your coming."

The herald persisted. "Yet we are here. Open the gates for his majesty, Prince Danly, son of the queen of Lanverness!"

Still they hesitated, the gates remaining stubbornly closed. Steffan spurred his stallion forward. "Open the gates in the name of the prince!" He made a sweeping gesture towards Danly, sunlight gleaming on his silver circlet. "At least admit the royal party. You dare not keep the prince waiting outside your walls in times of war." Steffan stared up at the ramparts, willing them to obey.

The bearded knight nodded. A command rang out. "Open the gates.

Steffan hid his smile, a thrill of triumph rushing through him.

Wood creaked and groaned and the great gates slowly swung open.

Steffan squared his shoulders and urged his stallion to a walk, the first to enter the enemy's stronghold. A hundred stares fell upon him, most of them curious, full of questions, but he felt no hostility. Passing beneath the barbican, he entered a large courtyard filled with soldiers, iron fists emblazoned on their golden surcoats. Troops loyal to the baron formed a defensive ring, shields and swords held at the ready. It seems their trust was not so easily won; yet the gates gaped open.

Hoof beats clattered behind as the royal party followed. Danly drew rein beside Steffan, the Priestess at his side. Six guards bearing crossbows rode at their back. The others waited outside as a show of trust.

Steffan surveyed the soldiers, searching for the baron, but none fit the description. "We seek the hospitality of Baron Rognald."

"So I've heard." The soldiers parted and a giant of a man stepped forward. His gray hair was sparse, a meager fringe wreathing a baldhead, but his dark eyes were sharp and keen. Moving with the prowling grace of a warrior, he kept his hand upon his sword hilt. "We've had no heralds announcing your arrival."

Danly shrugged. "Messengers are oft lost in times of war, yet we've arrived safe at your gates, a long ride from Pellanor."

The baron stood his ground. "I might have expected Prince Stewart, but not you." His gaze reeked of suspicion. "Why'd the queen send you?"

Steffan tensed, watching Danly from the corner of his eye. For a fleeting moment, anger blazed from the prince's face, but then he mastered himself enough to give the practiced answer. "The queen divides her heirs. While her majesty remains in Pellanor, Prince Stewart rides with the army, and I am sent to the stronghold of Lingard, a shell game of royals designed to confuse the enemy."

The baron locked stares with the prince, as if weighing his words. Tension rode the air, the horses sidling, biting their bits. Steffan considered intervening, but then the baron snorted a rude laugh. "That sounds like your royal mother, ever the strategist. I never could beat that woman at chess." He made a grudging half-bow toward Danly. "Welcome to Lingard, my prince." The baron's words were comely enough but his tone bristled with sarcasm.

Danly's face curdled, but before the prince could offer a rebuke the people raised a rousing cheer. "All hail the prince!"

Soldiers beat their swords against shields. "The prince of roses!"

Steffan hid his smile; the well-timed cheer made the people complicit in his ruse. The stupidity of crowds never failed to amaze him.

Danly puffed with pride, giving the people a princely wave.

A soldier stepped forward, holding the prince's horse. Danly dismounted with a flourish, his emerald cape rippling in the breeze. Steffan was quick to join him; careful to keep Danly on a tight leash, but the Priestess had the task well in hand. She cleared her throat, her voice demure, yet it reached the prince. "My lord, I need help from my horse."

Danly turned towards her, his face aglow. Grasping her by the waist, he eased her from the saddle. For a moment they stood close as lovers, a handsome couple with noble features and raven hair, but to Steffan's eyes Danly looked a fool while the Priestess was incomparable.

A second cheer erupted from the crowd. The prince responded like a mummer drunk on applause. Lifting his lady's hand like a trophy won at tournament, he presented her to the crowd. Tucking her hand on his arm, he escorted her toward the baron. "Baron Rognald, may I present the Lady Cereus." The Priestess gave the slightest curtsey, just enough to offer a better glimpse of her bosom. The baron's stare plumbed her cleavage, clearly enjoying the scenery.

"My pleasure," the baron's voice was a deep rumble, his gaze focused on the Priestess. "Welcome to Lingard. It's rare to have such beauty grace our castle."

So the old rogue is a lady's man, Steffan hid a grin, but then Danly broke the mood.

"And this is my counselor, Lord Steffan."

The baron sent him a frosty glance. "Yes, I'll hear your news from Pellanor. Dispatches from the queen have been all too few." The baron gestured toward the stone keep rearing above the heart of the city, but his gaze remained fixed on the Priestess. "Come, you'll want to change and then we'll dine, meat and mead to celebrate such fair guests. Despite the war, you'll find my cooks can set a comely feast."

The baron led the way through the throng of soldiers but Steffan interrupted, "My lord, our troops outside the wall?"

With a negligent wave, the baron answered, "Yes, yes, let them enter. They can barrack with my soldiers."

Steffan watched as a captain leaped to obey, one step closer to success, and then he followed the others up the cobbled lane.

Lingard proved a prosperous city, a prize waiting to be plucked. Shops flanked the street, most of them doing a bustling business despite the war. Everything seemed clean and well tended, the wide cobblestone streets smelling of sweet horse dung instead of sour pisspots, but it was the faces of the people that Steffan found most telling. Peering from windows and shop doors, they watched the procession of lords and soldiers with open curiosity instead of fear, so different from Coronth. And all the faces seemed well fed and content; more proof the harvest of Lanverness was sequestered behind Lingard's walls. Steffan hid his smile; the city was well worth the risk, provisions for his army, and souls for the Dark Lord, a bounty waiting to be harvested.

The cobbled streets curved up a small hill to the tower keep. Steffan walked half a step behind the others, letting the baron set the pace. The Priestess hung on the prince's arm, but the full brunt of her allure fell on the baron. Rognald succumbed to her charms, nattering on about his dreary lineage as he led the way through the cobbled streets. Steffan ignored the idle chatter, studying the city as they walked.

A fair-haired page approached at a run. The lad whispered a message to the baron and then scurried back toward the tower keep. Soldiers and citizens seemed to leap at the baron's slightest order, more proof the baron was a formidable leader, a thorn in the side of their plans, just as the Priestess predicted.

They reached the stone keep set atop a small hill, a tower surrounded by a second ring of crenellated walls. Guards in gold surcoats snapped to attention, but the portcullis was already raised, leaving the gate wide open, seduced by the peace of the city. Steffan hid a sneer, the people of Lanverness were so trusting they deserved to be conquered.

The royal party passed beneath the iron teeth, into a second courtyard.

"Welcome to the Fist." The baron gestured toward the great drum tower, a grin of pride on his face. "The stoutest tower in all the queen's domain. Lingard has never fallen while held by a Rognald."

"Never?" Steffan hid a smile, knowing there was always a first.

The baron gave him a frosty glare. "Never." Turning his back on Steffan, he made a welcoming gesture to the prince and his lady. "Come, let me show you the ancestral home of the Rognalds."

The Priestess made soft murmurs of appreciation while the baron ushered his guests into the tower. Stone walls thick as a man's height bespoke a tower built for war, but the interior proved surprising, a rare mix of elegance and martial pride. A massive oak table dominated the great hall, six silver candelabras gleaming along its length. Tapestries lined the walls with scenes of hunting and war, the embroidered heroes all showing a striking resemblance to the baron. A massive fireplace spewed heat while glowing candles filled the room with light. A dozen servants in gold livery stood in a line, bowing low. The oldest among them, a thin pinched-faced man with gray hair stepped forward. "Welcome to the Fist."

The baron waved toward the gray-haired servant. "This is Daschel, my seneschal. He'll see to your needs."

A dust-covered soldier stepped from the shadows, a courier's pouch strapped to his side. "My lord, may I have a word?"

The baron silenced the soldier with a raised hand, and then turned toward the prince, a congenial smile on his face. "Daschel will show you to your chambers. We'll sup in my private solar at seven."

Danly nodded. "I look forward to it." Placing a possessive arm around the Priestess, the prince followed the seneschal toward the staircase. Steffan fought the urge to linger, concerned about the courier, but his curiosity might raise suspicions, and suspicions were often the death of deceit. Nodding toward the baron, he followed the others up the spiral staircase, playing the dutiful counselor.

Five turns of the staircase brought them to a hallway lined with oak doors. The seneschal opened the first, his gaze fixed on Steffan. "This will be your room, my lord."

Small but well appointed, the chamber had a four-poster bed, a tapestry on the far wall, and a pair of arrow-slot windows fitted with mullioned glass.

"The privy chamber is just down the hall. I'll have a page bring a fresh basin of hot water."

"And my clothes chest?"

The seneschal nodded, his face prim. "Will be brought to you."

"Very well."

The seneschal gave a half bow and retreated to the hall, closing the door behind him. Steffan listened at the door, hearing the laughter of the Priestess as they moved away. He did not like being separated from the others but the ruse demanded it. Much depended on the Priestess keeping the prince in hand.

Steffan crossed the room and opened the mullioned windows. A gust of crisp wind swirled inside, tugging at his dark hair. He leaned out the window, studying the city below. The streets bustled with commerce, no sign of any alarm despite the dust-coated courier. Reassured, Steffan studied the forest beyond the city's greensward. The dense thicket of woods seemed peaceful enough. He'd have to trust General Caylib to play his part. Trust was never one of Steffan's strengths, but sometimes it was necessary. He lingered at the window, watching the sun set in a burst of fiery light, bathing the walled city in a red glow like an omen of flames.

A knock came from the door.

"Come."

A page entered, balancing a steaming basin. Behind him a pair of soldiers struggled to carry a well-worn travel chest. Steffan recognized the soldiers, two of his Black Flames hiding beneath emerald surcoats. "Put the chest by the window and the basin on the nightstand."

The page took careful steps, a hint of lavender rising with the steam. The lad settled the basin on the nightstand, laying a fresh towel on the bed. "Will that be all, sir?"

"Yes." Steffan tossed a coin to the page, watching as the wide-eyed lad bowed his way from the chamber. When the door shut, Steffan skewered the soldiers with a warning glance lest they betray the plot. "Have the men been fed and settled?"

The bearded sergeant grinned. "They gave us barracks near the east gate, just as you said."

"All of you together?"

"Yes."

"Good. Keep your swords sharp. Remember, you serve the prince." He moved toward the sergeant, lowering his voice to a whisper. "Tonight as planned."

"As you say, counselor." The sergeant flashed a grin as he strode from the chamber.

Steffan shut the door and leaned against it, satisfied that everything was going as planned. Deceit was so delicious, especially when the stakes were so high. He felt himself grow hard, needing the Priestess. Danger was such an aphrodisiac. Stripping to the waist, he washed at the basin, using a sharp razor to scrape the stubble from his chin. He nicked his throat, a brief slice of pain. "Damn." He missed Pip's attentive service, but mere counselors rarely merited their own valets. Wiping the blood on a towel, he opened the travel chest and chose a red shirt of the finest silk and supple black leather pants. He tucked an assassin's dagger in his right boot and another behind his back and then pulled on a thick leather belt with an embossed scabbard holding a fancy table dagger. At the bottom of the chest, he found a purse thick with golds, and tucked it into his belt. Twirling a black wool cloak around his shoulders, he strode to the window to wait. Twilight had come and gone, leaving an inky blackness overhead, yet lanterns glowed in the city below. Blanketed by night, the city seemed peaceful.

A knock came from the door.

"Come."

A page entered. "The baron invites you to sup in his solar."

Steffan smiled. "Lead the way." He found the prince and the Priestess in the hallway, both dressed in their best court finery. Danly gave him a leering grin, his silver circlet gleaming against his black hair. "Evening, counselor." His hands roamed the Priestess, his dark eyes glazed, drunk on wine, or sex.

Probably both, Steffan scowled. "My *prince*." He emphasized the title, hoping to put steel in Danly's spine.

"All is well." The Priestess gave him a subtle smile. A vision of curves in dark purple, she wore a kirtle of delicate gold chains over a velvet gown, a graceful table dagger hanging at her waist.

Steffan leaned forward, catching a whiff of her musky scent. "The prince is a lucky man. With you by his side, the night is sure to be intoxicating."

"So it begins." She licked her lips, her gaze laden with heat.

For half a heartbeat, he forgot the plan, falling into her stare.

"My lords?" The page interrupted, gesturing toward the staircase. "The baron awaits."

Steffan nodded. "And we are rude to delay the inevitable."

The lad gave him a puzzled look and then led the way up the stairs to the baron's solar. The page knocked, admitting them to a small chamber. Tapestries hung from the walls and silver service gleamed from a round table. Candles glowed in sconces, the smell of fresh baked bread filling the air. Warmth came from a fireplace crackling with pine logs, a cozy room for intrigue.

Baron Rognald rose from the table, his gaze fixed on the Priestess. Clad in an elegant doublet of gold, Rognald looked more like an aging courtier than a warrior lord. Beside him stood a big ruddy man in a gold surcoat, a soldier with red hair and a brawler's flattened nose, a sword belted to his side. Steffan recognized him from his talks with the Priestess; he prayed she knew the captain's appetites as well she knew his appearance.

The baron grinned, gesturing them toward the table. "Welcome to the hospitality of the Fist."

Three pages leaped from the shadows to hold chairs for the guests. The Priestess took a chair next to the baron, keeping the prince on her right. Once seated, a line of pages began the service. Steaming bowls of oxtail soup accompanied by fresh baked bread, deviled quails' eggs, and slivers of smoked duck in a savory sauce. Rich aromas swirled through the chamber, a princely start to a fine feast. When the first course was laid, the baron made the introductions. "This is Leonard Vengar, the captain of my guard. He's a dull fellow when he's not in his cups, but I wanted him to hear first-hand the tidings of war."

The Priestess leaned toward the baron, laying her hand on his sleeve. "Must we speak of war?" She gave him a playful pout. "It's been so long since we've had such courtly company."

"Or such a fine feast." The prince hefted his goblet. "War is a dirty business, for clods and dullards, not princes and lords."

Rognald speared the prince with a glare. "You always were the lesser prince."

Danly bristled. "But a prince no less, and you're but a baron, a lackey to a queen."

The two men locked stares like stags in rut. Steffan threw an angry glance at the prince, but the Priestess intervened, loosing her seductive charms on both men. Stroking the prince's arm, she fixed her gaze on the baron. "How is it you set such a fine table despite the war? I never expected such a feast outside of Pellanor."

The baron hefted his goblet, puffed with pride. "To a fine harvest and an even finer queen." They all drank to the toast. The baron leaned forward, spearing a sliver of roast duck with his table knife. "By orders of her majesty we've gathered all the harvest for leagues around. Lingard's granaries are full to bursting. We'll weather this storm of flames behind stout walls, waiting till the war burns out." Rognald grinned as if sharing a secret. "And when the enemy turns tail and runs for Coronth, the queen will find a way for Lanverness to profit, you mark my words."

The baron's bold-faced confidence intrigued Steffan. "You show a commendable loyalty, but don't you fear a siege?"

"A siege!" The baron snorted a laugh. "I see you're not privy to the queen's counsel."

Danly bristled but Steffan restrained him with a hand hidden beneath the table. "What do you mean? The army of the Flame is said to be legion."

"Exactly." The baron quaffed a goblet of wine and a page promptly refilled it. "The queen *wants* a siege! She's practically begging for it." His dark gaze gleamed with a hunter's delight. "Let the enemy bring their numbers against Lingard or Kardiff. A siege makes the coming winter an ally of Lanverness. Cold and hunger will whittle away their numbers, while we pummel them with our catapults. And when they're at their weakest, the Rose Army will take them from behind, trapping between steel and stout stone walls." His fist banged the table, as if crushing a gnat. "Let them bring their siege and the queen will have her checkmate."

Steffan swallowed a scowl, realizing the queen was a shrewd opponent.

Danly glowered. "My royal mother is not infallible."

"Aye, but she's a canny queen, and I've yet to meet the man who can match her at chess."

"War is not chess." Danly sulked in his cups.

Steffan sent a warning glance to the Priestess. Smooth as honeyed milk, she intervened, laying a distracting hand on the baron's arm. "Such a stalwart lord, it's why the queen sent us to Lingard, to the protection of her best baron."

"Her *best* baron." Rognald raised an eyebrow, his voice gruff. "I like the sound of that. I wooed her once, you know, back when we were both younger."

"You and the queen?" The Priestess feigned interest. "What was she like back then?"

"Ever the beauty. I won her favor at the tournament, no one could best me at the joust." The baron fell into vanity's trap, reminiscing about his younger days. The Priestess proved a rapt audience. Full of sultry looks and subtle praise, she worked her wiles on him, stroking his ego and puffing his pride, while keeping his goblet brimming with wine. Steffan eased back in his chair, content to let the Priestess lead, like watching a black widow spider weave a seductive web. And all the while the prince glowered in his cups but at least he did not spoil the plot.

Servants brought more courses and the candles melted to stubs. The hour grew late. Finally when the last course was consumed, the servants brought a voiding dish of apples.

The Priestess claimed the bowl, giving the baron a beguiling smile. "My lord, let me serve you."

The baron blustered. "There's no need."

"But I insist. It is the least I can do to show my gratitude for such a fine feast...and for such a splendid lord." Her gaze smoldered.

The baron flamed red.

"Dismiss the servants, for we've no need of them."

The baron nodded, issuing the order. The servants left, closing the door behind them.

Flames crackled in the hearth, sending a surge of heat through the chamber. The Priestess waited, as if gathering the men's stares, and then she stood, loosing her raven-black hair, the lush tresses cascading down her back. Her hands reached up, smoothing the velvet of her gown. Like lovers hands, she caressed her own body, cupping the curve of her breasts and then spilling down to her waist, slow and sensual as a dance. One hand reached for the jeweled dagger at her waist, slowly drawing it from the silver sheath.

Steffan leaned forward, his manhood stiff with need.

The baron groaned.

The Priestess licked her lips, full of suggestion. She leaned forward, her breasts straining against her gown, displaying a spill of cleavage. She selected an apple from the bowl, plump and golden. Slow and sensual, she sliced the apple in half. Giving the baron a searing look, she made another deft slice, carving a long thick wedge from the juicy apple.

Licking the juice from her fingers, her voice was low and sultry. "Apples are the fruit of temptation, don't you think?" Her lips puckered for a kiss. She took the first slice for herself, slowly forcing it through her pouting red lips. The entire length slipped into her ample mouth.

The baron groaned.

She cut a second slice and offered it to Rognald. "Do you want a bite of my apple?"

"Yes, oh yes!" He leaned forward, sweat beading his brow.

The Priestess held the slice to his lips, slowly sliding it in.

Steffan nearly came.

The baron took the slice, his gaze locked on the Priestess. He licked her fingertips, suckling them, making hungry noises. His arms reached for her, but the Priestess evaded his grasp. "Not yet." The baron sprawled in his chair, his eyes glowing with hunger.

The Priestess cut a third slice and offered it to the prince, sliding it along his mouth like a slow tease. Danly ate the apple. "More." His voice dropped to a moan. "Give me more."

Steffan watched, gripping the arms of his chair, nearly bursting with need.

The Priestess turned her gaze on the captain, her voice low and sultry. "Will you taste my apple?"

"Oh yes." The captain leaned forward like a man bespelled.

The Priestess speared another slice. She leaned across the table, the slice hovering at the captain's lips.

The baron began to choke, a loud hacking sound. He clawed at his throat, his face turning beet red, gasping for breath. *"Poison!"* He spat the word like a curse. Fingernails raking his throat, he drew streaks of blood. A coughing fit claimed him, his huge body convulsing. One hand gripped the tablecloth, yanking it toward him. Goblets and platters shattered across the floor. The baron struggled to stand, his eyes bulging, his face contorted. He gave a strangled groan, a death rattle, and toppled like a felled giant.

The captain sprang backwards, drawing his sword. "What have you done?"

Danly leaped from his chair, his face contorted in fear. *"Poison!* You never said anything about *poison! I could have died!"*

"Calm down." Steffan stood, his gaze locked on the captain, time to test the plan. He pulled the purse from his belt and threw it on the table. Heavy with golds, it hit the table with an impressive thunk. "A first payment."

The captain's face flickered with interest, but he kept his sword raised.

Steffan pressed his argument. "You can be rich, and on the winning side, or you can die."

"What do you mean?"

"A hundred of my soldiers are billeted at the eastern gate."

The captain gave a terse nod.

"By now, they should have control of the gate. By morning, the city will be teaming with soldiers of the Flame."

Fear flickered in the captain's eyes.

"Take the gold and live."

His gaze slid from the purse to the dead baron and back again.

"There's more gold where that came from, enough to make you wealthy. You owe no allegiance to the dead."

Vengar lowered the sword and took the golds. "What would you have me do?"

"Take control of the keep." Steffan gestured to the Priestess and the prince. "Protect us till dawn. The army of the Flame will do the rest."

"And if anyone stands in my way?"

"Kill them."

The captain scowled but he did not argue. "And what about him?" He gestured to the dead baron.

"The heart and soul of the city." Steffan moved around the table, nudging the corpse with his boot. "To take Lingard I merely needed to defeat one man and claim one gate. Put his head on a spike over the keep's gates. When the people see their baron's head on a spike, all resistance will crumble. Take away the leader and you take away their hope." Steffan smiled. "It really is that simple."

The captain hesitated, his sword hanging limp in his hand.

Steffan gave him a piercing stare. "You have work to do."

Vengar saluted and strode from the chamber. The door slammed shut behind him like a final heartbeat. Steffan gave the Priestess a slow smile. "You were magnificent."

Her dark eyes gleamed bright. "Poison is such a sweet seduction."

Flushed from the kill, Steffan thought she'd never looked more enticing.

A low moan broke the mood. Danly cringed with his back to the wall. "I ate the apple! I could have *died*."

Steffan bolted the door. "Calm yourself."

"*Poison!*" Danly stared at the Priestess. "You never said anything about poison! You could have made a mistake!"

"Never." She wiped her dagger on the tablecloth. "When it comes to poison, I *never* make mistakes."

Danly sputtered. "But how'd you do it? I saw you eat the apple?"

"An age-old trick." She lifted the dagger, showing the runnel on one side. "Two sides to the dagger, but only one side holds the poison." She flashed a knowing smile. "Taste the food yourself and the victim never suspects." Her smile deepened. "Killing is an art, a special form of seduction."

Steffan crossed the room and took her in his arms, her lush curves melding to his body. "I can't wait any longer." He clasped her close, his hands tugging at the annoying velvet. She wore nothing underneath, as if she'd anticipated his need. Engorged, he carried her to the baron's bed. Her lips tasted of apple. He could not get enough of her. She gave a throaty laugh as he took her over and over again.

Outside the window, a scream pierced the night. The killing had started; the city was theirs, another victory for the Dark Lord.

36

Jordan

Goaded by nightmares, Jordan set a hard pace. Her companions stayed close, three monks and six swordsmen, their allegiance hidden beneath leather armor and cloaks of butternut brown. They thundered down out of the mountains, galloping through the forests of Wyeth.

The trees wept leaves, autumn quickly turning to winter. Time choked her like a noose. Jordan urged her horse to a gallop, praying they were not too late.

Riding from dawn till dusk, they raced across the leagues, making good use of their spare mounts, but when they reached Lanverness, they slowed to a crawl. War ravaged the Rose kingdom, long lines of refugees clogging the roads. Jordan rode among them, hungry for news, but the names of villages burned and hamlets forsaken meant little to her. Told from the perspective of peasants, war was nothing but a chaotic hell. Jordan wished them Godspeed but had little else to offer. Anxious to make better time, Thaddeus led them off road, wending their way through fallow fields and empty pastures.

They kept to the back ways, slipping through the countryside like shadows. Twice they eluded marauders in red, taking refuge in the woods, but everywhere they saw the scars of war. Homesteads deserted, bloated corpses rotting in the fields. Peasants stumbled along muddy lanes, pushing carts of meager possessions. Whole villages lay ravaged, some burned to cinders, smoking ruins haunting the countryside. For the first time, Jordan saw the true wages of war, yet she knew this first payment was merely a token if Darkness prevailed. She gripped her sword hilt, praying for a way to thwart the Darkness.

They smelled it before they saw it, the reek of rot fouling the air. Thad wanted to turn away but Jordan insisted. They rode across the battlefield, red and green cloaks churned to mud, a putrid stench rising with the morning mist. Jordan slowed her horse to a walk, picking a path among the dead. Corpses littered the field, gory and rotting, her gaze drawn to those in emerald green. Her heart pounding, she studied every face, mud-streaked and pale, frozen in death. A knight with an emerald cloak and black hair sprawled facedown in the mud. Jordan slid from the saddle and knelt to roll him over, praying it was not him. Mud sucked at the body, leaving a bloody puddle. Jordan held her breath, her heart thundering...but it was not him, *not*

Stewart. Relief washed through her. She closed the stranger's eyes, whispering a prayer to Valin.

"Whom do you search for?" Rafe pulled his horse to a stop, staring down at her, but she did not answer. Jordan gathered the reins of her horse and kept walking, her gaze fixed on the slain.

Thaddeus approached, his black stallion skirting a corpse. "Only a skirmish. More red cloaks than green, looks as if the queen's men waged a good fight."

A pair of crows cawed, fighting over a severed hand. She kicked at the crows, sending the pair flapping into a steel-gray sky. "Only a skirmish yet over a hundred died." Jordan kept walking, needing to see them all.

"We're exposed here, lass. Better to move among the trees."

She heard the truth of his words, yet she could not stop her search.

"Scavengers will be here soon, we best be off."

Her gaze scanned the battlefield, noting the lack of weapons. "They've already come and gone." She pointed to the nearest corpse, a barefoot soldier sprawled in the mud. "This one's missing his boots." Scavengers always followed the brave, gleaning weapons and armor and coin, a despicable practice. They took what they wanted but buried none of the dead, leaving heroes and enemies as fodder for crows. It was a grim sight, a grim lesson.

"We should ride."

"I need to know."

His voice sharpened. "Is this about your visions?"

"No...yes!" She stared up at Thaddeus, grateful for his keen insight.

"How?"

"Because if he's..." her voice broke, choking on the words. Jordan took a steadying breath. "Because if he's here, then certain visions cannot be true." Her voice dropped to a whisper. "Or I've come too late."

Thaddeus gave her a measured look. "Then you best gain the answer."

She quickened her pace, walking among the dead, checking every emerald cloak save one. From a distance she spied blonde hair beneath a cracked helm. Relief washed through her, *not him,* not *Stewart.* "He's not here." Her voice firmed. "We need to find the red tower."

"Then we best be off. And pray your description matches my memory." They put spurs to their horses, galloping for the woods.

37

Stewart

Darkness finally fell, a nearly moonless night, perfect for his plan. Lying huddled with the others, Stewart held the broken spur clamped between his thighs, sawing his hands back and forth across the rowel. The spur proved sharp but the rope was thick and stubborn. It seemed to take forever, but then the last strand broke, a rush of pins and needles flooding his hands. Stewart grinned in triumph. Flexing his fingers, he passed the spur to Gedry and then turned his attention to the camp. A single sentry sat lulled by the campfire, the best chance they were likely to get. Snores came from the others, thirty sleeping guards against twenty-five desperate prisoners. The numbers weren't bad, till he considered his men were half-starved and beaten. Desperation and ambush were their only advantages; Stewart prayed it would be enough.

Feigning sleep, he kept watch while the spur passed from one prisoner to the next. Every man needed to be released before they made their move. Sweat beaded his forehead despite the cold, knowing they had but one chance to escape. He flicked a glance to the heavens, tracking the slivered crescent across the night sky, nervous of losing the dark. The plan was simple, Gedry would take the sentry, Timmons would secure the horses, and he would take the sergeant; otherwise it was every man for himself, kill or be killed.

The lone guard stirred, rising from his seat by the fire.

Tension rippled through the prisoners. They feigned sleep, more than a few faking shallow snores. Stewart wrapped the frayed rope around his wrists, praying the ruse worked. The guard walked along the huddled prisoners, stopping now and then to stare. Stewart kept his breathing slow and even, his eyes closed to narrow slits. The guard hesitated but then moved on, returning to his seat by the fire.

Stewart whispered an order. *"Wait till his head lulls forward."* A single mistake would get them all killed. Gedry was given the spur, the only weapon among them. Stewart flexed his hands, his gaze locked on the sleeping sergeant. Tonight he'd regain the seashell broach or die trying.

The guard's head drooped.

Stewart waited a hundred heartbeats. *"Now."*

They moved like wraiths, slithering through the churned mud. Stewart found a rock the size of a child's head, a much better weapon than bare hands.

He tucked it in the crook of his arm and kept crawling. Silent as death, they crept toward the guards, no chink of armor or weapons to give them away. Reaching the firelight, they paused, but the guards did not stir. Gedry rose to a crouch, slinking towards the lone sentry's back. Stewart tensed, the rock gripped in his hands, his heartbeat hammering. Gedry struck, driving the broken spur deep in the guard's throat while twisting his head. The guard made a wet gurgling noise, one leg kicking out, but then he slumped dead.

The other guards still slept.

Stewart stood, leading the others to the attack. Looming over the blanket-wrapped sergeant, he hefted the rock with both hands, such a terrible way to die. Hesitation cost him. The sergeant's eyes flew open. *Kill or be killed.* Stewart struck, pounding the rock down with all his strength. The rock hit with a sickening crunch, releasing a splatter of brains. The sergeant's body twitched and then lay still. Stewart lunged for the sergeant's belt. Desperate fingers found the seashell broach nestled in the cloth pouch.

A scream rent the night. Guards sputtered awake, reaching for weapons.

Stewart grabbed the sergeant's sword. *"For the queen!"* He leaped to the nearest guard, severing the man's arm before he could draw his blade. Blood and screams filled the night. Stewart whirled, searching for the nearest foe. Silhouettes against the fire, he charged into the fray. Stewart fought like a madman, buying time for his men to gain their own weapons. The battle became a nightmare, men with rocks attacking guards with swords and halberds, courage and desperation pitted against steel. In the flickering firelight, he saw Kerlin charge a halberd, taking the wicked blade in the chest. Kerlin flung his arms around the blade, holding it tight as a lover. *"Kill him! Kill him!"* his dying breath wheezed out. Stewart leaped forward, taking the guard's head as Kerlin sank to his knees, the fearsome blade still buried in his chest.

"Behind you!"

Stewart whirled, parrying the swipe of another halberd. The half-moon blade whistled as it cleaved the air. Fear shivered through him, the same weapon had taken him prisoner. The guard sneered, *"Infidel scum!"* Fear blazed to anger; Stewart launched a furious attack. Beating the halberd away, he leaped inside its reach, thrusting his sword into the guard's loins. A hideous scream answered his thrust. He yanked his sword free just in time to parry another attack. Sword against sword, he fought like a demon. The battle became a blur, his muscles aching, his back screaming in pain. Desperation lent him strength. He dispatched another foe and staggered to a stop.

A heart-pounding silence surrounded him. The clang of steel was ended, nothing left but the cries of the wounded. It was over, and he still stood. He raised his sword to the heavens. *"For the queen!"*

Silhouettes stumbled toward him, but so few. Only eight, *eight of twenty-five,* the losses staggered him.

"We did it, my prince." It was Owen, the one who'd claimed to be the baron of Lingard.

"Gedry?"

Owen shook his head. "By the fire."

"No!" He found the scout slumped by the fire, a fearsome gash across his abdomen, his face twisted in pain. "I'm done for, lord." Stewart wanted to argue, but they both knew it was true.

"It hurts something fierce." Gedry clutched at his stomach, a tangle of entrails peaking between fingers. He looked up at the prince, his eyes pleading. "End it."

"An honor to fight with you." Mercy came in the form of a swift dagger. Stewart's eyes glazed with tears but his hand held steady. "You will be remembered." He closed the scout's eyes, and arranged a blanket over him, almost as if he slept. "The Lords of Light be with you."

The others stood in a circle watching. Stewart climbed to his feet, feeling like he'd aged a hundred years.

"What orders, lord?"

"How many horses?"

"Three."

Only three, three horses for eight men, he'd expected more, but then again, he hadn't really expected to win. "How many guards escaped?"

"At least eight."

So the cowards broke and ran, the answer to his victory. "We need to be far gone before the night ends. Gather what you can, weapons, cloaks, food, and then we run, run and hide, till we find our own men." They scattered, doing his bidding, while Stewart made the rounds, ending the moans of the wounded. It was a terrible task, but he would not order another to do it. Most took it as a mercy, but it was still grim work. Exhausted, he sheathed the dagger and claimed a corpse's cloak.

Owen brought him a horse, a saddled gelding.

"Take the saddle off. We ride double, the less the horse has to carry the better."

They unsaddled the horses and then they were off, riding double with two men running along side. He held the horses to a slow trot, refusing to let any man fall behind. Stewart touched the seashell broach for luck. A desperate plan, a desperate escape, but he'd gained his freedom, a sword belted to his side, another chance to defeat the Flame.

38

Danly

E verything changed overnight. He'd ridden through the gates as a prince, delivering Lingard to his so-called allies, yet she'd fed him the apple. *A poisoned apple,* Danly scrubbed his sleeve across his mouth, nearly gagging at the memory. *He could have died like the baron.* His resentment built as he watched the other two. Steffan and Lady Cereus were both distracted, standing close as lovers, studying a map. Caught up in their victory, they talked as if he wasn't even in the room. Danly sat in the corner, watching as they held court, listening to their schemes. Anger pulsed through him. Slinging a cloak around his shoulders, he fled the chamber, making his way down the spiral staircase.

Soldiers in red tabards crowded the keep. Messengers ran up and down the stairs, but none gave him a second glance. He reached the ground floor unopposed. Red-cloaked officers gathered in the great hall, maps slung across the oak table, saddlebags and gear dumped along the walls. All the trappings of wealth were gone. Silver candelabras stuffed in saddlebags, tapestries pulled from walls, heirloom swords claimed as spoils. Like a plague of thieves, the army transformed the keep. By mid-afternoon, the great hall looked more like a barracks than a lord's residence.

Disgusted, Danly shouldered his way outside, seeking the crisp winter air, but he found no relief. Soldiers filled the courtyard, horses picketed along the far wall. Some turned to stare, their faces a mixture of curiosity and disdain. He lowered his head and crossed to the outer gate, careful to avoid the steaming piles of horseshit.

The portcullis was raised, Black Flames guarding the gate. They let him pass, but not without an escort. Two Black Flames followed him like shadows, a pair of minders for the traitor prince. Hatred boiled in Danly, knowing they were shackles of another sort.

Danly slipped beneath the portcullis, escaping the keep. Soldiers gathered outside, staring up at the crenellated walls. Danly turned to follow their stares and staggered back a step. Baron Rognald's bald head glared down at him. Impaled above the gate like a trophy, the gray-tinged face was frozen in a rictus of agony. *Poison,* the weapon of assassins and women. Danly shuddered, making the hand sign against evil. He'd eaten from the same apple. Taking a slice from her hand, he'd even licked her fingers. He could have died like the baron, writhing in agony, his head destined for a spike above the portcullis. Backing away, Danly turned and fled, running as if all the hounds of hell gave chase.

Later, much later, he staggered to a stop. Bent over, hands on his knees, he gasped for breath. His heartbeat slowed and he took stock of his surroundings. Sounds came to him first, screams and cries and laughter, coming from every direction, the ruthless clamor of conquest. He stood in a narrow lane, houses and shops made of stone. It could have been an alley in the poorer quarter of Pellanor, until he saw the bodies. Two women flung aside, their heads twisted at unnatural angles, their skirts pushed high around their waists, *rape and murder*. Danly backed away.

Laughter came from behind, cruel and menacing.

Danly whirled, his hands balled into fists.

Two Black Flames stood leaning on their halberds, ugly sneers on their faces. "Lost, prince?"

Danly ignored their gibe. At least they knew his rank. Straightening his doublet, he marched passed them, leaving the ally and walking straight into hell.

Chaos claimed the city. Soldiers in red flooded the streets, looting houses and shops, claiming the spoils of war. Doors were battered and broken, the inhabitants dragged into streets and slaughtered. Screams and laughter riddled the air, terror and cruelty locked in counterpoint. A pair of soldiers fought over a massive silver platter, while three more took turns raping a woman. A soldier staggered down the street holding a small wine cask aloft, spilling more than he drank. A cedar chest crashed from a second story window, breaking open against the cobblestones, spewing silken finery. Petticoats and dresses littered the street, trampled beneath the boots of conquerors. Excess was everywhere, and so was death. Danly lurched to the left, avoiding a puddle of blood. Bodies lay piled in heaps, rivulets of blood in the cobbles. A few corpses wore soldiers' surcoats but most were townsfolk, old men and women and children, dead eyes staring as he walked past, food for crows.

Danly walked like a man in a trance. He'd seen murder and rape, but never on this scale. The waste appalled him. Why conquer a city and then reduce it to hell? He staggered through the streets, shocked by the brutality.

A pair of drunken soldiers drew their swords. "Well, well, what do we have here? A lordling, ripe for the plucking."

Danly froze, nothing but a fancy table knife at his belt.

"Let's strip him naked and bend him over a cask."

Danly retreated a step. "No, I'm on your side."

The bearded soldier sneered. "Sure you are...all dressed in emerald finery like a lord of Lingard."

Danly stared down at his clothes, shocked to realize he wore nothing but emerald. "No, you don't understand."

One of the soldiers sneered. "Turn your pockets out, let's see what you have."

"Not this one." Two Black Flames appeared at Danly's back, halberds held at the ready. "He's under the protection of Lord Raven."

The drunks backed away, a shadow of fear on their faces. "How was we to know?" They turned and fled, disappearing into a side street.

Danly sagged in relief.

One of his minders gave him a sideways glance. "You'd best return to the keep, *lord prince*."

Courteous words but their tone was full of loathing. Danly gathered the shreds of his dignity. "Lead the way." Setting his face in a mask of stone, he followed his minders. With the Black Flames as guards, he walked unhindered through the chaos, his soul absorbing the sights. Soldiers caroused like beasts, indulging every desire. Half-naked women screamed as they ran from drunken mobs. Overturned carts and broken casks littered the streets, the detritus of pillage. So this was the pinnacle of war, the rape and sack of a once-great city. Danly drank it all in, both appalled and captivated by the spectacle. His voyeuristic side reveled in the visual orgy while the waste and the danger repulsed his sense of survival. He shuddered, realizing he preferred peace. He'd thought Pellanor was boring, but he yearned for the days when he took his pleasures in the best bordellos. War was too wasteful and far too dangerous.

"Make way! Make way for the sinners!"

Soldiers scattered, clearing a path.

A procession of red-robed priests strode through the street, incense burners releasing clouds of sickly sweet smoke. A mitered bishop carried a golden brazier aloft. Red-robed acolytes walked on either side, carrying flaming torches.

Danly and his guards moved to the side.

Carts rumbled behind the phalanx of priests, and in the carts stood people, jammed together like cattle, young and old, men and women, their hands bound, their faces full of fear.

"Make way for the sinners!"

A few captives stared at Danly, recognition lighting their faces.

"The *prince!*"

Danly staggered as if slapped.

Bound hands reached toward him, desperate faces flickering with hope. *"Prince Danly! Save us!"* Other captives took up the cry. *"Spare us from the flames! The Prince will save us!"*

Danly watched in horror. The same townsfolk who'd cheered him yesterday were bound for the flames. He'd enjoyed their cheers...but now this. There was nothing he could do. It wasn't his fault. If they wanted to live they need only convert. He'd done it himself, a few mumbled vows to save his own life, a cheap enough price. After all, what did the gods matter? One god was as good as another. No, it wasn't his fault, but he didn't want to watch. He turned away. "Not this way."

A hand clamped his shoulder, strong as steel. "Stay." The bigger of the two guards leaned close, his breath a foul stink of garlic. "You're their prince, you should watch."

Danly wanted to strike the brute but force was never his forte. His instinct for survival won out. Shackled by the guard's grip, he turned to watch the procession, enduring the entreaties of the damned.

"Help us, my Prince!"

"Spare us!"

"Mercy!"

Cries for help dwindled as more carts rolled past and Danly did nothing. Hope died, fading to despair, but in some, it sparked outrage, their glares full of accusation. Their stares burned him. One captive leaned forward, arcing a wad of spittle in his direction.

"Traitor!"

"You betrayed us!"

Their taunts hurt. The truth stung like nettles on his soul. Danly tried to pull away, but the guard held him fast, an iron grip biting into his shoulder. The last cart rumbled past and Danly sagged in relief. "I've seen enough."

The guard prodded him. "Follow."

Danly stood his ground. "No. You're my escort. Take me to the keep."

The Black Flame shoved him hard. "Follow."

Danly staggered forward, barely keeping his balance. Flushed with rage, he turned to argue, but his protest died in his throat. Both guards glared at him with fanatics' eyes. Eyes of evil, eyes tinged with madness, their malevolent stares stunned him, erasing all doubt. If he argued they'd kill him, or worse, throw him in the carts to burn with the townsfolk. Danly followed the procession.

A crowd thronged behind the carts. Mostly soldiers but a few citizens as well, converts wearing the brand of conversion.

"Burn the sinners! Cleanse the infidels!"

The converts screamed the loudest, as if they had something to prove.

The procession spilled into a large square, a mountain of kindling heaped in the center. Bishop Taniff and his priests stood in a crescent around the pyre. Clouds of incense billowed around them like a holy haze. Captives cried and begged as soldiers hauled them from the carts, prodding them up the wooden mountain.

Danly knew what was coming, such a gruesome way to die. He'd seen soldiers sacrificed in the army camp, but nothing like this, never so many, and never people he'd betrayed. Sickened by the spectacle, he tried sidling away, but the Black Flame gripped his shoulder. "Stand in front."

Herded by the burly guard, Danly forced his way forward, till he stood at the foot of the pyre. Close enough to see the captives' faces, men and women who'd welcomed him the day before. And then it hit him; this was his doing, his doom.

The priests finished their prayers. The bishop's voice boomed through the square. "For the last time, I give you the chance to repent, to drop to your knees and beg for the brand of conversion. Accept the Flame God or die for your sins!"

Even now the captives hesitated. Danly wanted to scream at them, to tell them to take the brand, but he was afraid to call attention to himself.

A few relented. Mostly women, their faces streaked with tears, they staggered down the pyre to kneel before the bishop. Soldiers took them away.

Bishop Taniff gestured to his acolytes. "Burn the infidels!" Torches touched wood, causing the kindling to erupt in flames. Danly closed his eyes tight, refusing to watch, but he could not block out the hideous screams, or the roaring heat. Screams and shrieks beat against him, growing more intense, a nightmare clawing at his mind. A terrible burnt smell roiled through the square. Danly coughed on the stench. A single piercing scream and then a grim silence prevailed, a shocking stillness. Danly opened his eyes.

A gruesome black cloud belched from the pyre, a signal of death.

The crowd roared in jubilation.

Danly stared at the people cavorting in the street. Evil danced around him, a primal force pounding against him. Gripped in ecstasy, the crowd howled like monsters. Danly shuddered; he'd never witnessed anything so consuming, so primal, yet somehow he stood apart. Understanding struck like a hammer blow. This was the evil that sought to supplant his mother's rule, an evil that would scorch Lanverness to cinders, destroying his pampered world. *An evil he'd made his ally.*

Smoke shifted, drenching him in the stench of burnt flesh.

Danly ran and no one cared. Through cobbled streets and back alleyways, he ran till his side hurt and his lungs ached, and then he collapsed, the stench of burnt flesh clinging to his clothes. Vomit roared out of him. He emptied himself over and over again, till there was nothing left, yet in his mind the faces of the dead stared back at him. Betrayer and betrayed, both condemned to hell. A sob escaped him, for everything he'd done, for everything he'd lost. He sagged onto the cobblestones, beaten by guilt.

"There you are." The Lord Raven strode toward him, a dozen guards at his back. "We searched the city for you. It wouldn't do to lose our prince." Steffan made a curt gesture. "Bring him."

Hands grabbed Danly, lifting him to his feet. They carried him between them, like an empty sack, a hollow prince, a mockery of a man. His feet dragged on the ground, bumping against the cobbles, but that did not stop them. They dragged him back to the keep, dragged him back to serve evil, but this time he'd find a way to resist.

39

Jordan

A cold morning mist swirled across the land, as if they rode through a veil. Jordan glimpsed it from a distance, a broken tower, the color of dried blood, rearing above an old growth forest. She stared, needing to be sure, but the silhouette did not match her visions. Doubt gnawed at her, but she kept her worries to herself.

Thaddeus led them into a gully, the horses splashing through a shallow stream. Six swordsmen, a warrior-princess, and three monks, they kept their weapons close, peering through the mist. Despite the dawn, they kept riding, following the stream to the northwest. The woods thinned and they found themselves on the edge of farmland. Fallow fields stretched in every direction, offering little cover. Like a greensward, the fields surrounded a single hilltop crowned with an old growth forest, and atop that hill loomed a red-stoned keep. Thaddeus pulled his horse to a halt and turned towards her. "Is this the tower of your dreams?"

Jordan stared across the farmland, her gaze fixed on the tower. The angle was different. And they were closer. She shivered at the sight. Like a blunt fist, the broken tower reared above the winter-naked forest, defying time and the gods. "Yes."

"The Crimson Tower," he gave her a knowing look, "the past has a way of reaching into the present."

"What do you mean?'

"These ruins are old, very old. The Crimson Tower was once a stronghold of the Star Knights."

The Star Knights, the words shivered against her like a destiny. "Then my dreams must be true."

"We'll see." His gaze turned to the others. "We'll cross the farmland, riding hard for the keep. The peasants say the tower is haunted, so it should make a safe haven from prying eyes." He put spurs to his mount. Jordan and the others urged their horses to follow.

They galloped through the thinning mist, crossing the farmland to enter the forest skirting the tower. Oak and maple and hawthorn, the trees crowded close, their trunks' thicker than a horse's girth, as if the forest had never felt a woodsman's axe. So tangled the branches, they dismounted, leading their horses through the thicket. An owl hooted in the depths, an eerie sound.

Thaddeus found a deer track and they followed it toward the hilltop. Jordan caught glimpses of the tower through the naked branches. Broken by war and time, the tower reared above the forest like a blunt finger accusing the gods. *Just like my dreams*, a shiver of recognition passed down her spine. She quickened her pace, keen for a better look.

Blood-red stones littered the forest floor, as if a giant had sundered the tower. They wove a path between the massive blocks, moss growing on their sides, reeking of age. Jordan could almost hear the clang of a ghostly battle, little wonder the peasants named the forest haunted.

Thad led them onto a weathered trail that spiraled up the hill. Cresting the hill, they entered the tumbled walls surrounding the broken tower. The others fanned out to explore, but Thaddeus stayed by her side. Jordan secured her horse to a fallen log, intent on the tower. Running her hand along the blood-red stones, she made her way to the heart of the ancient keep. A brace of birds whirled aloft, nothing but open sky and ruined stones, a hollow shell, yet a hint of majesty lingered, a grand whisper of another era.

"Look here." Thad pointed to a keystone set high above an archway, an ancient emblem chiseled in stone.

"The eight-pointed star." Jordan crossed to stand beneath the symbol. Balancing on a fallen block, she reached up, her fingertips brushing the carving, half expecting another vision. She held her breath, but the moment passed, nothing but weathered stone beneath her touch.

Thad said, "It's as if the Star Knights still keep watch over Erdhe."

"So you feel it too?"

"The Zward serves the Grand Master, but in truth we feel more kinship to the Knights." He turned away, as if he'd said too much, making his way through the tumbled stones.

Jordan followed, searching for other hints of the past. The thick walls and massive stones instilled an abiding sense of strength. She shivered, wondering at the power required to sunder the ancient keep.

One of the Zward approached, hailing Thaddeus. "We found something you might want to see."

Intrigued, Jordan followed Thaddeus and Benjin out of the ruins to a narrow pathway that spiraled down the far side of the hill. A cave burrowed into the hillside, the mouth wide enough for five horses. Ellis emerged, holding a burning branch aloft. "It's not what you think." She scraped moss from the cave wall, revealing red stone beneath. "The ancients hollowed the hill to build a stable, big enough to hold a hundred horses."

Thaddeus turned to Benjin, "Is this what you called me to see?"

"No, come." The stocky swordsman led them through the opening.

The air proved dank and musty, the torch casting an island of light in the dark. "Watch your step." Refuse littered the hard-packed dirt floor. Broken crockery, a thrown horseshoe, a musty bedroll, an abandoned kettle, a moldering pile of leaves, the remnants of past occupants strewn across the floor, proof that others used the cave despite the ghost stories.

A rustling noise came from overhead.

Jordan flinched, reaching for her sword.

Ellis raised the torch. "Bats." Small bats clung to the vaulted ceiling, a writhing mosaic of brown fur and leathery wings. "It's better in the back."

A hole in the far corner admitted a shaft of sunlight and a breath of fresh air. Light pooled on the floor, illuminating a circle of stones awash with spent ashes. Benjin knelt by the blackened fire pit. Unsheathing a dagger, he stirred the ashes, revealing a red glow. "Still warm."

Thaddeus swore. "How many?"

Benjin gestured towards the far side of the stables. "Plenty of fresh horse dung over there. Fresh but not warm, so I'm guessing they left yesterday. As to how many," he shrugged, "Twenty or more."

Thaddeus scowled. "Deserters."

"Or brigands"

"Or solders of the Flame, either way the odds aren't good." Thaddeus turned his stare towards Jordan. "You're certain this is the tower of your dreams?"

"Yes."

His hand tightened on his sword hilt. "Then we stay, but we keep close watch and we prepare for a fight." He glanced around the cavern. "We'll make camp here and picket the horses near the entrance. And we'll take turns keeping watch from the broken tower."

Jordan said. "I'll take first watch." She left them to set up camp. Making her way out of the stables, she climbed the hill to the broken tower. Tumbled stones formed a giant's staircase against the northern wall. The morning light burnished the stones to a crimson glow, like something out of myth or legend. She climbed to the top, gaining a view above the barren treetops. Her gaze swept the countryside, an island of forest surrounded by a sea of fallow farmland, a testament to the power of superstition.

A chill wind snatched at her short blonde hair, a breath of winter at her back. Jordan pulled her checkered cloak close and sat perched atop the cold stones, staring out across the treetops.

Footsteps came from behind. Thad climbed the fallen blocks, taking a seat by her side. "A good view of the countryside," he gestured to the ruined keep. "The tower is broken but still defensible. The ancients built well."

A flock of crows cawed as they winged above the forest, throwing a shadow across the land.

"Too many crows."

Thaddeus nodded. "They've come to feast on a kingdom."

"But we can't let them."

"No, we can't." He gave her a measured look, but he did not push. He was good like that, still waters beneath leather armor. They sat in companionable silence, keeping watch over the forest. Thad twirled the ring on the smallest finger of his right hand. All his men wore them, a simple silver signet inscribed with a fist holding a rampant sword.

"I've noticed your ring."

He covered it self-consciously. "A vain conceit."

"No, it means something. All your men wear them."

He hesitated, but then he answered. "The symbol of the Zward, sons of monks who find other ways to serve. We choose the sword over the scroll."

"Are there many of you?"

"Never enough."

She knew better than to pry, the Order held its secrets close.

"So lass, what will you have of us?"

She sighed, feeling the weight of decision fall on her shoulders. "Wait, watch, be ready."

He chuckled, "Sounds like the Order," yet he stared at her, waiting for something more.

Jordan shook her head. "It's all I know. I've obeyed the vision. We've reached the red tower before the first snowfall. We're in the hands of the gods."

"A tenuous position." Thaddeus stood. "We'll keep watch, and we'll be ready." He stepped onto the lower stone. "Yarl will soon have the quails roasting. I'll send Rafe up with your share."

"Thanks." She gave him a wane smile.

He took his leave, making his way down the giant stairway.

Wrapped in her checkered cloak, Jordan sat still as stone, staring out over the forest. So much depended on her visions. "Wait, watch, and be ready"...*and pray I haven't made a mistake.*

40

Liandra

Liandra abhorred weakness, yet for the sake of the child she remained abed. The confinement chaffed at her, but her healers had been adamant. *Rest in bed or risk the child,* her hands laced protectively across the growing swell. Liandra sighed, wanting this child so badly, and desperately needing another heir, but work beckoned. Queens could not afford to appear frail lest the wolves circle, but she took the healer's advice and endured the pampering of her women. Propped with a mountain of pillows, an ermine shawl draped around her shoulders, Liandra held court from her bed. "We will see him now."

They ushered the petitioner in. A slight man with pale white hair, he wore the clothes of a merchant, a velvet doublet and a thick wool cloak of autumn russet. "Majesty, thank you for seeing me." He made a courtly bow. "Master Numar at your service."

"They tell me you were quite persistent." Sir Durnheart and Master Raddock hovered close behind the merchant, vigilant as shadows. "A matter of great urgency, they said."

"Yes," he paused as if considering his words. "My associates grew concerned when Master Fintan did not make his appointment."

So he comes about the monk.

He took a step toward her, his voice dropping to a whisper. "May I speak in private?"

"You may speak plainly."

An annoyed look flashed across his face, his voice blunt with warning. "Treachery stalks your court. Master Fintan was not without resources."

Resources, an interesting choice of words. "Whom do you represent?"

"I come on behalf of the Kiralynn Order."

Another monk. "Yet you are a merchant within our capital city? An apothecary by trade?"

He gave her a half smile. "It is said that you are a queen who appreciates the value of knowledge."

"Knowledge yes, but spies are another matter." She'd always envied the monk's web of spies.

"A debate rages within our Order. Some argue for openness while others say the time has not yet come. With the death of Master Fintan you understand why I am reluctant to wear the blue."

"Yet you come anyway."

"The Light must be served."

"And your purpose?"

"A pair of wagons has reached your city. They bear a gift from the Grand Master."

Beware monks bearing gifts. "A gift?"

"A weapon from ancient times, ninety-two flasks of Napthos, a fire potion that burns with the heat of hell. Nothing will quench it. Legends say it will even burn on water. Unstoppable, it burns until it consumes itself, destroying everything it touches, eating flesh and bone, even cracking stone. It is a fearsome weapon, not to be used lightly."

A weapon, so the monks brought her hope. "And how is this weapon used?"

He removed a scroll from his belt pouch, handing it to her.

She fingered the scroll, a shiver of recognition running through her. The wax seal bore the signet of the Grand Master. "What is this?"

"Knowledge, a way to use the Napthos."

She broke the seal and found detailed drawings inside. It looked like a giant crossbow mounted on a wagon bed.

"It is called a scorpion, another weapon from ancient times. It can hurl a steel bolt twice the distance of the best catapult. With slight modifications it will hurl clay flasks of Napthos, raining hellfire on your enemies."

"Hellfire?" She gave the monk a shrewd smile. "A fitting end to the Army of the Flame."

"Just so." He nodded. "But be warned, there is only enough for one battle. One chance to turn the tide of war."

"You cannot make more?"

"The recipe is lost to us."

So the monks have their limits. "Yet you give us this weapon, to use as we see fit?"

"To strike a blow against the Dark."

"Yet your Order hides in the shadows?"

He gave her a knowing look. "You are a queen who understands the value of shadows."

"Just so." She felt an accord with the monks, a blaze of intellect driven by purpose and protected by subterfuge. "We thank the Grand Master for his most generous gift." Her voice dropped a notch. "And we deeply regret the death of Master Fintan."

"Be warned, Darkness stalks your court."

It was a warning she knew all too well. "Shall we see you again?"

He gave her a wry smile. "I trust your shadowmen will know how find me." He sobered. "But send only your best men, for Darkness hunts us as well.

In the meantime, we will watch and we will do what we can." He gave her a courtly bow, a swirl of russet, and then he left.

Her glance shot towards Master Raddock. "Have him followed, discretely. Send your best men, this is an ally we cannot afford to lose."

"As you wish." The master turned to leave, Sir Durnheart on his heels.

The queen sat abed, fingering the scroll. Such an impressive gift, a chance to turn the tide of battle, but only if she chose the right moment. She weighed the scroll, wondering what other secrets the monks held, what power they might wield if their Order ever came out of the shadows. But that thought was for another day. Liandra caressed the swell of her unborn child. She'd gained an ally and a powerful weapon. For the first time in a long time, Liandra felt hope, a slender chance to defeat the Flame and preserve her kingdom.

41

Steffan

"Your ruse worked, Counselor." The general poured himself a goblet of ale.

Ale in a silver goblet, always the barbarian, Steffan stifled a grimace. "Lingard fell with nary a fight, proving deceit is stronger than swords."

The general stabbed a hunk of roast duck, eating it from his dagger, grease staining his beard. "You need both, Counselor. Deceit won't work without swords to back it up."

"Then it's good I have both."

A grunt was the only reply.

Steffan tasted a puffed pastry filled with sticky apricots. "You've posted guards on the food supplies?"

"The granaries are full, the larders overflowing, and the wine cellars well stocked. Lingard is full to bursting with women, loot, and a fat harvest." The general grinned past a mouthful of duck. "We've gained enough supplies to feast our army all the way to Pellanor."

"But first we secure Lingard."

"Aye," the general refilled his goblet. "You best keep an eye on the Bloody Bishop. Those damn pyres of his burn day and night. Makes the converts nervous."

"The bishop is another matter. The Flame God must have his due."

A knock sounded on the door. Before Steffan could reply the Priestess burst into the chamber, three Black Flames in tow.

"You need to see this." She crossed to the table, luscious curves sheathed in a shimmering gown of dark purple. He might have been distracted were it not for the warning in her voice. "What is it?"

She gestured and one of the Black Flames set a sheathed sword upon the table.

The sword looked ordinary enough, the hilt wrapped in black leather. "So?"

She flashed a triumphant smile. "Unsheathe the blade."

The general reached for the sword, but Steffan felt the need claim it first. Quickness beat brute strength. Steffan snatched the sword and tugged on the hilt.

The general gasped, "*Blue steel!*"

The sapphire blade gleamed beautiful in the candlelight but Steffan guessed there was more to the sword. Unwrapping the black leather binding, he revealed the hilt. The details were breathtaking, roses crossed on the hilt, a crown on the pommel, and etched in the blade, he read the name aloud. "The Thorn of Roses." Steffan held the blade aloft, shimmering lethal in the candlelight.

The general stared like a love-struck swain "A hero's blue blade. A fitting sword to lead our army to victory."

Steffan flashed a sly grin. "You think too small, general." He set the sword onto the table, a flash of sapphire blue across the oak grain. "It's not just a blue steel sword. It's victory." He snapped an order to Pip. "Bring the prince." His gaze turned to the Priestess. "How?"

She gestured to one of the Black Flames, a big hulking sergeant with a fresh scar on his face. The soldier stood hunched, as if trying to hide.

Steffan drilled him with his stare. "How?"

The other soldiers stepped back, opening a space around their comrade, like a gaping chasm to hell. "It was only booty, plunder taken from a prisoner. We always loot the prisoners..."

Steffan cut him off. "Where's the prince that goes with this sword?"

The soldier looked befuddled. "*Prince, lord?*"

"*Fool!*" Steffan erupted in anger. "Does an ordinary soldier wield a blue steel sword? And why wasn't this brought to my attention? Did you think to keep it for yourself?"

The Black Flame cringed. "No, my lord, I didn't think."

"Start thinking or you'll lose more than your useless head." Steffan swept the blue sword from the table. The Black Flame flinched backward, but Steffan only used the sword as a pointer, punctuating each word. "I want the prince found. Dead or alive, I want him brought to me. And I'll have his signet ring, and anything else of value. Bring me the prince or I'll slice you to bits, starting with your manhood."

The Black Flame fled, the door banging behind him.

Steffan glared at the other two. "And if the rest of you know anything about the crown prince, I'll hear it now."

Neither man answered.

"Does the prince still live?"

Their silence echoed through the chamber like a grim rebuke.

Pip opened the door, ushering Danly into the room.

"Prince Danly," Steffan lifted the sword. "Is this your brother's sword?"

Danly stared wide-eyed, drawn toward the blade. "The queen commissioned three blue steel blades...but I never saw them." His gaze fixed on the hilt. "Crossed roses and a crown...it must be my brother's." His voice caught, a shrewd gleam in his gaze. "But how did you get it? Is Stewart captured...or killed?"

Steffan grinned like a cat tasting cream. "The how is not as important as the having."

General Caylib leered at the sword. "A blue steel sword should be wielded by a warrior worthy of the blade."

"Like you, my general?"

The general stood his ground. "Every soldier dreams of a blue steel blade. Wondrous and rare, lighter than steel, the blade forever sharp, a legendary sword forged for the best warriors."

"Why general, you sound like a bard."

"Blue steel is meant to be wielded in war."

"And it will be. But you think too small." Steffan shared a knowing glance with the Priestess. "You understand, don't you my dear?"

"Of course," her voice purred with delight, "with one blow, this sword will claim a kingdom."

"Exactly," Steffan hefted the blade, marveling at its feel. "Why risk an army when a single sword can wield the fatal blow? I want a troop of heralds outfitted with the fastest horses. I'll have this sword delivered to the Spider Queen."

A nasty hiss came from the general. "You'll give it back to the enemy?"

"I'll strike a heart-wound at the queen, sending a message that I've captured both her heirs. If the message does not kill her outright, then it will surely bring her to her knees, after all, she's merely a woman, with all the foibles of a mother." Steffan grinned. "With a single sword thrust, I'll gain a kingdom. Worth the cost of one blue blade, wouldn't you say, general?"

The general scowled. "I like it not. You give advantage to the enemy."

Steffan snorted. "I see advantages and I *multiply* them. A pity my councilors are so blind."

The general glowered.

"Don't you see the beauty of it? Once we take Pellanor, the sword will be plunder once more."

A grin spread across the general's face. "And then I'll wield it."

Steffan did not answer. "Go and assemble the heralds. I want them dispatched at once."

The general sheathed his table dagger. "As you wish."

The others turned to follow.

"Not you, my prince. I need your help crafting a message to the queen, something aimed at her heart, something from both her sons."

Danly took a seat at the table. "The Spider Queen doesn't have a heart."

"Nevertheless, we must find it."

Pip approached with a quill and parchment, setting them before the prince.

Danly took up the quill, a sly look on his face. "With Stewart dead, I'll be the sole heir of Lanverness."

"A crown prince sitting at my table," Steffan grinned, "it seems the dice always roll in my favor." Victory was so close he could taste it.

42

Jordan

Jordan found herself returning to the broken tower, drawn by the past as much as the view. Sunset brought out the color, the stones glowing a burnished red in the fading light. She passed beneath the archway, wondering what tales the tower could tell. Murky shadows and gleaming legends surrounded the history of the Star Knights, a patchwork past, difficult to tell the truth from a bard's fancy tales, yet she yearned to know. Her hand trailed across the red stones, feeling a strange kinship with the ruins. An owl hooted in the forest, announcing the onset of twilight. She climbed the giant staircase and found Rafe keeping lookout on the topmost stone.

"What do you see?"

"A land riven by war." He pointed west across the treetops. "No smoke rises from the nearest farmhouse, yet this is the time of day when families should be gathered around the hearth for supper." He pointed toward the gloom on the northern horizon. "While in the north, whole villages burn, scorching the sky with smoke." Rafe scowled. "Smoke's become a signal for war instead of hearth and home."

She sat cross-legged beside him, pulling her checkered cloak close. "I've never seen war before."

"Nor have I, but the histories are full of them."

She gripped her sword hilt, the words whispering out of her. "The Battle Immortal."

"What?"

"My father always says that life is a battle immortal, an eternal struggle between Light and Dark."

"And now it's our turn to fight?"

Jordan nodded. "Just so."

"At least you chose a good place to camp, as if the past keeps watch."

She stared at him, *so you feel it too,* but she did not say the words. "I'll take the first watch if you like."

"No need."

"What?"

"Once darkness falls, Ellis will seal the woods to intruders."

"Seal the woods, how?"

"Magic of course." He gave her a knowing smile. "You'll see tonight, Ellis is a moon weaver."

Magic, the word shivered down her spine, she'd gained such strange allies. "Why tonight?"

"Our first night with a defensible position. Magic is never used lightly. There's always a price."

She chewed on his words, another layer of mystery. The monks were cloaked in riddles. Jordan wondered if Rafe carried a magic of his own.

"What's that?" Rafe stood, pointing toward the northwest.

Jordan squinted into the gathering dusk. "Riders, two sets, a mob of twenty chasing three." Her heartbeat thundered, wondering if this was the reason the gods had brought her here.

Rafe put his fingers to his lips, whistling a trill of notes, a signal to the others.

Jordan watched the riders, straining to make out their colors, but twilight was tricky, bathing the land in a dusky lavender and the figures were still leagues away. "I can't tell their colors."

"If they keep to a straight heading, they'll ride just west of the forest's edge. Should we intervene, or stay hidden?"

The mob was gaining on the three, like watching hounds chase a desperate fox. Jordan gripped her sword hilt, praying the fox escaped.

Footsteps came from behind, scrambling up the giant stairway. Ellis, Yarl and Thaddeus, joined them on the top step. "What comes?"

Rafe pointed. "Riders nearing the western edge of the wood, twenty chasing three."

Thad turned his stare to Jordan. "Is this why we've come? Are we meant to intervene?"

Jordan shook her head, riddled with doubt. "I don't know."

"Yours to decide."

Questions beat against her. The odds were bad, twenty against their hidden ten, but what if this was the reason the gods had led her to the tower? She watched the dark streaks race across the fallow farmland, the hounds gaining on the fox. "It feels wrong to just watch."

"Then we act." Thaddeus took over, not a hint of doubt in his voice. "I'll take Donal, Benjin and Marcus out into the fields. The two archers can bleed the pack, getting their attention. We'll draw them into the woods. The rest of you wait in ambush." He turned to Ellis, "I'll need you to set a weaving. We dare let no one escape."

Ellis nodded. "None will leave the wood."

"What about me?"

Thad shot Jordan a stare. "Stay with Rafe, we'll need your sword for the ambush." And then he was gone, leaping down the staircase. They rushed to follow, scrambling down the hillside to the cavernous stables. The others waited at the mouth, a dozen horses already saddled. Thaddeus issued orders, "Benjin, Donal and Marcus, to me!" They swung into their saddles. Setting spurs to mounts, they galloped down into the forest.

Ellis mounted a dark gelding. "Set your ambush halfway between the tower and the forest's edge." And then she was gone, riding into the falling darkness.

"Come on." Rafe gripped his quarterstaff, leading the others into the woods. Jordan followed, her heart hammering. Leaves crunched beneath their boots, the last streaks of purple fading from the twilight sky. Night fell like a cloak. Darkness made the footing treacherous, a tangle of roots weaving the forest floor. Jordan scrambled over a fallen tree, avoiding a clump of brambles. She gripped her sword, straining to keep quiet, straining to hear the enemy. Every sound seemed sinister, a host of threats lurking in the dark.

"This should be far enough." Rafe whispered orders. "Spread out and set your ambush. Remember, the enemy will be mounted, best to fall on them from above."

The others melted into the darkness, their brown cloaks blending with the naked trees. Jordan scanned the woods, seeking an advantage. Sheathing her sword, she shimmied up a gnarled oak, finding a perch between a thick branch and the main trunk. Crouched in the wedge, she unsheathed her sword. Movement caught her gaze, a gleam of light behind her. A gasp escaped her. Straining to see, she nearly lost her perch. A pale ball of light shimmered though the forest, like a ghost riding through the woods. The spectral glow trailed a thin stream of light and then disappeared. Jordan stared, wondering if the forest was truly haunted.

Sounds came her way, the jangle of steel, the clop of hooves. She tightened her grip on her sword, all of her senses alert. Horses bulled through the thicket, men shouting in the darkness. "Where'd they go?"

"After them!"

"Watch out!"

Jordan gripped her sword, straining to catch a hint of color. Arrows twanged through the forest. A man screamed in pain, the sound of battle creeping closer. Jordan tensed, her heart thundering, knowing she'd never slain an enemy.

A horseman broke through the brush, too far from her tree.

She tensed, waiting, erupting in sweat despite the cold.

Moonlight broke through the clouds, casting a confusion of shadows.

Another horsemen approached, closer to her perch. A glimmer of moonlight revealed a red tabard. *An enemy within reach;* fear and exhilaration thrummed through her. The horseman looked left and right but he never looked up. Jordan leaped, bringing her sword down in a two-handed strike. Her blade of Castlegard steel bit deep. She cleaved the enemy's shoulder, putting all of her weight behind the blow. He screamed, twisting away, but his fate was already sealed, blood spurting from a fatal wound. Her sword had struck true, but she made an awkward landing, falling sideways off the horse's rump. The enemy fell with her, a dead weight impaled on her sword. The horse bucked in fear, ironshod hooves slashing overhead. Twisting away, Jordan wrenched her sword loose and slipped back into the tangled forest. *My first kill,* the words thundered through her mind, igniting a spark of elation. Strength rushed through her, a gift from Valin. A blooded-warrior, Jordan gripped her sword, hunting another foe.

Clouds hid the moon and darkness triumphed, making the tangled forest both terrifying and thrilling. Jordan stretched her senses, trying to be stealthy, but her heartbeat hammered, her breath blowing plumes of mist in the cold. The sounds of battle echoed through the woods, screaming men, clanging swords, snorting horses, a dance of death in every direction.

Moonlight glimmered on steel.

A mounted enemy reared out of the darkness. Jordan whirled to find a halberd keening towards her neck. She threw herself sideways, rolling to evade the blade. Gripping her sword, she sprang to her feet, dancing behind a massive oak.

A man's voice said, "Run him through, Garred, while I flush him from behind."

Two of them, one in front and one behind, Jordan circled the oak, desperate for protection.

The horseman was good, holding his mount to a tight turn, the fearsome halberd whistling toward her. A half-moon blade with the reach of a spear, she'd never fought such a ferocious weapon. Jordan ducked low, evading the blow and then attacked, stepping inside the halberd's reach. But the enemy was wily, hitting her with the butt of his weapon.

Pain exploded across her face, the taste of blood in her mouth. She fell hard, barely hanging onto her sword.

Hoof beats drummed from behind, the sound of death approaching.

Fear gave her strength. She gripped her sword and surged beneath the legs of the nearest horse, coming up on the far side of the halberd. With all her strength, she swung her sword at the enemy's knee. The blade bit deep, a spray of hot blood across her face. The enemy screamed and the horse reared.

Jordan used the confusion to flee, running into the forest. Naked branches grabbed at her hair, thorns plucking at her cloak. Something struck her in the side, *only a branch,* but she fell hard. Winded, she tried to gain control of her breathing, desperate to listen. The sounds of battle persisted, but nothing near.

Shaking, she wiped the blood from her face. Her nose was broken. She yanked hard, setting it straight, stifling a scream. When the pain receded, she gripped her sword and rose to her feet, running through the trees, uncertain if she was prey or predator. Clouds shrouded the moon, deepening the night to a dense black. Jordan lost all sense of direction, unsure if she was moving towards safety or battle. Screams echoed through the wood, followed by the clang of steel, the confusion of sounds making every shadow a threat. She stumbled over a log and fell, but the log turned out to be flesh, a body sticky with blood. Jordan shuddered and kept moving. A snap of twigs gave warning; she froze, peering into the darkness. A figure lurked ahead, this one unhorsed, his back toward her. Moonlight cracked through the clouds, revealing the color red. *Another enemy,* Jordan crept forward, her breath sounding loud in her ears.

A rustle of leaves betrayed her.

The enemy whirled, a sword slicing through the moonlight. She parried the blade with a resounding clang. Stroke and parry, she met his attack, but he drove her backwards, grunting with each stroke. "Who are you?" She risked an overhand stroke, but her sword caught on a branch. *It caught on a branch!* The enemy grinned, aiming a thrust at her heart. Jordan twisted sideways, yanking on her sword. Desperation lent her strength. Her sword came loose and she dropped to a crouch. Lunging upwards, her sword took him just below the gorget. A gurgled scream marked his death-throes, a spurt of hot blood spraying the night.

A sixth sense warned her to duck.

A halberd whistled where her head should have been.

She scrambled backwards, trying to gain some distance.

The halberd advanced, slicing the air with a whistling death.

Behind the enemy, she spied a ball of glowing moonlight, the same witch-light she'd seen before.

The halberd whispered close, nearly slicing her leathers. Fear shivered through her. Angry at her carelessness, she surged to the attack. Steel clanged against steel, her sword meeting the shaft of the halberd. The strength of the blow shuddered down her arms. Her sword twisted from her grasp. Disarmed, she lurched backwards. Her foot caught on a root. Jordan toppled and fell hard. Weaponless, she stared up at her killer's face.

He sneered, raising the halberd for a deadly strike. "Now you die!"

Witch-light tangled the enemy's legs like a whip. The light pulled tight, toppling him to the ground.

Jordan scrambled out of the way, searching for her sword.

A woman hissed. "Finish him!"

Her hand found the hilt. Jordan gripped her sword, bringing the blade down on the enemy's neck. The blow nearly severed his head. Wrenching her sword free, she staggered backwards, gasping for breath.

"It's over." The words whispered through the woods, and then she realized the sounds of fighting had fallen silent. Relief washed through her. The battle frenzy bled out of her, replaced by exhaustion. Jordan slumped to the ground, grateful to be alive.

A ball of witch-light floated toward her, eerie as a ghost. It gathered strength, glowing like a second moon. The silvery light revealed its source. Ellis held a crystal ball aloft, the unearthly glow illuminating the woods.

"It's you!" Jordan stared, entranced by the light. "I saw you before the battle, but I thought it was a ghost, a haunt from the past."

Ellis gave a strained smile. "Captured moonlight, an ancient magic, nearly forgotten."

Others appeared out of the woods, drawn by the light. Jordan sobered, waiting to learn the fate of her friends. Rafe came first, leaning on his quarterstaff. A nasty gash above his left eye streamed blood, but otherwise he looked whole. "It looks worse than it is." Thaddeus and Benjin came next, leading a string of captured horses. "I sent the others up to the tower."

Ellis nodded. "How many lost?"

"Two. Eric and Jonah are both dead. Harl took a nasty cut to the arm, but he'll live."

Jordan took a deep breath, a heavy loss to save three. "And what of the three we sought to save?"

"Donal took them to the stable."

Jordan nodded, longing to know if Stewart was among them, but she kept her hopes to herself.

Thaddeus turned his stare to Ellis. "Did any escape?

"None." Ellis shook her head. "I sealed the weaving once they passed." She lowered her hand and the glowing ball of light began to fade. Captured moonlight dwindled to a firefly flicker, and then it was gone, snuffed out, nothing but a glass ball the size of her palm. Ellis swayed. Thaddeus crossed the distance and swept her into his arms, cradling her against his chest. For the first time, Jordan wondered if there might be something between them.

Thaddeus said, "Back to the tower," his voice gruff.

Moonlight emerged from the clouds, striping the forest with shadow. They picked their way through the woods. Twice they came across dead bodies, the grisly wages of battle. The smell of death clung to the woods, making life seem all the more precious. Jordan quickened her pace, desperate to know if Stewart waited with the rescued men. She climbed the hill to the tower and found the stables aglow with firelight. Horses crowded the entrance, still saddled, sweat-stained and trembling with fatigue. She pushed through them, anxious to meet the strangers. The others sat slumped around the fire, exhaustion writ in every gesture. She rushed toward them, but then she stopped. All three strangers wore golden surcoats emblazoned with iron fists, *not Stewart*. Her heart plummeted.

One of the strangers looked up, a young knight with a strong jaw and a mop of dark hair. "So you're the one we have to thank." Pale and bloodstained, he looked exhausted, yet he gave her a courtly bow. "I'm Ronald, son of Rognald, erstwhile Baron of Lingard."

"Erstwhile?" Her thoughts seemed shrouded in fog.

"We held the last gate as long as we could." He took a deep breath as if his own words cut like glass. "Lingard has fallen to the Flame. My father is dead, his head on a spike."

The grim news cut through her confusion. "Lingard fallen?" She'd heard of the mighty fortress-city, a great blow against Lanverness. The war fared worse than she thought.

Ronald nodded, his face grave. "We rode to bring the queen the truth."

"What truth?" She stilled, sensing there was more.

His face twisted in hate. "The prince betrayed us. He came with heralds in emerald green, and we opened the gates, welcoming treachery with an open hand."

She gaped with disbelief, but then she remembered. "What prince?"

"Danly, the younger."

"And what of the crown prince?"

"There's been no word for more than a fortnight."

No word, she sank to the ground near the fire, but she did not feel the heat. The gods had led her to the tower for a reason, but in her heart, Jordan had hoped to find Stewart, to save him from the nightmares of her visions. Instead, she'd helped to save three strangers. *Three strangers instead of Stewart*. The gods worked in mysterious ways, but somehow it left her feeling betrayed.

43

Stewart

Hurting and hungry, they made a ragged band, eight men for three horses, but at least they had swords, and cloaks, and desperation as a shield. Stewart led them west, hoping to slip past the fighting and then turn south. Wary of the enemy, he kept the men alert, sending out runners to act as scouts. They scavenged as they rode, but found little to eat. The countryside proved just as ravaged as they were, homesteads burned, fields abandoned, villages empty, everything brown and dull and dead. The cursed Flame had much to answer for.

Timmons returned from scout duty, loping down the ridge. "There's a farmhouse on the other side, unburned, no sign of the enemy."

Hungry stares turned toward Stewart. Hollow-eyed and filthy, they waited on his command. He knew what they wanted, a chance to forage. After their escape, they'd gorged on salted pork and hard bread taken from their captors, only to spew it all up an hour later. Such a waste, but hunger was a fierce goad, nearly as dangerous as enemy swords. Stewart nodded. "Let's see what's there, but stay cautious."

They rode to the ridge top and surveyed the land below. A small farmstead surrounded by fallow fields and stands of naked woods. Nothing moved, not even a crow pecking at the harrowed fields. "Looks like death."

"But there's no sign of the enemy." Owen shared his horse, a big man, riven to skin and bones.

Stewart nodded. "True, but I don't like the look of it, yet we need to eat." He made his decision. "Jasper and Kennith, you two keep watch from the ridge top, and remember to look behind as well as in front. The rest of you with me and keep your swords handy." Stewart clucked to his horse, asking for a slow trot. Emerging from the trees, they rode down the ridge and out across fallow fields, everything still as a graveyard. A winter wind blew, cold and biting, but he caught no scent of rotting corpses. Riding passed the stone well, Stewart pulled to a stop in front of the clapboard house. He slipped from the horse and drew his sword. "Owen to me, the rest of you spread out and see what you can find."

The door gaped open a handbreadth, not a good sign.

Stewart kicked it in, the bang sounding loud in his ears. Pale light filtered into a room strewn with refuse. "Already ransacked."

"By the nine hells." Owen muttered a curse and followed him inside.

Broken crockery littered the hearth, an overturned table in the middle, a straw-stuffed mattress cleaved by a sword; a simple life sundered by war. Owen bulled his way through the mess, searching for anything edible. "Sometimes there's a root cellar."

Stewart righted the table and found a rag doll abandoned on the floor, button eyes and a calico dress, some child's precious companion lost to war. Something about the doll touched him, a piercing sense of loss. He set the doll on the hearth mantle, hoping it might be found by its child, a bit of bright calico against the smoky stone.

"There's nothing here." Owen gave him a hollow-eyed stare.

"Nothing but crushed dreams. Perhaps the others fare better." He sheathed his sword and moved outside, the first signs of twilight streaking the sky. "Timmons, Crocker, anything?"

"Nothing lord, not an ear of corn or a withered apple, but at least there's no corpses."

Stewart surveyed the fields, his stomach rumbling with hunger. "There has to be something. Keep looking." Circling the cottage, he found a small garden plot on the backside, a tangle of brown vines. Amongst the vines were small brown fruits, twice the size of his thumb. Most were withered and others blackened but Stewart was hungry. Plucking a brown one, he popped it in his mouth, and nearly gagged, spitting it out. Nothing but seeds and a soapy, bitter taste.

Owen laughed, tossing him a water skin. "Careful what you eat, you'll be trying worms next!" But Crocker came to look. "What'd you find?" The scout bent to examine the dead vines.

"Don't bother." Stewart spat out the foul taste. "Whatever it is, it's gone bad."

But the scout ignored him, digging with a dagger. "You're not meant to eat the seedpods." His hands delved the dirt. "My father was a farmer, there's a chance some are still left." Crocker kept digging.

"What are you looking for?

The scout grinned, "I thought so! These are potato plants!" He hefted a brown spud aloft like the crown jewels.

"*Potatoes!*" The others came running. Drawing swords, they knelt on the ground, digging for their supper, the prince among them. "Found one!" Some were misshapen, others nothing but nubs. A handful were ruined, blackened by rot, too far gone to eat, but they soon had a mound of sixty, a veritable feast. Stewart cleaned his sword and sheathed it. His men stood in a circle, staring at their trove. Stewart's mouth began to water, his imagination running rampant, "baked potatoes with butter."

Crocker said, "Hash browns fried with bacon."

"Mashed potatoes and gravy."

"Pan fried potatoes."

"Potato pancakes with sour cream."

Owen laughed. "Hell, I'll eat mine raw!"

They all began to laugh, an infectious roar that took them in the bellies and didn't stop till tears glistened from their eyes. As the men sobered, they turned to stare at Stewart. "What will it be, my lord?"

A fire was always risky, but it seemed fortune smiled on them. "It's nearly night." His gaze turned to the scout. "Go get Jasper and Kennith, no sense leaving them on the ridge. The rest of you build a fire in the hearth, we'll dine on baked potatoes tonight!"

A cheer erupted from the men. Smiling, they scattered to do his bidding. Wood was collected and a fire laid in the hearth. While the fire blazed hot, the men debated how to cook their precious find. Without pots or frying pans, they ended up nestling the potatoes amongst the glowing coals. Sitting on the floor in front of the hearth, they kept watch, using a sword as a poker. Stewart righted a chair and sat at the table. It seemed forever since he'd sat at a table, as if all the trappings of civilization had fled, nothing left but war. He shivered, suddenly feeling as if the cottage were a trap.

"Timmons, go spell Percy outside. And keep a sharp watch. We dare not be lulled by the promise of food and a roof."

"Yes, lord." The lanky soldier slipped outside, admitting a breath of cold air.

After countless days on the road, the cottage seemed a haven, snug and warm and dry, full of forgotten comforts. Stewart dozed in the chair, till the tantalizing smell of roast potatoes prodded him awake. "Are they done?"

Owen poked a potato with a sword, a grin splitting his swarthy face. "Yes!"

They ate roasted potatoes speared on daggers. No one spoke, other than a few vague moans of pleasure. Stewart nearly swooned at the taste, the outer skin hard as crackling, the insides soft and white and full of flavor. He gobbled the first; too hungry to slow, but he savored the second. Each man ate two; the others set aside to cool for the morrow. They sprawled in front of the hearth, content from the feast.

The door banged open. *"Riders coming!"*

"Bloody hell!" Stewart leaped from the chair, his sword whispering to his hand. He rushed out into the night, the others at his back. Blinking against the darkness, he crouched for a fight, but it was already too late. Twenty horsemen approached at a gallop, fanning out to surround the farmhouse.

Timmons hissed, *"I'll not be taken again, not again."*

Another voice whispered. "Quiet."

Stewart studied the riders, hoping for emerald surcoats, but fortune was not so kind. The riders were a motley crew. Cloaks of brown and red and green, the tattered scroungings of escaped prisoners, or deserters, or worse still, scavengers come to feed off the leavings of war. Two carried crossbows, cocked and ready, while the others bristled with swords and halberds, their hands near their weapons, a lethal pack of wolves.

"Whose side do you serve?" Stewart tensed, his sword held at the ready.

"Side? Who said anything about sides?" A one-eyed man with a scarred face and red beard nudged his horse a step in front of the others, staking a claim to leadership. A mitered cleric's helm combined with an emerald cloak sent mixed signals. He flashed a nasty grin. "We've come late to the party, boys. Seems this pigeon's already been plucked." Putting his hand on his sword hilt, his voice dripped with menace. "But since we have the numbers, we'll take the prize, food, coin, and swords, the lot of it. Surrender your gleanings and you just might live." He laughed, and his men laughed with him, an ugly twisted sound.

Scavengers, Stewart cursed his ill luck. *Twenty against eight,* the odds were bad, especially without the element of surprise, but staring up at the leader's nasty grin, Stewart knew death would follow surrender. "No need to fight." He relaxed his stance, dropping his sword to his side, hoping to gain a measure of surprise.

"I wasn't talkin' about *fightin',*" the one-eyed leader leered from the saddle, "I was talkin' about *takin'.*"

Stewart shrugged, moving a step toward the brigands. "You'll not find much among us, our true worth's in our sword arms. Let us join you."

"Join us!" The leader barked a rude laugh. "As if we need a bunch of half-starved scarecrows. You can't even feed yourselves."

"My men feasted on baked potatoes tonight, as many as they could eat," Stewart kept moving, slowly sidling toward the nearest crossbow, "can your men say the same?"

"*Potatoes!*" Anger rippled through the brigands, a jangle of armor and snorting horses, a mutter of discontent. "Stop your yammering," the leader growled at his men, his gaze returning to Stewart. "You sound like trouble."

Stewart took another step, hoping his men sensed his drift. "No trouble. We've plenty of potatoes to share." Another step and he was almost within striking distance. "Join forces with us."

"Stop where you are. Clem, Dink, skewer the bugger if he takes another step."

A pair of crossbows aimed his way. Stewart froze, knowing attack would be suicide.

The leader scowled, "You're wasting my time. Surrender or die."

Stewart played his last gambit. "I'll make you a better offer."

"I'm losing patience, scarecrow."

"Your weight in gold."

"My weight in gold!" The leader roared in laughter. "Where are you hiding it, up your ass?"

Stewart yelled to be heard. "Safe conduct for me and my men to the Rose Army and you'll be paid your weight in gold. Better wages than you'll find scavenging farmhouses and burnt villages. You'll never grow rich off the leavings of the Flame."

Their laughter stilled. The leader gave him a squinty stare. "And why will they pay such a ransom for the likes of you?"

Owen protested, "No, my lord! Don't trust them." but Stewart raised a hand, forestalling him. "Because I'm the prince of Lanverness."

The brigands snorted with laughter. "Scarecrow thinks he's the bloody prince of Lanverness!" but the leader kept his one-eyed stare fixed on Stewart. "Prove it."

"Take me to the Rose Army and they'll know me. Take me to the Flame and you'll get nothing but eight corpses."

"A scarecrow prince?" The leader gave him a scathing look.

"It costs you little to learn the truth and the reward is great."

The crossbowman muttered, "It ain't true. Don't trust him."

Another brigand said, "Yeah, but think of all that gold."

"Kill him and be done with it."

Stewart pressed his argument. "Send a messenger to the Rose Army and you'll see how keen they are to find me. They'll meet your price." His gaze roved the brigands, noting the naked greed on their faces. "A fortune in gold for such a small risk. You know the Spider Queen is good for it." Stewart's gaze returned to the one-eyed leader, willing him to agree.

The leader met his stare, cold and calculating.

The waiting seemed to last forever. Stewart could feel his men tense behind him. He gripped his sword, knowing he'd rather die fighting than surrender.

"Alright," the leader gave Stewart a crooked grin, "drop your weapons and we'll send the messenger."

Stewart shook his head, pressing his luck, his heart pounding. "We're in enemy territory. We'll keep our weapons, but we'll keep them sheathed. Any of my men draws sword on one of yours, you're free to kill him."

"Setting terms?"

"Protecting your prize." Stewart waited, locking stares with the one-eyed brigand. "If trouble finds us, you'll need our swords. We stay safe or you get nothing."

The leader scowled. "Alright. Keep your swords, but if any of your men step out of line, your lordship will be payin' the price." He flashed an ugly grin. "We've got ways of carvin' a man that don't involve killin'. Agreed?"

Stewart nodded. "Agreed." He sheathed his sword, and turned to watch as his men did the same.

The brigand leader swung down from the saddle, a jangle of arms and armor. "Name's Skarn the Bold, and now I'll be havin' some of your potatoes." They trooped back inside, crowding the small cottage. Stewart stood in the far corner with his men, watching as the brigands feasted on their potatoes. He'd taken a risk, making a bargain with the devil, but sometimes the devil was better than death.

44

Steffan

A delegation appeared at the gates of Lingard. Twenty men rode under twin banners, emerald green for Lanverness and snow white for parlay. Steffan watched from the tower window as a troop of Black Flames escorted them to the inner courtyard. The Priestess joined him, leaning on the sill, luscious in a low-cut gown of smoky velvet.

She gave him a sloe-eyed glance. "Surrender?"

Steffan chuckled. "Doubtful. It's too soon for the blue sword to have reached Pellanor, let alone for the heralds to bring a reply. Besides, they don't look like soldiers, more like a bunch of nobles and their guards. The heralds must have passed them in the dark."

She pursed her lips in a tempting pout. "If not surrender, then what?"

He grinned. "Mischief, skullduggery, deception. Whatever it is, we'll turn it to our advantage."

"Shall I summon the prince?"

Steffan considered her suggestion. "If he's not drunk in his cups, why not? A show of force, or perhaps deviousness." He flashed a grin. "Let them see the prince sitting at my left hand and let them wonder."

She gave him a siren's smile. "Lingard captured and Prince Danly turned, it should be more than enough to make them tremble."

"Just so," he considered the possibilities, "but tell the prince to hold his tongue. I won't tolerate his interference."

"As you wish." She left him to summon the others, while he sipped a goblet of merlot, a tasty vintage from the baron's own cellar.

Steffan kept the delegation waiting for two full turns of the hourglass, long enough for the loss of Lingard to be appreciated. Taking the lord's seat at the table's head, he put the Priestess on his right and Prince Danly on his left. The bishops and the general were excluded from the in the parlay. Sometimes subtlety was better left to small numbers. With a wave of his hand, the guards admitted the lords of the delegation, three men, all of them in their early thirties, ambition gleaming from their eyes despite their dust-stained doublets. From the cut of their cloaks, Steffan assumed they had money, or at least a rich patron, wealthy noblemen come to play at politics.

"Welcome to Lingard. My name is Lord Steffan Raven, the councilor to the Pontifax." He gave a careful introduction, claiming power while keeping his position vague. Sometimes murkiness had its advantages. "What brings you to the gates of Lingard?"

The tall blond-haired lord with a jowly face and thick whiskers stepped forward, offering a cautious nod instead of a bow. "My name is Lord Evon." He gestured to the other two. "With me are Masters Holton and Spitzer. We've come from Pellanor on a matter of great delicacy." His gaze darted to the prince and then snapped back to Steffan.

Delicacy, a word that so often doubles for betrayal. Steffan hid his smile. "Parlay deserves a certain careful consideration, thus I've kept my council small."

The lord glowered. "We did not expect to see Prince Danly at your table."

"Surprises are just as much a part of negotiations as war." Steffan's smile deepened. "I'll wager you did not expect to find me in Lingard either?"

The lord's face flamed red. "No."

"Yet here I sit." Steffan grinned. "Imagine where you'll find me in another moon turn?"

The lord's eyes bulged. "But war is so wasteful."

"That depends on your point of view."

Lord Evon lowered his chin, like a man about to take a punch. "There are some in Pellanor who view this war as a great waste, a senseless destruction of lives and property. Wars are always costly, for both sides. The lords of Pellanor wonder if it might be possible to find a more peaceful accommodation."

"The cost of war is always born by the loser." Steffan sipped the merlot, letting the lordlings sweat.

"Yes, but so much death and destruction, surely there must be a better way?"

"What do you have in mind?"

Lord Evon hesitated, sweat beading his brow. "Lanverness is wealthy, a treasury filled with gold beyond the telling. Perhaps a peace could be brokered in exchange for coin."

Steffan smiled. "It's something to be considered, but whom do you represent? The queen?"

"No," the lordling blustered, "but my patron sits upon the queen's council and is privy to information that could be of great value."

"Great value? Enough to end a war?"

"It is hoped."

"That would take a great deal of coin, more than most men could imagine, especially since the Flame is winning." Steffan fondled the golden goblet. "Tell me gentlemen, how much gold can you imagine?"

"The treasury of Lanverness."

Beside him, Prince Danly gasped. Steffan shot the prince a warning glance and then turned his attention back to the lord. "A tempting offer, if you assume that's all we've come for."

Lord Evon looked confused. "What more could you want?"

"The souls of your people."

The lordling's eyes went wide, like a horse about to bolt.

Steffan used his most soothing voice. "But enough gold might assuage the fervor of my bishops."

"Let us hope so." The lordling mopped a sheen of sweat from his brow. "We have no wish to live under the Flame, but we do seek an accord."

"You decry our god yet you'd make an agreement with us?"

"The affairs of other kingdoms are not our concern."

The lordling actually managed to sound offended. "What terms does your patron offer?"

Lord Evon hesitated. "The treasury of Lanverness is uniquely vulnerable. In exchange for the details, you will claim the treasury and then retreat back across the border, returning to Coronth to trouble us no more."

"But the Flame Army has already claimed a full quarter of Lanverness."

"Then keep what you've claimed but take no more."

How easily he ceded the northern farmland. "Including Lingard?"

Lord Evon spit the answer. "Yes."

"An interesting offer, but we suspect the difficulties might lie in the details." Steffan leaned forward, refilling his goblet with a deep rich merlot. "There are details, aren't there?"

"Yes." Lord Evon looked like he longed for a cup, yet Steffan offered none.

"You were about to tell me the details?"

"A handful of lords travel with the treasury, my patron wants them out of the way."

Now they were getting to the good part. "He wants them killed."

"Yes."

"And how many soldiers protect the treasury?"

"Two thousand."

A bold-faced lie, but Steffan let it pass. "And what else?"

"We've brought documents, a treaty for you to sign, ensuring peace between our two kingdoms." The man to the lord's left produced a sheaf of documents bound with an emerald ribbon. He laid them on the table like an offering upon an altar.

Steffan hid a grin, as if mere parchments would ever bind him. "And what is the name of your patron, this paragon of peace?"

Once more the lord hesitated, proving they'd finally reached the delicate part. "I prefer to tell you in private."

"This is as private as you're like to get."

The lord glowered, but relented in the face of stubborn silence. "His name is...Lord Mills, a member of the queen's high council."

Beside him, the prince did not stir, as if the name meant nothing to him. Steffan sent a questing glance toward the Priestess and received a knowing smile. So the Lord Mills really was a traitor, Steffan smiled, considering the possibilities. "An interesting offer, but we sense there is something else."

"Something else?" Lord Evon looked confused.

"What does your patron gain by such an accord?"

"Peace for Lanverness."

"How noble, but what does he gain for himself?"

The lordling darted a furtive glance toward Danly and back.

Steffan waited, making him say it.

"He seeks the crown."

"No!" Danly shot to his feet, his face a boil of anger. *"I am the rightwise heir to Lanverness!"*

The delegates retreated a step, but otherwise silence reigned. Danly turned on Steffan, frothing with anger. "I want these men arrested! They're traitors to my throne." Red-faced, the prince bellowed at the guards. "Arrest these men!"

But the guards did not move.

Steffan waited, letting the lesson sink in, a revenge of sorts for sharing the Priestess, and then he turned on Danly, his voice as cold as steel. "Sit and listen and earn a place among the new order...or the guards will have you removed."

Danly sputtered like a fish out of water, but he slowly sank into the chair.

Stifling a smile, Steffan turned his gaze back to the delegates. "The queen still lives. How does Lord Mills plan to claim the throne?"

"Peace will earn him the gratitude of the people, and the loss of the treasury will be blamed on the queen, turning the nobles against her."

"And the queen?"

Lord Evon smiled. "That's the brilliant part. Lord Mills need not sully his hands with royal blood. He'll let nature take its course."

Steffan's gaze narrowed. "How?"

The lord's grin grew licentious. "The queen is great with child."

Danly gasped, his face turning dead-fish white, his voice a strangled whisper. *"She seeks to supplant me!"*

Lord Evon ignored the prince, giving Steffan a knowing grin. "A woman of her age rarely survives the birthing bed."

Steffan thrummed with possibilities. "And a tincture of herbs might help her along?"

"Just so."

"And I take it, the birth would be a scandal?"

"Exactly," the lord smiled in triumph, "It's why Lord Mills has sworn the other lords to silence, giving the queen the appearance that her secret is safe. The longer it remains hidden, the greater the scandal will be."

"Delicious!" Steffan laughed out loud, feeling as if the Dark Lord himself stood by his side. Lanverness was falling into his hands, like fruit ripe for the plucking. He gave a low chuckle. "Despite her intelligence, the vaunted Spider Queen proves she is a mere woman after all. She's caught by the age-old trap, the eternal weakness of her sex. Her own nature will be her undoing." He barked a laugh. "But tell me, who tupped the queen?"

The lord looked sheepish. "No one knows."

"Even more delicious!" He gestured to the guards. "Bring wine for our new allies. I'll drink a toast to the downfall of the Spider Queen."

The guards leaped to obey.

Lord Evon stepped forward. "So you'll sign our treaty?"

"Bring your parchments and your quills, I'll sign them all, and together we'll redraw the map of Erdhe. And this time, there'll be no place for queens."

45

Liandra

Liandra paced in front of the hearth, shivering despite the fire's warmth. With Stewart captured and her unborn daughter still months from being born, the problem of succession preyed on her mind. She needed allies and she needed a spare heir.

A knock came from the door. Lady Sarah opened it, admitting her guest. Princess Jemma was radiant as always, dark hair framing a heart-shaped face. She curtseyed with a rustle of silk, elegant in the latest fashion. "You asked for me?"

"Yes." Liandra took a seat before the fire, arranging the pleats of her velvet gown. "Come join us, we miss the pleasure of your company."

The princess flashed a wry smile, taking a seat opposite the queen. "Time with you is always well spent, but it is never just for tea."

"You know us too well." Pleased to dispense with the pleasantries, Liandra plunged straight to the heart of the matter. "A messenger from Navarre arrived a fortnight ago, yet you have not come to us with an answer."

The princess paled. "Of course you would you know of that."

Liandra's voice was soothing. "We know of the messenger, not the message."

The princess hesitated, taking a careful sip of tea.

Liandra pressed the issue. "Reports from the battlefield say that Prince Stewart is taken by the enemy, but we believe he still lives."

The princess gasped, dismay writ across her face.

Liandra reached for her hand, putting steel in her touch. "We hold to the belief that Stewart still lives. And you must believe it as well." Conviction ruled her voice. "We will pay any ransom for his release. Our royal son will be returned to us. But this terrible turn of fate only makes his marriage more important. We must have heirs, we must have grandchildren, and there is no one we would rather have as our daughter than you." Her voice softened. "We have come to care for you, to see you as our own true daughter. In time you will make a great queen, a boon to the people of Lanverness." Liandra released the princess's hand, and leaned back in her chair. She studied her apprentice. "What word from the king of Navarre? Does he consent to the marriage?"

But the princess did not speak, her gaze fixed on the roaring fire.

"It is a simple question."

"But not a simple answer." The princess met her stare. "The king gives his consent."

The queen smiled in pleasure and triumph.

"But..."

A single word and the queen's smile was stillborn.

The princess took a deep breath, her face troubled. "When does the heart matter more than duty?"

The queen did not hesitate. "Never, if you are royal born."

The princess gave her a slanted look, but her words were softly spoken. "Yet you dare to bear a love child without a husband."

Liandra recoiled as if slapped. Anger rose within her, but she reigned it back, impressed by the young woman's courage. She waited till her anger cooled and then gave an honest answer. "The child is begot from love but the lack of husband is pure duty."

"Are you sure?"

So the rosebud has thorns. "Such audacity."

The princess had the grace to blanch.

"We serve our kingdom best without the yoke of a husband." The queen's anger subsided. "But we were speaking of you. We offer you the chance to sit on the throne of the wealthiest kingdom of Erdhe. What say you?"

"The king gives his consent, but only if *I* also consent. My father gives me the chance to choose."

The king's leniency surprised Liandra. Perhaps having so many children made Ivor soft. "Your sire is most generous. What do you choose?"

Emotions raced across the young woman's face, a strange mixture of longing and regret leavened with defiance. "The truth is I yearn for a chance to rule, to be a queen worthy of your example, but I will not gainsay love." She took a deep breath, a touch of steel in her voice. "I will speak to the prince when he returns. If he consents to the marriage, then we shall wed, if he chooses another, then I will stand aside."

Liandra's gaze narrowed. "You speak of your sister, the swordish one?"

The princess nodded.

"For the sake of your sister, you would set aside a throne?"

"Yes."

Resolve shown from the princess's face, reminding Liandra of her younger days. "Such conviction, however misplaced, will stand you in good stead when you wear a crown." Despite her disappointment, the queen decided not to argue, taking a different tack. "If Prince Stewart consents then you will wed?"

The princess burned bright red. "Yes."

Liandra nodded. "Then we shall trust duty to prevail."

The princess gave her a sharp look but she did not argue.

"Now that the succession is settled, let us speak of lighter things. We would hear the gossip of the court. Truths can sometimes be found in the smallest rumor."

As if on cue, Lady Sarah bustled into the chamber bearing a tray with a fresh pot of tea and raisin-baked scones. "I thought you might be wanting something to eat."

Liandra scrutinized the scones. Since the monk's murder, she'd grown fearful of poisons. "Have they been tasted?"

"Barty baked them for you himself and we both tasted them. They're really very good, especially the way he bakes slivered almonds within the pastry. Adds a nice crunch to the scone. And the raisins are plump and juicy, very sweet." She set the tray on a table and began pouring fresh cups of tea. "Will you have one? You need to keep up your strength."

A hard knock on the door interrupted her chatter. Without permission, the door burst open and Master Raddock appeared. "Majesty, a messenger from the north."

One look at his face and Liandra knew the message was dire. "More dark tidings." She steeled herself, praying Stewart remained alive. "Come."

Lady Sarah fled the chamber and the princess rose to leave, but the queen gestured for her to remain. Master Raddock returned leading a mud-spattered messenger, a young lad barely old enough to shave. Dust-stained and weary, he knelt before her, a lad sent to war before reaching full manhood, yet his eyes told her he'd already seen nightmares.

"Majesty," his voice croaked with weariness, "Lingard has fallen."

The words pierced her like a spear thrust. For a moment she could not breathe. *Not Lingard!* She felt the blood rush from her face, leaving her cold. The implications staggered her. Lingard was one of her greatest strongholds, stout walls and a large force of knights. It meant the enemy was stronger than she thought. And now they had food, food enough to feed an army. It meant the war was nearly lost. She made her face a mask of stone. "How did this happen?"

"Treachery, majesty."

She gripped the arms of her chair, like pulling teeth from a hen. "Tell us more."

"They say it was the prince, Prince Danly, come with an escort of a hundred men, all in emerald cloaks, flying banners of Lanverness. The baron had no reason not to welcome him. Once inside the traitors opened the gates."

"*Danly?* Prince Danly?" Her mind stumbled over the news.

The lad nodded, fear glinting in his eyes.

Liandra sagged back into the chair. Her second son was proving her bane, the spawn from hell. The midwives had wanted to smoother him in the crib for murdering his twin sister, yet she'd protected him. No matter how many times she spared him, he always held a dagger to her breast. "How did Danly come to ride with the Flame?" She cast a venomous glare at her advisors, at Master Raddock and Sir Durnheart, but they both looked bewildered. Her shadowmen had failed her. Liandra shook her head, gathering her wits, trying to make sense of the message. Her mind fastened on a single insight, like a rocky isle jutting from a storm-tossed sea. "You said treachery?"

The lad nodded.

So it was treachery not strength, perhaps there was still hope for guile to prevail. "And Baron Rognald?"

"Rumors say he was murdered."

Her stalwart baron, Liandra closed her eyes, mourning his loss. She took a deep breath, sorting fact from raw emotion. Within the wretched tale there was a truth to be learned. Her gaze snapped to Master Raddock. "Now we know how the Flame treats those it conquers. If our loyal lords kneel to the Flame they'll soon find their heads on a spike."

The master gave a grim nod.

The queen turned her gaze back to the messenger. "What else can you tell us?"

"Lord Ronald sent three of us to ride with all speed."

Three boys sent to war and only one made it. "And does Lord Ronald still live?"

A tear slipped from the boy's eye. "He was trying to hold the southern gate...but there were so many of them."

The lad was at his breaking point. "You have served us well. Sir Durnheart, will you see that our brave messenger gets a hearty meal and a warm bed?"

"Yes, majesty."

She held her ringed hand toward the boy. "Your service will be remembered."

The lad kissed her ring and was shepherded from the royal solar by her knight protector. When the door closed, the queen leaned back in her chair, closing her eyes against the terrible news. "Lingard fallen." Such an ominous loss, yet somehow she had to rally her kingdom. Opening her eyes, she stared at her deputy shadowmaster. "Some of our loyal lords have been badgering us to sue for peace."

Master Raddock gave a cautious nod.

"And our shadowmen report rumors that the Flame will be lenient to those who bend the knee."

"True," he nodded. "Pellanor is rapidly becoming a city of refugees. Minor nobles fleeing the Flame grumble that those who surrendered instead of fighting kept their lands as long as they swore fealty to the new religion."

"A rumor designed to goad surrender."

"Just so"

"But now Baron Rognald is murdered. We want the truth of Lingard spread through the city."

"But it might stir panic."

"Or stiffen spines. We will bet on the power of the truth. Hire bards to put the foul deed to song. We'll have this tale told. Let our soldiers and our people know that surrender leads to death. We fight for victory or we die."

Master Raddock said, "And Danly? Will the prince be in this tale?"

"Yes, oh yes. That was *our* mistake. We hid the truth of his treachery and now we pay the price. We pay dearly for it. But we shall pay no more." For too long she'd offered Danly mercy instead of justice. The queen straightened in her chair, summoning her most regal voice. "Henceforth, Danly, second son of the Queen of Lanverness, is named a traitor of the realm. His life is forfeit. He is to be killed on sight. So let it be known across our kingdom, far and wide."

Her words echoed like a death knell.

"We shall sign a royal proclamation and have copies sent throughout our kingdom. Justice will finally have its due." Her words sentenced her own son to death. If her courtiers thought her ruthless before, what would they make of her now?

Master Raddock bowed low, his face pale. "As you command."

"Leave us. We have much to consider."

The shadowmaster and the princess fled the chamber. Liandra was left alone with her thoughts. Danly's actions shocked her. She'd shown him mercy after mercy and it only came back to haunt her. Robert should never have interfered. Better to leave her errant son locked in the deepest dungeons where he could do no harm. A lesson learned. And then there was the baron, always a staunch supporter and a dear friend. So much death and betrayal, Liandra sat bereft, awash in loss. Despair threatened to swamp her, but she rallied against it. Queens could not afford despair. Her mind fastened on the problem instead. The loss of Lingard was a disaster, yet it proved surrender was a lie, and it reminded her of the value of guile. She missed Robert, missed his wisdom and his embrace, but he was also her master of shadows. Sometimes shadows served elsewhere. Everything she loved was at risk. Liandra stared into the crackling fire, a blaze of heat on her face. A sword could melt in the flames, or it could anneal, finding greater strength. Something hardened within her. By all the gods, she swore to find a greater strength, to find a way to save her kingdom.

46

The Priestess

The Priestess played at rape. She lashed him to the bed, spread-eagled beneath her, and then she had her way with him. Fingers and tongue, she teased and tortured, heightening every pleasure, bringing him to a fever pitch. Steffan strained against the bonds, but she made him wait for it, made him beg for it. Magic kept him rampant, but a mortal heart could only bear so much. When his need became intolerable, she rode him without mercy, taking her own pleasure with each ruthless stroke. He came in a bellow, collapsing back on sodden sheets.

Smiling, she released his bonds, nestling against his side. "You liked that."

He groaned in pleasure. "You're intoxicating. I can't get enough of you."

She trailed a finger down his chest, knowing he was ripe for her suggestions. The sated pause between sex and sleep was always the perfect time to seed a man with thoughts. "You best be careful."

"What do you mean?"

"There are two ways to lead, from the front and from behind."

"So?" He rolled on his side, staring down at her, the perfect blend of trust and interest in his dark gaze.

"You're a master at leading from behind, you proved that in Coronth, but leading from the front is different, more dangerous."

"More exposed?"

"Exactly. In council you give orders to the general and the bishops, there's no doubt who leads. But in times of war, armies always strike for the head."

He fondled her breast. "But I'm fighting against a queen. Women know so little of war, it's a man's province."

Anger sparked within her, but she kept it hidden. "There's another danger. Those who lead from the front are often blinded by arrogance. They miss the daggers aimed at their backs."

"And in Coronth, all the daggers were aimed at the Pontifax."

"Just so. Survivors lead from the shadows. Women know this, that's why we're so good at it." She reached past him, pouring a rich red merlot into a silver goblet. Taking a sip, she licked her lips, and offered him the cup, prompting him with a question. "But how do you lead from the shadows in times of war?"

"Create a figurehead."

She rewarded him with a lusty smile. "Bishop Taniff is quite the fanatic, a perfect blend of religious fervor and bloody battle lust."

Steffan answered her smile. "And fanatics are so single-minded, so predictable in a chaotic kind of way...unless they run amok."

"And then you kill them."

He leaned forward, licking the merlot from her lips. "You're so delicious."

"So you'll make better use of the bishop?"

Steffan murmured a distracted "yes." His kisses roamed down her neck, creating a line of silken pleasure.

She wound her hands through his hair, fascinated by the white streak at his temple, so startling against his dark locks. "We're running out of time."

"What do you mean?"

Visions from her scrying bowl assailed her mind, sending a shiver through her body. "The Mordant has regained his power in the north. Soon he will come south. As the oldest harlequin, he is not the type to share."

"So?" Steffan moved even lower.

"Power respects power, there is no other way to treat with the Mordant."

"We'll soon have all the power of the queen's treasury, the richest hoard in Erdhe."

"Wealth will not impress the Mordant." She rolled on top, pinning him to the bed, regaining control. "You don't understand. He's had a thousand years to perfect his evil. We must solidify our power before he comes south."

"And we shall. Lanverness is nearly ours." He reared up, kissing her full on the mouth. They shared a taste of merlot, a taste of passion. She enjoyed the kiss, a deep delving, a promise of more, but then she pulled away.

"How do you do that?"

"What?"

He strained toward her. "Always make me want more?"

She gave him a silken smile, indulging him in another lingering kiss.

When they broke apart, he had a question of his own. "So what do you know of this Lord Mills?"

"A councilor to the queen, a handsome face with darkness lurking in his heart."

"So we can trust him to play his part?"

"As much as you can trust any traitor."

He ran his fingers through her long black hair, holding it to his face and breathing deep. "How do you know these things?"

"Women have their ways."

"That's not an answer."

She smiled, distracting him with a whisper of fingertips at his manhood. "So you'll take the treasury and then take the rest of Lanverness?"

He laughed. "Did you see their faces when I signed their treaty! As if mere parchments could ever constrain the likes of us." His laugh deepened. "So stupid, so naïve."

"But useful"

"Hmmm," he mumbled an answer as he kissed his way south.

"So you'll march on Pellanor?"

He raised his head, staring the length of her body. "We have both princes and we'll soon have the treasury. Capture the heirs and the gold and the queen will capitulate. With the queen's surrender I'll march to victory not war." He flashed a wicked smile. "If Lord Mills doesn't kill her first."

"Your plan is flawed. You have *one* prince and a sword."

"But the sword will serve." He grinned up at her. "Sometimes a lie is even better than the truth." He lowered his head, his fingers and tongue stroking her need, indulging her pleasures. She writhed beneath his touch, taking everything he gave. Her magic built to a fever pitch, and then she rolled on top, pinning him to the bed once more.

His dark eyes flashed up at her. "You liked that."

"Yes." He was ready again, but she made him wait. "It's past time I gained my own power." She'd gained an alliance in Radagar, putting Razzur on his brother's throne, and now she helped Steffan claim Lanverness, both alliances sealed in bed, but she wanted more, much more. "You know what I want." Her voice was deep and throaty.

"We'll share power in Lanverness, the richest kingdom in Erdhe. You'll sit by my side, my queen, my consort, my royal temptress."

As if she wanted to share power with any man. She hid the contempt from her face. "I have a different destiny." Leaning forward, she kissed him, her dark hair surrounding him like a veil, "and we have an agreement."

"More than an agreement." He arched toward her, like a rampant lion. "Who fills you the way I do?"

She gave him a sultry smile, reminding him of their bargain. "Six thousand men," she ground against him, "none of them clerics," her fingers stroked his length, "two thousand of them mounted," she teased him to his fullest extent, "all of them ordered to do my bidding." She hovered above him, poised to descend, a sheath for his sword. "Do you so swear?"

He strained upwards, but she held him at bay.

"Do you so swear?"

"Yes." The word was a groan.

She plunged down, taking his full length, sealing the agreement with sex. Leading him on a wild rampant ride, the Priestess set her hooks deep into his soul.

47

Stewart

Stewart made a deal with the devil, but it did not include trust. As part of the bargain his men kept their swords, always sheathed, but always close at hand. By day, they rode bunched together, ever vigilant, a hard knot of loyal soldiers surrounded by brigands. At night, his men slept in a huddle, taking turns at keeping watch.

Mistrust ran both ways, like a river full of dangerous eddies. Bristling with weapons, the brigands kept a sharp eye on their captives. Stewart felt their stares, even when he went to the privy. Skarn's men proved an ugly bunch, killers and rapists and deserters, hardened outlaws who deserved to hang; yet Stewart intended to keep his bargain. Need made for strange allies, but he did not like it.

At least the odds improved slightly when Skarn sent two of his men south to hunt for the Rose Army. Eighteen brigands guarding eight loyal men, the odds were still deadly.

Skarn led them west at a steady trot, Stewart riding close by his side. They foraged as they rode, but the gleanings were slim, the men always on the knife-edge of hunger. For the most part the countryside was empty, burned farmsteads and abandoned fields, the grim wake of war, but on the third day they spied an ox cart burdened with the goods of three families, ragtag children and a milk cow lagging behind.

Skarn laughed. "Easy pickings, lads. We'll feast tonight."

Stewart pulled his horse to a stop. "Leave them be, Skarn."

The leader turned in the saddle, giving Stewart a baleful stare. "What's this, the lordling givin' orders?"

Ugly laughter swirled through the brigands, but Stewart's voice brooked no argument. "They've lost enough, leave them be."

"Or what?" Skarn's glare turned nasty, his hand moving to his sword hilt.

Stewart matched the brigand leader, gripping his own sword, but he kept the blade in the scabbard. "Or we fight."

Their stares locked in a dual of wills.

Their horses stamped and snorted sensing the tension, the men perched on the edge of battle.

Tensions tightened and Stewart feared it would come to a fight, but then Skarn snorted in derision. "You'd fight for the likes of these?"

"Always."

"Then you're a damn fool." Skarn spit the words, his voice full of venom. "Little wonder the Flames are winning." His horse shied, but the big man controlled the stallion with his knees. Skarn's smile turned nasty. "This wasn't part of our bargain, princeling."

"The gold will more than make up for it."

"It better." Skarn yanked his horse's head, putting spurs to the flank, and then they were riding again, galloping down a hillside and across a fallow field, but they rode wide around the farmers.

An angry tension rose through the brigands like a river rising to flood. Stewart's men stayed close, their hands on their sword hilts, wary of the foul glances sent their way, but they weathered the storm without incident. At twilight's first blush, they camped beneath the boughs of an ancient apple orchard. A faint cider-like smell lingered despite the winter. For hungry men, the smell proved maddening. A few went in search of apples, but they returned empty handed, nothing but rotting mush beneath their boots. The lingering smell proved a bitter tease, setting the camp on edge.

Their stomachs rumbling, they risked a fire, sharing cups of tea and strips of salted venison. With the potatoes long gone it was a meager meal, but then Skarn broke out a flask of rye whiskey and the mood lightened. Skarn's men shared the flask, swapping bawdy jokes about their exploits in bordellos, while Stewart's men sat close and silent, a hard knot of suspicion, refusing the whiskey.

At moonrise, Stewart and his men rolled themselves into their cloaks, sleeping close as wolves, huddled for warmth as much as for safety. Timmons took the first watch, while Stewart agreed to the second. The prince checked his dagger and his seashell broach, his sword by his side, and then he succumbed to sleep, taking comfort in the sounds of men's snores.

The twang of a crossbow pierced his dreams. Stewart woke with a start, his hand reaching for his sword.

"Steady!"

Stewart froze. A sword was held to his throat, close enough to shave. The brigands threatened his men. "What's the meaning of this?"

Owen said, "Timmons is dead, a quarrel to the heart."

Anger snarled through Stewart. "We had a deal, Skarn. Safe passage for me *and* my men!"

Skarn stared down at him, a crooked smile on his face, his breath fouled with whiskey. "Bargain's changed, lordling. Or did you think you ruled us, like you rule your soldier-slaves?" He gestured and a brigand knelt to search Stewart, removing his dagger and his sword.

Anger turned to rage. "You gave your word."

"I lied." Skarn shrugged. "Besides, you changed the bargain when we spared those farmers. Now they'll be one less of you to feed."

Skarn gestured and a brigand knelt to bind Stewart's hands, a loop of rough rope pulled tight around his wrists. The prince snarled in protest, but the sword at his throat kept him pinned. Fighting was hopeless, yet he refused to give up. "What about the gold?"

Skarn laughed. "I'll be havin' that too, even more than what you offered. I've decided to auction you off."

A cold fear shivered down Stewart's back. "What do you mean?"

"First I'll offer you to the emerald cloaks, to see if you're lying, and if they're truly interested, then I'll offer you to the red cloaks." Skarn flashed a crooked grin. "I'll sell ya to the highest bidder. To the winner go the spoils."

"You can't do this!"

"Gag him."

A filthy rag was thrust into Stewart's mouth and bound tight. The prince struggled against his bonds to no avail. His men received the same treatment, trussed like stoats for the market. A pair of brigands hauled Stewart to his feet, lifting him into the saddle. Bound and gagged, he rode through the night, a prisoner once more.

48

Liandra

Pain wracked the queen, like being torn asunder. It ambushed her in the dead of the night, squeezing her body into convulsions. A scream rode her lips. *"Too soon!"* Her women fled, seeking aid while Liandra fought the urge to push, desperate to keep her unborn child. Sweat ran in rivulets down her face, a torrent of hurt, and still she refused. *"Poison, it must be poison!"* Her hands gripped the sheets, her body twisting in agony. *"Save my baby!"*

Healers rushed to minister to her while her women daubed sweat from her brow. Potions were held to her lips, foul tasting brews. One after another she forced them down, desperate for relief. Urgency circled the great royal bed, but nothing eased her torment. Liandra writhed across silken sheets. Pain claimed her. The agony grew like a tidal wave, arching her back, convulsing her body till she felt like she'd burst.

The child came in a gush of fluids. *"No!"*

The convulsions eased to tremors, sweeping the pain out of her, but not the hurt. Spent and empty, Liandra collapsed on sodden sheets. The queen tensed, listening, but there was no gasp of breath, no first cry. Her heart sank with the grim silence. "My child?"

Healer Crandor hovered over her, kindly brown eyes set in a face of ancient wrinkles. "Stillborn, majesty, too young to live."

"No." The words pierced her heart, killing her unborn hope. "No, it cannot be."

But the master healer was persistent. "I'm sorry, majesty, the babe is gone."

Liandra refused to believe. "Show me."

Crandor hesitated, as if he might argue, but then he gestured and they brought the small bundle toward her. Still swathed in blood, the child was small, too small to live, yet perfectly formed, dark hair and delicate features, the daughter of her heart. The bitter proof drained the strength from her. They took the small bundle away and Liandra sagged back into a sea of pillows, letting them minister to her body, an empty husk.

A man's voice issued orders. "In the name of the queen you are all sworn to secrecy." Master Raddock strode into the chamber. "The queen is ill, nothing more. The bedding must be burnt, all proof removed." A shadow in black, he swooped in to claim the bundle. "The details will be seen to."

Details, the word pierced her heart. When did a dead child become a detail? When did love become shame? Her secret hope transformed to scandal in the eyes of her court. Was any king burdened with such chains? Was any crown worth it?

Crandor held a goblet to her lips, wine laced with poppy's milk. She drank it, seeking oblivion, but oblivion did not come soon enough. *The babe is gone,* the words thundered through her mind, creating a cavern of emptiness. How could the gods be so cruel? Danly a condemned traitor, Stewart captured, and now her precious daughter taken from her, the second daughter lost at birth. Agony of another sort speared her heart. So much loss, so much pain, and for what? Was this the price of being a woman, of being a queen? Liandra wanted to rail at the gods, but she did not have the strength.

A hand gripped hers, an anchor in a sea of oblivion.

"Majesty, do not leave us."

A woman's voice called her back. Liandra peered through tear-encrusted eyes. Lady Sarah knelt by the bed, gripping the queen's hand, her face lined with worry. "Majesty, do not leave us."

"Why?"

"Your kingdom needs you."

Duty, always duty. Liandra's voice was a mere croak. "Why?"

"For Lanverness, for your kingdom, for your people." Something shifted in her friend's face, her voice dropping to a hushed whisper, a spark of urgency in her grip. "For the hope of another child."

Hope, such a slender word. Duty laced with hope, perhaps that was all that was left to her, but perhaps it was enough. Despite the pain, despite the loss, Liandra discovered she was not done being queen. She took up the crown once more. "We shall not leave you." And then she succumbed to the poppy.

49

Jordan

Jordan fled the others, seeking solace in the ruins. She climbed the giant stairway, taking a seat on the topmost step of the ruined tower. Morning light illuminated the forest below. It seemed so peaceful from above, a tangle of branches hiding the dead. She shivered, pulling her checkered cloak close, almost overcome by exhaustion, but her thoughts plagued her, too many visions, too many choices.

Subtle footsteps came from behind. She turned to find Thaddeus climbing the stairs. "May I join you?"

She nodded and the swordmaster took a seat beside her. Wrapped in a cloak of brown, he sat cross-legged, staring down at the forest, his sun-leathered face giving little away. "It wasn't what you expected."

Confused, she groped for meaning behind his words. "You mean the battle?"

He shrugged. "Your first battle is *never* what you expect. The feel of your sword cleaving flesh, the stench of blood and bowels, the taking of life, the rampant confusion, the dance with death. The bards never get it right." His blue-eyed gaze held hers, his voice soft and sure. "But the bards also don't understand the elation afterward, the thrill of a righteous victory, the way the blood sings in your veins, the thunderous joy of being alive."

"Valin's blessing."

"You felt it, didn't you?"

She nodded, a remembered warmth rushing through her, leaving her buoyed with triumph.

"You were meant for the sword, but something else plagues you."

She looked away, her mind spiraling into doubt.

"I saw your face when we returned to the stables last night. The three we rescued, they weren't the ones you expected."

"No."

"So now you doubt your visions?"

"Yet I foresaw this tower," Jordan gestured to the ruins, "*a shattered tower, red as blood, rearing above a winter forest.*" She shook her head, her broken nose throbbing. "I don't know what to think."

He nodded, his face thoughtful, but he did not press for more. They sat in companionable silence, listening to the sounds of the waking forest. The sweet song of a morning warbler rose from the forest underscored by the faint drumming of a woodpecker, but the illusion of peace was shattered by the crows' hungry caws. Black wings fluttered through the naked trees, feasting on the dead.

Jordan shuddered. "Too many crows, too much death."

"Yet we live to fight, to make a difference for the Light. And the question remains, should we stay or go?"

Her voice dropped to a whisper. "I don't know."

"Your visions are a sword against the Darkness, a chance to turn the tides. You must have an answer. The gods must have given you a sign?"

Anger warred with frustration. "I didn't ask for these visions, and I'm not afraid to use them...but they don't always make sense." Anger bled out of her like a receding tide. "I don't know what to do." She needed someone to talk to; she needed advice. Stalling, Jordan smoothed her cloak across the ancient stone, the checkered velvet pulling her heart in two directions. Taking a deep breath, she considered her words, slow and measured. "I've seen visions of Navarre, of my home, of the dark castle on the edge of the sea." She risked a glance toward him. "If I don't go home then all my family will die." She waited, holding her breath, but somehow he knew there was more.

"What else?" He tugged on his russet beard, avoiding her gaze.

"And then there's Kath."

His gaze snapped toward her, sharp as a sword. "The crystal blade-bearer?"

Jordan nodded. "She's going to need the help of Navarre. If she doesn't come south, all will be lost."

His gaze drilled into her. "You never said you had visions of the blade bearer."

"My sword-sister." Jordan bit her lip, avoiding his gaze.

"But something holds you here?"

Jordan nodded, choking on her words. "I don't know if I'm seeing true visions or nightmares, but if we leave the bloody tower too soon, then there'll be no hope for the prince of Lanverness." She sent him a searching look, begging him to understand.

Thad sighed, raking his hand through his russet hair, leaving a disheveled mess. "My first instinct is to aid the blade-bearer...but the gods always give us choices."

"*Choices!*" She spat the word like a curse. "These *choices* are cruel! Why can't the gods just help?"

"The gods work in mysterious ways."

"Well I'm sick of mystery." She turned away, hugging her knees to her chest, a ball of misery.

"There must be an answer, something we're missing." Behind her, Thad began to pace, a soft whisper of leather on stone. At first the sound annoyed her, but after a hundred steps the soft steady tread began to lull her, quieting the tumult of her mind. Jordan nearly screamed when the footsteps stopped and his hand gripped her shoulder. "There has to be a clue in your visions."

He folded to the stone step, sitting cross-legged beside her, his blue eyes sharp as ice. "Perhaps there's an order to your visions?"

She shook her head. "They're always a jumble, one image jumping to the next, never the same order."

"But always the same images?"

"Yes, except for Stewart." Jordan shivered. "My dreams of Stewart are always different, as if his fate is uncertain, shifting in the wind." Her voice dropped to a whisper, revealing her secret fear, "or perhaps they're just nightmares, not visions at all."

"But the images of this tower, of these ruins, they're always the same?"

"Yes," she let the images claim her, "*a shattered tower, red as blood, rearing above a winter forest.*"

Thaddeus leaned toward the tower's edge, gazing down at the crumbled ruins surrounded by a skirt of forest. "A shattered tower, red as blood, rearing above a winter..." he stopped and turned to stare at her, "...*a winter's forest!*"

Jordan nodded. "Bare trees without a single leaf upon them."

"And snow? Is there snow in your visions?"

Her eyes widened. "A light dusting." She turned to look down at the forest, at a thousand shades of brown. "*No snow!*" Joy flooded through her. "We're meant to wait till it snows!" She leaped to her feet, too excited to sit, but then she saw the sharp look in his eyes and knew there was something else. "What?" Jordan stilled, settling her hand on her sword hilt, as if his gaze threatened her conviction.

His words were solemn. "We don't know if your vision shows the *first* snow, or something deeper in winter."

She sank back down to the stone.

"Jordan," his words seemed to come from a thousand leagues away, "we'll wait till the first snow, but we cannot tarry longer. We dare not risk an entire kingdom, and the crystal blade-bearer for the sake of a single prince."

"No, of course not." But her voice sounded dead.

He grabbed her, his strength flowing through his hold. "Jordan, don't give up, have hope. Perhaps he'll come with the first snow."

She took a deep breath, coming back to herself. "You're right, we can only hope." She gave him a tentative smile and he released her. "But there's something else you should know."

He turned, his full attention centered on her.

"In my dreams, in my nightmares, Stewart is always fleeing enemies, sometimes red-cloaked soldiers, sometimes mercenary rogues...but they always outnumber us, two or three to one."

He gave her a feral smile. "Good to know."

"You're not worried?"

"To be forewarned is to be forearmed."

"But two or three times our numbers?"

"Knowledge is a sword." He grinned like a wolf chasing prey. "We have the ruins, and the forest, and we're forewarned. We'll build traps and tricks to even the odds. The Zward is not without teeth." He stood and stretched, as graceful as a forest cat. For a heartbeat he reminded her of Duncan.

"Come." He offered her a hand up. "We've much to discuss with the others."

Jordan rose to follow him but he sensed her reluctance, giving her a warm smile. "Don't lose hope. The gods can be merciful."

"I'll never stop hoping." She followed him down the stairway, his words ringing in her mind, *the gods can be merciful.* But in her heart, she knew the gods could also be cruel.

50

The Priestess

The Priestess chose a cloak of midnight black, a whisper of wool gliding across the cobblestone streets. She kept the deep cowl pulled forward, hiding her face, nothing more than a silhouette in the dead of night. Braxus led the way, Otham and Hugo at her back, three of her most trusted men.

Torches glittered in the main streets, mostly empty save for a few drunken soldiers returning from a late night revel. Refuse littered the cobbles and the night air stank of piss and spilled ale. So much had changed in the once-proud city, everything turned topsy-turvy with the coming of the Flame. Bishops and clerics claimed the wealthiest homes, enjoying the luxuries gained by divine right. Officers and soldiers barracked in fine inns and taverns, while the townsfolk, those who evaded the Flames by taking the brand of conversion, found other places to live, refugees haunting their own city. Someone always paid for the power of others.

They reached a home of modest wealth, probably once owned by a merchant of sorts. Braxus knocked. The door was opened by a red-cloaked officer. After a murmured conversation, Braxus slipped inside, his hand on his sword hilt.

The Priestess waited, knowing Braxus would be thorough.

The door re-opened, casting a sliver of light, and Braxus returned. "He's here, mistress, awaiting you."

She nodded. "Lead the way."

The house smelled of wood smoke and leather, cavalry officers playing dice in the front parlor. They paused in their game, turning to stare, but the Priestess ignored them, remaining hidden in the depths of her cowl. Braxus led her up the stairs and down the hallway to a closed door. She nodded and he opened the door without knocking.

A single officer waited inside. A solidly built man with a barrel chest, strong arms, and thick black beard, but the feature she liked best about him was his dark eyes, keen and intelligent. "Major Tarmin?"

"Yes." He stood before the fireplace, dressed in the leathers of a cavalry officer.

She lowered her cowl and he gasped, his dark eyes lighting with interest.

"They said you would come...but they failed to describe your beauty."

Courteous as well as intelligent, she liked that in her men. "You have just been promoted to general." She gestured and Braxus offered the general a sealed scroll.

"Examine the seal." She watched as he studied the waxy imprint. "These orders come direct from the Lord Raven, you are to be given command of two thousand mounted soldiers and four thousand foot. You and your men are to be placed at my disposal. You can read, can't you?" He nodded. She waited while he read the parchment, his lips moving with the words.

"This scroll is the last time you will obey an order that comes from another." At her gesture, Hugo stepped forward, placing a bulging sack on the oak table. The sack clinked with the sound of gold. "A bounty for your service, to be shared among your men."

The general's eyes widened at the largess. The Priestess smiled. "You'll find I'm a generous master to those who serve me well."

"My lady, what would you have of me?" His voice was deep and rough, accustomed to command.

"Select and equip your men. But I will have no clerics or bishops among them, and weed out the devout. I want soldiers not fanatics." Her voice dropped to a purr. "When it comes to worship, I'll not have religion clouding men's minds."

His eyes darkened at the stroke of her voice.

"And send one of your men to Dyers' Alley. Most of the shops have been looted but one has bolts of blue wool hidden away in the back bins, a deep blue the color of the sea. Have your men cut a square of blue, a double hand span by a double hand span, and sew it to the center of their cloaks. From now on, you'll wear my colors."

"As you command." His keen eyes raked her face. "And then?"

Braxus produced a second scroll, this one bearing her seal.

"And then you ride. The route is marked on this map."

He broke the seal, studying the map. "But, my Lady, six thousand men will be stretched to take a kingdom."

"But they can take a city, especially one as poorly defended as Seaside. Take the capital city, take the royals, and you have the kingdom."

"And the castle? It's said to be damn near impregnable."

She gave him a sultry laugh. "Leave that to me."

He gave her a searching look, but then he bowed his head. "As you will."

She liked her new general, stalwart and honest, honest men always made the best tools. "Take plenty of provisions, for I'll not have you ransacking the countryside. This will be a different kind of war, not as wasteful as the one waged in Lanverness. I mean to have a kingdom worth ruling when I'm done."

"As you command, my Lady."

"And now that we have an understanding," her voice deepened, full of suggestion, "I'll take your oath of fealty."

The general's eyes widened, his gaze fixed on her face.

Braxus and Hugo disappeared, slipping outside to stand guard in the hallway. The fire snapped and crackled, the air suddenly close and warm and charged with heat. The four-poster bed loomed large in the small room.

"All of my men swear a different kind of oath, a special oath." Her gaze traveled the length of him, a slow and sensual inspection. Smiling, she watched the hunger rise in his face, knowing his body was primed for the task. "I call upon you to take my oath of fealty. Swear with your body as well as your soul, eternally binding your fate to mine." Loosening the tie of her cloak, she shrugged it from her shoulders, a puddle of dark wool at her feet. She stood naked in the firelight except for a sparkle of diamonds at her throat, a pear-shaped gem dangling between her breasts. "Will you take my oath?"

The general groaned, falling to his knees before her. *"My lady!"*

She took him in front of the fireplace, once with his leathers on, and once without. A big hairy man, he did not have the finesse or stamina of Steffan, yet he had a soldier's rough eagerness, an earthy lustiness she enjoyed. Her newly made general rutted like a bull in season, plowing her with fervor. His groans of pleasure shook the room, but all too soon they turned to snores. Sated with sex, he sprawled in front of the fireplace. The Priestess smiled, writing her true name in the sweat of his chest. Gathering her cloak, she slipped from the room, one step closer to claiming her destiny.

51

Danly

Danly became adept at slipping his minders. All it took was slumped shoulders, downcast eyes, and a change of clothing, an ordinary red cloak, the type any soldier would wear, and a brown jerkin stolen from a servant. So easy for the prince to become the peasant, it rankled his sensibilities. He despised the stolen clothing, reeking of another man's sweat, but he despised being watched even more, like a dog on a chain. So he endured the stink, slipping down the stairs and across the courtyard, fleeing the tower.

Rage smoldered within him, a rage so hot he was surprised others did not see it. His world was sundered, turned upside down, every advantage lost. His mistress offered him poisoned apples, while his ally, the Lord Raven, treated with traitors, promising them his throne. *His throne!* And then there was his royal mother, seeking to supplant him with another a child. *A child at her age, such a scandal!* Laughter erupted from him, a wild barking laugh tinged with madness. He couldn't imagine his royal mother big with child. The scandal would be incredible. Always so prim and proper, and now the queen was caught rutting like a common whore, Danly shook with laughter.

Sharp stares turned his way. Passing soldiers looked at him as if he were a crazed cur. Danly knew stares were bad, so he stifled his laughter and took the back ways, slinking through piss-puddled alleys.

It took him half the day, visiting seven taverns before he found the man he sought. A big man slumped at a corner table, empty flagons littering the tabletop like a field of dead soldiers. Danly watched from the shadows. His red beard had grown wild and his skin turned sallow, but it was the same man, yet somehow diminished and shrunken, his shoulder's hunched, his head bowed. Perhaps diminishment was the price of being a traitor, but Danly shied from the thought. Girding his courage, he lowered the hood of his cloak and approached the table. "Share a drink with me?"

"If you've got the coin, I'll drink the swill." Bloodshot eyes stared up at him, growing wide with alarm. *"You!"*

"Calm yourself." Danly hissed the order, flinging a fist full of gold coins on the table. "Barkeep, another flagon of your best red." He pulled his hood back up, hiding in the cowled shadows.

The barkeep grumbled till he saw the gold. "Yes, m'lord." The fat man hustled to set another flagon on the table, scooping the coins into his fist before retreating across the room.

Danly sniffed the captain's cup, sour ale, a poor-man's swill. "What happened to your gold?" He emptied the dregs on the floor and then poured a rich red, setting the cup before the captain. "The Lord Raven always pays well."

"Lost some in a fight. Drank the rest. Not enough wine to drown in. Not enough ale to forget." He wrapped his big hands around the cup, making it look small. "Why are you here? No one else can stand your stink?"

Danly ignored the slur.

"Can't stand my own stink." Leonard Vengar sniffed at his own armpits, a loud snuffling sound. "I reek," he frowned in disgust, "the sour stench of a traitor." His voice turned whiny, "but Lord Rognald was already dead, killed by poison, killed by that *bitch*." Hatred slurred his words. "What was I to do? City already lost, enemies inside the gate, my own lord dead at my feet, nothing for a man to do. So I took their gold." He glared across the table, a spark of defiance in his voice. "Any man would have done the same. Take the gold or die."

Danly's words were low and soothing, wondering if he could use the man. "I know. I was there."

"So you were." His bloodshot eyes narrowed. "That bitch offered you a bite of the apple. Could have been poisoned. Could have died like my lord. Should have been you instead of him." He raised his cup, downing the wine in one long swallow, pounding the empty back on the table. "So why you here? No one else can stand your stink?"

The captain was becoming a bore, but Danly needed an ally, someone who knew the city, someone who knew how to fight. Urgency made him desperate. Danly filled the captain's cup to the brim. "I want out."

"Out? Try the bottom of a wine cup."

Danly stayed the man's hand before he could swill another. "I want out of the city and I want you to take me." He set a purse on the table, heavy with the clink of gold. "Are you my man?"

"More gold." The captain's voice steadied, as if he was not quite as drunk as he let on. "Why me?"

"Because you've learned the same lesson I have." His voice dropped to a hushed whisper. "They duped us, and then they used us, and now they'll discard us like three-day-old fish."

The captain snuffed. "Red cloaks won't even drink with me. Can't stand the sight of me."

"That's why we have to get out, before they decide we're better dead."

Vengar gave him a sobering look. "And go where?"

"To Pellanor, to the queen."

"*You!*" Vengar snorted a laugh. "You're daft! As if she'd take *you* back!"

"I was captured, held against my will." Danly tasted the lie, noting how easily it rolled off his tongue. "They used me, just like they used you."

Disbelief stared from the captain's bloodshot eyes, but Danly ignored the look. Leaning forward, he pressed the argument. "The queen values knowledge even more than gold." His voice dropped to a low whisper. "I know the enemy's plans. I know what they're going to do." He leaned closer. "And better yet, I know their *lies!*" Danly nodded, reassuring himself as much as the captain. "The queen will pay for what I know, and better yet, we'll have the queen's gratitude. With her protection we won't be looking over our shoulders for a knife in the back or poison on an apple." He drilled the captain with his stare. "Do you want a second chance?"

"Rognald was a good lord, he deserved better than to die of poison."

"We all deserve better than we get."

"Do we?" The captain's stare held all the torments of hell.

Danly did not look away. "Do you want a second chance?"

"Yeah, I do." Vengar sneered, his voice full of self-loathing. "I guess you're the only lord I deserve. You've got yourself a captain." He reached across the table and scooped the purse into his hand.

"It's not for drink. I need you sober, or I don't need you."

Vengar scowled. "A little for drinks. I need to cut the pain. But most of it will be for bribes. We'll never get out of here without plenty of bribes."

Danly nodded, watching the gold disappear into the captain's jerkin.

"We'll be needing plenty more."

"I can get it."

"When are you wanting to leave?"

Relief washed through Danly. "Lady Cereus leaves in three days." Just saying it made Danly tense, for he trusted Lord Raven even less than his dark-haired mistress. "I mean to be gone just after she leaves."

"How many days?"

"Five or less."

"Five days doesn't give me much time."

"It's all the time we have."

Vengar nodded. "I'll find a way."

"Good. Where will I meet you?"

"Here." Vengar made a sweeping gesture toward the flagon-strewn table. "Here I'm nothing but a drunken sot. So meet me here on the morning of the fifth day and I'll tell you the plan."

Danly nodded, hoping he could trust the captain. "On the morning of the fifth day." He stood to leave.

"And bring more gold," Vengar flashed an ugly grin, "this won't be nearly enough."

"It's always about gold." Danly turned his back on the captain and made his way to the door, wondering how much his life was worth, but he knew the answer. Steffan's trick with Lingard would only work once, and the queen would never bargain for a eunuch second son. He had to escape the Flame or his life wasn't worth a beggar's copper.

52

Stewart

A prisoner once more, anger turned to rage as Stewart struggled against the ropes. Bound to the saddle, he fought to keep his balance. So foolish to trust a brigand like Skarn, but what choice did he have? He'd made a deal with the devil, and now he had to find a way to escape the price. He couldn't let Skarn sell him to the red cloaks, couldn't risk being held like a knife to the queen's throat. As crown prince he was supposed to protect the kingdom, not threaten it. Bound and gagged, Stewart clawed at his bonds.

Skarn set a hard pace, galloping through the chilly night. Across fallow fields and winter-naked woods, they rode at a treacherous pace. Stewart's horse stumbled and nearly fell. Desperate to keep his seat, he clutched the pommel, an image of Crocker's battered skull flashing through his mind. In the midst of the nightlong ride, the scout had fallen, but the brigands never stopped. Bound and gagged, Crocker dragged behind till his head collided with a tree trunk, crushed to a bloody pulp. The brigands laughed and cut the rope, leaving the dead for carrion. Stewart smoldered at the memory, another debt to pay.

Eighteen brigands guarding six prisoners, they rode through the silvery moonlight like phantoms haunting a ravaged land. At dawn's first light, Skarn called a halt at a burnt farmstead. Smoke lingered like a pall, nothing left but a jumble of blackened timbers. Stewart's gaze searched the yard; relieved to find no bodies, perhaps the farmers escaped the Flame's savage heat.

Skarn dismounted. "Walk the horses, and let the prisoners down. We'll break fast before ridin' on."

The brigands obeyed without grumbling, which seemed odd since there wasn't much chance of foraging. Horses stamped and snorted, breathing plumes of mist into the cold morning air. Stewart made an awkward dismount, his bound hands tethered to the pommel by an arm's length of rope. Leaning against the horse, he stretched, working the blood back into his legs, grimacing against the needles of pain.

Two of the brigands, Dink and Roland, made the rounds. One at a time, they loosed the prisoners from the saddles, herding them to the side of the ruined farmhouse, a chance to make their morning toilet. Stewart took his time, searching for a weapon. The ground was hard with footprints, the grass scorched by the blaze.

"Hurry up." Dink kicked Owen, prodding the big man with his sword.

Owen scuttled sideways, his pants around his ankles while the brigands barked crude japes. Stewart used the distraction to palm a small stone. Slightly smaller than a gold coin, it had one rough edge, just what he needed. Gripping his prize, he laced his pants.

"Get moving."

The brigands herded them back to the front of the farmhouse. Skarn and the rest took their ease around a small fire. Leaning on bedrolls, they supped on dried venison and flagons of water. Stewart's stomach rumbled; his mouth fouled by the taste of the gag. Watching them eat was a kind of slow torture. Hatred boiled within him, a black rage that threatened to choke him.

The brigands roasted a brace of rabbits, juices dripping into the flames, releasing a maddening smell. Stewart and his men sat huddled on the cold ground beyond the fire's warmth, watching as their captors ate their fill. Like a dog desperate for a fallen morsel, Stewart felt the saliva swamp his mouth. At least his men did not whine, but their plight only fueled his anger. He drilled Skarn with his stare, willing the rogue leader to feel his hatred, but Skarn seemed oblivious to the daggered glare.

The brigands finished eating, a few stretching out on bedrolls. *No food for the prisoners,* Stewart felt despair leach through his men. Sagging to the ground, his men looked away, their faces etched with hunger, resigned to misery, but Stewart refused to give up. Bound and gagged, the prince kept his daggered stare locked on Skarn, hoping to engage the brigand leader, but Skarn seemed impervious to the visual assault. With his mitered helm and emerald cloak, Stewart should have known the brigand had no honor, yet he hoped to prick his pride or rouse his anger, anything to engage the bastard. Just when he thought it was hopeless, Skarn's stare snapped in Stewart's direction, a shrewd look on his face, a predator studying his prey. So the brigand had felt his stare all along, playing a possum's waiting game. Stewart held Skarn's one-eyed gaze, refusing to flinch.

Skarn kicked one of his men. "Remove the princeling's gag and give him some water."

Dink grumbled but obeyed.

Stewart felt his men come alert, but they had the good sense to feign indifference.

Dink removed the gag, thrusting the stoppered flask into Stewart's hands.

Stewart licked his lips, his mouth parched dry as shoe leather, but he refused to drink. "We're no use to you dead."

Skarn nodded. "Drink your fill, princeling."

"Not unless my men drink as well."

Skarn gave him a lazy smile. "Haven't you figured it out yet, princeling? You're the only one worth feedin'."

Stewart's hatred flared but he kept it hidden. "A thousand golds."

A few of Skarn's men sat up, but the brigand leader remained indifferent.

"A thousand golds above my ransom for every man who's delivered safe."

"Is your tongue lined with gold, princeling?" Skarn's men laughed. "I swear it must be gilded, the way you keep promisin' riches."

More laughter but Stewart's gaze never wavered. "You have my word."

"Your *word*," Skarn sneered, "the word of a raggedy-ass scarecrow who claims to be a prince?" His voice turned deadly. "Words ain't worth much, princeling, its gold and steel that matters."

"Gold you'll have, if you can keep six prisoners fed and alive." Stewart held Skarn's gaze. "Easy wealth for a raggedy-ass band of brigands."

Skarn scowled, a storm building in his face, but some of his men began to mutter. "He's right, Skarn, they're easy golds."

"All we have to do is keep 'em alive till Duster and Clem get back."

"And we're close to our winter stores, plenty of food to tide us over."

"*Enough!*" Skarn roared to his feet, a curved sword gleaming wicked in his mailed fist. "I *rule* here! *One* leader, *one* command." He turned to glare at his men. "Do any of you carrion-feeders dare to gainsay me?"

The brigands shrank back, proving Skarn was still dangerous despite the silver in his beard.

Skarn kicked Hubble and then Dink. "Feed and water the prisoners." Before the men could rise, Skarn crossed the distance, the edge of his curved sword held to Stewart's throat. "You best not be lying, princeling, or I'll flay and gut your men, one at a time till only your royal ass is left." His voice dripped with threat. "And I'll take the longest with you."

Stewart dared not breathe lest the blade cut his throat, but he held Skarn's stare.

Rage burned in the brigand's one-eyed glare, a rage that bordered on madness. "My blade's keen, princeling, and so is my anger." He drew the blade across Stewart's throat, a stinging line of pain.

Stewart gasped, clutching his throat, but it was only a flesh wound, a shallow crease.

Skarn laughed, cleaning his blade. "A promise and a threat, princeling. Don't fool with Skarn or you'll die screaming."

Stewart averted his gaze, stunned by the turn of events. Skarn was mad, mad and dangerous. There would be no deals with the devil. Fight or die, it always came down to that. At least he'd won food and drink for his men, a chance to build their strength and fight another day. Stewart raised the flask to his lips, a flood of sweet water gushing down his parched throat. He drank his fill and ate everything they gave him, and then he settled down to feign sleep. His men huddled close. Consumed by exhaustion, they soon released a medley of snores. While the others slept, Stewart slowly scrapped the small stone across his rope bonds. So intent on his work, he was startled when the freezing cold first touched his face. He stared skyward, surprised to see the falling flakes, the first snow of the year. Winter had come to Lanverness. Stewart shivered, feeling an omen of death. Time was against him. He returned to his work, sawing the stone across his bonds. Fight or die, he had to find a way to escape.

53

Danly

anly took to roving the streets by day, feeling safer in the city than the tower keep. Pulling his cloak close, he hid beneath a peasant's garb, royalty clad in drab brown. He checked the sun's progress across the mid-day sky. Vengar should be waiting for him at the tavern. The captain claimed he needed more golds. Danly fingered the purse tied to his belt, knowing it held mostly silvers, but the captain would have to make due. He slipped through the back streets, anxious to learn how their plans progressed.

Turning a corner, Danly came to a sudden stop, shocked to find a crowd milling in front of the tavern. An angry buzz rode the air, yet there were no priests in sight. Danly hovered in the alleyway, intending to leave, but curiosity got the better of him. Pulling his hood up, he skirted the crowd. Everyone stared at the clapboard tavern, something scrawled in red on the wall. Angling for a better look, he edged sideways. And then he saw the words written in blood. *The Pontifax is dead. The Gods curse this war!"* Danly stood slack-jawed, staring at the bloody message.

Questions rumbled through the crowd, a mixture of rage and fear.

"Is it true?"

"He can't be dead!"

"I saw him walk through the Flames myself! A bloody miracle!"

"He's the beloved of god!"

"The Lord Raven would have told us!"

Something was happening here, something he did not understand. Sensing the crowd might turn ugly; Danly began to back away. He eased passed a pair of soldiers, but then he spied a familiar face. For the barest moment, he thought he saw a distinctive profile hidden in the hood of soldier's red cloak, a hawk-faced man with silver-gray hair, and then he was gone, disappearing into shadows. Fear spiked through Danly, as if he'd just seen death. He told himself it was a trick of the light, but he knew he'd seen true. Pushing through the crowd, he reached the open street and began to run. Spurred by fear, he ran all the way back to the tower. The Master Archivist was in Lingard. The queen's shadowmaster had found him. Death stalked the city's cobbled streets.

54

Steffan

S teffan finished with a final deep thrust and then rolled off the bed, lacing his pants. "Enough. Get out."

"But my lord?"

"I said, get out." He watched as Salmay scrambled for her clothes. Long flaxen hair and tight buds for breasts, she was a comely lass, but there was no fire in their coupling, no rush of heat in his loins, a pitiful substitute for the Priestess. A snarl rose to his lips. He'd summoned the lass just to prove he wasn't besotted with the dark haired temptress, but nothing seemed to cure the raging ache in his loins. Already two weeks gone and he still couldn't get the Priestess out of his mind. The seductress had sunk her claws deep. Angry, he hurled a purse at the girl. "Get out and don't bother coming back."

She made a deft grab, catching the purse at the expense of dropping her shift, giving him another clear look at her pert breasts. Her priorities proved she'd gained a new profession.

"Once a whore, always a whore." Steffan turned away, pouring a goblet of merlot, listening as door slammed shut. He fingered his manhood, trying to sooth the persistent ache. For the thousandth time, he cursed the Priestess, angry that she'd left. The woman was impossible. He'd offered her the consort's crown of Lanverness, what more did the dark-damned temptress want? He gulped the wine, nearly gagging on its bitterness, nothing but dregs. "Pip!" He hurled the goblet against the wall, shattering the glass and spilling red wine down the stonework. Nothing seemed right since she'd left.

The red-haired lad appeared at the door. "Yes, my lord?"

"The wine's gone off, nothing but dregs, and where's the bloody bishop?"

"I sent a runner for the bishop, and I'll fetch a fresh flagon." The lad cast a wary glance his way and then disappeared behind the door.

Steffan paced his solar, eager to be gone. He had a war to win, but armies took time to prepare. At least he could rely on the general to see to the details. Together they'd take the cavalry south, leading a lightning raid to capture the queen's gold, a boon from the traitors. With the treasury secured and both princes captured, the queen would be forced to surrender. Steffan grinned at the thought, the vaunted Spider Queen defeated by guile. He wondered what she'd be like in bed, another spoil of war. A smile graced his lips, *once a whore, always a whore.* Perhaps he needed a queen to quench his lust.

The door slammed open.

Bishop Taniff strode into the chamber; his breastplate burnished bright despite the many dents, his mitered helm held in the crook of his arm, his voice a snarl. "Are the rumors true?"

Steffan bridled at the bishop's anger, but he kept his voice as smooth as glass. "So my runner found you." Ruthless in battle, the bishop was a big man, a warrior cleric, his black beard forked, his dark hair plaited into braids, he seemed to fill the chamber with menace.

"Are the rumors true?" Fanaticism glowed from the bishop's eyes like burning coals. "Is the Pontifax dead?"

A chill raced down Steffan's spine, a premonition of disaster, yet he met the cleric's stare, putting steel in his voice. "Have you lost your faith?"

The bishop reared back as if struck, but the glow in his eyes did not fade. "Have you heard what they're saying in the streets? Is the Pontifax dead? Did he die in agony, a sinner roasted in the Flames?"

"You're a warrior of the Flame God, yet you'd let lies quench your faith?"

The bishop took a step back, fairly shaking with rage.

Steffan pressed his assault. "You've seen the Pontifax take the Test of Faith. You've witnessed the holy miracle half a hundred times. How can you believe the heretics?"

The bishop's gaze narrowed. "They're even saying you killed the messengers from Coronth to claim power for yourself."

The truth blindsided him, but Steffan never faltered. He spread his arms wide, innocence writ large across his face. "Am I a cleric? Or even a priest? No, I'm just a simple counselor, a servant to the Pontifax. The power of the temple could never belong to one such as me."

The bishop teetered on the edge of reason.

"Someone tries to subvert our faith."

The bishop's gaze sharpened, like a dog keen for the hunt. "Lies then, all lies."

Steffan nodded, lacing his voice with conviction. "Heretics have found their way among us. That's why I'm leaving you in charge of Lingard."

"Leaving?"

"Lingard is important but we dare not linger. We have a war to win."

"You're splitting the army? Why?"

"I'm taking the cavalry to capture the queen's treasury, a lighting raid to the south, while you stay here to hold Lingard and root out the heretics." The bishop was a true believer, a dangerous two-edged sword full of holy suspicions, hence Steffan's decision to leave him behind. "I need you to deal with the heretics, to keep the faith strong. The Flame God has no better warrior."

Mollified, the bishop sank to a chair, tugging on his forked beard. "But how in the nine hells did the heretics come among us?"

Steffan poured the bishop a goblet of wine, doubting the cleric would even notice the dregs. "Perhaps the taint comes from the people of Lingard. Or perhaps we're so consumed by war; we haven't spent enough time tending to the faith. Either way, the heretics must die."

"And many will die for the sake of their sins." The bishop swilled the wine. "But how do we catch them? The town folk have all taken the brand."

Steffan wondered at the heretics, wondered how they'd gained the truth. Their death could not come soon enough. "Order your most faithful soldiers to sweep the city at night, arresting anyone in the streets. Put the prisoners to the question, and then feed them to the Flames. When the lies stop, you've caught the guilty."

"Or scared them silent."

Steffan shrugged. "Either way, the faith grows stronger." He refilled the bishop's goblet. "And while I'm gone, you should hold more devotions to the Flame God. Get the pyromancer involved. Give the army omens of victory. It's the surest way to build morale."

"Yes, more devotions to the Flames. The men need to be rededicated to the faith." The bishop's voice turned sonorous, quoting scripture. "The Pontifax says a man shall love the Flame more than he loves his life." The bishop's gaze narrowed. "But what about that pet prince of yours? He reeks of disbelief."

Steffan hid a smile, so the bishop thought he could smell disbelievers. "The prince has his uses, although his time grows short."

"Give him to me."

"What?"

The bishop's gaze glowed with fervor. "What better way to worship the Flames than to roast a royal infidel?"

The bloodthirstiness of the faithful never ceased to amaze Steffan. Religious fanaticism seemed to attract the most ruthless bastards, but the bishop had a point, Danly had grown annoying, his usefulness nearly done. Steffan decided to toss the bishop a bone. "When I return from taking the treasury, we'll have a victory celebration. You can burn the prince then."

"Good, a fitting offering to the Flames."

"In the meantime, I need you to rule with an iron fist. Stop this plague of lies and strengthen the faith in Lingard. Find the heretics and put them to the Flame. And when I return, we'll march on Pellanor to claim Lanverness for the Flame God."

The bishop flashed a ruthless grin. "The path to heaven is paved with the ashes of infidels. It will be a righteous day."

"Truly." Steffan rose from the table. "And now I think we both have much to accomplish."

"For the sake of the Flame." The bishop made the sign of blessing and then rose, tucking his mitered helm under his arm.

Steffan waited till the door clicked closed. A grin of triumph broke across his face. Deception was such a sweet game and religion the perfect foil. There was nothing quite as satisfying as weaving a pack of lies and watching lesser men scramble to believe them. A dangerous truth had threatened to undermine his plans, but he'd taken the truth and twisted it back on the heretics. Steffan grinned, realizing deception felt almost as good as sex. He crossed the chamber to the arrow-slit window, staring down at the courtyard below. From the god's eye view he watched as the bishop left the tower, a swirl of red and burnished steel, striding across the courtyard like a man on a mission. He'd loosed a hellhound on Lingard. The bishop would burn and torture till the heretics were silenced. And every burning would fuel the fanaticism of his troops. By the time he returned, he'd have an army slathering for the kill. Victory was nearly his. He could feel the Dark Lord's pleasure. One lifetime was not enough.

55

Liandra

For three days the pain triumphed. Trapped between life and death, the queen remained abed, wracked by grief and agony, but duty finally claimed her. Her shadowmen brought warning. "Majesty, the enemy approaches."

The dire threat pierced the pain-wracked fog, proving more potent than any healer's potion. For the sake of her kingdom, she rallied, burying her grief and bridling the hurt, but despite her royal will, her body still needed time to heal. Liandra lingered abed for as long as she dared, waiting till the enemy neared the gates. A delegation of red-cloaked heralds rode toward Pellanor, emissaries from the Flame come to parlay. Given the loss of Lingard, Liandra expected them to carry terms of surrender, but by all the gods they'd find no surrender in her kingdom.

When the heralds drew within four turns of the hourglass, the queen forced herself from bed. Liandra swayed, silently cursing the enemy's timing. Her body still bled; wracked with stabbing pains from the loss of the child, but the heralds posed a problem only a monarch could counter. Clutching the back of a chair, she forced herself to stand straight, ordering her women to attend. Weakness was a state no monarch could afford, leastwise a queen.

Lady Sarah knelt. "Majesty, I beg you, stay abed and let your lords deal with this."

The request was heartfelt but duty called. "The heralds bring more than just a message, they threaten the very will of our people. They shall not succeed."

War brought so many disadvantages to Pellanor, the queen could ill afford to let fear claim her city. Ever mindful of image, Liandra had long planned for just such a threat. At the start of the war she'd commissioned a suit of armor, a masterwork of silver filigreed with gold, burnished to a bright glow. The breastplate and the helm were real enough, capable of stopping an arrow despite the shapely curves, but everything else was ornamental. Her fingers traced the gold filigree, the workmanship exquisite. Clad in armor, a warrior queen would ride out to meet the heralds, a show of defiance and courage, a message for the enemy as well as her own people.

Her women swarmed around, trying to make sense of the armor. Greaves and gorget, bracers and bucklers, she wondered how men fought in so much metal. "Make sure the straps are secure. It won't do to have something fall off." A wave of pain ambushed her. She bit her lip to stifle a moan. Her insides felt as if they'd been torn asunder, yet the enemy gave her no choice. "It's hot in here. Open a window." Liandra gripped the back of the chair, refusing to succumb.

Lady Sarah clucked her displeasure. "Majesty, it's too soon. You should still be abed."

"Yet the enemy is nearly at our gates. They'll find no weakness in the queen."

Healer Crandor hovered nearby, fretting like an old woman. "Majesty, you've lost too much blood. Remain abed till you regain your strength. Listen to the wisdom of your lady if not your healer."

Liandra closed her eyes, rallying her strength. They did not understand the threat. They did not see the chessboard the way she did. "We'll have no more argument." She made her voice implacable. "This must be done."

Lady Sarah struggled with one of the buckles. "Send one of your lords. Let them earn their keep."

"There is only *one* queen."

Master Raddock stepped from the shadows. "Where will you meet them? At the castle or the outer walls?"

"The Flame has already proved adept at treachery. We'll not offer them a chance to enter Pellanor."

"At the outer walls then. At least the northern gate is finished."

One gate out of six finished, Liandra shook her head. "Then today will be full of ruses." She glared at her deputy shadowmaster. "Ruses might work for heralds but not for the Flame Army. You best tell the men to work harder." At her command, a second wall grew around her capital city. Cobbled together from buildings and stoppered alleyways, with ironshod gates erected at the major roadways, she hoped the new wall might offer a thin defense. Pellanor was a city long in love with luxury and commerce, a ripe plum for an enemy army, yet she swore to weave thorns into the walls, to find a way to protect her capital and her people.

"Will you wear the helm?" Lady Sarah lifted a silver helm crowned with a wreath of gold roses.

Liandra gazed into the mirror. A warrior queen stared back. Sculpted in silver, she looked magnificent, like something out of legend. Gleaming in the candlelight, the armor lent her an aura of strength; she began to understand the appeal. She turned sideways, studying the effect. Mirror-polished to reflect the sun, the armor was perfect, but her face was pale, too pale, like a ghost called from the grave. "More rouge and no helm. We want our people to know their queen and to be assured."

"And the sword?"

The hilt was an heirloom, golden roses entwined to make a basket-weave hilt, but the blade was fresh-forged, a slender rapier, light enough for a queen to wield yet honed to a deadly edge. Liandra knew little about swords, yet she'd insisted on a real blade, lest she make a mockery of her men. She'd even practiced, brandishing it in the privacy of her solar. She felt ridiculous waving a sword through the air, but the demands of image knew no bounds, forcing herself to practice till the mirror told her she'd got it right. "Yes, the sword."

"Majesty let me." Master Raddock stepped from the shadows. Taking the sheathed sword from Lady Sarah, he knelt, his thick fingers fumbling with the belt. It should have been Robert girding the sword at her waist, but he was away, serving queen and kingdom in a risky gambit. *Oh, Robert, may the gods keep you safe!* She thought of the risks they both faced, of the dangers threatening her kingdom, and all the while her pug-faced shadowmaster fumbled the belt around her waist. He finished the buckle and stared up at her, his face rapt. "You're a vision!"

If only the enemy were so easily conquered.

Her women swarmed around, making last minute adjustments. Adding an emerald cape embroidered with golden roses and a pair of jewel encrusted gauntlets to complete the effect. Liandra shimmered as she moved, casting reflected light around the chamber. "We are ready."

The doors opened and the queen left her solar for the first time in days.

An honor guard snapped to attention. The men gasped to see their queen gird in armor. More than one stood with his mouth agape and his eyes agog. She drank in their admiration like a balm to her soul. "Come, we have an enemy to meet." She set a swift pace, a show of strength, but she soon regretted it. Sweat built beneath the armor and she felt dizzy on the stairs. Gritting her teeth, she forced herself to endure.

Guards leaped as she approached, opening the doors to the inner courtyard, admitting a welcome breath of cold. Trumpets blared and a hundred knights snapped to attention, arms and armor gleaming, horses snorting, emerald banners streaming. Liandra swayed on the steps, gathering her strength. Her squire held the bridle for her stallion, a massive eighteen-hand white warhorse named Delusion. Bred for battle, he looked fierce but in truth he was a sweetheart with a gentle mouth and a smooth gait, but on this day, still sore from the birthing bed, the horse looked impossibly tall, and the saddle a torture device. Sir Durnheart must have felt her trepidation, for he knelt, cupping his hands, offering to give her a leg up. With a gracious nod, she accepted. The tall knight nearly lifted her into the saddle. She threw her leg across, refusing to sit sidesaddle, needing to be seen as a monarch instead of a woman, but image had its price. Pain spiked through her. Gritting her teeth, she played with the reins, running her fingers through Delusion's beribboned mane, gaining time to master the agony.

Sitting straight, Liandra nodded and the castle's massive outer doors creaked open.

Her people lined the cobbled street, young and old, rich and poor, concern writ large across their faces. Their silence reflected their fears, like a millstone around her neck.

Liandra made the smallest of moves and Delusion answered, leading her knights into the street with a stately prance.

At first there was no response, just the clops of hooves on cobbles, the jangle of armor and bridles, the snap of banners overhead. She felt the stares of her people, weighing her, judging her, then someone gave a shout. "The Queen will save us! *Gloriana martial,* the Queen of Light! Long live the Queen!"

Others took up the chant. *"Gloriana martial!"* The shout echoed through the street like thunder. Their acclaim washed across her like a healing balm. Gratitude and strength flowed through her. Sitting straight in the saddle, the queen supped on their cheers. More than any treasure or riches, this was the reason she ruled, for the love of her people, for the sake of her kingdom. In Liandra's eyes, a sovereign's worth was best measured by the people's prosperity. Despite the war, despite all the dire threats, she felt rich by their acclaim and she swore by all the gods to keep her people safe.

Her people crowded both sides of the cobbled street. Women strewed dried flowers in the path of her stallion. Children raced alongside, smiling and laughing. Men doffed their hats and knelt as she rode by. And always there was the cheering, following her like a thundering entourage of approval. She hoped the enemy heard, hoped they trembled at the heart of her people.

All too soon, she reached the outer gates.

The crowd stilled to a hush and the soldiers snapped to attention.

Major Ranoth met her, holding the bridle of her stallion.

Gritting her teeth, Liandra swung down from the saddle. The first step was jarring, a jolt of pain. Sir Durnheart was there, offering an arm, but she waved him away; weakness was something she could leastwise afford.

She gave the troops a cursory inspection, and then she faced the stairs, a rickety affair clinging to the side of the building. Four flights to the top, her armor seemed to drag her down like an anchor, yet she refused to succumb. Biting her lip, she made it to the roof. The view was almost as demoralizing as the rickety stairs. Instead of a crenellated tower, she stood upon the flat roof of a squat stone building. Compared to mighty Lingard, the outer walls of Pellanor were a pitiful joke. The city's outer defense was nothing more than toothy blocks of buildings connected by hastily built walls. The patchwork defense fooled no one. It might be enough to break a cavalry charge, but a determined infantry could scale the walls with short ladders and grapples. Liandra suppressed a shudder; more proof guile was her city's best defense.

Major Ranoth intruded. "The heralds await."

She nodded, approaching the edge of the roof.

The enemy waited on the road below, thirty mounted soldiers, their red tabards defiant in the afternoon light. One wore a mitered helm, she guessed him a bishop, a hateful cleric of the Flame, but her gaze stumbled when she saw the hilt of a blue steel sword. Even without seeing the details, she knew. *My son's sword! How many children must I lose?* For a heartbeat her vision blurred, but then she took a deep breath, gathering her strength.

Cruel laughter echoed up from below. The mitered cleric rode forward, his deep voice pitched to carry. "So this is *mighty* Pellanor!" His words dripped with mocking. "A fitting fortress for a queen! But then women know so little of war." Thumping his chest, he gave her a lewd grin. "When we sack your city, I'll be the first to smash your portcullis."

Her men bristled at the insult, more than a few reaching for their swords. From the corner of her eye, Liandra saw one of her archers nock an arrow. "No." She pierced the young man with her stare. "The rules of parlay will be observed."

Sheepish, he loosed the tension on his bow.

She turned her stare back to the bishop. "What brings you to our gates?"

"I bring word that your cause is hopeless. You fight for an empty throne. House Tandroth has no heirs." His horse reared as he unsheathed the blue steel sword. Gasps of dismay echoed from her walls. The bishop leaned forward, driving the blue steel blade deep into the grass bordering the road. The sword quivered upright, proof of its mythic sharpness. The bishop turned his stallion in a tight circle, his voice loud and taunting. "Your crown prince is captured, his life forfeit, a prisoner of the Flame. His sword proves the truth of my words." He reached into a saddlebag and withdrew a sealed scroll. "And the younger prince, Danly, is sworn to serve the Flame, even delivering Lingard into our hands." Sneering, the bishop brandished the scroll aloft. "His own handwriting gives proof to my words." He tossed the scroll before the city gates, a contemptuous gesture. "I bring you proof. I bring you truth. And now I bring you terms." He stilled his stallion, staring up at her. "Surrender your city and your people will live. Surrender your throne and your royal son will be spared. Yield to the Flame or death will be your only legacy." He grinned up at her. "What say you?"

She kept her voice firm. "We'll see your proof first."

He made a mocking bow.

The queen gestured and the word was passed. The newly built gates slowly creaked open. Major Ranoth emerged, resplendent in burnished armor and cloak of emerald green. Tall and dignified, he strode toward the blue steel sword. Pulling the sword from the grass, he stooped to gather the scroll. Without a word, he returned to the gates.

The ironbound gates clanged shut.

The enemy horses snorted and stamped, the white and red banners snapping overhead.

The queen waited statue-still, like a figure carved in silver. A breeze stirred her cloak, like emerald wings at her shoulders.

The major returned. "It is his blade."

A sharp pain pierced her chest, but Liandra refused to believe it, fighting a mother's pain with a queen's logic. She took the sword, no mistaking the crossed roses on the hilt, the crown on the pommel. At least she had his sword back, a symbol of heroism to her people. "It is his sword."

Beside her, the major's voice quavered. "Is he dead?"

"No."

"But the sword?"

"Exactly." She filled her voice with conviction, knowing her words would be repeated. "His signet ring would be proof enough, a trifling compared to the value of the sword."

The major's eyes widened, a flush of hope on his face. "They don't have his ring?"

She nodded.

"A sword can be dropped in battle...but the ring..."

She finished his thought, "...stays with the man."

"And the scroll?"

"The scroll matters not. We have but one son."

Below, the bishop grew impatient. "What say you? Will you surrender?"

Anger smoldered within her, yet she kept her voice to a mere whisper. "Give him our answer." Her gaze flicked to the young archer. "One arrow only."

Quick as summer lightning, the archer loosed a single shaft. The arrow struck true, the feathered shaft lodging deep in the bishop's throat. The bishop clawed at the arrow, his horse rearing beneath him. He toppled backward, felled dead, his boot tangled in the stirrup. The red escort drew swords, staring up at the wall, their faces wary. One soldier dared to hail the queen, outrage in his voice. "You broke parlay! You killed the emissary!"

"For Lingard. The treachery of the Flame is repaid in kind." For the sake of her own soldiers, she added. "It's war not chess."

"You'll die! You'll all die for this!"

She stepped away from the edge. "Give them a warning shot. If they persist, they're yours."

Her archers grinned. A single bow twanged and then she heard hoof beats galloping hard. The heralds were in retreat, bearing her answer north.

Liandra gasped in pain. Her task done, her strength bled out of her. She turned and left the wall, making her way back down the rickety stairs. The armor proved perilous. Halfway down she nearly fell, a sharp pain stabbing her abdomen. When she reached the ground, she was almost faint with agony, but she dared not show it.

Sir Durnheart lifted her into the saddle. She took the reins, leading her escort back through the city. Her people remained standing along the street, as if keeping vigil, but their cheers had grown silent, their faces fret with worry.

Liandra had little to give them. She clung to the saddle, willing herself to remain erect, but when she reached the castle gates, she forced herself to make one last gesture. With a light touch of her knee, she turned her stallion to face her people. A thousand faces met her stare, like children desperate to be reassured. She raised her voice, pitched to carry. "Keep faith with your queen and Pellanor will not fall." She drew the rapier while asking Delusion for a rear. The great warhorse reared, massive hooves striking the air, while she brandished her sword to the heavens. "By the Light, we shall be victorious!"

"The Queen! The Queen!" Her people rushed toward her like a tide returning to the sea.

Pain stabbed her, nearly loosing her hold on the pommel. She turned her warhorse, asking for a gallop, desperate for the sanctuary of the castle. The great horse must have felt her need, galloping through the gates, across the courtyard, and up the very steps of the castle. "Close the gates." She issued one last order and then slid from the saddle, succumbing to darkness.

56

Stewart

Snow fell in flurries, big fat flakes muffling the clop of hooves, dusting the land with a cold blanket. Stewart hunched in the saddle, desperate for warmth, desperate to sever his bonds. Skarn kept them moving without a break, always on a westerly course. Stewart assumed the brigand leader sought some kind of bolt hole, a hideout of sorts. Once there the chances of escape would diminish. Stewart gripped the small stone, sawing back and forth, scraping the rope raw. The outer edge frayed but it was not enough, not nearly enough.

His horse perked up, increasing the pace, as if it sensed home. Stewart gripped the pommel, trying to keep his balance, while sawing at his bonds. The snow fell harder, obscuring the sky, a blur of white dimming to dusk. They cantered across a fallow farm field and entered a forest thick with old growth trees.

Pale light speared through gnarled branches, cold and forbidding, almost twilight. A breeze carried the faint stench of rotting bodies. The forest stank of death yet the snow was unsullied. Stewart shivered, glancing left and right, but the brigands seemed unconcerned. Skarn forged ahead, winding a path through the forest while the others fanned out behind, a jangle of armor and weapons. Stewart could only follow, his horse on a lead, his mouth gagged, his hands bound to the saddle, but a sixth sense screamed of danger.

A loud crack broke the snowy silence.

A huge log swung down from the branches. Suspended on ropes, it cut through the brigands like a battering ram. Three men went down in a bone-crunching thud. Horses reared and kicked, wounded men screamed, sparking a pandemonium of fear. The log swung back for a second blow, punching through their ranks like a massive fist. Men scrambled to get out of the way. Skarn yelled, *"Ambush! Scatter!"*

Roland yanked Stewart's horse to the left. The sudden swerve nearly threw Stewart from the saddle. He dropped his stone, clinging to the pommel. Branches wet with snow whipped across his face. Stewart ducked, desperate to keep his seat. They plunged through the forest at breakneck speed, the horses mad with panic. Suddenly the ground in front gave way, exposing a deep pit lined with stakes. Six men disappeared, horses and riders swallowed by the toothy maw. Tortured screams rose from the pit, the dying impaled amongst the dead. Stewart's horse reared, teetering on the edge. He felt the horse begin to topple, the ground crumbling beneath its hooves, a deadly fall toward the spikes. Stewart threw himself from the saddle, but the rope pulled short, tethering him to the horse. He dug his heels in, straining against the horse's weight. The mare screamed, eyes wide with fright, slowly toppling into the pit. Pulled towards death, his boots found purchase against a root. Every muscle screaming with strain, he fought to keep his footing...and then the rope snapped. *It snapped!* Flung backwards, he hit the ground hard, watching as the hapless mare fell into the pit. Squeals of pain pierced the forest, but he was alive.

He was alive!

Clawing apart the last of his bonds, he threw the hated gag into the woods. Finally free, he stretched his arms wide, gulping the chilly air. The brigands had wandered into an ambush but was it set by friends or foe? Crouching low, he tried to make sense of the chaos. Snow shrouded the forest, screams coming from every direction. Twilight fell hard, the dim light adding to the confusion. A drum of hooves approached. Stewart drifted to the left, keeping low, trying to stay out of sight. He tripped and fell, landing on something soft rotting beneath the snow. A bloated corpse half eaten by predators stared back at him. He stifled a scream and then looked again. The fading light revealed a hint of red, a soldier of the Flame. Desperate for a weapon, he searched the corpse. He found a sword belt, but the scabbard was empty. Swearing softly, he searched the ground.

Steel clashed nearby, the sound of swords clanging on swords.

Unarmed and vulnerable, his search grew frantic. He scrabbled through the snow, his bare hands numbed by cold. Just as the fighting drew near his hand closed on something sharp. He tugged hard, freeing it from the forest floor, and found himself holding an antler shed last spring. Three feet long with six sharp tines, he hefted it like a battleaxe. A snarl rose in his throat. Perhaps it was being armed, or the primitiveness of his weapon, either way he hungered for vengeance. Keeping low, he slunk through the woods, the clash of swords luring him toward the heart of the fight.

The gods must have heard his prayer.

He came up behind Skarn. The brigand leader battled a brown-cloaked stranger, a sword against a quarterstaff. Skarn fought with a feral intensity, the curved sword hacking bites from the quarterstaff, driving the stranger to the ground. Laughing, he raised his sword for the killing blow; moonlight glinting on his mitered helm.

Stewart stepped from the brush. "Fight me, Skarn."

The brigand leader swung around, but Stewart did not wait. Bellowing a fearsome yell, he charged with the antlers held high, driving the tines deep into the brigand's throat. Skarn gagged, frothing a gurgle of blood. *"You!"*

Stewart twisted the antlers. "Choke on this!" Skarn's sword fell from his hand, death glazing his eyes.

Stewart wrenched the antlers free, but something snapped within him. A pent-up rage erupted like molten lava. Standing over the body, he plunged the antlers down, over and over again, rending flesh, spattering blood, shredding his enemy like a beast run amok.

"It's over."

A hand gripped his arm.

Stewart whirled, the bloody antlers poised for battle. But instead of an enemy he saw a familiar face, a vision of pale blond hair framing a face from his dreams. Stunned, he staggered backwards. "Is it you?" His hand sought his seashell broach, as if caught in a dream, or perhaps battle madness. "Is it really you?" His voice sounded hoarse, gruff as a beast.

She gave a tentative smile. "The fighting's over, you're among friends."

Her voice, the vision had *her* voice, but she couldn't be here. He stumbled towards her, half afraid to hope. "Jordan, is it really you?"

57

Jordan

Jordan gaped at the wild man standing before her. Spattered with blood and holding an antler like a weapon, he looked more beast than man. Dead leaves tangled his dark hair like an avatar of the forest. His beard was matted with filth, his clothes little more than dirt encrusted rags, his face gaunt with hunger, and the stench, she held her breath against the stench...but his eyes, something in his eyes reminded her of the prince she loved. *"Stewart?"*

"My love!" He threw the antler aside. Rushing toward her, he scooped her into his arms, his beard rough against her face. The first kiss was tender, the second fierce. His arms held her tight, nothing but sinew and bone, more proof of his ordeal. A sob escaped her, wondering what trials he must have endured.

He stepped away, looking abashed. "I'm sorry."

She stared at him, her arms bereft. "Why?"

"I'm so..." he grimaced, looking down at himself and then at her, "I've gotten blood on you." He took a deep breath. "And I stink."

"Nothing water can't fix." His ordeal suddenly seemed like a wall between them.

He stared at her, a haunted look in his eyes.

She reached out, shyly taking his hand. "I'm not used to your beard." His hand was encrusted with dirt, the nails chipped and broken, so different from the hands of a prince, yet their fingers entwined, still a perfect fit. "We're together now."

"Yes!" His reply held a fierce longing, his hand gripping hers, an electric touch.

Need shivered through her. She drifted toward him, like iron to a loadstone. They might have kissed again, but Rafe stumbled towards them, his quarterstaff nicked and battered, his face bruised. "I owe you my life," his gaze dropped to their linked hands, his eyes flaring wide. "So this is your bonny prince!" He clapped Stewart on the back. "Never saw a man wield a better antler." The breeze shifted and the monk took a step backwards. "What's that smell? Like cheese gone bad...or something worse."

Stewart's gaze hardened. "My men! I need to see to my men."

The others emerged from the woods, Thaddeus gripping a bloodied sword, Ellis holding an orb of moonlight, Ronald looking stern in his golden tabard emblazoned with a mailed fist. And with them came three men in filthy rags, tattered scarecrows with haunted eyes. The largest strode towards Stewart and knelt. "My lord, we owe you our lives." The other two knelt as well, their heads bent in homage.

Stewart said, "Only three?"

The big man nodded. "Percy died in one of the pits. Dalt was crushed by the ram."

"Then arise, for henceforth, you three shall be my royal guard."

Jordan watched as pride transformed their faces. They'd knelt as wretched scarecrows, mere shadows of men, but they arose as royal guards, taking places of honor behind their rightwise prince. Jordan swelled with love. Despite his ordeal, Stewart had kept his honor and saved his men. Beneath the filth, he was still the man she loved. She offered him her hand. "Come, we have much to share." She gave him a wry smile. "And you need to bathe." She drew him towards the ruined tower, their hands locked, their fingers entwined.

58

Danly

Lingard's streets had grown dangerous, a hunting ground for fanatics chasing heretics, the blood sport of a religion run amok. Danly shivered against the cold, slinking down a back alleyway, a dagger clutched beneath a plain brown cloak. Every footfall seemed a threat. Soldiers turned fanatics, citizens turned informers, heretics turned rabid prey, Danly didn't trust the lot of them. Escape was the only thing that mattered. Somehow he had to find a way out of this religious cauldron, but his luck had soured. Even the weather had turned against him, snow dusting the streets, as if the gods tracked his very steps. Danly cursed under his breath, scurrying down a moonlit street.

The rhythmic tramp of hobnailed boots gave warning, a red-cloaked patrol searching the quarter. Danly scuttled back into the shadows. Hiding in a doorway, he held his breath, praying for the patrol to pass. Sweat trickled down his back despite the cold. Every foray into the streets seemed more perilous. Time was against him; he had to find a way out.

The tramp of boots receded, but Danly counted half a hundred heartbeats before venturing back into the street. Patrols randomly gathered fodder from the streets, keeping the dungeons full and the pyres fueled. With the Lord Raven gone, the Bloody Bishop was on a rampage. No one was safe, not even red-cloaked soldiers or a turned-cloak prince.

Danly crossed the street and slipped into the tavern, repulsed by the reek. Spilled ale and sweaty bodies, the vile smells clamped around him like a suffocating hand. The room was crowded, mostly with soldiers. It seemed hunting heretics was a thirsty sport. Keeping his hood raised and his shoulders hunched, he wove his way toward the back. Vengar sat in the corner, a flagon of ale on the table, more of Danly's gold wasted on drink.

Swallowing his anger, he took a seat opposite the red-haired captain.

"What kept you?" Vengar's words were slurred, but the captain's eyes were not bloodshot, perhaps he only feigned being drunk.

Danly kept his voice to a low whisper. "Why this place?" Vengar varied their meeting places, always a different tavern or a low-class brothel.

"Safer." Vengar poured another mug, spilling ale onto the table.

"*Safer!*" His voice hissed with anger. "Are you mad? This place is crawling with red-cloaks."

"Better to hide among the cats than the mice."

The captain had a point. Mollified, Danly reached for the flagon, pouring himself a mug. "When do we leave?" Danly took a long swallow and nearly gagged, spewing a mouthful onto the floor. Cheap ale cut with water, a foul combination.

Vengar laughed, slapping the table with a meaty hand. "Can't hold yer ale!" Lowering his voice, he hissed, "Don't make a spectacle of yourself."

Fear sliced through Danly like a knife. Wiping his mouth on his sleeve, he hunched in his chair, but his eyes shot daggers at the captain. "When do we leave?"

"Plans have changed. I need more gold."

"*More!*"

"Keep your voice down."

Danly gripped the table. "What do you mean more?"

Vengar leaned forward, holding his mug in front of his mouth. "The Lord Raven emptied the city of horses. None left except for the messengers and the high ranking bishops."

"So?"

"So it means we'll have to leave on foot."

On foot, in winter, the plan kept getting worse, but Danly was desperate. Religious mania gripped the city, a rabid dog capable of turning on anyone. And then there was the queen's shadowmaster. Danly shivered. "So when do we leave?"

"The Bloody Bishop has the fortress shut tight as a virgin's ass. The only way out is with one of the patrols."

Danly didn't like the sound of this. "A patrol?"

"A patrol is twenty men led by a sergeant or a captain. That means finding eighteen men I trust enough to bribe, plus a sergeant or a captain. That means more gold."

Eighteen men, the number felt like a noose around Danly's neck. "The more men, the more risk." One informant and they'd both burn in the flames.

Vengar sneered. "Yah, but it's my neck being risked, my *lord*."

Danly didn't like the man's tone...but he didn't have much choice. "I'll find a way to get the gold."

"Good. And you can pay for the ale."

Danly tossed a coin on the table while slipping a purse of golds onto the chair. The captain scooped the purse with a deft hand. They agreed on their next meeting place and then Danly left the captain to nurse his watered ale. Keeping his head down and his hood raised, he passed through the gauntlet of soldiers without attracting noticed. Reaching the door, he stepped outside, relieved by the cold kiss of night air.

The tromp of boots made his blood freeze.

Danly skulked in the doorway, tempted to slip back inside, but something made him wait. A patrol returned from a late-night round-up, thirty prisoners herded before them, a fresh catch for the dungeons. Danly watched the poor bastards as they passed, their faces stunned, marching towards torture and death. Most were soldiers, caught in the wrong place at the wrong time without gold enough for a bribe, but a few were citizens, even one woman, probably a low-class whore by the look of her. Perhaps she'd provide a bribe of another sort. He stared at the damned, startled when the torchlight gleamed on silver-gray hair. Danly's breath hissed. Among the prisoners he saw a familiar face, a hated face. They'd caught the Master Archivist. Triumph shivered through Danly, but then he stilled, considering. He wondered if the soldiers knew what they'd caught. The queen's spymaster appeared to be just another prisoner, a shark swimming with minnows, caught in a fisherman's net. Danly wondered how much the Flame might pay to learn the truth of their catch.

The tromp of boots receded. Danly felt compelled to follow. At first he thought the patrol was heading back to the dungeons at the keep, but then they turned into a side street, stopping at a guard barracks. So the rumors were true. Lingard's dungeons overflowed with heretics, so the soldiers had started keeping prisoners in the barracks, a way station to hell. Danly hid in the shadows, watching. The queen's shadowmaster was a valuable prize and a dangerous threat, yet the choice of prison proved the soldiers were ignorant of their catch. Danly grinned, feeling like his luck had change. Knowledge was power, the question was, who would pay more, the queen or the Flame?

59

Stewart

Stewart couldn't stop touching her. Couldn't believe he was free, and whole, and with *her*. Intoxicated by her nearness, he gently eased her pale blond hair behind her ear. "But however did you find me?"

They sat cross-legged on a bearskin rug, huddled beneath a tarp angled against the tower wall. Jordan's companions had hastily assembled the small shelter, giving the couple the boon of privacy. A brazier of coals emitted light and warmth while Jordan used a cloth to clean his wounds. She'd cried the first time she saw his ruined back, a crisscross of scars more suited to a slave than a prince. Her tears touched him, easing his own pent-up pain. Despite the ugliness of his ordeal, she never once shrank from him, even when he'd appeared like a wild man wielding an antler. Now, clean and shaven, he stared at her, unable to believe his own luck.

"It's a long story."

"I want to hear it."

She told him about the attack in the monastery and the monks' healing magic. He'd seen the jagged scar during their love making and he knew it should have been fatal. Stewart shuddered to think of how close he'd come to losing her.

"Once I woke from the healing spell, I started to have visions." She hesitated. "Some of the monks name it a gift from the gods." Jordan shivered, a mantle of weariness falling across her shoulders. "But all my visions are nightmares, warnings of treachery and death. Somehow I'm supposed to use the visions to make a difference but they don't always make sense." She stared at him, a tentative question in her gaze. "I feel pulled in a hundred different directions."

Visions and magic, it seemed like something from a bard's song, yet how else could she be here, waiting to rescue him. "I believe you."

Her eyes widened, searching his face.

"How else could you have found me?" He reached for her, pulling her close, needing to touch all of her. Sheltered from the snow, from the howling cares of the world, they talked and touched and talked again, consumed with the need to fill all the empty spaces. Their first coupling had been rushed, a desperate collision of needs, a primal proof of life. Their second was slow and tender and full of soft kisses building to a profound soul-shuddering ecstasy, like nothing he'd ever known before. Sated, they drank a rich red wine and ate slivers of salted ham. Stewart used a dagger to cut another slice, feeding it to Jordan. "And ham? Wherever did you get this ham?" He took another bite, nearly swooning at the rich salty taste, ambrosia to his starving body.

"Yarl found it." Jordan laughed, clearly sharing his delight. "Sometimes I think the monks are magicians, conjuring stuff from thin air."

He took another slice. "No, seriously, I really want to know."

"Yarl found a hidden doorway to a subterranean vault. The monks were all excited about a stone statue in a side chamber, a massive hand with an eye carved in the palm, but the real treasure was the stores, casks of food and loot, like a dragon's lair. We've been eating well ever since."

"Not a dragon, but a brigand's lair. Ill-gotten gains raped from the countryside, Skarn's winter stores."

Jordan sobered. "Skarn, the brigand you killed, the one with the mitered helm?" Her voice held a dangerous edge. "The one who was going to sell you to the Flame?"

Stewart nodded, his hands curling into fists.

"I'm glad you killed him."

"So am I." Stewart met her sea-blue gaze. "I've seen what the Flame can do. I know what's out there, what the queen keeps at bay." Conviction filled him. "We have to find a way to defeat them. Without the queen there is no law, no honesty, no chance for a decent life." His gaze burned into her. "I never understood before, but I do now. Whatever it takes, the queen *must* win."

"I know." The worries of the outside world crowded her eyes. "Lingard has fallen."

He hissed with disbelief. "No!"

She nodded.

"I wondered when I saw Ronald among you. The war does not fare well for the Rose."

"There's more." In a grim tone, she told him about Danly playing the prince at the gates of Lingard, a traitor in emerald robes, betraying the city to the ravages of the Flame. "Ronald says they opened the city gates for him. They gave him a royal welcome, inviting the traitors in."

Stewart swore. "By the Dark Lord's balls, the queen should have strangled Danly at birth."

Jordan let him fume.

"Lingard betrayed by my own brother." A killing rage gripped Stewart. "Danly has always been a trial." He struggled to quell his anger. "A filthy traitor, and my own brother! But you wouldn't know what that feels like."

"Oh yes I would," her voice was soft but deadly, "not my brother but my aunt. My family lives under the Curse of the Vowels. We know what it's like to be betrayed by one of our own. Nothing cuts deeper, or hurts more."

He'd forgotten about the curse. He took her hand, kissing her upturned palm. "And if we have children, will the curse follow us?"

She blushed, giving him a shy smile. "No, the curse only follows the crowned royals. It's tied to the magic of the tuplets." Her smile turned to a devilish grin. "But ever since childhood, I've been collecting names that begin with a K."

He made a mock groan. "So I won't have any say in our children's names?"

"Not unless you want to bear them." But the playful glint in her eye quickly quenched to sadness.

"What is it?"

"I must leave on the morrow."

Her words cut like a dagger. "But I've just found you!"

"I know." She took a deep breath. "I told you about my visions. And now that you're here, now that you're safe, I must hurry to Navarre." She shook her head, a grim look on her face. "I fear I've lingered too long." The words rushed out of her. "For the sake of my family, for the sake of my homeland...and for Kath, I have to leave."

He heard the resolve in her voice. Having been saved by her visions, he could not gainsay the will of the gods, no matter the price. "I long to keep you with me, but we're both warriors. And we've both been given a second chance."

She gave him a searching stare.

"You were saved by the monk's magic and I was saved by your visions. The gods gifted us with a second chance. We need to make that second chance count." He gripped her hands tight, needing to touch her. "Duty beckons. We both have battles to fight. We'll do what we must to win this war, for our sovereigns, for our kingdoms, and for the sake of our own future. And when it is over, we'll never be parted, I swear it to you." He laid a fervent kiss on both her palms as if to seal the promise, but when he met her gaze he found sadness clouding her eyes.

"What is it?"

She looked away, a glint of tears in her eyes.

His hands gently cupped her face, turning her back towards him. "What is it? It pains me to see you unhappy."

"It's my dreams, my nightmares. I'm not sure if they're visions or just fears plaguing my mind." Her gaze clung to his, as if desperate for relief. "I fear for you, for *us*, if you return to Pellanor."

"Pellanor? What danger lurks in the Rose Court?"

She took a labored breath as if burdened by a terrible weight. "In my dreams I see you crossing the checkerboard floor of the audience hall...married to Jemma."

"Jemma! But it's *you* I love!"

"And it's Jemma the queen wants as a daughter-in-law." She turned away from him, hugging her knees to her chest, a ball of misery.

"I swear to you, it will not happen!"

"My visions do not lie."

That rocked him back on his heels, but he refused to give up. "You said yourself it might just be a nightmare, not a true vision?" But she kept her back to him, a wall of hurt. "Jordan, talk to me. Together we can figure this out."

She slowly turned, a pair of tears marring her face.

It hurt to see her cry. "The monks say the gods give us a choice, right?"

She gave a tentative nod.

"Then perhaps your visions are a warning, a god-given chance to change our fate?"

She waited, watching him through tear-strewn eyes.

He knelt before her, taking her hands. "Then let's change our fate. Let's grasp our destiny. Marry me?"

A smile broke across her face. "I already said I'd marry you, we hand-fasted last Midwinter."

"Yes, but I'm asking you to marry me, here, now."

"Here? Now?"

He laughed. "Why not, surely the monks can perform a wedding. And what better place for a wartime marriage than a ruined tower?" He sobered, holding her hands tight. "Jordan, I'd lay down my life for queen and kingdom, but after all I've seen, after all I've endured, I will not give up my one chance for love." His voice deepened. "The gods brought us together. It's their visions that led you to this tower. So I ask you, here and now, marry me? Be my queen?"

"Yes."

The love in her voice overflowed his heart. He pulled her close. They kissed, long and deep, a promise of love, a promise of passion, but then he pulled away with a sigh, tucking her pale blonde hair behind her ear. "You'd best get ready."

"Ready?" Her voice was muzzy with passion.

He chuckled, a deep throaty sound. "For your wedding." Grinning, he pulled on his boots and strode from the tent. He left her in a blind panic, sorting through her clothes as he went in search of the monks.

60

Jordan

A crescent moon danced along the edge of the night sky, still a few hours from dawn. The wedding party assembled in the heart of the ruined tower, snowflakes falling amongst the tumbled stones, but Jordan did not feel the cold. Every snowflake, every star overhead, seemed like a boon from the gods, a blessing upon their marriage. Dressed in her checkered cloak and a borrowed tunic of midnight blue, she waited for the ceremony to begin.

The strum of a lyre echoed through the crimson tower. The wedding song faltered, fingers fumbling to find the right notes, causing Jordan to smile. Rafe was doing his best, but she'd always thought Justin would play at her wedding. She whispered a silent prayer, wishing her brother well, refusing to let anything mar the magic of the moment.

Thaddeus offered his arm. "Shall we?"

She took his arm, letting the sword master lead her into the ruins.

The others waited in the heart of the tower. Ronald and Owen stood behind Stewart, both men in burnished armor, standing surety for the groom. Stewart wore borrowed clothing, a mixture of brown and blue, a sword belted to his side, nothing to indicate his royal rank, but to Jordan's eyes, he looked handsome, his long dark hair cascading to his shoulders, his face alight with promise. Seeing her, he touched his seashell broach and gave her a radiant smile.

Warmth rushed through her, suffuse with joy.

Beside her, Thaddeus said the age-old words. "Who comes to claim this bride?"

"I do." Stewart stepped forward, offering his arm.

Thaddeus played his part, his voice gruff with warning. "Guard her well."

Smiling, Jordan signaled her acceptance, stepping from her friend to her love. Linking hands, they turned to face Ellis. In the wane moonlight, with her dark hair flowing past her shoulders and her robes of midnight blue, the monk looked like a priestess of old, invested with the all the power of the gods. Raising her arms to the heavens, her voice rang with the words of ancient ritual. "Heart to heart, hand to hand, mind to mind, will ye wed in the Light?"

They answered in unison. "We will."

"Then kneel and pledge your troth before the gods and man."

They knelt, staring up at the monk who served as a priestess.

"We gather here for the joining of two hearts and two royal houses, a sacred union of marriage." Ellis smiled at her. "Jordan, princess of Navarre, will ye bind your heart and body to Stewart, forsaking all others, so that Two may become One beneath the Light of the gods, for as long as ye both shall live?"

Jordan felt the solemn words wash across her like a balm. "I do."

"Stewart, prince of Lanverness, will ye bind your heart and body to Jordan, forsaking all others, so that Two may become One beneath the Light of the gods, for as long as ye both shall live?"

Stewart squeezed her hand, his grip as sure as his words. "I do."

Ellis raised the crystal orb to the night sky, summoning the moonlight. "By the power of the Light, I call upon all the gods to witness this sacred union." Moonlight coalesced in the orb, radiant as a captured star.

Beside her, Stewart gasped in wonder.

Jordan shivered, awed by the monk's power.

A soft silvery light filled the ruined tower, like a blessing from the gods.

Ellis held the glowing orb over their clasped hands. "Let this ring of light be proof of your sacred vows." She wove the glowing ball around their hands, weaving a trail of moonlight around their wrists. "Bound by the light of the moon, bound by the shine of the stars, bound by the favor of heaven, bound by eternal love." Jordan stared in wonder, her hand bound to Stewart's with shimmering ropes of moonlight. "Let these two be forever wed by the power of the Light." Ellis tied an intricate knot and then the orb darkened, returning to a ball of clear witch-glass, yet the glow around their hands remained bright. "You may stand."

Jordan stood, her hand still bound to Stewart's by ropes of light.

Ellis spread her arms wide in benediction. "Henceforth let it be known across Erdhe that Princess Jordan of House Navarre and Prince Stewart of House Tandroth are bound in marriage by the Light of the gods. What the gods have joined let no man put asunder."

A cheer erupted from the others.

Ellis smiled. "You may take your first kiss as husband and wife."

Jordan turned towards Stewart. They kissed, twice for love and once for passion, and then they both looked at the light binding their hands. Jordan gave Stewart a devilish smile and he grinned in reply. By unspoken agreement, they unlinked their fingers and tried pulling their hands apart, but the moonlight ropes held them fast, their wrists bound tight as steel. Gasping in surprise, Jordan looked at Ellis.

The monk gave her a wry smile. "I said it was for all eternity."

Jordan stared slack-mouthed, but Ellis only laughed. Reaching out, she touched the bonds and the moonlight faded away, melting into their skin. Jordan shivered, feeling a tingle run up her arm.

Ellis chuckled. "The bonds would have faded with the dawn's first light. Moonlight powers the weave."

"Kiss her! Kiss her! Kiss her!" the others grew impatient, taking up the age-old chant.

They turned to face their friends, and then Stewart swept her into his arms. Dipping her backwards, he gave her a deep passionate kiss that seemed to melt the bones from her body. When he finally let her up for air, she wavered on her feet. He nuzzled her ear, "My queen of seashells." A radiant smile broke across her face, realizing she was truly married.

Someone yelled, "Break open the ale!" and the celebrations began.

Stewart gazed down at her. "May I have this first dance?"

She answered with a smile and he swept her into a waltz. There was no music, no lilting harp or pounding drum, no ballroom floor, yet they danced to their own tune, twirling beneath the glittering stars. Stewart drew her close, a hint of concern in his voice. "Do you mind not having a court wedding?"

She gazed into his eyes. "Bound by moonlight, witnessed by the stars, what could be more perfect?"

He held her close. "Everything's perfect." They danced close as lovers, lost in their own intimacy.

But then a lookout's cry broke the merriment. "Look to the north!"

The revelry stilled and they turned to stare skyward. Dawn's red light broke across the east, revealing a great white frost owl winging toward the ruins. Flying from the north, the owl spiraled around the tower in a gentle glide, coming to rest atop the stairs. "*Whooooo?*" The owl shimmered and stretched into a blur of light, transforming into a blue robed monk.

Beside her, Stewart swore in surprise. "By the gods!"

Jordan whispered, "The magic of the monks."

He gave her a sharp stare. "These monks are full of secrets," and then they both turned to watch as the monk descended the stone stairway.

"I bring word of Lingard."

The others crowded the newcomer with warm greetings, but Stewart's voice cut through the welcome. "What word of Lingard?"

For just a moment, Jordan closed her eyes, resisting the tug of destiny, trying to hold onto her wedding bliss, but the call to arms was implacable. She watched as Stewart transformed from a bridegroom to a warrior prince. His hand on his sword hilt, his voice full of command, he cut through the others. "What word of Lingard?" And she, as a warrior princess, stood by his side.

The newcomer hesitated till the introductions were made. Hearing their names, his eyes widened, betraying a hint of surprise. "My name is Aeroth, a monk of the Kiralynn Order." He offered them each a half-nod. "The heir of Lanverness, a princess of Navarre, and the heir to Lingard, all gathered in the same place, proof the Crimson Tower remains a sanctuary for the Light. Truly the gods lend a hand." His gaze turned to Stewart. "Many are searching for you, while others name you dead."

Stewart's voice brooked little patience. "Yet you found us."

"The Kiralynn Order has its ways."

"So I've learned."

Thaddeus intervened. "The Crimson Tower is known to the Order. Aeroth came to find *us*, not you."

"Yet finding you here is a boon from the gods. We have much to discuss."

They left the ruined tower for the warmth of the stables. A small bonfire was lit in the corner, banishing the shadows. They settled around the blaze, sharing flagons of ale, smoked ham, a haunch of roast venison, fried potatoes, dried apples, a sack of walnuts, and a small bag of sugared plums. Jordan sat by her husband, watching as her wedding feast became a council of war.

Aeroth leaned forward, his gaze fixed on Stewart. "The Flame divides its forces."

Beside her, Stewart quickened like a hound to the hunt. "We've been waiting for this! We've never had the numbers to confront their whole army, always hoping to splinter the main force, but they never took the bait."

"Does the enemy keep Lingard?" Ronald's gaze held a haunted look.

Aeroth nodded. "The Flame still holds Lingard, but they've emptied the city of cavalry."

"Do they ride on Pellanor?" Tension leaped through Stewart like a taut bow.

"No. They ride at a hard canter towards the southwest, six thousand mounted men or more, but they ride without foot soldiers or supply wains."

Thaddeus joined the discussion. "Without foot or supplies, it sounds like they're in a hurry. A raiding party of some sort?"

Aeroth nodded. "Yes, but to what end?"

Stewart said, "Doesn't matter, as long as it's not Pellanor." He leaned forward, his gaze keen. "What matters is that they've split their army, giving us a chance to even the odds. Question is, should we chase the riders or go for the foot soldiers in the city?"

Thaddeus said, "*We?*"

Stewart answered. "The Rose Army, assuming the owl-man can find them."

Aeroth nodded. "The army can be found. From the air it's hard to hide so many men."

Jordan stared at the monk, considering the implications of his magic.

Ronald dragged the discussion back to Lingard. "What about the legion of tents surrounding the city?"

"Gone. Either they've ridden away, or they moved inside the walls."

"Damn them. We might have ambushed the enemy, trapping him against the outer walls, but once inside the fortress," Ronald shrugged, his face grim, "the walls of Lingard remain formidable, whether they're held by the Rose or the Flame."

"Unless someone opens the gates."

Owen cracked a walnut with his fist, the shells hissing in the fire. They grew quiet, thinking of the traitor prince.

Stewart looked to Ronald. "Any chance?"

Ronald shook his head. "Not likely. The bloody priests held a mass burning even before they took the last gate. Any loyalist was likely burnt or beheaded."

Thaddeus said, "Then you're best bet is to chase the cavalry and spring an ambush."

Stewart scowled. "But Lingard is the greater prize. The fortress is a thorn in our side, protecting the bulk of their army, surfeit with food and supplies. Lanverness can ill afford to let this war drag out. We need a decisive victory."

A grim silence settled across them. They sat mired in a dire puzzle that seemed to have no solution. Jordan felt Stewart's tension, his desperate need to turn the course of the war. She longed to help him, but her visions had never included Lingard. The bonfire snapped and crackled, spitting sparks. Jordan watched the blaze, the flames contained by a stone ring. An idea teased the back of her mind. "Perhaps we're looking at this the wrong way. Walls can protect...or they can imprison."

Stewart turned towards her. "What do you mean?"

She reeled the idea in, like a fish on a line. "Walls are built to protect, but if you seal the gates, they can also act as a prison, locking the enemy inside."

Stewart's gaze narrowed. "What good would that do?"

Jordan gestured to the bonfire. "Set fire to the city. Feed the Flame to the flames."

Thaddeus startled, sending a pointed glance toward Aeroth.

Stewart asked, "But how do we seal them inside?"

Jordan gestured to Ellis. "With a moon weaving."

"Abomination!" Ellis shuddered, her face turning pale. "Magic is not meant to be an instrument of war!"

"Yet you used it in the forest."

"To save a life, yes, or to protect my own, but not on such a scale, never against an entire city." She looked aghast. "What you speak of is a total abomination, a perversion of the way of Knowledge."

Rafe said, "But you know the Grand Master's decision? How can you say that?"

"The Grand Master agreed to use knowledge, yes, but not magic, not like that." Horror rode her face. "To use magic against an entire city...would be like the War of Wizards! I'll not be party to such an abomination!"

Jordan stared at the dark-haired monk. "So only the Mordant can use magic in warfare?"

Her words struck like a thunderclap. The monks stilled, their faces grim.

Jordan's voice dropped to a harsh whisper. "Are you part of this war, or merely watching? You need to choose a side, or all of Erdhe will fall to Darkness."

A stark silence descended on the stables, and then the monks erupted in argument.

Jordan took Stewart's hand. "Come." She led him outside, into the snow dusted morning. "They need time to talk, time to decide for themselves."

"Will they help?"

"Thaddeus and Rafe will help, but I'm not sure about Ellis, and she's the one you need." Jordan's voice turned grim. "Difficult to win if the monks won't help. You've seen their magic, and I suspect they're only showing us the fin on the shark."

"How many owl-men do they have?"

"I've only seen one other, a woman." Jordan shrugged. "The monks keep their secrets close."

Something shifted in his gaze. "And you, can I keep *you* close?" His hands caressed her arms, stroking a slow rhythmic temptation. He leaned close, his voice a husky whisper. "My warrior-bride."

Heat flashed through her. "I can only stay for the war council and then I ride for Navarre." His hands strayed to the ties on her tunic, his voice insistent. "Only for the council?" His lips set a burning trail down her throat. "Or will you stay to finish the marriage rites?" She was finding it hard to think. "What rites?" He slipped the belt from her waist. "The part where I make love to my wife." He swept her into his arms and carried her back to their lean-to. And for a while, nothing else mattered.

61

Danly

Danly retraced his steps, hastening back to the tavern, but Vengar was already gone. Cursing his ill luck, he returned to the streets, dodging late-night patrols as he sought every place he'd ever met the red-haired captain, but Vengar proved elusive. Hearing another patrol approach, he scrambled for a hiding place. Sweat poured out of him as he crouched behind a wagon. As the streets grew empty they grew more dangerous. Desperate to get out of the hunting fields, Danly tried one last place, a low-class brothel in the city's poor quarter.

Paying two coppers, he gained entrance to the tavern-turned-parlor. Patrons sat slumped at tables, sipping overpriced drinks while the whores made the rounds, exhibiting their wares. Danly scanned the room, but Vengar was not to be seen. Fearful of the streets, he took a table in the corner, keeping his back to the wall.

A gap-toothed whore with a low-cut bodice sashayed his way. She looked old, nearly thirty, her hair a straggle of dull brown, dark sags beneath her eyes. "What'll ya have, deary?"

Danly tossed a silver on the table. "Your best wine and don't water it."

Her smile widened, the coin disappearing into her bodice. "For another silver ya can have me as well, deary." She circled the table, leaning close to give him a better view of her cleavage. "All night if ya like." Her hand caressed the back of his neck, her breath foul.

Danly flinched as if touched by hot coals. "Just wine."

Rebuffed, she gave him a cold stare. "Oh, so you're one of those."

Anger warred with shock. "One of what?"

Her lips curled into a sneer. "One of those who just like to watch." She turned her back on him, the sashay gone from her walk.

Danly glowered. A eunuch in a brothel, anger warred with humiliation, but then he thought of the Master Archivist marching amongst the prisoners. Revenge was within his reach, such a sweet turn of fate. The queen's spymaster captured by the Flame, and it seemed the soldiers were unaware of their catch. Perhaps he should wait a while, giving the shadowmaster a taste of torture. The Flame priests were oh so zealous, especially with heretics.

A different whore brought a flagon and a cup, plunking them on the table, her lips curled in disdain. Whores got paid by the lay not by the cup.

Danly poured the wine, desperate for a drink. Sour swill but he drank it anyway, quenching his anger while he kept watch for Vengar. Maybe it was better this way, giving him time to think. Choices tumbled through his mind, such a delicious decision. Should he turn the spymaster over to the Bloody Bishop, or barter him to the queen for a promise of privilege? He'd planned to trade Steffan's secrets for protection and golds, but it might not be enough. Returning the queen's shadowmaster would be worth a considerable boon...but the queen was a long ways away. That left Danly with Bishop Taniff. He didn't trust the Bloody Bishop. Priests of the Flame made his skin crawl, especially the steely-eyed bishop. And then there was the man himself, the Master Archivist, the queen's shadowmaster. Hatred boiled within him, remembering the pain of the apothecary's knife. Danly shuddered, his teeth clenched. The spymaster deserved to have his balls cut, or better yet, shaved completely, cock and balls, nothing left of his manhood. Torture was too good for the queen's spymaster...but that left Danly trusting the Bloody Bishop. His head began to swim, a whirlpool of decisions. He took another drink, pounding down the wine despite its sour taste. But no matter how much he drank, the answer never appeared in the bottom of the cup.

He must have dozed.

Someone poked his shoulder, morning light seeping through the only window.

"Didn't expect to find you here."

Danly bolted awake.

Leonard Vengar stood over him, a sleep-tousled whore on each arm. "Looking for me?" Dismissing the whores with coin from his purse, the big man took a seat opposite Danly. "You look awful. Should have taken one of the lasses to bed."

Anger spiked through Danly. "Is this how you spend my golds?"

Vengar gave him an annoyed look. "The brothels are safe. They pay a hefty tithe to the soldiers and priests so they're never raided at night. Safest place to sleep in all of Lingard, but I forget myself," his face turned hard, "your lordship sleeps in the baron's keep."

Fear spiked through Danly, they'd be looking for him at the keep. He reached for the flagon, but it was empty. Gesturing to one of the women, he ordered another.

"So why are you here."

Why indeed? Danly decided to hedge his bets. "I'm thinking of changing the plan."

Vengar's gaze narrowed. "What do you mean?"

"The patrols have caught a prisoner valuable to the queen. It might be worth our while to take him with us."

Vengar paled. "Forget him. He's as good as dead. You'll never get a man out of Lingard's dungeons."

"He's not in the dungeons. They're holding him in one of the barracks, a makeshift prison."

Vengar turned thoughtful. "How valuable to the queen?"

"Very."

One of the serving women plunked a fresh flagon on the table. Danly was quick to fill his cup, gulping it down. The wine tasted like swill but it eased his headache.

Vengar leaned towards him. "Which barracks?"

Danly told him. "How many men do you have?"

"Counting the two of us, fourteen."

"Do you trust them?"

Vengar gave him a dead man stare.

"Can it be done?"

"Maybe. I need to take another look at the barracks. But if we do it, it'll have to be done in the small hours of the morning. We raid the barracks, dress in soldiers' tabards and then march straight for the south gate. I've been bribing the sergeant there, so my men get assigned to the patrol the woods beyond the castle." Vengar's voice lowered to a hush, his gaze as sharp as daggers. "We get one chance at this, prince. Is the prisoner worth the risk?"

That was the question, and Danly still did not have an answer. Danly poured another cup. "Take a look at the barracks and see if it can be done."

"Meet me here tomorrow, three turns of the hourglass before dawn."

Danly nodded, disliking the danger of such an early hour.

"And bring coin, gold and silver, anything for bribes. We'll need plenty to get out the gates. If we don't make the first patrol, we're dead."

Danly chugged another cup.

Vengar caught his arm. "Don't be late, prince."

Danly pulled away. "I'll be here."

"And don't forget to pay for the wine."

He reached for his purse, but the strings were cut. "*Bloody hell,* the whore stole my purse." Danly started to rise, but Vengar grabbed his arm. "Don't cause trouble."

"But my..."

Vengar speared him with a stare. "The brothels are a safe haven from the Flame. A haven you might need."

Danly sputtered, struggling to swallow his rage.

Vengar said, "I'll pay for the flagon." He flashed an insolent smile, releasing Danly's arm. "Next time, sleep with one of them. It's cheaper."

Danly straightened his cloak, struggling to regain his dignity. He strode from the brothel, stepping out into the dim morning light. A cold wind hit him like a slap. Even the weather was rude. Squinting against the sun, Danly pulled his cloak close and checked for patrols. At least the streets were no longer empty, the smell of fresh baked bread coming from somewhere down the lane. His mouth watered and his stomach growled, but Danly needed to return to the tower. Keeping his head lowered and his shoulders hunched, he made his way back through the maze of streets, and all the while he couldn't stop thinking of the danger. In the cold light of day, his decision seemed insane. Why risk his life for his enemy? Far better to trade the shadowmaster to the Flame and gain the bishop's favor. Perhaps the wine had gone to his head, a momentary lapse of judgment.

Danly neared the keep. Feeling the stares of red-cloaked guards, he lowered his hood and straightened his shoulders, nothing to do but brazen it out. The guards at the outer gates knew him, a flick of their eyes granting permission to enter. He crossed the courtyard, avoiding the horse dung, and climbed the steps to the keep. Three strides into the great hall, he froze.

Bishop Taniff skewered him with his stare. "Late night, prince?"

A hundred stares turned his way, a conclave of red-robed bishops and clerics filling the great hall. Danly suppressed a shudder. "Late night with a lady." He tried to add a grin of bravado, but it wilted under the bishop's steely-eyed stare.

"A sinner like you should spend more time on his knees and less time whoring."

Danly had no answer, sweat trickling down his back.

"And the Flame God shall judge them all, separating the faithful from the sinners." The bishop gave him a narrowed look. "Have you been judged, prince? I never see you at morning devotions."

Religion would be the death of him. Danly shrugged, trying to make light of it. "I'm a late riser."

The bishop's gaze smoldered. "You best spend more time on your knees, prince." His grin turned nasty. "You never know when the Flame God will come calling."

The threat sent a shiver down his back. With the Lord Raven gone, Danly knew he was vulnerable. He bolted for the stairs. Laughter followed him, chasing him up the tower like death nipping at his heels. He slammed the door shut, seeking the solace of his chambers. The bishop was a pious prick and Lingard was a cauldron of death. He hated the bishop, hated the religion of the Flame, but at least he had his answer. Better to take his chances with the queen than to deal with the devil.

62

Liandra

The queen read the scroll three times before consigning it to the flames. *Her son was safe.* Relief washed through her like a soothing balm. Lacing her hands across her empty womb, Liandra closed her eyes and eased back in the chair, holding a thousand worries at bay with a single message. *Her son was safe. Her throne had an heir.* She raised the words like a castle around her heart.

Pine logs snapped and crackled in the hearth, drawing her back to the decision at hand. She sat before the fireplace, a chessboard set up on the side table. White against black, she often played against herself, a distraction from the war. She fingered an ivory pawn, considering the board. The game had reached that tricky point, a delicate stalemate where a single move would trigger a trade of pieces, a slaughter of sacrifice leading to the final checkmate. Liandra studied the web of moves, weighing the options. Her gaze kept returning to a single piece. Sacrifice a knight to take a castle and white might win. But chess was so much simpler than war.

Stewart's scroll demanded a fresh decision. Opportunity gave advantage to the bold, but every decision carried a risk. The fate of her kingdom teetered on a knife-edge. The enemy had emptied Lingard of cavalry, offering a chance to retake the fortress-city. Stewart's plan was bold, a risky gambit fraught with many dangers, not the least of which was the risk to Pellanor. The queen sighed, weighing one risk against another. If she sent the wagons of napthos north then she'd improve the odds of retaking Lingard, but the move would leave Pellanor exposed. A castle for a castle, she never liked even trades.

And then there was Robert. She'd sent her spymaster north to stir a religious storm in Lingard, to wage a war of truth against belief. She hoped to set the Flame against itself, unleashing a firestorm of persecution, weakening Lingard from within. She'd had no word from him since his arrival at the fortress, no way to send a message. Doubt gnawed at her. How could she loose a maelstrom on Lingard knowing he worked within the walls?

But great battles were not won by the timid.

Decisions weighed on her like a millstone. The war grew complicated, so many pieces in motion, so many dire threats. She considered all the options but her choice seemed inevitable. Crowns were not held by the faint of heart.

She moved to her desk and wrote out the orders, a scratch of the nib across parchment, the power of the quill. Blowing the ink dry, she rang the hand bell on her desk.

Master Raddock appeared. "Yes, majesty."

She handed him the parchment, watching him read by the light of the fire, his eyes widening in surprise.

"But..."

"See that it is done." She brooked no arguments.

"Yes, majesty." He turned towards the door.

"And Master Raddock," he turned back, waiting. "Send another sweep through the countryside looking for archers and arrows."

"It's already been done."

Her patience snapped. "Then do it again. If war comes to Pellanor, archers may be our only hope."

"Yes, majesty."

"Any word from Navarre?" She knew the answer yet she had to ask.

"None, majesty."

Another worry. She waved him away in dismissal. Bowing, he closed the door. A gentle click of the lock, and she was alone again with her thoughts. Flames roared in the hearth, spilling light across the chessboard. Liandra studied the game, refusing to sacrifice the knight for the castle. She fingered the ivory piece, every detail exquisitely carved. War was not like chess. Every sacrifice hurt, yet strategy was her best weapon. She'd made her decision, put her pieces in play, and now she could only wait for the enemy's next move.

63

Steffan

Steffan rode at the head of an army. Six thousand mounted soldiers thundered at his back, armor and weapons jangling, battle banners snapping overhead. They carved a path through snow-crusted farmland, riding without supply wagons or foot soldiers, a lightning raid striking deep into the heart of Lanverness. Steffan laughed at the biting-cold wind, his black cloak flapping like a raven's wing at his shoulders. War was exhilarating, the power of life and death, the conquest of a kingdom. Power flowed through him, the favor of the Dark Lord. This was what he needed, to escape the petty squabbles of Lingard, to forget the Priestess, to ride to war, striking a killing blow at the enemy. Victory was nearly within his grasp. Steffan could feel it, like an elixir coursing through his veins.

They followed the traitors' map south by southwest, chasing the queen's caravan of gold. Steffan set a punishing pace, needing to catch the treasury wagons in open farmland. They stopped only to rest their horses and to pillage food. Steffan chaffed at every delay, pouring over the traitors' map, seeking the best vantage for an ambush. Riding from dawn till dusk, they set a furious pace, like hounds dogging the hind, hot on the scent.

Just when his men began to grumble with doubt, the scouts reported wagon ruts scarring the road. "The ruts run deep, my lord." The scout grinned, snow flecking his beard. "Heavily laden wagons pulled by teams of oxen, we've found the Spider Queen's gold!"

A cheer went up from the men, but a second scout brought warning. "The caravan is heavily guarded, ten thousand foot marching in ranks behind the wagons."

Beside him the general groaned, "*Ten* thousand!" He turned a scathing stare towards Steffan. "You've led us on a fool's chase. They've got us outnumbered. Even with the enemy afoot, the odds are too great."

"Did you expect the queen's treasury to be lightly guarded?"

"But ten thousand foot?"

Steffan turned his gaze back to the scout. "Tell me about the ten thousand. What banner do they fly?"

"They march under the twin roses, the banner of Lanverness...but the color of their tabards is wrong, pea green instead of emerald."

"And the device?"

The scout hesitated. "I thought I spied a coiled cobra on their tabards."

The general swore. "Dark-damned mercenaries from Radagar."

Steffan flashed a triumphant grin. "Exactly."

The general growled, "Explain."

"Sometimes treachery is stronger than swords." Steffan swiveled in the saddle, looking for his servant. "Pip, bring the ironbound chest."

"Yes, my lord." The redheaded lad nosed his mount through the officers, leading a single packhorse laden with a small ironbound chest.

"What's this?" The general gave him a hooded stare. "Magic?"

"Of a sort." Steffan smoothed the map across his thigh, studying the lay of the land. "I'll ride ahead with a small guard of a hundred and meet the caravan here. You flank the road on either side, hiding in the hills. If you hear the clash of steel, come charging."

"If I hear the clash of steel, you're dead."

"Don't bet on it." Steffan grinned. "We'll take the caravan without a fight."

"So you'll charm them into submission?"

"Something like that."

The general gave him a squinty stare. "Treachery is a slippery weapon, even for a bastard like you."

"Not for me, general. Not for me." Steffan gave the orders, choosing a hundred of the best men, a troop of Black Flames, half armed with halberds and the rest with crossbows. Setting spurs to his stallion, Steffan asked for a gallop. He led them south, chasing the queen's gold. Before sunset the treasury would be his, one step closer to victory.

64

Stewart

S tewart found himself retreating to the small lean-to, using it as a sanctuary of sorts. Her scent still lingered on the bearskin rug. His fingers combed the thick fur, hard to believe she was gone, but they both had duties that could not be denied. The Crimson Tower had grown crowded with soldiers, crowded but also empty, so achingly empty. Jordan was two weeks gone, taking the Zward and most of the monks with her, while he remained to plan an assault on Lingard, a chance to foil the Flame. War consumed his waking thoughts, but Jordan filled his dreams at night. He preferred the nights, always shocked to find his arms empty at sunrise.

Someone scratched on the tent flap. It seemed he could never get a moment alone. "Come."

Owen poked his head inside. The big man had traded his prisoner's rags for burnished armor and an emerald tabard, a gleam of pride in his dark gaze. "Lord Dane to see you, sir."

"Dane!" Stewart leaped to his feet. His boyhood friend entered, looking leaner and scruffier since the start of the war. Dane clasped him close in a rough embrace. "I thought you dead!"

"Turns out I'm not that easy to kill."

Dane stepped back. "We searched for you, but the mud and confusion..."

"I know."

"How did you get away?"

"Luck and desperation." Stewart grimaced, "mostly desperation."

Dane's gaze roved the lean-to. "What are you now, the hermit prince?"

"No, I'm married."

Dane's stare snapped back. "*What?* To whom, a woodland nymph?"

Stewart smiled. "To Jordan."

"The seashell princess? You found her? *Here?*" Dane looked incredulous.

"More like she found me. Sit down. You look like you need a drink."

They sank to the bearskin rug, sitting cross-legged, a small brazier throwing off heat. Stewart poured wine for both of them. Dane drank his in a single long swallow and then held the cup out for more. "A good vintage. I suppose that was just waiting for you too?"

"In a manner of speaking."

"You best tell me, I'm finding it hard to believe."

Stewart told his tale in simple words, from his capture, to his escape, to his ordeal with the brigands, to the ambush in the forest.

"So she really was waiting for you?"

Stewart smiled. "Sent by the gods."

"And you really married her?"

His smile deepened. "Let no man put asunder."

"Without the queen's consent?"

The question struck like a sword blow. Stewart winced. "I'll tell her after we win the war."

Dane barked a laugh. "Take the coward's way and send a messenger."

"You think?"

"It's your head."

Stewart considered the advice, but then his friend's face turned grim.

"My lord, I beg your pardon." Dane got to one knee, his voice full of remorse. "I should have never left your side. And afterwards," his dark eyes brimmed with pain, "we searched but there were too many footprints, too many directions. We attacked every convoy of prisoners, but you were never among them." His voice choked to silence.

Stewart clasped his friend's arm. "You only followed orders. I *ordered* you to leave, to lead the men out of ambush."

"But everything you endured..."

"Perhaps it was meant to be, now more than ever I know what we're fighting for."

"But..."

He gripped his friend's arm. "It's over. Let it go."

Dane sank back down to the bearskin rug. Stewart refilled their cups. They drank in silence, the brazier providing a comfortable heat.

"So why are you hiding here instead of returning to the army?" Dane's gaze sharpened. "And how did your messenger find us anyway?"

Stewart hated to lie but he'd sworn to keep the owl-man's secret safe. "I made a few guesses and sent out messengers. There's only so many places for an army to hide."

Dane's gaze narrowed. "And the ruins, why here?"

"As good a place as any to plan an attack on Lingard."

"*Lingard!*" Dane hissed in disbelief. "That fortress is damn near impregnable."

"The Flame took it."

"By treachery, I've heard the tale of your brother."

Stewart grimaced, like opening a raw wound.

"So are you planning some treachery of your own?"

"Not treachery, something else. We'll take the fortress with magic."

"*Magic!*" Dane made the hand sign against evil. "So now you're a wizard?"

"Not me. Did you see the woman down in the stables, the dark-haired monk in blue robes?"

Dane nodded. "The prickly one? Couldn't help but notice the comely curves, but her tongue's as thorny as a nettle bush."

"It's her magic."

Dane's eyes widened. "A *sorceress?*"

"And you best treat her with respect." Stewart ran his hand through his hair. "I'm still not sure if she's going to help. She claims magic should not be used as a weapon, but it's our only hope. That and the wagons."

"What wagons?"

"A gift from the monks. Clay flagons filled with some kind of rare potion that burns like hellfire, but there's only enough for one battle. The queen's agreed to send the wagons to Lingard, but it's a risky gambit." A kernel of fear gnawed at him. "It leaves Pellanor undefended, nothing but makeshift walls and a small force of knights. If the Flame captures the queen, the war's over." Stewart stared at Dane seeking reassurance. "And then there's Lingard. By using fire we risk killing our own people, but it's the only way to even the numbers. We dare not fight their army in a pitched battle." Stewart sighed, the weight of decision lying heavy on his shoulders. "Despite the risks, we have only this one chance to strike at Lingard, to tip the balance of the war, but if we fail..." He shook his head, not trusting his voice.

"Then don't fail." Dane's gaze was full of conviction, his boyhood friend and sparring partner, his brother-in-arms. "Tell me your plan."

Stewart unrolled a map, setting it between them. "We need to take them by surprise, and it must be done at night." He ran his hand through his hair. "It's all a matter of timing, timing, magic and luck."

Dane nodded. "I don't know about magic, but it seems the gods owe us some luck."

"Perhaps they do." Stewart stared at the map, desperate for a way to end the war. "We dare not lose."

65

Danly

The streets were most dangerous in the small hours. Danly's neck prickled in warning. He crept through the back alleys, straining to see in the darkness. Patrols prowled the city like starving wolf packs, as if they knew something was afoot. Danly dodged into a side street, a bugling sack hidden beneath his cloak. He'd ransacked the keep, taking everything of value. Coins, jewels, and silken finery, even the silver circlet he'd worn as a crown the day he'd brought down Lingard. *His crown,* mad laughter bubbled in his throat, but Danly choked it down. If the patrols caught him now he'd wear that crown to the pyre.

Another patrol tramped through the street, hobnailed boots striking the cobblestones. Danly hid behind a rain barrel, sweat running in rivulets down his back. In the dark of the morning, the soldiers' red cloaks looked almost black, sinister wraiths hunting for victims.

Danly shivered, making the hand sign against evil. Crouched behind the barrel, he waited a hundred heartbeats and then sprinted for the brothel, tapping the code on the scarred oak door. Relief rushed through him when it opened. He slipped inside to find Vengar waiting for him. The red-haired captain had shaved his bushy beard, taking ten years off his face. Danly almost didn't recognize him.

Vengar must have felt his stare. "Yeah, the beard." He fingered his smooth shaven face. "Too many turn-cloak converts guarding the walls. Without the beard they might not recognize me." Vengar turned. "Come on, the others are waiting."

They entered the back room to find eleven strangers bristling with weapons. *Eleven,* Danly counted again, his gaze turning to Vengar. "I thought you said fourteen, counting the two of us?"

Vengar gave a grim nod. "Kirkby has the flux."

Danly got a sick feeling in his stomach. "The flux or a turn-cloak?"

Vengar shrugged, his eyes bleak. "We'll know if we're caught."

It was not the answer he wanted.

Vengar turned away, his voice brisk with command. "Come on lads, check your weapons, take a last swill of ale, and we're on our way."

Danly felt like heaving. He sidled towards the door, but Vengar grabbed his shoulder, thrusting a sword belt into his hands. "For you."

So they expected me to fight, a chill shivered down his back. Danly took the belt, reluctantly buckling it around his waist. He'd never been much of a swordsman, relying on his guards to do the wet work. This plan kept getting worse.

"Alright lads, two at a time, out the back door, we'll meet at the barracks." Vengar surveyed his men. "Look sharp and keep to the shadows. By tomorrow we'll be free of the Flame."

A growl of approval echoed through the men, a desperate glint in their eyes.

The first two slipped out the door, a gust of cold wind blowing through the room like an ill omen.

Vengar turned towards Danly. "We'll go last. Stay close." His gaze narrowed. "What've you got there?" Vengar grabbed Danly's sack, rummaging through it, tossing the silken finery to the floor.

"My things." Danly watched as a samite cloak fell beneath the careless tramp of a muddy boot.

"Can't fight with a sack bulging beneath your cloak." Vengar found the silver circlet and held it aloft. Their eyes met like crossed daggers. "Can't use this as a bribe, not in Lingard. Show this to the wrong man and you'll buy yourself a bad death." Vengar thrust the circlet at Danly, his voice a low growl. "Best leave it."

Danly clutched the crown, watching as Vengar tied the sack to his own belt.

The big man flashed a wolfish grin. "The rest will be needed for bribes."

Danly felt like he'd just been robbed. He stared at the silver circlet, smooth beneath his hands, his only symbol of royalty. Bereft of everything else, he could not part with it. Snatching the samite cloak from the floor, he slashed a small square and bundled the crown into the cloth, tying the makeshift pouch to his belt.

Vengar watched, disapproval in his gaze. "That thing will be the death of you."

Danly refused to listen. Grabbing a flagon, he took a long swill of liquid courage. The ale tasted like piss but it settled his nerves.

The last man slipped out the door.

"Time to go, prince." Vengar twirled a brown cloak across his shoulders, his face hidden in a deep cowl. Opening the back door a crack, he peered outside. "Looks good." They plunged into the alley way. Vengar led, weaving a path through the back streets. Danly stayed close, his hand on his sword hilt. Darkness cloaked the city, still hours from dawn. The streets were eerily empty; Vengar had a gift for evading the patrols. All too soon, they reached the barracks. The others crouched in a side alleyway. One man carried a large sack, the others gripped their swords. Vengar grinned. "Time for a bit of revenge, lads. We attack hard and show no mercy. Kill every guard, release the prisoners and we're gone." Vengar stood, a sword whispering to his hand. "Let's go!"

The suddenness took Danly by surprise, but he dared not be left behind. Hurrying to catch up, he ran in the middle of the pack, his hand sweaty on his sword hilt, his heartbeat thundering in his ears. Vengar reached the barracks first. The door stood unguarded, more proof that fear ruled the city. Vengar eased the door open and slipped inside. A red-cloaked soldier sat slumped at a table, issuing soft snores. The big man crossed the room like a prowling lion. A single blow and the soldier died without a sound.

Danly followed the others, crowding into the room. Shutting the outer door, they listened. Muffled screams came from deep within the barracks, screams mixed with laughter. *Torture*, the word shivered through Danly's mind, threatening to loose his bowels.

"*Let's go!*" Vengar crashed through the inner door. The raid became a blur. Soldiers startled awake, fumbling for weapons while desperate brigands rushed to make the kill. Surprise availed them. Cutting a deadly swath through the barrack, they finally stumbled into a large room with iron cages affixed to the far wall. Tortured screams echoed through the chamber, masking the sounds of fighting. A trio of red-robed priests hovered over a shackled prisoner, the smell of roast flesh hanging heavy in the air.

Vengar snarled, "*Kill them!*"

Howling like demons, the brigands attacked. The priests tried to flee but there was nowhere to hide. The room became a slaughterhouse. Blood spattered the walls as the men slew the priests, dismembering their bodies.

Danly stood with his back to a wall, horrified by the slaughter. When the killing finally stopped, his sword was still clean.

Vengar turned towards him, his gaze flicking toward the prisoner chained to the table. "Is it him?"

The thing on the table was hardly a man. His nose was cut off, his eyes burnt out with coals. He writhed on the table like a worm, keening a twisted scream. The tortured mess had silver hair, but the chin was wrong and the body too flabby. Danly looked away. "Not him."

Vengar hefted his sword. A quick stroke and the screaming stopped. The sudden silence was horrible, a skin-crawling stillness. "Sometimes death is a mercy."

No one spoke.

Cool as night, Vengar surveyed his men. "Find the keys, open the gates and let the prisoners out."

Danly felt a hard stare burning into his back. He whirled, impaled by the daggered glare of the Master Archivist. The queen's shadowmaster gripped the cage bars, his soldier's tabard rumpled and soiled, but otherwise he seemed unharmed. Even imprisoned, he looked dangerous.

Hatred snarled through Danly. He crossed the room, thrusting his sword between the bars, the point pressed to the spymaster's throat. "*Your manhood or your life!*"

The master never flinched, never pulled away, his voice annoyingly calm. "I wondered if you saw me."

Danly pressed the point, drawing blood. "*Your manhood or your life!*"

"You gave Lingard to the Flame."

Danly sucked air like a bellows about to explode.

"You're still the queen's son. Have you come for revenge or redemption?"

The words struck like a slap. His sword began to shake. *Revenge or redemption?* Danly longed for revenge...but was redemption even possible? Aiding the Flame was wrong; he saw that now...yet he finally had a chance for revenge. His sword wavered.

Vengar yanked Danly's arm, pulling the sword away from the prisoner. "What are you doing?" Vengar hissed in surprise. "The queen's Archivist?" The big man sketched a half bow. "The prince never said it was you. We'll have you out of there in a nonce, my lord."

"No need for keys." The shadowmaster thrust his hands through the bars, plumbing the lock with a set of iron picks.

Defeated, Danly dropped his sword, the impotent steel clattering on the flagstones.

The lock clicked open and the shadowmaster stepped from the cage.

Kurt returned with the keys, releasing the other prisoners. Most were ordinary citizens, men of all ages, even women and children, scared and bedraggled, but mixed among them were soldiers in red tabards. The prisoners poured into the chamber, some stunned, staring with vacant eyes, others crying with gratitude.

Danly watched through haze-filled eyes.

Vengar spoke with the Master Archivist, their backs turned toward him.

Danly reached for his dagger, *revenge or redemption?*

Something stirred in the back of the cages, a churning madness. A handful of red-cloaked soldiers pushed from the rear, desperate to get out. Nearly trampling the others, they burst from the cages, their faces twisted in hate. "*Kill the infidels!*" Armed with nothing but fists and teeth, they attacked like rabid animals.

Danly stumbled backwards, staring in disbelief. Prisoners who'd faced torture mere moments ago now fought for the Flame? The insanity staggered him.

One of the madmen hurtled towards Danly, spittle flying from his mouth. "*Die, infidel!*"

Danly reached for his sword, but the scabbard was empty.

Clutching nothing but air, Danly watched in horror as a fist blazed towards his face. He tried to duck, but shock slowed his reflexes. Pain smashed his face. His nose crunched flat, a sudden spike of agony. Struck with the force of a bull, Danly's head snapped backwards, hitting the wall. Pain exploded in the back of his skull. His vision dimmed and his legs wobbled. Absolute darkness claimed him.

66

The Master Archivist

The Master Archivist lunged for a weapon, grabbing a sword from the floor. Twisting left, he brought the sword to bear, fighting against rabid men turned monsters. Howling like beasts, they burst from the cages, their eyes crazed with hate. Consumed by a religious contagion, they fought like demons, clawing and kicking, gouging at eyes and biting with their teeth, but flesh is no match for steel. The master slew two of them himself before the fighting came to a sudden halt.

He staggered to a stop, the torture chamber awash in blood. The other prisoners cringed against the walls, their faces frozen in horror.

The shadowmaster took stock of the survivors. Danly was down, slumped against the far wall, but Vengar seemed unscathed, surrounded by a handful of his men. He locked stares with the redheaded captain. "Get the prisoners out of here, before this insanity spreads."

Vengar nodded, herding the newly freed from the chamber. Sheathing his sword, the master crossed the chamber to kneel by Danly. Blood covered the prince's face, his nose smashed flat, but he still lived, a sluggish pulse at his throat. The master tried to rouse him, but nothing worked. Blood matted the back of Danly's head; perhaps the prince was hurt worse than he looked.

Vengar returned. "Does he live?"

"Knocked senseless, but he still breathes." The master eyed the captain, wondering how he'd survived Lingard's fall, but that was a question for another time. "I assume you have a plan to get out of the city?"

Vengar gave a curt nod. "We change into soldier's tabards and march for the south gate. I've bribed a sergeant to let us take the morning patrol, but we need eighteen men plus a captain, and we need to look like soldiers."

"Bluff and bluster."

Vengar gave him a desperate look. "Sometimes that's all you have."

The master nodded. "How many of your men survived?"

"Nine, counting myself."

"Then recruit the rest from the captives, we need to get out of the city." He gestured toward Danly. "I'll bring the prince."

Vengar stayed his arm. "If you can't rouse him, he stays."

"He deserves another chance."

Vengar looked away. "Maybe we all do."

So that's how it was. "We can't leave him."

"If he can't march then we can't take him. The ruse will never work with an injured man."

Vengar's words were as cold as iron, but they rang of truth. The master scowled. "If we leave him, he dies."

"I'll take him to Sandra's."

The master raised an eyebrow.

"A whore who owes me. She'll keep him hidden. It's the best we can do."

The shadowmaster nodded, struck by the irony. It seemed the eunuch-prince had come full circle, back in the care of whores.

"I'll take the prince, you organize the men and get them marching towards the south gate. Trust Kurt, the big blond with the scarred face, he's my second." Vengar untied a sack from his belt, thrusting it into the master's hands. "Take this for bribes."

The master nodded. "I'll see you at the south gate."

Vengar hoisted Danly onto his shoulder, carrying the prince like a sack of potatoes. The big captain made the prince look small. They made their way back through the carnage to the front room. Vengar whispered orders to Kurt and then slipped out into the street. The queen's shadowmaster took charge. He turned to face the released prisoners. "We're looking for men who want to escape the city." A few stepped forward, eager to flee the madness, but others had to be cajoled. In the end, he took two young women to fill out the numbers. "Bind your breasts tight and cut your hair and don't say a word. If just one of you looks wrong, we all die."

They ransacked the barracks for armor and tabards, sword belts and helms. Dawning a sergeant's tabard, the master urged them to hurry, every moment a strike against them.

Lining them up for inspection, he studied their appearance, straightening sword belts and adjusting armor. The red tabards proved fortunate, hiding more than a few bloodstains. "Pathetic, but it will have to serve." He hid the women at the rear. "March smart, hold yourselves like soldiers, and don't stop unless ordered."

They nodded, more than one face flushed with fear.

Darkness still held sway in the streets, a reluctant dawn creeping across the sky. Bold as brass, he marched them out of the barracks, two abreast, setting a quick pace. At first they stumbled, but he barked a cadence and the rhythm soon claimed them.

Another patrol approached, hobnailed boots pounding the cobbles.

With no choice but to brazen it out, the master snapped a salute and kept his troops marching. Feeling the chill of fear sweep through his men, he bellowed commands like a drill sergeant. "Backs straight, march tall, you serve the Flame God!" Their rhythm faltered, but then steadied under the tongue-lashing. They marched passed without incident. The master sighed, whispering thanks to the gods for the darkness.

They stayed on the main street, making their way toward the southern gates. Except for patrols, the streets stood empty, the storefronts shuttered, doors locked and windows barred, the city cowering in fear. He could almost smell oppression riding the air, the reek of religion run amok.

A shiver of warning pricked his neck, as if informers watched from the shuttered windows. He'd lost three shadowmen to the heretic hunters. Lingard was a dangerous tinderbox of desperate survivors and rabid believers. He'd come to stir the pot, hoping to ignite a revolt with word of the Pontifax's death, but the Flame religion proved impervious to the truth. Instead of an uprising, a fanatical frenzy gripped the city, inciting the clerics to rampant cruelty. Patrols combed the streets scrounging for heretics. The pyres burned day and night, choking the city with death. He'd spread the word but now it was time to get out. Religion coiled around Lingard in a deadly stranglehold. Swords would have to prevail where words could not.

The shadowmaster scanned the streets, searching for threats, every sense stretched taut. Taking a deep breath, he surveyed his men, yelling a cadence to bolster their courage. The march to the gate seemed to take forever.

Another patrol approached, the tramp of boots pounding a warning.

"Steady! Eyes straight!" They marched past, following the curve of the main street, gaining their first glimpse of the southern gates. Crenellated battlements soared towards the brightening sky, but the gates were closed, the drawbridge raised, the fortress-city shut tight as a madhouse.

Vengar slipped from a side street. Clad in a captain's tabard and red cloak, he joined their ranks, barking a command. "Patrol, halt."

They came to a raggedy halt, standing at attention. A poor showing, but given the early hour no one seemed to notice.

Vengar reclaimed the sack of bribes and then disappeared into the guard tower. A cold wind blew from the north ruffling their cloaks, more snow threatening the air. The waiting grew hard, giving his men too much time to think. They stood beneath the scrutiny of guards walking the battlements, knowing a single mistake could be their death. The master gripped his sword hilt. If caught, he'd fight to the death. Better a clean death under the morning sky than a trip to the torturer's table. He fingered the small signet ring on his left hand, a love token from the queen. Memories washed across him like a balm. He longed to hold her, but duty was a harsh taskmaster, the needs of the kingdom outweighing them all.

One of the men began to quiver and shake.

"Stand tall!" His words hissed like an arrow. They found their mark and the man straightened. The master scowled, willing Vengar to hurry, time was against them.

The door to the guard tower creaked open, drawing the master's stare. A stranger emerged, a captain from the look of his tabard. Casting a cursory glance their way, the captain sauntered towards the far wall. Turning his back on the street, he adjusted his clothes and then arched a golden stream towards the wall.

The master scowled, praying for the captain to leave.

Finished, the captain sidled over, his gaze drawn toward the sergeant's stripes on the master's tabard. "Haven't seen you before." He cast a questioning glance at the troops. "I thought Rothwell's boys had the dawn patrol?"

The name held no meaning for him. The master's mind raced, desperate for an answer. Religion came to his rescue. "Didn't you hear? Rothwell was named a heretic. Bishop Taniff ordered his arrest." The master gave the captain a piercing stare. "You a friend of Rothwell's?"

The captain backed away, his face turning ghost-pale. "No, not a friend, just asking." The captain fled towards the tower as if a plague nipped at his heels.

Sinners proved a contagion in a city ruled by religion. The master took a deep breath, staring at the brightening sky, praying they made their escape before the real patrol appeared.

The tower door banged open. Soldiers spilled into the courtyard, swarming the gate. Something was happening on the battlements. The master tensed, his hand gripping his sword, but then he heard a distinctive sound. Chains began to rattle, the creak of wood bearing a heavy strain, the sounds of the drawbridge being lowered. The master watched as soldiers shouldered the heavy crossbar unbarring the gate.

Vengar emerged from the tower without the sack. The red-haired captain took his place at the head of the troop. *"Attention!"*

The troop snapped to attention, hope threading through them like a current.

The city gates swung open, the drawbridge lowered across the moat.

Dawn cracked the sky, red and gold spearing the snow-laden clouds.

They began to march. They passed through the gates, beneath the iron portcullis, across the drawbridge and out into the snow-dusted greensward. Halfway between the fortress and freedom, the master's shoulders began to twitch, expecting an arrow, but none came. A shout rang out from the fortress, but they did not stop. They marched across the greensward and into the woods and then they ran, running for their lives, running from the Flame.

67

Steffan

Steffan chose the highest vantage point along the southbound road, a fitting stage for his latest treachery. Clad in black chainmail, his raven cloak billowing in the wind, he spurred his sorrel stallion to the hilltop.

Pip rode beside him, serving as his bannerman, a troop of Black Flames at his back. Reaching the snowy crest, he pulled his stallion to halt.

A caravan snaked through the valley below, toiling along the mud-churned road. A handful of nobles on caparisoned horses rode in the vanguard, glittering in their silvered armor and brightly colored silks. Shiny guards and a flutter of banners surrounded the nobles, a testament to their rank. Behind the nobility came the prize, twelve wagons piled high with ironbound chests. Pulled by teams of oxen, the wagons struggled through the mud, plowing deep ruts in the road, telltale proof of the gold within. Behind the treasure wagons came the muscle, a long tail of infantry marching smartly in ranks of four abreast, their pea-green tabards emblazoned with red cobras. Drummers beat a cadence and the wagons creaked with strain, the oxen blowing plumes of mist into the cold. The mercenaries of Radagar marched to the drum beat, an impressive show of strength and discipline. Even from the hilltop, Steffan could hear the tramp of their boots.

"A sight to behold." Steffan smiled. "Unfurl the banner, and make sure they see it."

The red-haired lad loosed the banner, a crisp snap of sky-blue silk adorned with a black scorpion. Pip held the banner aloft, catching the wind. "Why a scorpion instead of a cobra?"

"A change of kings in Radagar. Make sure they see the banner."

Pip stood in the stirrups, waving the banner high, a flutter of silk against the pale winter sky.

Needing to be seen, Steffan asked for a rear from his stallion. Unsheathing his sword, he brandished the blade to the heavens, a promise and a threat.

A shout rang from the road below. The nobles pulled their horses to a stop and the wagons ground to a halt, but Steffan kept his gaze on the mercenaries, a group of officers huddled in a knot, staring at the hilltop. Steffan grinned; it was time to roll the dice. He nudged his stallion to a walk, ambling down the hillside, giving the mercenaries plenty of time to decide. Pip kept pace beside him, the sky-blue banner snapping in the breeze. A handful of Black Flames armed with crossbows rode at his back, a surety against the nobles' misplaced pride.

Steffan kept his stallion to a slow walk, his hand away from his sheathed sword, an amiable smile on his face.

Twenty guards surrounded the nobles, swords bristling with threat, their emerald tabards bright against the snowy fields. "Halt or die."

Steffan ignored the threat, stopping within easy talking distance of the nobles. "Who leads this caravan?"

A pinch-faced lord clad in a showy surcoat, gold cockatrices prancing on a field of burnt orange, eased his horse forward. The gray-haired noble looked foolish in a knight's surcoat. "I lead here, Lord Lenox, the treasurer to the queen. Your banner is not known to me. Yield the road or face the consequences."

Another haughty lordling, drunk on too much pride. "I'll ask you again, who leads this caravan?"

A jangle of armor approached. Mercenary soldiers jogged from the back, taking a protective stance around the nobles. Bolstered by more swords, the Lord Lenox flashed a haughty smile. "*I* lead here. Now state your business or yield the road."

The lordling was quickly becoming annoying, but Steffan had the perfect remedy. "Wrong answer." He signaled with a flick of his hand. "The Lord Raven leads here."

Behind him, a crossbow hissed.

Thunk, the feathered bolt embedded deep in the Lord Lenox's chest, a trickle of blood on his surcoat. Surprise washed across the lord's face. He glanced down and then slid from the saddle, a fresh corpse sprawled in the road.

Panic erupted amongst the nobles. "Seize him!"

"Kill the rogue!"

"Capture him!"

But the mercenaries did not obey. To a man, they drew their curved swords and turned, encircling the nobles and their guards in a ring of steel.

The lords' bluster melted to silence.

Outrage changed to disbelief. The nobles stared in shock, their gaze bouncing from the Lord Raven, to the mercenaries, to the dead lord, and back again. A heavy-set lord in a plum-colored surcoat dared to break the silence. "Who *are* you?"

"Finally a question worth answering." Steffan made a mocking bow. "The Lord Steffan Raven, counselor to the Pontifax, and now your captor."

"And the mercenaries serve you?"

Steffan shrugged. "Deals change."

The lord seemed to consider the answer. "Our families will pay a rich ransom."

At least one of the nobles had a lick of sense. "And your name?"

"Lord Quince."

"Just a name, no fancy titles, I like that." The plump lordling was actually growing on Steffan. "I suppose one of you has the keys to the treasury?"

"In the saddlebag of Lord Lenox." Lord Quince paled. "The one you killed."

Pip scrambled from his horse and ransacked the dead lord's saddlebags, holding a thick ring of keys aloft. "Got em!"

A lone trumpet echoed through the valley, a mournful call. Riders in red tabards appeared on the two hills flanking the road, battle banners snapping overhead. Surrounded by the Flame, the nobles cringed together, drawing close like a hedgehog curled into a ball.

The mercenary captain tensed, stepping towards Steffan. "Trouble, my lord?"

"No, just the rest of my army. Keep the nobles penned and tell the rest of your men to stand down."

The captain saluted, snapping orders to his men.

A detachment of red-cloaked riders thundered down the hillside. They cantered towards Steffan, General Caylib in the lead. "So your ruse worked."

"Oh ye of little faith. The queen's treasury falls without a fight." Steffan flashed a triumphant grin. "Your timing is perfect. We were just about to inspect the gold. Pip, pick a wagon."

Pip chose the third wagon. Climbing onto the bed, he used a knife to cut the oilcloth. Three enormous ironbound chests filled the wagon bed, the seal of Lanverness emblazoned on their lids. Steffan began to salivate, imagining the wealth and power within his grasp. "Pick one."

The lad chose the middle chest, trying the keys one by one.

Soldiers gathered around, a mixture of the Flame and the Cobra. Even the captured nobles came to look, everyone gathered to witness the queen's treasure.

Steffan remained on his stallion, his manhood stiff with anticipation.

Pip worked through the keys. "Got it!" The key turned and the lock clicked open. Pip raised the heavy lid, throwing it back with a loud thunk. A stunned silence hissed through the men. Instead of gleaming gold...the chest held nothing but dull lead bars, dull, worthless, lead.

"No!" Steffan leaped from the saddle onto the wagon. Pushing Pip aside, he dug through the chest, hurling lead bars onto the wagon bed. "No!" His mind refused to believe. "Try another!" He grabbed the keys, jamming them into a lock till he found another match. The lock clicked and he threw back the lid. Nothing but lead. Rage roared through him. "No! The bitch tricked me! The god-damned Spider Queen!"

Laughter erupted from the nobles.

Steffan's rage found a focus. Cold as midnight, he turned his gaze on the nobles. "You knew."

Their laughter sputtered to silence. Lord Quince paled. "None of us knew, I swear by all the gods, we did not know. She tricked us, she tricked us all."

"She tricked you." His plans foiled by a woman, his rage turned deadly. "Kill them, kill them all!"

Soldiers of the Flame sprang to the attack, falling on the nobles.

Steffan drew his sword. Pulling the fat Lord Quince from the saddle, he attacked, striking over and over again. *"She tricked you!"* Screaming his rage, he slashed and hacked at the mewing lord till there was nothing left but bloody bits.

Gore splattered his face. Steffan staggered to a halt.

A grim silence pooled around him.

Sticky with blood, he stayed his sword. Dead nobles littered the ground, hacked to death in a fit of fury.

Someone clapped.

He whirled to find the general staring down at him. "So there really is a barbarian in you." The general's smile twisted to a malicious grin. "It just took the right woman to bring it out."

"The Spider Queen," the words hissed out of Steffan like a curse. He shuddered, drawing a deep breath, trying to quell his anger.

"Now what?" The general's voice was full of challenge.

Steffan stared at the dead nobles, at the wagons full of useless lead, and then his stare turned towards the mercenary captain. "Who leads your men?"

"I do." A tall bearded man in a gold-trimmed cloak stepped forward. "General Xanos at your service."

Steffan met his dark gaze. "I hold the scorpion banner. Do you know what that means?"

General Xanos nodded. "To turn our cloaks at first sight of the banner of House Razzur. To give the banner bearer one battle, one victory, and then return home."

"Will you honor those terms?" Steffan waited, knowing much depended on the answer.

The general glanced at the dead nobles.

Steffan said. "This hardly counts as a victory. You've not even bloodied your sword."

General Xanos gave a measured nod, his face solemn. "You'll have our scimitars for one battle...just *one* battle."

"One is all I need." Steffan raised his voice to a shout. "We march on Pellanor! *Death to the Spider Queen!*" The men cheered like wolves slavering for blood. Composed once more, Steffan swung into the saddle, his face a mask of stone, but in his soul he seethed.

68

Danly

Pain thundered through his head and his nose ached. Danly woke in a strange bed, naked beneath the sheets. *Naked!* The realization hit like a douse of cold water. Repulsed by his lost manhood, he *never* slept naked. Leaping from the bed, he found his clothes tossed on a chair. Rumpled and filthy, he hurriedly pulled them on despite the overpowering stink. Reeking of sweat and blood and fear, the clothes released an avalanche of memories. *Vengar and the shadowmaster!* His mind groped for more. Was he free of Lingard...or had they left him behind? Fear throbbed through him. After all he'd done, they couldn't have left him.

The door squeaked opened, admitting mingled scents of stale ale and cheap perfume.

"Well, deary, I see yer up." She gave him a gap-toothed smile, the same whore from the other night.

They'd left him! Horror drenched Danly. Shaking his head, he backed away, trapped in a nightmare. "I'm in Lingard."

"Where else would ya be?" The whore gave him a knowing wink, her gaze dropping to his crotch. "Now I know why ya only want to watch. Don't have the stones for it."

The bitch maligned his manhood, and worse, she dared to wear his crown. His silver circlet gleamed against her mouse-brown hair, an insult and a travesty.

Noticing his stare, she struck a pose, a despoiled vixen pretending at beauty. A cackle of laughter rolled out of her. "I look good in a crown, don't ya think?"

Something broke inside of him, a swell of madness compelling him to act. He lunged at her, his hands wrapping around her scrawny neck. He took her by surprise, his rage propelling them back through the door, into the hallway. They landed hard, Danly on top, a twisted parody of lovers. *"My crown! You dare wear my crown!"* His hands squeezed hard, choking her neck, banging her head against the floor, but she would not shut up. She thrashed beneath him, her screams beating against him.

Rage roared through him. *"Shut up and die!"*

Doors flew open, a rush of footsteps in the hall.

A pack of whores descended on him, kicking and screaming and biting. Like a plague of mosquitoes they penetrated his rage. He released the bitch, snatching the crown from her head, and then he ran. Down the hallway, down the stairs, he pushed his way through the tavern, desperate to escape. He catapulted through the outer door, into the cold light of morning, running straight into the arms of a red-cloaked patrol.

69

Liandra

Liandra knelt in the front pew, staring up at the many faces of the gods. Built long ago by her ancestors, the royal chapel was exquisite. A delicate confection of lace-work stone fanned across the soaring vault, giving the chapel an airy lightness, a masterpiece of masonry. Sunlight slanted through stained glass windows, casting rainbows of light across the marble floor. A faint cloud of incense hushed though the air, a hundred candles defeating the darkness. She prayed alone, only her ancestors for company, stone effigies of kings and queens and fabled knights topping their tombs. So much history, so much glory, yet it fell to Liandra to save her kingdom, a queen who ruled alone.

Destiny had almost caught her. She sighed and the sound echoed through the stonework. She'd played the game of war as well as she could, putting all her pieces in motion, plots within plots, but now all she could do was wait. The waiting proved hard, so much at stake, crowns and kingdoms, lives and loves, all hanging in the balance.

She felt the stare of the gods, their stone statues crowding the sanctuary. Perhaps they rebuked her for her laxness at devotions. She seldom came to pray, believing the gods helped those who helped themselves, but she'd done all she could, and now she needed more.

Her stare roved the pantheon, statues carved of luminous marble. Most people probably thought she prayed to Prosporo, the horned god of wealth and prosperity, but her gaze always sought winged Marut, the goddess of justice. It seemed to Liandra that women held a special place in their hearts for the winged goddess, feeling a keening need for justice. There was never enough justice in a world ruled by swords.

Liandra rose from the pew, sunlight glinting off her bejeweled hands. "We are not meant to kneel." She faced the gods as a queen, silently asking for succor, for victory, for justice.

The doors of the chapel creaked open. *So they found her even here.* Liandra turned, a whisper of emerald velvet across the marble floor. She waited in the sanctuary, the gods at her back.

Master Raddock and two shadowmen approached, striding down the short nave, three crows in black robes. "Majesty, forgive me, but we have urgent word. An army marches on Pellanor."

So her worst fears came calling. "How long?"

"Ten days."

She waited knowing there was more.

"Our scouts estimate nearly six thousand mounted soldiers of the Flame and ten thousand foot."

The numbers alone were damning, more than enough to take Pellanor, but the queen sensed there was more. "And?"

Her deputy shadowmaster cringed, the reluctant bearer of bad tidings. "The ten thousand foot are Radagar's mercenaries. They've turned cloak against us."

So her royal son was right not to trust mercenaries. "At least they are outside our walls rather than within." She considered the news, adding moves to the chessboard in her mind. "So they took the bait of our treasury, but our plot was only half successful." She began to pace, wearing a path beneath the gods. "We'd hoped the mercenaries might obliterate the Flame, but now it seems they're joined forces, turning against us. At least we succeeded in splitting their army."

"Majesty," Master Raddock interrupted, "you must recall the prince at once, the army needs to protect Pellanor."

The queen stilled, considering. "No."

"No?" The master made a strangled sound.

His shortsightedness irked her. "We expect our shadowmasters to look more moves ahead. We dared this gambit to split their army. If we recall the prince before Lingard is taken, then the Flame Army will surely give chase to the prince. Even divided, they have superior numbers. If the Rose Army is lost then the game is over." She considered the board from all angles. "Better the enemy comes to Pellanor than returns to Lingard before the fortress is taken."

Her shadowmaster sputtered. "But if they take the queen?"

"The queen must be the bait and Pellanor must hold."

"But the outer walls..."

The queen forestalled him with a raised hand. "It all comes down to timing. Timing, and luck, and an iron will. We shall send a royal scroll to the prince, but the messenger will be sworn to only deliver the message once Lingard falls. Till then, Pellanor must hold."

Her shadowmaster stared slack-mouthed, his shoulders hunched as if he walked into a storm.

"Alert Major Ranoth. And scour the city for food, moving everything into Castle Tandroth. If the outer walls fall, we shall hold siege within the castle."

"But majesty, Castle Tandroth cannot hold."

She gave him an implacable stare. "The castle walls will buy us time. While we have time, we have hope

"Majesty, as your deputy shadowmaster I must advise you to leave Pellanor. It is not too late to retreat. Seek safety in the fortress of Graymaris, where your knights can better protect you."

She felt as if her ancestors gathered close to listen. "Do you think us less than a king because we are a woman?" She pierced him with a winter-cold stare. "Would a king flee his people? Or would he stay and lead them to victory?"

Her shadowmaster retreated a step, his face flustered. "I think only of your safety."

"You have advised, we have considered. The queen stays."

"Yes, majesty."

"Now go, and ready our people for battle."

He sketched a hasty bow and turned to leave but she called him back.

"Master Raddock," her voice was as cold as a grave. "It is time to settle accounts with the traitors."

Her shadowmaster paled, his face hesitant. "But you said there was not enough evidence?"

"We gave them rope and they hanged themselves. How do you think the Flame learned of our caravan laden with treasury chests?"

A calculated look crossed his face. "You used them. You *knew* he would betray you!"

"We predicted their moves and wove them into our gambit. A good chess master never wastes a single piece, even a slimy traitor." Her voice turned chilly. "But our handsome lord must pay for his treason. It is time for accounts to be settled in full. Arrest Lord Mills and all of his associates. Consign them to the dungeons. Put Lord Mills in the traitor's hole."

"Without a trial?"

"The queen has tried them and found them guilty." She gave him a steely-eyed stare. "Justice will be served."

His face paled. "As you command."

"And one more thing," her shadowmaster waited on her word. "Assign one of your best men to guard Lord Mills. If Pellanor falls, the traitor shall not live to see it."

"It will be done."

She extended her hand and he knelt to kiss her ring. He stared up at her, his voice fervent. "Long live the queen!" Rising, he gave her a bow and then turned and strode down the nave, a flap of black robes in the chapel.

The doors closed and she was once more alone with the gods. The silence weighed heavy on her shoulders. She'd risked everything on this one gambit, a chance to snatch victory from defeat. Liandra turned to stare up at the god's faces chiseled in cold hard marble. "Victory or death, which shall it be?" But if the gods had an answer, they did not share it.

70

Danly

Danly skidded to a stop. Red-cloaked soldiers surrounded him, swords drawn in a ring of steel. "Well, well, what'll we have here? An early morning heretic?"

"No!" Danly cringed beneath their stares, fear slithering down his back. "I was just...just visiting a brothel."

The sergeant grinned. "Yeah right, broken nose, black eye, disheveled clothes, tell it to the priests." He made a rude gesture. "Take him, lads. One less heretic for our quota."

"No!" Danly flinched from their grasp. "I'm under the protection of Lord Raven!"

The sergeant barked a laugh. "Yeah, and my uncle is the Pontifax."

Another soldier said, "Sergeant, look at his right hand."

Danly stared along with the others; he'd forgotten the silver crown.

Several soldiers hissed, *"The traitor prince!"*

The sergeant reconsidered. "Maybe he does have the Raven's protection."

Relief washed through Danly, but it was short-lived.

"Take him to the Bloody Bishop. The bishop will know what to do with him."

Danly protested. "No, just take me back to the keep," but the sergeant had already turned away, leading his patrol up the street. A pair of red-cloaked soldiers grabbed Danly by the arms. "March, *traitor!*"

Convert soldiers! Brands marked their foreheads, a sure sign of cruelty. "No, leave me alone." He tried to pull away but the soldiers dragged him forward. A cold fist gripped Danly's stomach, wondering if they'd murder him in some back alleyway, a sword slit to his throat, leaving his body for rats. Slick with fear, he dragged his feet, but the soldiers pulled him forward.

They muscled him towards a shadow-shrouded alleyway. "In here."

"No!" Danly resisted till a sword changed his mind.

The stink of stale piss clogged the lane. A soldier shoved him forward. Danly staggered and almost fell. Pressing his back against a stone wall, he turned to face them. "Wait, you don't want to do this."

The soldiers sheathed their swords, their faces twisted in hate. "You betrayed our city! We opened the gates for you, *traitor-prince.*"

Flush with fear, Danly raised the silver crown like a talisman. "Take it, it's yours, just don't hurt me!"

One of the soldiers sneered. "You think we can be bought for silver?"

He wanted to rail at them, to say that they'd already been bought, selling their lives to the Flames, but he bit back the words, fearing retribution.

The first punch took his breath away. The second bent him double. Danly puked, hurling sour ale onto the muddy lane, but the soldiers did not let up. Blow after blow rained against him, a storm of hate. Danly fell to the ground, curling into the ball. And then they started kicking.

"*Enough!*"

The kicking stopped. The soldiers drew back.

"Get him on his feet."

Hands grabbed him, pulling him erect. Danly hung between the soldiers, wracked by pain.

A red-cloaked captain glared at him. "The bishop will be wanting his prize."

They lashed his wrists behind his back. One of them smashed the silver circlet down onto his head. "Your crown, your majesty." They dragged him out into the street.

People turned to stare, but no one raised a voice in protest.

"Help me!"

More people turned his way. A few hurled curses. Others made the hand sign against evil. "*It's the prince!*" Recognition bloomed in the crowd, their faces twisted with hate. Emboldened, an old man hawked a wad of spit.

The spit hit Danly in the cheek, running down his face. Outraged, he screamed. "I've done nothing to you!" Their hate filled stares said otherwise. Confronted by the truth, Danly began to shake, wondering if he had a single friend in the hell-damned city.

"Move, prince." A sword prodded his back.

Danly stumbled toward the keep, lost in a haze of pain. A flock of crows cawed a welcome, the dark birds pecking the spiked heads rotting on the keep's battlement. Danly refused to look aloft, refused to see the baron's desiccated head. His gaze scanned the gates, relieved to recognize one of the guards. "Hester, you know me! I don't deserve such treatment. Release me!"

But the guard looked away, a smirk on his face.

A sword pricked Danly's back. "Keep moving, prince."

Shattered, he stumbled through the gates, across the courtyard and up the steps to the keep. Instead of taking him to the bishop's chambers, they prodded him to a side alcove. "Wait here." Danly sank to the floor, his back against the wall. Leaning his head against the cold stones, he closed his eyes, lost in a blur of pain. He must have dozed. When he woke, beams of sunlight were slanting low through the arrow-slit windows, marking the lateness of the day.

A boot nudged his side. "On your feet, prince."

Danly struggled to stand, every part of him stiff and aching.

"So you caught a royal heretic."

The bishop's deep voice sent a chill down Danly's spine.

"On your knees, heretic."

A soldier pushed him to the floor, the flagstones hard beneath his knees. Danly gazed up at Bishop Taniff, desperate for a reprieve, but the cleric's dark gaze gleamed with the pious bloodlust of a fanatic. Danly struggled to swallow, his voice a hoarse croak. "I have the protection of Lord Raven."

The bishop barked a laugh. "You have *nothing!*"

"But I've served the Flame! I proved my loyalty by giving you Lingard!"

"Yet your heart is impure. I can smell a heretic, prince. You reek of disbelief."

"I took your oath! I'm sworn to the Flame God."

The bishop laughed, an ugly sound. "Then it's past time you took the Test of Faith."

"*No!*" A stream of hot urine ran down his leg. "Not that!"

"The Flame God will judge ye. The path to heaven is paved with the ashes of infidels." The bishop turned away. "Take him to the pyres. I'll conduct the rites myself, a royal offering to the Flame God."

Soldiers saluted, while others grabbed Danly by the arms, hauling him to his feet.

"*No! I know things! I know things that can help you!*" Danly screamed, but no one listened. Soldiers half carried, half dragged him out of the keep, across the courtyard, and through the streets. They took him to the square in the western quarter of the city, pyres of tinder already built, awaiting the nightly offering. Danly struggled and kicked, but it made no difference. The soldiers bore him to the central pyre. Forcing him up the mound of kindling, they chained him to the iron stake. Thick chains looped around his waist and ankles, binding him like a sacrificial offering, a prince chained atop the pyre.

"*Let me go! Take the silver crown and let me go!*"

The soldiers ignored him. Securing the chains, they left him screaming.

71

Stewart

Secrecy and stealth were essential to his plan. Stewart marshaled his forces for a desperate gamble. Deploying a screen of scouts, he marched his men hard by night, drawing a stealthy noose around Lingard. He split his army into three parts, dividing them between the three woods surrounding the fortress. Dane commanded the north wood, Major Batton the southeast, while Stewart took the west wood. The prince kept Ronald, the heir to Lingard, close by his side. Only three men in all of his army wore the golden surcoat emblazoned with the Rognald's iron fist. A proud emblem nearly extinguished by royal treachery, Stewart hoped it would once more reign in the fortress of Lingard.

Flanked by scouts, the prince crept through the forest, his sword in his hand. Snow crunched beneath his boots, the bows of the scouts pulled taut. They reached the forest's edge, gaining a clear view across the snow-dusted greensward. Viewed from an attacker's perspective, the mighty fortress looked damn near invincible. Tall walls surrounded by a deep moat, the crenellated battlements bristled with trebuchets. Rearing from the greensward, the fortress stood solid and defiant, a vision of martial strength reflected in still waters. Stewart studied the walls, finding no weaknesses. Lingard might fall to a lengthy siege but never to a conventional attack. Trickery or magic were his only options. His brother had tried the one, Stewart would try the other.

Surrounded by scouts and accompanied by his captains, Stewart crouched behind an oak tree. He scanned the sky, noting the scant hours till twilight. The wind shifted and he nearly choked on the stench. "What is that god-awful reek?"

Beside him, Ronald answered, "Heretics. They burn heretics at dawn and at dusk. The stench hangs over the city like a pall. It's been that way since the priests first took the city."

Stewart sketched the hand sign against evil, recalling how he'd been bound for the Flames. "Tonight we'll give them a taste of fire. We'll see how much they love the flames."

A steady clop of hooves approached, a lone rider on a dark horse threading her way through the winter forest. Stewart rose to greet the lady. Clad in midnight blue robes, Ellis wore her dark hair unbound falling below her shoulders, her face pale as ice in the waning daylight. Wrapped in an aura of power, she carried herself with a reserved dignity, as if a warrior-priestess of legend had sprung from history to ride among them.

Awed by the vision, Stewart gave her a courtly bow. "Thank you for coming."

Ellis gave him a cold stare. "I will ask you again to set aside this plan."

"There is no other way. Swords alone will not succeed."

She pursed her lips, her face stern, her voice as cold as a sepulcher. "Magic was not meant to be used in this fashion. It harkens back to the War of Wizards, to a time of great evil."

"Yet evil must be confronted. And somehow it must be defeated." Stewart pressed his argument, passion giving force to his words. "I've seen the depths of their depravity." His voice turned hard. "Take a deep breath. The very air carries the stench of their victims turned to ashes. How many more will die if you don't help?"

"Their deaths are not my doing."

"Yet you could save many."

Her stare pierced him, as if studying his soul.

Stewart held his breath, as if all of Erdhe depended on her answer.

Ellis sighed. "Two truths crossed like swords. We are both right, yet I fear what this night will unleash." She gave him the smallest of nods. "Evil must be confronted and the Flame defeated. My magic will join your cause for this *one* night, but in recompense, the prince of Lanverness shall swear to be beholden to the Kiralynn Order, required to grant a boon to our Grand Master." Her voice turned cold as winter. "Do you so swear?"

A warning shivered down Stewart's back. He did not like the open-ended nature of the boon, but he needed her magic. He gripped his sword hilt. "I so swear."

"So be it."

Stewart's skin prickled as if a geas had been laid upon him.

Ellis's horse stamped and snorted, but she controlled him with the pressure of her knees. "Know this, prince, the magic of the moon weaving will last till dawn's first light. You have but one night to retake the fortress and then the enemy will be able to open the gates."

"One night will be enough." Stewart prayed he had the truth of it.

"We shall not meet again." She gave him a piercing stare. "Once the weave is set, I will return to the Southern Mountains. My magic is too strong for the lands of Erdhe."

"I will grant you an escort."

"I want none."

"As you wish."

She turned her horse towards the depths of the woods.

Beside him, Ronald said, "Will it work?"

"Pray that it does, else we'll lose the war, not just Lingard." Stewart issued orders to his scouts, birdcalls whispering through the woods, and then he settled down to wait for the moon's rising.

72

Danly

Seven pyres for seven heretics, Danly stood bound to the central stake, railing against his fate. The others were chained to smaller pyres, four men and two women. They hung their heads in sullen silence, like sheep awaiting the slaughter, but Danly fought against his bonds. *"I don't deserve this! I'm a prince of royal blood! Release me or be damned!"* He howled his rage, and yelled his fear, but no one came to his rescue. Driven hoarse by his screams, he fell silent.

Staring at the sky, Danly watched the sun sink towards darkness, like watching his life slip through an hourglass, but the sun waits for no man. The fiery orb sank into the horizon, a blaze of red fading to purple, such a bloody sunset, such a bloody waste.

A crowd began to gather, come to witness the sacrifice.

Danly glared at them, hatred in his stare.

A small dark-haired lad crept to the base of Danly's pyre. "Look, mother, he wears a crown! It's the traitor prince!"

A rumble of anger swept through the watchers.

"He's the one!"

"You did this to us!"

"You gave us to the Flame!"

Someone hurled a rock, hitting him in the cheek. Danly shook with rage, screaming his hate. "You did this to yourselves! Did you fight? Are you fighting now? You're all sheep! You all deserve to die! At least *I* dared to reach for a crown!"

Someone yelled, "Traitor prince!" and the crowd took it up as a chant, *"traitor-prince, traitor-prince, traitor-prince."*

Danly sobbed, always the same accusation. He strained against his bonds, desperate to escape, but the chains held him fast.

Torches appeared in the far street, a procession of red-robed priests chanting prayers to the Flame God. Death paraded towards him.

The crowd stilled to a hush, parting to give passage to the priests. The procession circled the pyres, intoning prayers to the Flame God. Waving braziers smoking with incense, they muttered a litany of chants. Danly watched, his mouth as dry as a desert, desperate for a reprieve. After the third circuit, individual priests broke away from the others to climb the pyres.

A portly priest struggled towards Danly, drawing close enough to whisper his rum-soaked words. "Repent, my son. Repent and the Flames may spare you."

Wild laughter burst from Danly, ending in a strangled sob.

"Confess your sins, confess the names of your fellow heretics and go to the Flames shriven of your deeds." The priest reached out, dabbing Danly's face with holy ashes. "Confess and the Flame God will know you as one of his own!"

Danly flinched from the priest's touch. Straining against his bonds, he shouted his answer. "*I gave you Lingard!* I'm a prince of the realm! How can you do this to me?"

"It is written that all heretics shall face the judgment of the Flame. Your time has come."

Danly yelled, "Do you see this crown! I'm a prince of the realm! Release me!"

"Meet the Flame God with repentance in your heart and your end will be swift."

Sickened, Danly looked away, ignoring the blather. The priest made a final sign of blessing and then stumbled back down the pyre.

Hoof beats drummed on the cobblestone street. Bishop Taniff and his holy entourage thundered into the square. The crowd shrank backwards, like sheep before the wolf. Danly might have laughed if he wasn't so scared.

The Bloody Bishop dismounted, a mitered helm shining on his head, his red cloak billowing in the breeze, his great mace affixed to his belt. Tall and imposing, the warrior-cleric looked like an avatar of the Flame God. A priest held the bishop's smoke-gray stallion while another handed him a flaming torch. Raising the torch to the darkening sky, the bishop made the sign of blessing, his voice booming through the square. "And the Flame God shall know his own, separating the infidel from the faithful. For he that walks through the Flame without sin, shall be spared by the Fire, and those who sin shall be consumed."

The crowd murmured, "The Test of Faith."

The bishop strode toward the pyres, stopping below Danly. "Are you ready to be judged?"

Danly felt like pissing but his bladder was empty.

The bishop laughed, an ugly sound. "I'll save you for last, prince, a royal offering to our most righteous God. Watch the others as they burn. Hear their screams, smell their roasting flesh, enjoy their torment. May you find justice in the Flame God's embrace."

"You can't do this to me!"

The bishop laughed. "There's darkness in your soul, prince. You've always been destined for the Flames."

The words struck like a sword to his bowels. Danly emptied himself, quaking with fear. "I can be useful! I know things!"

But the bishop had already turned away. Striding to the first pyre, he set his torch to the kindling. Fire leaped to the wood, a hungry crackle of flames.

The flames embraced the kindling, racing up the pyre toward the sacrifice. The woman screamed and flinched away but she was bound fast. Fire touched flesh, releasing a tortured howl.

Fear pulsed through Danly. Sobbing, he heaved against his bonds, rattling the chains. Bound tight, he watched as the flames consumed the first and second pyres. Tears streaked his face, forgotten prayers on his lips.

Hooves drummed on the cobblestones. A red-cloaked messenger burst into the square. Dismounting, he rushed towards the bishop. *"My lord bishop!"*

Bishop Taniff turned, annoyance on his face, yet he paused to listen.

Danly strained to hear, but their words were drowned by tortured screams.

Whatever was said, it galvanized the bishop to action. "My horse!" A priest rushed forward, leading the bishop's smoke-gray stallion. Tossing his torch to the cobblestones, Bishop Taniff vaulted into the saddle, bellowing orders.

Danly's stare followed the torch. It landed a hand-span from his pyre. Horrified, he watched the flames, willing the wind to snuff them out.

The Bloody Bishop put spurs to his stallion, leading his entourage from the square. The remaining priests conferred in a huddle, while the screams of the heretics shrank to silence, consumed by the flames. A terrible stench filled the square, a lingering cloud of burnt flesh. The crowd began to mill, uncertain whether to stay or leave.

Danly's stare fixed on the burning torch, flickering flames reaching toward his pyre.

A soldier approached, stamping out the flaming torch.

Danly sagged in relief, wondering if it was a sign. Something had saved him, though he knew not what. Perhaps the gods had forgiven him, granting him a second chance. He watched from atop the pyre as the crowd melted away. Danly laughed and then cried, tears streaming down his face. "See, I told you I was innocent!" Bound atop the pyre, Danly muttered prayers to every god he'd ever heard of, begging for a second chance, begging to be released.

73

Stewart

Night fell hard, a harvest moon rising bright over Lingard. The fortress was shut tight as a coffin, the gates closed, the drawbridge raised, secured for the night, but the night would prove their downfall. Stewart gave the signal and bird calls trilled through the woods.

A lone rider cantered into the moonlight.

All along the wood, battle-hardened men crept to the forest's edge, come to watch a lone woman take on a fortress filled with evil.

Dark as midnight against the snow covered ground, the monk sat straight in the saddle, staring up at the moon-drenched sky. Horse and rider stilled. Cloaked in robes of midnight blue, the woman and the dark horse seemed melded together, like a mythical figure come to champion the Light. The moon hung low in the sky, full and bright and tinged with orange, a bloody moon, a harvest moon, rising like an omen of death. The wind died and the night stilled, as if the world held its breath. Ellis threw her head back, her right fist thrust toward the heavens. Stewart watched spellbound, his breath held in wonder. An ancient power seemed to shimmer around the monk. A gleam of moonlight appeared in her raised fist. A faint flicker at first, quickly growing in strength till the orb blazed star-bright.

Gasps of awe rippled through the forest.

Cries of alarm rang from the fortress.

Ellis drummed her heels against the stallion's flank. The horse leaped forward, galloping across the snow-crusted greensward. The monk circled the fortress, holding the glittering orb aloft, weaving a noose of moonlight in her wake. Thick as a man's arm, a shimmering strand of light trailed behind her, encircling the fortress. *Magic*, Stewart shivered in awe, knowing the moon weaving was stronger than steel.

Arrows thrummed from the fortress, arcing into the night sky, but none hit the lone rider.

Soldiers crouched at the forest's edge cheered as the monk rode out of sight.

A silence descended over the woods, nothing to do but wait. Stewart gripped his sword hilt, knowing everything depended on the monk. He began to pace, wearing a path between two trees. Time seemed to drag, an eternity of waiting. A shout rose from the woods. He turned to watch the monk emerge from the far side of the fortress, galloping across the moonlit greensward. Her dark hair streamed like a battle banner, her fist raised in defiance, a rope of light shimmered in her wake. Ellis blazed like a warrior-priestess anointed by moonlight. Completing the circuit, she returned to the start of the moon weave. Leaping from the saddle, she worked to bind a knot in the moonlight.

Arrows arched from the fortress, a deadly hail falling around her.

"*Guard her!*" Stewart roared the order and a dozen soldiers with shields ran towards Ellis. Standing in a crescent, they raised their oaken shields, a stout barrier protecting the monk.

Arrows thunked into upturned shields, skewering the ground, but the monk never faltered. Ellis finished the knot and then gathered the moon weave. Like a noose she pulled the moonlight rope taut against Lingard's walls, sealing the fortress. A shimmering ring of moonlight strangled the battlements, holding the drawbridges shut with magic. Ellis remounted her stallion. For a dozen heartbeats, she slumped in the saddle. Stewart feared she was shot, but then she straightened. Sending one last stare in Stewart's direction, she gathered her reins and rode south.

A hush descended on the woods, a reverence for courage melded with magic.

Stewart felt the awe as much as his men, but he had a fortress to reclaim. It was time for his men to do their part. He bellowed orders, "Bring up the scorpions! It's time to retake Lingard!"

An earth-shattering cheer erupted from his men.

Three wagons trundled through the forest, coming to a stop at the wood's edge. Soldiers leaped from the wagons, setting chocks to the wheels. Scorpions were affixed to the wagon beds. Giant crossbows fashioned of wood and sinew and steel, the scorpions were a marvel of military craftsmanship, another gift from the monks.

Stewart took a position near the center scorpion. "Test the range before you risk the Napthos." They dared not waste a single flask of the fiery brew. The queen had sent the entire hoard north, ninety-two ceramic flasks full of the ancient potion. Stewart prayed it would be enough.

A pair of soldiers muscled the scorpion into the bent position. A third loaded a ceramic flask filled with water. The captain yelled, "Loose!" A soldier released the tickler. The scorpion bucked with a mighty shudder, hurling the flask toward the fortress. Sailing like an arrow, the flask shattered against the ramparts, raising a cheer from the men, but Stewart knew the walls were not the target. "Reset the scorpion and try again."

On the third try, the flask sailed high over the walls, deep into the city's heart.

Stewart nodded. "Bring up the Napthos."

One at a time, flasks of Napthos were carefully carried to the scorpions. A soldier held a torch to the Napthos-soaked wick embedded in the stopper. The wick blazed bright, spitting flames. A lone soldier wearing blacksmith's gloves gingerly set the flaming flask in the firing slot. Another soldier released the tickler. The scorpion bucked, hurling its charge aloft. A flaming meteor soared over the fortress walls, sailing deep into the heart of the city.

Stewart waited, watching.

Flame erupted from the city, licking skyward. Screams followed the flames, a wail of pain and suffering.

Soldiers stationed in the woods remained statue still, as if captured by a premonition of dread.

Beside him, Ronald swore, "*By the gods!*"

Stewart worked the saliva back into his mouth. "Finish it! Set the city aflame!"

Soldiers sprang to their work, feeding the scorpions. The night sky became a weave of flaming meteors, arching a deadly path into the city. Stewart watched from the edge of the wood. From the north, the southeast, and the west, flaming meteors scored the night sky, as if a hoard of fire-breathing dragons attacked the city. It might have been beautiful, if not for the screams.

The Napthos quickly ran out, the scorpions stilled to silence.

The city burned. Towering flames licked skyward, bright as a false dawn.

A deep pounding throbbed through the night, as if the enemy took a battering ram against their own gates, but the moon-weaving held, keeping the fortress bound shut.

Enemy soldiers scrambled onto the ramparts. Shedding their armor, they leaped from the battlements, plunging into the moat. Others crowded the walls, poised to jump till they saw bloody bodies rippling the moat. Fresh screams rose from the murky waters, adding to the night's horror. Stewart cast a questioning glance towards Ronald.

"Razor eels."

Stewart shuddered, such a horrible way to die.

They kept vigil through the night, watching the great fortress-city burn. Stewart sickened at the sight, wondering if the monk had the truth of it, wondering if he'd loosed a great evil on the kingdoms of Erdhe.

Ronald stood by his side. "It was the only way, my lord. Evil consumed by evil. As if the Flame priests summoned their own doom."

"Thank the gods there's no more Napthos."

Ronald nodded. "Thank the gods the enemy never had it."

Their stares crossed, chilled by the thought. "Just so."

The fires burned till the small hours of the morning. A great black cloud belched over the fortress like a doom. At dawn's first light, the rope of moonlight dissolved, but none on the walls seemed to notice.

Stewart sent heralds cantering toward the gate. Horns blared into the grim stillness. Soldiers appeared on the walls. The heralds returned unharmed and the great drawbridge slowly lowered. The gates of mighty Lingard swung open. Soldiers and citizens staggered from the fortress. Their faces blackened with soot, they dropped to the snow-covered greensward, a total surrender to weariness.

Stewart mounted his stallion, appalled by the god-awful reek in the air. "Let's see what we've wrought." He rode towards Lingard. It did not feel like a victory yet it had to be done. The prince spurred his stallion toward the gate, claiming a fortress defeated by a single night of horror.

74

Danly

A meteor blazed across the night sky, falling into the city. Danly straightened, staring skyward. Bound to the iron stake, he watched from atop the pyre, wondering if he'd imagined the fiery streak.

Screams erupted from the city, a lick of fire belching toward the heavens. A second flaming meteor scored the night, and then a third. Like the wrath of an angry god, a storm of meteors fell upon the city. The fireballs came from three directions, arching across the ramparts, raining fire upon the rooftops and streets. Screams echoed through the city, the sound of a trumpet blaring from the outer walls.

Lingard was under attack! Hope thrummed through Danly; the enemy of his enemy had to be his friend. If he could just survive the attack, he'd be saved!

People rushed pell-mell through the square, bleating like frightened sheep.

"Release me! Release me!" Danly screamed, straining against his chains, but no one looked his way, intent on their own panic.

A flaming figure staggered into the square, his clothes alight, screaming like a banshee. *A human torch,* fear shivered through Danly. He watched the flaming drunk lurch across the square, like a figure sprung from the depths of hell. *"Keep away, keep away,"* Danly repeated the words like a prayer. The gods must have heard, for the man collapsed, a flaming outline twitching against the cobbles.

Another meteor hissed from the sky, hitting a nearby tavern. Danly watched in horror as fire burst across the rooftop. The flames spread like starving demons. In the blink of an eye, the entire tavern was ablaze. Heat beat across the square, fierce as a blacksmith's forge. Danly stared in awe, amazed by the fire's ferocious appetite. Appalled by its nearness, he strained against his bonds. Flames consumed the building and then leaped to another, but they did not enter the square. *They did not enter the square!* Surrounded by a moat of cobblestones, Danly realized he was safe atop his pyre. Fate had spared him! He laughed until he cried. All around him, the city burned, but not the square. He stared aloft, the rain of fireballs becoming a thing of beauty. Meteors scored the night sky, brighter than falling stars. Screams embraced the city. Lingard burned like hell come calling, but he was spared.

Danly grinned, reveling in the destruction. Relief and hatred broiled within him, an upwelling of wild emotions. Chained atop the pyre, he screamed his wrath at the city, damning them all to hell. "You worshiped the Flames and now your vengeful God has found you! He's found you! Take your Test of Faith! Justice has come calling!"

Like a brief summer storm, the rain of meteors came to an end. Danly stared skyward, the stars hidden by belching smoke. All around him, the city burned, yet he was safe, spared by the gods. Chained atop a pyre, *he* was going to live, while everyone else *died*! Danly burst with laughter. He'd cheated fate! He'd survived the pyre! The Bloody Bishop was wrong; he wasn't meant to die in the flames, he was meant to live!

One last fireball rose from the north, streaking across the smoke-filled sky.

It came towards him.

"No!" Danly stared in horror. "You spared me! I don't deserve this!"

The fireball ignored his plea. Like the flaming hand of god, it struck the square. Fire belched across the cobbles, licking towards his pyre.

"*No!*"

The flames found his pyre. Wood exploded in fire. Crackling flames raced up the mound, opening a portal to hell. "*No, not me!*" Embraced by fire, Danly screamed till Darkness came calling.

75

Stewart

Smoke blunted the rising sun to a dull orange. In the dawn's eerie light, Stewart led his men from the woods. The gates of Lingard gaped open. Beyond the battlements, the city fumed and hissed like a pit from hell.

Stewart urged his horse to a walk, leading his troops toward the fortress. They crossed the drawbridge, a hollow clop of hooves announcing the victors. Stewart's gaze was drawn to the gates. Deep dents in the ironshod wood proved the enemy had taken a battering ram to their own defenses, yet the gates had remained shut. *Magic*, such an awesome and mysterious force, for the hundredth time Stewart thanked the gods the monks were on their side.

They passed beneath the iron teeth of the portcullis and entered the city. Stewart unsheathed his sword, but there was no need. Citizens and soldiers lay collapsed in the cobbled streets, their faces blackened with soot, their clothes singed, succumbed to horror. Staring at him with hollow gazes, most did not bother to move.

Stewart drew his horse to a halt. "Who's in charge here?"

A soldier stirred. "The Bloody Bishop, Bishop Taniff, but I saw a fireball take him. The bastard burned to death, screaming like any sinner."

"And do you still believe in the Flame God?"

The soldier stammered, staring wide-eyed. "No sir, not any more, the god deserted us, if he ever was a god."

Stewart gave the soldier a steely stare and then nudged his horse to a walk, moving deeper into the city. Smoke billowed from blackened buildings, embers glowing in the depths like glimmers from hell. The dead were everywhere, blackened and burnt, raising a horrible stench. Most of the city was burned, glass and iron melted to distorted shapes, giving proof to the fierce heat of the flames. But amongst the cinders were islands of unscathed buildings, as if the flames had a selective appetite. So eerie to see homes and shops untouched, standing amongst the charred ruins, perhaps the gods had a way of protecting their own.

The cobbled street opened up into a large square, offering a nightmare of another sort. Pyres of sacrifice filled the square. Three were blackened and burnt, but on four of the pyres the prisoners still lived, their faces streaked with tears. "Release them." Shuddering, Stewart made the hand sign against evil. "So this is how they worship their twisted god."

Soldiers scrambled to obey, steel swords ringing against iron chains.

Stewart's gaze was drawn to the central pyre, so consumed by heat that the iron stake was distorted into a tortured sculpture of pain, chains melted at its base, the very bones of its victim devoured by flames, nothing left but ash. Stewart wondered what the poor soul had done to earn such a hellish fate. "Such a horrible way to die. Let's hope the Flame religion dies with you." Stewart turned away, his gaze falling on Ronald, the rightwise heir to Lingard. "You have much to rebuild. Lingard will rise from the enemy's ashes, a mighty fortress once more."

Ronald nodded, staring at the devastation, his face stunned. "At least the Flame is defeated."

"If any priests survived, have them beheaded. The queen will not suffer this foul religion in her kingdom."

Ronald saluted. "It will be done."

An emerald-cloaked messenger came running, "Lord Prince!"

Stewart recognized the young man, Cleary, a messenger from the queen's court. "Why are you here?

The young man thrust a sealed scroll towards the prince. "An urgent message from the queen. I was sworn not to deliver it till Lingard fell."

Fear spiked through Stewart. He checked the royal seal and then ripped the scroll opened. Reading it, he hissed in anger, his worst fears confirmed. "Trumpeter, sound the alert! The army rides for Pellanor and pray we're not too late."

76

Jordan

Jordan spurred the gelding, desperate for more speed. A cold wind lashed her face, the snow-dusted countryside passing in a blur, but it was not fast enough, not nearly fast enough. Her dreams chased her like wraiths, visions of death and betrayal hounding her forward. She dare not be late.

A gloved hand reached across, yanking her reins.

Startled, Jordan reached for her sword, but then the shouted words pierced her mind. *"You're killing the horses!"*

Shame struck like lightning. Jordan slowed her mount to a walk, shocked by the gelding's condition. Lathered in sweat, foam flecking his mouth, his lungs worked like a blacksmith's bellows, her mount staggered to a walk. *She'd nearly ridden him to death.* Jordan shuddered. "I did not know. I did not see..."

"Lass, you ride us all too hard, yourself most of all." Thaddeus rode beside her, his voice a soothing balm.

Her horse hung his head low, blowing hard. Chagrinned, she dismounted, loosening his girth. The others joined her, walking their lathered mounts.

Thaddeus kept pace beside her. "You ride like a banshee loosed from hell. What troubles you?"

Jordan flushed with shame. "My dreams are getting worse. Sometimes I get caught in them." Her voice dropped to a whisper. "If we don't get there soon, it will all be for naught."

"We'll get there, lass, the gods are on our side."

The swordmaster was so confident, she almost believed him.

Thad gestured to the north. "Chimney smoke scoring the sky, marking a small village or a large farmstead. Perhaps a chance to buy fresh mounts. These are spent."

"Perhaps." Radagar was a chancy kingdom to traverse. Jordan was never certain if she'd find a warm welcome or a sword held to her throat, but the Zward had a knack for avoiding trouble. For the thousandth time she thanked the gods for their company.

They kept the horses to a walk, breathing bellows of mist into the cold morning air. Four swordsmen, two monks, and a princess plagued by nightmares, they seemed a pitiful force in the face of her dreams, but she had to try.

Thad matched her stride. "What do you see that drives you so hard?"

She owed him an answer. Taking a deep breath, she struggled to explain. "My family, my home, a threat in the night, but the images always change, different nightmares, different outcomes. I just know I need to get to Castle Seamount by Royal Nachte or Darkness will prevail."

"Royal Nachte?"

"Founder's Night."

"And once we get there?"

She took a deep breath. "We fight."

He raised an eyebrow. "Just the seven of us?"

"We'll have better odds once we reach Navarre." She raised her right hand, the silver signet of Navarre gleaming in the morning light. "With this ring I can command fresh mounts and men from the border garrisons. By the time we reach the castle, we won't be riding alone."

"Will it be enough?" He gave her a shrewd stare, "or are you counting on magic?"

Her breath caught, as if he'd read her mind. Her gaze strayed to the two monks. "Does Yarl or Rafe wield magic?"

Thad's voice was sharp, cutting off her question. "That's *their* secrets. Theirs to share or to keep." His voice softened. "But lass, I must warn you, magic is rare, even among the monks. Their best weapon is knowledge. But I don't think it'll be knowledge that helps you defeat your nightmares."

"No, I guess not." She'd hoped for magic, but it seemed she'd have to prevail by swords and wits, yet her gaze kept straying to the two monks. "Why do the monks have such strange magics?"

He gave her a puzzled look.

"Lenore turning into an owl? Ellis with her moon weaving? They're not what I expected."

"You mean they're not lightning bolts and fire balls? Not the stuff of bard's songs?"

His question made her feel silly, yet she persisted. "Yeah, I guess so."

Thaddeus shrugged, his face thoughtful. "From what I hear tell, magic was plentiful before the War of Wizards, most of it better suited to peace than to war. Perhaps the peaceful magic survived." His face darkened. "But tales of the Mordant tell a different story. From what I've heard, the dark bastard's been collecting magic for nigh on a thousand years."

A chill shivered down Jordan's spine. "So *he's* got the fireballs and lightning bolts?"

"Mayhap."

His words seemed like a doom. "But surely the monks have powerful magic too?"

He gave her a steely-eyed stare. "The monks keep their secrets close."

"But owl-men and moon weavings?"

"You thought of a plan to retake Lingard using a moon weaver's power."

Her breath caught, thinking of Stewart, praying the gods kept him safe. "I wonder if it worked."

"So do I."

Jordan smiled, hearing the fervor beneath his words. "You like her don't you, you like Ellis?"

The big swordmaster turned as red as his russet beard. "She's a flinty woman, yet she knows how to strike sparks off a man."

"Sparks of anger, or passion?"

He grinned. "Both."

"Yet you're with me, instead of her."

His voice turned gruff. "The Grand Master tasked me with keeping you safe. The Zward lives to serve."

"Thank you."

He nodded, pulling a bramble from his horse's mane. "We've walked the horses long enough. I think they'll bear a trot."

They tightened the girths and swung back into their saddles. Nudging their horses to a weary trot, they rode towards the smoke piercing the sky. Jordan stared ahead, her mind beset by worries. Magic and nightmares, she tried to make sense of her visions. A feeling of doom cloaked her shoulders, a stranglehold of fate. Jordan clutched the reins, needing more speed. The gods gave warnings, but they never made it easy.

77

Steffan

Steffan drove his army hard, keen for vengeance. Tricked by a mere woman, the insult raged in his soul. *Empty treasury chests!* The memory ate like acid at his mind, but the gold had to be somewhere, most likely hidden in the bowels of Castle Tandroth. The Spider Queen had tricked him once, but vengeance would be his. He'd sack her city and rape the royal bitch, claiming the gold and the crown. Victory was his for the taking. He grew hard just thinking about it.

Ten thousand boots beat a fearsome rhythm at his back, the sound of invincibility heralding his victory. The numbers were still his, a mighty host claimed by treachery. Steffan rode in the vanguard with the general, red battle banners snapping overhead. By mid afternoon they topped a rise, gaining a view of the queen's capital city.

General Caylib barked a rude laugh. "So *this* is Pellanor! The Spider Queen is a fool! The woman has no sense for war. I've seen hill forts with better defenses."

"A prize waiting for a conqueror's fist." Steffan grinned, remembering the soft luxury of the queen's city. Spurring his horse off the road, he followed the general to the hilltop. They studied the capital from a conqueror's viewpoint. Castle Tandroth sat like a spider in a web of prosperity, shops and buildings sprawling around the castle walls, radiating in all directions. In times of peace, Pellanor was an impressive sight, the largest and most prosperous city in Erdhe, but in times of war it was laughable. Without battlements or a moat, the city was protected by nothing more than a series of blocky buildings strung together with hastily erected walls. The mortar was still fresh upon the walls, white glaring against the gray stone. Steffan smirked at the queen's shoddy attempt to erect a defense. The general had the truth of it. Pellanor had less protection than a hill fort, a ripe plum waiting to be plucked.

The general slapped his thigh, a twisted grin on his face. "Easy pickings. We'll take the city in less than a day."

The general's confidence proved contagious. "When will you attack?"

General Caylib surveyed the city, his warhorse pawing the ground as if eager to charge. "We'll set up camp in the nearest woods." He pointed to a hill crowned with forest, a vantage point overlooking the city. "We'll give the

mercenaries a day to rest and then we'll spend a day building ladders and
battering rams. On the third day we'll attack."

Three days, Steffan could wait that long. "Good."

The general gave him a piercing stare. "Will you send heralds to offer
terms?"

"Terms?" Steffan sneered. "The Spider Queen forfeited terms when she
tricked me with the treasury caravan."

"Good," the word was little more than a grunt. The general turned his
stallion, flashing a wicked grin. "After all this marching the men deserve some
bloodshed and rape."

"So does the queen."

The general barked a rude laugh. "I like you counselor. Despite your
fancy clothes, you're a barbarian at heart." He spurred his horse forward,
galloping towards the vanguard.

Steffan lingered on the hilltop, staring down at the queen's city. In three
days it would be his. A deep hunger gnawed at him, one lifetime was not
enough.

78

Liandra

Once more the queen donned armor. Greaves and gorget, breastplate and bucklers, Liandra assumed the silvered trappings of war. "Armor is fast becoming the fashion of our court."

Lady Sarah adjusted a buckler. "You wear it so well."

"Who would have thought? But we much prefer silks and velvets. Peace becomes us more than war." She studied herself in the mirror, sunlight reflecting off of silvered steel, lending her an aura of invincibility. "Yet it does have its own appeal. There is a certain power to it, a grand glory. Perhaps that's why men love it so." Noticing the grave faces of her women, the queen dared a quip. "It looks good, but it's devilishly difficult in the water closet."

Her women forced a laugh, but nothing could lighten the grim mood. Word of the approaching army had swept through her city like a plague. Her courtiers came calling, some pleading for surrender while others begged for protection. She summoned her officers but they gave little hope. Liandra decided she needed to see the enemy for herself. Clad in silver armor, a sword belted to her side, she became the warrior queen once more, a symbol to her people.

Lady Sarah fastened the emerald cloak at her shoulders, "Be careful, majesty."

Behind her, Master Raddock fretted. "Must you take the risk?"

"Yes, we must." The queen took a final look in the mirror and then swept out of her solar and down the stairs to the outer courtyard. A troop of mounted knights waited in the yard, serious warriors bristling with weapons, another sign that peace had fled her kingdom. The knights saluted, a brisk snap of mailed fists to armored breastplates. The queen acknowledged them with a regal nod. Sir Durnheart knelt to give her a leg up. Liandra mounted her white warhorse, struggling against the armor's weight. Taking up the reins, she arranged her emerald cloak and then gestured for the castle gates to be opened. With a slight press of her knees, she led her knights out into the city streets, sunlight glinting on armor.

Liandra rode forth from the castle without fanfare. No blaring of trumpets, or snapping of battle banners, just a small escort of knights, everyone else needed for the outer walls. Hoof beats clattered on cobblestones, her people scattered to get out of the way; gaping when they realized the queen rode among them. Doffing their hats, their stares followed her, their faces lined with worry. The queen rode past without a gesture or a wave. She wanted no lies between herself and her people. Instead of false hope she gave them steely determination. Liandra prayed it would be enough.

She reached the outer walls and found Major Ranoth waiting. He held her stallion while she dismounted, but they did not speak. The chill of his gaze told her more than enough. Steeling herself against the truth, she climbed the rickety stair to the rooftop that served as a gatehouse tower. Such a pitiful defense, but she kept her face a mask of stone.

Emerald-cloaked knights and officers awaited her on the rooftop. They bowed low, their faces grim. She stared past them, beyond her city, to the forested hilltop known as Crown Hill, a royal hunting preserve overrun by the enemy. Even from a distance, the plague of pea-green tabards and flame-red surcoats glared among the winter-naked trees. The enemy infested the wood, an army of evil come to claim her city.

In the stillness of the late afternoon, she heard a distant pounding. It sounded like a death knell. As she watched, a massive oak toppled, felled by the enemy's axes.

Beside her, Major Ranoth said, "Ladders. They're building ladders and battering rams. With such pitiful defenses, they won't need more."

Spoken aloud, the truth deepened the chill in the winter air. The queen gripped her sword hilt, finding a strange reassurance in the strength of steel. "When will they come?"

"Most likely on the morrow."

On the morrow, such a short amount of time. "Not at night?"

Major Ranoth shook his head. "They don't need the cloak of darkness. When the ladders and rams are built, they'll come calling."

"Do they only hold the wood, or do they surround our city as well?"

"Just the wood. If I were the enemy, I'd use all my forces to punch through a single gate and then forge a path straight to the caste. Just one gate is all they need and the city is lost, but the castle is the true prize. They'll have a tougher time with the castle."

Liandra nodded, feeling like a chess piece about to be toppled. Staring at the enemy, she hardened her resolve. "Then we'll meet their attack with all of our might. Save for a small skeleton force, pull every soldier from the other gates and station them here."

Major Ranoth hesitated, his voice a low whisper. "But majesty, to deplete the other gates is very risky. I could be wrong."

She gave him a steely glare. "Risk is all we have left. Give the orders."

"As you wish."

"And open Castle Tandroth to our people. Anyone who wants refuge shall be welcome. We'll take them all, even if we have to cram the hallways with them."

"But majesty, if it comes to a siege, it will be a strain to feed so many people."

Resolve filled her voice. "We are queen of *all* the people. We will have it no other way."

He gave her a deep bow. "Yes, majesty."

Liandra stared at the plague-infested wood. Time had nearly caught her. One more day and the enemy would be pounding on her gates, the hell of war loosed on her city. In her mind's eye, she saw a chessboard crowded with enemies, a lone queen backed into the corner. Liandra wracked her mind for a way to gain a stalemate. She'd long since played most of her gambits, but she still had a few slender tricks saved for the endgame. She wondered if they would be enough.

Movement caught her eye. A handful of riders galloped towards Pellanor as if chased by demons. Cloaks flapping in the wind, they presented a wild riot of colors. Red and brown and emerald, they wore the trappings of scavengers, yet something about the lead rider held her gaze. Riding low in the saddle, he urged his horse to a breakneck gallop, the man melded to the beast yet clearly the master. Her heart knew him, *Robert!*

The riders passed beneath the crown of forest, too near the enemy.

The wood broiled like a kicked anthill. A horn blared and a dozen red-cloaked riders galloped to the chase.

"*Protect them!*" Her heart clenched in fear. "Open the gates!"

Major Ranoth shouted orders. "Archers draw bows! Soldiers open the gates!"

Emerald-clad archers scrambled to the rooftops, bows bent with tension. Below the ironclad gates slowly swung open.

The queen watched from the rooftop, her fists clenched, her words a harried whisper. "*Hurry, Robert, hurry!*"

Lathered with sweat, the lead horse stumbled and nearly fell, but somehow her shadowmaster rallied the horse, coaxing more speed from the foam-flecked beast.

Beside her, Major Ranoth said, "He's killing the horses."

Her heart lurched. "They won't make it. Loose the arrows!"

Major Ranoth shook his head. "Still too far."

Red riders gained on the ragged few.

"Send out the guard!" Even as she issued the command, Robert's horse floundered, stumbling to its knees. Horrified, she watched as he leaped from the saddle. Tumbling across the ground, he came to rest facedown, sprawled in the road. The others thundered passed, yet he did not move. Terrified, she stared at him, willing him to rise. "*Get up!*" The gods must have heard her prayer, for he staggered to his feet.

Swords flashing, the red-cloaked riders galloped for the kill.

"*Protect him!*" but her words made no difference.

Unsheathing a sword and a dagger, he dropped to a fighting stance. The enemy attacked. Red-cloaked soldiers swarmed around him. Liandra stared in mute horror, unable to watch, unable to look away, wondering if her love would be killed before her very eyes.

Two of the brown-cloaked riders turned their horses, galloping back towards the skirmish, their swords raised to the attack.

"Kill them, kill them all!" The words whispered from her lips, sending a desperate plea to all the gods.

More riders burst from the gates, her escort of knights galloping to the rescue. Lances lowered, they charged into the fray. Liandra thought she'd never seen a finer sight.

More horns sounded from the distant hilltop, but Liandra's gaze was fixed on the fight beyond her gates. She strained for a glimpse of Robert, unable to tell if he still lived.

Lances couched, her knights struck. The power of their charge drove the enemy backwards, leaving her spymaster standing in the dust-choked road. *He lives! He lives!* The thought thundered through her mind like a paean to the gods.

More enemies poured from the wood, a larger force, spurring their mounts to vengeance.

Major Ranoth issued an order. "Sound the retreat!"

Trumpets blared along the city's makeshift walls.

Out on the field, her knights regrouped turning back toward the gate. Liandra watched just long enough to see her spymaster swing up behind a mounted knight. Consumed with longing, she raced across the rooftop and down the rickety stairs. Her heart pounding beneath the armor's weight, she reached the ground just as the gates clanged shut.

A thousand stares fell upon her. Liandra slowed to a walk, desperate to still her racing heart.

Her gaze sought his.

He swung down from the horse and strode towards her, a raggedy scarecrow in dust-strewn clothes. Gaunt and weary but otherwise unharmed, her heart swelled to see him safe.

"My queen!" He knelt and she offered her ringed hand.

With one touch, he sent a current of need spiking through her. Capturing her hand, he kissed her ring, much more fervent than mere duty. She struggled for composure, feeling the weight of so many stares.

As if he understood, he gave her a wolf's grin full of promise and then stepped away.

She felt bereft, but duty claimed her.

Another man knelt before her, a big broad-shouldered stranger with a thatch of wild red hair. "My queen, I beg your forgiveness and offer you my sword." Unsheathing his sword, he laid it at her feet.

She sent a questioning glance to Robert.

He gave her the smallest of nods.

"Your name?"

"Leonard Vengar of Lingard."

Liandra wondered at his story, but now was not the time. She touched the stranger's shoulder. "Your sword is accepted in our service."

The big man sighed, as if a great burden eased from his soul. "You'll not regret it."

"You have already earned our gratitude, for you were one of the riders who turned to fight when our shadowmaster was beleaguered." She raised her voice, addressing the knights and soldiers crowding the gate. "On this day, you have all earned the gratitude of your queen. By your bravery you snatched victory from the enemy's grasp! You have proven that Pellanor has teeth. Our lances are sharp and our swords are strong. What we do here this day, we shall do again!"

A cheer thundered through the men, their eyes glistening with pride.

A soldier knelt by her stallion and she accepted the leg up. With a flourish, she drew her sword and brandished it toward her soldiers, gaining a second cheer. A thousand stares followed her, but one man's gaze smoldered through her armor. Her face reddened. She turned her stallion, and asked for a trot. For the sake of image, she kept her white steed to a stately prance, but in her heart she longed to gallop, to reach the castle and be alone with Robert.

79

Liandra

Liandra struggled against her armor. *"Take it off!"* It suddenly seemed like a cage, a steel sheath strangling the breath from her body. *"Hurry!"* Her women swarmed around, releasing straps and buckles. Sculpted steel fell to the floor, like shedding an outer skin. Finally divested of the silvered armor, Liandra dismissed her women, all save Lady Sarah.

Her visit to the outer gate had proved that time was a desperate commodity. Liandra refused to waste a nonce. "Bring us the ivory nightgown, the one with the slender straps." She'd worn it before, on her first night with Robert. Shimmering in the candlelight, the silky softness was enticing. Liandra slipped into luxury. Silk was so different from armor, so richly feminine. Like a cool caress across her skin, she ran her hands down the silky sheath, smoothing every curve. Despite the loss of the child, she'd regained her figure, a lush hourglass beneath the ivory silk.

Lady Sarah brushed the queen's raven-black hair, a dark contrast to the ivory. Their gazes met in the mirror. "When will the attack come?"

"Most likely on the morrow. That's why we are going to him."

Lady Sarah raised an eyebrow. *"Going* to him?"

"Yes, for once we shall put off our crown and go to him." Liandra closed her eyes, remembering his desperate ride toward the gates. "We almost lost him today. He could have died before our very eyes." Liandra shivered in horror. "We shall not waste this last night." Impatient to be gone, the queen gestured towards a small cedar box on her bedside table. "Bring us our jewel box."

Taking the box in her hands, the queen pressed the subtle depression on the carved rose petals. A secret panel opened on the side. Reaching within, she removed two iron skeleton keys, both set on delicate chains of silver. She placed one around her neck, settling the key in her cleavage, a twinge of cold against her bare skin. The other she pressed into Lady Sarah's hands. "We entrust you with the key to the castle's hidden passages. We ordered two copies made in secret. Robert has one, and this is for you." Liandra clasped her friend's hands tight between hers. "If the castle falls, take our loyal women, and as many others as you can gather, and hide in the secret passages. You'll find food and water and weapons stored within, enough to endure a secret siege. Wait for rescue or a chance to escape."

Lady Sarah's eyes grew flinty with protest. "But majesty, not without you!"

"Rest assured, we shall do our best to join you. Taking the city is one thing, but if the Flame captures the queen, the game is over." Steel laced her voice. "We shall not surrender the board so easily."

Lady Sarah turned pale. "Then you expect the castle to fall?"

"We hope for the best and plan for the worst." The queen gave her a wry smile. "Pellanor has grown too fond of luxury, but Castle Tandroth has its secrets. We may yet win a checkmate from this game." The queen stood. "Now bring us our ermine cloak, we grow anxious for the night."

Lady Sarah wrapped the cloak around her shoulders, a warm shield against the winter chill. Pulling the robe close, Liandra took a lighted taper from a wall sconce, and then opened the secret door, releasing a breath of cold mustiness. The queen hesitated at the threshold, suddenly mistrustful of the dark. "Bring us the dagger by our bedside."

Lady Sarah returned with the jeweled dagger.

Unsheathing the blade, the queen gripped it in her right hand, the lighted candle in the other. "Wait for us. Let no one enter our bedroom. We will return before first light."

Lady Sarah smiled. "The blessings of Eros be upon you."

Anxious to be away, the queen entered the secret passage, the stone door whispering shut behind her. So cold and musty, the dark labyrinth entwined her castle like a secret web, a legacy from her ancestors. As a young child, she'd memorized the rhymes of passage. A single candle lit her way, her memory her only guide. Darkness lurked beyond the frail circle of candlelight, like a beast waiting to pounce. Chiding herself, Liandra gripped the dagger, studying the details as she walked. Stone faces stared back at her, all with onyx eyes, some with keyholes in their mouths. Twice she took the wrong turn, but eventually she found the visage she sought, a bearded man smoking a pipe, a look of contentment on his stone face. Liandra caressed the carving, hesitating at the onyx eye-plugs. She'd come to be with Robert, not to spy on him. Juggling the candle and the knife, she inserted the iron skeleton key, relieved when secret door whispered open.

She stepped from darkness into light.

Robert stood with his back to her, naked from the waist up, washing at a basin.

She'd entered without a sound, yet he whirled, a pair of daggers sprung to his hands.

His eyes grew wide in surprise. Straightening from a fighting crouch, his voice was a fervent whisper. "*My queen!*"

She drank in the sight of him; dismayed to find him gaunt from his mission, a mission she'd sent him on. For a moment, duty stood between them. "You survived Lingard."

Setting the daggers on the bedside table, he raked his hand through his steel-gray hair. "Lingard was worse than anything we imagined. Like hell come to Erdhe." His gaze sought hers. "Their so-called religion is an abomination. The Flame *must* be defeated."

"And the truth of the Pontifax's unholy death?"

He grimaced. "I tried, but it seems their foul religion is impervious to truth. Swords must succeed where words failed."

"That is why we took this gambit, risking Pellanor for a chance to defeat the Flame."

"Pellanor cannot stand alone. Prince Stewart *must* come."

"We have sent a message."

"Will it be in time?"

"Only the gods know."

The risks of tomorrow beat against them, stripping away rank and duty. His gaze traveled the length of her, stopping on the hollow of her belly. "The child?"

Sorrow pierced her. "A daughter, lost to poison."

He hissed in anger. "*Poison!*" He raked his hair and began to pace. "An assassin in the castle, I should never have left you."

"You were needed in Lingard. It was a gambit we had to try." She took a step toward him, longing for his touch. "*Robert!*"

He turned then, his face aflame. Crossing the chamber, he swept her into his arms, carrying her to the bed tucked in the corner. Such a small bed, but Liandra found she like it. His weight pressed down on her, his hands caressing her silken curves, a deft tease releasing a rush of heat. He cupped her face, his voice husky. "It's not a queen's bed."

"It's *your* bed." She reached for him, hungry with need.

He drew the silken straps from her shoulders, while she fumbled with the bindings on his pants. Too many clothes in the way, she yearned for his touch. Finally released, they came together. Skin to skin, they fed the hunger. Her nails raked his back, impatient to be taken. He entered her without preamble. She moaned at the sudden thrust, arching her back. He rode her hard, coming in a desperate rush. She shuddered with release, stifling a scream. Slick with sweat, he collapsed beside her, his voice a low growl. "I didn't mean to come so fast."

"It's what I wanted, what I longed for."

Entwined, they touched and talked and touched again, desperate to hold the morning at bay. The second time was much slower, an indulgence of delight building to a crescendo of passion. Liandra shook with the force of it, rocked by fierce waves of pleasure. Finally sated, she nestled against him. "I've missed you so."

"How long can you stay?"

She glanced to the window, the dark already thinning towards dawn. *So soon.* Liandra sighed in dismay; duty falling on her shoulders like a millstone. "The crown beckons."

His arms tightened around her. "If the castle falls, you'll do as we planned?"

"Yes."

He pulled her close. "And I will be at the gates, trying to hold this city for you."

She closed her eyes against his words, wanting to order him to remain within the castle, to keep him safe by her side, but she would not unman him, just as he would not unqueen her. "Promise you'll return to me?"

He caressed her cheek. "We both do what we must."

It wasn't enough. "Promise me?"

"I'll do what I can." He kissed her deeply, a lingering passion, and then he let her go.

She found her silken gown buried beneath the covers, while he searched for her slippers. Kneeling, he slipped them on her feet. For a moment, he held her captive, gazing up at her. "Be strong tomorrow, my queen."

"Tomorrow has already caught us."

"Duty becomes you." He settled the ermine robe around her shoulders and then gave her one last kiss. "My queen." She clung to him, loving the strength of his arms, wanting the kiss to last forever, but time intruded, the dawn's first light tapping impatiently at the window. "The crown beckons." Releasing him, she took up the dagger and a fresh candle and stepped back into the castle's secret ways. Despite the terrible odds, she had a war to wage and to win.

80

The Priestess

Moonlight glinted on a storm-tossed sea. Three dark-hulled boats battled the waves. Low and sleek with ten oars to a side, the raiders sliced through the bay like arrows loosed towards a prize. The Priestess rode the lead boat's prow. Dressed in dark leathers, her raven hair unfurled like a battle banner, she licked the salt spray from her lips, reveling in the taste. Waves slapped the boat, a prelude to a storm, but the Priestess only laughed. Her feet spread wide, she rode the rocking motion, accustomed to the moods of the sea. Fisherman claimed a stern trident-wielding god ruled the briny deep, but the Priestess knew better. The ocean bore a woman's temperament, all that suppressed rage lurking in the depths, something she knew so well. Gripping the wolf-carved prow, she leaned forward urging the rowers to greater speed, so close to retribution.

Castle Seamount reared ahead, a fist of black stone battered by salt spray. A formidable castle yet she knew its weakness. Spread in a crescent behind the castle, the city of Seaside gleamed white in the moonlight; limestone houses huddled on the hillside, cascading down to the night-dark sea. Black and white, she laughed at the image, as if Navarre had no understanding of gray. She'd always loved gray, that moral murkiness where any decision might hold sway. Tonight she'd test them all, pushing them into the gray, the first step towards Darkness.

Muscles strained and the oars bit deep, the raiders pulling towards the castle. Armor and weapons clanked as her soldiers readied for battle. All of her men wore black, a cloak of subterfuge against the dark. On any other night, she'd fear the castle lookouts, the glint of steel in the moonlight, the foam-flecked wake of a boat slicing the sea, but not this night. She could almost hear the drunken revelry from the city, Royal Nachte, the night when all of Navarre celebrated a dukedom raised to a kingdom. This close to midnight, every soldier in the castle would be nodding into his cups, drunk on celebratory wine. And if her women had done their work, subtle herbs added to the brew would see them sleep till dawn, leaving the castle ripe for the taking. The Priestess laughed, so fitting to stake her claim on Founder's Night.

A lantern waved from the tower window, proof her women had done their work. Seeing the signal, she urged her men to speed. *"Row! Row hard!"*

A single lightning bolt cracked the cloud-strewn sky, as if the heavens protested, but the Priestess only laughed, knowing she had a god on her side.

The lead boat neared the castle, angling toward the gaping portal at the base of the westernmost tower. The dukes of old had built for war, raising a castle of black basalt surrounded by pounding waves, but they'd also left themselves an escape route, a sea gate, protected by tides and tricks. The Priestess laughed at the irony. She'd spent a lifetime collecting secrets, a woman's way to power. The ancient builders thought themselves clever, but their traps and tricks only made the castle more vulnerable. "Slow the oars, and keep to the center."

The rowers battled the waves, aligning the boat with the gaping portal, a dark mouth cut in the tower's base. The portcullis was raised, probably rusted into place, iron teeth menacing the archway. As if fate favored her, the tides proved perfect and the boat slipped inside smooth as a lover. Waves slapped the walls, the sound booming through the man-made cave. Her rowers maneuvered the boat alongside the stone dock. One of her soldiers lit a torch. Light flared across basalt walls, the salty smell of the sea hanging heavy in the air. Barnacles, mussels and starfish encrusted the lower walls, jewels from the sea dripping with cold. The Priestess balanced on the prow. Timing her jump, she leaped onto the stone walkway. Her boots skidded on green slime, but she kept her balance.

Soldiers swarmed onto the dock, Otham and Hugo at her back. "There's no door."

"It's there, if you know how to find it."

Hugo studied the landing. "Why are swords embedded in the wall?" Buried halfway to the hilt, a dozen great swords impaled the side wall, as if waiting for the hand of a hero.

The Priestess gave him a knowing smile. "All part of the secret."

"I don't like it." Her captain growled. "Without a door, this portal becomes a trap." He scanned the arched ceiling. "There's murder holes overhead. If were caught here we'll die screaming."

"Do you doubt me?" Her voice struck like a cold lash.

"No, mistress."

"Then watch and learn." She snapped a command. "More light."

Soldiers jostled behind, producing a pair of torches. Flickering flames revealed the details. Twelve two-handed great swords protruded waist-high from the wall, their blades half buried in the slime-slick stone. Time and the sea had taken their toll. Rust coated the great blades, pitting the steel dark with age, but the hilts still displayed their intricate designs. The Priestess walked along them, lightly caressing their hilts. Each sword was different. A spiny sea dragon entwined the hilt of the first, while the second displayed a royal osprey with wings spread wide. Poetry forged into steel, the swords told a story, the legend of Navarre's founding. She fingered a hilt shaped like a crown, praying the ancient mechanism still worked. So much rust and neglect, peace had a way of eroding the weapons of war, but it gave her hope that the guards had not changed the secret order.

"Lady, we dare not tarry."

Her captain was beginning to annoy, but she heard truth beneath his words. "Start with the first, the sword closest to the sea."

Hugo stepped in front of the first sword, the hilt entwined with a sea dragon. "What would you have me do? Pull it from the stone?"

"Nothing so dramatic, merely push it down."

Dark runnels incised beneath each blade were barely visible in the gloom. Hugo grasped the hilt and pushed. At first the sword resisted, till Hugo brought his full strength to bear. Uttering a rusty groan, the sword levered downward, tilting toward the walkway. "Levers, the swords are levers!" He flashed a grin, moving toward the second sword. "Lower the swords and the door opens?"

"Stop."

He froze at her command, his hand poised above the second hilt.

"Nothing so simple. Only certain swords and only in a certain order. Choose the wrong sword and a warning bell tolls in the tower." She gave him a wicked smile, pointing to the ceiling. "Choose poorly and scalding oil will erupt from the murder holes. Castle Seamount is not without teeth."

Her captain sobered, backing away from the second sword. "Which sword?"

"The fifth, the sword of the invaders, the one with the dragon-prowed longboat for a cross hilt."

"Are you sure?"

The Priestess only nodded, her face a mask. She watched as he reached for the fifth sword, praying the order still held true. Hugo followed her instructions. One by one, he pitted his strength against the swords, till six were tilted down toward the walkway. And through it all the murder holes gaped empty and the warning bell remained silent, nothing but the cold slap of the sea marking time against the basalt walls.

"And now the last, the royal osprey of Navarre."

Hugo moved to the osprey sword. Grasping the hilt, he slowly pushed the blade down.

Stone ground against stone, and a dark door eased open, a secret way into the castle.

Relief washed through her. "The trusting fools never changed the order." The Priestess gave a throaty laugh. "Welcome to Castle Seamount."

81

Liandra

Dawn came with a grim relentlessness, as if the world could not wait for war. Liandra stood amongst her women, trading silks for cold hard steel. Silence held sway in her chamber, the gravity of the threat pervading her women. Piece by piece, the armoring of the queen held all the solemnity of a sacred ritual. Breastplate and helm, gorget and greaves, she gained a sheath of steel curves. Her reflection glittered in the mirror, her armor polished to a blinding brightness, yet her mouth tasted of ashes, war was such a bitter pursuit. Liandra stared at the silvered stranger. It seemed fate favored irony. Guile and gold, spies and strategy, beauty and wit, these were Liandra's best weapons, yet fate thrust a sword in her hand. She wondered if she'd die a warrior queen.

Lady Sarah knelt, girding the sword at her waist. "Be safe, my queen."

Her words snapped the queen's mind back to the chamber.

Her women knelt as if asking for a blessing, but Liandra had only warnings to give. "Listen for the trumpets. If the alarm sounds then know that one of the castle gates is fallen." Her gaze settled on Lady Sarah. "If a gate falls, you must seek sanctuary in the hidden passageways. Do not delay." As an afterthought, she added, "And take the royal jewels with you, we shall not cede them to the enemy."

Lady Lindsey began to cry.

The queen laid a gauntleted hand upon her head. "Be brave and heed our words, for you have served us well."

Liandra turned to leave but Lady Sarah grabbed her hand. "Come back to us!"

"We will see this game to the end." Burdened by their tears, the queen turned and left the chamber.

Sir Durnhcart and a handpicked guard of ten soldiers snapped to attention. The soldiers wore helms and shields and thick coats of mail. *Shields within Castle Tandroth*, another sign of the grim odds set against them. She gave them a royal nod and then led the way through the castle corridors.

Beyond the Queen's Tower, the castle hallways were choked with frightened citizens, refugees seeking succor from the war. They huddled along the walls, mostly women and children, a few gray-haired men among them.

Clutching their scant possessions, they stared as she passed, fear writ large across their faces, but she had no hope to give, only grim determination.

She reached an outer doorway and a guard leaped to open it. The queen stepped from the castle's warmth to the rampart's winter chill. A bitter wind snatched at her emerald cloak, a cold and forbidding morning.

Soldiers and archers snapped to attention, their faces pale but determined. She gave them a steely smile, infusing her voice with courage. "We are with you." Her words raised a cheer among the men.

Their conviction brought a tear to her eye. Such bravery deserved better than war, but evil must be defeated. Acknowledging their cheers, the queen made her way along the battlements to the barbican protecting the castle's north gate.

Princess Jemma waited on the rampart. Dressed in huntsman's leathers, with knee-high boots and a padded jerkin, the checkered shield of Navarre blazed proudly over her heart. The petite princess bore a shortbow, a quiver of arrows attached to her belt. The sight of the archer-princess brought a smile to the queen's face, steel melded with velvet, the perfect betrothal for her royal son.

"We see you are dressed for the hunt."

"We hunt the Flame. I'm told every bow will be needed." The princess flashed a smile of pride, her sweeping hand presenting a dozen Navarren guards ranged behind her, all of them with longbows. "There are no finer archers in all of Erdhe."

"Your bows are most welcome. As are you." Three times the queen had asked the princess to flee Pellanor and three times she'd refused. Liandra would not despoil her courage by asking again. Instead she said, "Your presence is dear to us. If the castle falls, stay close. We will retreat to the hidden passageways."

The princess gave her a grim nod. "Yes, majesty."

A trumpeter joined them. The queen had ordered one stationed above every gate.

A jangle of weapons and armor came from below, soldiers mounting horses in the castle's keep. The queen stared down at them, her gaze catching on one in particular, *Robert*. He'd traded his dark shadowmaster's robes, dawning burnished chainmail and a cloak of emerald green. So strange to see him in bright colors; war changed them all. He wore no helm, his silver-gray hair shimmering in the morning light, as if taunting the enemy. Fear shuddered through her, knowing bravery could be a doom. Liandra longed to call him back, to order him to her side, but instead her eyes drank him in, memorizing every detail. He looked dashing in armor, so confident and sure, vaulting into the saddle with the verve of a much younger man. Gathering the reins, he asked his dappled stallion for a trot, leading his men through the gate.

Liandra rushed across the narrow battlement, staring down into the cobbled street, refusing to lose sight of him.

He must have felt her stare, for he turned his horse, his gaze finding her on the battlement. From the saddle, he offered her a courtly bow. "We ride to your defense, my queen!"

Liandra tugged a silk scarf from her belt. "Wear our token to battle and bring it back to us!" She released the silk, a flutter of emerald embroidered with gold roses. The vagaries of the wind were kind, taking her token straight toward him.

He caught it in his mailed fist. Holding it to his face, he breathed her scent, and then tucked it beneath his chainmail, close to his heart. Unsheathing his sword, he asked his stallion for a rear. Brandished his blade aloft, he yelled, "For the queen!"

"*For the queen!*" The shout echoed through the street.

He flashed her one last smile, and then he turned, spurring his stallion down the cobbled street.

Her gaze clung to him, watching until he disappeared in the distance. Liandra leaned against the battlement. "And now we wait."

Princess Jemma moved to stand by her side, a comforting presence.

By the queen's order, the castle gates remained open, offering sanctuary to her people. Citizen's streamed toward the gates, the young and the old, sacks of belongings slung across their shoulders. She'd ordered her guards to let them bring nothing save food and blankets. Some wept in protest but the guards remained steadfast. A strange collection of belongs piled along the street, mounds of discarded clothing, a small wooden chest, a pair of silver candelabras, blacksmith's tools, a carpenter's saw, cast iron skillets, a child's cradle, all the precious gleanings of lives turned upside down by war. Liandra watched the pile grow high. "War is such a waste."

"Yet the world never tires of it."

"Just so."

Horns blared from the north, a harsh brazen sound. Liandra balled her gauntleted hands into fists. "And so it begins."

Cries of panic raced through the streets below, yet the queen stood firm upon the barbican, sword-straight, sunlight glinting on armor, a symbol to her people. She stared to the north, praying for the outer wall to hold. So hard to be far from the action, yet this was where she belonged. The day of destiny but all she could do was wait.

82

Steffan

The day dawned bright and crisp and clear, a perfect day for war. Pip served as Steffan's squire, arming his lord for victory. Black chainmail settled over dark leathers, the raven badge emblazoned on his chest, Steffan flexed beneath the weight, testing the fit. The weight felt comfortable, he'd grown accustom to war. He pulled on a pair of leather gauntlets studded with garnets while Pip affixed his black cloak to his shoulders. At his belt, he wore a rapier with a gleaming double-ringed hilt of gold and a pair of jeweled daggers, all of the finest steel. For a helm, he'd commissioned a special piece in Balor, an open-faced helm of dark metal with raven's feathers patterned in the steel. A golden beak protruded like a visor to shade his vision, a pair of garnets embedded in the steel feathers for the raven's eyes. Fierce and proud and forbidding, the helmet screamed of martial splendor. He'd saved the helm to mark a special victory. By day's end, he planned to despoil a queen and claim a crown.

Horns blared through the wood, calling his army to war.

His sorrel warhorse stood picketed outside his pavilion. Caparisoned in deepest black, the big horse breathed plumes of mist into the chill morning air. A major snapped a salute and Steffan swung into the saddle. Pip rode beside him, serving as his bannerman. A hundred Black Flames followed, a handpicked honor guard assigned to protect the future king of Lanverness.

The woods thrummed like a kicked hornet's nest, men arming for war, sergeants bellowing orders.

Steffan threaded his way through the camp, riding to the very edge of the winter-naked woods. He took a position on a small hilltop overlooking the queen's city, a perfect perch for the Lord Raven. Steffan was lucky at dice, but he felt no need to risk his life in battle. General Caylib and General Xanos were both paid to fight; he'd let them lead the charge. Besides, the sword was never Steffan's best weapon, always preferring to stab a dagger in his enemy's back. Leading from the rear had so many advantages. First among them was survival. Content to watch, Steffan settled in to wait.

Snow-covered fields surrounded the city, a perfect canvas for war. Even from a distance, Pellanor's patchwork walls presented a pitiful defense. Instead of battlements and a gatehouse, the soldiers of Lanverness stood on rooftops. The city's defenses were laughable. More proof the queen had little knowledge of war.

A flock of ravens landed in a nearby oak, releasing a raucous chorus. It seemed his namesake could sense the coming war. Steffan took it as an omen of victory.

Horns blared a second time. Soldiers of the Cobra and the Flame swarmed down out of the woods to assemble on the field. Ten thousand infantry supported by nearly six thousand cavalry, a formidable army drawn up in ranks, their tabards bright against the snow. Battle banners snapped overhead and burnished armor glistened in the morning light. Only in war did so many men work as one, a powerful force for death and destruction. Little wonder the Dark Lord loved it so. Yet seen from afar, there was a certain glory about it, the very image of the bards' heroic songs. The sight stirred Steffan's blood, especially with Erdhe's richest kingdom as the prize. His ambition soared, the crown nearly within his grasp.

Steffan's warhorse pawed the ground, as if eager for the charge. He settled the horse with his knees. "Watch, Pip, history is about to be made."

A horn sounded, shattering the romantic illusion. Loosed from their ranks, the mercenaries hefted ladders and charged. Howling like demons, they raced toward the city's walls. Defenders loosed arrows, staggering the line, leaving a trail of bloody corpses strewn across the snow, but the weight of numbers prevailed. Sidestepping the dead, the Cobra swarmed the walls, throwing up fresh-made ladders. Gouts of flame erupted along the walls, the defenders fought back with oil, a nasty weapon. Doused in burning oil, soldiers ran screaming through the lines, human torches spreading chaos across the field. The attack faltered, a stalemate of death. For a while, the outcome hung in the balance, the mud-churned snow spattered with bloody and burned corpses. The defenders put up a brave fight, repulsing the ladders, but the waves of mercenaries never slowed. Swords and ladders battled flames and arrows...but then the enemy ran out of oil. A shout of triumph rose from the attackers, a third wave charging the wall.

General Xanos ordered the battering ram forward, a massive oak felled from the queen's own forest. Twenty men carried the ram, shields strapped to their backs. They labored forward, defying the enemy's arrows. Like a giant's fist, the ram pounded the gate, demanding entry. Emerald archers swarmed the walls, raining a blistering hail of arrows. Men fell and others sprang to take their place, but the hail of arrows proved too fierce. Cowering under their shields, the men dropped the ram and fled. A mighty cheer rose from the defenders, but in truth, the ram was merely a diversion. While the enemy concentrated their archers at the gate, the mercenaries scaled ladders further down the wall. This time the ladders did not come down. Steffan watched as the Cobra swarmed over the western wall, like cockroaches raiding a larder. "It won't be long now. Unfurl my banner."

Pip obeyed, unfurling the silken banner, deepest black to honor the Dark Lord. In the center rode a blood red circle, and in the circle a black raven with wings spread wide, a golden crown upon its head. The wind caught the banner, snapping proudly against the sky, fresh colors for defeated Lanverness. Steffan laughed, feeling the Dark Lord's pleasure.

Shouts of triumph rang from the battlefield.

The gates swung open, captured from within.

A tide of mercenaries flooded the gate, poised to rape and sack a great city.

Beside him, Pip said, "Shall we go, lord?"

"Not yet, give them time to sweep the streets."

The Raven banner snapped overhead, dark against the pale winter sky. Destiny called to Steffan, finally a crown for his brow, another triumph for the Dark Lord.

83

Liandra

The sounds of battle carried, but not well enough. Fraught with worry, the queen stood high upon the northern barbican, straining to listen, desperate to discern the battle's ebb and flow. The castle ramparts overlooked a vast web of rooftops and cobbled streets. Her city sprawled in every direction, putting the battle almost half a league away. Banished from the outer walls by her commanders, the queen fretted at the heart of her city, a defiant symbol atop the castle ramparts. The waiting proved hard, yet the queen stood statue-still, her silver armor glinting in the cold morning light.

Enemy horns blared from the north, an ominous sound. Liandra strained to listen, imagining the clash of weapons and the rabid howl of attack. So far from the wall, she felt blind, straining to interpret every sound. Tension gripped her, uncertainty gnawing at her imagination. Liandra longed to pace, but she resisted the urge, intent on chaining her worry.

The sun climbed the sky to mid-morning and still they fought. Every hour that passed was a victory for her side.

Below, her people continued to stream through the streets, seeking sanctuary in the castle. At least they did not run, families holding their children's hands, maintaining a sense of order, holding panic at bay.

Gouts of flames erupted in the distance, belching columns of black smoke. Her soldiers used the oil, a terrible weapon, but war was a terrible business. Liandra wondered if she should have saved the monk's Napthos for Pellanor, but that gambit was long spent. She stared towards the north, hoping the oil prevailed. All too soon the flames stopped, leaving a lingering pall above the north wall. Her men were out of oil. A sick feeling pervaded her stomach. The queen clenched her fists, waiting.

A dull boom echoed from the north, *a ram at the gates*. Boom, boom, boom, the relentlessness pounding shuddered through the morning. A shiver of fear raced down her spine, as if the Dark Lord came knocking. The queen lost track of the beat...but then the ram fell silent. Either the gates were breached or the ram defeated. She waited poised on a knife-edge. A tease of sounds came her way. Liandra thought she heard a distant cheer; perhaps her men prevailed.

The queen sent a prayer to Valin, but something ominous stirred in the north.

An omen of fear gripped her. "What's happening?" But none around her knew.

The answer came from her people. Panic erupted in the streets. People dropped their scant processions, running pell-mell for the castle gates.

The truth was in her streets. "The wall has fallen." The words sounded like a death knell, yet the queen waited upon the barbican, needing to witness it all.

Her people rushed the gates, desperate for sanctuary, some trampling others, a riot of death. The clog at the gates slowed to a grind. Behind the crush of citizens, came the wounded, soldiers limping and bloody, their emerald tabards disheveled by war, their faces shocked by defeat. Liandra stared beyond them, fearing for Robert.

Horns blared, the awful sound of retreat.

And then the deluge came, a river of emerald retreating to the castle like a flood in ebb.

Liandra gripped the rampart, frantic for a glimpse of Robert.

And then she heard the clash of steel; fighting in her streets, proof her city was lost.

The sound pierced her heart like a cold lance of despair.

Sir Durnheart stepped to her side. "Majesty, we should close the gates."

"Not yet. They fought for us. Give them a chance to reach safety."

"But majesty, you risk the castle."

Anger pulsed through her. "They risked their *lives* for us. The gates stay open."

Beside her, Princess Jemma strung her bow, nocking an arrow. "The archers will buy them time."

The streets began to clear, like the awful calm before a terrible storm. The queen waited, a steel fist clamped around her heart.

The battle drew near, a terrible clash of steel. And then she saw them, a thin line of emerald, some mounted, some on foot, holding back a tidal wave of foes. Red mixed with pea-green, the traitorous Cobra fought along side the Flame. The soldiers in emerald battled like heroes, buying every step of ground, staining the cobbles with blood. Citizens joined the fray, wielding staves and rods, a frenzy of courage to protect their city. Liandra even saw a few women wielding cast iron skillets and rolling pins. The stalwart courage of her people sent a fierce shiver of pride through Liandra, but the outcome was inevitable, the weight of numbers too much to bear.

The queen gave the order. "Archers loose! Trumpeters sound the retreat!"

Princess Jemma raised her bow.

Arrows arched toward the enemy, a hail of death falling in the streets.

Trumpets blared, sounding the retreat.

Under the hail of arrows, the enemy faltered, while the thin emerald line turned and raced for the castle gates.

The queen gripped the stone ramparts, staring down at them, willing them to hurry. And then she saw him, fighting near the rear, a sword in one hand, a dagger in the other. So gallant, so brave, she watched him slay an enemy, her heart clenched in mixture of pride and fear. "*Hurry, Robert!*" One of the last to retreat, he put spurs to his dappled stallion, racing for the gates.

Sir Durnheart bellowed, "More arrows!"

A twang of bows loosed, a whistle of death skewering the air.

The enemy hesitated. Dead clogged the streets, but then a hungry roar burst from their ranks. They surged forward, chasing the stragglers to the gate.

"*Hurry, Robert, hurry!*"

Hoof beats on cobblestones, lathered horses raced for the gates.

"Majesty, you must..."

"Yes, begin to close the gates!"

The trumpeter called the signal.

The queen leaned forward, willing him to safety.

Robert rode at the rear, a handful of emerald riders racing through the streets, but the Flame was not far behind, death charging at their heels.

"*Save them!*"

Every detail was painstakingly clear, the racing horses, the swords poised to strike, the closing distance, a slim margin of life.

Beside her, Princess Jemma took aim. Her bow twanged and the lead rider for the Flame fell, tumbling in front of the others, slowing the chase.

The gap widened.

The emerald riders reached the gates, a thunder of hooves galloping into the courtyard.

Below, the ironclad gates clanged closed, a massive bar sealing them shut.

The enemy swarmed the gate, but her love had made it, *he'd made it.*

The queen's archers took aim, raining arrows on the clogged streets, but the enemy was too numerous, a sea of soldiers frothing at her gates.

Enemy archers answered, arrows soaring toward the ramparts. Liandra's guards rushed forward, shields raised to protect the queen. Arrows thunked among them, a guard screaming in agony.

"Majesty, you must leave the rampart!"

Liandra nodded, letting her guards lead her towards the tower door. A grim truth gripped her mind. The enemy was at the gates. Her city had fallen. The siege of Castle Tandroth had begun.

84

The Priestess

The secret door slid open and the Priestess entered the castle. Her soldiers followed, their swords drawn, but just as she predicted the corridor was empty. Trusting to their secrets, the Navarrens left the sea gate unguarded. Their trust would be their undoing.

A dank mustiness pervaded the rarely used hallway. So close to the sea, the walls wept moisture, clear as tears, as if the castle mourned her return. Her men raised their torches, the light flickering against black basalt walls, striping the halls with shadow. She led them deeper into the castle to an intersection of stairs going up and down. The lower ones led to the dungeons, the upper to the kitchens. She climbed the stairs to find a slight figure lurking in the shadows. The Priestess whispered a name. "Lydia?"

A dark-haired woman dressed as a cook's servant stepped into the torchlight, her handmaiden sent to poison the castle. "Here, mistress."

"Is it done?"

"Yes, mistress. A tincture of henbane added to the soldiers' ale. If they're not asleep by now, they soon will be."

"And the royals?"

"In the great hall, feasting. Tara was assigned as one of the servers to the high table."

"Good," the word was a purr, so easy to slip her handmaidens in amongst the extra help. Women were always overlooked, especially the servants. "What course are they on?"

"The seventh, mistress."

"Plenty of time for the royals to be truly entangled." The Priestess smiled. "You've done well, but now it is past time I joined the royals at their feast. So rude of them not to invite me."

Dismissing her handmaiden, the Priestess led her men through the winding corridors.

A soldier approached, wearing the checkered tabard of Navarre. Tottering in the hallway, he wobbled back and forth like a drunk. "Who are you?"

Hugo stepped past her, landing a solid punch on the soldier's jaw. The man flopped to the floor like a boneless fish.

The Priestess smiled. "Henbane, so reliable. Lydia did her work well." Sidestepping the soldier, she followed the succulent scents of roast sea bass and garlic scallops, a feast fit for royals. Torches began lining the hallways as they moved deeper into the castle, yet they met no opposition. Servants, pages, and soldiers began to appear, always slumped at their posts. A few white-smocked cooks sprawled across the floor, caught in the spell of henbane. The Priestess smiled, enjoying the proof of her plan, an entire castle caught in a drugged stupor, like a dark curse in a fairy tale run amok. Everyone slept except the royals. For the royals, the Priestess had something special in mind.

Led by memory, she strode through the castle's twists and turns. The hallways became more opulent. Rich tapestries adorned the walls, portraying scenes of conquest on the high seas, but the Priestess paid scant attention to the embroidered details, intent on reaching her prey. A cheerful melody echoed through the hallways, the soft strains of a lute pulling her forward. The royals dined by music, the merrymaking soon to become a dirge. She paused at the entrance to the great hall. Hiding in the shadows, the Priestess spied on the feast.

Tantalizing smells swirled through the chamber, belying the truth of the banquet. The royals feasted at the high table, an intimate family gathering celebrating the founding of the seaside kingdom. King Ivor sat in a throne-like chair, his frumpy queen sitting next to him. Such a pathetic pair, no style, no grace, no sense of royalty, not even a crown amongst them. And then there was Isador, the commander of the guard. He still cut a fine figure in his checkered surcoat, but his dark hair was salted with too much gray. Next to Isador sat Igraine, a mousy little woman with dreary scholar's eyes, always so boorish. Ian and Ivy sat on the far side of the table flanked by their spouses. Laughing at some shared amusement, the bowyer and the merchant captain sat close together, always thick as thieves. The Priestess swallowed her contempt. One big happy family, Royal Nachte brought them together, all the Royal Is seated at one table, but none of the youngsters. The heirs were missing. She'd so wanted to meet the Royal Js. The youngsters must be on their Wayfarings, a pity since she'd hoped to catch them all in one fell coup.

The Priestess lingered in the shadows, watching them feast and laugh and talk, as if they had not a care in the world. How foolish and how naïve, especially given the truth writ large on their faces. Time had nearly caught them. They all looked old. Gray dimmed their hair, lines creased their faces, and paunches bloated their waists, all of them worn by time while she remained forever young. Giving thanks to the Dark Lord, the Priestess ran her hands down a firm figure of sultry curves, reveling in her seductive allure. She laughed and the silken sound carried into the great hall.

Staying her soldiers with a hand signal, the Priestess sauntered into the hall. Smiling like a hungry cat, she stared at the royals, her skin-tight leathers showing off her curves, her every gesture brimming with brazen sexuality.

The music fell silent.

The conversation crashed.

The royals turned to stare.

"Royal Nachte, yet no one thought to invite me?" The Priestess circled the table, watching their faces, savoring their reactions. Questioning stares slowly changed to stunned disbelief.

"*Iris!*" Her true name whispered through the great hall like a curse.

Isador gasped. "It can't be you!"

The Priestess chuckled. "Very good, Isador, you were always the quick one." Her voice gained a sinister edge. "Quick to pry, quick to suspect, quick to accuse." Gliding behind his chair, she caressed his face, a parody of passion.

Isador flinched away, as if touched by hot coals. He sent her a baleful glare.

The king interceded. "We all thought you dead."

"Yes, how convenient for you, but I had other plans."

Igraine said, "But how did you stay so...?"

"Beautiful? Young? Breathtakingly gorgeous?" The Priestess purred. "Wouldn't you like to know?"

Igraine scowled, "What sorcery is this?"

The Priestess chuckled, a throaty sound. "Now you're nearer the mark."

Isador growled. "What do you want?"

"What I've always wanted. What you've always denied me." She continued circling the table, like a hungry shark scenting blood. "I've come for what should have been mine."

Isador stood, his hand on his sword hilt, his face aflame with hate. "*Murderess!* I named you before and I'll name you again." He stabbed an accusing finger at her. "You're a bloody murderess, a kin-slayer, the cursed one, and you deserve to die!"

At a gesture, her soldiers burst into the chamber, ringing the great hall. Clad in black, most of her men carried swords, but a few held crossbows. All the crossbows were aimed at Isador.

"Did you think I'd come alone?"

Isador quivered like a plucked bow, quaking with anger. Removing his hand from his sword, he slowly sank back into his chair. Setting his hands on the table, he gave her a hooded glare. "It's only a matter of time till the guards come."

"Don't fret, we have plenty of time."

Igraine gasped. "You killed them."

"Nothing so wasteful. My servants merely laced their ale with henbane."

"Henbane can kill."

"Only if taken in excess." The Priestess flashed a reaper's smile. "A few will die, mostly the drunkards, the sots who always overindulged. It's just as well to cull them now. Drunkards are of so little use to anyone. The rest will wake in the morning with nothing more than a vicious headache and a new liege lord."

Isador growled. "What do you want?"

"Isn't it obvious?" She sauntered around the table, stopping near the king. "I've come for my inheritance. But first we're going to play a little game."

Ian scowled. "A game?"

"Yes, I've thought long and hard about my homecoming. And you may not believe it, but in my own way, I've decided to be merciful." She cocked an eyebrow, waiting for a challenge, but none of them spoke. They stared at her as if watching an adder slither across the banquet table. She smirked. "I've decided to give you a choice, a test of your precious belief in the Light." Her voice turned hard. "Life is all about choices, a lesson I learned when I was so very young." She drew on her magic, a shadow of Darkness adding menace to her voice. Her words boomed through the hall. "Serve me and live. Embrace Darkness and thrive. Refuse me and die."

Silence held sway. They gaped like fish caught on hooks. The Priestess savored their fear, but she wanted them to make an honest choice. Loosing her hold on Darkness, she appeared mortal once more. Tension leaked from the chamber. The Priestess smiled, knowing a willing submission was always the most binding.

Isador was the first to recover, a sneer on his face. "So if we don't bow to you, you'll have us all killed?"

"You're already dying."

That got their attention. Pointed glances flew around the table, a mixture of thinly veiled fear and silent questions.

The Priestess laughed, a deliciously seductive sound. "Such a fine feast spread before you, a feast fit for royals." Her gaze lingered on the table heaped with silver serving platters, many of the dishes already consumed. "Whole sea bass stuffed with herbs, scallops seared with garlic, muscles drenched in butter, deep-fired clams, abalone on the half shell, pigeons cooked in a flaky piecrust, so many delicacies, so many ways to poison a royal."

Igraine gasped, her face turning pale. "*Poison?*"

The Priestess smiled. "See what I learned on my Wayfaring? A pity House Navarre never had a food taster."

The king said, "It's not our way."

"No, of course not," sarcasm riddled her voice, "so much more honorable to trust your servants. Honor is a conceit of the Light. And now it will be your undoing."

Isador snarled. "What do you mean?"

"Don't play stupid, it doesn't become you." The Priestess draped an arm across the king's high-backed chair. Leaning forward, she studied his plate. "The question is, where was the poison and how much did you eat?"

Isador hissed. "*Bitch!*"

"Exactly, and I'm so good at it." The Priestess gave her brother a nasty smile. "You were always fond of clams, Isador, filling your plate before anyone else got a first serving. Did you have clams tonight? I wonder if they were laced with nightshade, or did I save that for the sea bass? Perhaps a sprinkle of laburnum in the scalloped potatoes? A tincture of camas poured on the abalone, or hemlock baked in the pigeon pie? Did you have two servings of pie, Igraine? Perhaps you can already feel the telltale signs. Is your vision blurring? Can you feel a tingling in your feet? Have your legs gone numb? Has your throat started to swell?" She let them consider the symptoms, watching as their imaginations ran wild. "Who will be the first to die?"

King Ivor roared, "Stop this!"

"So the king speaks." The Priestess gave him a mocking bow. "Easily done, *sire*." She snapped her fingers and Hugo strode towards her carrying an alchemic flask sloshing with a dark amber liquid. "Behold the antidote." She held the flask aloft like a rare prize. "Regardless of the poison, this is life. Swear fealty to me, accept me as the rightwise queen of Navarre and you shall live. One oath, one sip, and your life will be spared." She lowered the flask. "But do not wait too long. Death already stalks you."

"You lie!"

Hatred boiled within her. "I was never the one to lie, at least not then, though none of you ever believed me." She reined in her hatred, burying it deep beneath a cold facade. "Time holds the truth. All we need do is wait." Her voice held a deadly edge, like a dagger at their throats. "How much time do you think you have?" Her gaze circled the table. "Ian, will you watch as your wife dies? Ivy, perhaps you've grown tired of your dear husband? After all, he is getting thick around the middle." Her gaze settled on the king. "Will your majesty sit and watch as your queen dies, the mother of your tuplets, writhing on the floor in agony, all because you would not bend the knee?"

The king glared at her. "End this."

"No, *you* end this. Bend the knee and take a sip, that's all you need do." She swallowed her anger and gave him a venomous smile. "It's one of those gray decisions. Take an oath and save a life, it really should be easy. And since you're all so honorable, I know you'll keep your word." She gave them a lethal smile. "Take one step into the gray and you'll soon find yourself embracing Darkness. You might even learn to like it. I know I did."

The Priestess settled into a side chair, the flask held in her lap. "And now we wait, giving the poison time to do its work. I wonder who will be the first to die?"

85

Steffan

Steffan entered the queen's city in triumph. His raven battle banner streamed overhead, a guard of Black Flames at his back. Corpses from both sides gave witness to his conquest. Piled high in mounds on either side of the gate, they stared with lifeless eyes as ravens fought among them, come for the gleanings of war.

One of his guards took offense, moving to strike the winged scavengers, but Steffan stayed his sword. "Let them feast." Like his chosen namesake, Steffan knew how to profit from death.

The city gates gaped open, unguarded by either side. The signs of war were legion, from the abandoned battering ram, to the mounds of dead, to the scorch marks on the walls, to the awful stench of death, more proof of the power of the Dark Lord. Steffan held his sorrel stallion to a walk, savoring the victory.

They rode through the city streets without fanfare or opposition. Most streets stood empty save for soldiers searching for spoils. Everywhere Steffan looked, he saw the same things. Shops shuttered. Homes abandoned. Doors nailed shut or left gaping open, like mouths startled in panic. Pellanor was well and truly conquered, a city drenched in fear. Steffan drank it in, so intoxicating.

Screams of rape and pillage punctuated the streets, heralding his progress. His army claimed its due reward. A few soldiers stopped in mid debauch to snap a hasty salute, but Steffan let the men have their way, a valuable lesson to the citizens of Pellanor. They'd soon feel his iron grip, so different from the queen's limp touch.

Keeping his stallion to a walk, he followed a trail of corpses, emerald and red tabards entwined. Like faithful guides, the dead led him straight to the city's heart. Sounds of fighting surrounded the queen's castle, besieging the last bastion of emerald green. His army swarmed the castle, trading arrows with the enemy. Even as he watched, soldiers in red gained the roof of nearby buildings. Archers dueled across the narrow space, a withering rain of death.

Steffan pulled his stallion to a halt, considering the prize. Pale white towers soared into the winter sky. Castle Tandroth was elegant and beautiful, a strange confection of luxury palace and military ramparts. Bound by the city on all sides, the castle had no greensward, or moat, or catapults, surrendering its military value to luxury. The inner towers shimmered with diamond-paned windows and elegant embellishments, a prize plum waiting to be plucked. Steffan could almost taste the fruit of his labors, a captured queen, a claimed crown, an elegant castle, and gold enough to make him the richest monarch in all of Erdhe. His army need only breach the gates and the prize was his.

General Caylib cantered toward him, a leer on his swarthy face. "So Counselor, you decided to join the war."

"Some of us aren't as blood thirsty as you."

"I only wield the sword; the plan was yours, and a good one at that." The general cracked a grin. "The defenders fought hard but the ram duped them."

"Never underestimate the value of deceit. And the castle?"

The general scowled. "Shut tight as a maiden's chastity belt."

"How long will it take you to find the key?"

"The walls are too tall for the ladders, so I've ordered the ram brought up. All we need is one gate and the castle is yours."

Steffan nodded. "Let me know when the gate is breached. And remember, I want the queen taken alive." The general began to turn away, but Steffan called him back. "And general, don't keep me waiting."

The general glared but then thought better of it, offering Steffan a nod.

Satisfied, Steffan turned his sorrel stallion away from the castle only to find General Xanos waiting for him. The mercenary general looked polished despite the battle, his mustache curled, his armor gleaming, his surcoat unsullied by blood, and then Steffan noticed the bulging bags affixed to his saddle, a silver candlestick protruding from beneath the flap. "I see the looting has gone well."

General Xanos grinned. "We're mercenaries. The spoils of war matter." He patted the saddlebag. "My orderlies know what to look for and the gleanings were rich." His gaze narrowed, his face turning serious. "We've given you your victory, the richest city in all of Erdhe. The terms of the king's agreement are fulfilled."

A spike of unease pierced Steffan. "The castle has not yet fallen."

"One victory was promised and one has been delivered."

"The victory is not complete until the castle falls."

"Surely your men can take one palace?"

Steffan did not like the way this was heading. "Help take the castle and you'll gain a share of the queen's gold."

"What gold?" The general barked a rude laugh. "I've seen the bars of dull gray lead gleaming in the queen's treasury chests. I'll not be tempted by the same dull lure."

Anger pulsed through Steffan. "You've seen the city's wealth. A rich city begets a rich monarch. The damn Spider Queen must keep it somewhere and the castle is the only place left to the bitch."

The general gave him a snide smile. "The castle is yours to take. And something tells me this Spider Queen will not be so easily captured. Spiders and women both have venom. Besides," the general flashed a wolf's grin, "our saddlebags are already bulging. We march on the morrow."

"But I thought profit mattered?"

"Only the king can broker our services. And with a new king on the Cobra throne, we must return home to swear fealty." The general turned his horse. "Our bargain has been kept, our saddlebags are full, we march for Radagar."

Steffan watched the general ride away, anger pulsing through him. He regretted losing the mercenaries, but he did not have the might to force them to stay. Turning his stallion, he watched the battle for the castle. With nearly six thousand men at his command, the outcome was assured. And he had all of Lingard at his beck and call. He'd already ordered the bishop to send the bulk of the army south. Once the rest of his army arrived, he'd consolidate power in Pellanor, extending his iron will across Lanverness, supplanting the Rose with the Raven. Steffan stretched in the saddle, banishing any doubts. The prize was nearly his. He'd seek out some luxury and wait for the castle to fall. Life was good in the service of the Dark Lord.

86

Jordan

A crescent moon winked from the clouds. The sinister grin loomed above the seaside city, as if the moon laughed at her, knowing she'd come too late. Jordan urged her horse to speed, a host of two hundred riders at her back. In their wild push across Navarre, Jordan had gleaned a handful of soldiers from every village and keep, gaining a patchwork of loyal men. They rode without battle banners or trumpets, bearing a hodgepodge of weapons and armor, a desperate host come to save their king.

Worry drove her hard. Jordan kept the Zward and the two monks close, but even their confidence could not dim her fears. Cold dread seized her heart. Her dreams had stopped a fortnight ago, as if the gods had given up on her. Or maybe they'd shown her all she needed to see. Either way she felt failure nipping at her heels.

The road turned steep, climbing the wooded hills that ringed the city. Jordan spied the first tower, set to keep watch for sea raiders. Six watchtowers crowned the hills skirting the city, white as shimmering swords, so tempting to stop and raise the alarm, but she'd only be warning the enemy. Her dreams had warned of a small army poised at the south side of the city, enemies waiting for word from the castle. Knowing surprise was her best weapon, Jordan led her men around the hills, entering the city from the north. But the long ride only lengthened the journey. Sweat trickled down her back, visions of death urging her forward.

They crested the hills and thundered down into the city. She breathed deep the salty sea scent, the smell of home urging her onward. Moonlight silvered the cobbled streets, a cascade of limestone houses descending to the sea. From every direction Jordan heard sounds of revelry, songs and merrymaking, a nightlong feast lauding the Royal Nachte. As a child she'd always loved the night of revels, Jordan prayed it would not be the last.

The streets twisted and turned amongst homes and shops, always leading downward. In Navarre's capital city all roads led to the sea. Jordan urged her horse to speed. The Zward stayed close by her side, the host galloping behind. With her goal nearly in sight, she pushed the horses hard, galloping for the castle at the heart of the harbor.

Black basalt towers rose from the night-darkened waves. Castle Seamount stood upon a rocky outcrop trust up from the sea like a sentinel. A narrow causeway linked the stalwart castle to the shore, but the tentative strip of barnacle-encrusted land was fickle, alternately swallowed and rejected by the tides. Jordan raced to the coast, praying the causeway remained passable.

They reached the harbor and followed the road to the causeway, but the tides had already won the race. Waves covered the narrow land strip, broiling around the castle like an unassailable moat.

Riding beside her, Thaddeus yelled, "We're too late!"

But Jordan refused to give up. "Keep riding. There's still a chance."

She led them to the very start of the causeway. Waves lapped the shore, but Jordan's attention was fixed on two stone ospreys perched like gargoyles on either side of the causeway. Chiseled from black basalt, the ten-foot ospreys marked the causeway's entrance, but they also served as a measure of the tides. Seawater lapped the ospreys, but the salty foam only reached their clawed talons. Hope surged through her. "We can make it!" She turned her horse, yelling orders to her men. "The tides hide the causeway but the water is less than a hand span deep. Keep on a straight path between the osprey and the castle gates and don't stop for anything."

Jordan turned her horse toward the castle, riding dead center between the two massive ospreys. Whispering words of encouragement, she urged her mare forward, but the horse balked, frightened by the sea. Running out of time, she jammed her spurs into the mare. Squealing in fear, the small horse leaped forward, bolting into the frothing waves. Finding solid footing just beneath the sea foam, the pale mare settled to a gallop, striding across the ocean like a horse sprung from legend.

Her host followed, racing the tide across the causeway, galloping hooves throwing up a salty spray. Ahead, the castle reared from the sea, a slime-slick ramp climbing to the ironshod gates. Jordan whispered to her mare, urging the horse across the churning causeway. They reached the base, the sea crashing against the breakwater. Her mare clattered up the ramp, but the gates were closed, barred from within. Unsheathing her sword, she pounded the hilt against the gate. *"Open the gates!"* but no one answered. Fear gripped her. Just like her visions, the gates were barred, the soldiers deaf to her entreaties. But then she realized there was one major difference. In her dreams the causeway hadn't been submerged. Either she was too late or something had changed.

Jordan erupted in cold sweat. She turned to the Zward. "We need the grappling hooks."

Thaddeus and Benjin dismounted. Removing ropes and grappling hooks from their saddle packs, the two Zward stepped away from the gates. Spinning the hooks in a deadly arc, they loosed the grapples towards the rampart walls. Thaddeus's caught on the first try, Benjin's on the second. Hand over hand, the two men began to scale the walls.

Jordan moved the horses closer to the castle gates, making room for others on the sea-slick ramp. Horses and soldiers crowded close, shivering against the cold. Strung out in a line along the causeway, the bulk of her host stood vulnerable to the tides. Dark waves lapped closer, climbing the ramp, greedy for land. The horses whinnied in fear, their eyes showing white in the moonlight. A soldier yelled, "There's something in the water!" A horse reared, falling backward off the causeway, man and beast spilling into the waves.

Fins sliced the dark water, a frenzied froth surrounding the swimmers.

Screams pierced the night.

"There's monsters in the sea!"

A rogue wave burst across the causeway, sweeping twenty men and their mounts into the frothing foam.

"Get back to the causeway!" Standing in the stirrups, Jordan yelled to be heard. "Hold your positions! Stand your ground!" Trapped between the waves and the castle, Jordan prayed she hadn't brought her men to a watery death.

Beside her, Yarl yelled. "Send the others back, before the sea claims them."

Jordan considered giving the order, but she knew they'd need the numbers to prevail. "I can't."

A grating noise came from the far side of the gate. "Stand back."

They forced the horses back down the ramp, into the swirling sea. Cold water crept up her leg, reaching halfway to her knee. The mare whinnied, close to panic, but then the gates began to creak open. She drew her sword, praying the Zward opened the gates and not the enemy.

Thad and Benjin pushed the gates wide, a welcome sight. Jordan spurred the mare forward, up the ramp and into the courtyard. Soldiers in the checkered tabards lay slumped at their posts, but she saw no signs of fighting.

Thaddeus rushed to her side. "All the soldiers are either asleep or dead drunk, just as you said. It's as if the castle's under a spell."

Instead of comfort, his words spurred panic. "We may be too late." Jordan swung from the saddle, pulling her sword from its sheath. "Time is against us, we need to get to the great hall." She sprinted for the nearest door, desperate to save her family.

87

The Priestess

The Priestess fondled the alchemical flask, life or death held within her hands. She watched her royal siblings, savoring their fear. They sat at the banquet table, glances passing between them, their faces full of questions, longings, pleas, and wavering resolve. Tension heated the room, like a cauldron set to boil.

Ian was the first to break. "Will you let Mary drink from the flask?"

His dark-haired wife flushed with a mixture of embarrassment and hope. "Not unless you drink as well."

The Priestess smiled. "Such devotion. Your wife has the truth of it. You are the royal, not her. Bend the knee, swear to me, and you shall both live."

Ian flared in anger. "But why kill her? It's senseless murder!"

"Anything but senseless." She flashed a cruel smile. "Your wife becomes a dagger at your throat. For the sake of love, will you swear an oath? Where do your loyalties lie? It's time to test the truth of your convictions." She held the flask aloft, sloshing the contents. "Time to choose."

"This is madness." Isador glared at her. "You're lying about the poison."

"Am I?"

Igraine chose that moment to choke, her face turning bright red. Clutching at her throat, her eyes went wide in surprise. *Help me!* Isador and Ivor leaped from their chairs, but it was too late. Poison claimed the scholarly woman. Her face turned purple, foam frothing at her mouth. She fell from the chair, writhing in agony.

Isador leaped toward the Priestess but Hugo barred the way, a sword held to the commander's throat.

Isador glared across the blade, his voice a snarl. "Save her!"

The Priestess shook her head. "Too late. The poison has her."

Igraine spasmed, bent nearly double with convulsions, her face twisted in torment. She gave a startled gasp and then fell dead, sprawled across the floor, the spark of life snuffed from her open eyes.

"You killed her!"

"She killed herself. She could have bent the knee and saved her own life." The Priestess stared at her dead sibling. "A shame about Igraine. I was hoping Isador would die first."

Isador snarled. "I'll kill you for this."

"You'll never get the chance. Now sit down and make your decision. Bend the knee or die by poison...or the sword."

The commander returned to his chair.

A brooding silence strangled the chamber. The royals sat hunched at the dining table. Death stood at their shoulders, stalking them one by one. The king broke the silence. "Let Megan drink from the flask."

The Priestess smiled. "Yes, if she swears allegiance to me."

Ian protested. "Why her and not my wife?"

The Priestess answered. "Because if the mother swears, if her life is held forfeit, then the Royal Js will follow."

The king speared her with his stare. "What will you do with the children?"

The Priestess gave him a benevolent smile. "One of them will be my heir." Her smile deepened at his surprise. "You see, my brother, the choice is not as hard as you think. Since I have no intention of ever playing the broodmare, I need an heir. So if you swear homage, your line will still inherit. Of course, it will be a long time before any of them ever gains the throne." She raised the flask, her voice filled with warning. "If you want to see your grandchildren born, you need to bend the knee. Time is wasting. Swear and save your life."

The king stared at his queen. "Do it for me. And for the children. I cannot bear to watch you die."

The queen stifled a sob. She hugged her husband and then stepped toward the Priestess. "What must I do?"

The Priestess leaned forward, suppressing a feral grin. "Kneel before me, and swear homage. Accept me as the rightwise queen of Navarre, and you shall live."

The queen crossed the distance, a frumpy woman in a gown of chestnut brown. She sent a questioning glance toward her husband and then knelt, her voice a hoarse whisper. "I, Megan of Navarre, acknowledge Iris as the rightwise queen of Navarre, and pledge...and pledge my loyalty to you."

The Priestess smiled, savoring the triumph. "Well done. Otham, a goblet."

The big man crossed the room. Snatching a pewter goblet from the table, he dashed the red wine to the floor. The Priestess uncorked the alchemical flask and poured a thumb's width of amber liquid into the goblet. "This should be enough." Like a holy celebrant, she handed the goblet to the queen. "Drink and live."

The queen drank the potion, her hands trembling as she lowered the goblet.

"Good." The Priestess swept the others with her gaze. "Now for the rest of you. Time is running out, for as surely as Igraine lies dead upon the floor, the poison works its will among you." She gave them a venomous smile. "Decide or die."

88

Liandra

Liandra should have been exhausted, but somehow danger sharpened every sense. Colors seemed brighter, the cold air seemed crisper, her lavender perfume more pungent, everything intensified, as if the nearness of death made life all the dearer. She climbed the castle's tallest tower, seeking an eagle's view of her city. Leaning on the battlement, she took stock of the situation below. Soldiers in red clogged the streets, a mortal blight upon her city, a bloody strangle choking her castle. An occasional scream drifted upwards, the sounds of battle drowned by an endless incessant pounding, the massive ram bludgeoning her gates, minions of the Dark Lord come calling. The queen shuddered at the thought. At least she'd had the foresight to strengthen all the gates with steel, but nothing was invincible. Given time, even steel failed.

"May I join you?"

His voice was a balm to her fears. Liandra turned to give him a welcoming smile. "So you found us."

"My shadowmen are never far from the queen." Dashing in emerald and armor despite the weariness etched in his face, Robert took his place by her side, staring down at the beleaguered city. They stood in silence, a bitter wind snatching at their cloaks, the grim truth blatant in the cold morning light.

She dared the question that hung between them. "How much time do you think we have?"

"Perhaps a day. Two at the most. Less if they dare use fire."

"They won't."

"How can you be so sure?"

"They want the prize intact, the castle and the queen."

He stiffened beside her. "They can have the one, but never the other."

She laid a gauntleted hand upon his, but armor was not meant for tenderness. Liandra was so weary of wearing steel. "And so it comes to this."

"There's always Tandroth's Gate."

So he remembered the secret of the passageways. She gave him a sharp look, the weight of the monarchy heavy upon her shoulders. "We will not abandon our people."

"No, I did not think you would." His voice held a tinge of sadness. "But I might."

"What?" She stared in shock.

He turned to face her, his gaze as keen as a blade. "I can serve you better from the shadows than the castle ramparts. Send me into the city and I will slay the one who wears the raven helm. Cut the head from the snake and the snake will surely die."

Her breath caught yet she listened. "One man?"

"In Lingard they spoke of a Lord Raven, although the bishop seemed the true monster in Rognald's city. Yet from Pellanor's outer walls, I spied a raven banner. He stood apart, surrounded by a troop of Black Flames, a raven helm upon his head. I believe the raven is the will behind the enemy. Send me to slay him. If we strike from the shadows, we may yet gain a victory."

It was something to consider, yet the thought of sending him once more into harm's way squeezed her heart. Twice she'd watched him escape death. A third time would be too much. "I don't think I could bear it."

"What, to send an assassin against the enemy?"

"No, to risk losing you."

His breath caught, understanding softening his face. "You will not lose me, my queen." He gestured to the city spread below. "This is *our* city. Shadows and secrets serve *us*, not them." His voice deepened. "Loose your shadowmen. Let us serve you."

"Send another."

"Yet *I* am your master of shadows."

Still she hesitated.

"Surprise will be our best weapon. One mistake and he will be surrounded by guards. You dare not let this chance pass by."

The woman in her wanted to refuse, but the queen could not. "For the sake of our people, we will send you. But you must not go alone. Take the best of our shadowmen. Slay the beast and return to us."

He knelt, kissing her gauntleted hand. "As you command."

A deep hunger surged through her. When he stood, she stepped close, wanting the strength of his arms around her. His chainmail clanked against her breastplate. A desperate laugh bubbled out of her. "There is always something between us."

He shared her mirth. "Armor has its drawbacks." His gaze sobered. "Yet you are a vision."

"*Majesty!*" A messenger burst upon the parapet.

Liandra stepped away from her shadowmaster. "What news?"

The lad sketched a hasty bow. "Major Ranoth sent me to find you. The mercenaries are leaving by the city's western gate!"

Hope sparked within her. Liandra rushed around the tower till she gained a view of the west. "It's true!" A long snake of pea-green marched from the city, battle banners streaming in the winter wind. "So the Cobra parts from the Flame, mercenaries deserting the fight." Hope beat wild within her heart. "That should even the odds."

Beside her, the Master Archivist said, "Now it's only five to one."

She gave him a silencing glare and then dismissed the messenger. "Tell the major, we will join him shortly."

The lad bowed and disappeared through the tower door.

Liandra turned back to the parapet, staring down at the enemy. "Finally the gods show us their favor."

"Yet a dagger in the back is still your best gambit."

"Perhaps."

His voice held an edge. "You must let me try."

She stood beside him, feeling duty come between them. "When will you leave?"

"In the dead of night, when shadows hold sway."

She nodded, knowing she would not sleep this night. "Who will you take?"

He did not hesitate. "Dartmore, Harrow, and Marstan."

"Send them to us before you go. We will speak to each of them."

"As you wish." His hand covered hers, gauntlet to gauntlet.

Below, the ram pounded the gate, an incessant threat of doom. Threats and risk tumbled through her mind. Liandra did not want to send him, yet his plan had merit. The queen stared toward the horizon, hoping for a better solution. She'd sent messengers in every direction, begging for aid. Time was running out, like sand slipping through an hourglass. If the gods owed her any favors, she needed them now.

89

The Master Archivist

The Master Archivist crouched in the doorway, waiting for his eyes to adjust to the dark. A crescent moon hung low on the night sky, winking in and out of a cloudbank. The heavens shifted and the clouds claimed the crescent. A rich velvety darkness settled across the queen's city, a perfect night for assassination.

Keen for the hunt, a feeling of exhilaration flowed through him, his senses stretched to a razor's edge. A feral smile filled his face, knowing his shadowmen owned the night. Clad in dark leathers and a cloak of deepest black, his face and hands were blackened with charcoal. He carried seven throwing knives and a garrote on his belt. A small crossbow hung across his back, but he carried no sword since he intended no fair fights. Stealth and secrecy were his best weapons, a queen's assassin sent to kill a single enemy.

A deep booming sound filled the city. Even in the dead of night, the battering ram kept up its infernal pounding. Like a malevolent heartbeat, the sound gave warning that he dared not fail. Time was running out.

He'd brought three of his best with him, Marstan, Harrow and Dartmore, a promise to the queen and a certainty to see the task done. Checking the alley one last time, he signaled the others to follow. Silent as death, four shadowmen crept through a city infested with red.

The master led them away from the castle, skirting the soldiers and the infernal battering ram. Despite the darkness, he knew every street and alleyway near the castle. Some he recognized by scent, the smell of fresh baked bread always lingering by the bakery regardless of the hour, the scent of heated charcoal by the blacksmith shop, but all too often the streets reeked of death. Entire families lay butchered in the streets, sprawled across the cobbles, left to rot. Anger burned within him, he would not let Pellanor become a second Lingard. The evil of Flame must be snuffed out, starting with the Lord Raven.

The crescent moon crept from behind the clouds, silvering the streets. Shunning the light, the master hugged the shadows. Crouched in an alleyway, he waited for darkness to return.

A patrol marched passed, halberds perched on their shoulders, enough moonlight to see the red of their tabards. They turned down a side street, but he waited till the tramp of boots fell silent. Clouds swallowed the sickle moon and the silky darkness returned.

Keeping to a crouch, he led his shadowmen through the craft district, heading for a single mansion in the city's affluent section. From the castle ramparts he'd kept watch on the Lord Raven till he found his lair. It seemed the raven had a penchant for luxury. Instead of barracking with his soldiers, he chose the opulence of a lord's mansion. The master smiled, hoping greed would be the raven's undoing, a trap of gilded luxury to catch a dark-turned bird.

Patrols appeared with greater frequency, more proof they neared the raven's lair. Twice they ducked into side alleyways, waiting for soldiers to pass, but they reached mansion undetected. Candlelight glowed from behind glass-paned windows, a half dozen guards picketed at the front door. The master led his men to the rear, seeking the servant's entrance. A single guard kept watch, a big man leaning against the side wall, his hands gripping a halberd. The master smiled. Just as he expected, the servant's entrance was neglected, proof the arrogant raven did not expect the conquered city to mount a threat. His confidence would be his undoing.

So close to the raven's lair, their assault needed to be flawless. At such a late hour, the back alley offered no distractions, so the master decided to create one. He whispered instructions to Marstan. The shadowman nodded and then slipped into a side street.

The master peered around the corner, keeping his gaze in the vague direction of the lone guard. He watched but he did not stare. Most people could feel a hard stare, even if they could not see the one who stared. He'd sent Marstan to the far side of the alley with orders to fasten a hard stare on the guard.

At first nothing happened, but then the guard began to fidget. Pushing away from the wall, he fingered his halberd, his gaze drawn to the opposite side of the alley. The master slipped a knife from his belt. He could have used the small crossbow, but he preferred the knife's silence.

The guard took the bait. Unnerved by the hidden shadowman's hard stare, he stepped from his post, peering into the darkness. "Who's there?"

The master flowed like liquid darkness. Harrow kept two steps behind. Silent as a wraith, he crept behind the guard. With one deft stroke he severed the guard's windpipe, holding him upright till his dying spasms ceased. Harrow leaped forward to catch the guard's halberd. Together they carried the corpse to the far side of the alley while Dartmore worked on the lock. Marstan joined them, keeping watch on the street.

Something moved in the darkness.

The master stilled, listening.

His senses warned him that someone else prowled the street, someone as sure and silent as a shadowman. He motioned his men back toward the alley, wondering if the Flame had assassins of their own. Crouched behind a barrel, he peered into the darkness, seeking the threat, but he saw nothing.

The creak of a bow sounded loud in the night.

The master froze.

Sliding a second dagger from his belt, he tensed, crouched to fight.

Moonlight chose that moment to brighten the alleyway and then he saw them, a dozen men in hunter's leathers, short swords belted to their sides, longbows nocked with arrows. They stalked the night with the stealth of shadowmen, but it was their eyes that sent a shiver of shock through him. Demon-eyes glowed golden-yellow in the moonlight, like a nightmare sprung to life.

"Why did you kill that guard?" They stared at him, their bows held taut, a finger's breath away from death.

Beside him, his shadowmen tensed to fight, but he made the hand signal for caution. "We're enemies of the Flame." Something made him add, "We've come from the castle. We serve the queen."

"Queen Liandra?"

Her named sounded odd on their lips, yet hope burned within him. "Yes."

"The Treespeaker sent us to aid the queen, but we do not know this city."

Allies in the night, unlooked for, yet so very welcome. Perhaps the gods lent a hand after all. "We need to silence the battering ram." He hesitated, torn between the ram and the raven. Clouds shrouded the moon and darkness returned to the streets, perfect for stealth and surprise. The raven or the ram, the master made his decision.

90

Steffan

S teffan startled awake. Something was wrong. His glance slid to the beveled windows, still dark outside. Beside him, the girl snored softly, exhausted by sex, a rumpled figure beneath the quilts. Steffan considered calling for Pip, but a sixth sense warned him to stay silent. Reaching beneath the pillow, he grasped the jewel-hilted dagger. Armed, he slipped from bed, padding barefoot across the bedroom.

He'd claimed a lord's mansion, a passing luxury till the castle fell. A comfortable bed, a well-stocked larder, a comely lass, he'd enjoyed the evening but now his senses screamed in warning. Despite the late hour, the house seemed too quiet. Embers glowed in the immense fireplace, a dull red light casting shadows across the four-posted bed. Straining to listen, he crept towards the door.

The doorknob turned.

Steffan ducked behind the door, his back pressed to the wall, holding his breath.

The door eased open.

Steffan waited, his heart pounding, the dagger poised to strike.

A tall lithe man dressed in black glided into the bedchamber.

An assassin, fear shivered down Steffan's back.

Moving like liquid darkness, the assassin slipped across the room, intent on the figure snoring beneath the quilts. Knowing surprise was his best weapon, Steffan did not hesitate. He leaped, attacking the intruder from behind. *The angle was wrong.* The blade skittered across leather armor, tearing a harmless slash in the dark cloak.

The assassin whirled, an angry snarl on his blackened face. A knife slashed towards Steffan's stomach, but he twisted away. The assassin pulled a second blade from his belt, two knives against one, but Steffan was no stranger to knife fighting. He feinted left and slashed right. The assassin was good, evading Steffan's attack. They circled the floor in a deadly dance, two scorpions poised to strike. Twice Steffan took cuts on his arms, but he always whirled away, staying a hair's breath from death. "Who are you?"

"The queen's assassin."

For a fleeting moment, Steffan worried about poison.

The girl woke screaming.

Steffan lunged towards the hearth. Grabbing the poker, he hurled it at the assassin's head. The assassin ducked, slinking left. Steffan charged, barreling into the man with his shoulder. They fell hard with Steffan on top. Grappling for control, Steffan pinned the man's left hand with his knee, while thrusting his blade towards the assassin's throat. The assassin parried the attack, blade against blade. The man was strong, keeping the jeweled dagger at bay, slowly forcing it away, but the dagger was a feint. Steffan pulled a second blade from the assassin's own belt and drove it into the man's groin. Close enough to kiss, he watched as the assassin's eyes widened in surprise, a gurgle of pain on his lips. Steffan drove the dagger deeper, twisting the blade. The assassin fell limp, the spark of life extinguished

Breathing hard, Steffan rolled onto the floor, a puddle of blood staining the carpet.

The girl screamed, clutching the quilt to hide her nakedness.

"Shut your mouth!"

But the bitch continued to wail. Steffan grabbed a dagger and leaped toward her. With one quick slice, he silenced her. "Stupid bitch," his voice was a harsh whisper, "where there's one assassin there's likely another."

Keeping watch on the open door, Steffan quickly dressed. His breathing sounded loud in his ears. Fear gripped his throat. Impossible to understand how the assassin had gotten past his guards...or out of the castle; perhaps Pellanor was far more dangerous than he'd thought. He grabbed the assassin's belt, five knives and a garrote, and then reached for his own sword. Swirling his raven cloak around his shoulders, he crept from the chamber.

Death filled the hallway.

A guard lay slumped outside his door, his throat cut, a puddle of blood on the floor. He found Pip dead in the next room, strangled by a garrote. Further down the hallway, he found another dead guard, a dagger in his back. Frantic to find allies, he raced to the stairs. Three more guards lay dead on the staircase, but at least they'd taken an assassin with them. Steffan kicked the black-cloaked body, making sure it was dead. Crouched in the shadows, he strained to listen, fearing more assassins lurked in the hallways.

Torchlight flickered from outside, a brace of guards standing at the front door. *But were they guards or assassins?* Needing to be certain, he crept towards the window and peer out. *Red tabards,* the guards wore red. Relief washed through him. But even as he watched, arrows thrummed through the night. The guards fell screaming, clutching their throats.

Steffan staggered away from the door. *The mansion was a deathtrap!* Shock warred with fear, but survival triumphed. He raced through the mansion, seeking the back door. More dead soldiers clogged the hallway, but Steffan did not stop. Desperate to escape, he burst through the back door into the night.

Trumpets blared a warning. He heard shouts and screams and a clash of steel. His city was under attack! Alone in the alleyway, he suddenly felt exposed, the darkness stalking him like a threat. Unease shivered down his back. He whirled, a sword in his hand, but no one was there. Needing to see the enemy, Steffan swallowed his fear and crept toward the front of the mansion. Hiding in the shadows, he peered into the street.

His guards were all dead, riddled with arrows, but he saw no sign of the enemy.

The crescent moon slipped from behind the clouds and then he saw them, archers slinking through the street, their golden-yellow eyes glowing in the moonlight.

Cat-eyed archers! Fear shivered down his back. Having grown up in Wyeth, he'd heard tales of the cat-eyed archers, the type of stories to seed nightmares in a young boy's mind. But how could this happen? His heartbeat hammered, a sheen of sweat erupting on his skin. Instead of a conqueror, he suddenly felt hunted. *Assassins and cat-eyed archers,* he needed to find a safe haven. Gripping his sword, Steffan slipped into a side alleyway, seeking to save his own life.

91

Jordan

Yanking the carved doors open, Jordan stepped into nightmares. Bodies littered the entranceway. At first she thought they were dead, but then the truth became clear. Soldiers slept at their posts, pale as candle wax, their faces slack, their breathing imperceptible, their bodies slumped across the floor like spent wax. She tired to rouse them to no avail. *Poison!* Fearing she'd come too late, she threaded a path between the fallen, the Zward and the two monks close behind.

Deeper into the castle, she found servants, pages, cooks and retainers, all sprawled across the floor, as if struck down by a terrible curse, the Curse of the Vowels. Jordan shivered, feeling evil reach across the generations.

So eerie and silent, the castle was still as a sepulcher, yet it all made a strange kind of sense. It was only a week ago that Jordan finally understood her dreams, like pieces of a puzzle falling into place. She knew the attack would come on Founder's Night, treachery used to disarm the castle. An insidious poison laced into the King's Dram, a toast made by every soldier and servant on Royal Nachte, their loyalty rewarded with a sleeping death. Jordan shuddered at the malevolence, fearing she was too late.

Setting off at a run, she led the Zward and the monks through the twisting corridors, leaving the others to follow. Tantalizing smells drifted through the hallways, like the remnants of a ghostly feast, yet the castle was eerily silent. So strange to return home in such a fashion, like an invader in the night. Jordan slowed her steps to a hush, needing the element of surprise. Rounding a corner, she slid to a stop, a pair of dark-cloaked soldiers guarding the hallway.

Startled, the guards looked her way, reaching for their swords.

Thaddeus and Benjin stepped forward, hurling throwing knives.

One of the guards issued a strangled gasp. The other crumpled forward. The two Zward raced forward. Finishing the kill, they lowered the dead to the floor.

Jordan froze, crouched sword in hand, expecting an attack, but the hallways remained quiet. Relieved, she gave the two Zward a grateful look. "We're nearly at the great hall. We have to take them by surprise." She turned to Thaddeus. "Keep the others back till you hear my call." Her gaze turned to the two monks. "Stay close. We need to take her alive and save the flask."

They gave her a grim nod.

Saying a swift prayer to Valin, she crept towards the open doorway, spying from the shadows. Soldiers ringed the great hall, perhaps sixty or more surrounding the chamber. *Sixty!* Jordan knew she needed to wait for own men, but the empty serving platters proved she was already too late. Her family sat at the high table, looking pale and drawn, the remnants of a forgotten feast spread before them. Aunt Igraine was already down, sprawled across the floor, claimed by poison. A sob caught in Jordan's throat. In her dreams, her scholarly aunt had still lived. Jordan's heart thundered, fearing she'd already failed. Her gaze fixed on the woman in black leathers, sitting like a queen on the far side of the room. So this was Aunt Iris, the cursed one. The family resemblance was uncanny, like a twisted version of Jemma writ on a larger, more voluptuous scale. Beautiful and malevolent, she exuded a sinister sexuality. Jordan shivered, making the hand sign against evil, wondering how someone from her own family could fall so far into Darkness.

Even as she watched, her father the king rose from his chair, moving towards the seductress like a supplicant.

Jordan took a deep breath, knowing it was time to act, praying her gambit would work.

93

The Priestess

The Priestess fondled the flask, playing a waiting game with death. She watched her siblings fret at the table, wondering who would break next. Ian began to tremble, a hint of panic in his voice. "I feel it! I feel the poison!" He bent double in his chair, groaning in pain.

The king took a step toward the Priestess, his voice as cold as a tomb. "If I swear, will you save the others?"

The Priestess swallowed a smile. Such a delicious moment, the culmination of so many dreams, so many plans, retribution finally at hand. "If you and Isador both swear, then all of you will live."

The king nodded, his face solemn. "For the sake of my family, I will swear."

The Priestess stood, feeling the pleasure of the Dark Lord surge through her like an elixir. "Then bend the knee and swear fealty to me."

"*Don't father!*"

A young woman dressed as a warrior strode into the great hall, a checkered cloak at her shoulders, a sword in her hand. Behind her stood two men, both cloaked in brown, one big and burly, gripping a quarterstaff, the other tall and thin and empty handed.

"Who dares to interrupt?"

"It's over, Aunt. Give them the potion and your life will be spared."

She studied the girl's features, finding familiarity in her face. "One of the Royal Js. You must be Jordan, the swordish one." The Priestess held the flask aloft, venom in her voice. "Don't meddle, child. Deeper powers are at work here." Her men stepped towards her niece, their swords raised, their crossbows cocked. "You're surrounded, you're outnumbered, and you're too late. The poison already works my will upon your family. I need but drop this flask and they'll all die. And then the crown will be mine, claimed by right of conquest. But you can save them. Bend the knee, and I will spare them."

Jordan pressed further into the room, the two brown robed men shadowing her. "Navarre will never kneel to Darkness."

The Priestess marveled at the girl's artless audacity, as if three could defeat seventy. "How naïve." She laughed, a chilling sound. "You think this is about swords, child? It's about wits. It's about power. *I* alone hold the power of life and death." She shook the flask, swirling the amber fluid. "Threaten me, and they all die. Bend the knee and they live."

Jordan shook her head, her face as pale as sea foam. "Navarre will never yield."

The Priestess narrowed her gaze. "Navarre has always been mine. Bend the knee and live."

"I did not come alone." The girl gestured and armed men crowded the far door. "Surrender and live."

"How dare you threaten me!" The Priestess raised the flask. "I hold the king's life in my hand!"

The girl yelled, "*Now!*" and lunged forward, as if to grab the flask.

Otham stepped in front. Grabbing the girl by the throat, he tossed her halfway across the room.

The Priestess stared in shock, surprised by the girl's recklessness attack, but then hatred claimed her. "You dare threaten me!" Screaming her vengeance, she hurled the flask to the stone floor. *"Then die!"*

A brown-robed man dove for the flask but he was too late. Glass shattered against stone.

Soldiers in motley armor burst through the far doorway.

A killing rage claimed the Priestess. *"Kill them! Kill them all!"*

Her men leaped to the attack, crossbow bolts thrumming the air.

More soldiers poured through the doorway, outnumbering her own. *Treachery*, the realization twisted in her mind like a dagger. The great hall erupted in fighting. At least her loyal men remembered her orders, aiming for the royals. She saw Isador take a bolt in the throat. Her hated brother died screaming, a minor consolation, while the others were doomed to death by poison, a pity she could not stay and watch. Turning, the Priestess fled toward the far doorway, Otham and Hugo and a handful of guards protecting her back.

Swords were never her forte. The Priestess raced up the steps, climbing towards Osprey Tower, but then she paused on the landing, listening to the battle below. She'd only brought seventy men; the rest of her army camped south of the city's hills, awaiting her signal. With the tides flooding the causeway, her army was beyond reach. She paced the landing, listening to the bloodbath below, wondering how her plans could have gone so awry.

Footsteps rang on the stairs. The Priestess whirled to face the victors. Bitterness gripped her throat.

Jordan paused on the stairwell, blood staining her sword. "Yield!"

For a moment, their stares locked, hard-won experience dueling with youth's foolish idealism. The Priestess sneered. "How little you understand."

Jordan hesitated, her face full of questions.

"As queen I could have protected Navarre." Irony riddled her voice. "I would have saved you all from a greater Darkness. A Darkness that is still to come." The Priestess saw doubt bloom in her niece's face. "You know of what I speak. You've seen it in your dreams...in your nightmares."

Jordan gasped, but then she shook her head, brimming with stubborn denial. "Surrender, Aunt."

The Priestess laughed, a tinge of madness in her voice. "You don't understand Darkness, child. There is never any surrender, only success or death." The Priestess whirled, Hugo by her side. The others stayed behind, a thin ring of swords blocking the stairs, buying her time.

94

Liandra

Liandra paced her castle ramparts, keeping watch through the long night. A crescent moon slipped from behind the clouds, illuminating her city. Such a jovial moon for such a dire night. The smiling crescent seemed to mock her, a sickle moon, a reaper's moon, an ill omen for a god-cursed night. She'd sent Robert into danger before, but this time seemed different. It seemed worse. An assassin sent to kill a raven, a desperate gambit for a cornered queen, yet she could not bear to lose him. Liandra wondered if desperation had made her foolhardy, leaving Robert to take the risk. For the thousandth time she considered the chessboard in her mind, wondering if she'd missed something. Pacing the ramparts, she cursed the necessities of war, so weary of waiting, so desperate to hold the enemy's checkmate at bay. "Stewart, where are you?" The question whispered out of her, as much a prayer as a plea.

An incessant pounding was the only answer. The battering ram boomed through the night, beating at the castle's northern gate, a relentless threat. Liandra massaged her temples, plagued by a throbbing headache. She couldn't remember the last time she'd slept.

"May I join you?"

A feminine voice, the petite princess hovered at the rampart's doorway. Still dressed in archer's leathers, Princess Jemma clutched her shortbow yet her quiver was empty.

Liandra offered her a smile. "Your company is always welcome."

The two women stood at the battlement, staring down at the incessant ram.

"Are you sorry you did not leave?"

The princess arched an eyebrow. "There's still hope."

Youth was ever optimistic. "Yet your quiver is empty."

She glanced down. "Yes, it seems we've run out of arrows."

More good news. "And the enemy?"

"Their archers have stopped as well. Perhaps they realize we only send their arrows back."

"Yet the ram never stops, never sleeps. How many soldiers will they spend to take one gate? How relentless is their evil?"

"Surely you have a plan?"

Liandra answered with a bitter laugh. "We have many plans. The question is, will any bear fruit, and do we have time to reap the harvest?"

"Help will come."

"We like your confidence."

Liandra continued to pace, roving the ramparts like a silvery ghost. The princess kept pace beside her, a reassuring shadow. The night seemed to last for an eternity, the ram pounding the gate, the sickle moon slipping in and out of the clouds. And then the ram stopped. *It stopped!* Liandra clutched the rampart, listening. Silence seemed to pound against her, and then she heard shouting. Fear shivered through her, *has the gate fallen?* Yet she'd heard no trumpet blaring a warning. Horns pierced the night, shrieking an alarm. *The horns of the enemy!* Hope burst through her. "Come, something stirs in the night!"

The queen led the way to the nearest door. They hurried down an endless spiral of steps, finally reaching the barbican above the northern gate. The queen stepped out onto the rampart, only to find the battlement clogged with soldiers, a crush of emerald staring down into cobbled street. One soldier saw her and snapped a salute. "The queen!" More soldiers turned, opening a path across the barbican.

Major Ranoth strode toward her. "My queen, the ram is down!"

"But who has come to our aid? Is it Prince Stewart and the army from the north?"

"I've seen no battle banners, only archers in huntsman's leathers."

Archers in leathers? A riddle in the night, yet any aid was welcome. She stared down into the street. A slaughter of red soldiers surrounded the ram. Skewered with arrows, they sprawled before the gate, the ram abandoned on the cobbles. If this was a ruse, it was a strange one, yet the queen refused to miss an opportunity. "Open the gate and lead the men out. This is our chance to defeat the Flame. Join the archers and take back our city!"

The major saluted, a wolf's grin on his face. "As you command."

Trumpets blared, calling the men to arms. Expecting a bitter defense, they assembled in the courtyard. When they learned the news, their cheers shook the castle. The gates opened and her soldiers rushed out, their swords flashing in the moonlight.

The queen stood upon the barbican, encased in steel, watching the battle for her city. She breathed deep the night scents, knowing dawn held all the answer. The last gambit was played, one night to wait, one night to win. The queen prayed for victory...while the woman in her prayed for Robert.

95

Steffan

Chaos ruled the night, horns blaring from every direction. Steffan kept to the back alleyways, but he did not know the city. Like a blind man, he groped his way through the streets, desperately seeking a safe haven.

Twice he came across battles and had to double back. All too often emerald soldiers and leather-clad archers clogged the streets, but never just soldiers in red, as if all the red had bled from the city. Steffan cursed his ill luck, and then he realized the ram had fallen silent. *Too soon for the gates to fall,* his plans were crumbling into chaos, like some misbegotten nightmare. Anger and rage warred with disbelief, this couldn't be happening.

Steffan stumbled and tripped, landing on something soft and putrid. *Old corpses,* the sickening stench assaulted his senses, so revolting, but then he froze.

Something prowled the street, a shadow against shadows.

Steffan hugged the ground, playing dead, a possum hiding amongst the slain. He held his breath, a trickle of sweat beading his neck. Born and raised in Wyeth, he'd heard tales of the cursed cat-eyed people, a foul crossbreed of man and animal, an abomination against the gods, yet rumors said they were uncanny hunters, especially in the dark. Taking shallow breathes, Steffan kept his head pressed to the corpse, resisting the urge to look.

The shadows passed him by.

He waited, counting to a hundred, and then he ran, the stink of the dead clinging to his clothes. Three streets later his luck changed and he found a cluster of red-clad soldiers. Steffan slowed to a walk, trying to keep the relief from his voice. "Who's in command?"

The soldiers bristled, swords raised until they saw his raven cloak. "Lord Raven," a young captain stepped forward, "Captain Bremmer at your service."

"Report, captain."

"We were billeted in a tavern when we heard the alarms." A bewildered look filled his face, his eyes shifting to scan the dark. "We reported to our post, but everyone was dead." His voice dropped to a hoarse whisper. "There's demons stalking the streets, cat-eyed archers, and the hell spawn don't miss." The soldiers stood in a huddle, facing outward, as if they expected an attack from any direction.

"And the general?"

"He was at the ram." The captain shook his head, his face grim. "We heard they're all dead, slaughtered by archers."

Fear gripped Steffan; it was worse than he thought, but at least he'd found protection. "We need to get to the stables. Do you know where they are?"

The captain nodded. "This way."

They set off at a run, Steffan keeping to the center of a dozen soldiers. Swords poised to strike, they raced through the back ways, every shadow laden with threat. It seemed to take forever, but in truth the stables were only a few streets away. The big doors gaped open, the guards gone, the stables deserted, but the horses remained. A horse whinnied in fright while others kicked at their stalls, as if sensing danger. "Saddle the horses and take spares." Steffan worked with the others, throwing a saddle on a piebald mare. Shouldering the horse, he cinched the girth, a flood of questions racing through his mind. Fight or flee? Should he rally his forces and try to retake the city, or should he flee and wait for dawn to learn the truth? Rumors said the cat-eyed people were most dangerous at night, attacking like demons in the dark. Adjusting the stirrups, Steffan vaulted into the saddle. Turning the horse, he faced the gaping doors, darkness brooding in the streets like a trap. His shoulder's twitched as if expecting an arrow. Fear forced his decision. "To me!" He drew his sword. "We ride for the north gates and the woods beyond! Stop for nothing! The enemy be damned!"

Steffan slapped the mare with the flat of his sword. Startled, the small horse burst from the stables. Running at a full gallop, they raced through the streets at a break-neck speed, hoof beats drumming on cobblestones. Arrows thrummed in the darkness. A soldier riding beside him fell screaming. Steffan bent low, urging his horse to a lathered sprint. The night was awash in confusion. Horns blared, soldiers shouted, and corpses sprawled the streets like barriers. Twice they rode through battles. Steffan hacked left and right with his sword, refusing to be slowed. Desperation lent him strength. They broke through and raced for the gates. Beyond the gaping gates, moonlight silvered the snowy countryside with the illusion of safety.

Steffan urged his mare to a desperate gallop. They burst through the gates, riding across the winter-white farmland. A cold wind flared his cloak, clearing the stink of the dead from his nostrils. Steffan reveled in the wind, urging his horse for more speed. Exhilaration rushed through him; he'd escaped the city and survived. But his elation was short-lived. Reality hit like a hammer stroke. Just yesterday, he'd entered the city as a conqueror, an army at his back. Now he fled the city with nothing but a handful of guards. Steffan slowed the mare to a trot. The small horse was lathered with sweat and breathing like a bellows.

He turned the spent mare toward the hillside, letting the winded horse pick its own path to the crest. Dismounting, Steffan tossed the reins to the captain. No one spoke. No one met his stare. He stood on the hilltop overlooking the city. Some of the soldiers slept curled in their cloaks, but Steffan stood vigil, waiting for the dawn.

Horns blared and the sound of clashing steel rose from the city, proof the fighting persisted. The sun rose in a bloody dawn and still he waited. He half expected to see battle banners raised above the gate, red or green proclaiming the victor, but the city walls remained barren. The waiting grew hard, doubt gnawing on his mind. Steffan was tempted to send a soldier to investigate, but he decided to be cautious, keeping his guard close.

"My lord, look!" The captain pointed toward the north.

Armor gleamed in the dim morning light, the tramp of thousands marching south.

The bishop, it had to be the Bloody Bishop! Elation thrummed through Steffan, expecting the army from Lingard...but then the colors became clear. *Emerald green,* the color choked his hope. Emerald battle banners fluttered above an emerald host, damning his fate. No matter the outcome of the fight in the city, he'd lost Lanverness. *He'd lost.*

His guards began to slip away, disappearing into the woods. Steffan did not try to stop them. Standing atop the hill, he watched the emerald host march south, the taste of ashes in his mouth. *He'd failed!*

He felt the Dark Lord draw near.

Retribution came swift and sure. A mighty fist of molten metal gripped Steffan's heart, the hand of the Dark Lord. *"No!"* Steffan clutched his chest, falling to his knees. Waves of agony poured through him. Steffan groveled on the ground, convulsing in pain. *"No!"*

You failed me. Defeated by a mere woman, now you pay with your soul.

Pain claimed him, assaulted by all the agonies of hell. His skin burned as if being torn in strips from his body. His back bent as if being racked. Every breath hurt as if his lungs were filled with fire. Writhing in agony, he begged for his life, for his very soul. *"No! Spare me, Lord, give me another chance!"* Steffan screamed as if his very blood boiled. The immortal fist closed tight, searing his heart...and then it released him.

One last chance. Do not disappoint.

Steffan lay sprawled in the snow, shivering from the nearness of hell. His mouth tasted like ashes, his muscles quivering in remembered agony, yet he was unharmed. Shuddering, he ate snow, desperate for moisture, desperate to cleanse the taste of hell. When he finally recovered, the sun was halfway across the sky. The others had deserted him; only the piebald mare remained. Wiping his face with snow, he struggled to his feet and then climbed to the saddle. At least he lived to fight another day. Darkness would never forgive, nor forget, but Steffan swore he'd find a way to reclaim his lost glory. Cursing the queen, he turned his horse toward the west and nudged the mare to a trot.

96

Jordan

The baldheaded giant blocked the stairwell, a mountainous man welding a sword in both hands. He straddled the stairs, a snarl of hatred in his voice. *"For the mistress!"*

Wary of the giant's strength, Jordan ducked the first strike. The second sword whistled towards her head. She parried the blow, hammered to her knees by the stroke's massive power. The second sword snaked towards her stomach. Jordan lurched sideways, the sword screeching a scar across her armor. Sweat bled down her back. Fearing his unnatural strength, she disengaged. Feinting left, she made a desperate lunge for his heart. Steel rang against steel. He parried her blow, forcing her sword to the stairs. Sneering, the giant trod on her blade, a snarl twisting his face. "Now you die!"

A crossbow thrummed from behind.

A feathered bolt sank into the giant's neck. Dropping his swords, he crumpled to his knees, his eyes wide in surprise.

Jordan yanked her sword free and struck the killing blow. "For Isador!"

Blood fountained across the stairs. The giant toppled sideways. Behind him, the enemy soldiers broke and ran.

Jordan withdrew her sword from the giant's chest. Sparing a glance behind, she was relieved to find Thaddeus and the Zward at her back. "Come on!" She raced up the stairs, needing to find her aunt, confused by the woman's choices. Retreating to the castle heights made little sense. Osprey Tower left her aunt no way to escape. Jordan climbed the stairs two at a time. A breeze laden with the sea's salty tang blew in from an open door. The doorway led to a battlement overlooking the sea, a trap of another sort. Jordan raced through the door and slid to a halt.

Iris stood balanced upon the castle ramparts. Her arms spread wide, her long hair billowing in the wind; she stood poised above the storm-clashed sea like a dark goddess. Her liegeman crouched beside her, divested of armor, a sword clutched in his hand.

Jordan took two steps toward her aunt. *"Don't!"*

Iris turned, her voice full of silken cruelty. "Why not?"

"I need more antidote."

"Your loss, my victory." Her eyes gleamed with dark malice. "Despite your swords, my poison works my will."

Jordan struggled for another argument. "It doesn't have to end like this."

"Who said it would end?" Her aunt gave a throaty laugh, but her eyes glittered cold as the sea. "Tempting death is all you've left me. I trust in the Dark Lord." She leaped from the rampart, like a cormorant diving for the sea. Her liegeman hurled his sword towards Jordan and then jumped.

Jordan ducked the sword and then raced for the ramparts. Clutching the cold stone, she stared below. Waves battered the tower's base, an impossible drop. Two bodies struck the frothing sea, one as clean as a knife, the other like a stone.

"Do they live?" Thaddeus crowded the rampart beside her. "Look there." Three small ships plowed the night-dark waters, rowers maneuvering towards the swimmers.

Jordan swore, a mixture of admiration and bitter regret. She'd hoped to capture her aunt, but Darkness proved slippery as an eel. She watched as the boats snatched the swimmers from the sea. Evil lived to hunt another day.

Struck by weariness, Jordan slumped against the battlement. She'd chased her aunt from the castle but the victory felt hollow. Dread claimed her, cinching her stomach, knowing the antidote was lost. Poison was such an insidious way to die. Turning from the battlement, she returned to the great hall, praying to Valin to spare her family.

97

Liandra

The night seemed to last forever, one long vigil plagued with a thousand worries. The queen paced the barbican, listening to the tides of battle, desperate to learn the outcome. Her imagination ran rampant, fraught with worry. She feared for Robert, she feared for her city, yet all she could do was wait. Waiting was a woman's lot, but as a monarch, Liandra found it nearly intolerable. She paced the castle ramparts, replaying the chessboard in her mind. All the pieces were in play, the endgame in motion, a desperate gambit to save her kingdom.

Dawn came in a rush of reds and golds bursting across the eastern sky and still the fighting continued. She'd ordered the castle gates closed, a precaution against the enemy, but that left her soldiers vulnerable, another worry to add to her burden. Clad in mirror-bright armor, she kept her face a confident mask, standing vigil upon the barbican, a symbol to her people.

At midday, the tenor of the fighting changed. Trumpets blared, a cavalcade of riders forging a path through the streets. Liandra strained to see their colors. *Emerald!* Elation thrummed through her. Emerald cloaks and emerald battle banners, Liandra clutched the ramparts, certain it was Stewart, but the battle remained a stalemate. Red-cloaked soldiers rushed to clog the streets, waging a fearsome fight. They pushed the emerald back, a broil of red surrounding the castle. Swords clashed and men screamed, the dead and the dying trampled beneath the fighting, a bitter struggle before the gates. The queen stood upon the ramparts, watching the battle tides ebb and flow, a desperate hope warring against a terrible fear. Twice the emerald guard surged for the castle, and twice they were thrown back, but on the third charge, the red broke and ran.

"Open the gates!" The queen issued orders from the battlement. And then she saw him, her royal son leading the final cavalry charge. Bloody and battered, yet he rode like a hero sprung from a bard's tale. Liandra closed her eyes and whispered a hundred prayers of thanks. Her city was saved; her son was safe.

Somehow she made it to the tower doorway, down the spiral stair and out into the castle courtyard. Chaos claimed the yard, a swirl of warhorses, armor, and steel, the able helping the wounded. Liandra watched them dismount, never so glad for so much martial glory. The chaos resolved to order and

Stewart strode towards her. Clad in bloodied armor, he removed his helm and knelt.

"Majesty, we came as soon as we could."

"And Lingard?"

"Restored to the Rognalds." He stared up at her. "Our plan worked."

His dark hair was too long and matted from his helm, his face too lean and unshaven, his eyes shadowed from lack of sleep, but he was whole and alive. She wanted to embrace him, to hold him safe in her arms, but instead she played the queen, giving him the dignity he deserved. "You have done well." She offered him her hand. "We are most pleased."

He kissed her gauntleted hand and then he stood, flashing a boyish grin. "You look good in armor, mother."

Liandra could not suppress a smile. "We prefer silk."

His face sobered. "I lost my blue steel sword."

"We have gained it back for you."

His face brightened, full of questions, but then a stranger stepped forward, a man in huntsman's leathers carrying a longbow. His eyes were startling, golden-yellow with vertical slits for pupils. Cat eyes in a man's face, the queen smothered her surprise. "And who is this?"

Stewart gestured to the stranger. "When we came to the city, we found allies fighting the Flame."

The pieces began to fall into place. "So you are the ones who silenced the ram?"

He gave her the barest of nods, as if his pride forbad him to bow. "I am Alwin of Clan Hemlock, a ranger of the Deep Green. The Treespeaker sent us to save a queen."

His words made little sense, yet Liandra was grateful for any allies, no matter how strange. "You have our thanks, but we would hear more of your people and your Treespeaker."

"Cenric speaks for the clan, but he is still fighting within the city."

"Then we will meet with him when the fighting is done."

Stewart stepped forward, his face anxious. "I must return to the battle. The city is not yet secure."

The queen nodded, reluctant to let him go, yet it was his duty to be crown prince, just as it was her duty to be queen. "We will await you in our chambers."

Stewart took his leave, leading half a hundred knights back into the streets, a thunder of hooves on cobblestones. The queen watched them ride out, confident in their victory, but one fear nagged her mind, she had not heard from Robert. Her heart quailed at the thought. Victory was rarely without sacrifice, but this was one price she refused to pay.

Mired in worry, the queen climbed the steps to her castle. Tired of scurrying through the dank military stairwells, Liandra needed to walk in her castle's marbled hallways, to feel the sunlight pouring through mullioned windows, to see her ancestors' faces embroidered in the great tapestries. A pair of guards rushed to open the gilded doors and then she saw them. Her people crowded the marbled hallways, their faces strained with a mixture of hope and fear. Most clutched weapons. A few held swords, but most carried makeshift arms, pokers, cast iron skillets, mallets, cudgels and staves. Despite their fear, she knew they stood ready to fight. Liandra studied their faces, the true wealth of her kingdom.

"The Rose Army has returned. Victory is nearly ours."

A cheer erupted from her people, a triumphant shout echoing through the gilded hallways.

The queen moved among them. Her people knelt, leaving an open path down the marbled hall. Hands reached out to touch the hem of her cloak. Liandra saw hope and resolve etched in their faces. She drew strength from her people, strength and confidence. A conviction grew in her heart. As long as her people stood against evil, as long as they dared to fight, then Darkness could not win.

"We shall never succumb to evil."

Her people cheered and she knew her kingdom was saved.

98

Liandra

L iandra paced her solar, wearing a path in the wool carpet. Victory was secured, yet she still had not heard from Robert. If the man was dead, she'd never forgive him, if he kept her dangling with needless worry, she'd kill him. "Where is he?"

Princess Jemma and Lady Sarah kept vigil with the queen, but neither woman dared an answer. The princess stood before the roaring fireplace, still dressed in huntsman's leathers, absorbing the fire's warmth, while Lady Sarah sat in a chair, her knitting needles clacking a distracting rhythm. Scones and tea sat forgotten on a side table. Still clad in armor, Liandra paced her solar, consumed with worry. She'd lost her unborn daughter to treachery; she could not bear to lose Robert to war. Surely the gods could not be that cruel.

An abrupt knock came from the door.

The queen tensed. "Come."

A page opened the door and then *he* was there. Striding towards her, he looked a fright, his face blackened with charcoal, his leather armor stained with blood, but she did not care. "*My queen!*" He swept her into his arms and kissed her hard. She clung to him, decorum be damned, but her armor was between them, a stiff reminder of her rank.

He gave her another kiss, a promise of the passion to come, "They'll be time for us," and then he stepped away, her shadowmaster once more.

The queen took a deep breath, struggling to regain her poise. "Is the raven dead?"

Her shadowmaster scowled. "I had to make a choice. I sent Harrow and Dartmore after the raven, while I led the archers against the ram." His face turned grim. "Later, after the ram was defeated, I found them both dead in the mansion. The lord's chamber was empty save for a woman, her throat slashed, naked in his bed. I fear the raven survived the attack, but perhaps the city caught him. Either way, the victory is yours."

Her city was safe, her kingdom secured, but if the raven still lived, he'd be keen for vengeance. "Question the prisoners. See if any know if the raven survived."

He nodded. "As you command. But I've also brought allies to meet with you."

"Now?"

"Yes."

"Then show them in." The queen took a seat in the gilded chair set before the fire. Stiff in her armor, she arranged the drape of her emerald cloak. Not her most attractive look, but perhaps it was best if she met these new allies as a warrior queen.

Three men in huntsmen's leathers entered her solar. Like a breath of wilderness come to her court, all three had yellow-gold cat-eyes, gleaming unnaturally bright in the firelight. *Yellow eyes, demon eyes*, Liandra's breath caught, suppressing the urge to make the hand sign against evil. They stood before her, tall and broad shouldered, their faces chiseled with pride despite the feral wildness of their eyes. One wore a cloak of peacock feathers, cascading to the floor. Turquoise eyes shimmering in the firelight, the feathered cloak lent him a strange mixture of regal luxury and exotic barbarism.

"I am Cenric, the leader of Clan Hemlock." The cloaked one gave her a nod, the barest hint of deference. "The Treespeaker sent us to save a queen."

"We bid you welcome to our court and we thank you for your aid."

Cenric cocked his head, as if listening to more than her words. "Yet you fear our eyes."

The queen stifled her surprise, amazed at his perception. She studied his face, trying to gauge the intent behind his strange golden eyes. Given his blunt challenge, she decided honesty was the best approach. "It is true that your eyes startle us. They remind us of children's tales, of demons stalking the dark, yet your actions name you allies. All too often people are judged by their appearance instead of their worth. As a queen, we understand this disparity all too well. Women are often overlooked, their deeds belittled or ignored. We shall not make that same mistake."

He stared at her, as if weighing her words, but then he nodded. "So the princess spoke true."

The conversation spiraled to a deeper level, like diving into a murky ocean. "What princess?"

"Princess Kath of Castlegard. She said that among the white-eyes only one queen ruled alone. A queen of uncommon wisdom who might welcome our bows despite our eyes."

Kath of Castlegard, a name she'd not thought of for many moon turns. The chessboard grew crowded with unexpected pieces, plots within plots. Liandra sensed a bigger game, as if all of Erdhe were drawn into a web, connected by strands of light and dark. "And how did you learn of our need?"

He gave her a knowing smile. "The trees drink deep, tapping into the roots of the world. An ancient evil awakes, threatening all of Erdhe." He withdrew a scroll from his pouch, handing it to her. "A messenger bid me give you this."

Liandra took the scroll. Her breath caught at the sight of the seal, dark blue wax imprinted with the Seeing Eye of the Kiralynn monks. She broke the seal and read the words. Just a few lines scrawled on parchment, yet they changed everything. A chill rushed through her, as cold and bleak as the worst winter. The parchment dropped from her hands. She'd barely saved her kingdom, only to face a worse doom. "The Knights of the Octagon have fallen. Raven Pass is taken. The Mordant marches south. The Battle Immortal has begun."

APPENDIX

LANVERNESS

Lanverness is an old kingdom, steeped in tradition, often relying on its wealth of natural resources and the shrewdness of its rulers to grow in prosperity and influence. Never fecund, the royal line of Lanverness has been forced to branch out several times over the centuries. The Rose Throne is currently held by the Tandroths. The Tandroths nearly lost the throne when the last king of Lanverness, King Leonid, failed to produce a male heir. The king survived a revolt and forced his noblemen to accept his only daughter, Liandra, as the heir to the Rose Throne on the condition that she marry a peer of the realm. Liandra is the only queen to rule a kingdom of Erdhe. Under Queen Liandra's stewardship, Lanverness has become the wealthiest kingdom in all of Erdhe.

The symbol of Lanverness is two white roses crossed on a field of emerald green. The seat of their power is Castle Tandroth, rising from the heart of Pellanor, the capitol city.

QUEEN LIANDRA TANDROTH, ruler of the Rose Throne, also known as the White Rose of Lanverness, also known as the Spider Queen
>-her husband, **PRINCE-CONSORT DONALD TERREL**, chosen from among the noble families of Lanverness, Lord Terrel was raised up to be the Prince-Consort to the queen on condition that he forsake his name and his lineage. He died in a hunting accident shortly after the birth of his second son. The heraldry of house Terrel is a red unicorn rearing on a field of green.
>-their children:
>**PRINCE STEWART**, heir to the Rose Throne, promoted to general of the Rose Army, wields a blue steel sword
>**PRINCE DANLY**, spare heir to the Rose Throne, a condemned traitor
>**PRINCESS ASELYNN**, died at birth

-her councilors:
>**LORD ROBERT HIGHGATE**, the Master Archivist, the queen's shadowmaster, right hand to the queen
>**MASTER RADDOCK,** deputy shadowmaster serving the queen, was once a condemned thief, rescued from the dungeons by the Master Archivist
>**SIR DURNHEART,** the Knight Protector, raised to a knight after the Red Horn rebellion, wields a blue steel sword
>**LORD TURNER**, a former member of the queen's council, boiled alive for treason, a harlequin of the Dark Lord
>**LORD LENOX**, Lord of the Treasury, replaces Lord Wesley on the queen's council

> **LORD SHELDON**, the Lord Sheriff, leader of the constable force of Lanverness
> **MAJOR RANOTH,** promoted after the rebellion, he serves as a military advisor to the queen
> **LORD SADDLER,** a goldsmith raised to a lord after the rebellion, the Master of Coin on the queen's council
> **LORD MILLS,** an ambitious and handsome lord raised to the queen's council after the rebellion
> **LORD HUNTER**, a skilled diplomat, used as a roving ambassador to the other kingdoms of Erdhe
> **LORD RICKMAN**, the Lord of Mines, responsible for the ruby, emerald and iron ore mines of Lanverness
> **LORD QUINCE**, Lord of the Hunt, Warden of the Royal Forests
> **LORD CADWELL**, Master of Letters, the secretary to the Royal Council
> **DUKE ANDERS,** a wealthy lord, fallen out of the queen's favor

-her ladies-in-waiting:

> **LADY SARAH JAMESON**, a distant cousin of the queen, principle lady-in-waiting to the queen
> **LADY MARTHA**, a lady-in-waiting to the queen
> **LADY AMY**, the youngest of the queen's ladies-in-waiting
> **LADY LINDSEY,** a lady-in-waiting to the queen

-other members of the court:

> **PRINCESS JEMMA**, a princess of Navarre, Wayfaring with the queen to learn the way of multiplying coins
> **SIR CARDEMIR,** fifth son of the Duke of Graymaris, the seahorse knight, sent by the queen as an emissary to the Kiralynn monks, murdered by the Mordant's treachery
> **FREDERINKO,** an emissary from the Empire of Ur, a chained servant of the twelfth-fold prince of Ur, come to the Rose Court bearing gifts, sent to prepare for the prince's arrival
> **CAPTAIN BLACKMON,** captain of the queen's guards
> **LORD EVON,** a minor lordling in Pellanor
> **MASTER HOLTON,** a nobleman in Pellanor
> **MASTER SPITZER,** a nobleman in Pellanor
> **HEALER CRANDOR,** a master healer of the Rose Court
> **MARSTAN,** a shadowman
> **HARROW,** a shadowman
> **DARTMORE,** a shadowman

THE ROSE ARMY

PRINCE STEWART, heir to the Rose Throne, General of the Rose Army, wields a blue steel sword
-his officers and soldiers:

> **LORD DANE,** eldest son of the Duke of Kardiff, fostered to the Rose Court at a young age, a sword brother to Prince Stewart, second in command of the Rose Army, the symbol of the Dukes of Kardiff is a rearing griffin holding a sword
>
> **KELSO,** serves as one of Prince Stewart's commanders
>
> **MATHIS,** serves as one of Prince Stewart's commanders
>
> **MAJOR BATTON,** a commander of the Rose Army
>
> **GEDRY,** a scout serving the Rose Squad
>
> **SAM,** a soldier captured by the Flame
>
> **TIMMONS,** a soldier captured by the Flame
>
> **DALT,** a soldier captured by the Flame
>
> **OWEN,** a soldier captured by the Flame, becomes a royal guard
>
> **JASPER,** a soldier captured by the Flame
>
> **KENNITH,** a soldier captured by the Flame
>
> **CROCKER,** a scout captured by the Flame, becomes a royal guard
>
> **PERCY,** a scout captured by the Flame
>
> **CRISPIN,** a soldier captured by the Flame, becomes a royal guard
>
> **KERLIN,** a soldier captured by the Flame
>
> **LEUTENANT AUBRY,** leads a troop serving to evacuate villagers
>
> **CARTER,** a guard assigned to Danly, a former Red Horn sworn to the queen
>
> **CAPTAIN TALCOT,** captain of the guards assigned to Danly
>
> **ATHON BAIRD,** a peasant turned soldier, assigned to guard Danly

LINGARD

Lingard is a fortress citadel, the second greatest fortress in Lanverness. The heraldic seat of the Rognalds, staunch supports and loyal lords serving Queen Liandra. Their symbol is an iron fist on a field of yellow-gold.

BARON ROGNALD, a peer of the realm of Lanverness, a friend and staunch supporter of Queen Liandra, the ruler of Lingard, he is a widower
-his officers, soldiers, and servants:

> **LORD RONALD ROGNALD,** eldest son of Baron Rognald, commander of the south gate of Lingard, heir to Lingard
>
> **CAPTAIN LEONARD VENGAR,** captain of the guard for Lingard
>
> **DASCHEL,** seneschal to Baron Rognald
>
> **KURT,** a soldier sworn to the baron, friend of Vengar
>
> **SANDRA,** a whore in Lingard, friend of Vengar

CORONTH

The kingdom of Coronth was long ruled by one of the oldest royal families in Erdhe. Tracing their lineage back to before the War of Wizards, the Manfreds struggled to maintain their kingdom despite the aftermath of chaos and famine caused by the magical war. Their descendents ruled in an unbroken line for over a thousand years until a preacher of the Flame God brought a new religion to the capitol city of Balor. Enthralling the crowds with the miracle of the Test of Faith, the Pontifax gained a rabid following. In less than a year, the new religion consumed the kingdom, making the Pontifax more powerful than the king. Ruling from the pulpit, the Pontifax declared that only a true believer of the Flame God could wear the crown of Coronth, forcing the king, his wife, and all of his children to submit to the Test of Faith. When the searing flames consumed the royal house, the Pontifax became the spiritual and secular ruler of Coronth.

The symbol of house Manfred was a golden lion rearing on a field of blue. The new symbol of Coronth is a golden flame on field of red, the symbol of the Flame God. The seat of power is the capitol city of Balor.

THE PONTIFAX, the supreme spiritual and secular ruler of Coronth, also known
as the Enlightened One, beloved of the Flame God
-his priests and counselors:
>**THE KEEPER OF THE FLAME**, Senior priest of the Flame, leader of the Confessors of the Flame, he becomes the ruler of Coronth and the leader of the faith after the death of the Pontifax, he remains in Balor

THE ARMY OF THE FLAME

LORD STEFFAN RAVEN, Counselor to the Pontifax, the leader of the Army of the Flame, his personal symbol is a black raven on a blood-red field
-his officers and servants:
>**GENERAL CAYLIB**, General of the Army of the Flame
>**BISHOP TANIFF,** also known as the Bloody Bishop, the senior cleric riding with the Army of the Flame, he is a religious fanatic and berserker warrior, he wields a spiked mace
>**PIP**, an orphan lad who serves Lord Raven
>**OLAFF**, a mute giant, a guard serving Lord Raven
>**ALAN JELLIKAN**, Pyromancer of the Flame
>**SALMAY,** a young woman who becomes a mistress to Steffan, a spoil of war

Officers, soldiers, and camp followers:

GALBERT, an army scout
TARNLEY, an army scout
CAPTAIN HUMBOLT, a captain in the army
MAJOR TARKIN, an army major sent by Steffan to spread lies in Pellanor
HESTER, a guard
SERGEANT DALBRIS, a sergeant serving on a prisoner detail
SERGEANT BERNIER, in charge of a prisoner detail
CAPTAIN ROTHWELL, a patrol captain
CAPTAIN BREMMER, a patrol captain
MELINDA, a camp follower serving as a whore

SCAVENGERS FOLLOWING THE FLAME ARMY

SKARN, also known as Skarn the Bold, leads a band of deserters and mercenaries scavenging the war torn lands for spoils. His only allegiance is to gold. His men wear a scavenged motley of red, green, and all shades of brown.
-his men:

CLEM, second in command after Skarn
DINK, mercenary
ROLAND, deserter of the Flame
HUBBLE, mercenary
DUSTER, mercenary

RADAGAR

Over five hundred years ago, fierce warriors from a distant desert kingdom followed the caravan route north and invaded Erdhe, carving out a vast new kingdom named Radagar. The proud conquerors maintained their desert culture, with the king and the royal houses taking many wives. The harems spawned an abundance of royal princes, all competing for the Cobra Throne. Treachery and poison became the tools of succession. Over time, the royal infighting caused the once great kingdom to dwindle in size and stature. Radagar is now known as a purveyor of mercenaries, poisons, and aphrodisiacs.

The symbol of Radagar is a red coiled cobra on a field of pea-green. Their seat of power is the capital city of Salmythra. The king of Radagar is known as the ruler of the Cobra Throne.

KING CYRUS, the king of Radagar, the ruler of the Cobra Throne, a descendent of the desert-born conquerors, a famed for his skills at wrestling -his lords:

> **PRINCE RAZZUR**, half brother to King Cyrus, a contender for the Cobra Throne, a proud descendent of the desert-born conquerors, leader of House Razzur, his symbol is a black scorpion a sky-blue field
> **GENERAL XANOS,** general of Radagar's mercenary army

-servants of the royal court:

> **MASTER SAL,** a eunuch "poison taster"

-people of Salmythra:

> **OLD LATHAM,** a merchant selling fresh ingredients for poisons and aphrodisiacs in the great market
> **RASHID,** a bearer hired by the Priestess
> **NEFFER,** a flute-playing snake-charmer boy, bought in the market by the Priestess
> **HAMID,** seneschal to Prince Razzur

NAVARRE

The youngest kingdom of Erdhe, Navarre was founded less than four hundred years ago by a daring adventurer, Alaric Navarre, who rescued the youngest daughter of the king of Coronth from a band of sea pirates infesting the Orcnoth Islands. Gaining the king's confidence, and his daughter's hand in marriage, Alaric earned a freehold of land running along the Western Ocean where he later established his kingdom. His domain includes the Orcnoth Islands.

While defeating the nest of pirates, Alaric discovered a long-forgotten focus. The magic of the focus renders the royal house very fecund, enabling the queens to bear six to ten children in a single pregnancy. After using the magic, both the king and the queen become sterile. The focus is the secret strength of the royal house of Navarre, the bedrock for the succession to the throne. Alaric abandoned the convention of primogeniture, declaring that all of the tuplets have an equal chance to the throne. He instituted the practice of Wayfaring, a type of fostering where the heirs develop their greatest interests, striving to become excellent at a skill, a knowledge, or a trade, so that they can bring this knowledge back to Navarre and thus enrich the kingdom. After the Wayfaring, the King, together with the royal council, chooses the successor to the throne based on the talents, skills, and temperament that best fit the needs of the kingdom at the time. Navarre is well known for its uncommonly wise rulers...but with every great boon there is also a cost, the hidden focus brings with it the Curse of the Vowels.

The symbol of Navarre is a white osprey soaring on a checkered field of red and blue. The seat of their power is Castle Seamount, perched on a rocky outcrop on the edge of the Western Ocean. Navarre has always had close ties to the sea.

KING IVOR NAVARRE, the eighth ruler of the kingdom of Navarre
 -his siblings:
 PRINCE IRWIN, died of poison, believed to be a victim of the Curse of the Vowels
 PRINCESS INGRID, fell from the rigging of a ship and died, believed to be a victim of the Curse of the Vowels
 PRINCESS IRIS, accused of murdering her two siblings, exiled to the Orcnoth Islands, she murdered her guards and then disappeared
 PRINCE ISADOR, Commander of the Army of Navarre, advisor to the king, nearly fell victim to the Curse of the Vowels
 PRINCESS IGRAINE, Counselor to the king, court historian, tutor to the Royal Js
 PRINCE IAN, Royal Bowyer, advisor to the king
 PRINCESS IVY, Captain of a royal merchant vessel of Navarre

-his wife, **QUEEN MEGAN**, a princess of Tubor

-their children known as the Royal Js:

> **PRINCESS JEMMA**, Wayfaring with the Queen of Lanverness to learn the way of multiply coins
>
> **PRINCE JUSTIN**, Wayfaring to become a bard, he receives permission from the King and Council to travel to Coronth to try and overthrow the Pontifax, also known as the Dark Harper
>
> **PRINCESS JORDAN**, Wayfaring with the Kiralynn monks to learn the art of war, felled by the treachery of the Mordant she is healed by the monk's magic, sword sister to Kath of Castlegard
>
> **PRINCE JARED**, Wayfaring with the Octagon Knights to learn the way of the sword
>
> **PRINCESS JULIANA**, Wayfaring with Navarre's merchant fleet to learn the way of the sea
>
> **PRINCE JAMES**, Wayfaring in Tubor to learn to become a vintner
>
> **PRINCE JAYSON**, Wayfaring in the Delta to learn the secrets of a new water wheel

his retainers:

> **MARY,** Prince Ian's wife
>
> **MASTER SIMMONS**, the royal healer

THE KIRALYNN MONKS

Founded over two thousand years ago by a group of scholars, knights, and wizards, the Kiralynn Order has always presented an enigmatic face to the world, a face that is open yet closed. One hundred years before the start of the War of Wizards the monks withdrew from the southern kingdoms, retreating to their monastery hidden deep in the Southern Mountains. As if erased from the minds of men, the monastery's location disappeared from the maps of Erdhe. The memory of the Kiralynn monks has slowly faded, becoming little more than legend and myth. Yet select rulers of the southern kingdoms still receive scrolls sealed with the symbol of the Order. History has proven that these scrolls contain an uncanny prescience. Kings ignore the advice of the Order at their own peril.

The symbol of the Kiralynn monks is a Seeing Eye in the palm of an Open Hand. Their seat of power is their mountain monastery. The motto of the Order is "Seek Knowledge, Protect Knowledge, Share Knowledge".

THE GRAND MASTER, the leader of the Kiralynn Order, his/her identity is a closely guarded secret
-monks and initiates of the Order:
> **MASTER RIZEL,** a Master of the Order
> **MASTER GARTH,** a Master Healer of the Order
> **BRYCE,** an initiate of the Order, he studied to take his vows to become a monk and a healer but was subsumed by the Mordant's Awakening, becoming a prisoner in his own mind
> **MASTER AEROTH,** an ambassador monk sent to the kingdoms of Erdhe
> **MASTER ZITH,** a Master of the Order, accompanies Kath as one of her companions
> **RAFE,** a sworn monk of the Order, he has worn the blue for five years
> **MASTER YARL,** a master of the Order, an expert with a quarterstaff
> **MISTRESS ELLIS,** a master of the Order
> **MASTER FINTAN,** a master of the Order serving as a Wanderer, an emissary to the Rose Court
> **MISTRESS LENORE,** a master of the Order
> **GILBERT,** a monk of the Order serving as a hidden Wanderer in Pellanor
> **ASTER,** a monk of the Order serving as a hidden Wanderer in Pellanor
> **MASTER NUMAR,** a master of the Order serving as a hidden Wanderer in Pellanor, posing as an apothecary

-visitors to the monastery:

PRINCESS JORDAN, a princess of Navarre, sent to the monastery for her Wayfaring, she was felled by the treachery of the Mordant and healed by the magic of the monks

THE ZWARD

The Zward are sons and daughters of Kiralynn monks who choose to serve by the sword instead of the scroll. An ancient and secret order, they serve the will of the Grand Master. Their symbol is a small silver ring emblazoned with a fist holding an upright sword.

THADDEUS TOKHEART, also known as Thad, a captain of the Zward
DONAL, a sworn member of the Zward
BENJIN, a sworn member of the Zward
MARCUS, a sworn member of the Zward

THE ORACLE PRIESTESS

Hidden in depths of the Great Southern Swamps, the Isle of the Oracle is an ancient wellspring of Darkness, a place of power where the Dark Lord reaches through the Veil to touch his dedicates. The Isle is currently ruled by a Priestess endowed with special gifts from the Dark Lord. At times of great prophecy, the Dark Lord releases his priest or priestess into the kingdoms of Erdhe to participate in his great dark designs.

THE PRIESTESS, the ruler of the Isle of the Oracle, the priestess to the sacred well, wielder of the Eye of the Oracle. She rarely uses her true name, but often goes by the name of Lady Cereus, a name given to her by Prince Razzur. Beyond the Isle, she takes the phases of the moon as her symbol, gold on a field of purple.
-her servants and soldiers:

> **OTHAM,** a baldheaded giant who serves as a guard, a seneschal, and a lover to the Priestess
> **HUGO,** captain of the guards, a lover to the Priestess
> **LYDIA,** dark-haired handmaiden to the Priestess
> **TARA,** blonde-haired handmaiden to the Priestess
> **BRAXUS,** a captain serving the Priestess, a lover to the Priestess
> **GENERAL TARMIN,** a major of the Flame Army, sworn to the service of the Priestess and promoted to the general of her army, a lover to the Priestess

THE DEEP GREEN

The Deep Green is an ancient power reborn from the ashes of the War of Wizards. Rising from the ruins of a great city, the forest grows with frightening speed. Trees at the heart of the forest are giants, growing to more than thrice the height of normal trees, while the dense tangle of underbrush forms a nearly impenetrable barrier. The forest protects its own, a race of people with golden cat-eyes. Calling themselves the Children of the Green, the cat-eyed people live within the boundaries of the forest in a confederation of clans under the leadership of the Treespeaker.

Outside of the forest, the cat-eyed people are shunned as evil abominations, said to be born from the perverse mating of man with animals. The cat-eyed people are persecuted across the kingdoms of Erdhe, and often put to death by the 'white-eyes'.

THE TREESPEAKER, as old as the forest, she is a seer, a witch, the embodiment
of the power of the Green. As the leader of the clans, she wears a cloak of snow-white swan feathers.
-her clan leaders:
    CENRIC, leader of Clan Hemlock, he wears a cloak of peacock feathers
        AGATHA, leader of Clan Aspen, she wears a cloak of blue jay feathers. She leads a faction that opposes dealings with the white-eyes
        BRAN, leader of Clan Ash, he wears a cloak of raven feathers
        CAMILA, leader of Clan Maple, she wears a cloak of orange kestrel feathers and is a member of the faction that opposes dealings with the white-eyes
        DEREK, leader of Clan Redwood, he wears a cloak of red woodpecker feathers and is a member of the faction that opposes dealing with the white-eyes
        CONRAD, leader of Clan Spruce, he wears a cloak of brown thrush feathers
        LANA, leader of Clan Oak, she wears a cloak of golden finch feathers

-her people:
        JORAH SILVENWOOD, a ranger of Clan Cedar, killed by fire
        RONAH, a ranger of Clan Hemlock
        JENKS, a patrol leader of Clan Hemlock
        MARTYN, an attendant to the Treespeaker
        ALWIN, a ranger of Clan Hemlock

Other books by Karen L Azinger

The Assassin's Tear- Explore the medieval kingdoms of Erdhe, raid the tomb of the first emperor of China, and unravel the enigma of Dark Space in this collection of fantasy and science fiction tales from the author of *The Silk & Steel Saga.* The two signature stories, *Prophecy's Twist* and *The Assassin's Tear,* are set in the fantasy realm of Erdhe. *Prophecy's Twist* discovers the dark deceit that started the War of Wizards, forever changing the kingdoms of Erdhe. *The Assassin's Tear* follows the exploits of a petty thief whose ambition leads him to unravel the dark secret of the Mordant's Citadel. *The Emperor's Shadow* is an international thriller in the style of Indiana Jones, combining the power of superstition with archaeology in a desperate attempt to end World War Three. *A Man's World* is a post-apocalyptic adventure set in Australia where coal miners discover all the rules have changed. *Pieces of the Truth* is a time travel story where a young physicist discovers a forgotten truth. In *Snakes and Ladders,* Lynn Gallant sets out to shatter the glass ceiling by taking a walk to the dark side of New Orleans. In *The God Planet,* universal dreams spark a religious frenzy, summoning humanoid kind to the riddle of Dark Space.

The Front Cover artwork was done by the award-winning Australian artist, Greg Bridges. Greg's artwork has appeared on the book covers of many well-known fantasy authors. His cover perfectly captures the seductive and poisonous nature of The Poison Priestess. To see more of his art or to contact Greg, visit his website at http://www.gregbridges.com/

The Maps and the Back Cover artwork was done by a graphic artist from Oregon, Peggy Lowe. Her illustration of the two maps helps to bring the kingdoms of Erdhe to life and the hand with the orb portrays the mystery and magic of moon weaving. Peggy can be contacted at her e-mail address, peggy@portfoliooregon.com

Look for **The Battle Immortal,** the fifth and final book in
The Silk & Steel Saga.

ABOUT THE AUTHOR

KAREN L. AZINGER has always loved fantasy fiction, and always hoped that someday she could give back to the genre a little of the joy that reading has always given her. Ten years ago on a hike in the Columbia River Gorge she realized she had enough original ideas to finally write an epic fantasy. She started writing and never stopped. *The Steel Queen* is her first book, born from that hike in the gorge. Before writing, Karen spent over twenty years as an international business strategist, eventually becoming a vice-president for one of the world's largest natural resource companies. She's worked on developing the first gem-quality diamond mine in Canada's arctic, on coal seam gas power projects in Australia, and on petroleum projects around the world. Having lived in Australia for eight years she considers it to be her second home. She's also lived in Canada and spent a lot of time in the Canadian arctic. She lives with her husband in Portland Oregon, in a house perched on the edge of the forest. The first four books of *The Silk & Steel Saga* have been published and she is hard at work on the fifth and final book, *The Battle Immortal*. You can learn more at her website, www.karenlazinger.com or at her Facebook page for The Steel Queen.

CPSIA information can be obtained at www.ICGtesting.com
Printed in the USA
BVOW042225280313

316769BV00002B/111/P